INTERNATIONAL SHORT NOVELS:
A CONTEMPORARY ANTHOLOGY

international short novels: a contemporary anthology

Edited by

LEO HAMALIAN
EDMOND L. VOLPE
The City College of the City University of New York

JOHN WILEY & SONS, INC.
New York, London, Sydney, Toronto

Copyright © 1974, by John Wiley Sons, Inc.

Library of Congress Cataloging in Publication Data:

Hamalian, Leo, comp.
    International short novels.

CONTENTS: Takeda, T. This outcast generation.—Lessing, D. The antheap.—Ekwensi, C. People of the city. [etc.]

1. Fiction—Collections. I. Volpe, Edmond Loris, joint comp. II. Title.

PZ1.H176In [PN6014]   808.8'3'1   73-18251
ISBN 0-471-34621-7

Printed in the United States of America

10 9 8 7 6 5 4 3 2 1

preface

"No college or university education for Americans can be complete without some systematically developed points of reference beyond the Western tradition."

Ward Morehouse, *Education for the
Revolutionary World of the Future*

"While the world is becoming a single great global community, it retains attitudes and habits more appropriate to a different technological age ... Before long, humanity will face many grave difficulties that can be solved on a global scale. Education, however, as it is presently conducted in this country, is not moving rapidly enough in the right direction to produce the knowledge about the outside world and the attitudes toward other people that may be essential for human survival within a generation or two. This, I feel, is a much greater international problem than the military balance of power that absorbs so much of our attention today."

Edwin O. Reischauer, *Toward the 21st
Century: Education for a Changing World*

About fifteen years ago, the editors of this anthology assembled a collection of European and American short novels. Although our intention was to bring together fiction of the highest literary quality, we realized as the anthology took shape that it had an internal thematic unity: the novels expressed the existential mood of our present century. We believe that this anthology was successful because it was responsive to then current trends of thought and to shifts of emphasis in the teaching of literature. Classroom discussion was replacing the traditional lecture, and courses developed along lines of genre began to attract more interest than the standard survey courses of English literature. The short novel proved to be admirably adapted to both of these trends.

Not long afterward, influenced by the growing sense of the world as a "global village," educators on all levels were engaged in reexamining the traditional curriculum in humanities, and undergraduate English departments were moving away from a rigid definition of their role as purveyors of English and American literatures only. More and more they were accepting as their province the whole Western literary tradition from Homer to Joyce. The clash of goals between those who continue to believe that an English department should teach only the literature written in English and those who believe the teaching of literature and literary appreciation in general are the responsibility of an English department is not yet resolved and probably will not be for many years. At the moment, however, there is a strong trend toward broadening the curriculum of English departments.

Three important forces have contributed to this trend. First, the United States has reached a point in its troubled history when Americans are no longer willing to suppress, for the sake of assimilation, their racial and ethnic consciousness and pride. Second, many of the small nations are discovering a sense of individual identity, and Americans are becoming aware of these rich cultures and traditions beyond the European. Finally, educators, particularly at the undergraduate level, are beginning to acknowledge that specialization has been carried too far. Just as old national boundaries are dissolving, the high walls between the various disciplines are crumbling. Literature is a humane art, but it is also involved with philosophy, psychology, sociology, anthropology, and science. It is an expression of the whole human being living in an often complex environment and many of us have come to realize that it must be taught, in the full context of human experience and knowledge.

This present collection of contemporary short novels from ten nations in different parts of the globe is, we trust, responsive to these trends, and we hope that as a result of reading these writers, the student will develop "points of reference" beyond the American and European tradition, which is readily available to him through other collections. The points of reference represented here are Japan, China, and India from the Far East; Israel and Morocco from the Middle East; Southern Rhodesia and Nigeria from Africa; British Guiana from the Caribbean; and Columbia and Chile from Latin America.

This selection does not mean, of course, that the influence of the European literary tradition is absent. Like the United States, the South American nations have firm cultural roots in the European past; and in many nations throughout the world, as these short novels clearly reveal, the impact of European and American thought and culture have both enriched the indigenous culture and produced many of the conflicts and tensions in these "emerging" nations. Taken together, these short novels present a world in transition, with national barriers breaking down and with modern, foreign customs and ideas clashing with ancient native traditions, or existing, incongruously, side by side with them. Many of the major issues—philosophical, moral, political, cultural, and social— that face twentieth-century life are dramatized in these novels.

In this century, Communist revolutions have altered the destiny and the existence of two major peoples: the Russians and the Chinese. Ma Chia's *Unfading Flowers* depicts the Chinese revolution in progress. Deliberately propagandistic, the story itself partakes in the struggle to win the support of the people to the revolutionary cause. Unsophisticated and perhaps even artistically gauche, Ma Chia's novel presents the old feudal barons and their supporters as the archvillains, and the dedicated, gallant, self-sacrificing revolutionaries as the unfading flowers of the future society. Although hardly representative of the great and subtle artistic achievements of China's rich and ancient culture, *Unfading Flowers* gives the "outside" reader a glimpse of the revolutionary spirit that has fired the youth of China and drastically changed this traditional society in which youth had always served old age. This novel, whatever its shortcomings, offers a true mirror of modern China in the making.

Like China, the rest of the world in this century has known few extended periods of peace. Global and local wars have altered the lives, individually and collectively, of millions of people and have left deep scars on the psyche of contemporary men and women. In this *Outcast Generation*, Taijun Takeda describes the dilemma of one such man, floundering morally and spiritually. Cut off by war from his homeland and humiliated by defeat, the poet-protagonist begins his account: "Perhaps it's easier to go on living than you think." His sense of nihilism, his indifference to almost everything until he becomes involved with another human being, precipitate a moral crisis very similar to the existential engagements recorded by the post-World-War II novelists in Europe who also had to pick up the pieces after surviving the experience of the holocaust. Indirectly, Takeda asks: After being submerged for years in the impersonal forces of war, how will human nature reveal itself in the private acts and emotions of uniformed robots who have become individuals again? The protagonist is overpowered by the discovery that it is possible to renew one's humanity even in the most inhumane of times, to discover the great chain of being that transcends the Darwinian "natural order of things."

Aharon Megged's hero in *The White City* comes to grips with a similar moral dilemma, even though he can enjoy the luxury of victory and not the despair of defeat. Passionately dedicated to the cause of Israel and convinced utterly of its right to defend itself against the enemies who besiege it, the soldier protagonist shrinks from the brutality and cruelty that war and violence demand. To seem uncowardly, he must kill his foes, but to kill his foes, he must regard them as murderers when he knows that they are people no different from himself. In the end, just as Segui in Takeda's novel understands that Karajima, his enemy, is a mortal being capable of suffering, of agony, of demise, so does the Israeli soldier find himself moved to a "wrong" compassion for his foe. One is reminded of the stories of that great Jewish writer, Isaac Babel, who foresaw the moral dilemma that so many young men would be forced to face in the century ahead.

During this century, peace has often seemed like war. We have had a cold war in which no battles were fought, and we have experienced the grim struggle for civil rights in our own country. Elsewhere, colonial nations have achieved precarious independence, often from reluctant masters. The internal political and economic problems produced by the relatively sudden freedom and responsibility have been staggering for many of these countries, but perhaps even more staggering have been the cultural and social dislocations that have followed on the heels of freedom. Rural, traditional cultures, with a different sense of time and a different pace of life have had to assimilate advanced technological developments and the alien ideas and habits that go along with abruptly different patterns of production and new life styles. There have been friction and fractionalism that must be resolved. In *People of the City*, Cyprian Ekwensi conveys the chaotic intermixture of modern ideas with ancient customs, the impact of rapid urbanization upon people who used to dwell in tribal villages, and the political strife that besets a developing nation like Nigeria as opposing factions vie for power. Amusa Sango, who in other times might have been a chieftan, is a crime reporter obsessed by the need for money. But if there is to be personal salvation for him in that "black city," it will probably come through the old power of love that he and his Beatrice are free to bestow on each other despite the turmoil of changing times.

Mohammed Mrabet's *Love with a Few Hairs* is an amusing, fascinating portrait of a world both familiar and strange to the Westerner. The protagonist, a young Arab named Mohammed, works for a Mr David, an Englishman who owns a small hotel. Mohammed serves him as both bartender and lover, and in his company, he adopts such Western customs as drinking hard liquor and running around in the boss's automobile. Despite such trappings of sophistication and modernity, Mohammed readily resorts to a primitive method of gaining the affection of a young girl he falls in love with. Because he does not follow the prescribed Moslem ritual for arranging a marriage, Mohammed suffers rejection by his family. The love potion works, the young couple are married, but because Mohammed has not followed the witch's instructions to the letter, the love potion mysteriously and magically ruins his marriage. There are things between Moslem heaven and earth that are not dreamed of in our rational Western philosophies.

The India of today is vividly presented in Bharati Mukherjee's *The Tiger's Daughter*. Wracked by the struggles of the poor for survival, torn by growing industrial pains and labor strife, yet profoundly defined by ancient traditions and rigid class distinctions, it is a rapidly changing land that must seem strange to the eye of a native who has returned after years of absence. Miss Mukherjee's story follows the fortunes of a young Indian girl who has been away at an American college where she met and married an American. While visiting her affluent family, she discovers that she is caught between two cultures, the Indian upper-class world, with its prescribed religious and social customs, and the American culture that ignores ritual and tradition for individualism. The record of her inner conflicts reflects the ambivalence of modern educated Indians. In this story, too, there is an existential theme, for not even the girl knows what kind of person will emerge from this experience. She knows only that she will be neither American nor Indian.

Perhaps the worst social evil created by the colonialism of the previous century was the caste system, a legacy that persists even today in many parts of the world. If the kind of abuse faced by American blacks differs from the kind that the blacks and "colored" of Southern Rhodesia and South Africa must endure, *The Antheap* by Doris Lessing reveals that no matter where they occur, anguish, humiliation, the waste of talent, and the expense of spirit are everywhere the same. The gold-mine where blacks are destined to labor in the white man's insatiable search for the yellow metal is the symbol of colonialism. As interpreted by the young black artist, Dirk, his "pit of death" becomes the equivalent of José Donoso's limitless hell, an inferno that sucks in the darkskinned and consumes them. At the end, the old Scottish mine owner feels defeated by something that "he did not begin to understand" as the two friends start "the long and difficult struggle to understand what they had won and how they would use it." Unfortunately, events in South and Central Africa do not bear out the implication that a new day may be dawning, and the victory at this moment—if there is one—appears to belong to the "angry old" white men like Macintosh.

While Doris Lessing places her hope for the future of her homeland in the educated new generation, Paule Marshall in *British Guiana* gives over the future to such young men as the vigorous, amoral Parrish. He has completely left the bush behind, but in doing so, he may have lost his bearings. His benefactor, Motley, even though he has risen to the top of his caste, has some sense of his own self-betrayal. Driving through the lush but ominous countryside outside of Georgetown, he feels the slow power of the land, hears ancestral voices calling from the bush, and for a moment, feels "the self he had long sought within his grasp." But the moment flickers and vanishes before he can fully understand its significance, and he returns to his old pursuits, more a neuter than a man. The car he drives is a mechanical version of the wild animal that once ranged the bush in unrestrained freedom, and the wicket of the cricket match that he interrupts with his car, standing incongruously in the muddy road, "like a sign of conquest," is as rooted in his soul as it is in the soil. Thus, the philososophical dilemma of modern men (and women, for Sybil is also a victim) caught in the conflicts generated by the caste system unfolds on the pages of Miss Marshall's Caribbean drama.

And finally, the more general philosophical dilemmas of contemporary people of different cultures is dramatized in the stories of two of Latin America's most gifted novelists. In the portrait of an old transvestite living in a brothel with a daughter he was bribed into begetting, José Donoso of Chile captures the loneliness and isolation of a human being trapped in a boundless inferno, where hell is daily fare. Like several of the short novels in this collection, *Hell Has No Limits*, beneath its bizarre setting and plot, deals with shifting identities, terror, and the possibility of redemption. In Donoso's inferno, the downtrodden oppress the downtrodden and the hunting dogs search out human prey. Many readers may feel that the title, taken from lines in Marlowe's *Doctor Faustus*, speaks—if not by design then by cryptic eloquence—for the prevailing conditions in Donoso's tragedy-saddled native land.

The central figure of *No One Writes to the Colonel* by Garcia Marquez of Colombia is also an old man. In this case, he is a decrepit old soldier, a sort of aged baby, a withered wonder child, wise and silly, who has been waiting twenty years for an official letter announcing that his military pension has finally been awarded to him. His son is dead, his wife asthmatic, his clothing in decay, his small mortgaged house falling into disrepair, and like Godot, the pension will never arrive. But each week the Colonel walks down to the dock to meet the packet boat bringing the mail to the small, lost village whose only contact with the outside world is through the weekly newspapers that accompany the boat. The Colonel's world is drab, hot, and mosquito-ridden, and his existence without purpose, yet he is sustained by the memory of a moment of glory and by his unflagging belief in possibility. Man, Marquez suggests, is a creature of hope and he endures, even in the dust and dung that the poor forgotten of Latin America are often forced to eat.

Although each of these ten short novels depicts the uniqueness of people living their particular daily lives in particular spaces, we recognize as familiar and even eternal their search for love or kinship, their loneliness and despair, their quiet courage under the crushing weight of disappointment and frustration, their moral and spiritual struggles as the shadows lengthen. Like the old Colonel, indeed like ourselves, these characters from contemporary fiction are enchanted and misguided by life, each in his own way. Their authors, even as they explore the differences created by time and place, lead us to remember the essential oneness of human beings, and this book, we hope, will introduce these writers and their work to a wider audience among college and university students who in their own lives have been seeking to relate the individual ego with a larger sense of community.

Leo Hamalian
Edmond L. Volpe

contents

about the authors

MA CHIA

Very little biographical information is available about the author of *Unfading Flowers*. He is known for an earlier novel called *Ten Days in Chiang-shan Village*. Written from 1945 to 1949 when there was quickened activity among the writers of the People's Republic of China, it celebrates the land reforms undertaken in northern China. The novelists of this period, including Ma Chia, turned for guidance to the popular Soviet novels then available in Chinese translation, such as Sholokhov's *Virgin Soil*, Gladkov's *Cement*, Ostrovsky's *The Tempering of Steel*, and Grossman's *People are Immortal*. The Chinese novelists paid tribute to the transformation of land and people in the standard social-realist style rather than in the manner suggestive of the return to "national forms" as defined by Mao Tse-tung in his series of highly influential books and pamphlets on the subject. After 1949, literary zeal was deadened by increasing party insistence on conformity with political ideology. Communist literary historians often survey this later period in terms not of literary achievement but of major ideological struggles. Thus, in fiction, the worker and the peasant soldier are the prevailing heroes. Soldier fiction like *Unfading Flowers* naturally turned for material to the Korean War or to the staple theme of the anti-Japanese wars of liberation. According to critics of Chinese fiction, few reputable novelists have produced good novels since the "freeze," although Ai Wu published in 1958 a highly acclaimed novel called *The Tempering of Steel*.

CYPRIAN EKWENSI

People of the City, originally published in 1954, is generally considered the first contemporary African novel. As Ekwensi's characters clearly demonstrate, the author believes that the tribal and cultural history of Africans has produced a unique character with special traits and temperaments. An Ibo, Ekwensi was interested in the cultural history of his people and collected Ibo folk tales under the title of *Ikolo The Wrestler and Other Ibo Tales* (1947). Ekwensi entered literature in a roundabout way. Born in 1919 in Minna, Northern Nigeria, he attended college in Ibadan and Ghana. Then he studied at the School of Forestry in Ibadan. A scholarship from the Nigerian government sent him to the University of London where he studied at the Chelsea School of Pharmacy. In London he discovered that his real interest was in writing. In 1947, he published his first novel, a sentimental, romantic tale written for the popular market, what is known in Africa as an Onitsha novel, named after a market town with an enormous output of such books. Since 1947, Ekwensi has published six full-length serious novels, seven children's books and Onitsha novels, two collections of short stories and numerous articles and stories in newspapers and journals. Translated into several languages, he is regarded as a city writer because *People of the City* and *Jagua Nana* are his best-known works. He has not, however, limited himself to the city. *Burning Grass* is a novel about cattlemen in Northern Savannah. Aside from writing, Ekwensi has devoted much time to radio broadcasting. At one time he was Head of Features for the Nigerian Broadcasting Company. During the Civil War, he became a prominent spokesmen for the Biafran cause and served as chairman of the Bureau for External Publicity in Biafra. Since the end of the war, he has worked to reorganize the Biafran radio station.

JOSÉ DONOSO

Short story writer, novelist, journalist, and teacher, José Donoso was born in Chile in 1923. An early interest in language led him to the Instituto Pedagogico at the University of Chile where he prepared himself to be an English teacher. Granted an award by the Doherty Foundation, he came to the United States to study at Princeton. After graduating in 1951, Donoso returned to Chile and taught. He had begun to write and publish short stories, and his first collection won him Chile's Municipal Prize. *Coronation,* his first novel and the first of his fiction to be translated and published in the United States, was awarded the Faulkner Foundation Prize for Chile in 1962. During the years before he was firmly established as a fiction writer. Donoso worked as a journalist, and his success at this type of writing brought him the Chile-Italia Prize for Journalism. Donoso has taught in the United States as well as in Chile. During the 1966-1967 academic year he served as Writer-in-Residence at the State University of Iowa. During the past few decades, Latin American writers have captured the attention of the world as some of the most imaginative and fertile creators in the field of contemporary literature. Donoso has helped to introduce Latin American writers to readers in the United States by serving as coeditor of the *Tri-quarterly Anthology of Contemporary Latin American Literature*, which was introduced in 1967, the same year in which his novel *This Sunday* was published. Donoso's latest novel, *The Obscene Bird of Night*, published in the United States in 1973, depicts as does *Hell Has No Limits* bizarre, lost characters. Currently, the novelist resides in Spain with his wife and daughter.

DORIS LESSING

Doris Lessing is neither a native of Southern Rhodesia nor of England. She was born in Persia in 1919, where her father, an Englishman, was director of a bank. Shortly after her birth, her father bought a huge farm in a sparsely settled district of Southern Rhodesia, where she spent a very lonely childhood, and her fiction bears the impress of her early and formative experiences in that country.

The Scots families, which were few and separated by great distances, owned the large farms worked by blacks. Being raised in Central Africa, she told an interviewer, meant that she was "a member of the white minority pitted against a black majority that was abominably treated and still is." She was still a teenager when she decided to leave the family farm and move into town (she has written a novella about this experience). Within a short time she married and bore two children. After her marriage broke up in 1943, she settled down to serious writing, and one book followed another in rapid succession. Within a decade two books of stories, a collection of short novels, and five full-length novels saw publication. These and the many books she has published since 1960 have won her an international audience. Although she eventually left Rhodesia and currently lives in London, her exposure to the injustices of racial discrimination bears its imprint on almost all of her work (sexual injustice is her other large theme). The situation in Southern Rhodesia mirrors the tragic condition of two-thirds of the people throughout the world, she believes, because only one-third of mankind enjoys the privileges and requirements of a decent, dignified existence. Doris Lessing's masterwork, a series of novels that she began in 1952 with *Martha Quest*, she has entitled *Children of Violence*. It concerns, she has said, the whole pattern in human existence of discrimination, tyranny, and violence. A recent novel, *The Summer Before Dark* (1973), resembles her first novel, *The Grass is Singing* (1950) more than any since: it is a simple narrative, simply told. Through dreams, through archetype and myth, the woman protagonist, Kate Brown, is related to the dark impersonal forces that underlie our lives.

TAIJUN TAKEDA

Born in Tokyo in 1912, Taijun Takeda enjoyed a happy childhood as the second son in a temple family of high rank. Although deeply influenced by his father, a man of simple tastes who taught Buddhistic philosophy, Takeda showed no interest in writing as a youth, and the account of Ryonosuke Agutagawa's suicide in 1927 led him to wonder why the death of a mere writer should cause such a stir.

In 1931, he entered the University of Tokyo to major in Chinese literature, but he was arrested in his first year for distributing propaganda leaflets for an anti-imperialist, leftist organization he had joined in high school. After serving a short term in prison, on his father's request he abandoned the leftist movement and left college on his own, but his continued association with a circle of scholars and students who opposed the government's China policies brought about a second arrest and confinement.

In 1937, he was called to military duty and sent to the battlefield of China for two years. After his discharge, he tried his hand at translating Chinese novels and in 1943, published his first serious work, *The World of Shi Chi*, while working in Shanghai for the Japan-China Cultural House. In 1945, he saw at firsthand what he regarded as the inevitable fall of his country's arrogant armies. The following year, he returned to Japan and taught Chinese literature at Hokkaido *National University*. *This Outcast Generation* (1945), his first full-length story, is based upon his Shanghai experience. It exposes the dangerous potentiality in all of us to become senseless killers. In a year when war criminals were hunted and confessions of guilt extracted by tribunals, this candid novel shocked the reading public and established its author alongside Tanazaki and Kawabata as an important postwar writer. In 1948, he gave up teaching to devote himself to writing, and in 1954, he consolidated his reputation with *Luminous Moss*, a novel about cannibalism in the Japanese army. One of Japan's most prolific writers, he has recorded his own experiences in an astounding number of stories, novels, and essays.

PAULE MARSHALL

Born in Brooklyn in 1929 of parents who had immigrated to New York from Barbados, Paule Marshall's childhood was shaped by a heritage that was both Afro-American and West Indian. As a second generation black American, she was to turn the problems of acculturation and racism that her parents and those like them confronted to literary use in her first novel, *Brown Girl, Brownstones* (1959), and again in her collection of stories, *Soul Clap Hands and Sing* (1961). Her second novel, *The Chosen Place, The Timeless People* (1969) also deals with cultural and racial conflict, but to this has been added a frankly political theme that envisions the emergence of the darker peoples of the world through revolutionary struggle.

After graduating as a Phi Beta Kappa from Brooklyn College in 1953, Ms. Marshall married, had a son, and worked in New York City libraries. Later she became a staff writer for the magazine *Our World*, traveling on assignment to Brazil and the West Indies—places that were eventually to provide her with the settings for many of her stories. After the literary success of her first two books, she received grants from the Guggenheim and Ford foundations, the American Academy of Arts and Letters, the National Endowment for the Arts, and the Yaddo Corporation. Having lived for considerable periods in the Caribbean, she now divides her time between New York and Haiti, the birthplace of her present husband.

Ms. Marshall's first novel, *Brown Girl, Brownstones*, examines the destructive impact of America's racism and materialistic values upon one immigrant black family, and is impressive for its insight into the psychology of its young heroine, its richly and densely evoked locale, and its poetic but functional prose. From the problems of acculturation and youth, Ms. Marshall turned in her next book to the problems of age. The protagonists of the four stories in *Soul Clap Hands and Sing*, from which this selection is taken, are not only caught in the physical and mental problems of their decaying bodies, but they are, on another level, symbolic of an old political and social order that is forced to give way to a new reality. In her most recent novel, *The Chosen Place, The Timeless People*, Ms. Marshall examines the heritage of slavery and revolt in a mythical West Indian village. The racial and cultural conflict between the villagers and the members of a visiting American aid team symbolizes the larger confrontation of the world's darker and lighter peoples, with the oppressed turning on their oppressors even when the latter pose as benefactors. In the author's prophetic vision, the time of the timeless people is at last at hand.

Ms. Marshall is presently at work on a novel tentatively titled *Little Girl of All the Daughters*, which deals with the spiritual odyssey of a middle-aged, middle-class black American matron back to the roots of her blackness and her true self.

AHARON MEGGED

Novelist and playwright, Aharon Megged was born in Poland in 1920 and came to Eretz-Israel at the age of six. After completing his secondary school education, he worked as a dock laborer, in the stone quarries and salt mines, and also as a farmer and fisherman. He now edits several literary reviews and supplements.

His novels, stories, and plays are distinctive for their humor as well as for the human compassion they convey. *Ruah Hayamin* ("Spirit of these days") is a collection of stories about Israeli fishermen, seamen, and kibbutz members, and about the life of the Arabs and the horrors of the War of Independence. In another book of stories, *Yisrael Haverim* ("Israeli comrades"), he deals with the problems of the former generation of settlers confronted with the new reality that has arisen in Israel. The novel *Hedva va-Ani* ("Hedva and I") describes the adventures of a kibbutz member who has gone to live in the city; through the eyes of this kibbutz idealist, it satirizes city life and the red tape instituted by the young state of Israel. In *Mikreh Ha Kessil* ("The Case of the Simpleton") the author satirizes the falsehood and hypocrisy of modern life and the individual's puny efforts to contend with the problems of his society, nation, and world at large. *Ha-Beriha* ("The Escape") is a grotesquely satirical description of the well-ordered life in a country where everything is planned by the ruling powers. One of these stories deals with the behavior of a group of people on a boat in which they have escaped from the doomed land. *El Ha-Yeladim Be-Telman* ("To the Children in Yemen") depicts Yemenite life. *H-Hai al Ma-Met* ("Living on the Dead") is a short story about the attitude of the younger generation toward the past and the resultant complication.

His plays, most of which have been performed in Israel theatres, include *Harhek Ba-Arava* ("In the Distant Steppes"), *Incubator a Ha-Sela* ("Incubator on the Rocks"), *Baderech le-Eilat* ("On the Road to Eilat"), *Ha-Het Ha-Rishon* ("The Primal Sin"), *Bereshit* ("In the Beginning") and *Hanna Senesh*—dramatic episodes in the life of the woman who parachuted behind the German lines in World War II. His only work to appear in translation in this country is *The Fortune of Fools* (1962).

GABRIEL GARCIA MARQUEZ

Probably the most fascinating place in Colombia today is a backwater called Macondo. Like thousands of other coastal towns in the heart of the hemisphere, it drips during rainy season and sizzles under the summer sun. It is however a very special spot: it is the invention of Gabriel Garcia Marquez, that extraordinary Faulknerian of Latin America.

Marquez was born there in 1928—on the map it is called Aracataca, a tiny village in the sweltering Atlantic savannah of Santa Maria, perhaps not unlike Macondo, which is named for a banana plantation he knew as a child. He grew up there. "I had a fabulous childhood," he says. He hardly knew his parents, and he met his mother for the first time when he was about seven. She had left him to be raised by his grandparents, who owned an enormous house full of ghosts that terrified the boy. His grandfather, who had fought in the civil wars, held a minor political post in the village. He was the boy's constant companion, "the most important figure in my life," says Marquez. The old man died when Marquez was eight. After that, he says, he felt rather jaded. "Growing up, studying, traveling, none of that particularly attracted me. Nothing interesting has happened to me since."

At the age of 12, he moved to Bogota to study with the Jesuits. An indifferent student, he flunked out of law school at the university, and began writing stories for the newspaper *El Espectador*. They were so good that he was hired as a reporter and editor. In 1954, he was sent to Rome and Paris as the paper's correspondent, and became interested in experimental films. He also began work on a book of several chapters, one of which was to become *No One Writes to the Colonel*.

In 1955, the Colombian government closed down the newspaper, leaving him penniless in Paris. In 1958, he returned to Colombia long enough to marry his sweetheart Mercedes, then transferred himself to Caracas, where he found work as a journalist. There he wrote *Big Mama's Funeral* (1962). In 1959, when Castro entered Havana, he was appointed to open an office for a Cuban press agency in Bogota, but he resigned when the militant element of the party began to criticize him. In 1961, he came to Mexico with $100 in his pocket. He finished *Hard Times* (1962), and until the publication of his great novel, *One Hundred Years of Solitude* (1967), he made a living by writing scripts for "new wave" movies.

Originally *No One Writes* was an episode in *Hard Times*, but as the Colonel grew in size and stature, he had to be given a separate life. Marquez has exhausted his Macondo mythography and is preparing a new opus to be entitled *Autumn of the Patriarch*, a dictator's long monologue as he stands trial in a popular court.

MOHAMMED MRABET

Paul Bowles, who transcribed and translated *Love With a Few Hairs*, writes of the author:

"Mohammed Mrabet was born in Tangier of Riffian parentage about 1940. (Since births were not registered at that time, there is no exact record.) After suffering through the usual turbulent Moroccan childhood, half of which was spent sleeping in the street, he began to work for an American who was employed at one of the American military bases in what was then French Morocco. He made two early visits to the United States and returned to Morocco, where he spent most of his time fishing. In 1966, after I had known him for a year, I suggested that he tape the folktales, legends and inventions he constantly told. The following year in London he published his first novel *Love with a Few Hairs*, and two years later a second novel, *The Lemon*, was published, also in London. Both books subsequently appeared in American editions. A volume of short stories, *M'Hashish*, was brought out by City Lights in San Francisco in 1969, and another collection of somewhat longer stories is scheduled for publication in November (1973) by Black Sparrow Press, *The Boy Who Set the Fire*. He made a third trip to the United States in 1968, this time to Los Angeles, which he disliked so heartily that he no longer has any desire to return to America. He is married, with two children, and lives in Tangier, where he still spends a good deal of time fishing."

Paul Bowles, a native of New York City, is a composer as well as an author. He has published many travel pieces, short stories, and the highly respected novels *The Sheltering Sky, Let It Come Down, The Spider's House*, and *Up Above the World*. He makes his home in Morocco.

BHARATI MUKHERJEE

The Tiger's Daughter is Bharati Mukherjee's first published novel. Calcutta, the setting of the novel, is the city in which she was born and raised. During her youth, she spent three years in English and Swiss schools, while her father, a chemist did research in those countries. She received her B.A. from the University of Calcutta and an M.A. from the University of Baroda before coming to the United States to study creative writing at the University of Iowa. She earned both an M.F.A. and a Ph.D. (in comparative literature) there and then taught literature at Marquette University. She is currently an associate professor and Director of the Graduate English Program at McGill University, where she lectures on the modern novel. She is married to the Canadian writer, Clark Blaise, and is the mother of two sons. She has published short stories and criticism in various publications in India and the United States, and is completing a second novel. She is also collaborating on a book with her husband based on a year of travel through India. Of the heroine of *The Tiger's Daughter*, Bharati Mukherjee writes: "Tara is a younger and far more helpless version of the girl I could have been . . . I like to think I am wiser than she, and could have avoided some of her defeats."

TAIJUN TAKEDA

this outcast generation[1]

1

—Perhaps it's easier to go on living than you think.

I had laid my pillow on the concrete platform used for drying laundry, and I was relaxing in the sun. I took a sunbath there every morning after coming out of my dim back room. In the corner, as usual, were two chickens pecking away at leftover rice and withered vegetables. From the alley below came the almost threatening voices of Chinese haggling over bargains from the Japanese. The voices of the Japanese were low, feeble, and confused, so their customers sounded even more overbearing in their abuse. Only the voices of Japanese children at play were full of energy and happiness. Oddly enough, those joyful cries made the parents even more irritable.

—Since everyone's apparently able to get along like this.

With my weak vision it looked to me as if the wall of a theatre beyond the house roofs stood out garishly white. It seemed to float radiantly white out of the blue winter sky.

—You can lose a war, see your country collapse. And still you can go on living.

Before I had realized it, the shop windows of even the Japanese were decorated with flags of Nationalist China and photographs of Chiang Kai-shek and his wife. I too had bought a small photograph from an old man peddling pictures of the couple. The snapshot had sold like hotcakes.

—All you need is a guardian angel.

To prepare for the inspection tours of the Chinese police, I had put the photograph between the pages of a notebook. When the Chinese national anthem was sung at the movies, the audience stood up and so did I, my eyes obediently on the flag and a framed picture of Sun Yat-

The Outcast Generation by Taijun Takeda is reprinted by permission of the publisher, Charles E. Tuttle Co., Inc.

[1]The Japanese title *Mamushi no sue* translates as *A Generation of Vipers*, an allusion to Matthew 23:33: "Ye serpents, ye generation of vipers, how can ye escape the damnation of hell?" But the translator decided not to use this title because Philip Wylie had written a novel with the title *A Generation of Vipers*.

sen. I had stood up apathetically, like a puppet, and then sat down, and the movie over, I had gone out through the crowds of Chinese teenagers pushing me around. I had merely listened indifferently as the agitated audience cried out simultaneously over a violently anti-Japanese film. Sometimes I had no expression on my face, sometimes I smiled reluctantly. Whatever the occasion, the only thing I really marveled at was my own ability to somehow continue living when I so easily might have been dead. At first, I believed that bearing the humiliation kept me going. But when I thought over the defeat and its aftermath, I felt no shame, nothing in fact. My blank face and reluctant smile were merely the mask by which I was simply living without any humiliation whatsoever.

I started to earn my keep by writing out documents in Chinese. There was no end of callers. Since my landlord was a broker, his customers of the past fifteen years came to me in a constant stream. They were so totally confused that they even talked respectfully to me! Even in defeat life marches on. As if to confirm this principle, clients came to me to lodge complaints of various kinds. A pale old man once asked me to help him after his employer had been robbed and kidnapped. Unless the police were notified immediately, his boss would be in for some real trouble. So urged, I had gone into my dark back room on the second floor. Even in broad daylight I turned on the electricity. I spread out my carbons on a tangerine crate. I sluggishly went about my task with the help of a Japanese-Chinese dictionary. And the job finished, I was paid off. I would hesitate in giving my fee. The currency of the puppet-government was still in circulation, and I had to figure out the price of four packs of cigarettes. The money I earned came out of human misery. Beautiful reflection that! It's a pity the thought lasted only two or three days after I had gone into my trade. I wanted my sake and rich food so that trouble and customers were an absolute prerequisite.

Someone would be evicted tomorrow. In one way or another, someone would have to move his belongings into the Japanese compound. A Japanese man desired Chinese citizenship in order to return to his family in Taiwan. A Japanese drafted to dive for salvage wanted to give written notice of illness—that was how eager he was to get home. Some Japanese wished to illegally convert the goods they had on hand into money, others to open street stalls. A Korean-born reporter came. A blind person came. A pregnant woman came. A Japanese merchant who promised to pay me anything I asked and a sick man hardly able to walk because of malnutrition, they came too. I undertook anything. I prepared documents audaciously. I wrote irresponsibly. All I cared about was getting my documents approved. Sometimes I chose expressions designed to move the heartstrings of officials in charge of us Japanese living in China. Sometimes I developed watertight arguments. I wrote grandiloquently. I wrote half-truths that favored my clients. I finally reached the point of writing barefaced lies. At the very least, however, what I did write was understood. That was why most of my documents got through. My customers came to offer their thanks. Before I realized it, I was gaining their confidence. Not only was I a popular transcriber, I began to be looked upon as a reliable guy!

My only thought was to get paid. I never felt I was working for the benefit of Japanese residents. Those that depended on me in this way I pitied. I found the world ridiculous in which a person as irresponsible, as incompetent as I, could still be useful. The world was too flimsy, too dissatisfying. Formerly, before coming to Shanghai and even later, I had studied hard, worked hard, thought hard. At that time not a soul had trusted me. After the end of the war I didn't study, didn't work, didn't think. But in people's eyes I was changing into a man of integrity, at least to the extent that I had never before been considered for the role. No longer did I have any ideals, any faith. I was merely breathing, and that, apparently, was what people expected of me. I fell into the habit of looking sober as a judge. No matter what the proposition, I wasn't surprised. That was the kind of person my customers were seeking advice from about their personal affairs. A man married to a Chinese woman wanted to know if he ought to get a divorce or not. A Japanese wife about to run off to her sweetheart just before her repatriation told me her scheme. Occasionally, therefore, I reached the position of the Catholic priest who lends an ear to confessions and vows.

One morning I was drinking some sake left over from the night before. I gulped down a cup. Though the wine was beginning to sour a little, I was in a hurry to get drunk. Then I intended to write a poem I had called "The Man Shot to Death." The execution of a German war criminal I had seen in a newsreel had made quite an impression on me . . . Shots. Inside the white smoke the upper part of the bound body jerked forward. With that it was over. It had really been simple. As plain as day. So truthful as to be intensely satisfying. In it was something beyond logic. It had pleased me immensely.

Upper torso in a forward fall—
Why?
Gravity's law.

As I was jotting down these expressions in bold strokes, my landlady called up to me that I had a visitor, a young lady who had come a few days before.

I put a padded robe over my wrinkled workclothes and went down. Young? Probably her, I said to myself, remembering one of my clients.

Her husband was an invalid, but the real estate company that owned their house had demanded they vacate in three days. There wasn't a thing she could do by herself, so she had asked me to write a petition to the authorities.

My visitors always waited inside the front door. The sunlight through the seven or eight sheets of glazed glass in the roof made the doorway brighter than my room. When I had first seen that woman in winter clothing standing in the pale light, a shudder had gone through me. What had impressed me was her tall, slim body, her white face, like some flower at evening, her attitude, shy in a lovely sort of way yet seductively coquettish. I had felt as if something I had forgotten over a long period of time had suddenly turned up, a fantasy I had once believed in when I hadn't lost my aim in life.

"I'll do it."

In an efficient businesslike way, I had learned the essentials from her and had gone upstairs and composed a beautiful piece of prose. I had handed her the document I was so proud of, and without smiling, I deliberately demanded twice my usual fee. My business was the writing of documents, and I had long ago become contemptuous of romantic sentimentality. I had given up any feelings of anxiety about matters not related to my trade.

"Is that enough?" she had said, taking some bills out of her patent leather bag and putting them down on the mats. "It's probably been very hard on you since you started doing this kind of work," she had said, her eyes large and friendly as she looked up at me standing there.

"I've often read your poems. My husband likes them too. He's always asking about you." It had seemed to me she was reminiscing.

"What's that?" I had said, embarrassed, as if the flow of blood in my body had suddenly reversed itself. Why, just as I was about to receive my fee, had she started talking about my earlier poems, those terrible sentimental pieces?

—Always asking about me, did she say? Listen to that!

"Take this to the Board and have them sign it," I had said roughly, gathering up the money.

She had thanked me, and when her beautiful legs were no longer in view beyond the dark door, I had tramped up the narrow staircase. I was so excited I felt dizzy. I had even bruised my right ankle as I missed a step.

Luckily I was drunk when she came again. After all, wasn't she a young wife, and even after the war, with plenty of money, was she really in need of anything?

"Well?" I asked rudely. "Did it get through?"

"Thanks to you, they made an immediate inquiry. We don't have to leave."

Her red and white checked sweater caused her white face to look even more dazzling. "Someone gave these to me," she said, holding out a pack of imported cigarettes. There was no sign she intended to return.

"Are you free now? I'd like to talk something over with you."

"Well? What is it?"

"It's difficult to talk here."

"In my room then?"

I took the cigarettes, worth several times my fee, and went upstairs. What a beautiful, graceful animal she seemed as she sat near me in my small dark room with its walls barren except for an electric light and a gas meter. Instantly my wretched back room was filled with scent and warmth, with something like the radiance of women. I spread out a dirty blanket and had her sit at the same time I did. Again I poured some wine into my cup from the half-gallon bottle.

"You men are lucky you're able to drink. You can forget everything."

I felt oppressed each time she moved her lovely legs in their silk stockings. I swore at myself, resisting, getting malicious even.

"We go on living, putting up with the humiliation. We're miserable. It's almost impossible to talk about."

"You don't say," I said with deliberate sarcasm.

"All we have is pain and humiliation." Suddenly her expression changed. She looked down, crying, her shoulders shaking. It annoyed me, yet I found her weeping charming enough. She was so gentle, so luscious, I couldn't help feeling sympathetic. Still, I wasn't going to let it get the better of me. She wasn't the only one that wanted to cry. If I could have, I might have tried a tear or two myself.

Yet her last remark, confirmed by her tears, had certainly turned out to be painful and humiliating for me too. I was drunk, but the pain I felt in her words refused to go away. I might reject them, ignore them, but I did feel their significance.

"I guess you know about Karajima. He was my husband's employer. What do you think of him, Mr. Sugi?"

Of course I knew how influential Karajima had been as a propagandist for the Japanese army. I had even seen him once, a handsome, well-built, fair-complected man. He was quite adept in his role as hero and gentleman. He wore tasteful ties, the best of clothes. In spite of myself, I could still accept his absolute self-confidence in treating others as sub-human. But I detested the way he played the sophisticate that knows every thought and emotion of the man he's with. It was stupid and depressing to be governed by such men of power. I had listened to his ranting voice and polished speeches, and even after spitting, I had been left with an aftertaste of something dirty. But when the war ended, I had forgotten him. I had forgotten his nastiness too. Once you started talking about nastiness, everything, yourself included, seemed nasty.

Her husband had worked in Karajima's printing division and later had been sent to Hankow. She had to remain alone in Shanghai. Karajima had offered to find her a room, and on the day they were to inspect it, she had gone to Karajima's office. When he had closed the door after her, he told her he had liked her from the first and violently threw his arms around her.

"Some of his workers ought to have been in the next room. I struggled and cried out, but no one came."

Though she might have been upset, she easily told me everything. Sometimes she stole a glance at me with those beautiful eyes of hers. Apparently she wanted to see if I was disturbed. I didn't let on that I was.

"He was like an animal," she said. Her words and look seemed to point an accusing finger at all men. I began thinking that if I had the power, I too—I even imagined that I was the one, not Karajima, who had those arms around her. What it had amounted to, at any rate, was that she had let him have her. She had lived on without even a thought of suicide.

"He had me every night after that." I kept staring at her body, and that searing pain I so patiently endured was possibly not unpleasant.

Out went a Karajima directive to Hankow, so her husband was stationed there until the end of the war. For the duration she had been Karajima's possession. Try as she might to hide from him, up he drove in his car. All the neighbors and her husband's friends knew about it, but no one stopped Karajima. When her husband had finally returned to Shanghai, he was totally emaciated from a terrible case of diarrhea. He was bedridden from the moment they had carried him off the truck. She was still kept by Karajima. He was generous with money and supplies. And sometimes he summoned her from the bedside of her stricken husband.

Her husband knew about their relationship and kept abusing her with it. She admitted the affair and asked him to forgive her. He refused to take the medicine purchased with Karajima's money, but without these funds they wouldn't have been able to afford electricity, water, even the sheets the invalid was lying on. He was tormented by the thought that his friends had so contemptuously forsaken him. It was even more painful to have her consoling him. He often kept telling her how detestable she was, yet he said she deserved pity.

"He's good. And so like a child."

She rolled her tear-drenched handkerchief into a ball, and opening her compact, she began putting on some make-up. She colored her slightly opened lips a fresh red, and as she powdered her face, her cheeks kept expanding and contracting. She was skillful, thorough.

"Well, how about now? Karajima I mean."

"I've definitely left him. I'm determined to hate him until I die. He'll be caught soon since he's a war criminal."

A cold, blunt expression was on her face. When she finished speaking, I picked up my cup. I felt my grim smile had somehow distorted my face. I couldn't explain why I felt only suspicious then.

Did she really despise Karajima? Wasn't there more pleasure than misfortune in having given herself to him? Her resolutions to the contrary, she had, however half-heartedly, kept up the relationship so that some desire other than monetary might have been behind it. In her eagerness to live comfortably, or if not that at least adequately, I doubted if there was any self-accusation or humiliation behind the affair.

I imagined she had the same detestable human instinct to survive by merely living, by forgetting all about pain and humiliation, especially when I was so well aware of that same instinct in me. The simple assault of her charm made me feel even more convinced of the truth of my observation. I felt sick, depressed.

"I believe in you. That's why I've gone into all of this."

She poured me some wine.

"But I really came on my husband's orders. He doesn't want to see any of his former friends. He's read your poems and believes in you. He wants to talk to you. Can you come just once as a favor to him? He'll be overjoyed. We're so miserable all the time! How about tomorrow? It's best to come early. The past few days he's been quite ill."

She had returned after making me promise to visit the next day. At the same time I was worrying about the dust blowing all over the concrete platform I was lying on, the particles sticking to my skin, which hadn't been exposed to a bath for a month, I kept wondering if I ought to go. It made little difference if I did or not. Of course, there was plenty to interest me. Yet whether I went or not didn't really matter. There wasn't a soul to accuse me of not doing something to help them out of their situation.

As I walked along, a youngster selling candy kept pestering me. I find these kids annoying except when I'm drunk. At a street corner I saw a Japanese having his hat stolen by a young delinquent. That troubled, weak-looking face should have evoked some sympathy in me, but all the same I couldn't help finding it disagreeable. He had run a few steps after the thief and had stopped, relinquishing his hat, stealing a glance at me. I couldn't help feeling disgusted by the sight of his helpless eyes.

I reached the woman's apartment, the Indian gatekeeper opening the iron gate for me. He looked sharply at my Japanese-resident armband. I rang the doorbell three doors beyond.

She seemed quite delighted as she ran down the stairs. It made me feel good to have caused that happiness in her. But I sensed the contradiction. She was too lively, quite out of keeping with the daily depression she had talked about.

As I took off my shoes at the threshold of the third floor apartment, I saw the signs of a sick person in the next room. He must have been lying in bed waiting for me. I felt the tension with which he must have waited. Perhaps it was a momentous interview for him. To me it shouldn't have meant a thing. I would have been disgusted with myself had I made it momentous when it was nothing of the sort.

She offered me a cushion to sit on, a colorful one.

The invalid was so very thin that the flatness of his covers made it seem as if his body wasn't under them. At first he turned sideways to look at me, but he glanced back up at the ceiling right away. At that very moment heavy wrinkles, like a monkey's or a baby's just after its birth, formed on his face. He was crying. It was embarrassing to see his neck and shoulders shaking as he tried to stop himself. His forehead and cheeks were an ugly red.

The tears made it difficult for him to speak. His voice often grew weak, gave out.

"At first he had only diarrhea, but then a bad case of pleurisy set in. The fluid's been accumulating, so his heart is slightly out of place."

Her own voice was clear and crisp as she handed her husband a handkerchief and forced him to take some water. I was surprised by the speed and energy of each of her actions. How conspicuously youthful the color of her arms, the roundness of her calves!

"I have no friends to confide in, so I thought . . . you . . . you would do me the favor of listening. It's . . . such a humiliating story . . . So humiliating I can't tell it to just anyone."

I forced myself to look at his face, which was too weak and dried up to convey the violence of his emotions. It wasn't a pretty sight, yet I was reminded of my own good health. It caused me to feel self-confident, even superior.

"I'm no saint. And I'm not a person you tell secrets to. But I thought I'd better come up to see you. It was rude of me just to drop in," I said.

"I . . . I don't expect you to do . . . anything in particular for me. I just wanted to talk to someone like you. It's unbearable to be lonely," he said.

He looked much younger than me. He had been good-looking. Those clear, nervous, agitated eyes seemed to be anticipating my thoughts way ahead of time. The slightest change in my face caused a shadow of fright to skirt across his eyes. For a fraction of a second a bright trace of insanity was glittering in that shadow.

"Lately my wife keeps saying she wants to die. Not me. I've . . . things I want to do."

"You have? I envy you. There's not a single thing I care to do."

"You're wrong. You don't realize . . . you're doing something already. I will too. I'll do . . . what I couldn't do during the war. I must do it! I've been totally useless . . . up to now. This time at least . . . I'll do what I want! I'll get strong! I'll do something . . . to destroy men like Karajima! If I can't . . . then I'm going to be a thousand times more evil than he is!"

The feverish and excited invalid had been overexerting himself by speaking. I knew he'd die soon. It was strongly foreshadowed by his yellow skin, by the bridge of his thin nose. It was obvious he'd never achieve any of his goals. I felt no pity, only oppression.

"I've no contact with anyone . . . any longer. They all . . . hate me. She's cheated on me, and . . . I'm living off the money she gets from him. It's not right . . . to let this pass! It's terrible . . . to be buried with such shame. Without wiping out even a small portion of it!"

Her husband's remarks about her made her glance at me, her beautiful eyebrows shaped into a frown.

"It's terrible . . . to be hated," he said, stopping momentarily to regulate his breathing. Then he recounted the dream he had the night before.

He had become a leper. The offensive odor given off by his mouth and body made him unbearable to his wife. Seeing her frightened face fill with hatred, he felt he was losing his mind. She ran away and he pursued her, catching her, holding her tight, that terrible odor coming out of his mouth and from his body so that he had finally become aware of his own stench. She spat at him, cursing him, then fled. His loneliness had made him cry out.

"When I woke up and found I'd only been dreaming, I felt I was lucky not to have leprosy. I really felt relieved my sickness was just ordinary."

"That's all you dream about, isn't it?" she said.

She looked tense as she prepared our tea. She was trying to smile but couldn't.

"My dream's about Karajima. I murder him in my dream."

She spoke casually, but her words sounded theatrical, melodramatic. They had the false ring of something feminine. Her husband's eyes became even more dismal.

"Mr. Sugi!" he suddenly cried out in a high thin voice. "I can't believe her! While Karajima's alive, I can't believe anything she says!"

Again he began crying. This time he didn't try to stifle it, crying openly, strange sounds in his throat mixed in with his words.

"You shouldn't talk like that in front of Mr. Sugi! It's too cruel! It's too much!"

"You keep on lying, that's why!"

"No matter what I say, you take it as a lie! I can't go on living like that!"

"You're living, aren't you? Aren't you living without a care in the world?"

His crying, staccato-like voice was a sick man's. But her tearful voice, even as she tried to suppress it, was bursting with the vigor of youth. Those two sobbing voices continued, sometimes intermingling, sometimes separating.

I took out one of the imported cigarettes I had received the day before. I had no matches, and she quickly pulled out a box of foreign-make from her pocket. She smiled, embarrassed by the tears on her cheeks.

"Oh, your tea's cold! Well, I'll serve you a nice lunch!"

I begged off since I wasn't feeling well. "It's my stomach."

"You're not going home!"

Her husband stopped crying, his expression changed, I imagined, since he thought I was about to leave at that moment. The look of sadness in his eyes seemed to indicate he didn't know what to do. It was as if I had suddenly struck him.

"I guess it's unpleasant to see something like this. But please stay. Just a little longer. We've no one to rely on. You're the only one we can trust."

"Oh, it hasn't been that unpleasant. It's just that I—" I wanted to say I couldn't stand being trusted. But I stopped for that would have sounded phony. In a situation of this sort, no matter how seriously I might have used such words, they would have been superficial. I had long stopped being in dead earnest about anything.

The couple recovered their composure and reverted to small talk. I sat ten more minutes before standing up.

"Can I join you for lunch next time? Frankly, the oysters I ate last night didn't agree with me."

The invalid was resigned, yet satisfied. A gentle expression was on his face.

"Please come again. I'll be waiting."

"I will. I'm glad I came. I like you both, more than I thought I would. I've really felt close to you."

That was true. I had sensed that they had been ashamed of themselves, that they were grappling, however hopelessly, with life in all seriousness. They had suffered between themselves long enough. After my words I saw a genuine look of pleasure light up the man's eyes. It wasn't an exaggeration to call it that. For quite a while I hadn't seen anything that simple and straightforward. He automatically offered me his thin hand, but he pulled it back fearfully.

She came with me when I was going downstairs. As she went alongside me, she was almost touching me.

"I was delighted you came today," she said, turning at once to face me before opening the downstairs door.

It seemed odd to hear her say, "Don't desert us, please. If you do, we won't forgive you! My husband will hold a grudge against you, and so will I!" Her words didn't sound that flippant, for apparently she had really given some thought to not being taken lightly. In fact, I found her words strangely profound.

"Don't be disgusted with me. Please protect me. Lend me some of your strength, and I'll come back to life again." She suddenly lowered her voice. "He may even die tomorrow. Understand?" Her eyelids narrowed over her eyes, which, ablaze with fever, were riveted on me.

As I went out the iron gate, firecrackers were going off everywhere, ringing in my ears. The next day would be the old calendar New Year. Red streamers were posted on the pillars and doors of every house. Some of the streamers had already been torn to shreds and were fluttering in the dust along the streets. Those fluttering scraps looked strangely vivid among the withered leaves and trash. A mother with her baby bundled up in a red cloth rode by on a rickshaw. Somehow those red colors seemed warm, mystical. As I walked back, I saw only the vivid reds of the festival. Men and women sat or walked or gathered in groups, their hands and faces dirty, their blue clothing worn out, filthy. Those men and women were trying to greet the New Year in some small way. For the first time apparently, I discovered that all these Chinese were living together, indifferent to me and other Japanese.

When I knocked at the back door, my landlady opened it. She smiled and then brought out a bottle of sake for me. It was a gift from the Japanese Self-Governing Council.

"You can celebrate the New Year," she said.

I took the bottle and went up to my room. The sake was sweet and thick. That night I had to finish a detailed report on a confiscated Japanese factory. I had to write in English or Chinese the name, serial number, and value of at least two hundred different kinds of precision machines. A catalogue and dictionary were on my crate. I made up my mind to buy some navel oranges with part of my fee. I would bring them as a gift when I visited the invalid.

By evening I was half-finished. I was drunk and tired. I felt a pain in my side, and my fingers could hardly move. My eyes kept getting weaker. Some men came into the alley to sell bread. A few came with pastry. All of them were Japanese reduced to becoming peddlers. No one bought anything from them.

Aoki dropped in. He wrote editorials for a Japanese newspaper.

"Why haven't you been to the Art Association meetings?"

"I haven't felt like it."

"The day after tomorrow the Cultural Division of the Chinese Control Office is calling everyone together. How about coming with me?"

"Can't. I've got documents to do."

I couldn't help feeling how superficial the word "culture" was. Aoki kept on talking about the Chinese People's Court and other topics. They didn't interest me either. All I could think about were those yellow oranges I had seen, lustreless, piled high.

When Aoki left, I crawled into bed and tried to doze off. It was windy out, and someone kept knocking at the back door. I had a hunch it was for me. It was annoying to be plagued with callers. I heard a woman's voice. The thought rushing through me that she had come drove away my heavy, uncomfortable drowsiness. I sat up in bed. She was coming, coming! I was drunk. There was no telling how callous or even violent I would become.

She opened the door, and I heard her brown raincoat rustling, her outer clothing visible through it. Small drops of water sparkled minutely on her coat. "Just a second!" she said. She stepped over my bedding on the mats, unfastened the window, and quietly opened it. The dark grating was drenched with rain. "It's all right. He didn't follow me." She closed the window after peering down into the alley. "I bumped into Karajima on the street. I told him I was going to your place, and he said he'd come with me. I broke away from him and ran here."

Her wet cheeks were pale. She looked tired.

"Is he still hanging around?"

"Yes. I even met him the last time I was here."

Her face was quite strained.

"He can't forget me. He said so himself. Strange, isn't it? —I brought you a snack. Have it with your sake."

"You came out just for that?"

"Yes. I really wanted you to have it." She took some teabiscuits from a black box. They were fried brown and looked homemade.

"Tomorrow's the New Year. I wonder if I can come see you?" she said.

I hadn't mentioned her sick husband, nor had she made the slightest reference to him.

"Quite free and easy, am I not?"

"Yes, free and easy."

"Perhaps I'm slightly insane."

"A little," I said.

But I had my mind on Karajima. I wanted a detailed account of him. In spite of her reluctance *he* was what fascinated me.

"He's really all steamed up about you after all."

"It looks that way." She showed her annoyance at my having mentioned it. "That conceited thing went so far as to ask *me* to save him! I was dumbfounded. It's too late for jokes like that. With the war crimes he's going to be charged with, he's really losing his mind."

"You mean he asked *you* to help him?"

"Odd, isn't it? A man asking a woman to help him out!"

That surprised me too. My only impression of Karajima was as the man of power you can't help despising. I had thought of him as an annoying insect, not as a man with feelings similar to my own. I didn't really loathe him—that is, I didn't really think about him. So I wasn't quite ready to accept her words at face value.

"It's not even a question of saving him. Since it's absolutely impossible for me to. Even if I could, I don't want to be dragged into the mess he's in. I definitely left him, you know, when the war ended."

She sounded phony to me. That was what she had said at our last meeting. I suspected her words were false, but she probably hoped they didn't sound that way.

"It strikes me he's not the type to scream for help. It's just that he needs you."

"I don't know about that. At any rate, I'm afraid. While he's alive, I can't sleep." She gave me the same look she had used at the door of her apartment. "Will you protect me? Will you love me? I love you."

"You mean—?" I might have felt overjoyed, but even then I wanted to equivocate. It was all so new. In contrast to me, she looked absolutely certain.

"I'm really in a difficult situation. You see that, don't you? So I'm quite serious. Don't lie. If you love me, say so. A half-hearted reply won't settle anything. I'm honestly in love with you."

"I love you. Of course I do. But maybe I can't protect you. I can't protect anyone."

"You love me then?"

"Yes."

"That's enough for me. That's fine. If *only* you do. Well, perhaps it's difficult for you to protect me." There was no malice in her smile. "You do seem lazy."

"I haven't had any experience along that line."

She grabbed my shoulders and stood up and kissed me. Her lips were quite soft. When she was about to move away, I put my arms around her and gave her a fairly hard kiss.

I felt she had planned this scene. I was certain she was following a script. But that didn't upset me. I didn't even feel I was being taken in. In fact, the thought that she was precious to me kept steadily increasing.

"But can you love me? Can you love a woman Karajima had?" Her eyes were riveted on me, her face oddly static, almost blank, because of her own passion.

"Love me! Think of me with pity! Oh, I want him killed! I wish someone would kill him now, right away!" Clinging to me and drawing her face close and sobbing quietly, she blurted out her threat. Apparently she couldn't control her feelings. All the while I continued holding her against me, I clearly recalled Karajima's face. He was no longer unrelated to me. Through her I was conscious of his body. He came so surprisingly close I could actually smell his breath.

"Before you said Karajima acted like he was coming here, didn't you?"

"Yes." She seemed caught up in some dark thought. "That's been his intention for a long time, I think. I'm sure of it."

"Alone? why?"

"Probably to talk something over with you."

"But I don't know him that well."

"I didn't know you either, did I? Isn't that true? He suspects I'm relying on you. He's quite desperate. We have no time to lose."

"Is it that bad?"

"Yes. You've never had your life hanging in the balance, have you?"

"Sure. But now it's different. Now I'm hanging only on the side of life. I'm not on a tightrope anymore."

"Sometimes a man risks his life even when he doesn't intend to. Can you kill Karajima?"

"... Yes. But I don't want to."

"Don't you think he deserves it?"

"I guess so. There aren't many men who don't deserve killing."

She smiled faintly and seemed to be even more lost in thought. In spite of her eager and naive way of speaking, that look came from the intense and instinctive way she was living, feeling. It seemed to me we were both saturated with darkness and violence.

"What's this? A poem?" She picked up "The Man Shot to Death" and read what I had written. Already it no longer appealed to me. Today I had fallen, collapsed. When I compared myself at this moment with the poem itself, I found it was annoyingly smooth and superficial. I had to make it deeper.

"What do you think about every day?" A trace of roguery was in her gentle smile. "Even *you* do some thinking?"

"No," I said, reluctantly smiling.

"Will you come see me again?"

I recalled the bedridden invalid. I saw she did too. "I'll bring him some oranges."

"Good. I'll be waiting." She pressed my fingers firmly. "But don't force yourself to since I'll be coming here."

"I'll definitely come at least once more." I deliberately kept myself from walking her back. I had had enough uniqueness for one day. It was already more than enough.

2

A Chinese sentinel rebuked me the day after New Year's. I was not only drunk. I was guilty. On the way to the Japanese Self-Governing Council is a post with a sentinel on duty. A regulation requires the Japanese to bow in front of him. I had often passed and bowed. If I was alone, it was an easy thing to do. But I was quite selfconscious when several men and women lowered their heads in rapid succession as they walked ahead of me or when I was talking to an acquaintance and happened to pass by. That was the moment I felt myself resisting. Many Chinese often came to a standstill and watched our performance. For the most part, the guards didn't give us any outlandish orders, didn't even shout at us.

That morning a well-built Japanese about thirty years old was walking ahead of me. Squaring his shoulders and apparently marching along steadily, he seemed charged with physical energy. He was wearing a business suit, but he looked like an ex-military man. His hat still on and with self-conscious dignity, he was about to go by the sentinel. Then the man violently cleared his throat, spat, and walked on. The short sentinel stopped just as he was about to shout at the man. That was when I came along. I was hatless. Not a soul was around, but I didn't bow. The sentinel called me to a halt. I crossed the street and came over to him. "Why didn't you bow? Stand there," he said. The voice of that short, young sentinel wasn't even threatening. He even looked like a nice young man. Standing at attention, I said in Chinese, "I'm very sorry." My drunkenness made me sway. "All right, move along," he said suddenly, turning aside. I didn't feel particularly embarrassed. In fact, standing at attention in the morning in front of a sentinel on a street in a strange land and bowing and apologizing seemed to exactly fit my personality. I understood the feelings of that young man who hadn't taken off his hat and had walked past the guard while purposely clearing his throat so strenuously. But those feelings could no longer exist in me. I had certainly broken the regulations often enough, but not because I had wanted to. I had simply been careless or lazy. I felt it natural to be rebuked and punished for violating laws. But even if I were rebuked or punished, I had almost become indifferent to it. I had made up my mind that I would often be scolded.

Immediately after the war I had frequently broken through blockades the authorities had set up. The crossroads were watched by groups of ten or more soldiers and policemen. I would cut through those blockades on my bicycle. They would shout at me from all sides and rush to grab my bike. Pedaling for all I was worth, I would shout back at them. All of a sudden the thick rope stretched across the road would strike against my arms. A burning pain. The skin would be scraped off my arms. The rope would slip away from me. So near would a few of the guards come that they almost grabbed my bike. I'd ignore them and make my bike race on. At that moment it would dawn on them that I was one of those half-cocked drunks. Then they'd only pretend they were after me. I'd escape with the night winds rushing by, and I'd end up at the edge of the French Settlement.

Sometimes they caught me. There were places, for example Japanese elementary schools, which, before we knew it, had been confiscated in order to house Chinese soldiers on their arrival from Chungking. Once I pedaled along a dark gravel road and was suddenly warned to halt. A gun-toting soldier stood in the dark. I kept on going right past him. Unfortunately, gravel roads aren't for fast riding. A soldier grabbed my handlebars. Instantly my bike fell sideways, and I rolled over on the ground. He held me by the arms and led me inside a gate. A table was set up in front of a tent, and someone, an officer apparently, was sitting there. Only that spot was glaringly bright.

"Who are you?"

"A Japanese."

"Japanese?"

Then his voice became mild. "What have you been up to?"

"Drinking at a friend's."

"Why didn't you stop when you were told to? Weren't you given an order? If you had stopped, we wouldn't be blaming you."

"No, you wouldn't."

They let me go and I went out the gate, picked up my bike, and rode on. Pedaling off after something like that, I always failed to keep my bike steady since I couldn't handle it as I wished. Somewhere one of its parts would be twisted or unfastened. But already I would have forgotten the incident. All I cared about was staying on that bike I could hardly control.

Right after the war I still had that childlike quality of performing such exciting feats, of having fresh adventures. Now, nothing like that remained in me. Those episodes were foolish acts that came from doing what was beyond my power. I had no physical stamina. I had no power by which to give blow for blow. I was only deluding myself in feeling I could do anything. Pretending to be strong is unnecessary when you know your pretense is useless. You can live even if you don't pretend you're strong. They'll pardon you if you apologize. Everything will work out all right if you just let the bowing stop being painful. And even if it is, everything will work out for you if you persuade yourself it's not painful. It's easier to live by obeying the regulations. At least it's essential to be thought of as someone who does. But when I'm drunk, I forget that injunction. I imitate the strong man. Then when I sober up, I'm contemptuous of my extravagant delusions. Still, I can't deny in my heart of hearts that I'm forever concealing a deep-seated desire to perform the actions of a superman. In some meaningful way living is related to strength. To live is to survive. In one form or another a man lives because of his strength. I had merely been existing in order to exist. But even in existing, I wondered if I hadn't been wanting, thirsting, for strength. "Can you kill Karajima?"

". . . Yes. But I don't want to."

A number of times since that night I had asked myself if I could kill him. I imagined various ways of doing it. I didn't feel I had to kill him, but it was hardly to be expected that I couldn't put him out of the way. Without letting myself get too keyed up, I had been able to feel the hardness of his head and chest, the thickness of his flesh.

That morning after I had been rebuked and pardoned, I went on toward the Self-Governing Council, and while walking alone, I suddenly began wondering if someone as worthless as me could kill Karajima. I could actually feel my strength, comparing it to the physical power of the young sentinel, the well-built Japanese who had passed without removing his hat, and Karajima. I imagined the weight of flesh and bone, the warmth and sweat and blood, charging into me. I felt how much life force I had even down to the most delicate parts of my arms and legs. Only then did I suddenly realize I was actually alive.

I stopped off at a market, a dreary, white concrete building two-stories high. Usually the square thick pillars lined up on the first floor were hidden by mobs of lively customers, but now those columns were nakedly exposed. Many of the Chinese shops inside were closed. The entire street was just about cleared of morning mist. It looked dead out. After I bought some of the oranges I had previously seen, I went up to visit the invalid.

"I was too upset last time," he said.

He was in better spirits. His wife had gone out. I found an unfinished pattern of brown woolen yarn still spread out where she had been sitting the time before. I imagined she was meeting Karajima somewhere.

I untied my package, took out an orange, and cut it with the jack-knife I kept in my pocket.

When the invalid bit into the slice I gave him, the juice trickled from his mouth to his chin. He was in bed, his face turned away to the side. The juice ran down onto the towel covering his ice-filled rubber pillow.

"Ever since you came to see me, I've felt better. I can probably sail on the hospital ship if I keep up at this rate."

"Sure you can. A ship's on its way."

I knew about these ships since I had been asked to write letters for embarkation.

"They said we'd be among the first to be sent back." That meant his wife would go as his attendant. It was natural she should, but somehow I couldn't picture her going with him.

"Haven't you any intention of returning yet, Mr. Sugi?"

"No. What would be the use even if I did? They say there's nothing to eat or drink in Japan."

"I live in the country. I don't expect to run short of anything. Stay with us for six months if you wish."

"Well, it's generous of you."

"Was your house destroyed?"

"Last March."

"What about your family?" he asked.

"There were two others, but they're dead. No one's left now."

My mother and younger sister were dead. After I got all mixed up during the war and even later, I couldn't remember what they looked like when I had met them the day before I had left for Shanghai. I had forgotten everything, the clothes they wore, what we talked about, whether we cried or laughed on saying good-bye. But when the invalid's frail voice had referred to my family, I suddenly felt I needed them. I was jolted, though only for a fraction of a second. I had no particular envy of the safe, peaceful homeland he was treasuring. In fact, I felt that kind of comfort couldn't last long. Feelings like that didn't belong to Shanghai. They were outside the turbulence of her everyday life, outside my own feelings in this turbulence.

He seemed quite sympathetic, but I was looking at the raincoat hanging against the wall. She had worn it when she had visited me.

"She's gone out shopping for a while, but she'll be back soon."

"Have you quarreled since?"

"Oh—quarreled?" The light vanished from his face. Suddenly he looked pathetically frail. "Yes. Even yesterday, late at night. Eventually she became . . . hysterical. Have you ever seen the face of someone that's hysterical? It's really horrible. The eyes turn up . . . the face gets white as a sheet. It becomes totally transformed. At these times they forget

about . . . being self-conscious. They shout. Their voices get terribly loud
. . . so loud the entire neighborhood can hear. The Chinese living across
the street from us . . . definitely heard her . . . since they opened their
shutters."

"Does she get that way often?"

"Yesterday was really unusual. She was almost like a savage. When
you see it . . . you actually get sick of human beings. You don't feel
hatred, but horror. No matter how much love or pity you try to feel, you
can't, just at that time only."

There were tears on his cheeks. Letting them fall calmed him.

"It's impossible to overcome her hysteria . . . unless you get that way
yourself. It's impossible . . . unless you believe she's not human . . . that
she's an animal. And inevitably that's just how I come to feel. Look
where she scratched me." He pointed to the side of his neck. "She tried
to strangle me. I threw a glass at her and a teacup. I'd have let her kill
me if she wanted to . . . but she didn't try to go that far. In fact, it
would have been a relief . . . to get rid of all the pain and sadness I've
felt. Sometimes it's unbearable . . . just to be quietly alone with her."

I handed him the towel by his pillow, and I sliced up another orange.
He had only eaten a quarter of his. I was sucking the juice of my
second.

"Sometimes I wondered . . . if she'd kill me. Even when there wasn't
the slightest clue she wanted to . . . I deliberately tried to think she did.
Of course I didn't have a single thing to go on since she was taking care
of me. Looking after me. And even while I wondered, I wasn't afraid,
perhaps . . . because I'd come so close to dying anyway. I merely thought
she'd have quite a job if she tried to. Instead of thinking about being
killed, I thought about the effort . . . it takes to kill. It didn't seem possible . . . anyone could go on living after killing someone. To be killed is
all right, but I couldn't stand the thought . . . of someone hating me that
much to do it."

"Does she hate you that much? I doubt it."

"You're right. She doesn't. It's the contempt I have for her that she
can't stand. If I stare absentmindedly at the ceiling, she says . . . I'm
showing my contempt. It's true that occasionally I've been thinking of
her affair with Karajima . . . sometimes even thinking she's so completely
satisfied with his body that I can see her performing the act. But I finally
end up forgiving her. Pitying her. But she can't believe that. The more
silent I am, the more I'm tormenting her . . . she says. She says that in
spite of my illness, I'm getting her so nervous with my deceptive silence
she can hardly breathe. She claims . . . that's how I'm getting my revenge.
True, sometimes I've had that kind of rotten feeling, sometimes getting a
real kick out of having tormented her. But more often than not, frankly,

I've just about had all the exhaustion I can take. It's humiliating to have to admit it, but I've even tried to forget everything that's happened. Tried to think nothing has. I've even forgiven Karajima. Once I return to Japan, I'll forget everything. Just the two of us will live on together. Erasing everything in our past. It's out of the question they'll allow Karajima to come back. So just the two of us will return . . . to our earlier peaceful years. That's the sort of weak, spineless, resigned state I'm in . . . most of the time. I pass my days in that hazy, quiet way. But she gets annoyed and eventually she's terrible. Like yesterday."

Again he started to talk, but stopped suddenly. A painful expression was on his face. It had really been an effort to come out with these difficult words.

"Yesterday . . . she went shopping for about an hour. She looked awfully ill . . . when she came back. I knew Karajima had got his hands on her. I asked her about it, but she refused to answer. All she said was that nothing was wrong. She boiled some water and prepared supper in the kitchen and brought it in. I tried to help her out . . . by talking about our living quietly once we returned, about everyone's suffering because of Japan's defeat, about it being better for those who can rest to take it easy. I even told her . . . I was getting to where I could love her again. My mind was getting back to normal, forgetting everything. And then in a joking way, I asked if Karajima hadn't merely done to her what I had. Wasn't it simply . . . a trivial act between a man and a woman? Suddenly she glared at me. She had been looking down, crying. All of a sudden she edged up to my pillow . . . and straining her voice . . . said, 'Let's separate please!' What? I asked. 'Let's separate! Right after we get home!' Did she realize . . . what she was asking? All she wanted was for us to separate. She'd get on the ship with me, but once we were home, she'd leave right away. I told her to stop being ridiculous. Hadn't I said . . . I'd forget everything . . . that we'd begin over again? But she didn't want that. She wanted a separation! Suddenly all I could feel was anger. The anger and pain I was feeling was all I could think about . . . when I realized the terrible things she was saying . . . to a sick man. I threw the water in my glass at her . . . and she stood up. Then I threw my glass and teacup at her. Abandoning me, aren't you? . . . I asked. That's right, isn't it! I understand! If you aren't, why begin saying such things. . . . when I'm this sick? If you feel that way, get out! Get out of here! She looked at me and threw off her jacket. Suddenly she turned toward me. Her face had already changed . . . to something rigid . . . as if she were glaring at me. She said . . . she'd just slept with Karajima. She pulled off her skirt. She said she hadn't wanted to . . . but that he'd come for her in his car. He'd done . . . all sorts of things to her. She was pressing against me from above the covers. She continued shouting out their sexual acts . . .

She recklessly let everything be known . . . saying once he'd done it one way, once another. Her weight against me . . . her terrible screams . . . they almost made me faint. I didn't care about the sordid details. But her shrill voice . . . and bloodshot eyes kept terrifying me. The way she exposed her teeth, her hot heavy breath! She began strangling me . . . and screaming, 'A man like you, like you!' I felt something superhuman . . . was attacking me . . . a primitive savage or an ape. Finally her voice got all choked up, her throat heaving, as if she were going to vomit. When she eventually stood up, she slipped on her coat, closed the door, and ran down the steps. I was so exhausted . . . I felt I'd stop breathing any moment. I was trembling so much . . . I thought I was going to pass out. My one regret was that I didn't have the energy to bring her back . . . as she walked through the streets—it's cold at night, you see. I fell asleep . . . crying. When I opened my eyes in the morning, she was changing the ice in my pillow."

For a while I heard loud firecrackers. It seemed as if they had ripped open the dry air.

"She kept herself busy working, as if she'd forgotten all about the night before. I didn't feel like saying anything. We glided over the surface of things with small talk. One step and we might have broken through that surface . . . and the confusion would have been endless. It was as if I'd already lost even the energy to suffer. The physical pain of sickness must be all I can suffer from. Yes, I'd return to Japan. At least she'd probably take me."

The languid sounds of an organ drifted by from the elementary school administered like the temple schools of old. The young girls were singing a melancholy Japanese song, an old one usually sung with the koto. As I listened to the invalid, I felt the profound human link between the sick man and his wife. That painful and intense link of suffering made me an outsider after all, completely separated from them. My own feelings at present were quite uninvolved in comparison. But to be as I was might have meant lack of depth, perhaps merely avoidance of pain. In avoiding pain, I was probably indifferent to it. I wondered if I could escape the consequences of that kind of attitude.

"You better go back to Japan. They say a ship's on its way and will be here within a week."

"Look, Mr. Sugi," the invalid said, his glistening eyes reflecting his feelings. "My wife's been wondering if you'd help us out by going back on the same ship with us."

"On a hospital ship? Is that possible?"

"Maybe. If an invalid's carried into the ship on a stretcher, apparently someone outside the family can go. Please come with us if it's not inconvenient, if you haven't anything to keep you here."

"There's nothing holding me back. It's just that it's useless to return."
"If it's convenient then, come to my home with us. Another thing—"
He broke off temporarily, averting his glance by looking at the ceiling.
" —My wife. She likes you."

I saw his lips tremble slightly. I remembered the softness of his wife's lips on that rainy day. I had the feeling he already knew about us. When he saw I was going to say something, he said hurriedly, "Lately, that's what she keeps telling me. Just to look at you makes her feel safe. It's an odd thing to say, but don't be offended . . . She really likes you."

"I like her too," I had to say. "I do, because she has some qualities that are just overwhelming."

"Oh you do like her, don't you?" His laugh was thin and weak. That laughing voice went through me far more coldly and ominously than his crying voice had. It revealed how close he was to dying.

I knew he was testing me. On the other hand, it was ridiculous to think he was. I was simply embarrassed in a fumbling sort of way. His words, in contrast to mine, were decisive, his voice low like the utterance of a prophecy or prayer.

"The words of the sick before they die are true. They keep thinking about things day and night."

I wanted to respond with something witty. But strong words, clever words, were futile. I merely wanted to conceal how uneasy and agitated I was. Yet that was futile too.

"I don't understand it," I said, "but the two of you and I have ended up in a relationship we can't get out of."

"Yes. You see that, do you? And with Karajima too, you've ended up that way."

I left the invalid before his wife returned.

Outside the New Year celebrating continued. Two men in gaudy red and green costumes were dancing on a riverboat. They looked like the strolling comic dancers we have in Japan. The audience of children, and the men themselves, seemed happy.

When I got home my landlady told me the woman had come. "About an hour after you left. She's quite pretty, that one!"

An artist-friend picked me up in the afternoon. We went out drinking, and instead of going home later, I walked to his house in the suburbs. Some reporters were there for an all-night drinking session.

The next day I toured the outskirts of the city with my friend. I noticed a beer company under British management, boats on the river, the extensive scenery of the desolate winter. Though we were in one of the areas where the Japanese were forced to live, it was far from the city, and the fields and creeks and roads stretched far into the distance under the movement of the vast sky. A long time had passed since I had seen the naked earth and trees in winter colors. It refreshed me to steep myself in them.

The artist was able to make dinner for us after selling a rug in his downstairs room. He got a hot bath ready for me by burning some sliding doors and clapboard. He had already received permission to return home and was merely waiting for notification of his departure. Everyone was talking about repatriation to Japan. Each of the Japanese zones was nervously agitated. In these lonely places in the suburbs, the tension of those returning or remaining was even more intense when they talked about it.

"What are you going to do?"

"I may find myself going back right away," I said. I hadn't forgotten the invalid's request. "But I'm not certain yet. It depends on the way things go."

"It's hard to leave. Shanghai's such a good place."

"It's not a question of good or bad. Somehow I feel I still have things I ought to do." As if warning myself, I had replied carefully. I felt that if I returned without doing something here, I'd have lost a precious chance. I had a premonition of the thrill I would feel in grabbing a heavy lump of truth dirtied with tears and blood. Before I went back, if I hadn't grabbed that unpleasant lump, limp like a pig's guts, it would disappear forever. I had only to take one step forward. And I was probably destined to take just one step more out of bounds. Generally no one has that kind of foreknowledge. But the invalid and his wife knew it, and I did too. Perhaps even Karajima did. With these thoughts in mind, I had been eating slowly, listening to the discussion of art that had been going on. In my drunken state I saw everything around me as charged with meaning. I continued drinking. And as I did, "human existence" revealed itself to me in colors far more thick and sensual than those brilliant touches in my friend's oil painting propped up in the corner. That image of "human existence" surrounded me, threatening me, glittering, making noises, burning in whirls. I decided to hurl myself into it.

I stayed two nights and returned to the city with the reporters in their three-wheeled car. Quite a few Chinese workers in gray overalls were sitting in the street in front of a theatre. The water-drenched asphalt glittered brightly. Pedestrians stepped quickly to the side to avoid the laborers. Twice as many soldiers as usual were opposite the theatre. With their pistols or rifles in hand, they had a murderous expression on their tanned faces. Some Japanese, talking together, looked on from behind an iron gate.

I left the car and went back home. My landlady told me the workers, who hauled lumber from the river, had been out to retrieve a group of laborers arrested by the Security Force. Guns had gone off, and some men had been wounded. I felt as if the stench of violent men and cruel disagreements was closing in on me.

"Right in the middle of everything that woman turned up again. Just when the guns were shooting."

My landlady was annoyed at my having stayed out two nights without notifying her. "She came yesterday and again today. It's a shame! Well, where've you been hanging out?"

She was fanning a fire under a small portable stove. Then, as if remembering something, she suddenly searched through her apron pockets. "By the way, this person showed up," she said, handing me his namecard. It was Karajima's. He had scrawled in pencil some instructions to meet him that night at the Golden Restaurant.

I went up to my room, crept under the bedding I had left spread out on the mats, and slept for about two hours. My room was cold and damp, and I was tired. I could still feel the jolt of the three-wheeled car as it ran through the streets jammed with excitement. But I was caught up in a calm sweet sleep. I had conceived a pure affection for the invalid's wife. I was gentle, obedient. The radiant, childlike smile on her face was totally innocent. Only the two of us were alive, no one else. Our minds were at rest. To be so much at ease was new for me. I wondered how that was possible. The odors, like those of a midsummer noon, were sweet. "It's all right," she said. "You don't understand? You do!" she said, frowning in her usual way, scolding me gently.

"I understand," I replied, but I really didn't. Then my dream ended. Sitting up in bed, I wondered why we had been so much at ease at that moment. I finally concluded we had probably died.

It was way past my seven o'clock appointment. The Japanese curfew was at eight. In the darkness I hurried to the tavern. The Golden Restaurant was quite small. Most of its customers were Japanese, and I had often gone there. It served cheap tidbits along with sake—beans, radishes, and the like. That was why the newspapermen made it their hangout. Sometimes you even had to stand and wait. But after the New Year even the line of regular customers had thinned out because no one had very much left to sell. That was why the tavern nowadays was deserted. The blank-faced owner and waiters were seen with nothing to do but rest with their hands holding up their chins.

As I pushed open the door and went in, I heard a deep voice shouting. A group of three waiters was looking in. The long tavern was so narrow that walking through was inconvenient. Light brown jugs were stacked to the ceiling on one side, and the remainder of the room had five or so square tables in it. At the innermost table were two Japanese quarreling. The one with his back toward me was clearly Karajima. The light kept me from recognizing the other at first, but on looking more closely, I saw it was Aoki. Karajima had grabbed the smaller man by the neck and was pressing him against the edge of a table. Aoki's small dark face had lost its color. Aoki, who was a born fighter, was making as much fuss as a child, his face as twisted as if he'd been crying.

"Maybe you think you've beaten me, but I won't admit to defeat by force!"

"By what then?"

Karajima's large, radiant profile was alive with arrogance. He turned in my direction. For the first time I noticed his shoulders and waist under the leather jacket he was wearing were really quite large. "All of you talk big, but you good-for-nothing bastards can't do a thing. What's there to win by if not by force? I'm busy. Get going."

After pulling Aoki close to him, Karajima shoved him toward the entrance. He bumped into tables and chairs and staggered toward the group of waiters. Then he fell backwards on the floor, but got up immediately. Grabbing one of the bottles of wine lined along the counter, Aoki screamed, "Bastard!" and again rushed at Karajima. The raised bottle was violently warded off, striking a wall and shattering. Some drops of wine landed on my face. Karajima, his own face red, grabbed Aoki by the shoulders and easily lifted him. With his feet flapping in the air, Aoki was thrown through the entrance and out into the street. All that time Karajima hadn't looked at me or the waiters. As he went back to his seat, his face was tense yet sullen. He sat down so violently his enormous body made his chair squeak. Noticing Aoki's hat on the table, he hurled it toward the waiters. His blunt "Take that!" sounded as if the waiters were inanimate, as if he were flinging a dog a bone.

"Warm some sake!" Karajima demanded, but the next moment, after rearranging his chopsticks and other things that had been upset, he tried to soften his expression. Then he offered me a seat.

On the table were many expensive side-dishes glittering with oil, dishes I had never been able to order. He poured some wine into his own cup from the lead bottle the waiter had brought him. "Lousy!" Karajima said after tasting a drop. He told the waiter to bring him something else. Karajima's way of speaking not only revealed his contempt for the waiter but indicated how the man was considered less than human. Karajima's words contained the extreme of indifference, as if he were flattening the waiter with a flyswatter. Once, during the war, a similar act of Karajima's at a publishers' convention had annoyed me. He had mounted the platform and had deliberately leered out at the gathered faces. Then he extended his arm to point to someone seated in a certain row. "Who are you?" Karajima had demanded. The youth, seventeen or eighteen, had apparently been sent to sit in during an interval one of the publishers couldn't attend. The substitute became thoroughly confused.

"Get out of here! Right away! Punks like you wouldn't understand even if you can listen! Get out!" Karajima looked as if he were about to spit or do something worse. He began his speech in a theatening tone, "The Japanese spirit . . ." Already he had forgotten his rebuke to the young man. Even the action of scolding, Karajima refused to acknowledge as an act. He exuded the self-confidence that he and the young man were totally separate, that the existence of persons not to Karajima's taste was not to be allowed. How I had hated the power behind his self-confidence, the eloquence of his speech, the authority he represented. I had felt his kind of individuality was phony, merely the dark, hopeless, reverse side of authority. Yet I had thought I myself was weaker than an insect, someone who couldn't even touch that authority with the tip of a finger.

But now, right in front of me, sat Karajima, who had lost his influence. If I felt hatred for him, it was for his individuality, not for the authority he had represented.

"Nice of you to come," he said, greedily munching on some roast pork and shrimp. "I know quite well the contempt you have for me."

When I emptied my cup, he filled it immediately.

"Please help yourself. You don't want to? Don't you want to enjoy my hospitality?"

I tried one of the delicacies. It dissolved at the tip of my tongue, spread over my entire mouth, and pleasantly disappeared down my throat.

He chuckled and smiled slightly. "You're interesting. I've always thought so." His sly, sharp eyes were feeling me out. "What's your opinion of me? I mean of me as a man?"

". . . During the war I didn't feel you were human. I hadn't the slightest interest in you. Recently, though, I have."

"How come?"

". . . Because of her, of course." I deliberately spoke as if it were troublesome to. He put down his chopsticks, emptied his cup, filled it again.

"You've heard everything? She's told you everything? Well. What do you think of my mistress?"

My face indicated I didn't want to talk about it.

". . . All right, if you don't want to tell me. Well, drink up!" He brought his face close to mine in the anxiously overpolite manner of a man with a trick up his sleeve. His skin had a quite healthy glow.

"What was all that about with Aoki?" I asked.

"Aoki? The bastard came in while I was drinking and sat himself down at a table near the entrance. He had the nerve to bitch in a low voice that I was still 'pissing around.' I kept warning him. He's a coward, you know, but he still does a lot of talking."

"He's probably not the only one surprised you're still 'pissing around.' "

Karajima came out with an angry crude look, but immediately returned to his pose of deliberately being nonchalant. The way he licked his lips, oily from the pork, you'd have thought he was trying to keep something nauseous from sticking in his throat.

"That's right! It's not just Aoki. All you bastards feel that way. All of you complain like feeble women. You know you'd be better off if I died. But not one of you bastards is brave enough to put me out of the way. Aoki's a punk, but at least he's stupidly frank. He challenged me even though he hasn't any physical strength. But you could see what he really was when he was working in the Rice Control Agency. He ran his ass off for the company tormenting the hell out of the Chinese by monopolizing the sale of rice. He was inefficient, stupid, scared. You can sum him up by saying he was being used, that he could never be in a position to use others. No matter what he does, he hasn't the power to control men. The way I see it, whether he lives or dies, his existence means nothing. How I despise bastards like him! But I won't allow them to despise me. I guess they'll charge me with war crimes. Maybe the Chinese government will throw the book at me. But you bastards can't. You never will. Understand? Never."

He came out with a slight laugh. Rather than call it an impudent laugh, I found it dismally profound.

"The way you bastards live is also meaningless. For the most part, you're penniless. Your retirement pay gets you nowhere. Each day prices are doubling. The best you can do is sponge off the crumbs of Chinese merchants and bank presidents. Guys come in for handouts even from me! I've some gold bars I've put away. If I dispose of them one at a time, I'll be able to enjoy myself for two or three years. If I deposit them with a few Chinese moneylenders, the interest alone will support me comfortably for the rest of my life. You heard about that Japanese who worked for the Chinese Railway and wrote some nonsense about dying of starvation, didn't you? A jerk writing that kind of stuff won't die like that in a million years. If you're dying of starvation, you starve in a corner somewhere without saying anything about it. First of all, what's the good of a real man stupidly announcing his own worthlessness by talking of starving to death? If he wants to die like that, why not? I've no money to hand over to bastards that want to go on living by capitalizing on death by starvation. Let them rail at me, hate me. They're free to. But what the hell can they do? Since they're weak, they're weak. That's all there is to it. Let them rationalize if they want to. But go anywhere in the world and you see that it's useless to rationalize. At any rate, I've my own power. They had none from the beginning. They're just ghosts that have nothing to do with money, with power— No matter how much they may have wanted to seize power, the fact remains they havn't been able to. I've lost my authority. Now I'm definitely the underdog. There's no comparing myself to what I was before. But the authority I had I got by my own strength. Do you see? Understand? That power remains in me undiminished!"

I found his words more plausible than his wartime speeches. But the voice was the same. His strident insistence hadn't changed. I briefly glanced at the waiters. Sometimes looking outside, sometimes wiping tables, they seemed to say, without revealing it on their faces, that the damn Japs were arguing again.

"That's enough. I don't want to hear anymore. I was fed up enough listening to your wartime crap."

My voice was comparatively quiet. The initial excitement had passed. The force of his conviction made me even wearier, more depressed.

"That's just like you. Always sarcastic. That's all you're good for."

"That's not all," I said.

"Not all? Well, then, what are you going to do?"

"I may be a weakling. But I don't feel you've any monopoly on power. You're not so different from me, are you?"

"No?" he said, laughing in finding me either contemptible or pathetic. "You mean I'm no different from any of you bastards? No? You're welcome to think so if you want. What a sweet guy you are! Me, in a few days from now I'm going to take her to the French Settlement and hide out there. I'll take her even if I have to drag her. I'll let you in on something. I don't have much longer to live. I've no regrets about that. But what I want to do I do. I'm in love with her. I really am. I'm not handing her over to anyone while I'm alive. Even if she hates me. She does already. She did from the first. But even while hating me, I probably gave her enough satisfaction. Now, though, it's different. She's changed. She keeps talking about some stupid nonsense that I don't have anything spiritual in me the way you have. Maybe that's how it is— But I can't give her up. That's why I'm locking her up."

"Do you think you can get away with it?"

"I haven't the slightest doubt about that. I still have four or five men working for me." He had the shrewd look of a detective or an MP or a public prosecutor. All over that magnificent face of his with its imposing features was an expression that easily and customarily subjugates the opposition.

"Some foreigners can help me hide out in the Settlement. I invited you today just to let you know. And depending on the circumstances, I intended to kill you. That's the truth. Even now I have that intention. And you probably came suspecting that. I had a feeling you did the minute I turned around while I was knocking the hell out of Aoki and I saw you come in. I'm a real expert on intuition. Besides, I'm not a fool. When I saw you come in, I thought of an honor student in elementary school boldly venturing forth to the home of the class troublemaker."

"And I thought of you as a high school bully picking on a freshman."
We laughed at the same time and stopped just as soon. For me the
situation was tense and awkward. It annoyed me to find I was becoming
too serious. Somehow I felt confused and couldn't think straight. The
humiliation of this face-to-face meeting and its uselessness confused me.
It embarrassed me not to know what to do. That was why I couldn't
become violent. If I couldn't hate him, that meant he wasn't on my mind.
I wondered if I hadn't already stopped thinking about him.

"During the war I acted the gentleman. There's no need to anymore.
To use a favorite phrase of you bastards—'to be other than myself' is no
longer necessary. Go on laugh. Sure I lectured on the Japanese spirit. So
often that people got fed up listening, like you said. But they did believe
in my speeches and they died. My younger brothers died. The dead
won't come back again. Definitely won't—"

He was drunker than I was. His large arms made the table shake.

"They can't return! Even in dreams! They're forgotten! At first slowly,
then completely! What do you think of this kind of world? Even with all
that crap about the Japanese spirit, I go on living. Even today I'm living!
And even if you can live quite well without the Japanese spirit, I gave
speeches that made those that didn't have it traitors! Bastards that took
those speeches at face value and joyfully believed in them and died! Sure,
there were other jerks like you and Aoki and her. What the hell's this
bitch of a Japan that's made up of me and bastards like that? Well,
what is it? Let them punish me with death. That's divine justice. And if
it's not, it's all right too. It's retribution. In a nutshell, it's the world's
retribution. Sure . . . okay with me. But even if they punish me, nothing'll be settled. Nothing. I'll be reborn. Perhaps as a Japanese. I won't
be any South Sea native. Probably not even a Frenchman. Because I'm
different. Racially different. It's better if they exterminate us Japanese.
Exterminated or not, we won't get away without paying for it. That's
impossible. The problem won't end with a reluctant smile. It won't end
with sarcasm. Better watch out! Even you intellectuals are involved!"

He stretched out the ending of "intellectuals." That pleased him, and
he repeated the word several times.

"Intellectuals, the conscience of the world! Right, ain't it? Maybe getting involved nauseates you, but it's your responsibility. Still, not one of
you intellectuals will be able to become the arms and legs and stomachs
and intestines of society! The best you can be is its nerves. Nagging
nerves fit for the scrap heap! You Japanese intellectuals, what's more,
are the nerve-endings of a strange and ridiculous race. Even if you get
your nerves up, you're useless. Not one of us, not the world either, feels
any vibration from you. To strain the metaphor, we're the blood-
pumpers. When we want to stop, we stop. Stop at our own sweet will!
You can't stop even if you want to!"

I kept eating the fried pork and shrimp and green peas, and I kept on drinking. Apart from what he was saying, I gradually noticed in the urgency with which he rattled on a seriousness of a different kind from his former eloquence, the seriousness of a man driven into a corner, squeezing out his almost breathless voice, cursing. It seemed to me he had reached the end of life. His cursing of the intellectuals didn't matter. What mattered to me was the force he was about to use on his mistress. I wondered if I had the nerve to speak about that. Despite all he had said, wasn't he really lonely? Now that she was his one hope, wasn't it loneliness to take by force what despised him? He derided the weak, but was he ultimately any stronger? Wasn't his strength merely the simplicity of derision, the sweetness of desperation? I tried framing these words, but I stopped. I had satisfied my hunger, and I was drunk and tired. To repeat what he had said, it's useless to rationalize, no matter what the situation. I no longer had any need to listen to his coercive words.

"I'm going home. How about giving me your address?" I said. He wrote it down and made a rough map on the back of his namecard.

"In any event, I'm taking her with me in a few days and disappearing!" he said forcefully. "Go on, interfere. But it'll be useless. You seem serious. More serious than I thought. But seriousness isn't the least useful. Pity, isn't it? Yes, it's true. You damn well better not come up with any fancy Japanese spirit!"

Bumping against tables and chairs, he saw me to the entrance.

"It just may be I'll kill you. Trivial perhaps, but unavoidable. You know, there are times when power becomes uncontrollable. See, I'm never serious. I—"

I went out the door the waiter held open for me. Karajima's voice vanished into the cold wind. Only the red charcoal from a soup stall on the street and the steam from the pots looked warm. Not a single Chinese, much less a Japanese, was to be seen. The only place with any life in the deadly silent surroundings was a recently opened bar. I was really beginning to feel drunk. Perhaps because of the moon and stars, the streets were brighter than when I had first come out. "We're nerves, you say?" I was walking unsteadily. "Just the nerve-endings of a strange and ridiculous race, you say? We can't even stop? Can't? Is that possible? We have to pay for it? Can't expect to get off scot-free? That's it! But the bastard'll kill me? Right! The main point above everything else. The heart's going to kill the nerves then. What for? Why?"

A bike brushed my sleeve and went off after almost colliding with me. The rider turned back to swear at me in Chinese. "The heart—the nerves? What the hell we doing?"

I raised my hands over my head. I saw my shadow fall on the asphalt as if a gorilla had just started walking. I deliberately bent my knees, and waving my hands above my head, I did a gorilla walk along the alley.

Three uniformed police were coming from the opposite direction. Their shoes sounded in unison. Their gold numerals glittered on their fresh blue collars.

"Hey! Cut that out. Can't do that," one of them said, mimicking me, gently rebuking me. "You Japanese?" the others said, peering at me. They walked off when I lowered my hands. Once they were out of sight, I again lifted my hands and bent my knees. Shadows from a row of tall shop buildings, their doors fastened ominously, darkened the entire street. I swaggered with each step planted firmly on the ground, and I walked through the darkness of overlapping shadows. I walked like a monster of superior physical strength emerging from the forest to the spot where blood was to be spilled. I was overflowing with confidence as if I were anyone but myself, a magnificent beast whose power went beyond mere nerves. Already the caution of the good citizen who lowers his head and obeys regulations had vanished.

3

The next day we crossed Garden Bridge. She had kept badgering me to, but I had also felt like taking a walk on the other side of the river. It was out-of-bounds for the Japanese, so we had removed our armbands. It had been a long while since we had last seen the streetcars, bikes, and rickshaws slowly mounting the steeply arched iron bridge so elevated at the center. Along the edge of the river rolled the yellow waves. I seemed to be trying to recapture the past, so greedily did I take in the trivial views of our former consulate, the junks and warships, the various national flags astir in the breeze. Up to the end of the war we had lived in the French Settlement, so now we hated the filthy streets of our district. As we walked, she joyfully held on to my arm. In the morning sun were brand-new cars and jeeps speedily racing along the road beside the river. So painfully dazzling was their speed that I saw the two of us as outcasts in this bright world of motion.

The police and street-vendors kept staring at her. That didn't restrain her—she was so buoyant over being liberated.

"Where have you been having such a good time the last two days? I was worried because I didn't know if you were hiding out."

Not a bit concerned about the congestion around her, she had begun talking about herself. A narrow but long park had been built along the Bund. We sat down on one of the benches facing the river. We stretched our legs on the railing before us. Although it was an ordinary railing, it was quite thick and long, but so solid that it almost looked ridiculous.

Yet merely seeing it along the Bund made me feel the tremendous power of the British Empire. I found it strange that the mere thickness of a piece of iron I hadn't even noticed until the end of the war seemed ample evidence of a power that was beyond coping with.

"We've permission to take a passenger. So even if you don't really want to, come back with us on the hospital ship. If you disappear when it's time to embark, I'll be quite annoyed!"

"I'll go if I can."

"If you can?"

"What about Karajima?"

"Don't worry about him. Once we're on board, it's over. Are you worried? Don't be since I'll take care of him."

"Is he that easy to handle?"

"Karajima? There's nothing we can do about him. You see that, don't you? Instead of worrying about him, concentrate on not changing your mind about leaving!"

Repatriation wasn't as light a matter with me as it apparently was with her. There was still the question of what Karajima was going to do. I imagined something bloody. That consideration aside, it was impossible for me to simply detach myself suddenly from Shanghai and return home. To go back to the Japan of old and to abandon the complexities of my Shanghai days would be cause for regret. I'd merely settle down. I doubted if I could look forward to any change, development, fear, desire.

"What's on your mind?"

"Something tells me I don't want to go back," I said.

"I know. I don't want to either."

A lingering puff of white smoke from a steamship drifted along the surface of the wide river. Some children around the bench next to ours looked eagerly down at the yellow waves dashing against the wharf below. Someone, perhaps a clerk, was leaning on the bench and idly watching the river. A few spectators stood up to leave. It suddenly occurred to me that these Chinese citizens, these men and women, knew nothing about such places as Japan. Most of them would never see Japan, and for the first time I realized that the two of us were foreigners linked together by our land. The clerk and those children were on a routine excursion to the park along the river. That was what they had come to see. But their geography ended there. At the proper time they would go back to their company or department store or tenement building. They would return to colleagues or families. But we were leaving Shanghai quite soon, never to return a second time. Perhaps our ship was already on the river. These thoughts, so filled with subjective meaning, made the scenes on the river close in on me.

"I thought we might hide out in the French Settlement. We'd be happy if we could."

"That's impossible," I said.

"But if we could, wouldn't we be happy?"

Her suddenly bringing up the French Settlement, as Karajima had, worried me. It was perfectly obvious she was as desperate as Karajima. Not only that. I couldn't believe in happiness. Cohabiting couldn't bring happiness. I was convinced that whatever was stable collapsed in time. I had never anticipated that happiness could materialize. Certainly the warmth of her happiness might be transmitted to me if we tried it. But I knew that possibility no longer appealed to me. It all boiled down to the fact that I was more familiar, more secure, with unhappiness. Something artificial in the word "happiness" itself lay behind her own use of the term.

"Oh I want to be happy!" she said.

"Can living with me make you happy?"

She was confident it could.

A clear indication of the unhappiness attached to the word itself was in the fact that someone in as precarious a position as hers, someone in the midst of danger, was all the more committed to happiness.

"I heard how bad your recent attack of hysteria was."

"What? Heard about it? I don't even know what I did." Her face looked lonely and embarrassed. It was delicate and lovely.

"You must have been quite disgusted with me after hearing about it."

"Not at all. For the first time I realized how justifiably beyond human control hysteria is."

"Then you did understand! You probably pitied me."

She took my hand and gripped my fingers and rubbed them with her hands. She seemed to enjoy caressing me in that old-fashioned, reserved way.

"A little while ago I asked you to protect me. That's all over. You don't have to."

"Why not?"

"Oh why! I also asked you to kill Karajima, didn't I? That's over too. Don't think about killing. You don't have to protect me with all your might! All you have to do is love me! Think of nothing else. Don't get involved anymore with Karajima. I tell you I'm worried. If anything should happen to you—if you should be killed, anything!"

She turned to me with that special look she used before her tears fell. She glanced down and wiped her eyes with her fingers. I held those fingers.

"It's nothing for Karajima to put you out of the way. So no matter what he writes, don't go to see him."

I hadn't yet told her of our meeting. I hadn't told her about his behavior, his words, the resolution he had revealed at the end of our talk. Possibly she knew already. She had a premonition of danger. And it was even stronger since she knew more about Karajima than I did. She was trying to protect me, at least trying to make me avoid any possible involvement. And I could have avoided it if I had felt like it. Obviously, as long as I didn't try to meet him again, things would pass without incident. But I felt that was impossible. If the event merely passed away without anything happening to me, that would mean I was an absolute zero. She'd be taken by force to the French Settlement, and the invalid would be left alone. Preventing this had nothing to do with justice. I didn't believe in justice. But I had become conscious of the fact that my withdrawal meant I'd become a nonentity. On meeting Karajima the night before, I was still only vaguely antagonistic. But my fear of being reduced to a zero was so very clear to me now that it was as if I had only just become conscious of the implications. As long as I lived by maintaining that fear, I couldn't become a nonentity. I had thought of myself as merely existing. But I now found that even in that state one inevitably has form and substance. When I held her fingers, moist from her tears, that awareness was physically represented to me through those fingers. I was surprised to find myself rejecting the possibility of becoming a zero. The tension I felt was as sharp as sitting down in ice cold water. Before I realized it, I was telling myself I could be killed and then even if I were, I deserved it. In a flash I realized I had decided my own destiny.

"I'd die if anything happened to you." Her large eyes were moist with tears.

I had never thought I'd hear such pathetic and dramatic words from a woman. Nor had I ever thought *she* would say them. I hadn't even known anyone could casually come out with such words.

"I wouldn't mind dying then," she said.

She laughed lightly. "Really, I wouldn't."

I recalled the words of a senior who had once told me of the frequency with which women use the word "die." Her profile after its earlier childlike radiance was now shrouded in the moodiness of the aged. Appropriate to this transformation, comparable to that of flower gardens in violent storms, her words gave the impression she was really ready to die. And those words, like a silhouette or an odor or a nuance that was beautifying her, had escaped through her lips and seeped through me.

"Leave it to me. It'll work out all right." She had suddenly returned to reality, had suddenly become businesslike.

"I know some men. Koreans and Chinese. If I ask them, they'll help me out one way or another. So don't worry. We'll be able to get back fairly soon."

All at once her earlier cheerfulness returned. It was genuinely spontaneous. Already I couldn't keep up with her mood.

Later she said she was meeting Karajima that evening. He had sent her a letter. In it he had informed her he'd be hiding out for a while and would give her all his ready cash. He had designated the time and place.

"It's probably a lie," I said at once.

"Not necessarily. That's the least he ought to do for me."

"But don't go," I said as if reprimanding her. For a moment she was silent, as though she were thinking it over.

"I won't go if you're worried. And if I don't, you shouldn't go to see him either. All right? Good! I'll have someone go for me tonight."

"Is there someone that can?"

"I think so."

"But it's not really necessary, is it? Just ask the Security Division to have someone stay at your house. Don't go out. In the first place, you're too careless. Don't even come to me. I'll go to your place. Don't go out at all until they call for the passengers to board."

She nodded obediently.

I took her back. On the way she said, "If only you hadn't started copying documents, you wouldn't be in this mess," and she laughed. Her words really struck home.

When I got to my place, I found two Chinese workmen removing steam pipes from the kitchen and my room. They were making quite a racket as they also took off the closet doors and carried them downstairs. Since my landlord had become ill at the end of the year, he had to sell junk of that kind. For the remainder of the day, in the middle of the dust from the demolished wall and the noise of separating the iron pipes and the boards, I continued copying at my crate. One of my jobs involved an old woman who desperately wanted permission to bring her electro-massage to Japan. Another of my clients, a factory owner, was being bothered by the demands of an official in spite of having completed the confiscation proceedings with another government clerk. It grew dark out while I was getting these headaches and others into documentary form.

I had the feeling she might go to meet Karajima that night. In spite of her words, it was a possibility. It was more than that judging from her character. I felt everything would be over between us if she did. The darker it became outside, the stronger grew my premonition. Finally, I had no more doubts about it. It hadn't been my intention to go after she had promised not to. But now that I was certain she would, I was forced into going too. I still had the faint but persistent feeling that I ought to save myself the trouble, that I ought to leave everything as it was. But in order to destroy that feeling too, I had to go tonight.

I imagined that as she was taking care of her sick husband, she was making the same kind of mental preparations I was. Lights on, supper finished, the small talk over. She was inventing some excuse or another, trying to leave. The invalid was suspicious. She sat down, stood up again. I imagined the meaningful passage of time, meaningful for her and for him. I was so tortured by these images that I could feel the pain in my guts.

Once Aoki had said to me, "Your room's just like Raskolnikov's in *Crime and Punishment*. He stole out with an axe. And he got back secretly without anyone recognizing him."

I glanced around my narrow, dark, miserable room. The dismantling that day had made the naked walls even uglier. The ceiling stains from the rain were dark yellow, shaped like foetuses without hands, their legs extended. There was only my dirty bedding except for sake bottles, carbon and writing paper, brushes and inkstone, several books. Yet as long as I was in my room, I had been able to carry out my daily tasks. To go out now would change everything beyond recognition. I lacked Raskolnikov's strong and resilient philosophy. My plan of action was no more than a childish impulse. Furthermore, I didn't have his minute calculation or cool preparation. Above all, I didn't have his depth. I was too dependent and impulsive. I could convince myself that if I went, things would work out somehow. But I didn't have the determination to work them out or do so at any cost even. I hadn't even thought about a weapon yet. "If only you hadn't started copying documents, you wouldn't be in this mess," she had said and laughed. She had spoken out of kindness. But it was the painful truth. After all, I did copy documents. I did them on request. That was how I made money. I was never serious myself. My customers were the only ones involved. I wasn't a hero. I was a bystander's bystander. When I recalled these things, I felt the task ahead of me slipping away in a flash, and I felt dizzy in trying to catch hold of it, my feet shaking, my power failing me.

I picked up a knife that had tumbled down by my books. Its blade was only four inches long. Its broken handle was wound with string. The face I saw reflected on the cold blade had an expression of absurdity rather than one of tragic seriousness.

"An axe!" My landlady had one to cut firewood for her small portable stove. The size would be convenient. When I went down, if she wasn't there, I would hide the axe in my overcoat pocket. First I put in the knife. Suddenly I remembered its make. *Chrysanthemum*. My younger sister had bought it for me. I recalled her face as if seeing it in a snapshot close up. It remained fixed, smiling. For the first time since coming to Shanghai, I had caught an image of my sister's face. I sensed that she probably intended to protect me. And I felt she might be able to.

No one was in the kitchen. The lights were on in my landlady's room, but it was quiet there. She opened the glass door and looked out. "Can you get me some medicine? Anything for a fever will do." She took some bills from her purse. "Drinking today too? Please come back soon," she said, entering her room and sliding the door shut. Quickly I picked up the axe from the box of charcoal and slipped the weapon into my overcoat pocket. I opened the kitchen door and went out.

The heavy axe was quite bulky. Its shape stuck out taut and hard so that it could certainly be observed under my thick coat. If Karajima noticed, he'd be on guard and would have an added incentive for murdering me. Not to use it would really be idiotic. My own unpreparedness and incompetence exasperated me. But my one hope lay in the axe. I was conscious of every man in the street at night, of every man loitering about. And each time I passed someone, I imagined the moment of raising the axe, of striking out. I'd cut at the flesh of one of these men, strike at his bones, spill his blood—these images so troubled me that slowly and steadily I felt the sweat seeping out of me. I actually was no more than a bundle of nerves. I felt I was walking in order to be killed. The appointed rendezvous spot was near a streetcar line beyond the Chinese residential area far past the shopping district. I stayed in the shadows of the houses on one side. Suddenly from second-story windows and from doorways yellow lights fell over my entire body. Then darkness again. I merely hurried on to my destination as if I'd forgotten the desperate situation of meeting Karajima, contending with him.

All at once, about thirty feet ahead of me, I heard a loud voice laughing. And then a Japanese said something. Then that laughing voice again. The two men were together. They were heading in the same direction I was and were walking slowly. One was definitely Karajima.

"That so? The wine was bad? I never thought it would be. I took the mud off the jug and opened it myself." Karajima's voice was as clear as ever.

"But it was tasteless," his companion said in a low voice. "It's a shame a man like you should end up drinking such stuff."

"Cut the crap! Something went wrong with the sake, not with me!" They laughed cheerfully.

At first I wondered if Karajima's companion was a subordinate. But apparently Karajima had simply met him on the way. At the next crossing they separated. They had proceeded along that street and then Karajima had turned right. "Give my regards to your wife," he had said and, glancing at his watch, had walked off quickly. He looked resolute, bursting with self-confidence. His proudly squared shoulders seemed especially large that night. I imagined him confronting me with his pompous and detached attitude. If I panicked for a fraction of a second even, it would be as deadly as if my entire body had been shattered. I decided to go on to my destination by proceeding one block ahead of the street he had turned on.

A deserted lot was at the end of the street I took. The scrap iron accumulated by the Japanese army was still piled up high there and enclosed by a rusty barbed wire fence. No one was in the vicinity. At that hour in the neighborhood, no Japanese would have been out. So when I reached the corner of the street, Karajima and I would have recognized one another despite the distance between us.

Near the end of the street, the lot, brightened a little by the moon, came into view. It was a peaceful night. Suddenly, from a fairly isolated spot, I heard gravel trampled underfoot. At the same time I heard light footsteps running at great speed, someone falling heavily to the ground.

I ran so fast the bones in my legs snapped. The axe was in my hand. Before I realized it, I was shouting out of breath, "Bastard!" I ran toward a shadow on a caved-in wall. Karajima rose toweringly to his feet. Until then he had been lying on the ground. With his face a grotesque mask of pain, he began grabbing at me. I swung my axe. It cut through the air. The second time it plunged deeply into his body somewhere. He caught hold of me. But what actually happened was that his heavy body had collided with mine, leaning against me. That caused me to fall violently, Karajima's body pinning me down. My head and the palms of my hands touched the cold ground. I struggled to get away. Then Karajima's body slid heavily away from on top of me. I jumped to my feet. Karajima was moaning. I was searching for my axe. He remained where he had fallen. He was lying face down. He twisted his body in jerks and starts. For the first time I could clearly see his face. A white face, a handsome face, but totally transformed from its usual appearance. Oily, lifeless. Exceedingly tense. Almost deranged. He was trying to stand up. I readied my axe, and when he had just about half-risen, I struck at the back of his neck. He fell face forward.

That was when I saw the knife in his back, a razor-sharp, long and slender knife used for cutting meat. It had gone through his coat, piercing his heart or lungs. That was why he couldn't shout or fight. Someone had already wounded him fatally before I had started my attack.

I couldn't do anything. I couldn't even bear to hold the axe in my hand. I hadn't the energy to fight or hate. The blood streamed out of Karajima's lacerated neck. From that spot alone the blood was spilling out over the ground. His face was twisted toward me. He was looking up at me. His pathetic eyes were terror-stricken, like a dog's, desperately pleading. He had been trying to pull out the knife. He kept attempting to, but had finally looked up at me. He wanted me to do it for him. Before I realized it, I had grabbed the black handle. I pulled it out with all my might. That was all I could have done at the time. Every limb of mine was exhausted, severely chilled. At my feet was a man I knew quite well, a man covered with blood, a man I had talked to only the night before. Afraid, trembling, I had only the urge to cry out or run away.

His eyes closed, then opened. Not the slightest trace of hatred was on his face. There was only fear. That fragile face was full of misery. The flesh on its cheeks contracted spasmodically. The color of his lips changed. They were distorted, apart. He called out her name in a low, inaudible voice, but I felt it had been uttered with a grotesque explosion. He kept calling it. I was bewildered by the fact that he was dying and that I was the only one watching him, that at the end he had called for her but I was the only one listening.

He was lying in agony on the cold mud I myself had been pushed onto a while back. If the assassin had not jabbed a butcher knife deep into Karajima's body, I would have probably been the corpse on that ground. Some water was flowing along the ground. It was gushing out from a conduit that had been left open close by. Some light was reflected on the brass faucet while the water gushed out, and the falling water, itself reflecting light, drenched the barbed wire and scrap iron and gravel.

I left without making certain Karajima had died.

Like Raskolnikov I washed the blood off my weapon. I scoured the axe and the butcher knife with sand and washed them again. Then I put them in my overcoat pockets and went back. I had wanted to rush to her as soon as I could, to find my way to her room where she and her sick mate were lying quietly awake in bed thinking about Karajima and me. Now the two of them were indispensable for me. I needed them to call out to me, to reveal their concern about my whereabouts, to help me in any way they could. But I had decided instead to return to my room. It gave me quite a jolt to see how absorbed I was in saving my own neck. Before I realized it, I was behaving as if I had to establish proof that I had nothing to do with Karajima's murder. Even the slightest suspicion was an apprehension comparable to the destruction of the universe!

"He's already dead. Already cold and stiff." At home, safely in bed, I repeated those words many times. But I continually dreamed he wasn't dead, not quite. My undershirt was soaked through. I kept sweating almost until dawn. I would feel hot, then cold. The sweat would be gone, then come again.

That day I walked in the rain to her house. It was past noon. On the way I heard some Japanese talking about Karajima's murder. Everyone already knew about it. "Just think. Someone with the guts to do a beautiful job like that!" "Was he Japanese or Chinese?" "I bet it was a thief." They were talking about it that casually. I had no idea who the real murderer was. I was so overwrought, so depressed by my experience, I had no energy for any kind of speculation.

"You're safe," she said, running down the steps and taking both my hands. "I thought you'd come! I bought some wine to celebrate!"

"You know, don't you?"

"Of course! I heard about it when I went shopping this morning."

"Did you really stay home last night?"

"Of course. Why?"

Her composure irritated me. It was so totally out of keeping with my own desperation. "I went out," I said in a serious, moody voice.

"I knew you had the instant I saw you come in. It's written all over your face. Did you kill him?

"No."

"Who then?"

"I don't know."

"You were there, weren't you? Why don't you know then?"

"I struck him with an axe. But someone else killed him. I don't know who. At any rate, someone stabbed him before I could."

"My husband's been saying you did it. I thought so too."

"But I didn't."

"It doesn't matter. Who cares who it was so long as someone did it!" She hugged me then, kissing me violently. "Now we're safe! Everything's fine now!"

She was pleased, radiant. I was depressed, uneasy, as if my hands were still dirty from the blood, as if I could still hear Karajima moaning. Not even her lips could bring me any relief. Everything was ugly, useless. I was too annoyed even to speak.

As she had indicated, the invalid was convinced I had killed Karajima. No matter what I said to the contrary, all he could do was smile his denial. He even thanked me with tears in his eyes. He was deeply moved. "Forgive me," he pleaded, "for making you do it." And he said, "You're a great man." I grew silent, merely drinking the wine his wife had prepared. I found it tasteless. I was feeling more and more depressed.

"How did he die?" the invalid asked.

"It wasn't the Karajima we knew. He was afraid, a coward."

"I see. Frightened, you say?"

"Like a child or an idiot. He was so miserable it was painful to look at him. What's more, he kept calling your wife's name."

When I said that, she looked up sharply. "That's a lie! A lie!" She spoke so intensely it made her husband glance back violently.

"I've no reason to lie."

"Well, it's annoying to hear he called my name. I can't believe it." The look of ill-humor she made was the same one has in brushing away a bug clinging to the body.

"He plagues me even after he's dead."

The invalid ignored his wife and began talking to me.

"When I heard the news this morning, all my energy suddenly collapsed. I felt . . . it would now be all right to die. I felt . . . my life was worthwhile . . . just to have heard the news. But as the excitement wore off, I gradually realized that everything was over, that I didn't have anything to wait for any longer. I was vacantly listening to my wife. Karajima . . . no longer existed. His life didn't have the slightest connection to ours anymore. The man that had dominated us up to now, hovering over us day and night like some demon, had, in a flash, ceased to be. That was the strange, empty feeling I was absorbed in. You see, I kept thinking I hadn't done it, that you had, that you had killed him while I had been lying in bed without moving a muscle! I thought of how irresponsible . . . and dependent . . . and sly it was of me . . . to have had you do it. I had suffered, but it was no more than that. I hadn't done a single thing. I had been trying to evade . . . as much as possible, trying to forget . . . as much as possible . . . trying to resign myself. My only thought was to get back to Japan. To be perfectly honest . . . I didn't think you had that much courage. And not merely you. I didn't feel a single man in Shanghai could kill him. I had hoped someone would. But I had believed that was absolutely impossible. Yet I woke up to find it done. But even though I had realized my one desire, it struck me unexpectedly . . . confusing me. I was overjoyed at being freed and revenged, but at the same time I was full of self-pity and shame. I wondered if it was right . . . to allow a human being to be killed . . . for the sake of a man like me, lying in bed, unable to do anything, dependent, irresponsible, a sly, selfish cripple! I wondered if a murder committed for me ought to satisfy me. I began crying, some sort of intensely painful tormenting thing full of shame and regret . . . all of a sudden coming over me. When I told my wife about it, she said Karajima had been trying to kill us, to kill her, you. But if we hadn't been miserable, if I hadn't been a cripple . . . unable to move, you wouldn't have had any trouble. I don't want to remain a cripple! I don't want the shame . . . of being dependent on others! I want to get well! To behave responsibly! I want to do . . . what I have to do, like you, at least once!"

His words were too much for me to take. His crying voice had never disturbed me as much as it did then. I felt he had deliberately selected each word to judge me with, hurling those words at me.

He kept repeating he wanted to live. He went so far as to indicate his desire to work with me after he got home, even noting the political party he wanted to join.

"Karajima's dead, so we don't have to hurry back to Japan," his wife joked while making cloth tags for their luggage.

Her casualness annoyed me.

It was at that moment they received word the returnees would meet at six the next morning and embark in the afternoon. The invalid's eyes brightened, his wife stood up in high spirits. I helped them pack quickly, and after that I purchased enough food for three days. Then I went home to get my own bags ready. On the way I bought the medicine my landlady had asked for. She was cooking when I entered the kitchen. In one hand she held the axe.

"I see. So tomorrow you're finally leaving. Well, congratulations!" she said smiling, the axe in her hand.

I wanted to leave Shanghai as soon as possible. I wanted to separate myself from the streets that had dirtied my hands with Karajima's blood. I didn't think about the fascinating complexity of Shanghai or the monotony of Japan. I wasn't even thinking about what to expect in Japan, about actual possibilities. I even forgot the sick man's feelings, the sentiments of his wife. All I could think of was my own part in Karajima's death. All I could think about was that I had attacked with the axe in my hand, that it had cut deeply into his neck, that I had seen the color of his eyes as he lay dying, had heard his groans at the end.

The next day it continued to rain. The roll call at the meeting place, the loading of baggage onto trucks, the luggage inspection at the depot, the reloading into trucks and unloading at the wharf, the transfer to the ship, the invalids on stretchers carried into sick bay—I had worked to the point of exhaustion.

The hospital ship was a rebuilt training vessel for a merchant marine school. In the evening the embarkation was completed. The student crew and invalids' attendants were covered with sweat and dust. We didn't even have enough energy to laugh. We even had to put the invalids on the floor of the dining salon.

Due to fog, our ship, which had set out, spent a day and night at the mouth of the Yangtze. When we were finally underway, the invalid and his wife were seasick from the high waves. So were most of the passengers. I wasn't, and I carried meals and contacted doctors and washed dishes and chamberpots. Most of the time I spent on deck. If the ship made any progress at all, it was only after a sharp incline of thirty degrees. It seemed as if the gray sea rose high above the deck and receded heavily, a portion of the ship's bottom exposed. The cloudy sky was without rain, and when I looked up, the tall, inclining mast cut across the lead-colored sky. The square, overly large life preserver installed on the mast ropes looked like the frame of an oil painting. Inside that white frame was the sea, an austere gloomy background, alternately appearing and disappearing.

I had no desire to talk to the invalid or his wife. The various emotions I had undergone had exhausted me. For companionship I desired only the spectacle of the enormous, heartless sea. The invalid's wife had wanted to talk to me, but I had somehow managed to avoid her. Behind her dragged the shadow of Karajima, and that shadow threatened me.

Passengers were even lying in the corridors. The serious cases were quiet. The frauds, their illnesses invented to get on board, talked enthusiastically. The officer in charge walked up and down the narrow sick bay corridor that pitched and rolled. During his all-night vigil he kept giving orders. That made any sort of intricate discussion impossible. But when I awoke in the morning and hurried up the flight of stairs, the invalid's wife looked at me with eyes that seemed to close in on me. When she smiled and touched up her hair, she gave me a meaningful look. Given the chance, she'd have grabbed me by the shoulder.

After lunch the third day out, the wind toying with her hair and the sun streaming down, she said to me, "Last night my husband mentioned something odd." Since the ship was on an incline, she was bracing her trousered legs, her transparent, white fingers twisted around some rigging.

"He said he's jealous of you. He's come to feel afraid of you. In spite of the gratitude he feels, he say it's unbearable to put up with the idea you're in love with me. He hasn't made anything out of the fact that I'm really the one in love, but that's all he's been thinking about now since Karajima's death. He's quite serious when he says that even though it amazes him, shames him, he can't get rid of that feeling. I asked him how he could say such things when he's so indebted to you. I told him that was what he really ought to be thinking about. He said he understands that quite well. But he's gradually come to hate you. He can't help it. He had to tell me since he feels guilty about keeping these feelings to himself."

She smiled as if to please me, but then she suddenly became sad and frightened and grabbed my arm.

"You're annoyed, aren't you? Annoyed that I'm just talking nonsense. You've come to dislike me. I'm a bother, aren't I?"

I shook my head as I watched the rising and falling waves.

"I'm just worried."

"Do you still love me?"

"I'm so weighted down I can't think of anything."

"What's worrying you so much?"

The waves struck the side of the ship, the sound muffled. The cold spray fell on my hands and face.

"Karajima? My husband?"

"Everything, everything that concerns my being alive."

The sunlight was pouring down brilliantly, and the silver-gray crests of the waves glittered. Pitching and rolling, they streamed away. Then the thick walls of salt water crumbled, rolling down hills, splitting into ravines. That huge movement was precise and sharp. But even the immense, clean-cut movement of that brilliant ocean couldn't drown my gloom. I felt, in fact, as if I were standing alone, steeped in a gloom fully exposed to the overflowing brilliant vitality of nature.

I continued to worry about what I had done, something heavy and uncomfortable clogged in my chest.

The ship's doctor had informed me the invalid wouldn't survive the trip. Undoubtedly the invalid himself knew. I too had seen the omen in the color of his weak eyes, in the movement of his throat when he drank water. Obviously he was afraid of me. Even if he wasn't, he'd get nervous and irritable each time I touched him. Without her having told me about it, I had easily guessed his change in attitude. I had neither hoped for his death nor waited for it. It had been settled he'd die. There was no need to hope or wait. I nursed him faithfully and calmly. His wife and I watched over him. In time he would just die. How agonizing it must have been for him to know the obvious. No longer did it matter to him that something had existed between his wife and Karajima, that Karajima had been murdered, that he thought I was the murderer, or even that the ship was continually getting closer to Japan. What must have been weighing on his mind second by second was that his wife and I watched over him while death was closing in on him, that we would stay alive, not die with him.

Once he had asked in a barely audible whisper, "When he died, you were looking at him, weren't you?"

As he spoke he was facing the wall in a corner of the room, but I was startled and stared at him. He hadn't intended to make anyone hear him, nor could his voice actually be heard. Yet in that feeble, hoarse whisper that had started talking about Karajima's death, I had sensed some hidden grudge against me. And yet, his words might have been explained as coming from a fever and exhaustion between sleep and waking.

"Seeing him die, did you understand what was on his mind? You see, I do. Completely understand. I understand . . . what . . . he was thinking . . . as about to die." I had felt as if the invalid's pathetically sunken eyes were faintly shining under his thin eyebrows.

"How strange . . . that as I'm dying, you're calmly alive. That's what he was thinking." The sick man tried to move his neck, probably to raise his head, but he couldn't.

"That's what I'm thinking now." Then he was silent. Contemptuously he shut his eyes as if he had achieved some great feat. He had made the last assertion of his life. At least he had made his point. His haggard features stubbornly and coldly indicated he had. His unrelenting maliciousness and uncompromising hostility oozed out over the entire surface of his discolored skin.

She had said he started hating me. That hadn't surprised me. What had been crushing me was his conviction that his thoughts and Karajima's were identical at the point of death. It was no surprise that he had guessed Karajima's mental state during those final moments. It was natural for the invalid to have said to me, "How strange that as I'm dying, you're calmly alive." Yet I couldn't believe that Karajima, who had suddenly been killed, and the invalid, slowly dying of illness, could reach the same thought, especially that the thought of two men who had been enemies should coincide. Obviously though, the invalid was drawing closer to Karajima and joining his camp of the dead. That, apparently, was the invalid's way of threatening us.

By the time we entered Kagoshima Bay, the waves had not yet quieted down. The ashes of Sakurajima trailed in the sky and made the streets of Kagoshima white and dim. We hadn't come across a single Japanese vessel until we entered the harbor. The sea without ships, the town covered with volcanic ash, everything looked dreary and spent. But the repatriates were quite thrilled. A farewell party with entertainment was going on. Halfway through the singing of "Oh! Who Thinks Not of Homeland!" I went out on deck. As I expected, the invalid's wife followed me, moving next to me, looking out at the sea at night.

"We've finally come home together," she said.

The chilly night had subdued her, or perhaps her relief on reaching Japan had. She was quite resigned. For her that was unprecedented.

"What do you intend to do? Separate at once, go away somewhere?"

"I've no place in particular to go," I said.

"It's all right if you want to break up." She smiled awkwardly. "But I've something I want to tell you and get it over with. I know who killed Karajima. I've been wanting to tell you."

She spoke quietly, gently. Her pale profile with its graceful curve didn't seem the least self-conscious. It seemed innocent and fresh.

"I asked someone to. Not a Japanese. A person you hire for murder. A person I knew. I couldn't help worrying about you. I didn't know whether or not I hated Karajima that much to kill him at the last moment. But I wanted to murder anybody likely to kill you. I couldn't help it. Even now I feel it was better to have had him murdered. Even though I instigated it, I don't regret it in the least. I'm not suffering for it. So you don't have to worry about him. You had no connection with it from the very first. I was the one that got you mixed up in it. The responsibility is only Karajima's and mine and my husband's. So there's no need for you to suffer. I'd never have done it if you were to suffer the least bit for it. I can only think of how sorry I am to have caused you any trouble. When you copied your documents and drank sake, you were quite happy. You were confident. You looked so different from us. I knew that when I came to you. How much better if I had ended only as your customer. Forgive me for involving you in our difficulties. But I was really fond of you. That at least is the truth. I'm a hopeless case I think. But I've never felt like tormenting anyone. I've never felt like doing that, not even to my husband, not even to Karajima. But before I knew it, I was tormenting them. I couldn't stand it if I've gone that far as to torment you. Since you came on board, I've been unhappy about your attitude, but I've thought and thought about it, and I've come to reconcile myself to the fact that I'm to blame. So you really can believe you've absolutely nothing to do with us. Absolutely nothing. I loved you, and that's all there was to it."

She wasn't even slightly agitated. Nor was she hysterical. She spoke quite sympathetically, as a beautiful nurse does in washing a wound with pure water. I hadn't expected that. It increased my feeling of tenderness for her.

"Still, you did go out to attack Karajima for me that night."

"I had to."

"Once you said you couldn't stake your life on anything, but it wasn't true after all, was it? In fact, you're probably the type that's anxious to throw his life away."

"Perhaps."

"Don't, please!"

Her face changed, as if she could no longer bear the strain.

"Live. Don't die. Please, please."

A chorus of voices rose from the deck below: *That's the mountain I knew when I was a child; that's the river.* The children and old men were singing in chorus. At times the wind made their voices weak, at times strong.

We heard someone running up the steps. The doctor in his white operating gown appeared on deck. He called out her name. He turned around and noticed us, and he came up, his slippers dragging. In a slow yet tense voice he told her the invalid had taken a turn for the worse.

DORIS LESSING

the antheap

Beyond the plain rose the mountains, blue and hazy in a strong blue sky. Coming closer they were brown and grey and green, ranged heavily one beside the other, but the sky was still blue. Climbing up through the pass the plain flattened and diminished behind, and the peaks rose sharp and dark grey from lower heights of heaped granite boulders, and the sky overhead was deeply blue and clear and the heat came shimmering off in waves from every surface. "Through the range, down the pass, and into the plain the other side—let's go quickly, there it will be cooler, the walking easier." So thinks the traveller. So the traveller has been thinking for many centuries, walking quickly to leave the stifling mountains, to gain the cool plain where the wind moves freely. But there is no plain. Instead, the pass opens into a hollow which is closely surrounded by *kopjes*: the mountains clench themselves into a fist here, and the palm is a mile-wide reach of thick bush, where the heat gathers and clings, radiating from boulders, rocking off the trees, pouring down from a sky which is not blue, but thick and low and yellow, because of the smoke that rises, and has been rising so long from this mountain-imprisoned hollow. For though it is hot and close and arid half the year, and then warm and steamy and wet in the rains, there is gold here, so there are always people, and everywhere in the bush are pits and slits where the prospectors have been, or shallow holes, or even deep shafts. They say that the Bushmen were here, seeking gold, hundreds of years ago. Perhaps, it is possible. They say that trains of Arabs came from the coast, with slaves and warriors, looking for gold to enrich the courts of the Queen of Sheba. No one has proved they did not.

But it is at least certain that at the turn of the century there was a big mining company which sunk half a dozen fabulously deep shafts, and found gold going ounces to the ton sometimes, but it is a capricious and chancy piece of ground, with the reefs all broken and unpredictable, and so this company loaded its heavy equipment into lorries and off they went to look for gold somewhere else, and in a place where the reefs lay more evenly.

For a few years the hollow in the mountains was left silent, no smoke rose to dim the sky, except perhaps for an occasional prospector, whose fire was a single column of wavering blue smoke, as from the cigarette of a giant, rising into the blue, hot sky.

Then all at once the hollow was filled with violence and noise and activity and hundreds of people. Mr. Macintosh had bought the rights to mine this gold. They told him he was foolish, that no single man, no matter how rich, could afford to take chances in this place.

But they did not reckon with the character of Mr. Macintosh, who had already made a fortune and lost it, in Australia, and then made another in New Zealand, which he still had. He proposed to increase it here. Of course, he had no intention of sinking those expensive shafts which might not reach gold and hold the dipping, chancy reefs and seams. The right course was quite clear to Mr. Macintosh, and this course he followed, though it was against every known rule of proper mining.

He simply hired hundreds of African labourers and set them to shovel up the soil in the centre of that high, enclosed hollow in the mountains, so that there was soon a deeper hollow, then a vast pit, then a gulf like an inverted mountain. Mr. Macintosh was taking great swallows of the earth, like a gold-eating monster, with no fancy ideas about digging shafts or spending money on roofing tunnels. The earth was hauled, at first, up the shelving sides of the gulf in buckets, and these were suspended by ropes made of twisted bark fibre, for why spend money on steel ropes when this fibre was offered free to mankind on every tree? And if it got brittle and broke and the buckets went plunging into the pit, then they were not harmed by the fall, and there was plenty of fibre left on the trees. Later, when the gulf grew too deep, there were trucks on rails, and it was not unknown for these, too, to go sliding and plunging to the bottom, because in all Mr. Macintosh's dealings there was a fine, easy good-humour, which meant he was more likely to laugh at such an accident than grow angry. And if someone's head got in the way of the falling buckets or trucks, then there were plenty of black heads and hands for the hiring. And if the loose, sloping bluffs of soil fell in landslides, or if a tunnel, narrow as an ant-bear's hole, that was run off sideways from the main pit like a tentacle exploring for new reefs, caved in suddenly, swallowing half a dozen men—well, one can't make an omelette without breaking eggs. This was Mr. Macintosh's favourite motto.

THE ANTHEAP / **49**

The Africans who worked this mine called it "the pit of death," and they called Mr. Macintosh "The Gold Stomach." Nevertheless, they came in their hundreds to work for him, thus providing free arguments for those who said: "The native doesn't understand good treatment, he only appreciates the whip, look at Macintosh, he's never short of labour."

Mr. Macintosh's mine, raised high in the mountains, was far from the nearest police station, and he took care that there was always plenty of kaffir beer brewed in the compound, and if the police patrols came searching for criminals, these could count on Mr. Macintosh facing the police for them and assuring them that such and such a native, Registration Number Y2345678, had never worked for him. Yes, of course they could see his books.

Mr. Macintosh's books and records might appear to the simpleminded as casual and ineffective, but these were not the words used of his methods by those who worked for him, and so Mr. Macintosh kept his books himself. He employed no book-keeper, no clerk. In fact, he employed only one white man, an engineer. For the rest, he had six overseers or boss-boys whom he paid good salaries and treated like important people.

The engineer was Mr. Clarke, and his house and Mr. Macintosh's house were on one side of the big pit, and the compound for the Africans was on the other side. Mr. Clarke earned fifty pounds a month, which was more than he would earn anywhere else. He was a silent, hard-working man, except when he got drunk, which was not often. Three or four times in the year he would be off work for a week, and then Mr. Macintosh did his work for him till he recovered, when he greeted him with the good-humored words: "Well, laddie, got that off your chest?"

Mr. Macintosh did not drink at all. His not drinking was a passionate business, for like many Scots people he ran to extremes. Never a drop of liquor could be found in his house. Also, he was religious, in a reminiscent sort of way, because of his parents, who had been very religious. He lived in a two-roomed shack, with a bare wooden table in it, three wooden chairs, a bed and a wardrobe. The cook boiled beef and carrots and potatoes three days a week, roasted beef three days, and cooked a chicken on Sundays.

Mr. Macintosh was one of the richest men in the country, he was more than a millionaire. People used to say of him: But for heaven's sake, he could do anything, go anywhere, what's the point of having so much money if you live in the back of beyond with a parcel of blacks on top of a big hole in the ground?

But to Mr. Macintosh it seemed quite natural to live so, and when he went for a holiday to Cape Town, where he lived in the most expensive hotel, he always came back again long before he was expected. He did not like holidays. He liked working.

He wore old, oily khaki trousers, tied at the waist with an old red tie, and he wore a red handkerchief loose around his neck over a white cotton singlet. He was short and broad and strong, with a big square head tilted back on a thick neck. His heavy brown arms and neck sprouted thick black hair around the edges of the singlet. His eyes were small and grey and shrewd. His mouth was thin, pressed tight in the middle. He wore an old felt hat on the back of his head, and carried a stick cut from the bush, and he went strolling around the edge of the pit, slashing the stick at bushes and grass or sometimes at lazy Africans, and he shouted orders to his boss-boys, and watched the swarms of workers far below him in the bottom of the pit, and then he would go to his little office and make up his books, and so he spent his day. In the evenings he sometimes asked Mr. Clarke to come over and play cards.

Then Mr. Clarke would say to his wife: "Annie, he wants me," and she nodded and told her cook to make supper early.

Mrs. Clarke was the only white woman on the mine. She did not mind this, being a naturally solitary person. Also, she had been profoundly grateful to reach this haven of fifty pounds a month with a man who did not mind her husband's bouts of drinking. She was a woman of early middle age, with a thin, flat body, a thin, colourless face, and quiet blue eyes. Living here, in this destroying heat, year after year, did not make her ill, it sapped her slowly, leaving her rather numbed and silent. She spoke very little, but then she roused herself and said what was necessary.

For instance, when they first arrived at the mine it was to a two-roomed house. She walked over to Mr. Macintosh and said: "You are alone, but you have four rooms. There are two of us and the baby, and we have two rooms. There's no sense in it." Mr. Macintosh gave her a quick, hard look, his mouth tightened, and then he began to laugh. "Well, yes, that is so," he said, laughing, and he made the change at once, chuckling every time he remembered how the quiet Annie Clarke had put him in his place.

Similarly, about once a month Annie Clarke went to his house and said: "Now get out of my way, I'll get things straight for you." And when she'd finished tidying up she said: "You're nothing but a pig, and that's the truth." She was referring to his habit of throwing his clothes everywhere, or wearing them for weeks unwashed, and also to other matters which no one else dared to refer to, even as indirectly as this. To this he might reply, chuckling with the pleasure of teasing her: "You're a married woman, Mrs. Clarke," and she said: "Nothing stops you getting married that I can see." And she walked away very straight, her cheeks burning with indignation.

She was very fond of him, and he of her. And Mr. Clarke liked and admired him, and he liked Mr. Clarke. And since Mr. Clarke and Mrs. Clarke lived amiably together in their four-roomed house, sharing bed and board without ever quarreling, it was to be presumed they liked each other too. But they seldom spoke. What was there to say?

It was to this silence, to these understood truths, that little Tommy had to grow up and adjust himself.

Tommy Clarke was three months old when he came to the mine, and day and night his ears were filled with noise, every day and every night for years, so that he did not think of it as noise, rather, it was a different sort of silence. The mine-stamps thudded gold, gold, gold, gold, gold. gold, on and on, never changing, never stopping. So he did not hear them. But there came a day when the machinery broke, and it was when Tommy was three years old, and the silence was so terrible and so empty that he went screeching to his mother: "It's stopped, it's stopped," and he wept, shivering, in a corner until the thudding began again. It was as if the heart of the world had gone silent. But when it started to beat, Tommy heard it, and he knew the difference between silence and sound, and his ears acquired a new sensitivity, like a conscience. He heard the shouting and the singing from the swarms of working Africans, reckless, noisy people because of the danger they always must live with. He heard the picks ringing on stone, the softer, deeper thud of picks on thick earth. He heard the clang of the trucks, and the roar of falling earth, and the rumbling of trolleys on rails. And at night the owls hooted and the nightjars screamed, and the crickets chirped. And when it stormed it seemed the sky itself was flinging down bolts of noise against the mountains, for the thunder rolled and crashed, and the lightning darted from peak to peak around him. It was never silent, never, save for that awful moment when the big heart stopped beating. Yet later he longed for it to stop again, just for an hour, so that he might hear a true silence. That was when he was a little older, and the quietness of his parents was beginning to trouble him. There they were, always so gentle, saying so little only: That's how things are; or: You ask so many questions; or: You'll understand when you grow up.

It was a false silence, much worse than that real silence had been.

He would play beside his mother in the kitchen, who never said anything but Yes, and No, and—with a patient, sighing voice, as if even his voice tired her: You talk so much, Tommy!

And he was carried on his father's shoulders around the big, black working machines, and they couldn't speak because of the din the machines made. And Mr. Macintosh would say: Well, laddie? and gave him sweets from his pocket, which he always kept there, especially for Tommy. And once he saw Mr. Macintosh and his father playing cards in the evening, and they didn't talk at all, except for the words that the game needed.

So Tommy escaped to the friendly din of the compound across the great gulf, and played all day with the black children, dancing in their dances, running through the bush after rabbits, or working wet clay into shapes of bird or beast. No silence there, everything noisy and cheerful, and at evening he returned to his equable, silent parents, and after the meal he lay in bed listening to the thud, thud, thud, thud, thud, thud, of the stamps. In the compound across the gulf they were drinking and dancing, the drums made a quick beating against the slow thud of the stamps, and the dancers around the fires yelled, a high, undulating sound like a big wind coming fast and crooked through a cap in the mountains. That was a different world, to which he belonged as much as to this one, where people said: Finish your pudding; or: It's time for bed; and very little else.

When he was five years old he got malaria and was very sick. He recovered, but in the rainy season of the next year he got it again. Both times Mr. Macintosh got into his big American car and went streaking across the thirty miles of bush to the nearest hospital for the doctor. The doctor said quinine, and be careful to screen for mosquitoes. It was easy to give quinine, but Mrs. Clark, that tired, easy-going woman, found it hard to say: Don't, and Be in by six; and Don't go near the water; and so, when Tommy was seven, he got malaria again. And now Mrs. Clarke was worried, because the doctor spoke severely, mentioning blackwater.

Mr. Macintosh drove the doctor back to his hospital and then came home, and at once went to see Tommy, for he loved Tommy very deeply.

Mrs. Clarke said: "What do you expect, with all these holes everywhere, they're full of water all the wet season."

"Well, lassie. I can't fill in all the holes and shafts, people have been digging up here since the Queen of Sheba."

"Never mind about the Queen of Sheba. At least you could screen our house properly."

"I pay your husband fifty pounds a month," said Mr. Macintosh, conscious of being in the right.

"Fifty pounds and a proper house," said Annie Clarke.

Mr. Macintosh gave her that quick, narrow look, and then laughed loudly. A week later the house was encased in fine wire mesh all round from roof-edge to verandah-edge, so that it looked like a new meat safe, and Mrs. Clarke went over to Mr. Macintosh's house and gave it a grand cleaning, and when she left she said: "You're nothing but a pig, you're as rich as the Oppenheimers, why don't you buy yourself some new vests at least. And you'll be getting malaria, too, the way you go traipsing about at nights."

She returned to Tommy, who was seated on the verandah behind the grey-glistening wire-netting, in a big deck-chair. He was very thin and white after the fever. He was a long child, bony, and his eyes were big and black, and his mouth full and pouting from the petulances of the illness. He had a mass of richly-brown hair, like caramels, on his head. His mother looked at this pale child of hers, who was yet so brightly coloured and full of vitality, and her tired will-power revived enough to determine a new régime for him. He was never to be out after six at night, when the mosquitoes were abroad. He was never to be out before the sun rose.

"You can get up," she said, and he got up, thankfully throwing aside his covers.

"I'll go over to the compound," he said at once.

She hesitated, and then said: "You mustn't play there any more."

"Why not?" he asked, already fidgeting on the steps outside the wire-netting cage.

Ah, how she hated these Whys, and Why nots! They tired her utterly. "Because I say so," she snapped.

But he persisted: "I always play there."

"You're getting too big now, and you'll be going to school soon."

Tommy sank on to the steps and remained there, looking away over the great pit to the busy, sunlit compound. He had known this moment was coming, of course. It was a knowledge that was part of the silence. And yet he had not known it. He said: "Why, why, why, why?" singing it out in a persistent wail.

"Because I say so." Then, in tired desperation: "You get sick from the Africans, too."

At this, he switched his large black eyes from the scenery to his mother, and she flushed a little. For they were derisively scornful. Yet she half-believed it herself, or rather, must believe it, for all through the wet season the bush would lie waterlogged and festering with mosquitoes, and nothing could be done about it, and one has to put the blame on something.

She said: "Don't argue. You're not to play with them. You're too big now to play with a lot of dirty kaffirs. When you were little it was different, but now you're a big boy."

Tommy sat on the steps in the sweltering afternoon sun that came thick and yellow through the haze of dust and smoke over the mountains, and he said nothing. He made no attempt to go near the compound, now that his growing to manhood depended on his not playing with the black people. So he had been made to feel. Yet he did not believe a word of it, not really.

Some days later, he was kicking a football by himself around the back of the house when a group of black children called to him from the bush, and he turned away as if he had not seen them. They called again and then ran away. And Tommy wept bitterly, for now he was alone.

He went to the edge of the big pit and lay on his stomach looking down. The sun blazed through him so that his bones ached, and he shook his mass of hair forward over his eyes to shield them. Below, the great pit was so deep that the men working on the bottom of it were like ants. The trucks that climbed up the almost vertical sides were like matchboxes. The system of ladders and steps cut in the earth, which the workers used to climb up and down, seemed so flimsy across the gulf that a stone might dislodge it. Indeed, falling stones often did. Tommy sprawled, gripping the earth tight with tense belly and flung limbs, and stared down. They were all like ants and flies. Mr. Macintosh, too, when he went down, which he did often, for no one could say he was a coward. And his father, and Tommy himself, they were all no bigger than little insects.

It was like an enormous ant-working, as brightly tinted as a fresh antheap. The levels of earth around the mouth of the pit were reddish, then lower down grey and gravelly, and lower still, clear yellow. Heaps of the inert, heavy yellow soil, brought up from the bottom, lay all around him. He stretched out his hand and took some of it. It was unresponsive, lying lifeless and dense on his fingers, a little damp from the rain. He clenched his fist, and loosened it, and now the mass of yellow earth lay shaped on his palm, showing the marks of his fingers. A shape like—what? A bit of root? A fragment of rock rotted by water? He rolled his palms vigorously around it, and it became smooth like a water-ground stone. Then he sat up and took more earth, and formed a pit, and up the sides flying ladders with bits of stick, and little kips of wetted earth for the trucks. Soon the sun dried it, and it all cracked and fell apart. Tommy gave the model a kick and went moodily back to the house. The sun was going down. It seemed that he had left a golden age of freedom behind, and now there was a new country of restrictions and time-tables.

His mother saw how he suffered, but thought: Soon he'll go to school and find companions.

But he was only just seven, and very young to go all the way to the city to boarding-school. She sent for school-books, and taught him to read. Yet this was for only two or three hours in the day, and for the rest he mooned about, as she complained, gazing away over the gulf to the compound, from where he could hear the noise of the playing children. He was stoical about it, or so it seemed, but underneath he was suffering badly from this new knowledge, which was much more vital than anything he had learned from the school-books. He knew the word loneliness, and lying at the edge of the pit he formed the yellow clay into little figures which he called Betty and Freddy and Dirk. Playmates. Dirk was the name of the boy he liked best among the children in the compound over the gulf.

One day his mother called him to the back door. There stood Dirk, and he was holding between his hands a tiny duiker, the size of a thin cat. Tommy ran forward, and was about to exclaim with Dirk over the little animal, when he remembered his new status. He stopped, stiffened himself, and said: "How much?"

Dirk, keeping his eyes evasive, said: "One shilling, baas."

Tommy glanced at his mother and then said, proudly, his voice high: "Damned cheek, too much."

Annie Clarke flushed. She was ashamed and flustered. She came forward and said quickly: "It's all right, Tommy, I'll give you the shilling." She took the coin from the pocket of her apron and gave it to Tommy, who handed it at once to Dirk. Tommy took the little animal gently in his hands, and his tenderness for this frightened and lonely creature rushed up to his eyes and he turned away so that Dirk couldn't see—he would have been bitterly ashamed to show softness in front of Dirk, who was so tough and fearless.

Dirk stood back, watching, unwilling to see the last of the buck. Then he said: "It's just born, it can die."

Mrs. Clarke said, dismissingly: "Yes, Tommy will look after it." Dirk walked away slowly, fingering the shilling in his pocket, but looking back at where Tommy and his mother were making a nest for the little buck in a packing-case. Mrs. Clarke made a feeding-bottle with some linen stuffed into the neck of a tomato sauce bottle and filled it with milk and water and sugar. Tommy knelt by the buck and tried to drip the milk into its mouth.

It lay trembling lifting its delicate head from the crumpled, huddled limbs, too weak to move, the big eyes dark and forlorn. Then the trembling became a spasm of weakness and the head collapsed with a soft thud against the side of the box, and then slowly, and with a trembling effort, the neck lifted the head again. Tommy tried to push the wad of linen into the soft mouth, and the milk wetted the fur and ran down over the buck's chest, and he wanted to cry.

"But it'll die, Mother, it'll die," he shouted, angrily.

"You mustn't force it," said Annie Clarke, and she went away to her household duties. Tommy knelt there with the bottle, stroking the trembling little buck and suffering every time the thin neck collapsed with weakness, and tried again and again to interest it in the milk. But the buck wouldn't drink at all.

"Why?" shouted Tommy, in the anger of his misery. "Why won't it drink? Why? Why?"

"But it's only just born," said Mrs. Clarke. The cord was still on the creature's navel, like a shriveling, dark stick.

That night Tommy took the little buck into his room, and secretly in the dark lifted it, folded in a blanket, into his bed. He could feel it trembling fitfully against his chest, and he cried into the dark because he knew it was going to die.

In the morning when he woke, the buck could not lift its head at all, and it was a weak, collapsed weight on Tommy's chest, a chilly weight. The blanket in which it lay was messed with yellow stuff like a scrambled egg. Tommy washed the buck gently, and wrapped it again in new coverings, and laid it on the verandah where the sun could warm it.

Mrs. Clarke gently forced the jaws open and poured down milk until the buck choked. Tommy knelt beside it all morning, suffering as he had never suffered before. The tears ran steadily down his face and he wished he could die too, and Mrs. Clarke wished very much she could catch Dirk and give him a good beating, which would be unjust, but might do something to relieve her feelings. "Besides," she said to her husband, "it's nothing but cruelty, taking a tiny thing like that from its mother."

Late that afternoon the buck died, and Mr. Clarke, who had not seen his son's misery over it, casually threw the tiny, stiff corpse to the cookboy and told him to go and bury it. Tommy stood on the verandah, his face tight and angry, and watched the cookboy shovel his little buck hastily under some bushes, and return whistling.

Then he went into the room where his mother and father were sitting and said: "Why is Dirk yellow and not dark brown like the other kaffirs?"

Silence. Mr. Clarke and Annie Clarke looked at each other. Then Mr. Clarke said: "They come different colours."

Tommy looked forcefully at his mother, who said: "He's a half-caste."

"What's a half-caste?"

"You'll understand when you grow up."

Tommy looked from his father, who was filling his pipe, his eyes lowered to the work, then at his mother, whose cheekbones held that proud, bright flush.

"I understand now," he said, defiantly.

"Then why do you ask?" said Mrs. Clarke, with anger. Why, she was saying, do you infringe the rule of silence?

Tommy went out, and to the brink of the great pit. There he lay, wondering why he had said he understood when he did not. Though in a sense he did. He was remembering, though he had not noticed it before, that among the gang of children in the compound were two yellow children. Dirk was one, and Dirk's sister another. She was a tiny child, who came toddling on the fringe of the older children's games. But Dirk's mother was black, or rather, dark-brown like the others. And Dirk was not really yellow, but light copper-colour. The colour of this earth, were it a little darker. Tommy's fingers were fiddling with the damp clay. He looked at the little figures he had made, Betty and Freddy. Idly, he smashed them. Then he picked up Dirk and flung him down. But he must have flung him down too carefully, for he did not break, and so he set the figure against the stalk of a weed. He took a lump of clay, and as his fingers experimentally pushed and kneaded it, the shape grew into the shape of a little duiker. But not a sick duiker, which had died because it had been taken from its mother. Not at all, it was a fine strong duiker, standing with one hoof raised and its head listening, ears pricked forward.

Tommy knelt on the verge of the great pit, absorbed, while the duiker grew into its proper form. He became dissatisfied—it was too small. He impatiently smashed what he had done, and taking a big heap of the yellowish, dense soil, shook water on it from an old rusty railway sleeper that had collected rainwater, and made the mass soft and workable. Then he began again. The duiker would be half life-size.

And so his hands worked and his mind worried along its path of questions: Why? Why? Why? And finally: If Dirk is half black, or rather half white and half dark-brown, then who is his father?

For a long time his mind hovered on the edge of the answer, but did not finally reach it. But from time to time he looked across the gulf to where Mr. Macintosh was strolling, swinging his big cudgel, and he thought: There are only two white men on this mine.

The buck was now finished, and he wetted his fingers in rusty rainwater, and smoothed down the soft clay to make it glisten like the surfaces of fur, but at once it dried and dulled, and as he knelt there he thought how the sun would crack it and it would fall to pieces, and an angry dissatisfaction filled him and he hung his head and wanted very much to cry. And just as the first tears were coming he heard a soft whistle from behind him, and turned, and there was Dirk, kneeling behind a bush and looking out through the parted leaves.

"Is the buck all right?" asked Dirk.

Tommy said: "It's dead," and he kicked his foot at his model duiker so that the thick clay fell apart in lumps.

Dirk said: "Don't do that, it's nice," and he sprang forward and tried to fit the pieces together.

"It's no good, the sun'll crack it," said Tommy, and he began to cry, although he was so ashamed to cry in front of Dirk. "The buck's dead," he wept, "it's dead."

"I can get you another," said Dirk, looking at Tommy rather surprised. "I killed its mother with a stone. It's easy."

Dirk was seven, like Tommy. He was tall and strong, like Tommy. His eyes were dark and full, but his mouth was not full and soft, but long and narrow, clenched in the middle. His hair was very black and soft and long, falling uncut around his face, and his skin was a smooth, yellowish copper. Tommy stopped crying and looked at Dirk. He said: "It's cruel to kill a buck's mother with a stone." Dirk's mouth parted in surprised laughter over his big white teeth. Tommy watched him laugh, and he thought: Well, now I know who his father is.

He looked away to his home, which was two hundred yards off, exposed to the sun's glare among low bushes of hibiscus and poinsettia. He looked at Mr. Macintosh's house, which was a few hundred yards farther off. Then he looked at Dirk. He was full of anger, which he did not understand, but he did understand that he was also defiant, and this was a moment of decision. After a long time he said: "They can see us from here," and the decision was made.

They got up, but as Dirk rose he saw the little clay figure laid against a stem, and he picked it up. "This is me," he said at once. For crude as the thing was, it was unmistakably Dirk, who smiled with pleasure. "Can I have it?" he asked, and Tommy nodded, equally proud and pleased.

They went off into the bush between the two houses, and then on for perhaps half a mile. This was the deserted part of the hollow in the mountains, no one came here, all the bustle and noise was on the other side. In front of them rose a sharp peak, and low at its foot was a high anthill, draped with Christmas fern and thick with shrub.

The two boys went inside the curtains of fern and sat down. No one could see them here. Dirk carefully put the little clay figure of himself inside a hole in the roots of a tree. Then he said: "Make the buck again." Tommy took his knife and knelt beside a fallen tree, and tried to carve the buck from it. The wood was soft and rotten, and was easily carved, and by night there was the clumsy shape of the buck coming out of the trunk. Dirk said: "Now we've both got something."

The next day the two boys made their way separately to the antheap and played there together, and so it was every day.

Then one evening Mrs. Clark said to Tommy just as he was going to bed: "I thought I told you not to play with the kaffirs?"

Tommy stood very still. Then he lifted his head and said to her, with a strong look across at his father: "Why shouldn't I play with Mr. Macintosh's son?"

Mrs. Clarke stopped breathing for a moment, and closed her eyes. She opened them in appeal at her husband. But Mr. Clarke was filling his pipe. Tommy waited and then said good night and went to his room.

There he undressed slowly and climbed into the narrow iron bed and lay quietly, listening to the thud, thud, gold, gold, thud, thud, of the mine-stamps. Over in the compound they were dancing, and the tom-toms were beating fast, like the quick beat of the buck's heart that night as it lay on his chest. They were yelling like the wind coming through gaps in a mountain and through the window he could see the high, flaring light of the fires, and the black figures of the dancing people were wild and active against it.

Mrs. Clarke came quickly in. She was crying. "Tommy," she said, sitting on the edge of his bed in the dark.

"Yes?" he said, cautiously.

"You mustn't say that again. Not ever."

He said nothing. His mother's hand was urgently pressing his arm. "Your father might lose his job," said Mrs. Clarke, wildly. "We'd never get this money anywhere else. Never. You must understand, Tommy."

"I do understand," said Tommy, stiffly, very sorry for his mother, but hating her at the same time. "Just don't say it, Tommy, don't ever say it." Then she kissed him in a way that was both fond and appealing, and went out, shutting the door. To her husband she said it was time Tommy went to school, and next day she wrote to make the arrangements.

And so now Tommy made the long journey by car and train into the city four times a year, and four times a year he came back for the holidays. Mr. Macintosh always drove him to the station and gave him ten shillings pocket money, and he came to fetch him in the car with his parents, and he always said: "Well, laddie, and how's school?" And Tommy said: "Fine, Mr. Macintosh." And Mr. Macintosh said: "We'll make a college man of you yet."

When he said this, the flush came bright and proud on Annie Clarke's cheeks, and she looked quickly at Mr. Clarke, who was smiling and embarrassed. But Mr. Macintosh laid his hands on Tommy's shoulders and said: "There's my laddie, there's my laddie," and Tommy kept his shoulders stiff and still. Afterwards, Mrs. Clarke would say, nervously: "He's fond of you, Tommy, he'll do right by you." And once she said: "It's natural, he's got no children of his own." But Tommy scowled at her and she flushed and said: "There's things you don't understand yet, Tommy, and you'll regret it if you throw away your chances." Tommy turned away with an impatient movement. Yet it was not so clear at all, for it was almost as if he were a rich man's son, with all that pocket money, and the parcels of biscuits and sweets that Mr. Macintosh sent into school during the term, and being fetched in the great rich car. And underneath it all he felt as if he were dragged along by the nose. He felt as if he were part of a conspiracy of some kind that no one ever spoke about. Silence. His real feelings were growing up slow and complicated and obstinate underneath that silence.

At school it was not at all complicated, it was the other world. There Tommy did his lessons and played with his friends and did not think of Dirk. Or rather, his thoughts of him were proper for that world. A half-caste, ignorant, living in the kaffir location—he felt ashamed that he played with Dirk in the holidays, and he told no one. Even on the train coming home he would think like that of Dirk, but the nearer he reached home the more his thoughts wavered and darkened. On the first evening at home he would speak of the school, and how he was first in the class, and he played with this boy or that, or went to such fine houses in the city as a guest. The very first morning he would be standing on the verandah looking at the big pit and at the compound away beyond it, and his mother watched him, smiling in nervous supplication. And then he walked down the steps, away from the pit, and into the bush to the antheap. There Dirk was waiting for him. So it was every holiday. Neither of the boys spoke at first of what divided them. But, on the eve of Tommy's return to school after he had been there a year, Dirk said: "You're getting educated, but I've nothing to learn." Tommy said: "I'll bring back books and teach you." He said this in a quick voice, as if ashamed, and Dirk's eyes were accusing and angry. He gave his sarcastic laugh and said: "That's what you say, white boy."

It was not pleasant, but what Tommy said was not pleasant either, like a favour wrung out of a condescending person.

The two boys were sitting on the antheap under the fine lacy curtains of Christmas fern, looking at the rocky peak soaring into the smoky yellowish sky. There was the most unpleasant sort of annoyance in Tommy, and he felt ashamed of it. And on Dirk's face there was an aggressive but ashamed look. They continued to sit there, a little apart, full of dislike for each other, and knowing that the dislike came from the pressure of the outside world. "I said I'd teach you, didn't I?" said Tommy, grandly, shying a stone at a bush so that leaves flew off in all directions.

"You white bastard," said Dirk, in a low voice, and he let out that sudden ugly laugh, showing his white teeth. "What did you say?" said Tommy, going pale and jumping to his feet. "You heard," said Dirk, still laughing. He too got up. Then Tommy flung himself on Dirk and they overbalanced and rolled off into the bushes, kicking and scratching. They rolled apart and began fighting properly, with fists. Tommy was better-fed and more healthy. Dirk was tougher. They were a match, and they stopped when they were too tired and battered to go on. They staggered over to the antheap and sat there side by side, panting, wiping the blood off their faces. At last they lay on their backs on the rough slant of the anthill and looked up at the sky. Every trace of dislike had vanished, and they felt easy and quiet. When the sun went down they walked together through the bush to a point where they could not be seen from the houses, and there they said, as always: "See you tomorrow."

When Mr. Macintosh gave him the usual ten shillings, he put them into his pocket thinking he would buy a football, but he did not. The ten shillings stayed unspent until it was nearly the end of term, and then he went to the shops and bought a reader and some exercise books and pencils, and an arithmetic. He hid these at the bottom of his trunk and whipped them out before his mother could see them.

He took them to the antheap next morning, but before he could reach it he saw there was a little shed built on it, and the Christmas fern had been draped like a veil across the roof of the shed. The bushes had been cut on the top of the anthill, but left on the sides, so that the shed looked as if it rose from the tops of the bushes. The shed was of unbarked poles pushed into the earth, the roof was of thatch, and the upper half of the front was left open. Inside there was a bench of poles and a table of planks on poles. There sat Dirk, waiting hungrily, and Tommy went and sat beside him, putting the books and pencils on the table.

"This shed is fine," said Tommy, but Dirk was already looking at the books. So he began to teach Dirk how to read. And for all that holiday they were together in the shed while Dirk pored over the books. He found them more difficult than Tommy did, because they were full of words for things Dirk did not know, like curtains or carpet, and teaching Dirk to read the word carpet meant telling him all about carpets and the furnishings of a house. Often Tommy felt bored and restless and said: "Let's play," but Dirk said fiercely: "No, I want to read." Tommy grew fretful, for after all he had been working in the term and now he felt entitled to play. So there was another fight. Dirk said Tommy was a lazy white bastard, and Tommy said Dirk was a dirty half-caste. They fought as before, evenly matched and to no conclusion, and afterwards felt fine and friendly, and even made jokes about the fighting. It was arranged that they should work in the mornings only and leave the afternoons for play. When Tommy went back home that evening his mother saw the scratches on his face and the swollen nose, and said hopefully: "Have you and Dirk been fighting?" But Tommy said no, he had hit his face on a tree.

His parents, of course, knew about the shed in the bush, but did not speak of it to Mr. Macintosh. No one did. For Dirk's very existence was something to be ignored by everyone, and none of the workers, not even the overseers, would dare to mention Dirk's name. When Mr. Macintosh asked Tommy what he had done to his face, he said he had slipped and fallen.

And so their eighth year and their ninth went past. Dirk could read and write and do all the sums that Tommy could do. He was always handicapped by not knowing the different way of living and soon he said, angrily, it wasn't fair, and there was another fight about it, and then Tommy began another way of teaching. He would tell how it was to go to a cinema in the city, every detail of it, how the seats were arranged in such a way, and one paid so much, and the lights were like this, and the picture on the screen worked like that. Or he would describe how at school they ate such things for breakfast and other things for lunch. Or tell how the man had come with picture slides talking about China. The two boys got out an atlas and found China, and Tommy told Dirk every word of what the lecturer had said. Or it might be Italy or some other country. And they would argue that the lecturer should have said this or that, for Dirk was always hotly scornful of the white man's way of looking at things, so arrogant, he said. Soon Tommy saw things through Dirk; he saw the other life in town clear and brightly-coloured and a little distorted, as Dirk said.

Soon, at school, Tommy would involuntarily think: I must remember this to tell Dirk. It was impossible for him to do anything, say anything, without being very conscious of just how it happened, as if Dirk's black, sarcastic eye had got inside him, Tommy, and never closed. And a feeling of unwillingness grew in Tommy, because of the strain of fitting these two worlds together. He found himself swearing at niggers or kaffirs like the other boys, and more violently than they did, but immediately afterwards he would find himself thinking: I must remember this so as to tell Dirk. Because of all this thinking, and seeing everything clear all the time, he was very bright at school, and found the work easy. He was two classes ahead of his age.

That was the tenth year, and one day Tommy went to the shed in the bush and Dirk was not waiting for him. It was the first day of the holidays. All the term he had been remembering things to tell Dirk, and now Dirk was not there. A dove was sitting on the Christmas fern, cooing lazily in the hot morning, a sleepy, lonely sound. When Tommy came pushing through the bushes it flew away. The mine-stamps thudded heavily, gold, gold, and Tommy saw that the shed was empty even of books, for the case where they were usually kept was hanging open.

He went running to his mother: "Where's Dirk?" he asked.

"How should I know?" said Annie Clarke, cautiously. She really did not know.

"You do know, you do!" he cried, angrily. And then he went racing off to the big pit. Mr. Macintosh was sitting on an upturned truck on the edge, watching the hundreds of workers below him, moving like ants on the yellow bottom. "Well, laddie?" he asked, amiably, and moved over for Tommy to sit by him.

"Where's Dirk?" asked Tommy, accusingly, standing in front of him.

Mr. Macintosh tipped his old felt hat even further back and scratched at his front hair and looked at Tommy.

"Dirk's working," he said, at last.

"Where?"

Mr. Macintosh pointed at the bottom of the pit. Then he said again: "Sit down, laddie, I want to talk to you."

"I don't want to," said Tommy, and he turned away and went blundering over the veld to the shed. He sat on the bench and cried, and when dinnertime came he did not go home. All that day he sat in the shed, and when he had finished crying he remained on the bench, leaning his back against the poles of the shed, and stared into the bush. The doves cooed and cooed, kru-kruuuu, kru-kruuuuu, and a woodpecker tapped, and the mine-stamps thudded. Yet it was very quiet, a hand of silence gripped the bush, and he could hear the borers and the ants at work in the poles of the bench he sat on. He could see that although the anthill seemed dead, a mound of hard, peaked, baked earth, it was very much alive, for there was a fresh outbreak of wet, damp earth in the floor of the shed. There was a fine crust of reddish, lacey earth over the poles of the walls. The shed would have to be built again soon, because the ants and borers would have eaten it through. But what was the use of a shed without Dirk?

All that day he stayed there, and did not return until dark, and when his mother said: "What's the matter with you, why are you crying?" he said angrily, "I don't know," matching her dishonesty with his own. The next day, even before breakfast, he was off to the shed, and did not return until dark, and refused his supper although he had not eaten all day.

And the next day it was the same, but now he was bored and lonely. He took his knife from his pocket and whittled at a stick, and it became a boy, bent and straining under the weight of a heavy load, his arms clenched up to support it. He took the figure home at suppertime and ate with it on the table in front of him.

"What's that?" asked Annie Clarke, and Tommy answered: "Dirk."

He took it to his bedroom, and sat in the soft lamp-light, working away with his knife, and he had it in his hand the following morning when he met Mr. Macintosh at the brink of the pit. "What's that, laddie?" asked Mr. Macintosh, and Tommy said: "Dirk."

Mr. Macintosh's mouth went thin, and then he smiled and said: "Let me have it."

"No, it's for Dirk."

Mr. Macintosh took out his wallet and said: "I'll pay you for it."

"I don't want any money," said Tommy, angrily, and Mr. Macintosh, greatly disturbed, put back his wallet. Then Tommy, hesitating, said: "Yes, I do." Mr. Macintosh, his values confirmed, was relieved, and he took out his wallet again and produced a pound note, which seemed to him very generous. "Five pounds," said Tommy, promptly. Mr. Macintosh first scowled, then laughed. He tipped back his head and roared with laughter. "Well, laddie, you'll make a businessman yet. Five pounds for a little bit of wood!"

"Make it for yourself then, if it's just a bit of wood."

Mr. Macintosh counted out five pounds and handed them over. "What are you going to do with that money?" he asked, as he watched Tommy buttoning them carefully into his shirt pocket. "Give them to Dirk," said Tommy, triumphantly, and Mr. Macintosh's heavy old face went purple. He watched while Tommy walked away from him, sitting on the truck, letting the heavy cudgel swing lightly against his shoes. He solved his immediate problem by thinking: He's a good laddie, he's got a good heart.

That night Mrs. Clarke came over while he was sitting over his roast beef and cabbage, and said: "Mr. Macintosh, I want a word with you." He nodded at a chair, but she did not sit. "Tommy's upset," she said, delicately, "he's been used to Dirk, and now he's got no one to play with."

For a moment Mr. Macintosh kept his eyes lowered, then he said: "It's easily fixed, Annie, don't worry yourself." He spoke heartily, as it was easy for him to do, speaking of a worker, who might be released at his whim for other duties.

That bright protesting flush came on to her cheeks, in spite of herself, and she looked quickly at him, with real indignation. But he ignored it and said: "I'll fix it in the morning, Annie."

She thanked him and went back home, suffering because she had not said those words which had always soothed her conscience in the past: You're nothing but a pig, Mr. Macintosh . . .

As for Tommy, he was sitting in the shed, crying his eyes out. And then, when there were no more tears, there came such a storm of anger and pain that he would never forget it as long as he lived. What for? He did not know, and that was the worst of it. It was not simply Mr. Macintosh, who loved him, and who thus so blackly betrayed his own flesh and blood, nor the silences of his parents. Something deeper, felt working in the substance of life as he could hear those ants working away with those busy jaws at the roots of the poles he sat on, to make new material for their different forms of life. He was testing those words which were used, or not used—merely suggested—all the time, and for a ten-year-old boy it was almost too hard to bear. A child may say of a companion one day that he hates so and so, and the next: He is my friend. That is how a relationship is, shifting and changing, and children are kept safe in their hates and loves by the fabric of social life their parents make over their heads. And middle-aged people say: This is my friend, this is my enemy, including all the shifts and changes of feeling in one word, for the sake of an easy mind. In between these ages, at about twenty perhaps, there is a time when the young people test everything, and accept many hard and cruel truths about living, and that is because they do not know how hard it is to accept them finally, and for the rest of their lives. It is easy to be truthful at twenty.

But it is not easy at ten, a little boy entirely alone, looking at words like friendship. What, then, was friendship? Dirk was his friend, that he knew, but did he like Dirk? Did he love him? Sometimes not at all. He remembered how Dirk had said: "I'll get you another baby buck. I'll kill its mother with a stone." He remembered his feeling of revulsion at the cruelty. Dirk was cruel. But—and here Tommy unexpectedly laughed, and for the first time he understood Dirk's way of laughing. It was really funny to say that Dirk was cruel, when his very existence was a cruelty. Yet Mr. Macintosh laughed in exactly the same way, and his skin was white, or rather, white browned over by the sun. Why was Mr. Macintosh also entitled to laugh, with that same abrupt ugliness? Perhaps somewhere in the beginnings of the rich Mr. Macintosh there had been the same cruelty, and that had worked its way through the life of Mr. Macintosh until it turned into the cruelty of Dirk, the coloured boy, the half-caste? If so, it was all much harder to understand.

And then Tommy thought how Dirk seemed to wait always, as if he, Tommy, were bound to stand by him, as if this were a justice that was perfectly clear to Dirk; and he, Tommy, did in fact fight with Mr. Macintosh for Dirk, and he could behave in no other way. Why? Because Dirk was his friend? Yet there were times when he hated Dirk, and certainly Dirk hated him, and when they fought they could have killed each other easily, and with joy.

Well, then? Well, then? What was friendship, and why were they bound so closely, and by what? Slowly the little boy, sitting alone on his antheap, came to an understanding which is proper to middle-aged people, that resignation in knowledge which is called irony. Such a person may know, for instance, that he is bound most deeply to another person, although he does not like that person, in the way the word is ordinarily used, or the way he talks, or his politics, or anything else. And yet they are friends and will always be friends, and what happens to this bound couple affects each most deeply, even though they may be in different continents, or may never see each other again. Or after twenty years they may meet, and there is no need to say a word, everything is understood. This is one of the ways of friendship, and just as real as amiability or being alike.

Well, then? For it is a hard and difficult knowledge for any little boy to accept. But he accepted it, and knew that he and Dirk were closer than brothers and always would be so. He grew many years older in that day of painful struggle, while he listened to the minestamps saying gold, gold, and to the ants working away with their jaws to destroy the bench he sat on, to make food for themselves.

Next morning Dirk came to the shed, and Tommy, looking at him, knew that he, too, had grown years older in the months of working in the great pit. Ten years old—but he had been working with men and he was not a child.

Tommy took out the five pound notes and gave them to Dirk.

Dirk pushed them back. "What for?" he asked.

"I got them from him," said Tommy, and at once Dirk took them as if they were his right.

And at once, inside Tommy, came indignation, for he felt he was being taken for granted, and he said: "Why aren't you working?"

"He said I needn't. He means, while you are having your holidays."

"I got you free," said Tommy, boasting.

Dirk's eyes narrowed in anger. "He's my father," he said, for the first time.

"But he made you work," said Tommy, taunting him. And then: "Why do you work? I wouldn't. I should say no."

"So you would say no?" said Dirk in angry sarcasm.

"There's no law to make you."

"So there's no law, white boy, no law . . ." But Tommy had sprung at him, and they were fighting again, rolling over and over, and this time they fell apart from exhaustion and lay on the ground panting for a long time.

Later Dirk said: "Why do we fight, it's silly?"

"I don't know," said Tommy, and he began to laugh, and Dirk laughed too. They were to fight often in the future, but never with such bitterness, because of the way they were laughing now.

It was the following holidays before they fought again. Dirk was waiting for him in the shed.

"Did he let you go?" asked Tommy at once, putting down new books on the table for Dirk.

"I just came," said Dirk. "I didn't ask."

They sat together on the bench, and at once a leg gave way and they rolled off on the floor laughing. "We must mend it," said Tommy. "Let's build the shed again."

"No," said Dirk at once, "don't let's waste time on the shed. You can teach me while you're here, and I can make the shed when you've gone back to school."

Tommy slowly got up from the floor, frowning. Again he felt he was being taken for granted. "Aren't you going to work on the mine during the term?"

"No, I'm not going to work on the mine again. I told him I wouldn't."

"You've got to work," said Tommy, grandly.

"So I've got to work," said Dirk, threateningly. "You can go to school, white boy, but I've got to work, and in the holidays I can just take time off to please you."

They fought until they were tired, and five minutes afterwards they were seated on the anthill talking. "What did you do with the five pounds?" asked Tommy.

"I gave them to my mother."

"What did she do with them?"

"She bought herself a dress, and then food for us all, and bought me these trousers, and she put the rest away to keep."

A pause. Then, deeply ashamed, Tommy asked: "Doesn't he give her any money?"

"He doesn't come any more. Not for more than a year."

"Oh, I thought he did still," said Tommy casually, whistling.

"No." Then, fiercely, in a low voice: "There'll be some more half-castes in the compound soon."

Dirk sat crouching, his fierce black eyes on Tommy, ready to spring at him. But Tommy was sitting with his head bowed, looking at the ground. "It's not fair," he said. "It's not fair."

"So you've discovered that, white boy?" said Dirk. It was said good-naturedly, and there was no need to fight. They went to their books and Tommy taught Dirk some new sums.

But they never spoke of what Dirk would do in the future, how he would use all this schooling. They did not dare.

That was the eleventh year.

When they were twelve, Tommy returned from school to be greeted by the words: "Have you heard the news?"

"What news?"

They were sitting as usual on the bench. The shed was newly built, with strong thatch, and good walls, plastered this time with mud, so as to make it harder for the ants.

"They are saying you are going to be sent away."

"Who says so?"

"Oh, everyone," said Dirk, stirring his feet about vaguely under the table. This was because it was the first few minutes after the return from school, and he was always cautious, until he was sure Tommy had not changed towards him. And that "everyone" was explosive. Tommy nodded, however, and asked apprehensively: "Where to?"

"To the sea."

"How do they know?" Tommy scarcely breathed the word they.

"Your cook heard your mother say so . . ." And then Dirk added with a grin, forcing the issue: "Cheek, dirty kaffirs talking about white men."

Tommy smiled obligingly, and asked: "How, to the sea, what does it mean?"

"How should we know, dirty kaffirs."

"Oh, shut up," said Tommy, angrily. They glared at each other, their muscles tensed. But they sighed and looked away. At twelve it was not easy to fight, it was all too serious.

That night Tommy said to his parents: "They say I'm going to sea. Is it true?"

His mother asked quickly: "Who said so?"

"But is it true?" Then, derisively: "Cheek, dirty kaffirs talking about us."

"Please don't talk like that, Tommy, it's not right."

"Oh, mother, please, how am I going to sea?"

"But be sensible Tommy, it's not settled, but Mr. Macintosh . . ."

"So it's Mr. Macintosh!"

Mrs. Clarke looked at her husband, who came forward and sat down and settled his elbows on the table. A family conference. Tommy also sat down.

"Now listen, son. Mr. Macintosh has a soft spot for you. You should be grateful to him. He can do a lot for you."

"But why should I go to sea?"

"You don't have to. He suggested it—he was in the Merchant Navy himself once."

"So I've got to go just because he did."

"He's offered to pay for you to go to college in England, and give you money until you're in the Navy."

"But I don't want to be a sailor. I've never even seen the sea."

"But you're good at your figures, and you have to be, so why not?"

"I won't," said Tommy, angrily. "I won't, I won't." He glared at them through tears. "You want to get rid of me, that's all it is. You want me to go away from here, from . . ."

The parents looked at each other and sighed.

"Well, if you don't want to, you don't have to. But it's not every boy who has a chance like this."

"Why doesn't he send Dirk?" asked Tommy, aggressively.

"Tommy," cried Annie Clarke, in great distress.

"Well, why doesn't he? He's much better than me at figures."

"Go to bed," said Mr. Clarke suddenly, in a fit of temper. "Go to bed."

Tommy went out of the room, slamming the door hard. He must be grown-up. His father had never spoken to him like that. He sat on the edge of the bed in stubborn rebellion, listening to the thudding of the stamps. And down in the compound they were dancing, the lights of the fires flickered red on his window-pane.

He wondered if Dirk were there, leaping around the fires with the others.

Next day he asked him: "Do you dance with the others?" At once he knew he had blundered. When Dirk was angry, his eyes darkened and narrowed. When he was hurt, his mouth set in a way which made the flesh pinch thinly under his nose. So he looked now.

"Listen, white boy. White people don't like us half-castes. Neither do the blacks like us. No one does. And so I don't dance with them."

"Let's do some lessons," said Tommy, quickly. And they went to their books, dropping the subject.

Later Mr. Macintosh came to the Clarkes' house and asked for Tommy. The parents watched Mr. Macintosh and their son walk together along the edge of the great pit. They stood at the window and watched, but they did not speak.

Mr. Macintosh was saying easily: "Well, laddie, and so you don't want to be a sailor."

"No, Mr. Macintosh."

"I went to sea when I was fifteen. It's hard, but you aren't afraid of that. Besides, you'd be an officer."

Tommy said nothing.

"You don't like the idea?"

"No."

Mr. Macintosh stopped and looked down into the pit. The earth at the bottom was as yellow as it had been when Tommy was seven, but now it was much deeper. Mr. Macintosh did not know how deep, because he had not measured it. Far below, in this man-made valley, the workers were moving and shifting like black seeds tilted on a piece of paper.

"Your father worked on the mines and he became an engineer working at nights, did you know that?"

"Yes."

"It was very hard for him. He was thirty before he was qualified, and then he earned twenty-five pounds a month until he came to this mine."

"Yes."

"You don't want to do that, do you?"

"I will if I have to," muttered Tommy, defiantly.

Mr. Macintosh's face was swelling and purpling. The veins along nose and forehead were black. Mr. Macintosh was asking himself why this lad treated him like dirt, when he was offering to do him an immense favour. And yet, in spite of the look of sullen indifference which was so ugly on that young face, he could not help loving him. He was a fine boy, tall, strong, and his hair was the soft, bright brown, and his eyes clear and black. A much better man than his father, who was rough and marked by the long struggle of his youth. He said: "Well, you don't have to be a sailor, perhaps you'd like to go to university and be a scholar."

"I don't know," said Tommy, unwillingly, although his heart had moved suddenly. Pleasure—he was weakening. Then he said suddenly: "Mr. Macintosh, why do you want to send me to college?"

And Mr. Macintosh fell right into the trap. "I have no children," he said, sentimentally. "I feel for you like my own son." He stopped. Tommy was looking away towards the compound and his intention was clear.

"Very well then," said Mr. Macintosh, harshly. "If you want to be a fool."

Tommy stood with his eyes lowered and he knew quite well he was a fool. Yet he could not have behaved in any other way.

"Don't be hasty," said Mr. Macintosh, after a pause. "Don't throw away your chances, laddie. You're nothing but a lad, yet. Take your time." And with this tone, he changed all the emphasis of the conflict, and made it simply a question of waiting. Tommy did not move, so Mr. Macintosh went on quickly: "Yes, that's right, you just think it over." He hastily slipped a pound note from his pocket and put it into the boy's hand.

"You know what I'm going to do with it?" said Tommy, laughing suddenly, and not at all pleasantly.

"Do what you like, do just as you like, it's your money," said Mr. Macintosh, turning away so as not to have to understand.

Tommy took the money to Dirk, who received it as if it were his right, a feeling in which Tommy was now an accomplice, and they sat together in the shed. "I've got to be something," said Tommy angrily. "They're going to make me be something."

"They wouldn't have to make me be anything," said Dirk, sardonically. "I know what I'd be."

"What?" asked Tommy, enviously.

"An engineer."

"How do you know what you've got to do?"

"That's what I want," said Dirk, stubbornly.

After a while Tommy said: "If you went to the city, there's a school for coloured children."

"I wouldn't see my mother again."

"Why not?"

"There's laws, white boys, laws. Anyone who lives with and after the fashion of the natives is a native. Therefore I'm a native, and I'm not entitled to go to school with the half-castes."

"If you went to the town, you'd not be living with the natives so you'd be classed as a coloured."

"But then I couldn't see my mother, because if she came to town she'd still be a native."

There was a triumphant conclusiveness in this that made Tommy think: He intends to get what he wants another way ... And then: Through me ... But he had accepted that justice a long time ago, and now he looked at his own arm that lay on the rough plank of the table. The outer side was burnt dark and dry with the sun, and the hair glinted on it like fine copper. It was no darker than Dirk's brown arm, and no lighter. He turned it over. Inside, the skin was smooth, dusky white, the veins running blue and strong across the wrist. He looked at Dirk, grinning, who promptly turned his own arm over, in a challenging way. Tommy said, unhappily: "You can't go to school properly because the inside of your arm is brown. And that's that!" Dirk's tight and bitter mouth expanded into the grin that was also his father's, and he said: "That is so, white boy, that is so."

"Well, it's not my fault," said Tommy, aggressively, closing his fingers and banging the fist down again and again.

"I didn't say it was your fault," said Dirk at once.

Tommy said, in that uneasy, aggressive tone: "I've never even seen your mother."

To this, Dirk merely laughed, as if to say: You have never wanted to.

Tommy said, after a pause: "Let me come and see her now."

Then Dirk said, in a tone which was uncomfortable, almost like compassion: "You don't have to."

"Yes," insisted Tommy. "Yes, now." He got up, and Dirk rose too.

"She won't know what to say," warned Dirk. "She doesn't speak English." He did not really want Tommy to go to the compound; Tommy did not really want to go. Yet they went.

In silence they moved along the path between the trees, in silence skirted the edge of the pit, in silence entered the trees on the other side, and moved along the paths to the compound. It was big, spread over many acres, and the huts were in all stages of growth and decay, some new, with shining thatch, some tumble-down, with dulled and sagging thatch, some in the process of being built, the peeled wands of the roof-frames gleaming like milk in the sun.

Dirk led the way to a big square hut. Tommy could see people watching him walking with the coloured boy, and turning to laugh and whisper. Dirk's face was proud and tight, and he could feel the same look on his own face. Outside the square hut sat a little girl of about ten. She was bronze, Dirk's colour. Another little girl, quite black, perhaps six years old, was squatted on a log, finger in mouth, watching them. A baby, still unsteady on its feet, came staggering out of the doorway and collapsed, chuckling, against Dirk's knees. Its skin was almost white. Then Dirk's mother came out of the hut after the baby, smiled when she saw Dirk, but went anxious and bashful when she saw Tommy. She made a little bobbing curtsey, and took the baby from Dirk, for the sake of something to hold in her awkward and shy hands.

"This is Baas Tommy," said Dirk. He sounded very embarrassed.

She made another little curtsey and stood smiling.

She was a large woman, round and smooth all over, but her legs were slender, and her arms, wound around the child, thin and knotted. Her round face had a bashful curiosity, and her eyes moved quickly from Dirk to Tommy and back, while she smiled and smiled, biting her lips with strong teeth, and smiled again.

Tommy said: "Good morning," and she laughed and said "Good morning."

Then Dirk said: "Enough now, let's go." He sounded very angry. Tommy said: "Goodbye." Dirk's mother said: "Goodbye," and made her little bobbing curtsey, and she moved her child from one arm to another and bit her lip anxiously over her gleaming smile.

Tommy and Dirk went away from the square mud hut where the variously-coloured children stood staring after them.

"There now," said Dirk, angrily. "You've seen my mother."

"I'm sorry," said Tommy uncomfortably, feeling as if the responsibility for the whole thing rested on him. But Dirk laughed suddenly and said: "Oh, all right, all right, white boy, it's not your fault."

All the same, he seemed pleased that Tommy was upset.

Later, with an affectation of indifference, Tommy asked, thinking of those new children: "Does Mr. Macintosh come to your mother again now?"

And Dirk answered "Yes," just one word.

In the shed Dirk studied from a geography book, while Tommy sat idle and thought bitterly that they wanted him to be a sailor. Then his idle hands protested, and he took a knife and began slashing at the edge of the table. When the gashes showed a whiteness from the core of the wood, he took a stick lying on the floor and whittled at it, and when it snapped from thinness he went out to the trees, picked up a lump of old wood from the ground, and brought it back to the shed. He worked on it with his knife, not knowing what it was he made, until a curve under his knife reminded him of Dirk's sister squatting at the hut door, and then he directed his knife with a purpose. For several days he fought with the lump of wood, while Dirk studied. Then he brought a tin of boot polish from the house, and worked the bright brown wax into the creamy white wood, and soon there was a bronze-coloured figure of the little girl, staring with big, curious eyes while she squatted on spindly legs.

Tommy put it in front of Dirk, who turned it around, grinning a little. "It's like her," he said at last. "You can have it if you like," said Tommy. Dirk's teeth flashed, he hesitated, and then reached into his pocket and took out a bundle of dirty cloth. He undid it, and Tommy saw the little clay figure he had made of Dirk years ago. It was crumbling, almost worn to a lump of mud, but in it was still the vigorous challenge of Dirk's body. Tommy's mind signalled recognition—for he had forgotten he had ever made it—and he picked it up. "You kept it?" he asked shyly, and Dirk smiled. They looked at each other, smiling. It was a moment of warm, close feeling, and yet in it was the pain that neither of them understood, and also the cruelty and challenge that made them fight. They lowered their eyes unhappily. "I'll do your mother," said Tommy, getting up and running away into the trees in order to escape from the challenging closeness. He searched until he found a thorn tree, which is so hard it turns the edge of an axe, and then he took an axe and worked at the felling of the tree until the sun went down. A big stone near him was kept wet to sharpen the axe, and next day he worked on until the tree fell. He sharpened the worn axe again, and cut a length of tree about two feet, and split off the tough bark, and brought it back to the shed. Dirk had fitted a shelf against the logs of the wall at the back. On it he had set the tiny, crumbling figure of himself, and the new bronze shape of his little sister. There was a space left for the new statue. Tommy said, shyly: "I'll do it as quickly as I can so that it will be done before the terms starts." Then, lowering his eyes, which suffered under this new contract of shared feeling, he examined the piece of wood. It was not pale and gleaming like almonds, as was the softer wood. It was a gingery brown, a close-fibred, knotted wood, and down its centre, as he knew, was a hard black spine. He turned it between his hands and thought that this was more difficult than anything he had ever done. For the first time he studied a piece of wood before starting on it, with a desired shape in his mind, trying to see how what he wanted would grow out of the dense mass of material he held.

Then he tried his knife on it and it broke. He asked Dirk for his knife. It was a long piece of metal, taken from a pile of scrap mining machinery, sharpened on stone until it was razor-fine. The handle was cloth wrapped tight around.

With this new and unwieldy tool Tommy fought with the wood for many days. When the holidays were ending, the shape was there, but the face was blank. Dirk's mother was full-bodied, with soft, heavy flesh and full, naked shoulders above a tight, sideways draped cloth. The slender legs were planted firm on naked feet, and the thin arms, knotted with work, were lifted to the weight of a child who, a small, helpless creature swaddled in cloth, looked out with large, curious eyes. But the mother's face was not yet there.

"I'll finish it next holidays," said Tommy, and Dirk set it carefully beside the other figures on the shelf. With his back turned he asked cautiously: "Perhaps you won't be here next holidays?"

"Yes I will," said Tommy, after a pause. "Yes I will."

It was a promise, and they gave each other that small, warm, unwilling smile, and turned away, Dirk back to the compound and Tommy to the house, where his trunk was packed for school.

That night Mr. Macintosh came over to the Clarkes' house and spoke with the parents in the front room. Tommy, who was asleep, woke to find Mr. Macintosh beside him. He sat on the foot of the bed and said: "I want to talk to you, laddie." Tommy turned the wick of the oil-lamp, and now he could see in the shadowy light that Mr. Macintosh had a look of uneasiness about him. He was sitting with his strong old body balanced behind the big stomach, hands laid on his knees, and his grey Scots eyes were watchful.

"I want you to think about what I said," said Mr. Macintosh, in a quick, bluff good-humour. "Your mother says in two years' time you will have matriculated, you're doing fine at school. And after that you can go to college."

Tommy lay on his elbow, and in the silence the drums came tapping from the compound, and he said: "But Mr. Macintosh, I'm not the only one who's good at his books."

Mr. Macintosh stirred, but said bluffly: "Well, but I'm talking about you."

Tommy was silent, because as usual these opponents were so much stronger than was reasonable, simply because of their ability to make words mean something else. And then, his heart painfully beating, he said: "Why don't you send Dirk to college? You're so rich, and Dirk knows everything I know. He's better than me at figures. He's a whole book ahead of me, and he can do sums I can't."

Mr. Macintosh crossed his legs impatiently, uncrossed them, and said: "Now why should I send Dirk to college?" For now Tommy would have to put into precise words what he meant, and this Mr. Macintosh was quite sure he would not do. But to make certain, he lowered his voice and said: "Think of your mother, laddie, she's worrying about you, and you don't want to make her worried, do you?"

Tommy looked towards the door, under it came a thick yellow streak of light: in that room his mother and his father were waiting in silence for Mr. Macintosh to emerge with news of Tommy's sure and wonderful future.

"You know why Dirk should go to college," said Tommy in despair, shifting his body unhappily under the sheets, and Mr. Macintosh chose not to hear it. He got up, and said quickly: "You just think it over, laddie. There's no hurry, but by next holidays I want to know." And he went out of the room. As he opened the door, a brightly-lit, painful scene was presented to Tommy: his father and mother sat, smiling in embarrassed entreaty at Mr. Macintosh. The door shut, and Tommy turned down the light, and there was darkness.

He went to school next day. Mrs. Clarke, turning out Mr. Macintosh's house as usual, said unhappily: "I think you'll find everything in its proper place," and slipped away, as if she were ashamed.

As for Mr. Macintosh, he was in a mood which made others, besides Annie Clarke, speak to him carefully. His cookboy, who had worked for him twelve years, gave notice that month. He had been knocked down twice by that powerful, hairy fist, and he was not a slave, after all, to remain bound to a bad-tempered master. And when a load of rock slipped and crushed the skulls of two workers, and the police came out for an investigation, Mr. Macintosh met them irritably, and told them to mind their own business. For the first time in that mine's history of scandalous recklessness, after many such accidents, Mr. Macintosh heard the indignant words from the police officer: "You speak as if you were above the law, Mr. Macintosh. If this happens again, you'll see . . ."

Worst of all, he ordered Dirk to go back to work in the pit, and Dirk refused.

"You can't make me," said Dirk.

"Who's the boss on this mine?" shouted Mr. Macintosh.

"There's no law to make children work," said the thirteen-year-old, who stood as tall as his father, a straight, lithe youth against the bulky strength of the old man.

The word law whipped the anger in Mr. Macintosh to the point where he could feel his eyes go dark, and the blood pounding in that hot darkness in his head. In fact, it was the power of this anger that sobered him, for he had been very young when he had learned to fear his own temper. And above all, he was a shrewd man. He waited until his sight was clear again, and then asked, reasonably: "Why do you want to loaf around the compound, why not work and earn money?"

Dirk said: "I can read and write, and I know my figures better than Tommy—Baas Tommy," he added, in a way which made the anger rise again in Mr. Macintosh, so that he had to make a fresh effort to subdue it.

But Tommy was a point of weakness in Mr. Macintosh, and it was then that he spoke the words which afterwards made him wonder if he'd gone suddenly crazy. For he said: "Very well, when you're sixteen you can come and do my books and write the letters for the mine."

Dirk said: "All right," as if this were no more than his due, and walked off, leaving Mr. Macintosh impotently furious with himself. For how could anyone but himself see the books? Such a person would be his master. It was impossible, he had no intention of ever letting Dirk, or anyone else, see them. Yet he had made the promise. And so he would have to find another way of using Dirk, or—and the words came involuntarily—getting rid of him.

From a mood of settled bad temper, Mr. Macintosh dropped into one of sullen thoughtfulness, which was entirely foreign to his character. Being shrewd is quite different from the processes of thinking. Shrewdness, particularly the money-making shrewdness, is a kind of instinct. While Mr. Macintosh had always known what he wanted to do, and how to do it, that did not mean he had known why he wanted so much money, or why he had chosen these ways of making it. Mr. Macintosh felt like a cat whose nose has been rubbed into its own dirt, and for many nights he sat in the hot little house, that vibrated continually from the noise of the mine-stamps, most uncomfortably considering himself and his life. He reminded himself, for instance, that he was sixty, and presumably had not more than ten or fifteen years to live. It was not a thought that an unreflective man enjoys, particularly when he had never considered his age at all. He was so healthy, strong, tough. But he was sixty nevertheless, and what would be his monument? An enormous pit in the earth, and a million pounds' worth of property. Then how should he spend ten or fifteen years? Exactly as he had the preceding sixty, for he hated being away from this place, and this gave him a caged and useless sensation, for it had never entered his head before that he was not as free as he felt himself to be.

Well, then—and this thought gnawed most closely to Mr. Macintosh's pain—why had he not married? For he considered himself a marrying sort of man, and had always intended to find himself the right sort of woman and marry her. Yet he was already sixty. The truth was that Mr. Macintosh had no idea at all why he had not married and got himself sons; and in these slow, uncomfortable ponderings the thought of Dirk's mother intruded itself only to be hastily thrust away. Mr. Macintosh, the sensualist, had a taste for dark-skinned women; and now it was certainly too late to admit as a permanent feature of his character something he had always considered as a sort of temporary whim, or makeshift, like someone who learns to enjoy an inferior brand of tobacco when better brands are not available.

He thought of Tommy, of whom he had been used to say: "I've taken a fancy to the laddie." Now it was not so much a fancy as a deep, grieving love. And Tommy was the son of his employee, and looked at him with contempt, and he, Mr. Macintosh, reacted with angry shame as if he were guilty of something. Of what? It was ridiculous.

The whole situation was ridiculous, and so Mr. Macintosh allowed himself to slide back into his usual frame of mind. Tommy's only a boy, he thought, and he'll see reason in a year or so. And as for Dirk, I'll find him some kind of a job when the time comes . . .

At the end of the term, when Tommy came home, Mr. Macintosh asked, as usual, to see the school report, which usually filled him with pride. Instead of heading the class with approbation from the teachers and high marks in all subjects, Tommy was near the bottom, with such remarks as Slovenly, and Lazy, and Bad-mannered. The only subject in which he got any marks at all was that called Art, which Mr. Macintosh did not take into account.

When Tommy was asked by his parents why he was not working, he replied, impatiently: "I don't know," which was quite true; and at once escaped to the anthill. Dirk was there, waiting for the books Tommy always brought for him. Tommy reached at once up to the shelf where stood the figure of Dirk's mother, lifted it down and examined the unworked space which would be the face. "I know how to do it," he said to Dirk, and took out some knives and chisels he had brought from the city.

That was how he spent the three weeks of that holiday, and when he met Mr. Macintosh he was sullen and uncomfortable. "You'll have to be working a bit better," he said, before Tommy went back, to which he received no answer but an unwilling smile.

During that term Tommy distinguished himself in two ways besides being steadily at the bottom of the class he had so recently led. He made a fiery speech in the debating society on the iniquity of the colour bar, which rather pleased his teachers, since it is a well-known fact that the young must pass through these phases of rebellion before settling down to conformity. In fact, the greater the verbal rebellion, the more settled was the conformity likely to be. In secret Tommy got books from the city library such as are not usually read by boys of his age, on the history of Africa, and on comparative anthropology, and passed from there to the history of the moment—he ordered papers from the Government Stationery Office, the laws of the country. Most particularly those affecting the relations between black and white and coloured. These he bought in order to take back to Dirk. But in addition to all this ferment, there was that subject Art, which in this school meant a drawing lesson twice a week, copying busts of Julius Caesar, or it might be Nelson, or shading in fronds of fern or leaves, or copying a large vase or a table standing diagonally to the class, thus learning what he was told were the laws of Perspective. There was no modelling, nothing approaching sculpture in this school, but this was the nearest thing to it, and that mysterious prohibition which forbade him to distinguish himself in Geometry or English, was silent when it came to using the pencil.

At the end of the term his Report was very bad, but it admitted that he had An Interest in Current Events, and a Talent for Art.

And now this word Art, coming at the end of two successive terms, disturbed his parents and forced itself on Mr. Macintosh. He said to Annie Clarke: "It's a nice thing to make pictures, but the lad won't earn a living by it." And Mrs. Clarke said reproachfully to Tommy: "It's all very well, Tommy, but you aren't going to earn a living drawing pictures."

"I didn't say I wanted to earn a living with it," shouted Tommy, miserably. "Why have I got to be something, you're always wanting me to be something."

That holiday Dirk spent studying the Acts of Parliament and the Reports of Commissions and Sub-Committees which Tommy had brought him, while Tommy attempted something new. There was a square piece of soft white wood which Dirk had pilfered from the mine, thinking Tommy might use it. And Tommy set it against the walls of the shed, and knelt before it and attempted a frieze or engraving—he did not know the words for what he was doing. He cut out a great pit, surrounded by mounds of earth and rock, with the peaks of great mountains beyond, and at the edge of the pit stood a big man carrying a stick, and over the edge of the pit wound a file of black figures, tumbling into the gulf. From the pit came flames and smoke. Tommy took green ooze from leaves and mixed clay to colour the mountains and edges of the pit, and he made the little figures black with charcoal, and he made the flames writhing up out of the pit red with the paint used for parts of the mining machinery.

"If you leave it here, the ants'll eat it," said Dirk, looking with grim pleasure at the crude but effective picture.

To which Tommy shrugged. For while he was always solemnly intent on a piece of work in hand, afraid of anything that might mar it, or even distract his attention from it, once it was finished he cared for it not at all.

It was Dirk who had painted the shelf which held the other figures with a mixture that discouraged ants, and it was now Dirk who set the piece of square wood on a sheet of tin smeared with the same mixture, and balanced it in a way so it should not touch any part of the walls of the shed, where the ants might climb up.

And so Tommy went back to school, still in that mood of obstinate disaffection, to make more copies of Julius Caesar and vases of flowers, and Dirk remained with his books and his Acts of Parliament. They would be fourteen before they met again and both knew that crises and decisions faced them. Yet they said no more than the usual: Well, so long, before they parted. Nor did they ever write to each other, although this term Tommy had a commission to send certain books and other Acts of Parliament for a purpose which he entirely approved.

Dirk had built himself a new hut in the compound, where he lived alone, in the compound but not of it, affectionate to his mother, but apart from her. And to this hut at night came certain of the workers who forgot their dislike of the half-caste, that cuckoo in their nest, in their common interest in what he told them of the Acts and Reports. What he told them was what he had learnt himself in the proud loneliness of his isolation. "Education," he said, "education, that's the key"—and Tommy agreed with him, although he had, or so one might suppose from the way he was behaving, abandoned all idea of getting an education for himself. All that term parcels came to "Dirk, c/o Mr. Macintosh," and Mr. Macintosh delivered them to Dirk without any questions.

In the dim and smokey hut every night, half a dozen of the workers laboured with stubs of pencil and the exercise books sent by Tommy, to learn to write and do sums and understand the Laws.

One night Mr. Macintosh came rather late out of that other hut, and saw the red light from a fire moving softly on the rough ground outside the door of Dirk's hut. All the others were dark. He moved cautiously among them until he stood in the shadows outside the door, and looked in. Dirk was squatting on the floor, surrounded by half a dozen men, looking at a newspaper.

Mr. Macintosh walked thoughtfully home in the starlight. Dirk, had he known what Mr. Macintosh was thinking, would have been very angry, for all his flaming rebellion, his words of resentment were directed against Mr. Macintosh and his tyranny. Yet for the first time Mr. Macintosh was thinking of Dirk with a certain rough, amused pride. Perhaps it was because he was a Scot, after all, and in every one of his nation is an instinctive respect for learning and people with the determination to "get on." A chip off the old block, thought Mr. Macintosh, remembering how he, as a boy, had laboured to get a bit of education. And if the chip was the wrong colour—well, he would do something for Dirk. Something, he would decide when the time came. As for the others who were with Dirk, there was nothing easier than to sack a worker and engage another. Mr. Macintosh went to his bed, dressed as usual in vest and pyjama trousers, unwashed and thrifty in candlelight.

In the morning he gave orders to one of the overseers that Dirk should be summoned. His heart was already soft with thinking about the generous scene which would shortly take place. He was going to suggest that Dirk should teach all the overseers to read and write— on a salary from himself, of course—in order that these same overseers should be more useful in the work. They might learn to mark pay-sheets, for instance.

The overseer said that Baas Dirk spent his days studying in Baas Tommy's hut—with the suggestion in his manner that Baas Dirk could not be disturbed while so occupied, and that this was on Tommy's account.

The man, closely studying the effect of his words, saw how Mr. Macintosh's big, veiny face swelled, and he stepped back a pace. He was not one of Dirk's admirers.

Mr. Macintosh, after some moments of heavy breathing, allowed his shrewdness to direct his anger. He dismissed the man, and turned away.

During that morning he left his great pit and walked off into the bush in the direction of the towering blue peak. He had heard vaguely that Tommy had some kind of a hut, but imagined it as a child's thing. He was still very angry because of that calculated "Baas Dirk." He walked for a while along a smooth path through the trees, and came to a clearing. On the other side was an anthill, and on the anthill a well-built hut, draped with Christmas fern around the open front, like curtains. In the opening sat Dirk. He wore a clean white shirt, and long smooth trousers. His head, oiled and brushed close, was bent over books. The hand that turned the pages of the books had a brass ring on the little finger. He was the very image of an aspiring clerk: that form of humanity which Mr. Macintosh despised most.

Mr. Macintosh remained on the edge of the clearing for some time, vaguely waiting for something to happen, so that he might fling himself, armoured and directed by his contemptuous anger, into a crisis which would destroy Dirk for ever. But nothing did happen. Dirk continued to turn the pages of the book, so Mr. Macintosh went back to his house, where he ate boiled beef and carrots for his dinner.

Afterwards he went to a certain drawer in his bedroom, and from it took an object carelessly wrapped in cloth which, exposed, showed itself as that figure of Dirk the boy Tommy had made and sold for five pounds. And Mr. Macintosh turned and handled and pored over that crude wooden image of Dirk in a passion of curiosity, just as if the boy did not live on the same square mile of soil with him, fully available to his scrutiny at most hours of the day.

If one imagines a Judgment Day with the graves giving up their dead impartially, black, white, bronze, and yellow, to a happy reunion, one of the pleasures of that reunion might well be that people who have lived on the same acre or street all their lives will look at each other with incredulous recognition. "So that is what you were like," might be the gathering murmur around God's heaven. For the glass wall between colour and colour is not only a barrier against touch, but has become thick and distorted, so that black men, white men, see each other through it, but see—what? Mr. Macintosh examined the image of Dirk as if searching for some final revelation, but the thought that came persistently to his mind was that the statute might be of himself as a lad of twelve. So after a few moments he rolled it again in the cloth and tossed it back into the corner of a drawer, out of sight, and with it the unwelcome and tormenting knowledge.

Late that afternoon he left his house again and made his way towards the hut on the antheap. It was empty, and he walked through the knee-high grass and bushes till he could climb up the hard, slippery walls of the antheap and so into the hut.

First he looked at the books in the case. The longer he looked, the faster faded that picture of Dirk as an oiled and mincing clerk, which he had been clinging to ever since he threw the other image into the back of a drawer. Respect for Dirk was reborn. Complicated mathematics, much more advanced than he had ever done. Geography. History. "The Development of the Slave Trade in the Eighteenth Century." "The Growth of Parliamentary Institutions in Great Britain." This title made Mr. Macintosh smile—the freebooting buccaneer examining a coastguard's notice perhaps. Mr. Macintosh lifted down one book after another and smiled. Then, beside these books, he saw a pile of slight, blue pamphlets, and he examined them. "The Natives Employment Act." "The Natives Juvenile Employment Act." "The Native Passes Act." And Mr. Macintosh flipped over the leaves and laughed, and had Dirk heard that laugh it would have been worse to him than any whip.

For as he patiently explained these laws and others like them to his bitter allies in the hut at night, it seemed to him that every word he spoke was like a stone thrown at Mr. Macintosh, his father. Yet Mr. Macintosh laughed, since he despised these laws, although in a different way, as much as Dirk did. When Mr. Macintosh, on his rare trips to the city, happened to drive past the House of Parliament, he turned on it a tolerant and appreciative gaze. "Well, why not?" he seemed to be saying. "It's an occupation, like any other."

So to Dirk's desperate act of retaliation he responded with a smile, and tossed back the books and pamphlets on the shelf. And then he turned to look at the other things in the shed, and for the first time he saw the high shelf where the statuettes were arranged. He looked, and felt his face swelling with that fatal rage. There was Dirk's mother, peering at him in bashful sensuality from over the baby's head, there the little girl, his daughter, squatting on spindly legs and staring. And there, on the edge of the shelf, a small, worn shape of clay which still held the vigorous strength of Dirk. Mr. Macintosh, breathing heavily, holding down his anger, stepped back to gain a clearer view of those figures, and his heel slipped on a slanting piece of wood. He turned to look, and there was the picture Tommy had carved and coloured of his mine. Mr. Macintosh saw the great pit, the black little figures tumbling and sprawling over into the flames, and he saw himself, stick in hand, astride on his two legs at the edge of the pit, his hat on the back of his head.

And now Mr. Macintosh was so disturbed and angry that he was driven out of the hut and into the clearing, where he walked back and forth through the grass, looking at the hut while his anger growled and moved inside him. After some time he came close to the hut again and peered in. Yes, there was Dirk's mother, peering bashfully from her shelf, as if to say: Yes, it's me, remember? And there on the floor was the square tinted piece of wood which said what Tommy thought of him and his life. Mr. Macintosh took a box of matches from his pocket. He lit a match. He understood he was standing in the hut with a lit match in his hand to no purpose. He dropped the match and ground it out with his foot. Then he put a pipe in his mouth, filled it and lit it, gazing all the time at the shelf and at the square carving. The second match fell to the floor and lay spurting a small white flame. He ground his heel hard on it. Anger heaved up in him beyond all sanity, and he lit another match, pushed it into the thatch of the hut, and walked out of it and so into the clearing and away into the bush. Without looking behind him he walked back to his house where his supper of boiled beef and carrots was waiting for him. He was amazed, angry, resentful. Finally he felt aggrieved, and wanted to explain to someone what a monstrous injustice was Tommy's view of him. But there was no one to explain it to, and he slowly quietened to a steady dulled sadness, and for some days remained so, until time restored him to normal. From this condition he looked back at his behavior and did not like it. Not that he regretted burning the hut, it seemed to him unimportant. He was angry at himself for allowing his anger to dictate his actions. Also he knew that such an act brings its own results.

So he waited, and thought mainly of the cruelty of fate in denying him a son who might carry on his work—for he certainly thought of his work as something to be continued. He thought sadly of Tommy, who denied him. And so, his affection for Tommy was sprung again by thinking of him, and he waited, thinking of reproachful things to say to him.

When Tommy returned from school he went straight to the clearing and found a mound of ash on the antheap that was already sifted and swept by the wind. He found Dirk, sitting on a tree trunk in the bush waiting for him.

"What happened?" asked Tommy. And then, at once: "Did you save your books?"

Dirk said: "He burnt it."

"How do you know?"

"I know."

Tommy nodded. "All your books have gone," he said, very grieved, and as guilty as if he had burnt them himself.

"Your carvings and your statues are burnt too."

But at this Tommy shrugged, since he could not care about his things once they were finished. "Shall we build the hut again now?" he suggested.

"My books are burnt," said Dirk, in a low voice, and Tommy, looking at him, saw how his hands were clenched. He instinctively moved a little aside to give his friend's anger space.

"When I grow up I'll clear you all out, all of you, there won't be one white man left in Africa, not one."

Tommy's face had a small, half-scared smile on it. The hatred Dirk was directing against him was so strong he nearly went away. He sat beside Dirk on the tree-trunk and said: "I'll try and get you more books."

"And then he'll burn them again."

"But you've already got what was in them inside your head," said Tommy, consolingly. Dirk said nothing, but sat like a clenched fist, and so they remained on the tree trunk in the quiet bush while the doves cooed and the mine-stamps thudded, all that hot morning. When they had to separate at midday to return to their different world, it was with deep sadness, knowing that their childhood was finished, and their playing, and something new was ahead.

And at the meal Tommy's mother and father had his school report on the table, and they were reproachful. Tommy was at the foot of his class, and he would not matriculate that year. Or any year if he went on like this.

"You used to be such a clever boy," mourned his mother, "and now what's happened to you?"

Tommy, sitting silent at the table, moved his shoulders in a hunched, irritable way, as if to say: Leave me alone. Nor did he feel himself to be stupid and lazy, as the report said he was.

In his room were drawing blocks and pencils and hammers and chisels. He had never said to himself he had exchanged one purpose for another, for he had no purpose. How could he, when he had never been offered a future he could accept? Now, at this time, in his fifteenth year, with his reproachful parents deepening their reproach, and the knowledge that Mr. Macintosh would soon see that report, all he felt was a locked stubbornness, and a deep strength.

In the afternoon he went back to the clearing, and he took his chisels with him. On the old, soft, rotted tree trunk that he sat on that morning, he sat again, waiting for Dirk. But Dirk did not come. Putting himself in his friend's place he understood that Dirk could not endure to be with a white-skinned person—a white face, even that of his oldest friend, was too much the enemy. But he waited, sitting on the tree-trunk all through the afternoon, with his chisels and hammers in a little box at his feet in the grass, and he fingered the soft, warm wood he sat on, letting the shape and texture of it come into the knowledge of his fingers.

Next day, there was still no Dirk.

Tommy began walking around the fallen tree, studying it. It was very thick, and its roots twisted and slanted into the air to the height of his shoulder. He began to carve the root. It would be Dirk again.

That night Mr. Macintosh came to the Clarkes' house and read the report. He went back to his own, and sat wondering why Tommy was set so bitterly against him. The next day he went to the Clarkes' house again to find Tommy, but the boy was not there.

He therefore walked through the thick bush to the antheap, and found Tommy kneeling in the grass working on the tree root.

Tommy said: "Good morning," and went on working, and Mr. Macintosh sat on the trunk and watched.

"What are you making?" asked Mr. Macintosh.

"Dirk," said Tommy, and Mr. Macintosh went purple and almost sprang up and away from the tree-trunk. But Tommy was not looking at him. So Mr. Macintosh remained, in silence. And then the useless vigour of Tommy's concentration on that rotting bit of root goaded him, and his mind moved naturally to a new decision.

"Would you like to be an artist?" he suggested.

Tommy allowed his chisel to rest, and looked at Mr. Macintosh as if this were a fresh trap. He shrugged, and with the appearance of anger, went on with his work.

"If you've a real gift, you can earn money by that sort of thing. I had a cousin back in Scotland who did it. He made souvenirs, you know, for travellers." He spoke in a soothing and jolly way.

Tommy let the souvenirs slide by him, as another of these impositions on his independence. He said: "Why did you burn Dirk's books?"

But Mr. Macintosh laughed in relief. "Why should I burn his books?" It really seemed ridiculous to him, his rage had been against Tommy's work, not Dirk's.

"I know you did," said Tommy. "I know it. And Dirk does too."

Mr. Macintosh lit his pipe in good humour. For now things seemed much easier. Tommy did not know why he had set fire to the hut, and that was the main thing. He puffed smoke for a few moments and said: "Why should you think I don't want Dirk to study? It's a good thing, a bit of education."

Tommy stared disbelievingly at him.

"I asked Dirk to use his education, I asked him to teach some of the others. But he wouldn't have any of it. Is that my fault?"

Now Tommy's face was completely incredulous. Then he went scarlet, which Mr. Macintosh did not understand. Why should the boy be looking so foolish? But Tommy was thinking: We were on the wrong track . . . And then he imagined what his offer must have done to Dirk's angry, rebellious pride, and he suddenly understood. His face still crimson, he laughed. It was a bitter, ironical laugh, and Mr. Macintosh was upset—it was not a boy's laugh at all.

Tommy's face slowly faded from crimson, and he went back to work with his chisel. He said, after a pause: "Why don't you send Dirk to college instead of me? He's much more clever than me. I'm not clever, look at my report."

"Well, laddie . . ." began Mr. Macintosh reproachfully—he had been going to say: "Are you being lazy at school simply to force my hand over Dirk?" He wondered at his own impulse to say it; and slid off into the familiar obliqueness which Tommy ignored: "But you know how things are, or you ought to by now. You talk as if you didn't understand."

But Tommy was kneeling with his back to Mr. Macintosh, working at the root, so Mr. Macintosh continued to smoke. Next day he returned and sat on the tree-trunk and watched. Tommy looked at him as if he considered his presence an unwelcome gift, but he did not say anything.

Slowly, the big fanged root which rose from the trunk was taking

Dirk's shape. Mr. Macintosh watched with uneasy loathing. He did not like it, but he could not stop watching. Once he said: "But if there's a veld fire, it'll get burnt. And the ants'll eat it in any case." Tommy shrugged. It was the making of it that mattered, not what happened to it afterwards, and this attitude was so foreign to Mr. Macintosh's accumulating nature that it seemed to him that Tommy was touched in the head. He said: "Why don't you work on something that'll last? Or even if you studied like Dirk it would be better."

Tommy said: "I like doing it."

"But look, the ants are already at the trunk—by the time you get back from your school next time there'll be nothing left of it."

"Or someone might set fire to it," suggested Tommy. He looked steadily at Mr. Macintosh's reddening face with triumph. Mr. Macintosh found the words too near the truth. For certainly, as the days passed, he was looking at the new work with hatred and fear and dislike. It was nearly finished. Even if nothing more were done to it, it could stand as it was, complete.

Dirk's long, powerful body came writhing out of the wood like something struggling free. The head was clenched back, in the agony of the birth, eyes narrowed and desperate, the mouth—Mr. Macintosh's mouth —tightened in obstinate purpose. The shoulders were free, but the hands were held; they could not pull themselves out of the dense wood, they were imprisoned. His body was free to the knees, but below them the human limbs were uncreated, the natural shapes of the wood swelled to the perfect muscled knees.

Mr. Macintosh did not like it. He did not know what art was, but he knew he did not like this at all, it disturbed him deeply, so that when he looked at it he wanted to take an axe and cut it to pieces. Or burn it, perhaps . . .

As for Tommy, the uneasiness of this elderly man who watched him all day was a deep triumph. Slowly, and for the first time, he saw that perhaps this was not a sort of game that he played, it might be something else. A weapon—he watched Mr. Macintosh's reluctant face, and a new respect for himself and what he was doing grew in him.

At night, Mr. Macintosh sat in his candlelit room and he thought or rather *felt*, his way to a decision.

There was no denying the power of Tommy's gift. Therefore, it was a question of finding the way to turn it into money. He knew nothing about these matters, however, and it was Tommy himself who directed him, for towards the end of the holidays he said: "When you're so rich you can do anything. You could send Dirk to college and not even notice it."

Mr. Macintosh, in the reasonable and persuasive voice he now always used, said, "But you know these coloured people have nowhere to go."

Tommy said: "You could send him to the Cape. There are coloured people in the university there. Or Johannesburg." And he insisted against Mr. Macintosh's silence: "You're so rich you can do anything you like."

But Mr. Macintosh, like most rich people, thought not of money as things to buy, things to do, but rather how it was tied up in buildings and land.

"It would cost thousands," he said. "Thousands for a coloured boy."

But Tommy's scornful look silenced him, and he said hastily: "I'll think about it." But he was thinking not of Dirk, but of Tommy. Sitting alone in his room he told himself it was simply a question of paying for knowledge.

So next morning he made his preparations for a trip to town. He shaved, and over his cotton singlet he put a striped jacket, which half concealed his long, stained khaki trousers. This was as far as he ever went in concession to the city life he despised. He got into his big American car and set off.

In the city he took the simplest route to knowledge.

He went to the Education Department, and said he wanted to see the Minister of Education. "I'm Macintosh," he said, with perfect confidence; and the pretty secretary who had been patronising his clothes, went at once to the Minister and said: "There is a Mr. Macintosh to see you." She described him as an old, fat, dirty man with a large stomach, and soon the doors opened and Mr. Macintosh was with the spring of knowledge.

He emerged five minutes later with what he wanted, the name of a certain expert. He drove through the deep green avenues of the city to the house he had been told to go to, which was a large and well-kept one, and comforted Mr. Macintosh in his faith that art properly used could make money. He parked his car in the road and walked in.

On the verandah, behind a table heaped with books, sat a middle-aged man with spectacles. Mr. Tomlinson was essentially a scholar with working hours he respected, and he lifted his eyes to see a big, dirty man with black hair showing above the dirty whiteness of his vest, and he said sharply: "What do you want?"

"Wait a minute, laddie," said Mr. Macintosh easily, and he held out a note from the Minister of Education, and Mr. Tomlinson took it and read it, feeling reassured. It was worded in such a way that his seeing Mr. Macintosh could be felt as a favour he was personally doing the Minister.

"I'll make it worth your while," said Mr. Macintosh, and at once distaste flooded Mr. Tomlinson, and he went pink, and said: "I'm afraid I haven't the time."

"Damn it, man, it's your job, isn't it? Or so Wentworth said."

"No," said Mr. Tomlinson, making each word clear, "I advise on ancient Monuments."

Mr. Macintosh stared, then laughed, and said: "Wentworth said you'd do, but it doesn't matter, I'll get someone else." And he left.

Mr. Tomlinson watched this hobo go off the verandah and into a magnificent car, and his thought was: "He must have stolen it." Then, puzzled and upset, he went to the telephone. But in a few moments he was smiling. Finally he laughed. Mr. Macintosh was the Mr. Macintosh, a genuine specimen of the old-timer. It was the phrase "old-timer" that made it possible for Mr. Tomlinson to relent. He therefore rang the hotel at which Mr. Macintosh, as a rich man, would be bound to be staying, and he said he had made an error, he would be free the following day to accompany Mr. Macintosh.

And so next morning Mr. Macintosh, not at all surprised that the expert was at his service after all, with Mr. Tomlinson, who preserved a tolerant smile, drove out to the mine.

They drove very fast in the powerful car, and Mr. Tomlinson held himself steady while they jolted and bounced, and listened to Mr. Macintosh's tales of Australia and New Zealand, and thought of him rather as he would of an ancient Monument.

At last the long plain ended, and foothills of greenish scrub heaped themselves around the car, and then high mountains piled with granite boulders, and the heat came in thick, slow waves into the car, and Mr. Tomlinson thought: I'll be glad when we're through the mountains into the plain. But instead they turned into a high, enclosed place with mountains all around, and suddenly there was an enormous gulf in the ground, and on one side of it were two tiny tin-roofed houses, and on the other acres of kaffir huts. The mine-stamps thudded regularly, like a pulse of the heart, and Mr. Tomlinson wondered how anybody, white or black, could bear to live in such a place.

He ate boiled beef and carrots and greasy potatoes with one of the richest men in the sub-continent, and thought how well and intelligently he would use such money if he had it—which is the only consolation left to the cultivated man of moderate income. After lunch, Mr. Macintosh said: "And now, let's get it over."

Mr. Tomlinson expressed his willingness, and, smiling to himself, followed Mr. Macintosh off into the bush on a kaffir path. He did not know what he was going to see. Mr. Macintosh had said: "Can you tell if a youngster has got any talent just by looking at a piece of wood he has carved?"

Mr. Tomlinson said he would do his best.

Then they were beside a fallen tree-trunk, and in the grass knelt a big lad, with untidy brown hair falling over his face, labouring at the wood with a large chisel.

"This is a friend of mine," said Mr. Macintosh to Tommy, who got to his feet and stood uncomfortably, wondering what was happening. "Do you mind if Mr. Tomlinson sees what you are doing?"

Tommy made a shrugging movement and felt that things were going beyond his control. He looked in awed amazement at Mr. Tomlinson, who seemed to him rather like a teacher or professor, and certainly not at all what he imagined an artist to be.

"Well?" said Mr. Macintosh to Mr. Tomlinson, after a space of half a minute.

Mr. Tomlinson laughed in a way which said: "Now don't be in such a hurry." He walked around the carved tree root, looking at the figure of Dirk from this angle and that.

Then he asked Tommy: "Why do you make these carvings?"

Tommy very uncomfortably shrugged, as if to say: What a silly question; and Mr. Macintosh hastily said: "He gets high marks for Art at school."

Mr. Tomlinson smiled again and walked around to the other side of the trunk. From here he could see Dirk's face, flattened back on the neck, eyes half-closed and strained, the muscles of the neck shaped from natural veins of the wood.

"Is this someone you know?" he asked Tommy in an easy, intimate way, one artist to another.

"Yes," said Tommy, briefly; he resented the question.

Mr. Tomlinson looked at the face and then at Mr. Macintosh. "It has a look of you," he observed dispassionately, and coloured himself as he saw Mr. Macintosh grow angry. He walked well away from the group, to give Mr. Macintosh space to hide his embarrassment. When he returned, he asked Tommy: "And so you want to be a sculptor?"

"I don't know," said Tommy, defiantly.

Mr. Tomlinson shrugged rather impatiently, and with a nod at Mr. Macintosh suggested it was enough. He said goodbye to Tommy, and went back to the house with Mr. Macintosh.

There he was offered tea and biscuits, and Mr. Macintosh asked: "Well, what do you think?"

But by now Mr. Tomlinson was certainly offended at this casual cash-on-delivery approach to art, and he said: "Well, that rather depends, doesn't it?"

"On what?" demanded Mr. Macintosh.

"He seems to have talent," conceded Mr. Tomlinson.

"That's all I want to know," said Mr. Macintosh, and suggested that now he could run Mr. Tomlinson back in town.

But Mr. Tomlinson did not feel it was enough, and he said: "It's quite interesting, that statue. I suppose he's seen pictures in magazines. It has quite a modern feeling."

"Modern?" said Mr. Macintosh. "What do you mean?"

Mr. Tomlinson shrugged again, giving it up. "Well," he said, practically, "what do you mean to do?"

"If you say he has talent, I'll send him to the university and he can study art."

After a long pause, Mr. Tomlinson murmured: "What a fortunate boy he is." He meant to convey depths of disillusionment and irony, but Mr. Macintosh said: "I always did have a fancy for him."

He took Mr. Tomlinson back to the city, and as he dropped him on his verandah, presented him with a cheque for fifty pounds, which Mr. Tomlinson most indignantly returned. "Oh, give it to charity," said Mr. Macintosh impatiently, and went to his car, leaving Mr. Tomlinson to heal his susceptibilities in any way he chose.

When Mr. Macintosh reached his mine again it was midnight, and there were no lights in the Clarkes' house, and so his need to be generous must be stifled until the morning.

Then he went to Annie Clarke and told her he would send Tommy to university, where he could be an artist, and Mrs. Clarke wept with gratitude, and said that Mr. Macintosh was much kinder than Tommy deserved, and perhaps he would learn sense yet and go back to his books.

As far as Mr. Macintosh was concerned it was all settled.

He set off through the trees to find Tommy and announce his future to him.

But when he arrived at seeing distance there were two figures, Dirk and Tommy, seated on the trunk talking, and Mr. Macintosh stopped among the trees, filled with such bitter anger at this fresh check to his plans that he could not trust himself to go on. So he returned to his house, and brooded angrily—he knew exactly what was going to happen when he spoke to Tommy, and now he must make up his mind, there was no escape from a decision.

And while Mr. Macintosh mused bitterly in his house, Tommy and Dirk waited for him; it was now all as clear to them as it was to him.

Dirk had come out of the trees to Tommy the moment the two men left the day before. Tommy was standing by the fanged root, looking at the shape of Dirk in it, trying to understand what was going to be demanded of him. The word "artist" was on his tongue, and he tasted it, trying to make the strangeness of it fit that powerful shape struggling out of the wood. He did not like it. He did not want—but what did he want? He felt pressure on himself, the faint beginnings of something that would one day be like a tunnel of birth from which he must fight to emerge; he felt the obligations working within himself like a goad which would one day be a whip perpetually falling behind him so that he must perpetually move onwards.

His sense of fetters and debts was confirmed when Dirk came to stand by him. First he asked: "What did they want?"

"They want me to be an artist, they always want me to be something," said Tommy sullenly. He began throwing stones at the tree and shying them off along the tops of the grass. Then one hit the figure of Dirk, and he stopped.

Dirk was looking at himself. "Why do you make me like that?" he asked. The narrow, strong face expressed nothing but that familiar, sardonic antagonism, as if he said: "You, too—just like the rest!"

"Why, what's the matter with it?" challenged Tommy at once.

Dirk walked around it, then back. "You're just like all the rest," he said.

"Why? Why don't you like it?" Tommy was really distressed. Also, his feeling was: What's it got to do with him? Slowly he understood that his emotion was that belief in his right to freedom which Dirk always felt immediately, and he said in a different voice: "Tell me what's wrong with it?"

"Why do I have to come out of the wood? Why haven't I any hands or feet?"

"You have, but don't you see . . ." But Tommy looked at Dirk standing in front of him and suddenly gave an impatient movement: "Well, it doesn't matter, it's only a statue."

He sat on the trunk and Dirk beside him. After a while he said: "How should you be, then?"

"If you made yourself, would you be half wood?"

Tommy made an effort to feel this, but failed. "But it's not me, it's you." He spoke with difficulty, and thought: But it's important, I shall have to think about it later. He almost groaned with the knowledge that here it was, the first debt, presented for payment.

Dirk said suddenly: "Surely it needn't be wood. You could do the same thing if you put handcuffs on my wrists." Tommy lifted his head and gave a short, astonished laugh. "Well, what's funny?" said Dirk, aggressively. "You can't do it the easy way, you have to make me half wood, as if I was more a tree than a human being."

Tommy laughed again, but unhappily. "Oh, I'll do it again," he acknowledged at last. "Don't fuss about that one, it's finished. I'll do another."

There was a silence.

Dirk said: "What did that man say about you?"

"How do I know?"

"Does he know about art?"

"I suppose so."

"Perhaps you'll be famous," said Dirk at last. "In that book you gave me, it said about painters. Perhaps you'll be like that."

"Oh, shut up," said Tommy, roughly. "You're just as bad as he is."

"Well, what's the matter with it?"

"Why have I got to be something? First it was a sailor, and then it was a scholar, and now it's an artist."

"They wouldn't have to make me be anything," said Dirk sarcastically.

"I know," admitted Tommy grudgingly. And then, passionately: "I shan't go to university unless he sends you too."

"I know," said Dirk at once, "I know you won't."

They smiled at each other, that small, shy, revealed smile, which was so hard for them because it pledged them to such a struggle in the future.

Then Tommy asked: "Why didn't you come near me all this time?"

"I get sick of you," said Dirk. "I sometimes feel I don't want to see a white face again, not ever. I feel that I hate you all, every one."

"I know," said Tommy, grinning. Then they laughed, and the last strain of dislike between them vanished.

They began to talk, for the first time, of what their lives would be.

Tommy said: "But when you've finished training to be an engineer, what will you do? They don't let coloured people be engineers."

"Things aren't always going to be like that," said Dirk.

"It's going to be very hard," said Tommy, looking at him questioningly, and was at once reassured when Dirk said, sarcastically: "Hard, it's going to be hard? Isn't it hard now, white boy?"

Later that day Mr. Macintosh came towards them from his house.

He stood in front of them, that big, shrewd, rich man, with his small, clever grey eyes, and his narrow, loveless mouth; and he said aggressively to Tommy: "Do you want to go to the university and be an artist?"

"If Dirk comes too," said Tommy immediately.

"What do you want to study?" Mr. Macintosh asked Dirk, direct.

"I want to be an engineer," said Dirk at once.

"If I pay your way through the university then at the end of it I'm finished with you. I never want to hear from you and you are never to come back to this mine once you leave it."

Dirk and Tommy both nodded, and the instinctive agreement between them fed Mr. Macintosh's bitter unwillingness in the choice, so that he ground out viciously: "Do you think you two can be together in the university? You don't understand. You'll be living separate, and you can't go around together just as you like."

The boys looked at each other, and then, as if some sort of pact had been made between them, simply nodded.

"You can't go to university anyway, Tommy, until you've done a bit better at school. If you go back for another year and work you can pass your matric, and go to university, but you can't go now, right at the bottom of the class."

Tommy said: "I'll work." He added at once: "Dirk'll need more books to study here till we can go."

The anger was beginning to swell Mr. Macintosh's face, but Tommy said: "It's only fair. You burnt them, and now he hasn't any at all."

"Well," said Mr. Macintosh heavily. "Well, so that's how it is!"

He looked at the two boys, seated together on the tree-trunk. Tommy was leaning forward, eyes lowered, a troubled but determined look on his face. Dirk was sitting erect, looking straight at his father with eyes filled with hate.

"Well," said Mr. Macintosh, with an effort at raillery which sounded harsh to them all: "Well, I send you both to university and you don't give me so much as a thank-you!"

At this, both faced towards him, with such bitter astonishment that he flushed.

"Well, well," he said. "Well, well . . ." And then he turned to leave the clearing, and cried out as he went, so as to give the appearance of dominance: "Remember, laddie, I'm not sending you unless you do well at school this year . . ."

And so he left them and went back to his house, an angry old man, defeated by something he did not begin to understand.

As for the boys, they were silent when he had gone.

The victory was entirely theirs, but now they had to begin again, in the long and difficult struggle to understand what they had won and how they would use it.

CYPRIAN EKWENSI

people of the city

chapter one

Most girls in the famous West African city (which shall be nameless) knew the address Twenty Molomo Street, for there lived a most colourful and eligible young bachelor, by name Amusa Sango.

In addition to being crime reporter for the *West African Sensation*, Sango in his spare time led a dance band that played the *calypsos* and the *konkomas* in the only way that delighted the hearts of the city women. Husbands who lived near the All Language Club knew with deep irritation how their wives would, on hearing Sango's music, drop their knitting or sewing and wiggle their hips, shoulders and breasts, sighing with the nostalgia of musty nights years ago, when lovers' eyes were warm on their faces. Nights that could now, with a home and family, be no more. While those who as yet had found no man would twist their hips alluringly before admiring eyes, tempting, tantalizing . . . promising much but giving little, basking in the vanity of being desired.

Of women Sango could have had his pick, from silk-clad ones who wore lipstick in the European manner and smelled of scent in the warm air to the more ample, less sophisticated ones in the big-sleeved velvet blouses that feminized a woman.

Yet Sango's one desire in this city was peace and the desire to forge ahead. No one would believe this, knowing the kind of life he led: that beneath his gay exterior lay a nature serious and determined to carve for itself a place of renown in this city of opportunities.

His mother had seen to it that he became engaged to "a decent girl from a good family, that you might not dissipate your youth, but sow the seed when your blood is young and runs hot in your veins . . . that I might have the joy of holding a grandchild in my arms."

Many of Sango's sober moments were spent in planning how he would distinguish himself in the eyes of his mother, an ailing woman in the Eastern Greens whose health had steadily broken down since Sango's father died two years previously. She was no longer young. Sango did not know how old she was, but he was twenty-six and an only son. Every letter of hers expressed anxiety that Sango had to work so far away from home, and cautioned him about a city to which she had never been.

He had received one of them only yesterday, just before he met another of those girls he had been begged to avoid. And he had fallen. To make up for this lapse and to prove that from now on he really meant to be "good," Sango had been up since 4:20 a.m., working on the report of an inquest. Now it was nearing 6:30 a.m., and he knew that if he did not wake his servant Sam his morning bath would not be served and he might be late for the office.

The door was slightly ajar and Sango was startled to hear a furtive knock. The room had already darkened and the caller stood behind the half-open door waiting to be invited in, yet too polite to intrude.

"Who's that? Come in, if you're coming in!"

"Are you alone, Amusa?"

A female voice, a female hand, elegant: a girl, ebony black with an eager smile. She smiled not only with her teeth and her eyes, but with the very soul of her youth. She wore one of those big-sleeved blouses which girls of her age were so crazy about. Really, they shouldn't, for the *bubas* were considered "not good" by the prudes: loose, revealing trifles, clinging to the body curves so intimately that the nipples of the breasts showed through. Certainly not the most comfortable sight to confront a young bachelor on a morning when he had just made noble resolutions, Amusa tried to appear unmoved. Her large imitation-gold ear-rings twinkled in the dim light. She moved across the room gracefully. Sango felt the vitality of the girl and it tantalized him.

She came over to the edge of the table where he was working and rested her hands. This simple movement had the effct of throwing up her bust, so that it swelled within the loose blouse. She smiled.

"Don't you ever rest? Last night you were playing trumpet at the club."

"Don't remind me about that one; I must get on with my report. By the way, where are you going all dressed up like this?"

"I've come to see you." The smile had vanished and Aina seemed suddenly aware of herself.

"Very kind of you, Aina; but my mother will not be pleased to hear that I spend my time in this city receiving pretty girls in my room at seven in the morning!"

She looked away. She looked down at her slender, shapely hand. She looked into his face. He saw the tears in the dark eyes and thought: now, now . . . not this morning!

"Come, come, Aina! I didn't mean to speak harshly. You're looking so very pretty this morning. I love your *buba* and the careless ease with which you always dress. Aina, you're a man-killer. Ah, now you smile. But I see a darkness in your face. Tell me, what is it?"

"I—I—No! Let's leave it till another time."

"Please tell me. Do you want something? Is there a way I can help?"

"No, Amusa. Let's leave it like that. Please fetch me some paper. For wrapping."

Amusa found her some paper. He was wondering when she would come to the point. She took it from him and went to the corner of the room. He saw her quickly take something from the folds of her cloth and wrap it up. Then the crackling of paper ceased and she came to him once more, smiling.

"Thank you, Amusa. I want to ask you something. Amusa, will you always love me as you did yesterday, no matter what happens?"

"Like what? I don't understand."

"Answer me. Will you always love me?"

"Yesterday?" Sango asked.

To him the past was dead. A man made a promise to a girl yesterday because he was selfish and wanted her *yesterday*. Today was a new day. He had met her at one of those drum parties they always held on Molomo Street. Almost any night you could walk in among the singers and drummers. A marriage. a christening, a death: no matter what it was, the incandescent lamp always shed its rays on the girls who hovered around the glitter like moths. Sometimes the girls danced and then the young men would pinch one another and point to something appealing in a new girl. Sango had been bored with the party until he had seen Aina standing alone, tall and graceful, waiting, he imagined, for the man who could stimulate her imagination.

He had been that man. It had not been easy, for Aina had come to the city and was attracted by the men, yet very suspicious of them. Not even the festive throbbing of the drums could break the restraint which her mother, and the countryside, had instilled in her. But Sango was the city man—fast with women, slick with his fairy-tales, dexterous with eyes and fingers. It had required all his resources, and when they had parted, a little after midnight, Sango had known the intensity of her passion. To be reminded of last night's abandon so early the next morning was like being faced with a balance sheet of one's diminishing prestige.

"Amusa, do you like me still? Do you love me? If anything happens, will you always love me? We are both young, and the world is before us . . . All I want is your word."

"Is it important?"

He saw the struggle in her eyes. What could this mean? Could there be something else? What did she want of him? Her fingers were restless. Her firm bosom heaved against the clinging blouse. Again that mad longing to touch her welled up in him.

Suddenly she met his gaze squarely. "Have you no feeling at all?"

Before he could answer she turned swiftly and was out of the room. He heard the crunch of her retreating crêpe soles on the gravel.

This girl must be treated like the others. She must be forgotten. She must not be allowed to be a bother to him. Every Sunday men met girls they had never seen and might never see again. They took them out and amused them. Sometimes it led to a romance and that was unexpected; but more often it led nowhere. Every little affair was a gay adventure, part of the pattern of life in the city. No sensible person who worked six days a week expected anything else but relaxation from these strange encounters. Aina must know that. Sango had his own life to lead, his name to make as a band-leader and journalist. All else must be subordinated to that. Nothing must be allowed to disturb his plans.

Yet he was disturbed. Now that she had gone and the scent lingered in his room, he wanted her. He went to the door and called: "Sam!"

Sam came quickly enough, wiping his hands on the seat of his khaki shorts. His red shirt was unbuttoned all the way down the front, revealing the hard muscles of his chest. He could be fifteen or fifty. He had the youthful gaiety of a boy of fifteen and the cunning of a grandfather.

"Is she gone?"

"Who, sah?"

"Come on, Sam! You saw her."

Sam smiled cunningly. He had that ideal quality of a bachelor's houseboy: a complete and thorough knowledge of the women with whom his master associated. Their names, their addresses, their real cousins and false cousins, their moods. . . . Not only did he know how to deliver a letter to a prospective mistress without embarrassing her, but he could also read faces and guess the innermost thoughts of the lady's heart. And these unique qualities covered up his other faults and rescued him from the bane of unemployment.

He scratched his head. "I am in the kitchen, washing plates. I don't see anyone, sah!"

"I believe you, Sam."

"I'm sorry, sah."

"Okay!"

Sam hesitated a moment.

"Coffee or tea, sah?"

"Coffee, and make it black."

Sam took the percolator from the table in the corner and went out of the room. Sango could hear him asking the two street women who lived next door whether they had seen anyone leave his master's room and pass along the corridor.

Sango sighed. "Shan't be bothered about her any more. A funny girl. She's the one in dire need of something. But rather than ask for it, she'll bluff and put on a mystery act, expecting *you* to go down on your knees and beg her. And if you don't, then you're hard-hearted. That's life. That's women all over. Yes, I've begged and coaxed . . . when I'm in need. But this morning? No, I must be good."

He pulled his chair closer to the table and settled down to writing his report:

"Popular opinion does not incline favourably towards this verdict of suicide. During the investigations it seemed as if a foregone conclusion had been arrived at. The prosecution tried to prove its theory of suicide. And it appeared as if the learned judge co-operated with them. I ask, what had the judge to fear? Why did he suppress—or gloss over as if in haste —all the evidence which tended to create the faintest suspicion of doubt as to what really happened?

"That a gun lay beside the body of the managing director has been firmly established. That it bore his fingerprints is beyond question, and that he was in financial difficulties (as his books show). But do all these necessarily add up to suicide?

"The West African Sensation *can now reveal a phase of Mr. Trobski's private life unknown to the police. Mr. Trobski came to West Africa in the war years when Government was looking for just such a man . . ."*

He chewed his pencil. Should he throw this bombshell on the city? Yes, in all fairness he must. Too often had murderers been left to go scot-free.

There comes the dreaded city noise, Amusa. You live with it so you don't notice it any more. Sounds of buses, hawkers, locomotives, the grinding of brakes, the clanging of church and school bells. . . .

The city was awakening.

When Sango first moved into Twenty Molomo, the faintest noise would bring him racing to the street. And he would get there to find the crowd pressing on the central characters. Once he had seen a husband dragging his wife by her hair because—he had never found out why. All the answers he got were in Yoruba and Sango did not speak the language. Now the scenes had lost their novelty, and whatever he missed he could always pick up at the barber's shop.

The noise grew louder. Something *was* happening. This noise had a hysterical urgency that frightened Sango. Even the cars were checking and now the yelling was rising above the hum of the engines. He decided to remain where he was and finish his report.

He heard the sound of running feet along the corridor. There was a rude and demanding knock.

"*Mr Sango!* Sango, are you in?"

A slippered foot peeped into the room, then a gilt-edged fez cap with golden tassels. Lajide was chewing the end of a cigarette and puckering up his big chocolate-brown face to avoid the fumes getting into his eyes.

"Come here, please." He beckoned.

How that one-inch of ash remained at the end of his cigarette without dropping off fascinated and annoyed Sango. He got up from his report reluctantly.

"Anything wrong, sir? Haven't I paid my rent? You are the landlord, but you've never spoken to me so early in the morning. There *must* be something nasty . . . anyway I've switched off all lights before going to bed, so it can't be the electricity bill."

"I just want you to see something for yourself; because of next time."

Sango regarded Lajide as his one great obstacle in this city, and Lajide in turn often called Sango a vandal, sent by the devil to destroy his property at Twenty Molomo Street. Everything was in order between landlord and tenant except good feeling. Sango took care to make no advances to any one of the extremely attractive harem of eight wives with whom Lajide surrounded himself and flooded his premises.

"Just go up Molomo Street," Lajide said. "Go and never mind about your work; you'll come back to finish it." He squinted through the haze of cigarette-smoke. "Go, you will see something interesting." The challenge and the implied insult were intriguing.

Sango was puzzled. "I'd like to go, but can't you just tell me what it is? It's getting late, and my report—"

Lajide smiled. The cigarette-ash was now one and a half inches long and had not yet fallen off. It had curved slightly. "Just go up the road . . . " The noise suddenly increased. "You hear that?" He was jubilant.

Sango did not like unpleasant surprises in the morning before breakfast. From what he could make of it, the voices appeared to be children's. But underlying that was something sensational. Sango could feel it.

"Another husband beating his wife? Are there no police in this city?"

"Is all right, Sango. If you like, you go. You don't like to see your gal frien' naked in de street. When I talk, you say I talk too much—"

"Which gal frien'? Tell me, which gal frien'?"

Sam appeared and said, "Is true, sah. I tink is the gal who jus' lef' here. People gather roun' her and laugh at her. Some even slap her, sah!"

On Molomo Street, the traffic was in a jam. Sango made his way through a seething mob of raving lunatics, jeering with excitement. He was quite unprepared for the surprising sight which met his eyes.

A girl was seated on a stone, and for all the world she looked like a model posing for a group of drunken artists who yelled and threw missiles at her. Only, these mad people were no artists. They were people who had wanted her and had not got her. They were revelling in her humiliation. She sat there on the stone paralysed, defenceless and scornfully beautiful. A child came near and with a stick dealt her a blow across the shoulders. She winced. Everyone shouted and booed.

"Thief! Thief! *Ole! Ole!*"

Could this be the same girl in the blue velvet wrapper and the imitation-gold ear-rings? He had suspected that she had something on her mind, but she had been too proud to say just what. Sango pinched himself to make sure he was not dreaming. Aina was seated there on the stone, fully alive to the stone-throwers and the yelling mob. He must do something. It would be foolish to face the mob.

"*Ole! Ole!*" (Thief! Thief!)

"A thief? What has she stolen?"

"She's sitting on it . . . that green cloth."

"*That one?* But—"

"Yes!"

"But it is worthless."

"She stole it."

"Look at her lover! I know him."

Someone was pointing and Sango knew he had been identified.

"Yes, that is her lover—the lover of a thief-woman. These Lagos gals. When they make up you don' know thief from honest woman."

"Ha, ha!"

Now Sango understood why Lajide had been so insistent that he should see things for himself. At the other end of the street a policeman was pacing up and down, quite unconcerned. Sango ran towards him.

"Constable—" He tried to catch his breath. The traffic drowned his voice. "Constable—"

"I'm a corporal," said the man.

"Oh, sorry. Corporal. Are you going to stand there while they kill the girl?" He pointed down the road at the crowd. "Please help her quick. Only your uniform can save her."

"I'm on point duty here. What girl? Not that street girl?"

"This is no time for that, Corporal. Protect her first, then judge her. It's your duty!"

"What did she do?"

"Stole a cloth, they say!"

"You think that if she had husband and family, she would go and steal? Is because she's a street walker. The devil finds work for the idle."

"Please, now! They're stoning and beating her."

"Softly, my friend. Why so hot? Or is she your girl, eh? Is she your girl? Tell me why you're so hot!" He waved his arm. The oncoming traffic stopped. He was working and talking at the same time. To Sango it appeared as if they had been talking for hours. The corporal went to a little post near by, opened a metal box, took out a phone.

He turned to Sango. "Why didn't you ring 999?"

"Because I saw you so near. I just wanted protection for her, that's all."

"*Hello* . . . Corporal Daifu here . . . Molomo Street . . . Yes, proper street gal . . . They want to kill her with stones. Send patrol van to pick her up quick." He winked at Sango. "Over to you. Over." He hung up, closed the metal box.

"Go now!"

"Thank you." Even before Amusa Sango could turn round, the 999 van with the letters POLICE was wheeling into Molomo Street, and the young officers were leaping out while the vehicle was still in motion.

Amusa was pleased.

"I tol' you," smiled the corporal in triumph. "But lissen. Man to man, go and warn your gal. Yes, I know she's your gal. You see, person who's not careful, the city will eat him!" He laughed.

The arrival of the van had created a definite sensation. Aina was still there. She was standing now and hugging the gay cloth which she had tied firmly under her armpits, covering her breasts from searching eyes. The young men sighed regretfully. A group of policemen were questioning her, and the crowd, all ears and eyes, pressed against them.

Amusa's arrival created another stir. Elbows dug into ribs. Lips whispered into ears. "That's the boy friend!"

They parted before him; away from the touch of a man who had loved a thief. Near the policeman, Amusa stopped. Aina looked up from her humiliation and their eyes met. The accusation in her eyes made Sango feel awkward. She seemed to say: "Didn't you promise you would always love me?" To which question Sango could find no answer in his mind. He heard the policemen questioning her.

"What's the matter? Can't you answer the question?"

Aina was silent. Everyone was silent. The policeman barked out: "Can't you talk? I said what's the matter?"

An elderly corporal said: "You girls of nowadays, you're too proud. You won't learn something useful, you won't marry; and you're proud. I'll teach you sense!" He turned abruptly. "To the station!"

"To the station! Yeh! They are taking her to the station!" yelled the crowd.

Aina scowled as if to intimate that she was prepared to face the worst. They bundled her into the car. The crowd booed and sighed. *"Ole! Ole!"*

A woman said: "I'm sorry. Such a beautiful girl!"

"Listen, the thief is saying something. She's talking. Listen to her!"

"Amusa, come and save me! Come and save me, I beg you. If you love me, come and save me! Don't mind what they're saying . . . Come and save me!"

"No," Amusa said to himself. "I can't go. I really can't. I was impulsive. I liked you. We had an affair. Let's forget it, Aina . . ."

He looked round and saw the woman standing near him. Tears were coursing down her face. Amusa looked away. To the left of him he heard sneers, whispers, giggles. It would be silly to listen to them or to take offence. They would only laugh all the more and make a fool of him. These were the men who would give anything to have her. Were they not satisfied with her misery as it was?

At the entrance to Twenty Molomo, a man in a gilt-edged cap with golden tassels was waiting. He seemed to be admiring his floral slippers. When Sango approached he looked up.

"You see now?"

"See what?" Sango mumbled in his irritation.

Lajide's cigarette bobbed up and down as he spoke, but the ash did not drop off.

"The girl . . . didn't I warn you about city women? They're no good. They dress fine, fine, you don't know a thief from an honest one. Just be careful, Mr. Sango. Don't bring more thieves here. I don't want them on my premises. Hear that?"

Sango forced a smile. "Thank you, Lajide. Aina will not come here any more. That is, if she gets out of this mess."

Sango went back to his report. He read over what he had written, chewed his pencil, and continued:

"The public must be satisfied that he could have died by no other means than suicide. Otherwise that feeling of unsafety will always lurk in the citizen's mind. After all, it is the citizen who pays the tax that pays the police. Therefore he must be protected from gangsters, hooligans, robbers, rich men who flaunt authority . . ."

He looked over the last sentence. There was something there. The public liked a paper which spoke up. The Trobski murder had something unsavoury about it, and the *West African Sensation* would not let those concerned make a mess of things. People would speak of the *Sensation* as the fearless paper.

chapter two

Sango did not hear the knock but looked up when the doorway darkened. The tall woman who came in could have been fifty or sixty or eighty. Her jowls were shrunken, and a pathetic expression lingered in the depths of her wine-red eyes. She was a total stranger to Sango.

"Take a seat," he said with reverence. He was afraid.

She sat down very slowly, assessing him. Something in her manner chilled the beating of his heart.

"She sent word to you . . ."

"Who?"

"My daughter, Aina."

Sango flopped into an arm-chair. He could not see the resemblance between Aina and the old woman. But he felt the slow, confident grip of her power over him. The word "witch" occurred somewhere in his subconscious, but he quickly dismissed it as out of date. She was behaving with the air of a mother-in-law in the tenth year of her daughter's marriage.

"She said you should come and bail her . . . they want to put her in jail."

Amusa Sango bit his lip.

"You have been very kind to her so far . . ."

Amusa jerked himself up from his seat. "Me?"

"She hides *nothing* from me. She is my daughter, and I trained her, since she was like this . . ." She made a motion to show Aina's height at the age of taking the first steps.

How much did this woman really know? What was at the back of her mind? Amusa thought of her age, of the generation in which she had grown up, and he became afraid. *I wish my mother were here to match her magic against your magic, if that's what you're trying to use against me. You know I am young. I may be able to read and write, I may work in a big office, but I am as a child where your worldly wisdom is concerned. I wish my mother were here.*

"So, Aina told you about this place?"

"Yes; and your servant, Sam. He comes from near our village. You know we are not Lagos people. We only come here for a while."

Your servant Sam. But—no, Sam wouldn't do that. He wouldn't take a powder from you to sprinkle over my breakfast beans. I have been very kind to him. So that's out of the question. You cannot poison me through Sam.

"Well, I'll think about it. I'll see if I can help her." He tried desperately to sound all-powerful and authoritative. "But if she has really stolen that cloth—"

"Don't listen to them." The energy behind her words startled him.

She had absolute faith in the honesty of Aina. She rose. "I want to tell you this: I may leave the city without notice. My work involves travelling to Abeokuta. I sell cloth, you see."

"The same thing here," said Amusa. "It is going to be as if I run away, if I bail her and leave the town. That is against the law."

She did not understand. Her wine-red eyes were regarding him malevolently. He broke off, his mouth half open. In that moment he felt the full impact of the woman's power. He knew he had no other choice than to obey.

He called at the charge office after breakfast. Aina was not there. A policeman told him that along with other prisoners—

"Prisoners? Magistrates Court No. 2? What are you talking about?"

"Yes. Her case will be tried this morning."

When Sango got to the magistrate's court, the magistrate had not arrived. A number of men and women sat inside and outside the court, waiting. Some of them had waited six months for their cases to be heard. And yet Aina's case was being heard so very soon.

Sango saw the Black Maria standing under the mango tree. It was empty. Looking upstairs he saw a window with stout iron bars. A dangerous-looking man with a grizzled beard tried to bend the bars. What if he did? Could he survive a fifty-foot fall to the traffic below? Sango looked at the next window and saw only women. An overwhelming flood of shame swept over him. Aina would be with them. But why did he feel ashamed? What was different about her case? He had often come here to this same court and it had meant nothing to him. He went back into the court and sat in the wooden chair and looked at the magistrate. This was Dirisu, a man feared for his cold-blooded strictness. Around the table a handful of police inspectors, plain-clothes detectives of the C.I.D., shuffled papers. They looked important, with that power to grant or remove personal freedom.

The prisoners began to trickle in, but Sango was looking for a particular one. Suddenly there was a hum. Aina was led into the court. Amusa felt a lump rise in his throat. He should have done something to save her, but hadn't. As it was, she stood alone against a city determined to show her no mercy. She would never win. Sango could hardly bear to look at her face, grey and drawn with suffering, the sheepishly straining eyes, one of which appeared to be swollen.

From the wtiness box she was repeating after the policeman: "I promise to speak the truth, the whole truth, and nothing but the truth, so help me God."

It all looked so formal with a constable standing behind her in the witness box. "On 26 March at 0430 hours you, Aina, did enter and break into the residence of Madam Rabiyatu Foleye of 19A Molomo Street and at the said time did remove, without her prior knowledge or consent, one wearing apparel valued at £30. Do you plead guilty or not guilty?"

"Guilty!" came the faint voice. This must have been what the young policeman told her the night before. Do not say "not guilty" because that will complicate things and annoy the magistrate. Plead guilty and he will be lenient. You will be fined, that's all. A few pounds at the most. Her voice came up again. "I—I stole the cloth. I am guilty."

"You are guilty?" There was a sneer on the magistrate's face.

"Yes, your worship."

A moment's silence as heavy as the entire twenty years of Aina's life. What would happen now? Sango wanted to disappear immediately.

"Three months!" The magistrate's voice was like a whiplash. "Next case!"

And immediately an old woman at the back of the court broke out in a wail. Two policemen seized Aina. She fought violently, kicking their shins, clawing, biting. "O, my mother! My mother, come and save me. O Lord, I am dead—O!"

But the stalwart men had been hand-picked and she might just as well have saved her breath. "Ha," they laughed. "Your mother did not follow you on *that* day! Ha!"

Amusa sat cowed. His limbs were heavy and inactive, his throat parched. He needed a drink. He got up ponderously; walked out of the court. Under the mango tree, the Black Maria was leaving. He caught a glimpse of the policeman with the rifle at the back door, Aina's slim waving hand through the bars. She still clung to him even when condemned.

An old woman shuffled beside Sango. She stopped, and said: "Thank you for all you did, and may God bless you."

He did not need to look at her, could not bear it. He heard her footsteps as she walked up to the mango tree, mumbling in her dejection; and then he was alone.

chapter three

When Sango got to the *Sensation* office, McMaster, editorial adviser, had not yet arrived. Amusa talked to the art sub-editor about the poor quality of the sports pictures that had appeared in recent issues of the paper. He saw the night editor, Mr. Layeni, shuffling towards them with sleepy eyes. Sango looked at him, said good morning, and continued talking to the sub-ed.

Layeni stopped. He was one of the old school of Africans who believe that the younger generation were getting too cute. They were rude, did not bow to their elders as of old. They called it "education," but he had another word for it. They lacked "home-training." He would show them. He always showed them.

"Why didn't you greet me?" he demanded of the art sub-ed. "That's how the younger people disregard your seniors. I don't profess to be very educated, but I'm your senior in age."

"But I said good morning; Sango, did you not hear me?" The art sub-editor stared helplessly round the office. Protesting and apologizing voices were raised from all tables. The art sub-ed was told to say good morning again, which he did, but Layeni continued to harass him at the top of his thin voice. He was now in the position of a man who has started a row for which no one has any use. He was merely talking to keep face. No one listened to him. He had become a nuisance.

All of a sudden his manner changed. He stopped near the stairs, looking down. Sango followed his gaze. The man coming upstairs wore a gilt-edged velvet fez with golden tassels. He was smoking a cigar, and smoking it as only a big man knows how. His robes radiated wealth.

"That's Lajide coming," Sango said.

"Perhaps he wants to insert an advert in the *Sensation.*"

Lajide waved his cigar. "Hello! How is everybody?" His voice was warm and friendly.

Everybody was all right. Everybody waited to know the source of this sudden display of goodwill. Ladjide joked. He laughed at the inconvenience of leaving one's home at night to work for somebody. But people had to do it. It was the same in all countries. If people did not work at night, things would not go on. Layeni laughed, but Sango could see that he was nervous about something.

"Well," Layeni stammered. "I—I must be going now." He looked about him, smiling uneasily.

Lajide blocked his way. "It's you I've come to see. That's why I'm up so early."

"Me?" said Layeni.

"I've come to collect my money."

"Ha, Lajide! Give me some more time!"

Lajide's whole manner changed. The warm and friendly smile vanished into the hot morning air. On his face appeared that cold metallic sheen so familiar to financiers. He had become a snake contemplating his hypnotized victim.

"Every day you say give me time, but I don't see a penny. And you are paid every month."

"I'll pay . . ."

"That's what you always say."

"End of this month," Layeni pleaded. He looked quite subdued and sober standing there, his feet arrested and frozen in a movement contrary to the direction he was facing. All the blustering and bullying had faded from him.

In the office, they whispered about him.

"Drinks too much . . ."

"What does he do with his money? He earns a fat salary yet he owes. Everywhere he's in debt! God save us!"

"And we, his juniors, can manage on our poor salaries . . ."

"But you haven't a wife and children."

"Children! Does he pay their school fees? Don't you see them coming here every day to ask for fees? I wonder, such a man! And he claims to be old and sensible!"

Lajide said: "I'm waiting, Layeni."

"The old drunkard," someone muttered. "He doesn't respect himself, and he expects us to respect him."

The phone rang. Sango went over.

"West African Sensation."

"May I speak to the editor, please?" The voice was strained, excited and high-pitched. Sango could feel the tension.

"Not in the office."

"Any reporter there?"

"Amusa Sango, crime reporter. Who's speaking, please?"

The office became silent. Even Lajide and his debtor had frozen and were staring at the telephone with expectant mouths. Sango knew the smell of news. It always gave him a kick. The breeze blew in from the windows, scattering the papers. No one tried to pick them up. The telephone voice was louder, more tinny than ever, clear enough to be heard by all in the room.

"If you want something for your paper, come at once to the Magamu Bush, and you'll get it. Never mind who I am."

"Magamu Bush. Where are you speaking from? Hello, Hello . . . He's gone, hung up! I must get out to the Magamu Bush at once."

He went across to the map and stared at it. It was an uninhabited part of the city on the road that led from the wharf. Sango had a vision of a broken motor road lined on both sides by dense woods, swamps and bogs. How often had the *Sensation* drawn the attention of the authorities to the need for developing this area! The crimes committed there were becoming tiresome and monotonous.

"Be careful, Sango," someone said, as he put on his hat at the rakish angle he loved. The typewriters were clattering again, someone was picking up and sorting out the scattered papers. Lajide was saying: "Attend to me, Layeni. I'm a busy man, you know that!"

He went outside and hailed a *Sensation* van. In half an hour he was at the railway crossing. The gates had just closed in front of him. Sango fumed and got out. It was always like this. The gates always closed when he was in a hurry. A single shunt engine steamed up. It stopped in the middle of the road and rail junction. The driver in his blue jeans wiped his forearms with waste and smiled. He got down and a woman in blue, with a child strapped to her back brought him a tray and he began to extract the plates of food. His fireman leaned out, shovel in hand, and said something.

Sango looked back. The queue of traffic was now a mile long, awaiting the pleasure of the shunt engine driver and his wife (or mistress).

"They killed somebody in the Magamu Bush—"

Sango heard the words distinctly. He was furious with impatience. The shunt engine belched smoke. The driver's wife (or mistress) moved away. She and her child waved at Papa. Papa climbed slowly back and the engine moved away. The gates swung open. Everyone wanted to get through at the same time. Some day the city would learn to build rail and road crossings on different planes as they did in sensible cities. Sango's van was not the last in the queue of cars, vans, trucks, wagons, bicycles, motor-cycles and scooters. Bells were clanging, horns were screeching and blasting, the entire junction had been transformed into a mixture of fire engines and ambulances in a hurry to get to a church and school where all the bells were ringing at the same time.

"Drive fast," Sango begged, but it was unnecessary. The mad noise was enough command.

Magamu Bush was not difficult to locate. As they neared it, Sango saw the number of cars parked close by. The van parked on the side of the road and Sango stepped into the bush. People who met him had grave and frightened faces. They picked their way with awe. He barged his way through the crowd and arrived at the front of the huge crescent.

She was lying on the floor, dead. They had killed her, and her child too. Must have torn the poor thing from her back in a fury. Evidence of foul play was there on the floor beside her: two rough-looking clubs. The police in cork helmets and white cuffs took measurements, glanced at their watches. They entered figures methodically into their black notebooks while a photographer flashed lights at the bodies.

"Some people are heartless," someone said. "I can't understand it. Kill the woman, yes. But the innocent child—no! That's too much!"

"Too bad," said an old man. "And she don't do them nothing." He folded his arms across his brown jumper.

"You mean they killed her for fun?" Sango asked.

"What else!" The old man shot back. "What is a gramophone that they will kill someone for? Of course they were drunk. But does that mean they should kill her? For her own thing?"

"No," Sango said. "But in this world many people die defending 'their own thing,' whether it is a material thing, or just a belief." He hurried back to the office and wrote:

"I have just witnessed the most gruelling murder since I became crime reporter for the West African Sensation. *In Magamu Bush, I saw her, a woman of twenty-five, lying with face twisted. And beside her lay her child, condemned in all its innocence by a gang of drunks. I saw also the two brutal clubs with which she had been done to death. The question I must ask the people of the city is this: Why? Why was the young woman killed in this heartless manner? And why the child too? The answer is simple: greed. The men who killed her borrowed a gramophone of hers. When she went to collect it, they would not part with it, but lured her into the Magamu Bush. The young woman, unsuspecting, followed the drunkards. And having defiled her in bacchanalian triumph, they clubbed her to death and strangled the child.*

"Let me assure these criminals that the whole of the Metropolitan Police, crime branch, is out in full force, looking for them. Let me assure the people of this city that the West African Sensation *will give the police every support to bring the criminals to justice and to safeguard the life and property of the law-abiding citizens."*

The weeks of investigation that followed only confirmed much of what Sango had written. The woman had been killed by drunken men for a quite trivial reason. The two men arrested were bachelors who lived on the outskirts of the city. They had come to the city from a fishing district in the delta of the Great River. They had known Muri as a girl, and now that she was married and lived in the city they looked at her with the same eyes of their childhood.

Her husband worked for a coastal vessel and was often away from the city. They persuaded her to lend them the gramophone while he was away. But Muri heard he was on his way back, and quickly went to them to return the gramophone lest her husband make trouble.

She found them drinking. One of them, Thomas, persuaded her to come with him to a neighbouring bush—the Magamu Bush. "That is where the repairer lives," he told her.

"Repairer?"

"Something went wrong with your gramophone. I gave it to him to repair."

Muri would not go. "I left no one in the house. Is only me and the child here, and—"

"Come on! We won't take long."

A little maid who saw Muri leave her home went to the police after a restless night, waiting for her to return. What had actually happened between Muri and the drunken Thomas in that lonely strip of bush no one would ever know.

Sango did not often sit at his typewriter with satisfaction. As Crime Reporter, he had seen the beginning of many crimes that made the headlines, but never the end. In this case, it was different, and hence his smile: MAGAMU BUSH MURDER SOLVED BY CITY POLICE, ran his headline.

"Readers of the West African Sensation *will recall my scathing remarks in these columns some weeks ago about the way the police handled the murder case of Mr. Trobski. Well, I must now hand it to the police for their brilliant performance in the Magamu Bush murder. The man who perpetrated the atrocity, who defiled the mother, strangled and killed the child, this* devil *has now been apprehended by the police. If only the police in this city were as hardworking as the corporal who handled the case, life and property would be much safer in this city, and in the country as a whole."*

He paused and looked up. One of the reporters had just come in, and turning to Amusa Sango, he smiled.

"Mystery calls are not always safe—or true."

"Mine was," Sango said.

"I just received one of those mystery calls. A complete hoax. Spent the last six hours roaming the wilds." He looked it, too. He blew at his open shirt while fanning himself with his reporter's notebook.

Sango smiled and continued with his story.

Sango made a routine call at the pathology laboratory near the hospital. From the pathologist's window he had a clear view into the prison yard. As he came down the steps a note was thrust into his hand by a stranger in warder's uniform. Aina wanted to see him, the note said.

"I take you there," said the male warder, and Sango followed him. He tried hard to imagine what she would look like, but failed.

In a little separate group from the out-patients stood a number of women in numbered white frocks. They all looked alike. Sango saw the female warder in her austere khaki holding a book and checking her stock of mixtures. Beside her stood a pharmacist.

How had the male warder got hold of Aina's message? Were there love affairs behind the barbed wire between prisoner and captor? Sango stood thinking about Aina's power over men and he could not but hand it to her. From an adjoining store a girl—also in a numbered white uniform—came in carrying a freshly-filled winchester bottle of medicine. Amusa's heart missed a beat.

"Aina!" He almost shouted out the name.

She was quite changed. It was incredible, but she was becoming plumper, more seductive. There was a new and wicked glint to her eye. He steeled himself against the choking sensation in his chest. Her suggestive curves showed even in a uniform designed to reduce feminine charms to the barest minimum. Few women with their hair shaved off could have been exciting as Aina was.

The female warder who had brought them down was standing with the other prisoners in the waiting-room, checking stocks. Sango went over towards her, but before he spoke she fixed him with a hostile look.

"I'm sorry," she said, in answer to his request. "You cannot see Aina. It is forbidden. Law-abiding citizens are not allowed to speak to prisoners. You may see her on visiting day, next Sunday."

Sango had seen the flash of eager joy in Aina's eyes. Her eyes were downcast when she knew Sango could not see her. But between the crime reporter and the girl a smile of understanding had passed. Sango felt the sadness and mystery of the whole episode.

chapter four

All day long and all night long, wherever he went, the thought of Aina obsessed him. It seemed as if, in going to jail, she had left behind her something more distracting than her own presence: the silent accusation that he had deserted her in her moment of need. When the knock sounded on his door, he half expected to see her or her mother and would have been grateful to put aside the article he had been trying to work on so unsuccessfully.

It was Bayo. He had a habit of dropping in on Sango whenever he felt like jazz. Sometimes he came alone, sometimes with his friends in their narrow trousers, pointed shoes and dark sun goggles.

He breezed in now. "Amusa Sango!"

Sango in a shirt and loin cloth was chewing the end of his pencil and puzzling out an article on "Sporting Criminals." He looked up grudgingly.

"Hello, Bayo!"

"Always busy!"

Bayo unbuttoned his coat, displaying his zebra-striped shirt. He fanned his face with a newspaper.

"I've got a dame with me," he confided. "She's crazy about jazz. I've told her about your records."

"Where's she? So few people appreciate real jazz—"

"Don't start lecturing yet. May I go and fetch her? I left her at the street corner. Thought you'd be too busy to have us."

"Not at all."

"Shan't be long!" Bayo went out. Sango got up to tidy the room. His working table was in a hopeless mess. The armchairs were untidily set on the lino. He straightened the cushions. There was a knock at the door and they came in.

"Sango, Miss Martins—Dupeh Martins."

"How're you?"

She smelt sweet. Sango took her soft hand gently in his, looking into the black eyes. She was a girl in that dangerous age which someone has called "the mad age": the mid teens. Her eyes held nothing but infatuation for Bayo. This was a girl who belonged strictly to the city. Born in the city. A primary education, perhaps the first four years at secondary school; yet she knew all about Western sophistication—makeup, cinema, jazz . . . This was the kind of girl whom Sango knew would be content to walk her shoes thin in the air-conditioned atmosphere of department stores, to hang about all day in the foyer of hotels with not a penny in her handbag, rather than live in the country and marry Papa's choice.

As she sat down, Sango put her age definitely at sixteen. Do not be deceived by those perfectly mature breasts. Girls ripen quickly in the city—the men are so impatient. But why did she put rouge on her naturally blooming cheeks? She was pretty enough without it; and besides, it did not blend.

"Well, what will you have?"

"Beer," Bayo said. "Brandy for the girl."

He rose and shuffled towards the gramophone. Sango went out to give Sam instructions. From the corridor he could hear *Basin Street Blues*. Bayo lost no time. He commented: "One thing I like about Armstrong—he's very original."

"Sure," Sango agreed. "Some good scat singing there."

"Listen to that! Listen!" He waved his hand to the music. *"Cau!* That's the part I like best. Terrific!"

The girl smiled. "It send me—oh!"

Sango said: "There's plenty more there."

"We're going to enjoy ourselves." Bayo lounged in the divan. "By the way, Amusa, I've got a job with the Medical Department; an uncle's influence did it for me. The pay is not bad either."

"Congrats, then! I hope you keep it."

"Things will soon be all right with me."

"Yes," Dupeh added cryptically. "If you don't keep running after girls. You have let them turn your head!"

"Now, now!"

Sango said: "I'm now going to play a record made in 1906, and I would like you to compare the original dixie-land style with the modern version."

He put on a record which began with a noise that made Dupeh's face twist.

"Sango," Bayo said. "Do you still play at the All Language Club? What's happened to your band?"

"It's there when I can find the time."

"When next are you playing?"

"Well, I have an engagement—"

"Turn it off, please," Dupeh said.

"Why, don't you like it?"

"Play something modern. I'm crazy about modern jazz."

"I'll find you something. Yes, I have an engagement at the All Language Club; crime reporting for the *Sensation* is not enough. But when I return at night, I'm sometimes so tired that—"

Sam came in with four bottles of beer and a packet of cigarettes. "Ah use the change to buy biscuits, sah."

He produced a small parcel loosely tied with green paper. As he fidgeted, five biscuits fell to the floor. They were cabin biscuits.

The girl began to laugh. Bayo joined. Sango could not repress a smile. It was all very embarrassing to Sam. He did not see the joke.

"You expect my visitors to gnaw cabin biscuits?"

Bayo wiped the tears in his merry eyes.

"What's wrong with that, Sango? You eat cabin biscuits, don't you?"

"For myself, yes. For my visitors, no!"

"I'm no stranger," Bayo said. He glanced at Dupeh.

"I'll eat them," she said. "I like them with beer."

"Shame on you, Sango," Bayo laughed. "Your boy Sam is very clever and understands our needs."

Sam was pleased. "T'ank you, sir and madam. God bless." He went out.

"A very good boy," Dupeh said. "I like him."

"I'm lost without him," Sango confessed.

"He's sweet and honest," said Dupeh. "I can see that."

The beer put them at ease. Dupeh and Bayo began with slow lilting dances, clinging together like drowning people. Sango saw that he had become one too many and went back to his typewriter. There were three words at the top of the paper. "Sports and Crime." He thought it over, and began to write.

"There comes a time when—in contemplating any crime, especially the

*large-scale, carefully planned type—one has to sit back and muse over
the question 'Isn't there an element of sport in all this?' "*

"*This thought has come to me because the truly great crime loses its
sense of sin and becomes nothing more than a matching of wits—in all
fields of human knowledge including superscience—between the law on
one side, and the outlaw and socially unacceptable on the other side. The
fact still remains that there is as much thrill in pursuing a criminal
across winding roads, in making one move ahead of him, as there is in
watching a football match or a motor race. One difference, though: in a
football match the stakes involved are far less gruesome . . .*"

He glanced up and saw the faith in Dupeh's eyes. Dupeh obviously
believed implicitly in Bayo. She must fancy herself in love with him.
A girl of that age would believe in the first attractive liar who spoke
love to her: therein lay the danger for all unguided teenagers.

Just at that moment Bayo paused, opened his zebra-striped shirt, and
blew into it. "My it's hot! Sango, I wanted to ask you: what about that
girl?"

"Who?"

"The one who stole a cloth that Sunday morning?"

"You mean Aina? Haven't you heard? She's in the white college now."

"Tell me!"

"Serving three months' hard labour. I saw her about five days ago.
They had gone to collect medicines at the hospital. D'you know, I
wasn't allowed to speak to her?"

"So sorry." Bayo became suddenly serious. "Sango, what are your
plans about Aina?"

"What d'you mean?"

"I mean . . . but can't you appreciate love? The girl is crazy about
you."

"Well, I'm not crazy about her!"

"You were telling me last time that many women do worse things
than Aina, but are never caught—"

"Yes—"

"Is it because she's a—"

"It's not because of anything. I just can't think of marrying her."

Bayo smiled. "If I were you, since she has sacrificed so much . . .
I mean . . ."

Dupeh cut in: "Sango, have you got that new record . . . forgotten
what it's called . . . er *Kiss me before I fall asleep and dream of you* . . .
something like that."

"That's what we were just discussing, Dupeh. I'm not all that romantic.
I only collect jazz."

"You're out of date."

"Didn't I tell you," Bayo smiled.

Dupeh came over and linked her hands with Bayo's. She caressed him, spoke to him tenderly. Sango saw that his presence had become unwanted.

"You've bothered me so much about Aina," he said. "Now I'm going to visit her mother. I want to see how she's taking it."

Sango took his hat and went into the street. He called at Aina's but was told to come back in the evening.

· · ·

Sango was to play at the All Language Club that evening. Towards eight in the evening First Trumpet arrived. While he sat reading a music magazine, Sango changed into the band's uniform: draped flannel coat, black trousers and black shoes. The green ribbon in his buttonhole distinguished him as bandleader.

"Look, Trumpet! I must go out. Just down the road. When the others come tell them I shan't be long. In any case we're not playing until nine."

First Trumpet winked knowingly.

"Don't be funny. I'm not going to see a girl."

He walked down Molomo Street. At night the street had a rare mysterious quality that never failed to excite him. Veiled women slipping from hazy light into the intense darkness of the corners; young girls leaving their buckets at the public water-pumps and stealing away under the trees where the glow of a cigarette-end told of a waiting lover and the headlamps of a passing car would suddenly reveal embracing couples. "Put out your lights!" the screams and curses would come. "Put out your lights, you clot!"

Sango stood near the public pump for a moment. He watched the traffic; crossed the road. A few minutes' walk brought him to the house where Aina's mother lived.

It had looked drab enough in the sun, but now the darkness gave it a quality of musty poverty. The only light came from a street lamp some fifty yards away, though the two houses that flanked it fairly glittered with their own lights. On both sides of the main entrance, groups of old women sat, indistinguishable in the gloom. One of them was selling petty things in a wooden cage. On the cage was a hurricane lantern.

"Good evening," Sango said. He felt on the brink of an important discovery. "I've come to see Aina's mother."

"Go in!"

He could not see his way forward. With hands outstretched he groped towards what might be a door. His head caught against something and he ducked. He was in. He could feel that the room was large, like a low-ceilinged hall. In one corner a light flickered. A dark figure approached behind the light. The figure entered a side room. The light faded.

"Welcome," said a voice, and Sango was startled. "Welcome again . . .

You asked for Aina's mother? I'm here. Move towards this corner. Watch your step!"

He tried to move, but something caught his step and he staggered. Then he realized that the entire floor was covered with sleeping bodies. He was in a kind of bedless open dormitory. Everyone but the old woman slept on the floor. Old, young, lovers, enemies, fathers, mothers, they all shared this hall. From early childhood Aina had listened to talks about sex, seen bitter quarrels, heard and perhaps seen adults bare their passions shamelessly like animals . . . From early childhood she had learnt the facts of life without being taught.

The old woman said, "Have you seen her?"

"Er, yes."

"The time is passing . . . Twenty years is not for ever."

"So you're counting the days?"

"What else is there for me to do?"

"Yes, she'll soon be out all right."

The old woman coughed. "Aina had bad luck, too much. People always dislike her, for no reason."

"You still believe she did not steal the cloth?"

"You're a small boy . . . You know book, you work in a big office, but you are a small boy. You do not know yet the blackness that lies in men's hearts. Such a one as Aina who is young and lively and beautiful. Some wish her nothing but evil."

Sango was silent. The voice from the dark bed went on: "One day, I'll tell you what happened, the real truth. But not now."

Sango asked himself: why did I come here at all? Morbid curiosity, that's all. And now this woman is bluffing. She is going to try blackmail next.

A bicycle grated against a wall outside. A man stood silhouetted against the door. Sango could make out nothing but a heavy dress, and around his shoulders what looked like a thick rope, looped, for climbing palm trees. The man brought into the room a strong smell of alcohol. He marched past Sango and disappeared into the gloom. Sango concluded that he was a wine-tapper back from his work.

The old woman resumed her insistent demands. "What have you brought for your old woman? You know Aina is gone and now—" She checked herself. "I am living in hunger. No one to support me." When he did not respond she went on.

"Aina was working for those Lebanese cloth merchants. She used to give me money every month when they paid her. Now she is in jail, no one gives me money. I am old."

Sango felt the remark was an accusation. He thrust his hand into his coat pocket and brought out a wad of notes. It was the band's money, and goodness knew from where he hoped to replace it. He tossed the notes on the bed and got out fast.

chapter five

By ten o'clock the All Language Club was full, and still more people came. They liked what the Club was trying to do. No bars—social, colour, political, or religious. There were two bars, though; a snack bar, and one plentifully supplied with all percentages of alcohol right up to a hundred.

Some people came because they liked Sango's music, or the music of the Hot Cats Rhythm, or the Highlife drumming of the unsophisticated Nigerian bands. They came in couples, they came alone and unescorted and sat under the palm trees and smoked and watched the bright lights.

Sango in his spotless jacket announced the next number. He winked at one or two girls. They winked back and trailed on after their wealthy and influential escorts.

Sango's trumpet caressed his lips. The notes came tumbling out, slickly, smoothly, with all the polish of a Harry James; yet sometimes they were clear, high and tremulous with passion as if this young city lad were modelling his style after Louis Armstrong. Nobody noticed; nobody bothered. In the middle of a clever solo, Sango noticed Bayo and Dupeh enter the Club. They were selecting a table while a waiter hovered around them.

Yet more people came. Towards the small hours they poured in from the cinemas, from the other clubs with early-closing licences. A very short man was trotting beside a girl who might have come from the pages of a South Sea travel book. Yet Sango knew she was a West African. Everything about her was *petite*, delicate. Her almost transparent dress was cleverly gathered at the waist. Her ear-rings and smile shone.

"Who is she?" Sango asked, with a heart now beating faster. His eyes followed her to her seat.

"I don't know," said the First Sax. "My, my!"

"Who is she?"

Faces lifted from music scores. Heads shook. "Don't know her . . . Must be new! Yes, sir!"

Sango was conscious of that strange excitement which had possessed him that night when he first saw Aina. The symptoms were the same: an insistent restlessness, a desire to be near this creature, to bask in the radiance of her beauty. He could restrain himself no longer, and during the interval went over to Bayo. Behind the dum palm, Bayo was making a scene. He was a little drunk, and Dupeh was having the worst of it.

"I've told you I don't want to be interfered with! If you love me, love my ways! That's my policy."

Sango stood for a moment, surveying the scene with amusement. Bayo, talking of policy! His sports shirt open at the neck, he was pacing up and down before the table, bellowing and waving his arms. Dupeh sat still, her head drooping. A handkerchief was pressed against her nose. She was crying. A number of men were trying to tell Bayo not to hurt the girl.

"Bayo, come here!" And when he came, Sango spoke in low tones. "Stop this wretched show you're making of yourself. There's something you must do for me. Look! That girl over there . . ." He indicated her without moving his arm.

"Pale blue dress, sort of off-the-shoulder?"

"Gipsy ear-rings too . . . they're always in the fashion, aren't they? Which reminds me. I have an ear-ring to return to Dupeh! And the condition you left my room in! Sam will never forgive you!"

"Forgive me, Sango; I'll expain. Now what about the girl? Champagne on her table! He must be somebody, then!"

"Find out who they are. Okay?"

"Trust me. Got a match?"

Sango walked between the tables back to his band and struck the cymbals. The band boys began to return from various parts of the club. In a few minutes, Bayo came across.

"Her name is Beatrice; the man is called Kofi something or other: a timber-dealer from the Gold Coast. He also runs an over-land transport to Accra."

He paused, pulling at his cigarette.

"You're fast, Bayo."

"Was that all you wanted to know?"

"What is she in this city?"

"I don't know what she does . . . she's new. I've never seen her before. They say her mother is here, but I don't know. She's hot stuff, Sango. Keep clear. The Europeans are crazy about her. I hear tales of disputes settled out of court on her behalf. If you're looking for trouble, well . . . remember Aina!"

"I'm not falling for Beatrice, make no mistake. But she looks so much like my fiancée back home in the Eastern Greens. She attracts me."

Bayo tapped him on the shoulder. He went back to the little table under the palm tree and took Dupeh's hand. Sango was pleased to see them dancing happily together.

But Sango was not being honest with himself. The fleeting picture of Beatrice was giving him no respite. He saw her when he went to sleep.

She was with him in his dreams, his waking hours, his band practice. And night after night, Amusa came to the Club. He wanted to meet Beatrice again. He wanted it so badly, he even took to playing for the Hot Cats Rhythm. When he was too early, he passed his time playing darts, or ping-pong, or talking to the barman.

The proprietor had been in the Civil Service when the idea of the All Language Club occurred to him. He wanted to take a practical step towards world unity, he said. To create a place where men and women of all languages and social classes could meet and get to know one another more intimately. It was his earnest desire that the spirit of fellowship created here would take root and expand.

"But as you can see, one cannot do very much without adequate funds." He smiled. "Still, we are trying."

Beatrice came there one night—but not alone. The Englishman who came beside her was a well-known engineer named Grunnings. He lived on Rokiya Hill, a wooden area outside the city. Sango learnt that Beatrice was married to Grunnings—according to African law and custom.

"She has three children for Grunnings," the barman told him. "They all go to St. Paul's School."

Sango said. "When he completes his usual eighteen months tour, does he take her to England with him?"

"No; she goes to her home in the Eastern Greens. Grunnings has just returned from leave in England, as a matter of fact. She has been waiting for him. He's a bit late this time."

In well-cut evening dress, with his hair well brilliantined, Grunnings was examining the menu and smiling at Beatrice. Grunnings looked fit and attractively tanned. He was about thirty-eight, of medium build, and his smile was friendly. Beatrice was smiling back with an eagerness that made Sango jealous.

He felt sad. "To think I've spent all my time dreaming in vain!"

Never once did her eyes leave Grunning's face. If only she could dote on me like that, Sango thought bitterly. But it brought him no comfort. What could they have to talk about at such length? Was her life really complete and full? Had she, in marrying Grunnings, a man with a wife and children in England, realized her purpose?

Sango went to the bar to console himself. He climbed on to a stool. Various resolutions were forming in his mind: *I should never come here again; I must forget her—completely.* He must have been there a long time when he noticed her sitting at the other end of the counter. She had a straw between her lips and was sucking an ice-shake.

Her bare arms lay on the counter, while one leg dangled above the chrome-plated rungs. It would be wrong to speak to her, because he did not know her. Even as the thought flashed through his mind her eyes were on his, dancing with a joyful light; and she was smiling. His heart warmed and he was encouraged.

"My husband knows I like this place," she said. "He always lets me sit at the bar and suck a cold drink—by myself. You are not playing today?"

"We play when we're engaged."

"I enjoy your music; I've always wanted to see you more closely . . . My husband has just returned from England, and is very busy. I wish he would bring me here more: I like night life."

Sango said: "An engineer who works all day would like to sit with his wife and family; not go hunting bright lights."

She sighed. "Grunnings has changed. Whenever he comes back from leave it is always like that. But this time, I shall do something about it."

She was talking half to herself, half to him; more like someone thinking aloud. Sango had little time to ask himself: why is she telling me all this? Her manner was so engaging. Add to it the fact that a beauty to whom he had attached so much importance should prove human, with her own worries, and the whole dazzling incident became numbing to his reason.

"He's a nice fellow; he loves me very much. But lots of men also love me and I'm going to leave Grunnings . . . Sango, do you know where I can find a room? I want to move from Rokiya Hill."

"A room?"

"The place is a grave; too quiet and lonely. I like noise; it is not so boring as silence. And I like high life and drinks and music."

"Let me think . . . My landlord might be able to help you—a man called Lajide. He's a housing agent and lives at Twenty Molomo."

She raised an eyebrow and smiled. "Housing agent! I have no money."

"Your beauty will see you through, Beatrice. Lajide is a man who likes beautiful women. He has eight wives, but they're not enough. And it will save you wasting a lot of time looking around. In any case, you can always move if you are not satisfied with his offer."

"You are very kind, Mr. Sango. When I live on my own, I'll be happy. I came here to live and enjoy life. For a short while I enjoyed my life, went to big functions, night clubs . . . I always wanted to be free. Then I met Grunnings and he married me. You will not believe it when I say that he was surprised to find me a complete girl who had known no man before him."

Sango started. He looked more closely at her. Her eyes were a little too bright, but her voice was low and steady. It was just possible that the champagne, the bright lights, the heady wine and lilting music had affected her a little.

"But now, I have given him three children and I know he can never be a real husband to me, so I'm quitting. I have thought over it a long time!"

She slipped to her feet, smoothly, delicately. No one would ever give this young woman up lightly. She left him and the astounded barman and walked back to her table. Sango could never tire of watching her walk. In his mouth was that sharp taste peculiar to an awakened but unsatisfied craving. At last he had met Beatrice and spoken to her. But what impression had he made on her? He watched her stop at a table. All eyes were on her glittering pearls. Her right arm flashed as she lifted her fingers and placed them gracefully on her forehead. It did not occur to Sango then that something unusual was about to happen.

In the next few minutes the All Language Club was disrupted by one of those dramas which take place so often and are so easily forgotten. Beatrice tried to move on. She couldn't. She began to sink to her knees. As she fell, Sango bounded towards her.

But Grunnings was there before anyone else and had taken her hand tenderly.

"You're not getting your attack again, Beatrice?" He peered critically into her face. "I'll take you home."

"I—I just felt giddy . . . I'm all right."

She seemed to have shrunken of a sudden. Her hair looked sodden. The lipstick had caked on her lips and her smile was wooden. Never had Sango seen such a rapid transformation. She put her arm round Grunning's shoulder. Grunnings led her to their seat, collected her handbag and helped her out of the Club.

A waiter ran after them with a bill. Sango stood rooted, perplexed. Could there be so much unhappiness wrapped up in a single person? The waiter joined him, still waving the unsettled bill.

"That woman, one day she will die—like this!" He snapped his fingers. "She get some bad sick inside her. When them tell her, go home, she no go. One day she go die for this city."

How true that prophecy proved to be! And how saddened Sango was to dwell on the enigma that was Beatrice. There seemed to be little more to do at the club that night, or perhaps morning. For already it was 2 a.m. Walking home through the streets of the city, Sango met his First Trumpet who had gone to play at an exclusive club on the island.

They fell into step, as both of them lived on the same side of the city. On Molomo Street Sango suggested a late cup of coffee and First Trumpet thought it a good idea. The whole of Twenty Molomo was unaccountably gloomy. It almost reminded Sango of the dingy courtyard in which Aina's mother lived.

"Careful, First Trumpet. We're early sleepers here."

He led the way. In the corridor, Sam crawled out of his bed, got the keys from his master and helped him open the door. He had that rare quality of continuing to behave like a wide-awake person even though he was fast asleep on his feet.

"There's no light, sah."

Sango tried the switch himself, in vain. He went out and surveyed the adjacent houses on Molomo Street. Lights were burning gaily in them. It couldn't be a breakdown, then.

"Lajide has started his meanness."

"It is annoying," said First Trumpet. "And we've been out all night. To get home now, hungry and in the dark: what kind of economy is that?"

Sango found a brush and with the pole end began to bang on the ceiling above him.

"Light please!" The idea of Lajide, comfortable and happy with eight women around him rankled in his brain. "Put on the light, I've paid my rent!"

"He must be out," said First Trumpet, after a moment's silence.

"Somebody must be in. Lajide, please put on the light; I beg you, put on the light!" The sound of his own voice, ignored, angered him the more.

Sango peered into the darkness and saw a man standing there. "You have no light too?"

"Yes, I've just come back from the Club. I've been out all evening so no one can accuse me of having wasted current!"

"I have no light, too. I'm the engine-driver living at the other end. I've never seen you, I'm always away on line, but I knew when you moved in."

Sango could now see the dim outline of the man's heavy overalls and the cap which showed a peak when he turned his face sideways,

"How do you do?" Sango said, shaking his hand. "An odd meeting, eh?"

First Trumpet said: "The electricity undertakings have increased their fees by thirty-three per cent. Perhaps that's why you have no light."

"And the landlords have increased their rent by three hundred per cent, so it balances—with plenty to spare."

Just then it started to rain. At first one could neglect the drizzle, and then it intensified, pouring with all the vengeance of a tropical tornado.

The woman Rose, who lived next door, produced a hurricane lantern. There was nothing for it but to accept her kind offer and light himself into his room. It was the first time Sango had ever spoken to the prostitute. Now everyone in Molomo Street was awake. At the far end of the passage, the engine-driver was cursing in a venomous stream. Rose came into Sango's room, giggling. She was enjoying the situation immensely. Sango thanked her for her lantern and as soon as she left he and First Trumpet were again plunged into darkness.

"It is not many hours to breakfast," Sango said. "You'll have to sleep here, First Trumpet. I want to talk about Beatrice, to pass the time. If you go home now, you will have to wake *your* landlord who may have locked the gate against thieves—"

"I'll stay here," said First Trumpet. "But I must be away first thing in the morning. I've got to go to work."

"Take the bed, then. I'll make myself comfortable on the sofa. And please don't argue with me. I'm dead tired and disappointed with life as a whole."

"Good night, Sango."

"Good night, Trumpet."

Sango awoke. The door was open and the sunlight was streaming in. First Trumpet was gone. On the floor at Sango's feet was a note addressed to him in a feminine hand. Sango picked it up.

He read the copy-book script, no doubt written by a girl—Lajide's lady clerk:

"With respect to your attitude last night, it is, and always ever will be, an outstanding rule, that lights should be switched off by 6 every morning, and on the dullest days 6:30 a.m. I am still having 22 points of light and when all the lights are operating I have more dues to pay.

"Had I not the utmost patience, you are sure you provoked me to the last yesterday. I have been waiting to receive from you a notice to quit.

"But now I must give you one month's notice from this date."

Over his breakfast, Sango tried once again to make sense out of the involved memo. One thing was clear. He had been given notice to quit. This could be more than serious. A man thrown out of his lodgings in the city could be rich meat for the ruthless exploiters: the housing agents and financiers, the pimps and liars who accepted money under false pretences. This matter needed very careful thinking out. If only his nerves had not been in that awful state last night.

Before he had lowered his third cup of coffee, the engine-driver stood at the door. He was in his blue overall and a blue cap.

"Going to work?" Sango asked.

"Yes . . . Look at this."

"Oh," said Sango. "You got one, too!"

Sango took the note and read:

"I, A. O. Lajide, your landlord, do hereby give you notice to quit and deliver up possession of the room with the premises and appurtenances situated and being to No. 20 Molomo Street, which you hold of me as tenant hereof, one month from the service of this notice. . . ."

Written in the same feminine hand, it was signed with the same bold scrawl.

"Lajide has not been hanging round the courts for nothing." He handed over the note, rubbed his head reflectively. "This is really serious, you know. Where have I the time to search for new lodgings?"

"It's not easy," said the engine-driver. "I'm going on line now; I return next tomorrow."

Sango said, "Now we shall see how overcrowded the city really is, with the trains bringing in more and more people every day."

"I'm not going to sleep in the gutter," the engine-driver said with confidence. "New houses are being built every day."

"For you?" Sango sneered. "The owners want money, my friend! How much can you pay? A European is able to offer five thousand pounds cash to a landlord, and he gets a tenancy for five years. He takes a whole courtyard that can house one hundred Africans . . . and we are driven to slums like Twenty Molomo."

The engine-driver said: "But the Africans are the brothers of the landlords. They can't do that, surely!"

"Brotherhood ends where money begins."

"I'm going to find a room, all the same."

"Best of luck! And if you have one to spare, think of me."

He marched down the corridor in his heavy boots and Sam came in to clear the table. His back was expressive as usual, and he was most sympathetic. He would tell his brother and all the others, but would Master consider going to beg Lajide? He might yet change his mind and that would save a lot of trouble.

Sango smiled. "Not me, Sam!"

Almost everybody on Molomo Street had heard of the landlord's behaviour of the previous night. They came to see Sango and to sympathize with him. Once it was generally known that he did not send them back, yet more of them came. There was the woman who sold rice to the loco workers. Sango had often seen her sitting under the almond tree. He was surprised to find that she could be quite smart when she got out of her oily working clothes. Then there were the two sisters who lived down Molomo Street. The baby-faced one was appealing in a maternal way with folds of fat everywhere and a face that was sweet and peaceful. Sango, as more and more of them knocked and told him they were sorry he was leaving, said to himself: "I never knew I was the darling of Molomo Street! How the people love me—especially the women."

He lay on his back in the night, unable to sleep. This was his usual time for work, when the city traffic had thinned down to a mere trickle and comparative silence descended on Molomo Street; but on this particular evening he did not feel like work. He rolled over and over, gazing at the ceiling. When he heard the knock, it was so faint he could not be sure. But it came again, a mere brushing of the hands against the woodwork. The lines of a poem he had composed flitted through his mind:

You who knock so secretly
Sidling up the door, your eyes in veils
Your feet on pads of silence
Your manner furtive
Your breath held in suspense
Who might you be?
A thief—that fears to waken
A household fast asleep?
And when 'tis asked who knocks
Why slide you mutely out of sight
Waiting in concealment
Hearkening for the voice of whom you seek?

Perhaps you know he knows your knock
And would not raise a voice
For fear your call would scandalize the moral world
So patiently you wait
And hearing steps that only you can hear
Your eyes light up with love
As he with stealth transcending yours
Slides back the bolt and in his arms
Takes your sweetly scented arm
And savours more the fruit that, forbidden,
Delights the more . . .

He lingered with pleasure on the lines, saying again the more delightful ones: *Your feet on pads of silence* . . . But now the knock had become persistent. He groaned and got out of bed. When he opened the door, he drew back in surprise. A girl was standing there, nestling against the wall.

She could not be more than fourteen, but her breasts were taut and large with ripeness. She had sleepy eyes, a husky voice and soft lips. Sango had often seen her hawking lobsters, a Molomo Street delicacy. Her deep croaky voice set his blood afire.

"Doctor . . . Doctor . . ." He was not a doctor, and only the devil's temptress could tell him where she had got the idea, but it pleased him. He looked up and down the corridor and saw that no one was in sight. This was temptation. She pushed her breasts against the door.

Sango kept the tremor out of his voice.

"What is it?"

"Doctor," she breathed, and cleared her throat. She made eyes at him. "Doctor, I heard you are going . . ." Her bare smooth shoulders and rounded arms invited his fingers. He held back.

"Now, girl, go to bed. Quick. All girls of your age are lying in their mother's beds."

He shut the door. "Phew!"

> You who knock so secretly
> Sidling up the door, your eyes in veils
> Your feet on pads of silence . . .

He listened. She was still there. He could hear her moaning to be let in. He went to sleep still hearing her calling croakily, "Doctor . . ." and brushing her hands against the door, "I want to tell you something. . . ."

chapter six

That afternoon Sango began to search for new lodgings. He found little luck. After cycling miles and miles, he met Dele on the crest of a hill. He had not seen Dele since college days and now he found him virtually unchanged, carrying a Bible, smiling and shy.

"Dele, I'm looking for a room," Sango told him when they had overcome their mutual surprise.

"A room? Now let me see . . ." He stroked his chin and looked thoughtful. "Would you like to live in this area?"

Sango looked around him, and saw the logs floating on the lagoon. Logs that would soon be loaded into cargo boats and sent on their journeys to Europe and America. Logs that trapped the still waters and made a happy breeding ground for mosquitoes and malaria.

"I'm looking for a room, Dele, not an area!"

"Then come along! I'm just back from the office. But we may be lucky enough to meet the man I want."

Sango followed him and learnt that, as the time for the Town Council elections was very near, candidates were willing to consider any proposals that might win them votes. As it happened, the man they were going to see was an election candidate and might help them. He was also an intimate friend of his father's. Dele pushed his bicycle and talked of old days.

So wrapped up were they in comparing notes that Dele overshot his mark and they had to wheel back to find the right door. Dele knocked. While they waited Sango had a glimpse of an expensive cap not unlike Lajide's. But the man who wore it was much darker, stouter and more pleasantly disposed.

"Dele, is that you? Ha, ha! Come in!"

Sango's heart warmed towards the man. He was at a table littered with small cards, labels, posters, pamphlets. Sango could read the inscription on some of them:

YOUR CANDIDATE FOR "A" WARD IS . . . VOTE FOR HIM: WE WILL DELIVER THE GOODS . . . OUR POLITICAL MANIFESTO . . . AFRICANIZA-TION OF THE CIVIL SERVICE . . . SELF-GOVERNMENT NOW . . . AWAY WITH EXPATRIATES

The words seemed to shout frantically from the very pages. On a large poster was a photograph of the candidate himself, looking dignified in his robes.

Dele said, "This is my friend, Amusa Sango. We were at school together, after which he went to teach for some time; now he is a journalist."

"How are you, Mr. Sango?"

They shook hands. It was a warm, confident hand, Sango thought. Dele smiled.

"Yes, sir, as I was saying, he's a journalist. I would like you to help him. Maybe he can write something good about you in the *West African Sensation*. You see, sir, he's looking for a room. As a man who reads a lot, he would like a place that is not noisy; that's why I have brought him to you. Because I know you can help him."

Sango admired Dele's acting. In his loose but well-cut English suit, he looked boyish. He spread his palms upwards, rolled his eyes, bent his head this way and that in an appealing manner. His gestures were expressive. One would think that Sango was not the one in need but Dele himself.

He paused now, his eyes focused on the election picture. To Sango he said: "He's the candidate for your ward. The elections are coming on. He's very busy as you can see."

"Yes," said the Councillor, beaming. "I pray I get in. My party fights for the people, for the poor. There are poor men in every tribe and race, therefore my party is the Universal Party. But my rivals!" Here he snorted. "They're out to line their own pockets! They're out to capture all the highest posts. We must defeat them and have things our own way—for the people's good."

"I think you'll get in, all right, sir!"

"It's not so easy: the candidate for the other party is not sleeping. He says he stands for the workers—the liar! He tells them I am deceiving them, that I am an aristo. And he gives them money, so they believe him—that's the worst of it! They do not know they are selling their freedom, their birthright, everything decent in them! Oh!"

"He will not get in," Dele assured him. "We are voting for people, not parties. The British have given us a new constitution. It is for us to select the best *men* to work it. That is our first and last step towards self-government. You have done a lot for this area. Look at Grave Street. Two years ago, it was all swamp. Not a light anywhere. Now we have water, electricity . . ."

"Oh yes! but when people pass along Grave Street, they don't bother to think. Still, one does not have to wait for thanks. That's a politician's lot. Do the right and leave it at that; that's my motto. And it gets things done."

He rubbed his chin and beamed. He was pleased. His work was appreciated by the two young men. Sango thought guiltily of his assignment for the *West African Sensation*. But the politician would not come straight to the point.

"I remember when I was a teacher some years ago, things were quite different."

"Quite so, sir."

"No African Education Officers, Principals . . . where would you find them? But now things are different. Yes, things are gradually passing into African hands. Soon all the power will be in our hands. It's worth fighting for."

"You love politics, I can see that," Sango said.

"Politics is life. Look at it now. After these elections, life will be different. With every election things change. And so it will go on changing, all the time, and one day we'll get what we're fighting for: complete autonomy!"

"Things can't be the same," Dele said.

"And that's politics. We want our own Government. They will decide what money you may have, what food you may eat; what hours you may sleep; what films you may see: all this is life. Politics is life. I like it."

"Politics is not for young men like ourselves. For you, it's good. You worked for years under the British Government. Now you have retired. You have your pension. Your children are at the University. What more? You have nothing to risk. But we young men, we are only just starting our lives."

The Councillor sighed. "Too much guts. That is the trouble with young politicians. They see one cause, one belief, and they stake their whole life on it, regardless of consequences. An older man tempers belief with tact—that's why he gets through."

The liberation of his ideas had brought a new and more promising light to his eyes.

"Dele, you know my son."

"Yes, sir."

"Well, he returns to the University in October. That's in a few weeks time. He's occupying a room here. Why doesn't your friend share the room with him till he leaves, and then he can have the room to himself. And I don't want any rent from him. If he's in difficulty about meals, my wife is there to help."

Sango was overwhelmed by the kindness of the Councillor; but knowing his own irregular hours, he did not see how he could live as part of a family. He was silent enough to compose his thoughts.

"I don't know how to begin," he said and glanced at Dele.

"You're going to accept, of course! The Councillor has been very generous."

"Thank you," said the Councillor. "It is my plan to devote the rest of my life to sacrifice."

"I mean—" Sango said. "I—I wanted to say that I cannot accept your offer. I wish I could, but—"

"As you wish!" The Councillor waved his arm. "You're under no obligation."

"Thank you. I—I hope you win your seat."

Sango was embarrassed and confused by Dele's stare of surprise. Once outside he breathed deeply, filling his lungs with air and sowly puffing it out.

"You surprise me, Sango." Dele did not even wait to get out of ear-shot.

"It's simple. I like freedom. Not too much politics. Not too much moral guidance. You know the sort of life I lead. Jazz ... girls ... late hours. Odd assignments. Queer visitors at awkward times. I don't want to be too much under observation. It might change my character completely. At Twenty Molomo it's not like that."

"I can't understand it," Dele said. He tried to smile as he shook hands with Sango, but for once his acting ability failed him. He was sore as a child.

Since Bayo could not put through his plan at his own home, he decided to use Sango's room. He had called in the afternoon and Sango was out looking for a room; and now it was evening, and still Sango was out, which suited him.

"Come and open the door, please," he told Sam. "I want to sit down and wait for him . . . by the way, did a man with a black bag call here for me? Like a doctor."

"Man with a black bag? I don' see anybody, sah."

Very reluctantly, Sam opened the door. Bayo's hand trembled but he did not let Sam see it. Every time he thought of his get-rich-quick plan, his heart gave a leap of fear. Something might still go wrong. No, the nurse would not doublecross him. He was a reliable fellow.

"Sam, trust me. I shall steal nothing. I'll just play some music till my friend comes."

"All right, sah. When you want to go, let me know."

Bayo was impatient. He walked to the corridor, peered outside, came back. He could not sit still for one moment. He thumbed through a magazine, put it down, searched his pockets for cigarettes. There were none. He sat down again.

This could be a very dangerous business. The penicillin racket had made some people and broken others. He wished he had not posed as a doctor. He wished he had not told that old woman that penicillin would cure all her ills. But there was a matter of five guineas to be considered.

There was a knock and a man carrying a leather bag came into the room. He put his raincoat on the arm of a chair and sat facing the door. He was the "nurse" whom Bayo had engaged to administer the drug.

The man said impatiently: "Where's the woman? I thought you said eight-thirty. Well, it's time."

"She'll soon be here. Give me a cigarette, please."

"I don't trust this place. I don't know why, but I feel a bit scared." The nurse glanced nervously round. "Suppose she discovers I'm no nurse, but a quack?"

"Give me a cigarette."

"I don't smoke."

"You sound annoyed. Why, now?"

The nurse glanced about the room. At every footfall he rose and went to the door. "I thought it was our patient . . ."

"She'll be bringing the whole five guineas," Bay said. "She'll give me the money and we'll split it. You will have—"

"You will have one pound ten shillings. That's what we agreed, Bayo."

"I'm having two-twelve-six!" Bayo said, his eyes flaring. "But keep quiet. We don't want Sam to know what we're doing. If possible too,

I don't want him to know what we've done. Sango is very queer. He may disapprove."

They turned when they heard the knock. Aina's mother had entered the room. "Where is . . . the other man? The one who lives here?" She sounded disappointed.

"Do you want the man, or do you want your medicine?" Bayo asked. "Don't worry about the man who lives here. Me and my friend will attend to you. My friend is a famous nurse."

She looked about her suspiciously. "I was here—once. When Aina fell into trouble."

"You . . . must be Aina's mother? Lord save me!" Bayo did not like this new turn of events. So this woman knew that Sango lived here, knew perhaps that the racket was against the law. And with the painful plight of her daughter in mind, what could she not scheme?

"Five guineas, not so?" She fumbled in her cloth and produced a little envelope. "Here is your money."

Bayo and the nurse exchanged glances. It was the easiest thing ever. Ten cases like this, twenty cases, a hundred . . . and they would be rich. Bayo took the money from her, checked the notes expertly, almost contemptuously.

The woman rose. "Excuse me, I've just remembered something. I'll be back just now."

She was out of the room before they could stop her. Bayo and the nurse again exchanged an uneasy glance. Bayo went to the table, poured himself a glass of water. He raised it to his lips, then stopped. An idea had struck him. Suppose this woman did not return before Sango came back?

And then, by one of those odd things that happen once in a lifetime, Bayo in returning the glass to the table upset it. The water poured on the notes which the woman had given them in payment.

Immediately they became an intense violet. On the back of each note appeared the letters C.I.D.

"Nurse! We're finished. Betrayed! The woman has gone to call the police. Look, marked notes. Get your bag and let's run!"

Sango paid off his taxi at Twenty Molomo Street and got in quickly, hoping to rattle off the story of the *Apala* dance in good time to catch tomorrow's edition. He felt that he had stumbled on one of the mysteries of the city. This was his chance to catch McMaster's attention with his handling of the assignment. Two women go to a dance, and while dancing one of them collapses and dies. There is no explanation. She has been in a state of elation before her sudden death. The dance has taken her into a kind of trance and she is foaming at the lips. Why? What is the significance? The more he thought of the woman's face, her eyes glazed, staring about her unseeing, her tongue lolling out of her mouth, the more terrified he became. Everyone had sat forward, waiting in suspense. They knew she was possessed. Even the drumming had ceased, and yet she continued to dance—without the music. He could never forget it.

The pathologist had said something about the woman "at the time of her death . . . undue physical exertion . . . advanced state of myocardial degeneration . . ." or some such jargon, very convenient but still leaving the mystery uncleared.

He glanced at his watch. It was past nine. The story could not possibly get through now for tomorrow's paper. In the corridor he met Sam carrying a cooking-pot and Sam told him: "Your friend Bayo is here. Himself with some strangers. I think C.I.D."

He stopped, his heart leaping into his mouth. What could he have done? He was no politician, or youth leader. He knocked at his own door and went in. Apart from Bayo, Sango could not say where he had seen the other before. One of them was slender and badly tailored. He had the air of a man on the verge of panic and his fever tended to be contagious. His trousers were greasy and unlined. He showed dirty teeth when he smiled. He held his card and Sango saw he was from the police.

"We are searching your room."

Another man, robust, in dark sun-goggles even in the room, looked at his watch.

"We have found nothing in the room. Now I'm afraid we must search the clothes of the two gentlemen."

Sango's heart sank. He saw Bayo close his eyes. The robust policeman patted the bulges on his dress.

"You're sure you haven't got them in your shoes?"

Sango slumped into the nearest seat. He heard the other policeman say, "I've found something! On the floor!"

He was holding a note marked with the letters C.I.D. "Who owns this?"

Bayo opened his eyes.

"I've never seen that before!"

"I must ask you both to come to the station," the stout man said. "Nothing much, just formalities."

"Sorry about the inconvenience, Amusa . . ."

"You know my name!"

"Amusa Sango, crime reporter *West African Sensation*. The most eligible bachelor along Molomo Street. But take care women don't land you in trouble." He showed his dirty teeth.

They went out.

Sango could not get his grip on things. He knew he must write his report but try as he would he could not concentrate. Sam came into the room. "Lajide is very annoyed with you, sah. He say he never get C.I.D. men in this house since he built it. He and the men talk for long time before they take Bayo away in the 999 van."

"Not very good news, Sam; we don't want anything to annoy Lajide now."

"Jus' so, sah. That Bayo is a bad boy. You better be careful of him, sah. He will put somebody in big trouble."

"What d'you mean?"

"I will show you somethin', sah."

Same went out and in a moment returned with the cookingpot which Sango had seen him carrying a moment ago. "Master, look what they give me to take to barber and keep. I no meet barber in the shop . . ."

He opened the pot.

"What!" exclaimed Sango on seeing the hypodermic syringe and the phials of penicillin. "Go and throw that into the lagoon, quick! You want to put us all in prison?"

Carefully Sam wrapped the dangerous goods in paper, threw a cloth over his shoulder and stepped out into the street, whistling.

Sango did not find out the full details of this incident until, out of sheer habit, he dropped in at the All Language Club. It was past midnight and Sango felt entitled to the treat, since he had already dispatched his copy to Layeni, the night editor of the *Sensation*.

"Amusa Sango!" It was First Trumpet. He looked up from a music score as Sango entered the club. "Where have you been? Since eight we have been waiting for you and now it's over midnight? Or you forgot?"

"I'm sorry, First Trumpet! You carry on. Lead the band for a change. Let me have an instrument."

There was a clarinet which Sango took over; and, for the first time since he owned a band, he played sitting down. But his mind was not on his music. He was thinking generally of himself in the big city. What had he achieved? Where was he going? Was he drifting like the others, or had he a direction? Whatever that direction was, he did not feel at this moment that he was progressing along it. Certainly his mother would not be proud to see how he was making out. Crime reporter for the *West African Sensation*. Leader of a band in a night club. The old woman would think he was lost. As far as money was concerned, there was little of it being put aside for the rainy day; and then there were the girls, every one with her own problems and thrice as interesting as the last. Something must have happened to his noble resolutions.

The number was a hot one, and he rose and took a bouncing solo, registering the twisting, writhing bodies, the glittering jewellery, the shuffling feet and wiggling hips. He could smell the mixture of dust, perfume and sweat. The excitement rose to a rollicking climax topped with cheers. He looked up and saw his friend Bayo, just entering the Club and performing a late jig at the entrance.

During the interval, Bayo came and apologized for his irresponsible action. "Sango, I didn't want you to know at all. I needed money, you know . . ."

"You were joking with a hundred pounds' fine or two years' imprisonment, or both, so the books say."

"You know when they were searching me, I was shivering . . . I prayed and prayed. I was lucky they found nothing on me. You know what happened to the "nurse"? He was detained. No bail allowed."

"You'd better learn your lesson, Bayo. If I find you mixing with any more of the underworld, I shall never have anything more to do with you. You have angered Lajide, my landlord. He is very annoyed. Sam told me."

"Sango, I'm sorry. The mistake was mine. I did not know that woman was Aina's mother. She arranged with the police! What, the malice that woman has against you! You better be careful yourself. The trouble was not meant for me, but for you. I advise you to leave Twenty Molomo before they plan something else."

"Aina's mother? Of course! But didn't you know? You were playing with fire. The first time I saw her I thought she was a witch. Honestly."

"Where's the syringe?"

"Don't worry about that. It's safe."

At that moment the band began to stir to life once more. Sango took himself off and went back. First Trumpet was mustering forces for a *Highlife*. One, two! and away it went, soft, lilting . . .

Molomo Street was dead. Gone were the lingering lovers under the almond trees. The water-pump in the street dripped unnoticed. Sango's steps were loud, clear and lonely. He turned into Number Twenty, a tired man.

The corridor was completely impassable. Arm-chairs, stools, books and lino cluttered up the passage. At first Sango thought that a new tenant had just moved in. He got to his door and tried to open it. The key would not fit. It was only then that the truth dawned on him. He looked more closely at the furniture in the corridor. He recognized, with gradually increasing shock and anger, his own bookshelves, his own radio and gramophone.

Sam emerged from the gloom.

"Welcome, sah!"

"What's this, Sam?"

"I tol' you, Lajide is annoyed with you, sah. He remove all your thin' and put his wife in your room. I been to police office to report him, but he bribe everybody; they will do nothing."

Sam handed Sango a note which he read by the glow of a distant light. It said simply: I FINISH WITH YOU.

Considering how involved the whole procedure would be in taking Lajide to court, and the risk of having the penicillin racket dug up all over again, Amusa decided to let sleeping dogs lie.

The door of his own room opened and one of Lajide's wives poked her head out.

"Too much noise. You won' let me sleep!"

Sango bit his lip to keep back the torrent of angry words. "I don't blame you—but don't rejoice too soon. You will be the next one in the corridor—and you will never come back!"

chapter seven

As far as Sango was concerned, Beatrice could not have chosen a worse time to call at Twenty Molomo. This girl, whom he had wanted to impress with his importance and charm, dismissed her taxi in front of Lajide's house and stepped delicately into the courtyard. A wide-brimmed straw hat with trailing ribbons framed her face. Her eyes were hidden by the latest fad in glasses, silver-rimmed and so flattering that Sango stood confused and unable to fathom the eyes behind the dark shields. Her cool blue frock moulded a body that cried out to be wooed and she carried a black bag, while the gloves summarized her sophistication.

It was impossible that Beatrice had failed to notice the *omolanke* or hand-cart which stood outside while Sam loaded his master's possessions on to it. It was common knowledge in the city that your method of shifting lodgings depended on your means. A poor man employed head porters; a man of average means hailed the hand-carts and trailed behind them with the more precious things. But a man who had posed as a bandleader would naturally be expected to go one step better and engage a lorry.

Beatrice had stretched out her hand, and as Sango took it she smiled, and said "At last, I've found it. I was trying to follow your description from the All Language Club."

"I see! Welcome. It's not all that difficult—"

"For someone always locked up in Rokiya Hill it's not so easy." She seemed then to notice the cluttered-up passage. "Are these your things? You are not packing? No, of course, you would have used a car . . ."

"I've been thrown out, Beatrice."

He caught the breath of her perfume and it went to his head. "I'm not all that well off, Beatrice. And as you've chosen to come at such an awkward time, I can offer you no hospitality."

"All right! Let me go and see Lajide. Wish me luck!"

She smiled and walked up the stairs. He was watching her swinging hips. Suddenly he felt angry at the way he was getting on in the city. Something must be done about it soon, for he was certain now that the good things were eluding him. He was actually getting nowhere, come to think of it. He was still crime reporter, *West African Sensation*, and bandleader at the All Language Club. If that was status, then he must be sadly mistaken.

Beatrice had been offered a seat in Lajide's sitting-room. One look at the carpets, the expensive curtains, the large pictures and ebony carvings, had confirmed her first impression. This was a man who loved finery. He was not likely to be stingy in spending money on a woman he fancied. He was not economical either, or he would not leave the fluorescent lights on in the room. The window blinds had been tactfully drawn, lending a touch of enchanting glamour and romantic isolation to the room. She had to remind herself that it was afternoon, and hot. This was the reception-room of a man who might be called upon to make love at short notice by any of eight women. A glance in the mirror revealed that her spider-web of a dress had acquired a new and dazzling colour reflected by the lights. This was the sort of setting that made her most seductive.

Lajide came into the room as she was sitting down. He threw himself into a couch and stared at her with no attempt to hide his admiration. Even as he sat down, one of his wives, Alikatu, came into the room, carrying a large bowl of some aromatic fluid. She set it down and eyed Beatrice with all the venom of a possible rival and disappeared, no doubt to go and gossip with the others.

It has started, Beatrice thought. She has already come to assess me. I am a woman and I understand.

Lajide sipped the fluid. "Welcome, Madam. What can I do for you?"

"I'm looking for a room."

"Oh. What happen to the ol' one?"

"I'm not happy there . . ."

"Finish? You're not happy there, so you want to leave? Come on, tell me the truth! You have quarrelled with your husband, not so? *Omashe-O!*" He shook his head.

"Not that," Beatrice protested. "It is not healthy for me. I'm always sick there. I suspect somebody is trying to poison me, so I wan' to leave the place."

In his eyes she saw the brightening glow of desire. His face looked crafty; his lips twisted with a smile. "If I give you room, you will be my woman?" He rose, opened a nearby cupboard, produced a bottle and two small glasses. He walked to the centre of the room, poured and downed a drink; then poured her one. "I like you; I like you very much."

She took the drink, but his hand trembled so that it spilled on the floor. The fire in his eyes had settled into a steady glow, undisguisable. She could feel the almost boundless passion of the man: an insatiable lust that made him lord of eight women.

"You like me . . . what of your wives? I don't want any trouble." She sipped her drink and found it was whiskey, very welcome in her present mood.

"Never mind about them. You have your room. I won't stop you from anything, but you must be my woman. You will be free, and live outside. You hear me. I will keep you outside; you won't mix with the others—here. Don't bother about the rent . . ."

The terms were worth considering.

Lajide moved closer so she could smell his thick whisky breath. He must have been drinking the whole day. "When I say a room, I mean a good room. You see, is no good living in a hole; no, not girl like you. One Lebanese is coming to see me this night about my fine house at Clifford Street. I will give you a room from there. What say you?"

"Do you want a reply now?"

Lajide shrugged. "As you like. People are rushing for the house . . . I can reserve one room for you, but if you waste time—" He waved his arm, the arm of the giver and the taker.

"Reserve a room for me, Lajide. But I'll think of the other part."

"What you have to think about? Is not many women I will say, I want you to be my woman, and they begin think. Fancy that!"

"Perhaps my husband will like to see you about the room first." Beatrice smiled very sweetly.

Lajide's face drained of colour. "Your husband! That's all right! That's all right, I don't worry. Come, I take you home in my car." He reached for his bunch of keys.

Beatrice hesitated.

"Come now—"

"Just a minute, Mr Lajide. That young man downstairs, Mr Amusa Sango. What did he do to you?"

"Leave him alone. He's a very bad young man. I give him notice long time, then he want to put me in trouble. He bring C.I.D. men here. Better for him to go now in peace before big trouble meet him in my house."

"Can't you give him a room in your new house?"

Lajide's mouth opened in surprise. "*Me?*" and he laughed.

Down the stairs Beatrice went, with the man in the voluminous robes trailing close behind her. She noticed that the corridor was now clear and that Sango was gone. Lajide was talking incessantly, about his wealth, his influence in the city, and the stupidity of certain tenants.

At the door of Twenty Molomo a maroon car of American make, streamlined, with chromium streaks, glided to a stop nodding proudly. The door opened and a Lebanese in a white shirt and shorts slid out.

Lajide whispered to Beatrice: "Tha's the man who want to buy my new house." He raised his voice: "Hello, Muhammed Zamil . . . I just goin' out."

"Lajide, is the house ready?"

"Almost ready."

"Every day almost ready; every day almost ready—"

"I want to do fine job; have patience, you will like the place when I finish."

"Is all right for me now."

"*Oya!*" said Lajide suddenly. "Let's go now. We see the house, then you sign!"

Finishing touches were being put to the house at 163B Clifford Street West. The painters, electricians and carpenters had been working hard in the last few weeks. It was painted in a sun- and rain-resisting cream on the outside, the inner walls in a very pale green. The garage was spacious enough to take Zamil's car without its tail preventing the doors from closing. There were quarters for the "small boy," cook and steward.

Beatrice thought it was a much more useful house than the one she shared with Grunnings on Rokiya Hill. But where in all this scheme did she fit in? She decided not to accept a room here, if Lajide gave her one. She might just as well be Zamil's mistress.

Zamil got into his car, and held the door open for Beatrice to come in and sit beside him. And there she sat between two men, each trying to please her, while her mind dwelt on Amusa Sango and his plight.

They drove into a side street and Zamil who had been showing signs of impatience burst out: "What's matter, is this Clifford Street?"

"We go and see my solicitor. Have patience!"

Lajide drew his pouch, selected a cigarette and lit it. "You want the house, or you don't want the house? Ah-ah! I never see hot temper man like you. If you don't want the house any more, let me go back!"

"I'm sorry, Lajide. I thought—"

"Park your car and follow me. Beatrice, you wait for us."

She watched them go up a narrow lane. When they emerged a long time afterwards, smelling faintly of alcohol, the agreement to lease 163B had been signed, sealed and delivered.

Beatrice heard Lajide say: "The house will be your own for five years now."

He took out a cheque from his pocket-book and looked at it once more. He acted like a man slightly tipsy, waving it in Beatrice's face and saying with his drunken breath: "Five thousand pounds on this paper. Ha!"

Zamil said: "Lajide, we must celebrate. I want you to come with me for a bite—anywhere."

He drove to the department store by the lagoon. Gingerly Beatrice walked along the pavement between the two men. As usual the snack bar was crowded with people of the city out to relax and look at the lagoon. They were mostly girls of the Dupeh type, fashion plates of the most devastating type—to young men. With every swing of the doors, the restaurant filled more than it emptied.

They sat down and made their orders. Beatrice could see at once that Lajide felt ill-at-ease, and shortly after the steward had taken their orders he begged to be excused.

"I'll see you later, Beatrice. I got business at home."

Beatrice looked up and saw a man, notebook in hand, just coming in through the swing doors. It was Amusa Sango. He had not seen her. Her heart fluttered till she was giddy.

"Is a big day for me," came Zamil's voice beside her. She was not listening. "Name anything you like downstairs in the shop and is yours . . ."

The waiter arrived with a tray full of orders for three. Beatrice looked beyond the waiter and saw that Amusa had come in with a girl. Who was she? She could not see the face behind the make-up and sunshade.

"I must leave you now," and she got up, smiling, and walked across the restaurant conscious of admiring eyes. Sango looked up as she approached.

"Beatrice!"

She took the only vacant seat next to Sango, beaming happily. "What brings you here?"

"You want to hear my hard-luck story? Well, I couldn't find a place in the city. My work has to go on, so what did I do? I took my things to the railway station and deposited them in the Left Luggage Office, and here I am!"

"And your boy—what did you do with him?"

"Sam has gone back to his younger brother. His brother is a trader. Lives in a tiny room just off Twenty Molomo. I'm sorry I had to lose him, but—" He shrugged his shoulders.

"Amazing! Do you sleep at the station, too?"

"Not yet. I'm now a hanger-on till I can find a place. My First Trumpet has invited me to share his little room with him."

"Is not easy," Beatrice said, and told him how Lajide wanted her to be his woman.

"When you're a man," Sango said, "they want six months' or a year's rent in advance. When you're an attractive woman, single, or about to be single, they want you as a mistress. That's the city."

"What am I to do, Sango?"

"If I were not engaged, I would say, marry me. As it is, I can only advise you to stick to Grunnings. He's much nicer than either of those two men—Lajide or Zamil. He's responsible, at least." He stopped when he noted her obvious disappointment. He looked at her and felt a strong desire to protect her as a woman in danger.

"I don't know what to do with my life," she said. She glanced round nervously as if to see if anyone had overheard.

Sango said, "Let's go somewhere quiet and you can tell me about it. Do you mind if we pass by the offices of the *West African Sensation*? I have a report to hand in to the editor."

"I don't mind, Sango. But where's the girl with you?"

"Disappeared. Don't worry. She was just a pick-up." He folded his notebook, paid his bill. Together they walked through the thick cigarette fumes. He was flattered by her loyalty to him.

They passed by Zamil's table and he looked up in surprise. Once out by the lagoon, they found a park bench under a coconut palm looking out at the ships anchored in the lagoon. A woman with a child strapped to her back was buying fish from a canoeman. Near by a man was dragging his nets out of the lagoon and pouring hundreds of silvery little fish into a canoe.

Beatrice talked freely, with little interruption from Sango. He listened, and as her story unfolded he asked himself: what is the secret of getting ahead in the city? Beatrice had disclosed that she came to the city from the Eastern Greens, from the city of coal. She made no secret of what brought her to the city: "high life." Cars, servants, high-class foods, decent clothes, luxurious living. Since she could not earn the high life herself, she must obtain it by attachment to someone who could. But she was not so well, and having found Grunnings, who did not quite satisfy her, she had to stick to him.

"But I'm tired of him and want to leave. But should I agree to what Lajide suggests? I do not like him very much."

Sango thought it over. His mind was confused. Her total trust in him had diverted his original desire for her. He could think of her now only as a sister. He forgot that he ever wanted her.

What he was too blind to see was that Beatrice had fallen in love with him. He talked to her about sticking to Grunnings and she looked only into his eyes and held his hand with tenderness.

Then he realized that she was not listening and had started dozing in the soft sea breeze.

Day by day thousands of copies of the *West African Sensation* rolled off the huge presses, were quickly bundled into waiting green vans that immediately struck out north, east, west, covering the entire country from the central point of the city. In the last few months of his present tour, McMaster's policy of giving local writers free rein was beginning to pay off. The *West African Sensation* was becoming a part of life, something eagerly awaited for its stories of politics, crime, sport, and entertainment.

For Sango, life had settled down to a routine and he seemed to be looking for some excitement to brighten up his page. Sometimes he had to remind himself that however exciting crime was, it brought tragedy to someone. But it was his function to report it, and to him it had become something clinical, with neither blood nor sentiment attached.

Unexpectedly, his chance came one afternoon with a strange phone call; and it very nearly altered his whole life. The caller had said that a body had been found floating on the lagoon. McMaster had instantly detailed Sango to cover the assignment.

Sango found on his arrival at the beach that a huge crowd had gathered in the manner of the people of the city. The police vans blared at them through loudspeakers, urging them to keep clear and to touch nothing. The shops and offices had emptied and there were clerks with pencils stuck to their ears, fashionable girls with baskets of shopping slung over their arms, ice-cream hawkers pedalling bicycles, motorists tooting their horns. The coconut palms waved their lazy fronds over the body draped in white and lying on the sands.

Sango went over and took a bold look at the face. It was the body of a man in the prime of life, and, as it turned out later, he had taken his own life. His name, Sango discovered, was Buraimoh Ajikatu. He had been missing from home for about three days. He was a clerk in a big department store and he was married, with four children.

They said he had been finding it increasingly difficult to support his family. To him the city had been an enemy that raised the prices of its commodities without increasing his pay; or even when the pay was increased, the increased prices immediately made things worse than before.

Buraimoh's plight was not alleviated by a nagging wife. He complained aloud and a friend at the office who worked no harder but always enjoyed the good things of life, said: "Have you not heard of the *Ufemfe* society?"

He had not heard and the friend told him about Lugard Square at midnight. There was to be a meeting. He went, and was enrolled. They promised him all he wanted. And strangely enough, life became bearable. He could not understand why his salary was increased, or why he was promoted to stores assistant, but it was not in his place to question. There was even a promise of becoming branch manager within one month. Why had it not happened all the time he was not an *Ufemfe* member? That too he could not answer. But he had been initiated and he now knew the secret sign of *Ufemfe*; this revealed to him that he had been the only non-member in the department store.

One night the blow fell. This was the unexplained portion of the pact. They asked him in a matter-of-fact manner to give them his first-born son. He protested, asked for an alternative sacrifice, and when they would not listen threatened to leave the society. But they told him that he could not leave. There was a way in, but none out—except through death. He was terrified, but adamant.

He had told no one of his plight, and that was when he vanished from home. Now that the good things of life were his, he would not go back and tell his wife. All this Sango learnt, and much more besides. For him it had great significance. By uncovering this veil, he had discovered where all the depressed people of the city went for sustenance. They literally sold their souls to the devil.

Even so, when things became much too unbearable for him, Sango often thought it would not be the worst thing in life to join the *Ufemfe*. And he would remember that swollen body with its protruding tongue and bulging eyes, a body that had been rescued from the devil's hands and given a decent Christian burial. And yet the tragedy remained.

PEOPLE OF THE CITY / 143

chapter eight

Sango had heard of the coal crisis which broke out in the Eastern Greens, of the twenty-one miners who had been shot down by policemen under orders from "the imperialists." To him it had a faint echo of something happening in a distant land.

He was somewhat taken aback when McMaster called him into the office and told him that a passage had been booked for him to travel to the Eastern Greens and bring back reports.

Sango was not happy to leave the city where he was still unsettled, sharing a room with First Trumpet, having his meals outside. But worse still he was afraid he might see his mother and find her worse than ever. He had just sent her twelve pounds—all the money he had kept to deposit as advance payment for a room.

The plane was taking him towards the Eastern Greens, nearer the source of his poverty, of his ambition to seek his fortune as a journalist and musician west of the Great River. Until he landed and visited the mines and saw the scene of desolation he could think of nothing else but his mother in hospital, and the girl Elina in the convent. He would try, if possible, to visit the two of them. It did not seem possible to visit the two places in the little time that would be available.

He saw the Great River below, broad and brownish with here and there a canoeman—a mere dot many thousands of feet below. Instantly his past life seemed to flash before his eyes. He saw his own poverty and his youthful ambition and found that he must work still harder to give happiness to his dependants.

As the plane touched down Sango saw the expectant group standing at the air terminal. One of them would be Mr Nekam, President of the Workers' Union. Sango had not met him but had seen pictures of him in the *Sensation*. Indeed Nekam was there, bearded and in a bush shirt.

"You'll be staying with me," he said to Sango, shaking him warmly by the hand. "So, better you cancel your hotel booking."

Sango, who wanted to see both sides of the dispute, told Nekam: "You'll give me a free hand, I hope, not try to influence my reports in any way."

They drove through unmade roads into the workers' quarters and Sango noted immediately the atmosphere one experiences in a town under the iron boot. Policemen were everywhere. Not the friendly unarmed men he had been used to in the city, but aggressive boot-stamping men who carried short guns, rifles or tear-gas equipment. There were African police and white officers and they all had that stern killer look on their faces. The shadow of death had darkened the people's faces as they went about their daily business, and though Sango listened hard, he could hear no laughter.

He decided to go—not to the president's house—but to the famous valley of death at the foot of the hills where the coal was mined. Here he saw the thorn scrub where many wounded miners had crawled in agony to die of bullet wounds. At the Dispensary many of the miners were being treated for head injuries and fractures in thigh and arm.

Sango spoke to them and their story was full of lament. They told how an outstanding allowance, amounting to thousands of pounds, had been denied them. How frequently labour disputes arose, and how the mine boss—an overbearing white man—would not listen. The background to the shooting had been simply—strained feelings.

Back in the home of the workers' president, Sango found that Nekam occupied a little compound with two rooms and one kitchen, that his wife raised chickens and rented a stall in the market where she sold cigarettes, tinned foods and cloth. The children had been sent away into the village because of the emergency.

Sango got down immediately to work. Nekam showed him copies of telegrams from the West African Students' Union in London, the President of the Gold Coast, the League of Coloured Peoples in New York . . . and one from a President in South America, urging Nekam to bring the matter up at the United Nations. Some of the telegrams were unrealistic but heartening.

At a Press conference the following day, Sango discovered that this shooting had become a cementing factor for the nation. The whole country, north, east, and west of the Great River, had united and with one loud voice condemned the action of the British Government in being so trigger-happy and hasty. Rival political parties had united in the emergency and were acting for the entire nation. Sango was thrilled.

In his report he was loud in praise of the new movement and caustic in his comment on the attitude of the British. His youthful fire knew no restraint and he wrote about the bleeding and the dying, the widowed and the homeless; the necessity to compensate these men who had sacrificed so much that the country's trains might run, its power-houses function, and its industries flourish. No other correspondent had been so brave and forthright, and the *Sensation* was eagerly bought and read for "the real truth about the coal crisis in the Eastern Greens."

For Sango the great question was: why do politicians have to wait for a period of crisis before they can sink their selfish differences and unite? Why can it not always be like this, what can we do to hold this new feeling? Even as he tortured himself with these questions he knew that as soon as the crisis was over the leaders would all go their different and opposite ways, quarrelling like so many market women.

At night he was at the airport to see the arrival of dark troop-planes from Great Britain. His report on the arrival of these reinforcements drew forth an immediate denial from the Government. The troops had nothing to do with the coal crisis, they said. And now the coal city was drained of women and children, black and white. Only the able-bodied men remained to face the terror.

Thanks to the unity of the politicians a way out was found. In the leaders Nekam placed all his confidence. In him the workers, in their turn, believed. The result was that the politicians said to Nekam:

"We must do things in a constitutional manner. It is hard, but that is the best sign of maturity. We don't want any more demonstrations or violence. Go and get your miners back to work and leave all negotiations with the British to us. Do we represent you or do we not? That is the first question."

"You do!" grunted Nekam.

Nekam, who had faith in the politicians, told the workers, who surely still had faith in him. He spent all night negotiating with the gang leaders who accused him of back-pedaling. By early morning he was fagged out. He invited Sango to the railway station where the workers took their train. If they did return to work, his task had been performed. If they did not, then something else must be tried; he could not now tell what.

They stood looking down at the valley below. The mist of morning cleared from the hills. In the east the sky reddened and the redness oozed into the valley. Sango peered, then held Nekam excitedly. Nekam followed Sango's eyes, but said nothing. His lips were pursed. Down there, there was movement—in groups. Neither Sango nor Nekam dare say the groups were composed of miners coming to work. It was best to wait. Soon the train would come.

The first man arrived with pick and Davy lamp, followed by others and soon the station was humming with mumbling men. They had come. He had succeeded. With hearts too full for words, Sango and Nekam boarded the train which took them down to the mines.

Sango followed them inside, into the abyss of the earth where heat reigned supreme, and reverberations threatened the teak props. There was ever present a sense of death, danger, disaster. Yet the men who risked all worked in sweat and courage.

Sango heard a rumbling ahead of him and went forward to investigate. The gang leader pulled him back. "Look out! Coal coming up!"

Sango stepped aside, just in time. A chain of automatic wagons loaded with coal clattered by. The striking miners had produced the first fruits of their toil and of Nekam's negotiations.

That same afternoon, a telegram was delivered to Sango. He tore it open with blackened hands. Nekam was peering over his shoulder.

COME BACK BY LORRY STOP YOU CAN GET FAST SERVICE FROM
JIKAN TRANSPORT STOP REGARDS MCMASTER

"You going back?" Nekam said.
"The job is done, isn't it?"

Daybreak found Sango and Nekam at the lorry station. Knowing how
"fast" the lorry service could be from the Eastern Greens, Sango made
sure that the driver of Jikan Transport would stop in the village near
the convent where Elina was. It would be a good opportunity to see her.

While the lorry was being loaded up with passengers, dried fish, yams
and oil, Nekam talked of his ambitions to see the country progress as a
whole till it took its place in the front rank of self-governing countries
within the British Commonwealth. There was still a lot to be done, but
this crisis was only the beginning of national unity.

"Keep up the struggle, Sango. We workers at this end will never
give up."

Sango had listened to this kind of serious talk once before: that bright
day when he had been at an identical motor station, and his father, an
old man, now no more, had come to see him off. The hairy Nekam was
less gentle, more full of fire.

The lorry horned. "That's the signal to go aboard, Nekam. Thank you
for your hospitality. You've made me see the whole business from the
inside as a real reporter should. I'd like you to be a little patient. I'm
sure the National Committee for Justice which the politicians have
formed will do something. The bereaved will get full social compensation. And when the Commission of Inquiry arrives from Britain, I hope
I shall be here again to listen to the evidence."

Nekam stood back, while Sango walked towards the lorry and took
a seat in the second class—a little partition shielded from the driver.
He sat with his knees bunched up, counting the miles between him and
the village where Elina was.

The lorry backed away and there stood Nekam under a tree, his arm
raised. Sango waved back. It had taken a national disaster of the mag-
nitude of shooting down twenty-one unarmed men to bring together
leaders from north, east and west, to make the country realize as never
before where its real destiny lay. What catastrophe, Sango wondered,
would crystallize for him the direction of his own life? Soon—perhaps in
another twelve months—he might be called upon to marry Elina; certainly his mother would insist on this to protect him from the gold-
digging women of the city. But would he be ready?

A fat woman sitting on his right sighed. He turned and looked at her face, radiant and attractive. Before the lorry had moved three miles, she was fast asleep, using Sango's back as a pillow.

When the lorry at last pulled up at the little village, Sango found that his second-class seat had been worth having after all. The other passengers in the third class were covered from head to foot in red dust.

The convent was beautifully situated: about a mile or two from the main motor-road, it overlooked an arm of the river. Sango walked across the village and beyond the market-place till he was well out in the woods. Peace and quiet such as he could never dream of, were here in the scented air, and the music of unseen birds. It was incredible, this idealized setting which had been chosen for a convent. Less than a hundred miles from the scene of death, desolation and the shattering of amities, yet this place stubbornly refused to see the evil in the world, talked only of the good and the pure. The sadness came when the girls graduated, as Elina would. Then rude shocks were theirs in the words, thoughts and deeds of the outside world.

Sango's steps were already becoming reluctant. He knew before the gate swung back and admitted him that some purification treatment must be meted out to him before he could dream of being worthy of Elina.

One of the girls led him round the beautifully kept lawns to the waiting-room, where she showed him a school bench and told him to wait. It was siesta time, she explained, and Elina must not be disturbed. Sango, confronted with pictures of the Madonna and Child, the Sacred Heart of Jesus radiating mercy to sinners like himself, saw no hope of his own salvation. He knelt down suddenly and made the sign of the cross.

At that moment he vowed to spend the rest of his life doing good, and cared nothing for the fact that the lorry driver up at the village had told him as he poured palm-wine into his drinking horn: "Don' keep long."

It took some time before a delicate rustle startled Sango out of his reverie. The Mother Superior, for she it must be, in her whites and black hood, clear-skinned and graceful in her old age, came into the little waiting room.

"You sent a letter some time ago from the coal city? It is an awkward time to come, for the girls are at rest."

Sango could see numerous heads peering into the room from dormitory windows. Such a commotion did a male visitor cause in a girls' establishment.

He said, "Yes, Mother Superior."

"But I'll treat this as a special case, since you live so far away." Once again she questioned him about his name, religion, and occupation. She talked at length about Elina and, sweeping up her robe to avoid dust, she walked gently down the steps. Sango looked into the dormitory windows: the heads had vanished.

Elina was a tall girl, quick-smiling, but somewhat gawky in appearance. Looking at her as she hung timidly on the arm of the head-girl who led her in, Sango felt his heart contract with pain and disillusionment. Pure she must be, innocent, a virgin no doubt; but one whom Sango could never see himself desiring. He smiled back at her, hoping she could not by some mysterious means fathom his thoughts. He cursed himself for his city background which had taught him to appreciate the voluptuous, the sensual, the sophisticated in woman. Elina was none of these. What did he want for a wife, anyway? A whore? Perhaps not; but he knew what he did not want. This must be the most awkward moment of his life. He was tongue-tied, and the presence of a chaperone choked back any warmth he might have shown.

On the other hand this was a beautiful moment, full of significance for them both. He was the man from the city who would one day be her husband. She was the pure girl, brought up according to the laws of God and the Church, unadulterated and therefore totally ignorant of the realities of life, looking forward to a life divine with him. Could anything be more impossible, he asked himself?

How the interview ended he never could tell, but he found himself walking back across the village to the impatient lorry, now on the point of departing without him. Now something had gone out of his life's purpose. As an ideal, unseen and alive only in his imagination, Elina had been an incentive. But now he felt that urge gone. He was alone with no idealized plan. And there was his weakness for the city woman with no restraining factor, nothing to check his lasciviousness. Whatever happened he was determined that his mother must not know of his disappointment.

If only this lorry journey were ten times as long, he would have time to work it all out before returning to the city.

PART TWO
When all doors are closed

chapter nine

This was no homecoming, because even though the taxi stopped in the lane where he shared a little room with First Trumpet, he had no feeling of ownership, let alone of freedom and privacy.

First Trumpet was dressed to go out, and in the band's uniform too. "Ha, Sango, welcome!" He was polishing his trumpet. "How you left us like that?"

And before Sango could answer: "We read all your dispatches in the *Sensation*. But were you not afraid? That was hot news! How was the rioting out there?"

Sango put down his box in a corner and flopped into a chair. "That's the first time I've relaxed in two weeks! Where are you going, all dressed up like this?"

"You've forgotten about the elections! Our band is playing for one of the parties. I don't care about their politics, but they pay well. Don't you see how I've been running the band in your absence?"

"Very good indeed." He yawned. "Well done! So I'm back with parties again. I thought we'd finished with parties as from last week. What's the use of all this nonsense when we are being led by the National Committee for Justice? I hope this election does not create a split. I'd hate to see the politicians split up once again."

First Trumpet had his instrument under his arm and one foot on the doorstep. "No . . . have no fear. They'll remain together, they won't split. You know how they act at election time. They make foolish promises, they abuse themselves. It's politics. Well! I must be off to Lugard Square; the band will be waiting."

"Whom did you say you were playing for?"

"The S.G.N. Party." He was already on the street.

Sango knew the S.G.N. (Self-Government-Now) Party as the one which claimed to represent the interests of the working man. Most of its members were people like Mr Nekam of the Eastern Greens. They were fanatics in their cause, and strongly opposed to the R.P.—the Realization Party—which helped "realize their dreams."

Sango wished Sam were here to help him unpack his suitcase. First Trumpet had gone without even asking him whether he had had a meal recently. It was not strictly his business, but it would have been comforting to hear. Sango set about having a bath and a change of clothing. When he returned to his room, he found Bayo sitting in an armchair, a warm smile on his face.

"Sango! Ah-ah! You just flew away like that! This your job is terrible. But what have you been eating in that place? Your skin looks so fresh!"

Sango's heart warmed. Now he knew he was really back. "I have plenty of news for you, Sango. Just wait. A lot has happened. Do you know, I saw your gal—the one who went to jail."

"Aina?" Sango was thrilled to hear her name, the very mention of it. In one reckless moment, he forgot the pain of Elina. When he saw that Bayo had observed his eagerness, he feigned anger. But Bayo smiled.

"I saw her on Beecroft Bridge, selling cigarettes."

"Oh?"

"But Sango, you don't sound interested. What's wrong? You're not like your old self. Or is the suffering you saw there still with you? Forget it, man!"

"I'm my old self, Bayo. It's nothing."

He was putting on his cleanest shirt and selecting his best tie. Why, he asked himself? Why? Must he impress an ex-jailbird like Aina? "You have no feeling," she had once told him.

"I don't blame you, anyway," said Bayo. "Those policemen are wicked. Shooting down their own brothers like that! Just because they wanted to be paid extra money. They'll not die well!"

He rambled on in his usual manner and soon the hardluck story came up. "I too, have changed. D'you know . . . Don't you see how thin I have become?"

Sango looked at him. If there was anything thin about Bayo that evening it was the colour of his tie. His hair was permed as usual and the nylon ankle-socks that peeped out under the narrow trousers were ablaze with colour. The basket shoes had three tones.

"Sango, I've suffered too much in this world, and now I have made a decision. I made it when you were away, because I had no other friend in the world. Look, I said to myself. Bayo, everybody is becoming something. Our country is fighting for self-government. Our boys and girls are going to Britain and America, they are learning new things to make our country greater. I must become a serious man and move with the times."

Sango looked at the face of his faithful friend. "Do you really mean that, Bayo?"

Bayo sat forward with a show of indignation. "Only the other day a lady bought me a new suit and gave me ten pounds on top. She is about forty-five, very wealthy, but no child. She has married, thrice, but no children. She wanted me to fulfil her desire, but I refused."

"True, you mean that?"

It was certainly surprising for Bayo to act in this manner. Something must have happened. Sango was quite sure now. It could be the encounter with the police; but something must have happened. Bayo was restless, unable to sit still. He got up, went to the door, came back.

"I don't know why things always happen like this. I've gone out with a lot of girls; they've spent pots of money on me. Yet I never spend one mite on them; it doesn't pay to do so. All those girls were nothing to me—"

"What are you talking about, Bayo?"

"Do you know a girl called Suad Zamil? She's a Lebanese, sister of a cloth merchant."

"Never heard of her. What's she to you?"

"I want to marry her; we've fixed everything for next month."

"Does she love you?"

"You don't appear surprised, Sango. That's why I like you. You do not blame me when I make a mistake. Have I made a mistake? Tell me, Sango. Everyone is blaming me. They say the marriage is impossible between me, an African, and this Suad, a Lebanese. Do you know, Sango, what frightens me is that the girl cannot sit down or think or even eat or sell her brother's cloth in the shop, she's thinking of Bayo— oh my love! She is always at the window. I pass there one hundred times in one day and it is still not enough for her. She is not afraid of African food. She says she is prepared to eat even sand with me and if necessary live in our slum. Anywhere, so long I'm there. Do you think she is mad?"

"D'you love her?"

"Why d'you think I've been racking my brain in the last few weeks? Why d'you think I've been trying to make money on my own? Only you were not in town to advise me, that's what saddened me."

Sango laced his shoes. This was one of those blinding love affairs into which Bayo was always falling, only to forget them entirely in a matter of days. He listened without attaching any importance to the words, and this attitude only made Bayo strive to impress him with his seriousness.

"She's the most beautiful girl in the whole world, and oh, so gentle! About nineteen, I should say, with very thick hair. You'll like to run your fingers through her hair, Sango. She does not speak any English, so we speak Yoruba. Yes, she's a native. She was born here . . ."

Bayo relapsed into a moody silence. Sango, who had finished dressing, said, "Aina! Where can I find her?"

"Beecroft Bridge. As soon as you cross the bridge, look among the cigarette sellers. You'll see her."

Beecroft Bridge was at least half a mile long. No one would sell cigarettes on the bridge, so Sango looked in the stalls outside the taxi park. It was already getting late and the shops were closing. Sango bade good-bye to

Bayo on the bus and got down near the bridge. He began to search for Aina among the handful of girls selling cigarettes, but in this rush-hour din he could identify none of them. He had become a target for the final appeals of the late hawkers.

"Penny bread! . . . Sugar bread! . . . " they cried from all sides of him. He was irritated but trapped. *"Banjo"* (auction) *"akowe"* (envelopes) *"Banjo, akowe! . . . "*

The cars and lorries and buses were trying to press forward in the slow traffic-stream by tooting horns. "Pip-pip! Paw-paw!"

Sango wanted to escape. He glanced desperately about him. Slippered feet rushed among the traffic, yet none belonged to the girl he sought. And the drone of the heavy diesel engines threatened to drown his voice.

Suddenly, everything seemed to stop, as if by an order. At that moment Sango caught just one glimpse: a girl straining upwards, trying to sell cigarettes to passengers through a bus window. He crossed the street, breaking through the tormenting chains that bound him prisoner.

"Aina!"

Her face was flushed with excitement, and she turned and looked into his eye. The change she was offering to the passenger on the bus slipped and rolled between the wheels. The cloth tied round her hips broke loose. Sango in one leap stood beside her.

She was panting with wonder. "What do you want? Twenty years is not for ever. Did you think I would die in jail?"

"Let us go to the Hollywood, Aina. I'll call a taxi and we'll go and eat. Where's your stall? Have you anyone to look after it for you?"

It was a way of life she liked. The glamorous surroundings, the taxis, the quick drinks. This was one reason why she had come to the city from her home sixty miles away: to ride in taxis, eat in fashionable hotels, to wear the *aso-ebi*, that dress that was so often and so ruinously prescribed like a uniform for mournings, wakings, bazaars, to have men who wore white collars to their jobs as lovers, men who could spend.

"I can't. I—"

"You must, Aina! After all, this meeting calls for some celebration. We may become enemies after that, but just let me give you this welcome. After all, I've been away and returned only this afternoon. How was I to know that you had come out of—"

A taxi drew alongside. He said: "The Hollywood!"

They were in and he was sitting beside her. Suddenly all the restraint he had imposed on himself broke loose and he held her in his arms and hugged her. She pushed against him like a naughty child, but he saw the tears in her eyes and he was sad. Yet the next moment she was laughing, teasing him derisively till all the pent-up desire he had for her broke over him and he knew he was still putty in her hands, this street walker with the dark, smooth face and white smile. Could it be for her sake that Elina had ceased to appeal to him? What was the magic of this unbreakable spell?

Outside the hotel he paid his fare and took her upstairs to the restaurant. He chose a seat near two large mirrors where Aina could have ample scope to admire her reflection. He tried to find out what the prison had taught her. She was bitter against him, that he could see. But she was also bitter against everybody, against the very city that had condemned her. She had become hardened. Where previously Aina might have stalled or hesitated, or used a tactful word, she now spoke bluntly. Amusa was shocked by her cynicism.

"It's money I want now," she said.

He nodded understandingly.

"I'm coming to visit you, Amusa, so get some money ready."

His heart sank. "Er . . . Lajide sacked me . . . er—"

"Said he doesn't want thieves and jailbirds, like me—eh? Don't deny, I know!"

He swallowed. She had got him wrong, but why reveal to her his present address?

"Well, I'm a thief! I've been to jail, and I'll still come to Twenty Molomo Street, and I shall visit you! Nobody can stop me, not even Lajide!"

Sango looked round nervously. "People are listening, Aina—"

"I don't care!" The waiter was standing behind her. Sango ordered chicken stew with rice.

There could be no guarantee that it did her any good, because throughout the meal she kept stabbing at him with her bitter explosions. It is said that a pleasant and cheerful disposition aids digestion. Aina apparently had not heard of this.

"I tried to bail you," Sango said. "Really, I did, Aina."

"Marry me, now, Sango. Don't you know I love you very much? Sango, I'll die for you."

He heard that warning again. The warning voice of his mother, about the women of the city. Letters from her were usually written by a half-literate scribe, but that warning was never in doubt.

"Aina, but—"

"You are very wicked, Amusa." She was smiling, and that made matters worse, because her smile always melted his heart. "If someone had told me that you would do this to me, after that night on Molomo Street and the way you said you loved me—"

"We're still friends, Aina."

She was still smiling. He tried to make it easy for her. But how could he make her see that their paths diverged from the very beginning?

"I want to ask you a favour," she said, as the waiter cleared the table.

Sango lit her cigarette and after she had inhaled deeply, she said: "I want new clothes: the native Accra dress . . . really special. The clothes I had before I went to jail, they're no use to me now. From now on I want to be wearing glamour specs. Nor for my eyes—my eyes are okay— but for fancy. And a gold watch. I have suffered for three months *hard labour*. Now I must enjoy all I dreamed of at night in my cell."

"But Aina, you know how broke I am, always!" He took out his wallet and found some pound notes which he offered her.

She took them from him without one word of thanks. Nor did she smile. It was then he knew that nothing could alter the bitterness she felt towards him.

Aina regretted not having gone with Sango. She watched his taxi swing into the traffic till it was hidden away by a mammy-wagon. Soon he would be at Lugard Square to see the soap-box orators. Aina looked at her clothes and decided that election time was fashion time, and one way to make certain she would be noticed was to get herself something smart. With only five pounds in the folds of her dress, she had a problem.

On High Street she noticed the sign SALE in large letters on every window of Zamil's shop. Zamil himself was standing knee-deep among the rayons and organdies, the printed cottons and velvets—just the very materials Aina would have loved. He was overwhelmed by customers and so was his sister at the other end of the counter. Dark-haired and pretty in a dark way, she had a large pair of scissors beside her on the counter.

"Suad! Mind the money!" shouted Zamil and fired away the rest of the sentence in rapid Arabic. Without looking up, Suad continued to zip out the cloth by the yard. There was no one else in this shop but Zamil, his sister, and the customers. It was a family business in which little out-side help was employed. Aina glanced round and saw bargains by the dozen. One caught her fancy—a rich plum velvet. She imagined herself wearing a dress of this material, cut by a dressmaker along Jide Street, frilled with lace at the bust-line, around the sleeves . . . the sleeves must be very short, to show off the roundness of her arms. Aina was over-come. It dawned on her that no one was watching.

"Steal it, Aina!" came that irresistible urge. "They're all looking away!"

She propped herself against the wall. If she took it, she could conceal it in the folds of her dress, sneak out quickly. The customers would still be yelling as they were doing now, Zamil and his sister would still be cutting cloth and piling the pound notes on the counter. Ten yards of material—no more; light enough. . . . Quickly now, before someone comes to buy it! No, they would be too frightened of the price.

Aina moved forward. She stopped. A silence reigned in the shop. She looked up and saw that a man in blue robes with a light blue gilt-edged cap had arrived. Lajide.

"Any more velvet cloth? I want twenty, thirty, forty yards; no fifty yards. Let me see . . . eight wives each one six yards, tha's forty-eight . . . give me fifty yards."

Everyone in the shop had stopped bargain-hunting. There was a gap of silence, which Zamil immediately tried to fill. "My sister Suad—she will open a new bale for you. Suad!" And he rattled off in rapid Arabic. Suad left her own customers and came across, smoothing back her rich black hair.

Zamil took a ready reckoner and thumbed through it shortsightedly. "Twenty-three . . . pounds . . . two an' six, that's the cost of fifty yards."

"Twenty poun'," said Lajide with confidence, but Zamil would not give in. The haggling began. The crowd piled nearer the two men.

Lajide sat down, crossed his legs, lit a cigarette. He said: "Zamil, how you enjoy the new house? Perhaps some of your brothers, they want fine place like that, eh? I got a new house for sale!"

Zamil's manner changed. "You have a house for sale? I been looking for a house for one of my brothers!"

The daily papers had been featuring long articles about what they called the "Syrian Invasion," in which they claimed that more and more Syrians and Lebanese were coming into the city and putting the small African trader out of business. They were also depriving him of living accommodation. One of them would take a whole compound and pay the rent demanded five years in advance, while ten Africans would squeeze into one room, musty, squalid and slummy.

"This morning, I got wire from home . . . One of my brothers is also coming. . . . Myself, my sister, and servants in Clifford Street, we're so crowded."

Lajide laughed. He was obviously one of those unscrupulous men who meant to cash in on the situation. He threw back his head and rocked in a manner that brought a frown to Aina's pretty face.

"The house is not for sale. No! For lease, yes. And is ten thousand. No, we talk about that sometime."

"Tha's all right for me."

"There you are! What did I say? You do me good, I do you good." He regarded Zamil questioningly.

"Pay twenty pounds," Zamil said, slapping the financier familiarly on the shoulder. "You are my friend."

Suad was prompt with scissors and brown paper, and in a few minutes, the full fifty yards were under her brother's arm and he was taking the cloth himself to the jeep and Lajide was having a few final words with him.

Aina did not breathe till she felt the air was freer. She dared not show her face from behind the pillar. She heard the jeep drive away and was almost grateful for what had *not* happened. Suad was shouting about closing time, and already Zamil was half-shutting the doors.

Aina, as she left the shop, was challenged by Zamil who quietly insisted that his sister Suad would search her. It was an embarrassing moment for her when she was led into a private room and stripped to her undergarments. In the folds of her dress Suad found the five pounds Sango had given her.

"Mus' be some mistake," Zamil apologized later, when Aina rejoined him in the shop. The shop was now quite empty. All doors were closed, except one left open, no doubt for her departure. Zamil was acting queerly, Aina thought.

"But Lajide told me . . . he said . . . are you not the girl who go to jail for shop-lifting."

"So that's what you were talking when you went to the car with him, eh?" Aina straightened her cloth. "Now listen. Lajide is telling lies! You can go and tell him I said so. I work for a Lebanese two years. Baccarat! I never steal one penny in my life. When people don' like you, they can say anything!" Aina gazed steadily into his eyes.

"Most sorry," Zamil said. "If I can do anything to help—"

"No! Not you—or Lajide!"

She pushed back the door and was out in the streets. For her it was a proud moment. She wished she could always hold her head as high. She wished she could overcome once and for all that itch to lift things. Then, and only then, would Sango, the man she dearly loved, take her seriously.

Lugard Square was packed to overflowing, and long before Sango had actually arrived at the square he heard the music of First Trumpet floating about the hubbub. He listened for a moment to the hoarse and false promises for better working conditions, improved medical services, more and better houses . . . The speaker was a man from the S.G.N. Party. Many of the audience milled around in groups of their own, some selling cigarettes, many with an eye for a sucker on whom to pull a confidence trick or two. At a bookstall at the entrance to the square Sango bought a copy of the party's booklet for sixpence.

There was no doubt that the S.G.N. Party would win the largest number of seats in the Town Council during the coming election. How the Realization Party was faring Sango found out the same evening. In a narrow lane beside the Methodist church, a man stood on a stool, his features dramatically lit by the dazzling glare of a gas lamp. He was saying much the same thing as the speaker of Lugard Square, namely, more houses, more food, more water and more light for the people.

"He's deceiving us," said a man on the fringe of his audience. There could not be more than thirty people listening to him.

Sango looked more closely and something in the speaker's manner arrested his attention. It was the kind politician who offered him a room he would not take. Now, Sango thought, was the time to help him.

After his speech, Sango told him how he had enjoyed his argument, and how he was taken by the R.P.'s ideas. "You want more listeners. The way to get them is to have some music, some attraction. Let something be going on while you talk."

"I've tried; I can't get a good band."

"I'll play for you."

The politician took off his glasses and looked closely at Sango. "Young man . . . Oh, it's you! I was wondering where I'd met you! Dele's friend!"

Throughout that week Sango and First Trumpet with the rest of the band toured the streets of the city. Large banners fluttered from their lorry with the words: THE REALIZATION PARTY WILL REALIZE YOUR DREAMS. They stopped at street junctions and one of the representatives would speak to dancing listeners. Very often they wanted to know in advance where the next speech would be.

First Trumpet did not entirely agree with Sango. He thought Sango was a fool not to play for money. But Sango told him: "We have our weekly engagement with the All Language Club. That will pay for our needs."

But that Saturday, arriving as usual at eight, Sango heard music coming from the bandstand. He asked for the manager of the Club and was shown into a tiny room by the Club's garden.

The manager seemed to be going through his books. He looked up when Sango knocked and said, "Ah, Mr. Sango. Sit down!"

Sango felt it coming.

"Now, Mr. Sango; I've engaged the Tropic Rhythms Band to play for me, until you stop this nonsense."

"I don't understand."

"For the last five days, you've been playing election music for the Realization Party. I, as manager of this Club, am not in agreement with their policy."

As he spoke he fingered an envelope lightly. "I'm paying you fifteen guineas for tonight and fifteen guineas for next Saturday in lieu of notice."

"But—really, this is ridiculous! I—"

Sango took the envelope and walked across the premises, seeing nothing. First Trumpet joined him.

"Sango, d'you know what I heard? The manager of this Club is broke. He's selling out—and Lajide is to be the new owner!"

"Mere rumour. Don't believe it."

"It's true. One boy from the Tropic Rhythms told me; it must be true."

"Okay! Anyway, jus' call the band together, First Trumpet. We've been sacked; so we mus' begin to look for another boss. First let's share our money."

All this meant some inconvenience. Sango could not think where they would hold their rehearsals from now on. The manager of the All Language Club had been so very kind to them; but now there was no more question of using the club in the afternoons.

Sango was in a blue mood as he walked about the city, drifting with the aimless ones, looking but not seeing. He walked longer and longer into the night because he did not like the thought of going home and also because the lights and the noise created in his guts a restless desire to be part of it.

He hoped that one day he would become editor of the *Sensation*, and settle down with a girl from within this city. But so far, no progress. To him it mattered, for he believed that a man had to have a home behind him if he must build. At the moment, not even the foundations had been laid.

Nothing penetrated his gloom, not even the cruel snort of a bus that nearly ran him over.

"Sango!" It was the voice of a girl.

She was still wearing the same dress she had on when he left her at the Hollywood. "Where are you going, this night? Better be careful. Some drivers are mad!"

"I'm taking breeze," said Sango, still startled.

The traffic spun dizzily across where she stood and, when it had calmed down somewhat, she crossed the street to meet him, moving in that way that gave him the greatest pleasure. She linked her hands with his and they walked and talked.

"You look sad. What has happened?"

"Nothing, Aina."

She was not to be put off. "When somebody loves you, you do not know, because you are proud. All right! If you like, tell me. I will not worry you."

He was touched, and he said: "It won't interest you. There's a place not far from Molomo Street called the All Language Club. You know the place? Well, we used to play there. But now we have been sacked. They gave us our money and told us never to go there again. That's why I'm sad. What I want now is a place where myself and the boys can meet and practise. We can still find work, but we must continue to practise together."

She smiled. "Is that all? And you say it won't interest me; but why now?" She puzzled over it for a moment. "Sango, there's a place on Molomo Street—near your own house. No one uses the place. It is a large compound. In the daytime, the *Alhaji* teaches Muslim children. But in the afternoons, there's nobody there. I can speak to the *Alhaji* for you."

Aina led the way confidently into a kingdom where Sango felt a complete stranger. He could not believe they were still on Molomo Street till he had gone and sat in the revolving chair in the barber's saloon. Aina left him there and went about her mission.

The barber came limping in, and winked knowingly. "You take up with her again? I tell you, the girl like you too much."

Sango smiled. "Where's Lajide?"

"I see him in his car with that new woman. They say he buy some new place—All Language Club. You know the place?"

"I use to play there, barber."

Now it was clear. If Lajide had become the lover of Beatrice, it could only mean that she had put the idea of buying the Club into his head.

Aina came back to say that all would be well. The *Alhaji* had given permission. He was very pleased with the idea because he thought Sango's band would make the school popular. Sango and his men could go there twice a week—Mondays and Thursdays—to practise. She smiled happily and said: "Let us go to the beach by the lagoon and play."

Again the barber winked, a little more knowingly this time.

Sango had not noticed the moon till he saw the shadows of the coconut fronds waving against the sky. The surf beat with violence and the courting couples were dark clumps on the sands. There was a faint breeze with a tang in it.

"Don't be sad any more," Aina said, leaning against him.

"No more. I'm happy."

"Because of me? Sango, do you love me now?"

He was silent, trying desperately to collect his thoughts, to marshal his forces against the wiles of this seductress. He looked at her face, serene, with long lashes and pouting lips. In the eyes he read admiration.

Just for this once, he decided to be defeated. He held her to himself and she sighed the sigh of love in triumph.

chapter ten

Bayo it was who brought the news about the battle for Beatrice. Lajide, as owner of 163B Clifford Street, was at war with Muhammad Zamil, the tenant—or so it seemed. How else could he explain what had happened? Zamil, after buying the house, had allowed Lajide to let one of the rooms to the girl; but he could visit Beatrice only by day. Sleeping in her room was out of the question for a man who had eight wives.

"Tha's where the trouble began," Bayo said. "You know that Zamil is a bachelor, always home in the evenings—and Beatrice is the kind of girl that foreigners like." Bayo glanced round the crowded restaurant where Sango had taken him for lunch and continued: "I know all this because when Beatrice was there she helped me a lot. I used to meet Suad in her room and no one would know."

"Wait a minute. 'When Beatrice was there,' you said just now. You mean—she's no longer there?"

"She left. I don't know where she is now. Perhaps she's gone back home to the Eastern Greens. I heard she was very ill lately."

"Home is the place for her," Sango said.

"I wish she had not left Zamil," Bayo said. "It has upset all my plans. I've not seen Suad for three weeks now. When I go to the shop I cannot meet her, and at their home it is so difficult."

He sipped his lime-juice. He had not touched his steak. It was unlike Bayo to show no appetite. "Sango, what am I to do? I love this girl very much!"

"It will pass away," Sango said. "I'm sure it will. She's not taking you seriously. And you are only kidding yourself. Come off it! When that girl meets some young man from her home, you think she'll remember you?"

Bayo sat back in his chair, but his depressed mood remained. Sango could not get him to talk about anything else but Suad Zamil.

Beatrice had become the thorn in Lajide's flesh, the one woman his vanity and money could not conquer in a city where women yielded to money and influence. He could not understand the girl, because their backgrounds were so different. Beatrice came from a poor but proud family where values still mattered. Right was right, but wrong met its punishment. The end was not the most important thing, but the means. Lajide had lived too long in the city to care about right or wrong, so long as the end was achieved. And that end was so often achieved by money that it was inconceivable to him that money could ever fail in anything or with anybody.

Lajide went to see her in the department store. She had told him of her desire to work there and within a week he had made the desire a reality. He boasted to his friends: "One of the girls in the department store is my gal!"

He saw her now in the top rung of the ladder, fetching down a packet of something for a white woman. She looked ultra-smart in the close-fitting uniform with the "D.S." above the breast. Her eyebrows were cleverly pencilled and she wore lipstick.

"Choose one scent—for yourself!" Lajide said impulsively as the white woman made her purchase and left. "You look too fine, Beatrice!"

"Lajide, please!"

"Ready to close now," he said possessively.

"Remain half an hour."

"Beatrice, you vex with me? I go to the restaurant till the time reach."

"You know that men are not allowed to stand about talking to girls in this store. You must be buying something or moving on. Unless you want me to be sacked?"

"No, no!" he said quickly, and went up into the restaurant above the store.

As he entered, Bayo pinched Sango and said: "Look! That's Lajide, your former landlord. Let's ask him. Perhaps he has seen Beatrice."

"Forget it," said Sango.

Neither of them could imagine the mental torture through which Lajide was passing. The girl was far too stubborn and independent. He was prepared to go any length to make money and yet more money, to consolidate his position with her. It was all strange to him, because he took it for granted that he was master where all women were concerned.

He did not get back home till late in the evening. He was tired. He had a wash, changed into a light cloth, and called Alikatu. She was his third wife. But it was Kekere, Lajide's eighth wife, who came to say that Alikatu was not yet back from the market. She brought him a drink, and curtseying, offered it to him.

Lajide was bored. "Sit on my knee and amuse me," he told Kekere.

She was the youngest of them all, about eighteen, with very round eyes. He called her Kekere, which means "small" because in position she was the most junior of them all. He never did this till he was in a playful mood or wanted some favour from her. Her soft fingers rested on his cheek.

"Why have you been so angry lately? You have neglected all of us . . . Or are we going to be *nine*?"

"Me? Angry? *Nine!* Ha, ha! . . ."

"Where are you going, Kekere?" Lajide said, as she rose laughing from his knee.

"To put on some music."

"Not too loud! The compound has been very quiet since that Sango left this place. I don't want any noise. My head aches."

She gave him a saucy look. "All right! But I'll play my favourite record."

He watched her bare shoulders. For a girl so young she looked very mature. Her bosom trembled beneath the cloth as she moved. He was excited by the soft freshness of her well-made body.

"Is all right now. Come and sit here." He tapped his knee.

Beatrice would never obey such commands; and now even Kekere was being naughty. She went forward and twisted her hips, dancing a wiggle dance to the music. Lajide watched the cloth, fearing it would soon drop off.

"Stop that! I want to think! What'll you say if a stranger enter here and see my wife with her cloth off?"

"No one will come."

She laughed and continued to tease him with her dance. He was discovering her for the first time. Did he really have a girl like this here, under his own roof and yet—

"Come and sit here, Little One!"

"I hear, my Lord!" She moved, noiseless on her toes, and stood with hands behind her back. "I'm here."

"Is this madness?"

She laughed and sat on his knee. He held her close, imagining desperately that she could be Beatrice. He did not see the strangers enter.

Kekere whispered: "They want you."

"Who are they?"

"I can see them: two men."

Lajide had never seen them before, yet they called him by name. Instantly he was on his guard. He pinched Kekere. "Go into the bedroom. I'm coming . . ."

"So you always say, and you won't come to me. You'll go outside to that woman."

"Go, I'll meet you. Truly."

She went. It was not often that love came her way. At the bedroom door, she turned and made eyes.

One of the men carrying a brief-case came into the room. "We have come to discuss business." As he spoke his partner entered and they both sat down. "It is like this. We have five lorries, big, nice, in good condition. We want to sell them, and we want one thousand five hundred pounds for them—spot cash. You can repaint them and sell them at eight hundred pounds each. The timber merchants will grab them quick." He produced a cigarette and lit it.

Lajide watched him. The directness of the offer left him gasping. He had always thought that no one could excel him in blunt talk. He stroked his chin. Why had they picked on him? On the other hand . . . Beatrice! Here was a chance to spend some real money on her and stun her. That five thousand he had received from Zamil, where was it? Gone . . . he must have some more cash.

"Excuse me gentlemen. Kekere! Kekere! come and get beer for the gentlemen. We can talk better with drinks."

"Just so, sah!"

Kekere bustled about the inner room. She came out, carrying a tray with bottles and glasses. She set the tray down near them and left. Their eyes followed her.

"You have a very beautiful wife," the one with the brief-case said.

"And young," the other added.

"Women are trouble," said Lajide, thinking about Beatrice. But he could not disguise his pleasure.

"Women soften life. Life is too hard," said the man with the brief-case.

"Yes; when you have one wife it may be true. But a man like me, I have eight."

Lajide filled his glass. "Of course they come and go. Today, six, tomorrow eight. I use to worry myself about them. Not now." Kekere came out now and wandered about the room. She picked something and slipped back behind the curtains. The men licked their lips.

"Where are these lorries?" Lajide asked.

"Not far from here."

"What kind of lorries?"

"Very good ones, have no fear. Ex-Army. Used by the Americans and the British during the war. Very good for the timber business."

While they talked, Lajide kept thinking how he could double-cross these men. The idea did not come all at once. Slowly he rose and went indoors to change.

Kekere lay in bed, half-draped. She looked up. "Are they gone? Have you come?"

"Pss! Listen! This is what I want you to do. If you bungle things, I won't come to you any more . . ." In a few quick words he gave her his orders and said, "Now, don't waste time."

Again and again he warned her that she must do as she was told. Then he went out and met the robbers, who had been waiting impatiently.

It was one of those moonlit nights when a man has to peer into a face to identify it. Lajide approached the men who took him to inspect the lorries. To his amazement he discovered that the lorries were sound: that they needed mere paint—in fact, these men were dealing with him as honestly as one rogue with another. But that did not alter his plan. He, too, needed the money and knew well the risk involved.

If Kekere had done her share, the police should be here now. He peered into the darkness, but saw nothing. Then he began to haggle with them, to fill in the time. His ears were tuned for the faintest sounds, and he identified the crunch of boots before anyone else.

A group of men broke into their conversation, two of them in police uniform. Lajide saw the glint of moonlight on handcuffs. The robbers cursed him, but his own men (so he thought) were there awaiting his orders.

"Take these lorries to the Eastern Greens and sell them. You must travel only by night."

"What are you talking?" asked the uniformed man.

Lajide peered into the face, a strange one and very likely that of a real policeman. Kekere had bungled his plans. He had instructed her not to summon the real police but his own accomplices disguised as policemen. Kekere's stupidity would cost him thousands of pounds.

He drew back. "I don't speak to you. Am laughing at the thief-men."

"You done your duty well," said the policeman, gleefully. He turned to the lorry thieves and said harshly: "Inside!" As they clambered into the police van he shook Lajide by the hand. "Well done!"

Lajide forced a smile and mumbled something but his thoughts were fixed on how best to discipline the frivolous Kekere. When he got home she was nowhere to be found and she did not show up until Providence dealt Lajide a blow.

His third wife, Alikatu, returning from market one evening, had a stroke. By morning there had been a relapse and she lay in a coma—not alive, not dead, not suffering. Lajide was distraught. He dared not leave Alikatu to go and visit Beatrice.

The news spread quickly. The financier's wife was dying. Sango heard it in the *Sensation* office and booked a van to take him to Molomo Street. As he stepped out of the lorry he recognized the leader of the Realization Party who had offered him a free room, rushing round in his siesta jumper and cloth as if trying to shake the sleep from his eyes. From the neighbouring houses women poured into Lajide's compound, pressing their noses against the windows. This whole part of the city seemed to be agitated and anxious as the last moments ticked by in the life of someone they knew and liked.

Sango squeezed through till he could see Alikatu lying on the bed. Her face was pallid. Gone was the radiance that made her one of Lajide's favourite wives. The head wife, fat and busy, pushed him aside and took Alikatu's head in her lap, like a baby's.

She pressed a tumbler to the sick woman's lips. "Drink it!"

Alikatu gurgled and turned away. "Drink it," echoed the politician. Alikatu gurgled again, spat out the liquid and lay still.

Lajide's head wife looked into the sky with the palms of her hands facing her Creator and called out, "*Olorun-O!*" in this manner offering to God all her prayer for more help and possibly a miracle.

"I think we better fetch a taxi, before is too late!" said the politician. The word taxi was taken up till it was echoed outside. "Taxi is here!" someone shouted from the streets. An argument arose and in the end the politician said: "Tell the taxi to go! Is best not to move her. We'll send for a doctor."

Lajide arrived and saw Sango. "I don't want you here! Go away. You and that Lebanese thief Zamil, you worry the life out of me. Everywhere I go I see you. Have I no private life?"

The politician held Lajide back, for he was advancing with clenched fists. Sango stood his ground. Tender hands managed to calm Lajide, who sat beside Alikatu and held her head in his arms.

"Alikatu!" he called softly. The feeling he injected into that whispered word, the loving care with which he held his wife, created a restlessness and pain in all present. The man was laying bare his soul before them. He kept glancing behind him expectantly.

Almost on his heels a tall and well-dressed man in European clothes walked into the room and put down his bag. He took out a stethoscope, pressed it to the woman's heart. They watched him in silence. His face betrayed nothing.

He took his bag and went downstairs accompanied by the politician. Sango listened to their whispered conversation. He heard nothing. The doctor continued down the stairs and had hardly gained the street when a wailing cry broke out from the room where Alikatu lay. The story was there—plainly written on every face. But in every face was also engraved that stubborn shade of hope . . . that there might still be just the barest chance . . . that the body lying there—the body of Alikatu—was not *dead*, only resting. She would still breathe, surely. She would answer when called loudly by name.

A tense crowd hovered in hushed silence along the corridor. Now a man with a black bag—a doctor in the African manner trained by tradition in the ways of the past—this man went down the stairs and began to chalk up the ground and to spatter the blood of a chicken about the house, muttering incantations. He made a great show of the ceremony while the gentle wind blew the feathers about the compound. To Sango it was rather early to begin to frighten off Alikatu's ghost from Twenty Molomo. The herbalist seemed to be giving the final order to the ghost, to be tilting the balance in a particular direction.

"Alikatu!" Everyone knew now. People threw themselves down into convulsions, crying: "Alikatu!"

The lament in that cry could tear the heart out of a stone. It chilled Sango's blood. As he stood there and listened to the wailing and the moaning, he could also hear the prayers, exhortations, wishes, rebukes, regrets. His soul was stirred. The sobs and sighs shook the frail rafters of Twenty Molomo. Something in the ritual reminded him of the terrible night at Lugard Square, the night of the *Apala* dance. Why, if Alikatu's spirit still hovered around this place, did it not have pity on the poor mortals and re-inhabit the body where it belonged? O, pitiless death.

The mourners came in groups. Sometimes Twenty Molomo was so quiet that one could hardly guess it was inhabited by even a single soul. Then a new and noisy group would come and start the wailing and the moaning and the deafening cries.

What Sango noticed specially was that not one of the people who had been at the festive party at the All Language Club set foot in Lajide's house. They must have heard of his bereavement. Instead they sent flowers. It must be the sophisticated thing to do. They were too busy to come, too busy to hearken to the voice of death which must one day call them one by one.

· · ·

Sango went to the "Waking" because Bayo had promised him there would be lots of girls. A waking in the city was a sad affair, but the living had eyes to the future and many a romance had been kindled in the long-drawn-out hours between night and morning, when resistance is at its minimum and the whole spirit is sympathetic and kindly disposed.

It was no surprise to Sango when, moving among the mourners, the drummers, and those who drank palm wine, he saw Aina. She had indeed bought and tailored her Accra dress and it heightened her charm. Plum velvet it was, bordered with white lace and sewn in the latest style. The blouse showed off the roundness of her arms, and the skirt, a long piece of material artfully tied round the waist, showed off just so much tantalizing thigh, and no more. Sango wondered how the men could keep their minds on death, with Aina so very vibrant with life.

Only one moment before that, Sango had seen Lajide sitting motionless, unaware of the world about him. Lajide's head had been sunk on his breast while Zamil came in briefly to console him. The fact that Lajide had not lifted his head, that he was surrounded by a group of friends who were chosen to prevent him from trying to take his own life, showed Sango the depth of his grief.

The contrast between his attitude and Aina's was clear. Aina had not come to mourn. She was not dressed like the others, in the *aso-ebi*, the prescribed dress of mourning.

She too had seen Sango and she now came towards him, bright-eyed. Some feet away, Sango caught a whiff of her perfume and the dry feeling came immediately to his throat. He desired her immediately. With shame in his eyes he tried to look away, to ignore her presence.

"Hello, Sango, I called at yours several times after that night!"

"Aina, not here! We have come to mourn, not romance!"

"I heard something; is it true that you went home to marry? They said when you went to the Eastern Greens during the crisis you paid the bride-price on your future wife. Is it true she will join you soon?"

Sango smiled. "Aina! But why are you so angry about it?"

"Don't you know why? It means you have been deceiving me!"

"But did I ever promise to marry you?" He left her abruptly and mingled with the crowd. He wished he could have seen Beatrice, but she was not here, neither was she at the funeral which took place in the afternoon.

Because of the death at Number Twenty, Sango was not allowed to practise with his band at the Muslim School on Molomo Street. The manager of the school, a good friend of Lajide's and a devout Muslim, told Sango that practice was out of the question for a long time to come. There were ceremonies still to be performed at Number Twenty, and again the *Ramadan*, their own festival, was very near and the school premises would be used for rehearsals during the next month or two.

The boys in Sango's band had already begun to disperse to undertake free-lance assignments. Another door had been closed in his face.

chapter eleven

By polling day all energy had been spent. The politicians were now tired of making promises and had taken their proper places—in the background. Clerks, motor drivers, butchers, market women, shopkeepers, who as responsible citizens had previously registered their names, went to the polling stations that dotted the city, and cast their votes. For that single day, the power was in their hands and the politicians waited with beating hearts and speculating eyes for the results.

It turned out that out of the fifty seats in the Town Council the Self-Government Now Party had won thirty-nine, leaving eleven seats for the Realization Party. This meant that the government was now in the hands of the S.G.N. Party and that they would elect a mayor from one of their leaders.

There had never been a mayor in the West African city and now the first one was to be an African. It was a great triumph for the S.G.N. Party. The *West African Sensation* had been working hard on the elections with such leaders as:

WHO WILL BE MAYOR?
CHOICE OF MAYOR CAUSES SPLIT IN SELF-GOVERNMENT NOW PARTY
TIME TO REDEEM ELECTION PROMISES
REALIZATION PARTY THROWS BOMBSHELL
NATURAL RULERS AND THE NEW CONSTITUTION

Sango found himself with less and less work to do. Lately he had developed a habit of leaving the office for longer than he should, searching for a place of his own, and a place for his band. Money was the limiting consideration. They were asking for too much, and he had very little.

The crime boys seemed to be taking a rest and the pages of the *Sensation* were losing their spice. McMaster called him into the office and told him to turn his hand to other assignments. There was a shortage of good men and it was a loss to the paper to have a man of Amusa Sango's calibre counting the minutes and doing nothing.

Then the great opportunity came. It was on a morning when the rain had added to his irritations and he had come into the office soaked. He remembered stamping his shoes as he entered the office. Layeni, the night editor, had not left. They were all discussing a subject of national importance.

"A great shock for the nation . . . but anyway, he was an old man . . . Good-bye to the wizard of statesmanship, the inspiration for the new movement . . ."

"Without him, there would be no nationalism today on the West Coast . . ."

Sango knew they were talking about De Pereira, the greatest nationalist of all time. He was eighty-three and though he did not involve himself now in the physical campaigns and speechmakings he was the brains of the S.G.N. Party. For the last twenty years he had been the spiritual leader of the party and the party dramatized his ideals. Sango listened to the idle talk. He did not know as he stood in the *Sensation* office what this would mean in his life. How could he? He was not detailed to cover the item: McMaster selected a special political correspondent. Most offices broke off for the day, and Sango could have gone home if he chose. Instead, he listened.

And as he heard more and more he found what he had missed by not being an active nationalist. The city, the whole country, rose together to pay tribute to De Pereira. Almost within the hour the musicians were singing new songs in his name; merchants were selling cloth with imprints of his inspiriting head. Funeral editions of the *Sensation* featured his life story from the time of Queen Victoria of England to Queen Elizabeth II, in whose reign he died. They asked the question: in view of De Pereira's death at so critical a time in the history of the S.G.N. Party, who would guide them to ultimate victory for the whole nation? This was too much of a loss for African nationalism. Who else had the experience, the wizardry, the insight, the centuries-old diplomacy of this man who had so long defied death?

During the funeral not a single white man was to be seen in the streets of the city, or anywhere near the Cathedral Church of Christ where his body lay in state. Even those who lived near the Cathedral were shut off by those overflowing crowds that vied for one peep at the magnificent coffin. In the trees above and around the Cathedral people hung like monkeys. Some had even defied the captains of ships anchored in the lagoon and climbed on deck, bravely trespassing, unmoved by the heavy smoke pouring from the funnels.

Sango was seeing a new city—something with a feeling. The madness communicated itself to him, and in the heat of the moment he forgot his worldly inadequacies and threw himself with fervour into the spirit of the moment.

He was one of the suffocated and crumpled men who groaned and gasped to keep alive in the heat and the pressure of bodies half a mile from the Cathedral. He strained to get nearer, and though it was barely two o'clock and the funeral service would not be due for another two hours, he knew he could never get near the coffin.

"Since morning, I stand here!" groaned a man in the crowd. "I don' know that people plenty like this for this city!"

The heat made time stand still. It was baking hot. It was irritating and unbearable. Two hundred thousand people forming themselves into an immovable block of fiery nationalists who jammed the streets, waiting, hoping to catch one glimpse of the coffin. Death had glorified De Pereira beyond all his dreams.

And Sango was there, more dead than alive, completely stifled by the sweat and squeeze of bodies. He was almost raving mad with irritation. When the wave of movement began from the foot of the Cathedral it came in a slow but powerful wave and beat against the spot where Sango stood. The current reminded him of a river overflowing its banks. Before this pressure the strongest man was flung irresistibly backwards like cork on an angry sea. Amusa staggered, off balance. At the same time he heard a faint cry. A girl in an immaculate white dress was in trouble. She had slipped, and if he did not do something about her that merciless crowd would trample her to death. And she would be the day's sacrifice to the spirit of De Pereira.

He sweated. He tried to disentangle his limbs. The pressure never relented. With his veins almost bursting he managed to bend over, to draw her to her feet. His eyes bulged so much he feared they would burst. His head cracked with pain. He stuck his elbows out so as to receive the surging crowd on a sharper point, shepherded the girl to a lane. Even the lanes were overflowing with people. He managed to push her into a little crevice and then looked at her face. It was tired, but attractive.

She was breathing in short gasps. "Oh! . . ."

She held her sides. "I hope you're not hurt," Sango said quickly. "Smooth out your dress—they've made a mess of it."

She leaned against him, bruised and shaken. There was nowhere he could take her to, for all the eating and drinking places had been closed.

"You—you saved my life!"

"Quiet, first. We must still get out of this madness."

Far down the Marina, by the lagoon, was a little promontory over which the broad leaves of a coconut palm waved. It was quiet and deserted and the wind blew sweet and cool. Sango made her sit down. She looked at him gratefully, not saying a word, and he felt a pain in his heart.

She had unbuttoned her blouse so that the breeze caressed her young body. "I'll soon be all right," she said. "There's going to be an important speech at the graveside."

"You're not strong enough now, Miss—"

"Beatrice is my name."

"Beatrice!" A thousand tunes hummed in his brain. "This is very odd!" He took her hand and now the touch of her hand had a magic enchantment for him.

The fresh air had partly revived her. Slowly they walked for mile after mile, and for Sango it could have gone on for ever without his noticing, so strange was the pleasure which her company gave him and so elated his spirit.

When they caught up with the funeral procession it was still difficult to break through to the front row. And Beatrice the Second—as Sango called her—insisted on remaining till the end. She was indeed showing him what nationalism meant for the people of the city.

"It's like the death of Gandhi," Sango said. "De Pereira was, after all, our own Gandhi!"

There had never been anything like this. It was impossible to move one step in any direction. They were obliged to give up and stand about for an hour, rooted to the spot. From somewhere a movement of bodies started. The funeral was over. A new song was born at that moment. It rent the air. Sango, ashamed of his ignorance of the words, could only mumble the most conspicuous word, "Freedom . . ." which seemed to be the recurrent theme.

"Did you see the coffin?"

"No, but they say it was an expensive one: covered with gold."

"I thought they said there would be a funeral speech?"

"We'll read it in the papers tomorrow."

Beatrice the Second was holding a handkerchief to her nose. All about them people were weeping with genuine grief. Sango was disturbed. He felt out of step with the city. A lump rose in his throat and a mist came to his eyes. He turned away in shame, swallowing hard and blinking, embarrassed by a new and softer side of himself.

"Don't cry, Beatrice!" He squeezed her shoulder.

But everybody was crying. Handkerchiefs were going to noses. And the sun was slowly setting on two hundred thousand mourners.

"There must have been something about that graveside speech! It has stirred everyone to lament. Beatrice, let's be going back now. Where do I drop you?"

Sango hailed a taxi. His conscience troubled him, as he thought: *You have no home, Sango; you have no money; your goods are still at the railway station; you want all the money you can put aside for that six months' rent in advance.* He ignored his misgivings. He tried to think of something to say, but no words could express how he felt. His response to this girl made him feel they had been friends all his life. He held her hand.

It was a slow drive through the chaotic city. Sango was irritated by the closeness and the dust, but he was pleased because he could talk to Beatrice the Second and get to know her. She was quite frank about herself.

"I have a fiancé in England. He's a medical student in his third year. I love him very much."

The words hurt Sango.

"I'll join him soon," she said. "I'll do nursing and midwifery. And when we return, we'll have our own hospital in the remote interior. No city life for us! I think they have quite enough hospitals and medical attention here. We'll go to the bush, where we are needed."

"Good idea," Sango said. "But you'll not make much money."

"I agree. But that's not all there is to it. We will be doing something, giving something . . ." As she talked, she brightened. A new glow came to her cheeks. Her eyes danced. She became a new girl. Sango was full of admiration.

"The city is overcrowded, and I'm one of the people overcrowding it," Sango said. "If I had your idea, I would leave the city; but it holds me. I'm only a musician, and a bad one at that. A hack writer, smearing the pages of the *Sensation* with blood and grime." He saw the interested way in which she leaned forward when he talked about himself.

Lights shone in the streets and long cars began to steal effortlessly through the night, freed at last from the traffic restrictions. The city was gradually recovering from its shock, exerting its everlasting magic.

"I wish I could see you again!"

Sango saw her hesitation. "I'm grateful to you. I'll tell my father all you did for me . . ."

"I'm sorry, I have no address at the moment, except Crime Reporter, *West African Sensation*. I used to play at the All Language Club, but that road is now closed."

The taxi pulled up before an old-type house, probably Brazilian. Beatrice the Second stepped gingerly down. She was much recovered now, and the shock was gone.

"I'll see you again," she said. He took her hand and squeezed it.

He watched her walk away and there was a sadness in his heart. *There is the girl for you, Sango. If you could win her, you would find a foothold in this city and all your desires would focus on a new inspiration. How different she is from them all: Aina, Elina, Beatrice the First. Have you ever felt anything like this beautiful feeling before? But it's hopeless. She herself told you she is engaged and loves her fiancé.*

Sango thought of Beatrice the Second as he sat down in the *Sensation* office to write his report. His despondency filtered into the general tone of his account of the De Pereira funeral. He was poring over the typewriter, a cigarette dangling from his mouth, when he heard footsteps in the corridor. McMaster poked his head into the room and said to Sango: "A moment, please!"

The telephone was ringing as McMaster entered his office. All the *Sensation* telephones had been ringing incessantly throughout the day. McMaster had the telephone in his hand when Sango entered and with one hand he waved him into a seat.

Sango wondered what it was all about.

"I've had my eyes on your work for some time," said McMaster when the conversation was over. "The coal crisis, the Lajide funeral, the election campaigns, and so on. But with the De Pereira affair, I think we're set for your most important achievement. I've had it hinted that you might be offered the post of Associate Editor, depending what the Board of Governors thinks . . ."

Sango went deaf. He opened his lips and no words came.

"Of course, it may be that you prefer the adventure of reporting. This will be an office-chair job. You may like to go and think the whole thing over . . ."

He was still sitting there after the conversation, and one thought was uppermost in his mind: Beatrice the Second. He was becoming a man, fit for a girl of her class. Beatrice the Second . . .

"All right now, Sango."

Lajide had not gone to the De Pereira funeral. He was alone; probably the only living being on Molomo Street. But his wives had gone. Nothing could keep them indoors these days. He lifted the glass to his lips, made a face, belched. Lately he had developed a habit of talking aloud to himself: "Since my wife died, everything has changed. Everything! Beatrice —she has no ear for my words. Kekere—she goes out openly to the street lamp on the corner. There she talks to young men. She thinks I do not see her. Ha, ha! Young men on bicycles! She must think I'm a fool. I know all, I see all; only, I don't talk!"

He drank more. That was another new development. The law called this liquor illicit gin, because it was distilled without licence. But the brewers who lived in timber shacks by the lagoon, they called it O.H.M.S. in honour of the Queen of England. The irony of it! Breaking the law to honour the Queen! Of course, they did not let the liquor mature like genuine distillers; that would take too long. But it was still alcohol. If you were not prejudiced you would not be able to distinguish the taste from that of pure gin.

He tossed the glass aside. No good would come of too much thinking. Alikatu—she was dead and gone. The five thousand from Muhamad Zamil was gone and he had not lived at 163B for three months yet. And this new four thousand from the timber deal? When you were in a prominent position and you lost your wife, four thousands pounds *might* see you through all the ceremonies and sacrifices—if you were the showy type like Lajide.

"I must do something . . . I must do something. . . ."

The timber business? He had tried that. He was still on the list of the city's exporters of logs. Everybody was timber-crazy and he might as well take his chance.

His gaze focused suddenly on the door. A strange woman was standing there, in a big-sleeved blouse, a velvet cloth about her waist. No, it could not be Alikatu. Alikatu was dead. Alikatu was dead . . . dead. She would not wear her cloth the wrong way round . . . She always dressed correctly. *Alikatu!* He stood up and reached for her. She was smiling.

"Alikatu!" His throat worked and his eyes bulged. She was smiling defiantly. She was beyond his reach. "What are you saying? Your lips are moving. I cannot hear you. I cannot hear—No! Not yet . . . I'll join you when my time here is up. Truly, I'll come . . . You have always been my favourite wife . . . I'll come, in *Olorun's* name, I will . . ."

She was no longer standing there, but instead Kekere was at the door and saying something. "I thought I heard you talking . . . Who was it? Who was it?"

Lajide crept back to his seat, not speaking. One by one his other wives were coming into the room, rigged and preened like courting birds. They were coming from the crowd, from the city and its noise.

"What's wrong, Kekere, tell us. You were here with him!"

"No, I've just returned. I came in. As I was coming in, I thought I heard somebody talking."

They looked at her suspiciously. She was the youngest of them all and completely frivolous. In her low-cut blouse, which showed far too much of her firm breasts, she seemed capable of anything.

"Truly," she said. "I'm not lying. When I came in, I—I thought he was looking at—at me. I was standing there, at the door. And I asked him whether he was talking to somebody and he did not answer."

"If you have done nothing to him, why does he look so queer? Better speak the truth now!"

"Lord receive my soul!" Kekere swore, noisily slapping her skirt. "Me? What could I possibly do to him?"

The six women sensed a mystery. Of course no one mentioned the word poison. Where each woman sought the husband's affection, a love potion might be given with good intentions.

Soft hands found the husband's armpits . . . wrapped round his knees . . . around his waist . . . Sweet breaths were indrawn and the aroma of delicate perfume filled the air . . . and as feminine silk rustled, the seven wives, now burdened with the snoring husband, bore him as lightly as they might into the bedroom.

"You'd all better go and change your clothes," said the fat woman, the Number One wife, taking charge. "I'll watch over him."

chapter twelve

"It's all my fault," Bayo said. He trudged beside Sango on their way to the left luggage shed where Sango's things were kept. He was in such a state that he followed Sango wherever he went, trying to get a word in about his love affair. "Sango, the girl Suad warned me all the time to be quick and marry her. She warned me. Truly, she did; but I was unable to marry her. No money. I kept postponing. And now, Sango. Can you believe it? What she said is coming true! Her brother wants to fly her back to Syria. But is that really possible? Just because the poor girl is in love with me?"

"When is the flight?"

"On Monday! Today is Saturday. What can I do? Too late! Oh Lord. My dear, loving Suad Zamil. She has cried so much! Her brother said he'd disown her if she so much as mentions my name again in his ears. She doesn't care. Goes on calling Bayo, all the time."

Sango found his box and now fumbling for his keys, opened it and began to remove an old script. He took out the clothes he wanted and together they went to a gents' near by to change.

"Sango, you mean this is where you actually keep your things? You haven't found a place? Of course the room of First Trumpet is too small to contain both your things. But this is awful. I'm very sorry. Where do you practise with your band? How can a man live like this?"

Sango said not a word. He was gradually changing his clothes, and Bayo was still talking. "They're keeping her away from me. Muhamad Zamil is watching over her with a loaded revolver. He doesn't let her out of his sight. Beatrice is no longer there. If she had been there, I could have some excuse of visiting the place. I'm very worried, Sango."

"How did this matter leak out in the first place?"

"I can't tell you the whole story, Sango. But I suspect Beatrice has something to do with it. You remember Zamil took her to "wife." Well, jealousy can do a lot, you know. And revenge too. You see, it was Beatrice who introduced Suad Zamil to me and we fell in love. She became jealous because the girl liked me at once. Of course we used to meet in her room and she was kind to us. But I never once suspected she would betray us. You see, she and Suad quarrelled. Suad did not like the idea of her brother merely keeping an African woman, and yet *she* was in love with me! I can't understand it all, Sango. It's complicated. But anyway, Zamil knows now, and is guarding her. This thing has gone to high quarters." Bayo wrung his hands.

"Have you been to the Welfare Office? Tell them you want to marry the girl; that the girl is old enough to decide things for herself, but her guardian will not let her do her will."

"I've been there!" Bayo said furiously. "Red tape was against me. They even said they were closing for the holidays. By the time they re-open the girl would be safely home!" He flung his cigarette-butt on to the lavatory floor. That gesture of despair touched Sango. A man came in and they went out on to the station platform. Idly, Sango and

Bayo watched a shunting engine. When you lived near a railway station the noise of the engines ceased to sound in your ears.

"Why not go away on a train?" Sango suggested. "Take the girl and run away. It's romantic! Don't laugh, people do it. At least, you'll leave Zamil alone to look after his shop; and when he cools off, you come back. After all, the girl has her own life to lead. And if you're the man she's chosen, you must see she is happy."

Bayo's condition was pitiful to see. Dull were his shoes, wrinkled his tie; and the hair of this erstwhile dapper youngster was for once uncombed. Was this the same Bayo who trifled with women's hearts? So terrified of everything that might hurt Suad Zamil? Bayo who was usually so confident in such affairs?

"Just think of Zamil," he went on bitterly. "How many girls does he 'marry' in a year? I know of Beatrice. Now he's taken another—a half-caste called Sybil. But she's not so new; they were 'husband' and 'wife' long before he met Beatrice. She has two daughters for him. Zamil makes Suad unhappy by all this and she wants him to settle down. He pays the girls good money if they are virgins. Then he throws them away after his curiosity has been satisfied. What future have girls like Sybil and Beatrice? What decent man will ever take them into their own homes and keep them? Yet, just think! It is this same Zamil who must hold Suad from me! It is he who must guard her morals . . ."

"When last did you see Suad?"

"Before I went to that waking . . . you remember? When Lajide's wife died."

"That's about two months ago. How then has this thing suddenly flared up? Okay, Bayo! If they're taking her away from you, we must make one last effort to see her. We're going there—this night, Bayo!"

"She told me to get a special licence. I went to the magistrate and he insisted on seeing her in person. There can be no marriage without a bride, or someone to give the bride away! One thing, Sango! I do not want to make this girl suffer for my sake. I love her too much. Please do not come with me tonight. It's too dangerous for two people."

"I'll come, Bayo. I want to see this girl Suad. Do you realize I've heard so much about her, yet do not know the future bride of my best friend?"

They walked on through the city, wrapped in this problem. Round and round they talked on the same topic: how wrong-doing is a hill, and how one mounts this hill and descries that of another: Zamil and Suad, Bayo and Beatrice, Sango and Aina. . . . And as Sango kept his eyes open for the notice ROOM TO LET, he was thinking how different life would soon be. Associate Editor, *West African Sensation*: but then he remembered the way Beatrice the Second had said "I have a fiancé in England . . . I love him very much."

He began to walk faster.

A little after midnight, two figures crept into the garden at 163B Clifford Street West. Lights were still on in the main building. From one of the rooms, the radio was blaring forth Arabian music.

"Which one is her room, Bayo?"

"We can't get in . . . it's at the back."

"We'll try. I have a little plan. This is all the money I've been saving for that new room: just ten pounds. I'll give some to the night watch. That'll put him on our side. After all, how much does he earn in one month?"

He disappeared. Bayo stood looking at Suad's window. It was in darkness. She couldn't have fallen asleep. She must be as troubled as he was. Just two nights more in the city, then she would embark on that forced journey back home—to what? A dull life, at best. Her love, her life was here in the land where her brother had been all but naturalized. But would she be ready to elope with him now? The reckless thought frightened him.

Sango came back. "She's sitting in the lounge. Bayo, she's a beauty! She's worth any sacrifice! But that fool Zamil is there too. And a strange woman—perhaps the Sybil you told me about. Some children too. No one seems to go to bed in this house. Wonder what we can do. This is a little harder than I expected."

They crept into the yard. The steward was drying his hands on a napkin. He took Bayo aside and for a long time they argued and sighed —in whispers. Then the steward took a trayful of glasses into the large house. "Zamil is drunk. We may be lucky. I'll try for you, if it can be possible."

They waited. Soon he was back. "I have made signs to Suad. Is best for you to wait her in the cotton bush, behind the window. No one will see you there."

Bayo went there and waited. Amusa went back to the night watch. Time crawled. He tried to imagine how the girl would be feeling now. Then he heard a rustle, delicate and light. A white figure in a pink dressing-gown flitted by. He saw the eagerness with which the two lovers embraced each other. Sango looked away with a sigh of pleasure. This alone, this abandon was enough reward for their effort.

Suad lifted her face to be kissed. She was breathing with some pain as if the tears choked her throat. "The licence? You have got it?"

"They said you must come. And two witnesses."

"What we can do? I fly in two days. My brother, he has made all the arrangements. This night, tomorrow night, that's all! Oh! I don't want to leave you, my Bayo! My African love!" She took his face between her hands with all the tenderness of a mother fondling a baby.

"Do you love me, Bayo?"

"I cannot sleep because of you."

"I love you too much. Bayo, kiss me!"

Bayo took her in his arms and kissed her with all the hunger of repressed love. Her lips were warm in their mad response.

"Bayo!" she whispered.

They were silent, treasuring the precious moments of their love. She it was who said, "Bayo, maybe we can run away! Yes, we can, my love!"

"Can you come—now? No, Suad! Do not come. It will be too much suffering for you. And—"

"I have some money. We can run away and never return. Never, never! Then Zamil will suffer."

"Enough talk! You are afraid, no?"

"I'm not afraid." He could not bear to see her dejection. "Suad, I'll die for you! In the whole world there's no girl like you, Suad," he said impulsively. "Go and get your clothes." He was very muddled about it all, but there was no way out now, only forward. "Go get your things."

At that moment the steward appeared. "Missus. I don' know what's wrong with Master. He's searching everywhere for you."

"You haven't seen us, steward. Understand?"

"Suad!" came the harsh call. "Suad!" It was Zamil.

Suad nestled quickly in Bayo's arms, wringing from their brief meeting all the joys of persecuted young love. His fingers sought her soft hair. Her frenzied lips searched fervently, not merely for his lips, but for his soul, probing for signs of assurance . . . searching for the slightest hint of fear or lack of constancy. "Good-bye, Bayo, kiss me, my love, and let me die."

"No, Suad. We go together. Without you, I die. Pack your things, let's ecape."

"Bayo, it is impossible. Embrace me, sweetheart, before I die."

"Hands off!" Zamil had emerged from the bushes, dishevelled wild. In his fist a dark object rested.

"Muhamad, don't be silly. Put that gun away."

A shudder ran through Bayo. "Keep still, Suad." His body vibrated with a new surge of joy and courage. "Your brother is a coward, and will do nothing. He's strong only with a gun. Here, let me have the gun."

"Where are you going? Bayo, be careful. He's drunk—"

Zamil stood his ground, but Bayo leapt. Two cracks split the air.

Bayo groaned, clutching his stomach. Suad screamed. This was the final moment. The life was ebbing fast from him. The warmth glowed upwards but down below all feeling drained and faces of evil menace, void and empty, ricocheted with the night in a kaleidoscope of grimaces. Death had ceased to be a stranger. Suad clung to him, and lifeless and tangled together both of them crashed to earth.

The gun dropped with a clatter. Zamil's eyes had become clear as drinking water. His madness had vanished with the slaughter of the two lovers who were too happy to know or care.

Sango had seen and heard the shooting. Desperately he hoped that no great harm had been done. He clutched his stomach, resolutely trying not to be sick, but up it came. He could not help it. There was a tap by, and when he had soaked his head and rinsed his mouth Sango felt a little better. When he got up he went to the public telephone and made a call to the police.

The speed with which their van arrived surprised him. Yet Zamil was nowhere to be seen. His car had vanished from the garage. The Inspector waited patiently, convinced by the bloodstains in the cotton bush and the deep marks on the floor where the bodies had apparently been dragged that there *had* been a killing here.

"Is it not the same Zamil of the counterfeit case? The one who was apprehended near Magamu Bush some time ago." The inspector was surveying the garden, flashing his torchbeam on every blade of grass. "We've had our eyes on him for some time. He hasn't escaped us this time. We'll get him!"

On Clifford Street West the loco workers who had a morning shift at 6:30 had begun to assemble. By dawn 163B Clifford Street West was the focus of the city's speculations. A love crime! Still Zamil did not show up. Even the steward had vanished.

By 10 a.m. a call came through. It was from the Emergency Ward of the General Hospital, and the inspector recognized the voice as belonging to one of his colleagues. A man had just been admitted with severe head injuries. It was suspected that he had tried to take his own life by shooting himself. He had been found about five miles away at Elizabeth Beach, lying unconscious in his own car. The fisherman who saw him had taken him by canoe across the lagoon to the General Hospital.

"Describe him!" said the inspector, drawing Sango near the receiver so that he too might hear.

The description tallied with what Zamil would look like with severe head injuries. But the inspector would not take the hospital's word for it.

"I'll be right over," the inspector said.

And Sango went with him. This will be my greatest story, he thought, as they got into the police van.

"I'm sorry to have to take so drastic a step, Sango," said McMaster. He was being very much the editorial adviser, Sango's boss sitting in the editorial chair in the offices of the *West African Sensation*. He was not the friend that Sango had worked with for two years. "You understand how it is—a matter of policy. The *Sensation* does not stand for playing one section of the community against the other. Personally I have nothing against you or your writing in this tragic affair. . . . But I do not own the *Sensation*—"

Sango fingered the letter of dismissal. He was not really listening to McMaster. He was thinking in confused circles: Beatrice the Second, First Trumpet, Lajide, Twenty Molomo; and back to that terrible midnight, small-hours shooting. His rage and disgust; his oath of vengeance. It had now worked in reverse. He had been fired.

"Amusa, less than a week ago, I thought we were all set for something really big: something you deserved. I'd always wanted you to take over the editorship when the need arose; with your drive, your fluent style of writing, your initiative—"

"Must we go over it all again? You've paid me off, you've given me a decent testimonial—"

"Personally I have nothing against you, Sango. Look, I don't often go into details in matters of this kind. But I feel I owe you an explanation for purely personal reasons. You're a good journalist—perhaps the most original in the city. All your writing invariably presents a fresh viewpoint. But in your handling of the Zamil murder case, you seemed to overreach yourself. You made an issue of it, and not a very satisfying one at that. Bayo fell in love with Suad Zamil. Right! The brother, Muhamad Zamil, objected, wanted to fly the girl out of the country. Bayo decides to elope with the girl. Zamil, drunk, shoot Bayo, wounds the girl who later dies in hospital. Zamil runs away, and is later found lying on the beach with bullet wounds in his head. That's your story-line . . ."

Sango smiled. "As far as you were concerned, that was my story-line. But don't forget, Bayo was my personal friend. And I was present when Zamil shot and killed him, and the girl he loved. The least I could do—"

"Was to fight him in the Press?" McMaster flicked away an ash.

"Naturally."

"I see . . . Now it's a little clearer why you let yourself go to the extent you did. I'm not sure it was the best way you could have won public sympathy. But I know how it feels to have your best friend killed right before your eyes. It happened to me in France during World War One. Well, you've won your fight. Zamil will die of his wounds; or if not, he'll be hanged. But your reports were most embarrassing. The Board of Governors employed all tact and influence to avoid legal action. As you know we have never been popular either with the *Daily Challenge* or the *Daily Prospect* who regard us disdainfully as the voice of the British Government. A fine mess we're getting into!"

There was little more to be said. As Sango walked down the steps, he heard Layeni saying loudly to the others: "Yes! . . . These rude college boys! They have no respect for their seniors! Imagine writing things like that for all to read! I've been with the *West African Sensation* fifteen years yet I wouldn't dare . . ."

Sango stepped quickly into the street, tearing himself from the people and the place to which he had become attached. On the lagoon a fisherman was taking advantage of a break in the rains to dry his nets. Beatrice the Second! He had begun to plan how they would both benefit from his new promotion; and now . . .

chapter thirteen

Sango was sitting under his favourite coconut palm by the lagoon looking at the ships and cargo vessels. It was a busy afternoon. Down the road came lorries from the hinterland, loaded with produce to be stacked in the adjoining warehouses. It was the usual afternoon scene on this part of the lagoon and Sango caught himself dozing in the still, oppressive air. Looking up for a brief moment he saw a lorry careering down the road. Something about this particular lorry caught his attention.

It could be the sign, painted in yellow letters on a black background: TRAVEL TO GOLD COAST OVERLAND. Or the numerous flags which fluttered from all parts of the lorry. But the real fact was that it was completely out of tune with its surroundings.

"Amusa! Amusa Sango!" came the sharp cry of a female voice, and at that moment the lorry pulled to one side.

Sango could see no one. From the lorry, a short and stocky man came down, followed by a girl whom Sango immediately recognized as Beatrice the First.

"She recognized you first," said the stock man.

Beatrice was smiling. A large raffia hat shielded her head and shoulders from the sun and through her dark goggles Sango could not see her eyes. Yet it seemed to him then that something had gone out of Beatrice the First. This could not be the same girl who had set his blood aflame in those nights when his band had pride of place at the All Language Club.

"Sango, this is Kofi. He's a transport owner who travels between here and Accra."

Kofi extended his hand. "I've heard so much about you. I feel I actually know you."

Beatrice linked her hands with Kofi, and Sango thought: So now it's Kofi. Happiness at last. You will now forget Zamil and Lajide.

She was pale and very thin and when she coughed Sango could not bear the sound.

"Beatrice has been ill and is only just recovering."

"I'm all right," said Beatrice brightly. "Sango, I went to look for you at the All Language Club."

"You know I don't play there any longer. Not since the manager sold it to Lajide."

"I was hoping to call at the offices of the *West African Sensation*."

"You wouldn't find me there, either. Lost my job. Fired. Just this morning. It's a fine day, isn't it? A fine day to lose one's job."

"I'm sorry, Sango."

"Beatrice is a very good girl," Kofi said. "She's been with me for a little while, and we've been happy. No so, Beatrice?"

"Yes, and you've furnished our flat wonderfully. Kofi, don't forget, you will drop me near Ladjide's house . . . I want to see him alone. Perhaps Sango is coming our way—or is he too busy?"

"I'll come," said Sango.

They drove through the streets till they came to the turning where Beatrice would get down. Kofi got out to help her down.

"D'you want me to come with you?"

"No, Kofi. I shan't be long."

She kissed him on the cheek and as she walked down the street, Sango sighed. She could still be the heart-snatching Beatrice he used to know.

"She's a funny girl," said Kofi tenderly. "I have never understood her and never shall." He stood still until Beatrice turned the corner.

Kofi climbed back into the lorry. "D'you mind coming to my place? We live on the outskirts of the city. You'll like it. We can have a drink, and talk about you, and—"

"Beatrice!" Amusa laughed. He liked Kofi and in a way was sorry for him. That dog-like attachment to Beatrice!

"I'll tell you something: a moment ago, you said you lost your job. I think you need a holiday. Why not come to the Gold Coast? It will be a real change for you."

"The Gold Coast? But I don't know anyone there."

Kofi laughed and turned on the engine. The lorry responded with a throaty rhythm. "You know me. Look! We will talk about it a little more." The lorry was moving through the streets. "My lorries run to the Gold Coast every week. Whenever you want to go, let me know. Here is my card. We are going to my house now, and you will know where we live."

The idea was appealing. Sango thought the Gold Coast would be a good place for a honeymoon. He took the card and slipped it into his pocket.

Lajide, draped loosely in a floral cloth—his own version of a pyjama suit —walked into the sitting-room to find Beatrice already seated. A full row of his seven wives occupied the divan on the other side of the room. He waved an impatient hand at them.

"What are you all doing here? Get out and let me speak to my visitor!"

He drew a chair and said: "Welcome, Beatrice."

She fanned her face with the straw hat. "I have come to see you about Sango. I've just seen him and he told me he would like to play for the All Language Club—"

"I don't want to hear anything about Sango. I thought there was something else . . ."

Beatrice hesitated. "There *was* something else . . ."

Lajide looked up. "What?"

She opened her handbag, took out a bundle of papers. For three days she had been carrying these papers. "Do you know Messrs Tade and Burkle?"

"Timber dealers? Yes, I know them."

"They're planning to put you to court." He looked surprised, and she added: "They say you altered the marks on some timber they sold to an American firm—"

"Ah! But I bought the timber from them . . ."

"You have altered the marks and put your own marks." She waved the papers. "These are the real receipts of the actual buyers."

Lajide smiled. "You got those from Tade and Burkle. Never mind. Let them put me to court. I have my own receipts too. Two hundred tons of timber at twenty-five pounds a ton. Is that all, Beatrice? Thank you. You have done well. I was annoyed with you at first for leaving me because of that transport lorry-driver. Yes, I know all about that. I have seen you in his lorry. But now, I see that it's me you love. Beatrice, won't you come back to me? I'll treat you well this time. That timber man is not better than I am."

Beatrice smiled. "Money is not everything. A man can have money and still not be a gentleman."

"I am a gentleman! More gentleman than Sango or the lorry-driver."

"You're mistaken. No gentleman calls himself by the name. Let people see your deeds and judge."

"Beatrice, you drive me to hell! I don't know what I see in you. With my position, and all my wives! What you're doing to me, is it good, Beatrice?"

She rose. "I must be going home now."

"Back to that man?"

"I just heard about Tade and Burkle and I thought to come and warn you. I don't want you to go to jail."

He moved near and held her hand. He must have caught a whiff of her perfume, for he tried to press his attentions on her.

"Not here, Lajide! Take your hands off! Now look what you've done to my clothes!"

She went to the long mirror and straightened her dress. "I'm going, Lajide. Good-bye!"

One thing she knew. Lajide would never be able to find those receipts. The fact was that Tade and Burkle had made a silly mistake. They had sold the mahogany logs to Lajide at a ridiculous price, only to discover that an American dealer was paying much better money for them. To protect themselves they had to recover Lajide's receipt, and to Beatrice had been assigned the task. Beatrice had been able to obtain the receipt from Lajide's clerk, but for days she could not get herself to take them to Messrs Tade and Burkle because she still felt a sense of loyalty to the financier. She decided to give him one last chance. If he would compromise on the Amusa Sango situation, she would not betray him.

On her way down the steps she paused at Sango's old room, then with firmer steps she walked into the street.

Beatrice was waiting for her taxi under the almond tree when the seven women made straight for her. She saw them coming but could not run for it. They beat her with fists, tore her clothes, scratched her skin till the paint and powder ran with blood and sweat. All the concentrated venom and fury, all the hatred which her open intrusion into their household had awakened—she had it all back in that devastating free-for-all.

"Come and see Lajide's mistress!" The cry was taken up all along Molomo Street, and in some ways it reminded them of the cries of "Thief! Thief!" that had greeted Aina when she emerged from Amusa Sango's room.

Beatrice screamed for help, but no help came. She fell to her knees and no one raised her. Kekere arrived, carrying a bowl. She dipped her hands into the contents and viciously rubbed them over Beatrice's eyes. Cayenne pepper! While the other wives held Beatrice down, Kekere rubbed the pepper into her nostrils, mouth, and—on an impulse—into her most private parts. Then and only then did they leave her to writhe and wriggle in shame and humiliation, disgraced, deprived of every vestige of attractiveness that had led their lord and master astray from them. She had received the treatment normally due to "the other woman."

When Lajide heard news of the beating-up he was angry, then miserable. He could not openly declare his support for Beatrice. In some ways he felt she had got her due. But he still loved her. Over and over again, he exclaimed: *"Women!"* with such an accent that those who knew all the facts felt sorry for him. He went into his bedroom, away from it all.

Somewhere in the compound of Twenty Molomo Street, his wives were chanting and wiggling their hips in triumph.

chapter fourteen

The invitation from Beatrice the Second was at least two weeks old. It had missed its way all round the world and finally found Sango.

"I shall dress up and just go; that's what I'll do," Sango murmured while knotting his tie.

His coat lay on the table beside the invitation. He had almost forgotten how nice it felt to be neatly dressed and to smell of talcum powder.

"Amusa, are you in?"

The question was followed by a knock and Aina came into the room.

"Aina! Who showed you my place?"

"You don't worry about me, so I say let me come and find you." She was enjoying his embarrassment.

"Very kind of you."

She sat down without being asked, familiarly, possessively. "Since I came out of prison, you don't care to send me anything."

"Like what?" Sango asked, straightening his tie.

"Twenty years is not for ever, Amusa. I have come out of jail. I didn't die there—"

"Come to the point, Aina. You always go round and round. Always. When you want paper for wrapping, you go round. When—"

"I want you to help me because . . . I am pregnant!"

"What!" All the drowsiness vanished from his eyes. Even First Trumpet got out of bed and opened the window. The bed was too narrow for one, but it was the only one in the room and he and Sango used it in turn. When they returned in the early hours of the morning after an all-night vigil at some den, they cared for little else than to crawl in there and remain till morning. This evening, Sango was sacrificing his usual all-night stand for the pleasure of Beatrice's company. He looked at Aina and said: "So you're pregnant. And you think I am the father—"

"Since *that night* at the beach, I have not been feeling well. I didn't want to come till I was sure."

"Enough!"

Sango did not wish to be reminded of that night when he had walked with her in the moonlight, when she had tried to be kind to him because his band had nowhere to go for practice.

"My mother is prepared to take you to court to claim damages if you refuse to marry me." She kept her eyes on him and smiled. "Perhaps you'll let us have about ten pounds to maintain ourselves till the child is born."

"At a time like this! And you have the guts to smile. Oh, what a fool I've been!"

"But everybody knows you're my lover, Amusa; it's only you that keep making a fuss. What's in it, after all?"

"So every time I raise my head in the world, every time I collect a few hard-earned pounds, you, Aina, come and stand in my way—with a new misfortune! Look, do you know this is blackmail? I could take you to the police—they know your record."

"I'm not afraid of them. What do I care?"

Which was not the same for Sango. He cared for Beatrice the Second —so much that she must not sully her ears with this nonsense. And there was his mother to think of. He had heard nothing as yet from her. This was a bad situation, whichever way he looked at it. There was no way out.

"I'll give you what I can now, Aina. And I beg you to keep away from me—for good! The baby cannot be mine, and you know it! I'm helping you because . . . well, because of memories!"

She took the money—all he had saved—and First Trumpet turned as she was leaving.

"What are you going to do, Sango?"

"The child is not mine! Certainly not, and she knows it. If that girl continues to pester me, I shall . . ."

"Kill her? Then you'll hang. For such an irresponsible creature, too! The law doesn't ask about that. At the same time, you cannot afford a second scandal. Your mother, for instance: have you thought of her?"

"But I have no more money! Something must be done. I know she'll come again. Someone is behind this scheme!"

"We've got to think it over," said First Trumpet. "You'd better hurry. You're getting late for your appointment."

Sango thought First Trumpet sounded as if he himself were personally affected. He was a good friend.

"Ah—Mr Sango," said a grey-haired old man, rising. He was very much a part of the Brazilian-type house, one of the legacies of the early Portuguese invasion of the city. His handclasp was crushing for one of his age. Over his shoulder Sango could see large framed diplomas that proclaimed his membership of the *Ufemfe* society. "Sit down and make yourself at home. Beatrice and her mother will soon be here."

Sango walked on the welcoming carpets with some gravity. This was no rent-grabbing type of house but a real home. He felt uneasy in his stiff collar and bow tie. There was too much starch in his white coat so that it creaked like a rusty door every time he craned his neck to speak to Beatrice's father. He envied the man in his bright robes and handsome necklet of beads.

"I've been anxious to make your acquaintance since that day when you saved my daughter's life. She speaks highly of you."

Sango smiled. "She's a wonderful girl; I've never met anybody like her."

A servant entered, bearing a bowl of kola nuts. He set this down on the little table on which stood decanters and all kinds of drinks.

"Yes," said the old man, offering Sango a nut. "She's a wonderful girl! Just like her two sisters—they're married now. One married an engineer and the other a lawyer. Beatrice is the youngest and we dote on her. Yes, we do. But we can't keep her too long. Her fiancé, who is studying medicine at Edinburgh, is pressing for her to join him. It will break our hearts to lose her."

No words could have torn Sango's heart into more painful shreds. He lost all hope of ever winning Beatrice. He cursed himself for ever having linked his ambitions with hers.

Beatrice's mother had a beaming countenance that spelt happiness. She was plump, but her loose blouse and beautiful jewellery gave her a dignity that stirred all Sango's feelings for a home. She stood for a moment by the large velvet curtains, then came in and shook Sango's hand, warmly appraising him. At that moment all Sango's past despondency vanished and was replaced with a new desire: to be one of this proud family.

"So *you* are Amusa Sango! Welcome, thrice welcome!"

But if Sango had hoped to have Beatrice the Second to himself—even for two minutes—he was soon disillusioned. She came in a few moments before the meal was served: a younger edition of her mother—slighter of build, therefore looking taller. Less gold and jewellery about her throat and bare arms, and a haircut like a boy's. She smiled very sweetly when her eyes met Sango's but often he caught her in a brown study.

She sat on her father's right, while Sango sat on her mother's right and felt honoured but tantalized. They had *jolof* rice and smoked antelope. Beatrice's father was one of the few men in the city who believed in bush meat. He criticized the offerings of the butchers' stalls as "tough and stringy."

"How do you expect meat to taste good when the cattle walk eight hundred or more miles to the slaughter-house? I have my own hunter!"

He talked about his youth and the days when the Portuguese and the Brazilians, the French and the Dutch, the British and the Germans were fighting for trade supremacy on the West Coast of Africa.

"I was a small boy then, and never dreamed of marrying my wife. Now, after fifty-odd years of British rule, we hear talk of self-government."

He believed in the Realization Party, though people accused it of belonging to the "upper classes." And why not? Was he himself not of the upper classes? When, after a chieftaincy battle, he had fled across the mangrove swamps of the Gulf of Guinea to this city—all the way from Dahomey—had he not himself been a chief over thousands?

"I believe in the past," the old man said, when the meal was over. "It is when you know the past that you can appreciate the present. We need something like the Realization Party to preserve our kingship, our music, art and religion!"

"You have come with your old talk, Papa Beatrice! The young man wants to talk to Beatrice. Let us leave them to play music and talk in their own way."

Sango's ears stood open expectantly.

"Yes, Mama Beatrice, that is right. But this is a thinking young man— that is why I talk in this manner. Is that not so, Mr Sango? Are you tired of my company?"

"No, no, no! Not in the least. I enjoy listening to our history from a man who has lived through it!"

"Fine!" He smiled triumphantly and tapped his snuff-box. "In my days when a man went to marry a woman it was a family affair. For instance, this medical student who is engaged to Beatrice. I know his father and mother. They are people who matter. They can offer my daughter security. I am proud to link my name with theirs, and they in turn are flattered. People talk loosely of love! Lovers cannot exist in a vacuum but in a society. This society demands certain things of them . . ."

He went on, harping on his point till Sango became suspicious. This old man was trying to discourage him; but at the end of the evening, he was more resolved than ever to win her, obstacles notwithstanding.

When he got home he wrote to his mother about Beatrice. Then he took the first step towards reinstating himself in a job. He wrote to various government departments—the last thing he had vowed to do in his life. It was all a farce, and when later on the replies came to say there were no vacancies he was not surprised or disappointed. Now he was well and truly up against the city which attracted all types. He had been very smug in his job as crime reporter for the *West African Sensation*.

At night he stood in for other people in their own bands. His motto had become money, money, money. This was the way the people of the city realized themselves. Money. He saw the treachery, intrigue, and show of power involved. Sometimes he earned twenty shillings a night for blowing his trumpet within smelling distance of a wet and stinking drain. He discovered the haunts of the sailors whose ships had anchored off the lagoon for a mere five days.

In these dens the girls were slick with too much of everything: too much lipstick, so that their lips were either caked or too invitingly moist: too much hips, too much of their thighs showing beneath their unfashionable skirts, too much breast bursting the super-tight blouses.

"But I have to stick it," Sango murmured, and tightened his mind against the sordidness of his surroundings. "Beatrice the Second must never know my humiliation."

One evening, in the heat of jiving and jostling a white man slipped in. He was by no means the only white man there for most of the sailors were white, but this stranger had the rare look of a gentleman and was decidedly out of place. Where everyone had on a loud coat-type shirt outside pole-clinging trousers and pin-point shoes, he came in evening dress with the Savile Row cut, and worn in that way peculiar to the well-bred Englishman away from home. He certainly could not be expected to "dig" the others.

With due respect they gave him a seat in an isolated corner, and as he sat down, Sango saw his face: "Grunnings!"

A steward came towards him and took his order. When he returned with the drinks and cigarettes, Grunnings pointed at the dance floor. The steward nodded; then went over to a tall girl in red jeans and scarlet lipstick that contrasted rudely with her chocolate skin. He whispered in her ear. Some moments later, she was sitting opposite Grunnings and smoking his cigarettes.

She was such a contrast to the elegant Beatrice the First that Sango could not disguise his shock. What had become of Grunnings's taste? Had his desire for a bed-partner driven him to the lowest sex-market?

When Grunnings left, Sango learnt that he had come here in search of Beatrice the First. The girl in the red jeans said: "Why he come ask me? I be sister of the girl? Me don' know where she stay!"

Sango was touched. Grunnings had actually loved Beatrice the First— more than she knew or cared. His playing acquired a plaintive note, and before dawn he was too exhausted to do more than drag himself into bed. Over and over again, he thanked his stars that in this city he had a friend like First Trumpet. But for him, life as it now was would have been unbearable.

chapter fifteen

The railway platform was crowded with Muslims in robes and turbans who had come to welcome a pilgrim from Mecca. Sango strolled among them, but soon found a remote seat and brought out the telegram. He read it again:

A RELAPSE: COMING TO CITY FOR OPERATION.

It was from his mother and he was afraid this time. When the train arrived, Sango was admitted into the special compartment where she lay. Blue-grey light filtered into the air-conditioned cell, and as the door shut behind him the yelling, chattering and sobbing from the platform was switched out with a click.

"My son," she murmured.

She was very thin, but her skin was well preserved. In her face Sango could see a gentle rebuke in the helpless expression that suffering had given it. He was stimulated tenderly. He realized suddenly the deep bond that existed between him and her; and through her the customs that were of the older generation—like his having to marry Elina. All this flashed through his mind in one revealing moment as he gazed calmly on her face.

"You are well and strong?"

"Yes, mother."

It was all that concerned her. So long as he was well and strong, there was hope. He felt that hope surge through him. His troubles paled before her presence.

"Elina and her mother came with me. Have you seen them? They are in the third class."

This was awkward. It meant that his mother was tired of talk and had brought the girl with her to make sure that her son was now safely out of danger from the women of the city.

The stretcher-bearers did not leave them much longer. With care they took her out of the carriage and into the ambulance that waited outside the station. Sango caught a bus to the General Hospital to make sure how she was looked after and how things were fixed for the next few days. A nurse told him he could not go in, but he was satisfied that she was in C.6 and that her bed was screened away from curious eyes.

In the corridor he bumped into a fair-skinned girl chaperoned by an elderly woman.

"I'm Elina!"

"You!" She had grown from the scraggy, timid girl he had seen in the Eastern Greens into a kind of "poster" girl. No one advertising the Girl

Guide Movement or the Women's this or that service could afford to overlook her. She had an air of calm repose and confidence that put one at ease.

Sango explained how it was that he could not take them to his home. They were not used to hotels and restaurants either, and were frightened of the idea of going to eat and talk in public. Finally Sango suggested a seat by the lagoon; they could at least watch the canoes and the ocean liners moving about. At least for people who had been inland all the time the sea had its fascination.

They sat long on those benches talking, and eventually someone mentioned the dreaded word "marriage." Sango looked up sharply and said he was not planning to marry for the next ten years. There was something about Elina which made him feel she just did not "belong."

"Elina can go into the convent," Sango said. "The convent in this city is good enough and she'll learn quite a bit."

She shook her head. "Elina is going nowhere. She'll look after me and that's enough. I do not intend to let her out of my sight *in this city*!"

"I could stay here for ever watching the lagoon!" Elina said, and her mother looked at Sango triumphantly. "Didn't I tell you?" her eyes seemed to say. "This city is no good for a girl so young—unless, of course, she has a husband!"

He saw them home. They had arranged to stay with a relation till Sango's mother got well, and they would go back to the Eastern Greens. Their relation turned out to be a clerk in the Survey Department. With a wife and child he occupied two spacious rooms with a kitchen at the back. The quarters were clean and well planned for clerks in the civil service, but the occupants complained of being remote from the centre of things.

When Sango left them he went immediately to search for Beatrice the Second.

The junction of Jide and Molomo Streets was perhaps the most central spot in the whole city. Someone had once said that if you remained long enough in the barber's shop, you were bound to see the people who mattered in the city. On this morning, Sango sat down and revolved the chair so that he had eyes on the street. It was a dull morning, threatening, but never seeming to rain. The sun was invisible, but the air was cool and crisp without being sticky.

In the distance, Sango saw a lorry bearing the colourful letters:

TRAVEL TO GOLD COAST OVERLAND

He sat up. It was Kofi. He ran into the street, waving. The lorry slid clumsily to the left side of the road and stopped. Kofi came down.

"Sango, is that you?"

"What's wrong, Kofi? Where's Beatrice? Why are your eyes so red?"

He took out a handkerchief and pressed it to his eyes. Sango was embarrassed. The poor man was weeping.

"Dead . . . she died last week." He coughed and blew. "And what pains me most . . . she was buried as a pauper. No one to claim her. I—I——" He could say no more.

They crossed the street to the barber's shop. Kofi found a seat. He was breathing deeply as though trying to compose his feelings.

"I have often asked, why do girls leave their happy homes and come here on their own? No brothers, no knowledge of anything, no hope . . . They just come to the city, hoping that some man will pick them up and make them into something. Not just one man. You can't find him at the right time. But *many men*. And some disease, something incurable picks them up. You see them dressed, and they are just shells. Hollow and sick . . ." He did not lift his head as he talked.

"But she was happy with you, Kofi! When I saw you on that day, you were just returning from the Gold Coast—"

"That's what you saw. We looked happy. You did not understand what was underneath. How could you? The girl was finished, man." He looked up and Sango could not bear to see his red eyes. "Finished, I say. I was trying to help her back. She was finished, I tell you; and I was the last man, and too late. The helping hand had come too late. Look, man to man, I have my own wife at home on the Gold Coast, and I rent a house here. And these your girls, I can't resist them! They're too beautiful. And I can't bring my own wife here. Of course she does not know about Beatrice, how can she? But now I must stop all that nonsense; it is not sweet when you lose a woman you love. You know, I did not know I could love her. It was a business arrangement, pure and simple."

He stared into the street. A woman carrying oranges swung her hips and made eyes. She had balanced the oranges precariously and was peeling one. Kofi looked at her, then turned to Sango.

"Tell me, why did she come to this city at all? Why did I have to know her?"

"I'll tell you why she came, Kofi. She was not content with poverty. Remember, not many people like to remain where fate has placed them. I have known the home of Beatrice. I can tell you. And if you have been there yourself, you would not condemn her actions. She was runing away from it."

Kofi shook his head slowly no less than a hundred times. The truth was sinking in. "But she threw her life away. The city eats many an innocent life like hers every year. It is a waste of our youth! It must stop."

Sango laughed. "Secret societies eat a lot more. But what do the People of the City care? Nothing whatever. They have created the flitter and they are content to live in it. Yes, yes. The irony of Fate. The strange turns of justice . . ."

Kofi was weeping again. If he continued in this manner he would never be able to see the road for tears. He sat with Sango and they talked and talked and still he wanted to know why Beatrice had come to the city. He would never be satisfied with any answer because he was not really seeking an answer, only venting his bitterness at the loss.

When Sango accompanied him across the street he was talking to himself like a man distracted. It was something very sad to see.

She rose when he entered; tied the cloth more firmly about her hips, swelling out her breasts as she did so. She walked vainly to the table, poured herself a glass of water. There was a time when Sango would have thought the dimples at the back of her knees nice and soft, but not now. When she turned and faced him he recognized her for what she was—the dark temptress who was such a threat to his happiness, especially now that his mother was here.

"What are you doing here, Aina?"

"No need to shout, Sango. I've come to rest. I'm short of money, so I came."

"Short of money? Is this the bank? And did I not give you some money a short time ago?"

"Five pounds will not last for ever. I tried to manage it, but I have a lot of things to buy, to prepare myself for the coming baby—"

"Quickly now! I don't want you here again!"

Nothing showed the condition she claimed to be in; in fact, if anything, she had grown more attractive. Sango admitted this grudgingly and at the same time decided what he must do. It must have shown in his eyes.

"Amusa, why do you look at me so? You frighten me with your eyes! Oh, let me go before you kill me!"

"Quickly!"

"I beg you—let me tie my wrapper properly before entering the street." She was at the door.

"Aina, come back! You silly fool."

He moved quickly and seized her garment from the rear. He heard it wrench. All the pent-up madness snapped in his brain and he slapped her face till his hands hurt.

"Let me go!" she cried.

In her panic she was clawing and biting noisily, and as she wrenched herself free, Sango saw with alarm how she held her sides in pain. Her knees buckled . . . she collapsed and fell. Incredible! He had not hurt her, surely! A thousand fears raced through his brain. He was in real panic. Suppose she died in this room?

When First Trumpet returned, Aina was still in a coma, and there was much water on the floor of the room. All the savagery had now died out of Sango and he wondered how she had provoked him into such brutality.

"What have you done?" First Trumpet moaned in dismay. "Now we're both in the soup."

"My nerves! I must have lost my head."

"I know a private doctor," said First Trumpet. "I'm going to fetch some help."

Sango heard him later in the street hailing a taxi.

He could not decide whether to be pleased or sorry, for Aina was having a miscarriage. That she was in great pain he knew and did not like to contemplate the degree of her suffering. At the same time he did not completely forget the unsatisfied desire to avenge the injustice he had suffered at her hands. He was glad she might live, glad she had not involved him in a sensational accident.

He prayed that Aina would live. If she did, he vowed once and for all to end this evil relationship with the temptress who always awakened the meanest traits in him. Ultimately everything would depend on Aina's not passing away during this misfortune, because everything could easily be traced back to that quarrel. The lawyers (who had not been present) would describe in detail how Sango—"all six feet of him, and he's not a weakling either"—had brutally assaulted this girl of delicate and feeble build . . . No! A disheartening picture which he did not like to pursue. On the other hand, if she lived, her mother might want to claim damages. She was that kind of shrewd woman who pressed her rights to the very end.

At visiting time he called at the shady little hospital accompanied by Beatrice the Second. They waited for a moment in the sitting-room overlooking a congested drain.

"You've come to see Aina," said a nurse, opening the door. "Come in —but only for a few minutes. The patient must not be disturbed. Please do not wake her. I believe she's asleep. Follow me."

She closed the door behind them. There was only one chair in the room. Beatrice sat on it. The air was close and antiseptic. There was so much white linen around that Aina looked like a saint. She was very pale.

"Look," said Beatrice. "She's stirring. We promised—"

Aina's eyes flickered open. "Sango, my love. Are you here? Hold my hand."

Beatrice looked awkwardly at them both. "Go on, Sango. Hold her hand."

"What have you brought me?" Aina said, seizing Sango's extended hand.

"Fruits," said Beatrice. She raised the basket for Aina to see.

"Sango, who is this girl? Your new wife? The one you went to marry in the Eastern Greens?"

"We're not married—yet!"

"You can marry now. What are you waiting for? You see, Amusa, we girls love you so much. I don't know why. You do not treat us so well, but we love you. I wanted you to marry me. And this girl, it is in her eyes."

Sango found the room particularly hot at that moment. He did not know where to turn his gaze. "You're weak, Aina. Don't worry yourself too much—"

Aina began to sob. "The women go for you, and you only hurt them as you hurt me . . ." She was sobbing loudly now.

The nurse came in. "You must leave now." She was angry. "Didn't you promise not to wake her? Next time—"

On the street, Beatrice held Sango's hand. "You know something: what this girl said is true. The girls go for you. I am very worried myself. Recently, I have been feeling very lonely when you're not with me. I can't concentrate. I do things I have never done before—like telling lies to my father so that they don't know I've come to see you . . ."

Sango was beside himself with joy. There was hope for him, then! He did not want to dwell on it because he did not see how Beatrice could ever be his—with all that family matchmaking her father had talked about.

"Have courage, Amusa. All will be well for you—and for me!"

"Good night, dear B."

He stood on the street corner until she climbed the steps of her father's house.

Sango was told by a nurse in a white mask and rubber gloves that visitors were not allowed anywhere near the theatre. Everything would be all right, she said, and he need not worry.

He walked in the hospital garden among the mango trees. If only he could go in there and see his mother. No. That would not do. It would make Soye too self-conscious. Soye had said. "I'll do my best for you," and that was good enough. Soye was a brilliant surgeon, one of the few select Africans with an F.R.C.S. to his name. Still, he was no god. He could still be handicapped by lack of facilities.

He went back to the waiting-room. There was a girl in a pale blue frock sitting at the other end of the bench. It was no time to notice girls, but Sango's heart began to race much faster. And when the girl turned her face, he was sure.

"Beatrice! Beatrice the Second!"

"Oh, Amusa! How's your mother?"

He could not believe his eyes. Beatrice the Second had a sad tale to tell. Her fiancé, around whom she had built all her plans, had been flown back home from England. His condition was critical. He had been found in a gas-filled chamber at the hostel soon after the results of his examination had been announced. Of course he had always been of a brooding temperament, taking things far too seriously. Beatrice told how his greatest ambition had always been to be a doctor and how he had worked far too hard with far too little success. Beatrice was too distressed to speak about her problems in full. Nor did Sango question her too closely. It was enough to know that they were partners in sorrow. A nurse called Beatrice into one of the wards.

Hours later, it seemed, Dr Soye came out. One glance at his face and Sango knew the worst. The doctor pressed his hand.

"Very sorry; she was getting so well before the relapse."

Relapse . . . relapse . . . the ugly word again. He could not make out exactly what was happening in the tottering world around him. Everybody was having a relapse. The nurse in spotless white was smilingly telling him how sorry she was. Beatrice was holding his hand, leaning close to him.

"Had you come when you got the message?" said the nurse.

"What message? This is just a routine visit. Nobody told me anything."

"Your mother wanted to see you," said the nurse. "Of course, that was shortly after the woman left her bedside."

"I know of no woman. Can you describe her?"

The world began to reel round in circles. Sango put the pieces together as she spoke and the pieces made only one picture: Aina's mother. The blackmailing woman of the tempting daughter. God alone knew what she had told the poor woman to bring about the relapse that killed her.

Hand in hand, he and Beatrice walked down the corridor. "Who was the woman, I mean the visitor?"

"Later on, Beatrice. Later on." Before they parted he said, "I'm going to be busy with arrangements. Can you come to the funeral? Tomorrow at four."

He saw the tears in her eyes and did not wait for an answer.

Sango had no pretext on which to enter Twenty Molomo Street. Not now, after all that had happened. All he could do in his off moments was to go there and sit in the barber's shop. It was always restful and anyone who sat there saw the city unroll before his eyes, a cinema show that never ended, that no producer could ever capture—the very soul of man.

It was his old boy Sam who told him that Lajide had drunk himself to death. "Yes sah! He die wonderful death. Everybody wonder how he die . . . they don' know what ah know. The man drink too much! Gin—every time. O.H.M.S.—illicit gin, the one they make in the bus."

Lajide's end had come suddenly. Like this—he got up in the morning, put on some clothes. He was to go to court that morning. Then he complained that he felt queer. He stretched himself on the bed, fell into a coma and was taken to hospital. There he passed peacefully away without ever recovering consciousness.

The thought of death terrified him. I must see Aina tonight at *that* address. The words hammered in his brain. Tonight, at that address. Who knows—perhaps she's dead! There's too much death now among the people of the city. It is as if they have all played at the big cinema show and are coming to its conclusion. After seeing Aina, if she's still alive, I must play at *that* wretched Club. They'll now pay only seventeen and six a night. Still, I must recover my funeral expenses.

Sam was telling him about a brother of Lajide's—a farmer who had a limp and rode a bicycle. A bicycle—when Lajide changed cars once a year. The whole compound was locked and bolted and all the wives had gone home to their mothers. With a sly wink Sam explained how the wives had refused to be taken over by the limping brother.

"Ha, ha! He take all his brother's things; but he no fit to take the wives!"

As they spoke a man riding a bicycle dismounted and began to limp toward the entrance.

"Tha's him, sah. Tha's Lajide's brother."

Not long after that, a car which looked like Zamil's drew up. A Lebanese in dark glasses strode towards Number Twenty, brought out a bundle of keys and let himself in, followed by Lajide's brother.

"Them say he done sell him brother house," Sam whispered. All the people in the street seemed to have gathered, and though it was no business of theirs they were whispering and pointing and watching every move.

Sango would always love Molomo Street. Nothing could ever be secret here, and it made nonsense of taking life too seriously. They were all—

each and every one of them—members of one family, and what concerned one concerned all the others.

chapter sixteen

Because Beatrice the Second had lost her fiancé, because she had tried once—unsuccessfully—to run away from home, because her mother thought the girl was old enough at twenty-two to marry whom she chose and her father could not bear the thought of his illustrious name soiled by a scandal, because the name "Amusa Sango" had rung in the ears of father and mother every minute for the last six months (banned though it had been), because of all this and much more, it was decided that the wedding should take place as quietly as possible.

Sango did not waste much time. The old man's whims were unpredictable and he could withdraw his consent at any moment. Beatrice had again affirmed her desire that her life be Sango's with no further delay.

They took a special licence at Sant Amko's magistrate's court, and the reception was held at Jogun Lane, where Beatrice's parents lived.

Sango's old friends came in their remaining force: the barber, limping as usual, casting curious eyes at Aina and her mother. "Ah-ah! But Mr Sango," he whispered in an aside. "Why you don' marry Aina? The gal like you too much. Why you don' marry her?"

Sango merely smiled. If only the barber knew the depth and complications of their relationships! If only he knew what Sango had escaped by that fleeting love affair begun under the shadows of Molomo Street!

But God must be praised for bringing back Aina's life. The private doctor had done his bit, of course, and had got his pay. But it had been precarious. That borderline between life and death: Aina had hovered on it threateningly for many a soul-searing night. If she had crossed, who would have believed that he never meant to harm her in the first place? Or that the child she had, belonged to another man? Who—in this wide city?

He looked at her. She was smiling. Still pale, her coming here showed that she was a sport, a good loser. Perhaps life had taught her that: perhaps she still hoped . . . The gramophone was playing and those who felt happier than Sango were dancing and drinking beer.

These did not include the father of Beatrice, who sat like a statue, apparently moaning his loss. Now and again he eyed Sango challengingly—a challenge Sango vowed in his young heart to accept in the smallest detail. It was not only those who were born into high society who became somebody. Sure, they began with a bigger advantage, but that did not mean they ended with their breasts against the winning tape.

"I'll show him. Or rather—we'll show him!"

And he looked at the face of Beatrice and from it drew all the courage he desired. At his request she had put on a cool blue frock—simple, without frills. He knew her preference for native wear which added a little more fullness to her figure and with it a little more dignity.

Elina and her mother must be far away now. They had caught the first train to the Eastern Greens and would probably almost be there. Sango wondered why he thought of them at this moment. And he wondered too, what it would have been like to see Elina sitting at a sewing-machine in that room with the lace curtains, idly making a dress while around her sat her friends, sipping lime-juice and eating chicken, a mixture of bashfulness, joy and sorrow.

"Amusa! Amusa!" It was Beatrice.

On hearing the happiness in her voice, everyone seemed to feel her longing for the man she loved. And they began to leave.

In the corridor, Sango found himself face to face with Aina's mother.

"Sango, your mother was a wonderful woman. She loved you so much! Do you know she died of *happiness*? When she heard you were to be a father, she was so glad. She said, 'Thank God, he is becoming something at last.' So she said, and I swear to you I am speaking the truth. She told me to fetch you at once, that she might see you. She was very glad! But I didn't know where to find you then. You must forgive me, Sango," she said and pressed the edge of her cloth to her eyes. "You see, I went there to spoil your name before your mother. Because of Aina. But your mother was above it all!"

Sango saw her to the door. Aina stood there, crestfallen. There were genuine tears in her eyes and a hint of rebuke. She had broken down at last. Sango looked at her, embarrassed.

"Travel to Gold Coast, Overland!"

"Kofi! Hello, Kofi. You just coming when everybody is leaving!"

"Travel to Gold Coast Overland," said the boisterous man. "Come with me, and bring your bride."

"Who told you, Kofi?" said Sango.

"There's no secret in this city. You took a special licence, and you tried to hide yourself. You think no one will know . . . Listen, Amusa. I'm all right now. I've recovered from the loss of my Nigerian girl friend. I'm not so sad as last time when we met. It was horrible then."

Sango looked at Beatrice and smiled. "Our secret is out, B!"

"Let's go to the Gold Coast. I have always wanted to go there." There was a plea in Beatrice's voice.

"Yes. We want a new life, new opportunities . . . We want to live there for some time—but only for some time! We have our homeland here and must come back when we can answer your father's challenge! When we have *done* something, *become* something!"

"Travel to Gold Coast Overland! By Kofi Transport! It is safe, sure and slow." Kofi by now had a glass of beer in his hand and was behaving as though the contents had taken effect. "But it will get you there—in peace."

"Not in pieces," Beatrice and Sango laughed together.

Beatrice had slipped her hand under Sango's arm. "Amusa, let's snatch happiness from life *now*—now, when we're both young and need each other." She was smiling and her eyes searched his face.

Yet contradicting that smile was the tiny pearl of a tear which he saw stealing down her cheek. He embraced her tenderly, murmuring into her hair.

"God bless you—and *us*!"

GARCIA MARQUEZ

no one writes to the colonel

The colonel took the top off the coffee can and saw that there was only one little spoonful left. He removed the pot from the fire, poured half the water onto the earthen floor, and scraped the inside of the can with a knife until the last scrapings of the ground coffee, mixed with bits of rust, fell into the pot.

When he was waiting for it to boil, sitting next to the stone fireplace with an attitude of confident and innocent expectation, the colonel experienced the feeling that fungus and poisonous lilies were taking root in his gut. It was October. A difficult morning to get through, even for a man like himself, who had survived so many mornings like this one. For nearly sixty years—since the end of the last civil war—the colonel had done nothing else but wait. October was one of the few things which arrived.

His wife raised the mosquito netting when she saw him come into the bedroom with the coffee. The night before she had suffered an asthma attack, and now she was in a drowsy state. But she sat up to take the cup.

"And you?" she said.

"I've had mine," the colonel lied. "There was still a big spoonful left."

The bells began ringing at that moment. The colonel had forgotten the funeral. While his wife was drinking her coffee, he unhooked the hammock at one end, and rolled it up on the other, behind the door. The woman thought about the dead man.

"He was born in 1922," she said. "Exactly a month after our son. April 7th."

She continued sipping her coffee in the pauses of her gravelly breathing. She was scarcely more than a bit of white on an arched, rigid spine.

Her disturbed breathing made her put her questions as assertions. When she finished her coffee, she was still thinking about the dead man.

"It must be horrible to be buried in October," she said. But her husband paid no attention. He opened the window. October had moved in on the patio. Contemplating the vegetation, which was bursting out in intense greens, and the tiny mounds the worms made in the mud, the colonel felt the sinister month again in his intestines.

"I'm wet through to the bones," he said.

"It's winter," the woman replied. "Since it began raining I've been telling you to sleep with your socks on."

"I've been sleeping with them for a week."

It rained gently but ceaselessly. The colonel would have preferred to wrap himself in a wool blanket and get back into the hammock. But the insistence of the cracked bells reminded him about the funeral. "It's October," he whispered, and walked toward the center of the room. Only then did he remember the rooster tied to the leg of the bed. It was a fighting cock.

After taking the cup into the kitchen, he wound the pendulum clock in its carved wooden case in the living room. Unlike the bedroom, which was too narrow for an asthmatic's breathing, the living room was large, with four sturdy rockers around a little table with a cover and a plaster cat. On the wall opposite the clock, there was a picture of a woman dressed in tulle, surrounded by cupids in a boat laden with roses.

It was seven-twenty when he finished winding the clock. Then he took the rooster into the kitchen, tied it to a leg of the stove, changed the water in the can, and put a handful of corn next to it. A group of children came in through a hole in the fence. They sat around the rooster, to watch it in silence.

"Stop looking at that animal," said the colonel. "Roosters wear out if you look at them so much."

The children didn't move. One of them began playing the chords of a popular song on his harmonica. "Don't play that today," the colonel told him. "There's been a death in town." The child put the instrument in his pants pocket, and the colonel went into the bedroom to dress for the funeral.

Because of his wife's asthma, his white suit was not pressed. So he had to wear the old black suit which since his marriage he used only on special occasions. It took some effort to find it in the bottom of the trunk, wrapped in newspapers and protected against moths with little balls of naphthalene. Stretched out in bed, the woman was still thinking about the dead man.

"He must have met Agustín already," she said. "Maybe he won't tell him about the situation we've been left in since his death."

"At this moment they're probably talking roosters," said the colonel.

He found an enormous old umbrella in the trunk. His wife had won it in a raffle held to collect funds for the colonel's party. That same night they had attended an outdoor show which was not interrupted despite the rain. The colonel, his wife, and their son, Agustín—who was then eight—watched the show until the end, seated under the umbrella. Now Agustín was dead, and the bright satin material had been eaten away by the moths.

"Look what's left of our circus clown's umbrella," said the colonel with one of his old phrases. Above his head a mysterious system of little metal rods opened. "The only thing it's good for now is to count the stars."

He smiled. But the woman didn't take the trouble to look at the umbrella. "Everything's that way," she whispered. "We're rotting alive." And she closed her eyes so she could concentrate on the dead man.

After shaving himself by touch—since he'd lacked a mirror for a long time—the colonel dressed silently. His trousers, almost as tight on his legs as long underwear, closed at the ankles with slip-knotted drawstrings, were held up at the waist by two straps of the same material which passed through two gilt buckles sewn on at kidney height. He didn't use a belt. His shirt, the color of old Manila paper, and as stiff, fastened with a copper stud which served at the same time to hold the detachable collar. But the detachable collar was torn, so the colonel gave up on the idea of a tie.

He did each thing as if it were a transcendent act. The bones in his hands were covered by taut, translucent skin, with light spots like the skin on his neck. Before he put on his patent-leather shoes, he scraped the dried mud from the stitching. His wife saw him at that moment, dressed as he was on their wedding. Only then did she notice how much her husband had aged.

"You look as if you're dressed for some special event," she said.

"This burial is a special event," the colonel said. "It's the first death from natural causes which we've had in many years."

The weather cleared up after nine. The colonel was getting ready to go out when his wife seized him by the sleeve of his coat.

"Comb your hair," she said.

He tried to subdue his steel-colored, bristly hair with a bone comb. But it was a useless attempt.

"I must look like a parrot," he said.

The woman examined him. She thought he didn't. The colonel didn't look like a parrot. He was a dry man, with solid bones articulated as if with nuts and bolts. Because of the vitality in his eyes, it didn't seem as if he were preserved in formalin.

"You're fine that way," she admitted, and added, when her husband was leaving the room: "Ask the doctor if we poured boiling water on him in this house."

They lived at the edge of town, in a house with a palm-thatched roof and walls whose whitewash was flaking off. The humidity kept up but the rain had stopped. The colonel went down toward the plaza along an alley with houses crowded in on each other. As he came out into the main street, he shivered. As far as the eye could see, the town was carpeted with flowers. Seated in their doorways, the women in black were waiting for the funeral.

In the plaza it began to drizzle again. The proprietor of the pool hall saw the colonel from the door of his place and shouted to him with open arms:

"Colonel, wait, and I'll lend you an umbrella!"

The colonel replied without turning around.

"Thank you. I'm all right this way."

The funeral procession hadn't come out of church yet. The men—dressed in white with black ties—were talking in the low doorway under their umbrellas. One of them saw the colonel jumping between the puddles in the plaza.

"Get under here, friend!" he shouted.

He made room under the umbrella.

"Thanks, friend," said the colonel.

But he didn't accept the invitation. He entered the house directly to give his condolences to the mother of the dead man. The first thing he perceived was the odor of many different flowers. Then the heat rose. The colonel tried to make his way through the crowd which was jammed into the bedroom. But someone put a hand on his back, pushed him toward the back of the room through a gallery of perplexed faces to the spot where—deep and wide open—the nostrils of the dead man were found.

There was the dead man's mother, shooing the flies away from the coffin with a plaited palm fan. Other women, dressed in black, contemplated the body with the same expression with which one watches the current of a river. All at once a voice started up at the back of the room. The colonel put one woman aside, faced the profile of the dead man's mother, and put a hand on her shoulder.

"I'm so sorry," he said.

She didn't turn her head. She opened her mouth and let out a howl. The colonel started. He felt himself being pushed against the corpse by a shapeless crowd which broke out in a quavering outcry. He looked for a firm support for his hands but couldn't find the wall. There were other bodies in its place. Someone said in his ear, slowly, with a very gentle voice, "Careful, Colonel." He spun his head around and was face to face with the dead man. But he didn't recognize him because he was stiff and dynamic and seemed as disconcerted as he, wrapped in white cloths and with his trumpet in his hands. When the colonel raised his head over the shouts, in search of air, he saw the closed box bouncing toward the door down a slope of flowers which distintegrated against the walls. He perspired. His joints ached. A moment later he knew he was in the street because the drizzle hurt his eyelids, and someone seized him by the arm and said:

"Hurry up, friend, I was waiting for you."

It was Sabas, the godfather of his dead son, the only leader of his party who had escaped political persecution and had continued to live in town. "Thanks, friend," said the colonel, and walked in silence under the umbrella. The band struck up the funeral march. The colonel noticed the lack of a trumpet, and for the first time was certain that the dead man was dead.

"Poor man," he murmured.

Sabas cleared his throat. He held the umbrella in his left hand, the handle almost at the level of his head, since he was shorter than the colonel. They began to talk when the cortege left the plaza. Sabas turned toward the colonel then, his face disconsolate, and said:

"Friend, what's new with the rooster?"

"He's still there," the colonel replied.

At that moment a shout was heard:

"Where are they going with that dead man?"

The colonel raised his eyes. He saw the Mayor on the balcony of the barracks in an expansive pose. He was dressed in his flannel underwear; his unshaven cheek was swollen. The musicians stopped the march. A moment later the colonel recognized Father Angel's voice shouting at the Mayor. He made out their dialogue through the drumming of the rain on the umbrella.

"Well?" asked Sabas.

"Well nothing," the colonel replied. "The burial may not pass in front of the police barracks."

"I had forgotten," exclaimed Sabas. "I always forget that we are under martial law."

"But this isn't a rebellion," the colonel said. "It's a poor dead musician."

The cortege changed direction. In the poor neighborhoods the women watched it pass, biting their nails in silence. But then they came out into the middle of the street and sent up shouts of praise, gratitude, and farewell, as if they believed the dead man was listening to them inside the coffin. The colonel felt ill at the cemetery. When Sabas pushed him toward the wall to make way for the men who were carrying the dead man, he turned his smiling face toward him, but met a rigid countenance.

"What's the matter, friend?" Sabas asked.

The colonel sighed.

"It's October."

They returned by the same street. It had cleared. The sky was deep, intensely blue. It won't rain any more, thought the colonel, and he felt better, but he was still dejected. Sabas interrupted his thoughts.

"Have a doctor examine you."

"I'm not sick," the colonel said. "The trouble is that in October I feel as if I had animals in my gut."

Sabas went "Ah." He said goodbye at the door to his house, a new building, two stories high, with wrought-iron window gratings. The colonel headed for his home, anxious to take off his dress suit. He went out again a moment later to the store on the corner to buy a can of coffee and half a pound of corn for the rooster.

The colonel attended to the rooster in spite of the fact that on Thursday he would have preferred to stay in his hammock. It didn't clear for several days. During the course of the week, the flora in his belly blossomed. He spent several sleepless nights, tormented by the whistling of the asthmatic woman's lungs. But October granted a truce on Friday afternoon. Agustín's companions—workers from the tailor shop, as he had been, and cockfight fanatics—took advantage of the occasion to examine the rooster. He was in good shape.

The colonel returned to the bedroom when he was left alone in the house with his wife. She had recovered.

"What do they say?" she asked.

"Very enthusiastic," the colonel informed her. "Everyone is saving their money to bet on the rooster."

"I don't know what they see in such an ugly rooster," the woman said. "He looks like a freak to me; his head is too tiny for his feet."

"They say he's the best in the district," the colonel answered. "He's worth about fifty pesos."

He was sure that this argument justified his determination to keep the rooster, a legacy from their son who was shot down nine months before at the cockfights for distributing clandestine literature. "An expensive illusion," the woman said. "When the corn is gone we'll have to feed him on our own livers." The colonel took a good long time to think, while he was looking for his white ducks in the closet.

"It's just for a few months," he said. "We already know that there will be fights in January. Then we can sell him for more."

The pants needed pressing. The woman stretched them out over the stove with two irons heated over the coals.

"What's your hurry to go out?" she asked.

"The mail."

"I had forgotten that today is Friday," she commented, returning to the bedroom. The colonel was dressed but pantsless. She observed his shoes.

"Those shoes are ready to throw out," she said. "Keep wearing your patent-leather ones."

The colonel felt desolate.

"They look like the shoes of an orphan," he protested. "Every time I put them on I feel like a fugitive from an asylum."

"We are the orphans of our son," the woman said.

This time, too, she persuaded him. The colonel walked toward the harbor before the whistles of the launches blew. Patent-leather shoes, beltless white ducks, and the shirt without the detachable collar, closed at the neck with the copper stud. He observed the docking of the launches from the shop of Moses the Syrian. The travelers got off, stiff from eight hours of immobility. The same ones as always: traveling salesmen, and people from the town who had left the preceding week and were returning as usual.

The last one was the mail launch. The colonel saw it dock with an anguished uneasiness. On the roof, tied to the boat's smokestacks and protected by an oilcloth, he spied the mailbag. Fifteen years of waiting had sharpened his intuition. The rooster had sharpened his anxiety. From the moment the postmaster went on board the launch, untied the bag, and hoisted it up on his shoulder, the colonel kept him in sight.

He followed him through the street parallel to the harbor, a labyrinth of stores and booths with colored merchandise on display. Every time he did it, the colonel experienced an anxiety very different from, but just as oppressive as, fright. The doctor was waiting for the newspapers in the post office.

"My wife wants me to ask you if we threw boiling water on you at our house," the colonel said.

He was a young physician with his skull covered by sleek black hair. There was something unbelievable in the perfection of his dentition. He asked after the health of the asthmatic. The colonel supplied a detailed report without taking his eyes off the postmaster, who was distributing the letters into cubbyholes. His indolent way of moving exasperated the colonel.

The doctor received his mail with the packet of newspapers. He put the pamphlets of medical advertising to one side. Then he scanned his personal letters. Meanwhile the postmaster was handing out mail to those who were present. The colonel watched the compartment which corresponded to his letter in the alphabet. An air-mail letter with blue borders increased his nervous tension.

The doctor broke the seal on the newspapers. He read the lead items while the colonel—his eyes fixed on the little box—waited for the post-master to stop in front of it. But he didn't. The doctor interrupted his reading of the newspapers. He looked at the colonel. Then he looked at the postmaster seated in front of the telegraph key, and then again at the colonel.

"We're leaving," he said.

The postmaster didn't raise his head.

"Nothing for the colonel," he said.

The colonel felt ashamed.

"I wasn't expecting anything," he lied. He turned to the doctor with an entirely childish look. "No one writes to me."

They went back in silence. The doctor was concentrating on the newspapers. The colonel with his habitual way of walking which resembled that of a man retracing his steps to look for a lost coin. It was a bright afternoon. The almond trees in the plaza were shedding their last rotted leaves. It had begun to grow dark when they arrived at the door of the doctor's office.

"What's in the news?" the colonel asked.

The doctor gave him a few newspapers.

"No one knows," he said. "It's hard to read between the lines which the censor lets them print."

The colonel read the main headlines. International news. At the top, across four columns, a report on the Suez Canal. The front page was almost completely covered by paid funeral announcements.

"There's no hope of elections," the colonel said.

"Don't be naïve, Colonel," said the doctor. "We're too old now to be waiting for the Messiah."

The colonel tried to give the newspapers back, but the doctor refused them.

"Take them home with you," he said. "You can read them tonight and return them tomorrow."

A little after seven the bells in the tower rang out the censor's movie classifications. Father Angel used this means to announce the moral classification of the film in accordance with the ratings he received every month by mail. The colonel's wife counted twelve bells.

"Unfit for everyone," she said. "It's been about a year now that the movies are bad for everyone."

She lowered the mosquito netting and murmured, "The world is corrupt." But the colonel made no comment. Before lying down, he tied the rooster to the leg of the bed. He locked the house and sprayed some insecticide in the bedroom. Then he put the lamp on the floor, hung his hammock up, and lay down to read the newspapers.

He read them in chronological order, from the first page to the last, including the advertisements. At eleven the trumpet blew curfew. The colonel finished his reading a half-hour later, opened the patio door on the impenetrable night, and urinated, besieged by mosquitoes, against the wall studs. His wife was awake when he returned to the bedroom.

"Nothing about the veterans?" she asked.

"Nothing," said the colonel. He put out the lamp before he got into the hammock. "In the beginning at least they published the list of the new pensioners. But it's been about five years since they've said anything."

It rained after midnight. The colonel managed to get to sleep but woke up a moment later, alarmed by his intestines. He discovered a leak in some part of the roof. Wrapped in a wool blanket up to his ears, he tried to find the leak in the darkness. A trickle of cold sweat slipped down his spine. He had a fever. He felt as if he were floating in concentric circles inside a tank of jelly. Someone spoke. The colonel answered from his revolutionist's cot.

"Who are you talking to?" asked his wife.

"The Englishman disguised as a tiger who appeared at Colonel Aureliano Buendía's camp," the colonel answered. He turned over in his hammock, burning with his fever. "It was the Duke of Marlborough."

The sky was clear at dawn. At the second call for Mass, he jumped from the hammock and installed himself in a confused reality which was agitated by the crowing of the rooster. His head was still spinning in concentric circles. He was nauseous. He went out into the patio and headed for the privy through the barely audible whispers and the dark odors of winter. The inside of the little zinc-roofed wooden compartment was rarefied by the ammonia smell from the privy. When the colonel raised the lid, a triangular cloud of flies rushed out of the pit.

It was a false alarm. Squatting on the platform of unsanded boards, he felt the uneasiness of an urge frustrated. The oppressiveness was substituted by a dull ache in his digestive tract. "There's no doubt," he murmured. "It's the same every October." And again he assumed his posture of confident and innocent expectation until the fungus in his innards was pacified. Then he returned to the bedroom for the rooster.

"Last night you were delirious from fever," his wife said.

She had begun to straighten up the room, having recovered from a week-long attack. The colonel made an effort to remember.

"It wasn't fever," he lied. "It was the dream about the spider webs again."

As always happened, the woman emerged from her attack full of nervous energy. In the course of the morning she turned the house upside down. She changed the position of everything, except the clock and the picture of the young girl. She was so thin and sinewy that when she walked about in her cloth slippers and her black dress all buttoned up she seemed as if she had the power of walking through the walls. But before twelve she had regained her bulk, her human weight. In bed she was an empty space. Now, moving among the flowerpots of ferns and begonias, her presence overflowed the house. "If Agustín's year were up, I would start singing," she said while she stirred the pot where all the things to eat that the tropical land is capable of producing, cut into pieces, were boiling.

"If you feel like singing, sing," said the colonel. "It's good for your spleen."

The doctor came after lunch. The colonel and his wife were drinking coffee in the kitchen when he pushed open the street door and shouted: "Everybody dead?"

The colonel got up to welcome him.

"So it seems, Doctor," he said, going into the living room. "I've always said that your clock keeps time with the buzzards."

The woman went into the bedroom to get ready for the examination. The doctor stayed in the living room with the colonel. In spite of the heat, his immaculate linen suit gave off a smell of freshness. When the woman announced that she was ready, the doctor gave the colonel three sheets of paper in an envelope. He entered the bedroom, saying, "That's what the newspapers didn't print yesterday."

The colonel had assumed as much. It was a summary of the events in the country, mimeographed for clandestine circulation. Revelations about the state of armed resistance in the interior of the country. He felt defeated. Ten years of clandestine reports had not taught him that no news was more surprising than next month's news. He had finished reading when the doctor came back into the living room.

"This patient is healthier than I am," he said. "With asthma like that, I could live to be a hundred."

The colonel glowered at him. He gave him back the envelope without saying a word, but the doctor refused to take it.

"Pass it on," he said in a whisper.

The colonel put the envelope in his pants pocket. The woman came out of the bedroom, saying, "One of these days I'll up and die, and carry you with me, off to hell, Doctor." The doctor responded silently with the stereotyped enamel of his teeth. He pulled a chair up to the little table and took several jars of free samples out of his bag. The woman went on into the kitchen.

"Wait and I'll warm up the coffee."

"No, thank you very much," said the doctor. He wrote the proper dosage on a prescription pad. "I absolutely refuse to give you the chance to poison me."

She laughed in the kitchen. When he finished writing, the doctor read the prescription aloud, because he knew that no one could decipher his handwriting. The colonel tried to concentrate. Returning from the kitchen, the woman discovered in his face the toll of the previous night.

"This morning he had a fever," she said, pointing at her husband. "He spent about two hours talking nonsense about the civil war."

The colonel started.

"It wasn't a fever," he insisted, regaining his composure. "Furthermore," he said, "the day I feel sick I'll throw myself into the garbage can on my own."

He went into the bedroom to find the newspapers.

"Thank you for the compliment," the doctor said.

They walked together toward the plaza. The air was dry. The tar on the streets had begun to melt from the heat. When the doctor said goodbye, the colonel asked him in a low voice, his teeth clenched:

"How much do we owe you, Doctor?"

"Nothing, for now," the doctor said, and he gave him a pat on the shoulder. "I'll send you a fat bill when the cock wins."

The colonel went to the tailor shop to take the clandestine letter to Agustín's companions. It was his only refuge ever since his co-partisans had been killed or exiled from town and he had been converted into a man with no other occupation than waiting for the mail every Friday.

The afternoon heat stimulated the woman's energy. Seated among the begonias in the veranda next to a box of worn-out clothing, she was again working the eternal miracle of creating new apparel out of nothing. She made collars from sleeves, and cuffs from the backs and square patches, perfect ones, although with scraps of different colors. A cicada lodged its whistle in the patio. The sun faded. But she didn't see it go down over the begonias. She raised her head only at dusk when the colonel returned home. Then she clasped her neck with both hands, cracked her knuckles, and said:

"My head is as stiff as a board."

"It's always been that way," the colonel said, but then he saw his wife's body covered all over with scraps of color. "You look like a magpie."

"One has to be half a magpie to dress you," she said. She held out a shirt made of three different colors of material except for the collar and cuffs, which were the same color. "At the carnival all you have to do is take off your jacket."

The six-o'clock bells interrupted her. "The Angel of the Lord announced unto Mary," she prayed aloud, heading into the bedroom. The colonel talked to the children who had come to look at the rooster after school. Then he remembered that there was no corn for the next day, and entered the bedroom to ask his wife for money.

"I think there's only fifty cents," she said.

She kept the money under the mattress, knotted into the corner of a handkerchief. It was the proceeds of Agustín's sewing machine. For nine months, they had spent that money penny by penny, parceling it out between their needs and the rooster's. Now there were only two twenty-cent pieces and a ten-cent piece left.

"Buy a pound of corn," the woman said. "With the change, buy tomorrow's coffee and four ounces of cheese."

"And a golden elephant to hang in the doorway," the colonel went on. "The corn alone costs forty-two."

They thought a moment. "The rooster is an animal, and therefore he can wait," said the woman at first. But her husband's expression caused her to reflect. The colonel sat on the bed, his elbows on his knees, jingling the coins in his hands. "It's not for my sake," he said after a moment. "If it depended on me I'd make a rooster stew this very evening. A fifty-peso indigestion would be very good." He paused to squash a mosquito on his neck. Then his eyes followed his wife around the room.

"What bothers me is that those poor boys are saving up."

Then she began to think. She turned completely around with the insecticide bomb. The colonel found something unreal in her attitude, as if she were invoking the spirits of the house for a consultation. At last she put the bomb on the little mantel with the prints on it, and fixed her syrup-colored eyes on the syrup-colored eyes of the colonel.

"Buy the corn," she said. "God knows how we'll manage."

"This is the miracle of the multiplying loaves," the colonel repeated every time they sat down to the table during the following week. With her astonishing capacity for darning, sewing, and mending, she seemed to have discovered the key to sustaining the household economy with no money. October prolonged its truce. The humidity was replaced by sleepiness. Comforted by the copper sun, the woman devoted three afternoons to her complicated hairdo. "High Mass has begun," the colonel said one afternoon when she was getting the knots out of her long blue tresses with a comb which had some teeth missing. The second afternoon, seated in the patio with a white sheet in her lap, she used a finer comb to take out the lice which had proliferated during her attack. Lastly, she washed her hair with lavender water, waited for it to dry, and rolled it up on the nape of her neck in two turns held with a barrette. The colonel waited. At night, sleepless in his hammock, he worried for many hours over the rooster's fate. But on Wednesday they weighed him, and he was in good shape.

That same afternoon, when Agustín's companions left the house counting the imaginary proceeds from the rooster's victory, the colonel also felt in good shape. His wife cut his hair. "You've taken twenty years off me," he said, examining his head with his hands. His wife thought her husband was right.

"When I'm well, I can bring back the dead," she said.

But her conviction lasted for a very few hours. There was no longer anything in the house to sell, except the clock and the picture. Thursday night, at the limit of their resources, the woman showed her anxiety over the situation.

"Don't worry," the colonel consoled her. "The mail comes tomorrow."

The following day he waited for the launches in front of the doctor's office.

"The airplane is a marvelous thing," the colonel said, his eyes resting on the mailbag. "They say you can get to Europe in one night."

"That's right," the doctor said, fanning himself with an illustrated magazine. The colonel spied the postmaster among a group waiting for the docking to end so they could jump onto the launch. The postmaster jumped first. He received from the captain an envelope sealed with wax. Then he climbed up onto the roof. The mailbag was tied between two oil drums.

"But still it has its dangers," said the colonel. He lost the postmaster from sight, but saw him again among the colored bottles on the refreshment cart. "Humanity doesn't progress without paying a price."

"Even at this stage it's safer than a launch," the doctor said. "At twenty thousand feet you fly above the weather."

"Twenty thousand feet," the colonel repeated, perplexed, without being able to imagine what the figure meant.

The doctor became interested. He spread out the magazine with both hands until it was absolutely still.

"There's perfect stability," he said.

But the colonel was hanging on the actions of the postmaster. He saw him consume a frothy pink drink, holding the glass in his left hand. In his right he held the mailbag.

"Also, on the ocean there are ships at anchor in continual contact with night flights," the doctor went on. "With so many precautions it's safer than a launch."

The colonel looked at him.

"Naturally," he said. "It must be like a carpet."

The postmaster came straight toward them. The colonel stepped back, impelled by an irresistible anxiety, trying to read the name written on the sealed envelope. The postmaster opened the bag. He gave the doctor his packet of newspapers. Then he tore open the envelope with the personal correspondence, checked the correctness of the receipt, and read the addressee's names off the letters. The doctor opened the newspapers.

"Still the problem with Suez," he said, reading the main headlines. "The West is losing ground."

The colonel didn't read the headlines. He made an effort to control his stomach. "Ever since there's been censorship, the newspapers talk only about Europe," he said. "The best thing would be for the Europeans to come over here and for us to go to Europe. That way everybody would know what's happening in his own country."

"To the Europeans, South America is a man with a mustache, a guitar, and a gun," the doctor said, laughing over his newspaper. "They don't understand the problem."

The postmaster delivered his mail. He put the rest in the bag and closed it again. The doctor got ready to read two personal letters, but before tearing open the envelopes he looked at the colonel. Then he looked at the postmaster.

"Nothing for the colonel?"

The colonel was terrified. The postmaster tossed the bag onto his shoulder, got off the platform, and replied without turning his head:

"No one writes to the colonel."

Contrary to his habit, he didn't go directly home. He had a cup of coffee at the tailor's while Agustín's companions leafed through the newspapers. He felt cheated. He would have preferred to stay there until the next Friday to keep from having to face his wife that night with empty hands. But when the tailor shop closed, he had to face up to reality. His wife was waiting for him.

"Nothing?" she asked.

"Nothing," the colonel answered.

The following Friday he went down to the launches again. And, as on every Friday, he returned home without the longed-for letter. "We've waited long enough," his wife told him that night. "One must have the patience of an ox, as you do, to wait for a letter for fifteen years." The colonel got into his hammock to read the newspapers.

"We have to wait our turn," he said. "Our number is 1823."

"Since we've been waiting, that number has come up twice in the lottery," his wife replied.

The colonel read, as usual, from the first page to the last, including the advertisements. But this time he didn't concentrate. During his reading, he thought about his veteran's pension. Nineteen years before, when Congress passed the law, it took him eight years to prove his claim. Then it took him six more years to get himself included on the rolls. That was the last letter the colonel had received.

He finished after curfew sounded. When he went to turn off the lamp, he realized that his wife was awake.

"Do you still have that clipping?"

The woman thought.

"Yes. It must be with the other papers."

She got out of her mosquito netting and took a wooden chest out of the closet, with a packet of letters arranged by date and held together by a rubber band. She located the advertisement of a law firm which promised quick action on war pensions.

"We could have spent the money in the time I've wasted trying to convince you to change lawyers," the woman said, handing her husband the newspaper clipping. "We're not getting anything out of their putting us away on a shelf as they do with the Indians."

The colonel read the clipping dated two years before. He put it in the pocket of his jacket which was hanging behind the door.

"The problem is that to change lawyers you need money."

"Not at all," the woman said decisively. "You write them telling them to discount whatever they want from the pension itself when they collect it. It's the only way they'll take the case."

So Saturday afternoon the colonel went to see his lawyer. He found him stretched out lazily in a hammock. He was a monumental Negro, with nothing but two canines in his upper jaw. The lawyer put his feet into a pair of wooden-soled slippers and opened the office window on a dusty pianola with papers stuffed into the compartments where the rolls used to go: clippings from the *Official Gazette*, pasted into old accounting ledgers, and a jumbled collection of accounting bulletins. The keyless pianola did double duty as a desk. The lawyer sat down in a swivel chair. The colonel expressed his uneasiness before revealing the purpose of his visit.

"I warned you that it would take more than a few days," said the lawyer when the colonel paused. He was sweltering in the heat. He adjusted the chair backward and fanned himself with an advertising brochure.

"My agents write to me frequently, saying not to get impatient."

"It's been that way for fifteen years," the colonel answered. "This is beginning to sound like the story about the capon."

The lawyer gave a very graphic description of the administrative ins and outs. The chair was too narrow for his sagging buttocks. "Fifteen years ago it was easier," he said. "Then there was the city's veterans' organization, with members of both parties." His lungs filled with stifling air and he pronounced the sentence as if he had just invented it:

"There's strength in numbers."

"There wasn't in this case," the colonel said, realizing his aloneness for the first time. "All my comrades died waiting for the mail."

The lawyer didn't change his expression.

"The law was passed too late," he said. "Not everybody was as lucky as you to be a colonel at the age of twenty. Furthermore, no special allocation was included, so the government has had to make adjustments in the budget."

Always the same story. Each time the colonel listened to him, he felt a mute resentment. "This is not charity," he said. "It's not a question of doing us a favor. We broke our backs to save the Republic." The lawyer threw up his hands.

"That's the way it is," he said. "Human ingratitude knows no limits."

The colonel also knew that story. He had begun hearing it the day after the Treaty of Neerlandia, when the government promised travel assistance and indemnities to two hundred revolutionary officers. Camped at the base of the gigantic silk-cotton tree at Neerlandia, a revolutionary battalion, made up in great measure of youths who had left school, waited for three months. Then they went back to their homes by their own means, and they kept on waiting there. Almost sixty years later, the colonel was still waiting.

Excited by these memories, he adopted a transcendental attitude. He rested his right hand on his thigh—mere bone sewed together with nerve tissue—and murmured:

"Well, I've decided to take action."

The lawyer waited.

"Such as?"

"To change lawyers."

A mother duck, followed by several little ducklings, entered the office. The lawyer sat up to chase them out. "As you wish, Colonel," he said, chasing the animals. "It will be just as you wish. If I could work miracles, I wouldn't be living in this barnyard." He put a wooden grille across the patio door and returned to his chair.

"My son worked all his life," said the colonel. "My house is mortgaged. That retirement law has been a lifetime pension for lawyers."

"Not for me," the lawyer protested. "Every last cent has gone for my expenses."

The colonel suffered at the thought that he had been unjust.

"That's what I meant," he corrected himself. He dried his forehead with the sleeve of his shirt. "This heat is enough to rust the screws in your head."

A moment later the lawyer was turning the office upside down looking for the power of attorney. The sun advanced toward the center of the tiny room, which was built of unsanded boards. After looking futilely everywhere, the lawyer got down on all fours, huffing and puffing, and picked up a roll of papers from under the pianola.

"Here it is."

He gave the colonel a sheet of paper with a seal on it. "I have to write my agents so they can cancel the copies," he concluded. The colonel shook the dust off the paper and put it in his shirt pocket.

"Tear it up yourself," the lawyer said.

"No," the colonel answered. "These are twenty years of memories." And he waited for the lawyer to keep on looking. But the lawyer didn't. He went to the hammock to wipe off his sweat. From there he looked at the colonel through the shimmering air.

"I need the documents also," the colonel said.

"Which ones?"

"The proof of claim."

The lawyer threw up his hands.

"Now, that would be impossible, Colonel."

The colonel became alarmed. As Treasurer of the revolution in the district of Macondo, he had undertaken a difficult six-day journey with the funds for the civil war in two trunks roped to the back of a mule. He arrived at the camp of Neerlandia dragging the mule, which was dead from hunger, half an hour before the treaty was signed. Colonel Aureliano Buendía—quartermaster general of the revolutionary forces on the Atlantic coast—held out the receipt for the funds, and included the two trunks in his inventory of the surrender.

"Those documents have an incalculable value," the colonel said. "There's a receipt from Colonel Aureliano Buendía, written in his own hand."

"I agree," said the lawyer. "But those documents have passed through thousands and thousands of hands, in thousands and thousands of offices, before they reached God knows which department in the War Ministry."

"No official could fail to notice documents like those," the colonel said.

"But the officials have changed many times in the last fifteen years," the lawyer pointed out. "Just think about it; there have been seven Presidents, and each President changed his Cabinet at least ten times, and each Minister changed his staff at least a hundred times."

"But nobody could take the documents home," said the colonel. "Each new official must have found them in the proper file."

The lawyer lost his patience.

"And moreover if those papers are removed from the Ministry now, they will have to wait for a new place on the rolls."

"It doesn't matter," the colonel said.

"It'll take centuries."

"It doesn't matter. If you wait for the big things, you can wait for the little ones."

He took a pad of lined paper, the pen, the inkwell, and a blotter to the little table in the living room, and left the bedroom door open in case he had to ask his wife anything. She was saying her beads.

"What's today's date?"

"October 27th."

He wrote with a studious neatness, the hand that held the pen resting on the blotter, his spine straight to ease his breathing, as he'd been taught in school. The heat became unbearable in the closed living room. A drop of perspiration fell on the letter. The colonel picked it up on the blotter. Then he tried to erase the letters which had smeared but he smudged them. He didn't lose his patience. He wrote an asterisk and noted in the margin, "acquired rights." Then he read the whole paragraph.

"When was I put on the rolls?"

The woman didn't interrupt her prayers to think.

"August 12, 1949."

A moment later it began to rain. The colonel filled a page with large doodlings which were a little childish, the same ones he learned in public school at Manaure. Then he wrote on a second sheet down to the middle, and he signed it.

He read the letter to his wife. She approved each sentence with a nod. When he finished reading, the colonel sealed the envelope and turned off the lamp.

"You could ask someone to type it for you."

"No," the colonel answered. "I'm tired of going around asking favors."

For half an hour he heard the rain against the palm roof. The town sank into the deluge. After curfew sounded, a leak began somewhere in the house.

"This should have been done a long time ago," the woman said. "It's always better to handle things oneself."

"It's never too late," the colonel said, paying attention to the leak. "Maybe all this will be settled when the mortgage on the house falls due."

"In two years," the woman said.

He lit the lamp to locate the leak in the living room. He put the rooster's can underneath it and returned to the bedroom, pursued by the metallic noise of the water in the empty can.

"It's possible that to save the interest on the money they'll settle it before January," he said, and he convinced himself. "By then, Agustín's year will be up and we can go to the movies."

She laughed under her breath. "I don't even remember the cartoons any more," she said. The colonel tried to look at her through the mosquito netting.

"When did you go to the movies last?"

"In 1931," she said. "They were showing *The Dead Man's Will*."

"Was there a fight?"

"We never found out. The storm broke just when the ghost tried to rob the girl's necklace."

The sound of the rain put them to sleep. The colonel felt a slight queasiness in his intestines. But he wasn't afraid. He was about to survive another October. He wrapped himself in a wool blanket, and for a moment heard the gravelly breathing of his wife—far away—drifting on another dream. Then he spoke, completely conscious.

The woman woke up.

"Who are you speaking to?"

"No one," the colonel said. "I was thinking that at the Macondo meeting we were right when we told Colonel Aureliano Buendía not to surrender. That's what started to ruin everything."

It rained the whole week. The second of November—against the colonel's wishes—the woman took flowers to Agustín's grave. She returned from the cemetery and had another attack. It was a hard week. Harder than the four weeks of October which the colonel hadn't thought he'd survive. The doctor came to see the sick woman, and came out of the room shouting, "With asthma like that, I'd be able to bury the whole town!" But he spoke to the colonel alone and prescribed a special diet.

The colonel also suffered a relapse. He strained for many hours in the privy, in an icy sweat, feeling as if he were rotting and that the flora in his vitals was falling to pieces. "It's winter," he repeated to himself patiently. "Everything will be different when it stops raining." And he really believed it, certain that he would be alive at the moment the letter arrived.

This time it was he who had to repair their household economy. He had to grit his teeth many times to ask for credit in the neighborhood stores. "It's just until next week," he would say, without being sure himself that it was true. "It's a little money which should have arrived last Friday." When her attack was over, the woman examined him in horror.

"You're nothing but skin and bones," she said.

"I'm taking care of myself so I can sell myself," the colonel said. "I've already been hired by a clarinet factory."

But in reality his hoping for the letter barely sustained him. Exhausted, his bones aching from sleeplessness, he couldn't attend to his needs and the rooster's at the same time. In the second half of November, he thought that the animal would die after two days without corn. Then he remembered a handful of beans which he had hung in the chimney in July. He opened the pods and put down a can of dry seeds for the rooster.

"Come here," she said.

"Just a minute," the colonel answered, watching the rooster's reaction. "Beggars can't be choosers."

He found his wife trying to sit up in bed. Her ravaged body gave off the aroma of medicinal herbs. She spoke her words, one by one, with calculated precision:

"Get rid of that rooster right now."

The colonel had foreseen that moment. He had been waiting for it ever since the afternoon when his son was shot down, and he had decided to keep the rooster. He had had time to think.

"It's not worth it now," he said. "The fight will be in two months and then we'll be able to sell him at a better price."

"It's not a question of the money," the woman said. "When the boys come, you'll tell them to take it away and do whatever they feel like with it."

"It's for Agustín," the colonel said, advancing his prepared argument. "Remember his face when he came to tell us the rooster won."

The woman, in fact, did think of her son.

"Those accursed roosters were his downfall!" she shouted. "If he'd stayed home on January 3rd, his evil hour wouldn't have come." She held out a skinny forefinger toward the door and exclaimed:

"It seems as if I can see him when he left with the rooster under his arm. I warned him not to go looking for trouble at the cockfights, and he smiled and told me, 'Shut up; this afternoon we'll be rolling in money.'"

She fell back exhausted. The colonel pushed her gently toward the pillow. His eyes fell upon other eyes exactly like his own. "Try not to move," he said, feeling her whistling within his own lungs. The woman fell into a momentary torpor. She closed her eyes. When she opened them again, her breathing seemed more even.

"It's because of the situation we're in," she said. "It's a sin to take the food out of our mouths to give it to a rooster."

The colonel wiped her forehead with the sheet.

"Nobody dies in three months."

"And what do we eat in the meantime?" the woman asked.

"I don't know," the colonel said. "But if we were going to die of hunger, we would have died already."

The rooster was very much alive next to the empty can. When he saw the colonel, he emitted an almost human, guttural monologue and tossed his head back. He gave him a smile of complicity:

"Life is tough, pal."

The colonel went into the street. He wandered about the town during the siesta, without thinking about anything, without even trying to convince himself that his problem had no solution. He walked through forgotten streets until he found he was exhausted. Then he returned to the house. The woman heard him come in and called him into the bedroom.

"What?"

She replied without looking at him.

"We can sell the clock."

The colonel had thought of that. "I'm sure Alvaro will give you forty pesos right on the spot," said the woman. "Think how quickly he bought the sewing machine."

She was referring to the tailor whom Agustín had worked for.

"I could speak to him in the morning," admitted the colonel.

"None of that 'speak to him in the morning,'" she insisted. "Take the clock to him this minute. You put it on the counter and you tell him, 'Alvaro, I've brought this clock for you to buy from me.' He'll understand immediately."

The colonel felt ashamed.

"It's like walking around with Holy Sepulcher," he protested. "If they see me in the street with a showpiece like that, Rafael Escalona will put me into one of his songs."

But this time, too, his wife convinced him. She herself took down the clock, wrapped it in newspaper, and put it into his arms. "Don't come back here without the forty pesos," she said. The colonel went off to the tailor's with the package under his arm. He found Agustín's companions sitting in the doorway.

One of them offered him a seat. "Thanks," he said. "I can't stay." Alvaro came out of the shop. A piece of wet duck hung on a wire stretched between two hooks in the hall. He was a boy with a hard, angular body and wild eyes. He also invited him to sit down. The colonel felt comforted. He leaned the stool against the doorjamb and sat down to wait until Alvaro was alone to propose his deal. Suddenly he realized that he was surrounded by expressionless faces.

"I'm not interrupting?" he said.

They said he wasn't. One of them leaned toward him. He said in a barely audible voice:

"Agustín wrote."

The colonel observed the deserted street.

"What does he say?"

"The same as always."

They gave him the clandestine sheet of paper. The colonel put it in pants pocket. Then he kept silent, drumming on the package, until he realized that someone had noticed it. He stopped in suspense.

"What have you got there, Colonel?"

The colonel avoided Hernán's penetrating green eyes.

"Nothing," he lied. "I'm taking my clock to the German to have him fix it for me."

"Don't be silly, Colonel," said Hernán, trying to take the package. "Wait and I'll look at it."

The colonel held back. He didn't say anything, but his eyelids turned purple. The others insisted.

"Let him, Colonel. He knows mechanical things."

"I just don't want to bother him."

"Bother, it's no bother," Hernán argued. He seized the clock. "The German will get ten pesos out of you and it'll be the same as it is now."

Hernán went into the tailor shop with the clock. Alvaro was sewing on a machine. At the back, beneath a guitar hanging on a nail, a girl was sewing buttons on. There was a sign tacked up over the guitar: "TALKING POLITICS FORBIDDEN." Outside, the colonel felt as if his body were superfluous. He rested his feet on the rail of the stool.

"Goddamn it, Colonel."

He was startled. "No need to swear," he said.

Alfonso adjusted his eyeglasses on his nose to examine the colonel's shoes.

"It's because of your shoes," he said. "You've got on some goddamn new shoes."

"But you can say that without swearing," the colonel said, and showed the soles of his patent-leather shoes. "These monstrosities are forty years old, and it's the first time they've ever heard anyone swear."

"All done," shouted Hernán, inside, just as the clock's bell rang. In the neighboring house, a woman pounded on the partition; she shouted:

"Let that guitar alone! Agustín's year isn't up yet."

Someone guffawed.

"It's a clock."

Hernán came out with the package.

"It wasn't anything," he said. "If you like I'll go home with you to level it."

The colonel refused his offer.

"How much do I owe you?"

"Don't worry about it, Colonel," replied Hernán, taking his place in the group. "In January, the rooster will pay for it."

The colonel now found the chance he was looking for.

"I'll make you a deal," he said.

"What?"

"I'll give you the rooster." He examined the circle of faces. "I'll give the rooster to all of you."

Hernán looked at him on confusion.

"I'm too old now for that," the colonel continued. He gave his voice a convincing severity. "It's too much responsibility for me. For days now I've had the impression that the animal is dying."

"Don't worry about it, Colonel," Alfonso said. "The trouble is that the rooster is molting now. He's got a fever in his quills."

"He'll be better next month," Hernán said.

"I don't want him anyway," the colonel said.

Hernán's pupils bore into his.

"Realize how things are, Colonel," he insisted. "The main thing is for you to be the one who puts Agustín's rooster into the ring."

The colonel thought about it. "I realize," he said. "That's why I've kept him until now." He clenched his teeth, and felt he could go on: "The trouble is there are still two months."

Hernán was the one who understood.

"If it's only because of that, there's no problem," he said.

And he proposed his formula. The other accepted. At dusk, when he entered the house with the package under his arm, his wife was chagrined.

"Nothing?" she asked.

"Nothing," the colonel answered. "But now it doesn't matter. The boys will take over feeding the rooster."

"Wait and I'll lend you an umbrella, friend."

Sabas opened a cupboard in the office wall. He uncovered a jumbled interior: riding boots piled up, stirrups and reins, and an aluminum pail full of riding spurs. Hanging from the upper part, half a dozen umbrellas and a lady's parasol. The colonel was thinking of the debris from some catastrophe.

"Thanks, friend," the colonel said, leaning on the window. "I prefer to wait for it to clear." Sabas didn't close the cupboard. He settled down at the desk within range of the electric fan. Then he took a little hypodermic syringe wrapped in cotton out of the drawer. The colonel observed the grayish almond trees through the rain. It was an empty afternoon.

"The rain is different from this window," he said. "It's as if it were raining in another town."

"Rain is rain from whatever point," replied Sabas. He put the syringe on to boil on the glass desk top. "This town stinks."

The colonel shrugged his shoulders. He walked toward the middle of the office: a green-tiled room with furniture upholstered in brightly colored fabrics. At the back, piled up in disarray, were sacks of salt, honeycombs, and riding saddles. Sabas followed him with a completely vacant stare.

"If I were in your shoes I wouldn't think that way," said the colonel.

He sat down and crossed his legs, his calm gaze fixed on the man leaning over his desk. A small man, corpulent, but with flaccid flesh, he had the sadness of a toad in his eyes.

"Have the doctor look at you, friend," said Sabas. "You've been a little sad since the day of the funeral."

The colonel raised his head.

"I'm perfectly well," he said.

Sabas waited for the syringe to boil. "I wish I could say the same," he complained. "You're lucky because you've got a cast-iron stomach." He contemplated the hairy backs of his hands which were dotted with dark blotches. He wore a ring with a black stone next to his wedding band.

"That's right," the colonel admitted.

Sabas called his wife through the door between the office and the rest of the house. Then he began a painful explanation of his diet. He took a little bottle out of his shirt pocket and put a white pill the size of a pea on the desk.

"It's torture to go around with this everyplace," he said. "It's like carrying death in your pocket."

The colonel approached the desk. He examined the pill in the palm of his hand until Sabas invited him to taste it.

"It's to sweeten coffee," he explained. "It's sugar, but without sugar."

"Of course," the colonel said, his saliva impregnated with a sad sweetness. "It's something like a ringing but without bells."

Sabas put his elbows on the desk with his face in his hands after his wife gave him the injection. The colonel didn't know what to do with his body. The woman unplugged the electric fan, put it on top of the safe, and then went to the cupboard.

"Umbrellas have something to do with death," she said.

The colonel paid no attention to her. He had left his house at four to wait for the mail, but the rain made him take refuge in Sabas's office. It was still raining when the launches whistled.

"Everybody says death is a woman," the woman continued. She was fat, taller than her husband, and had a hairy mole on her upper lip. Her way of speaking reminded one of the hum of the electric fan. "But I don't think it's a woman," she said. She closed the cupboard and looked into the colonel's eyes again.

"I think it's an animal with claws."

"That's possible," the colonel admitted. "At times very strange things happen."

He thought of the postmaster jumping onto the launch in an oilskin slicker. A month had passed since he had changed lawyers. He was entitled to expect a reply. Saba's wife kept speaking about death until she noticed the colonel's absentminded expression.

"Friend," she said. "You must be worried."

The colonel sat up.

"That's right, friend," he lied. "I'm thinking that it's five already and the rooster hasn't had his injection."

She was confused.

"An injection for a rooster, as if he were a human being!" she shouted. "That's a sacrilege."

Sabas couldn't stand any more. He raised his flushed face.

"Close your mouth for a minute," he ordered his wife. And in fact she did raise her hands to her mouth. "You've been bothering my friend for half an hour with your foolishness."

"Not at all," the colonel protested.

The woman slammed the door. Sabas dried his neck with a handkerchief soaked in lavender. The colonel approached the window. It was raining steadily. A long-legged chicken was crossing the deserted plaza.

"Is it true the rooster's getting injections?"

"True," said the colonel. "His training begins next week."

"That's madness," said Sabas. "Those things are not for you."

"I agree," said the colonel. "But that's no reason to wring his neck."

"That's just idiotic stubbornness," said Sabas, turning toward the window. The colonel heard him sigh with the breath of a bellows. His friend's eyes made him feel pity.

"It's never too late for anything," the colonel said.

"Don't be unreasonable," insisted Sabas. "It's a two-edged deal. On one side you get rid of that headache, and on the other you can put nine hundred pesos in your pocket."

"Nine hundred pesos!" the colonel exclaimed.

"Nine hundred pesos."

The colonel visualized the figure.

"You think they'd give a fortune like that for the rooster?"

"I don't think," Sabas answered. "I'm absolutely sure."

It was the largest sum the colonel had had in his head since he had returned the revolution's funds. When he left Sabas's office, he felt a strong wrenching in his gut, but he was aware that this time it wasn't because of the weather. At the post office he headed straight for the postmaster:

"I'm expecting an urgent letter," he said. "It's air mail."

The postmaster looked in the cubbyholes. When he finished reading, he put the letters back in the proper box but he didn't say anything. He dusted off his hand and turned a meaningful look on the colonel.

"It was supposed to come today for sure," the colonel said.

The postmaster shrugged.

"The only thing that comes for sure is death, Colonel."

His wife received him with a dish of corn mush. He ate it in silence with long pauses for thought between each spoonful. Seated opposite him, the woman noticed that something had changed in his face.

"What's the matter?" she asked.

"I'm thinking about the employee that pension depends on," the colonel lied. "In fifty years, we'll be peacefully six feet under, while that poor man will be killing himself every Friday waiting for his retirement pension."

"That's a bad sign," the woman said. "It means that you're beginning to resign yourself already." She went on eating her mush. But a moment later she realized that her husband was still far away.

"Now, what you should do is enjoy the mush."

"It's very good," the colonel said. "Where'd it come from?"

"From the rooster," the woman answered. "The boys brought him so much corn that he decided to share it with us. That's life."

"That's right." The colonel sighed. "Life is the best thing that's ever been invented."

He looked at the rooster tied to the leg of the stove and this time he seemed a different animal. The woman also looked at him.

"This afternoon I had to chase the children out with a stick," she said. "They brought an old hen to breed her with the rooster."

"It's not the first time," the colonel said. "That's the same thing they did in those towns with Colonel Aureliano Buendía. They brought him little girls to breed with."

She got a kick out of the joke. The rooster produced a guttural noise which sounded in the hall like quiet human conversation. "Sometimes I think that animal is going to talk," the woman said. The colonel looked at him again.

"He's worth his weight in gold," he said. He made some calculations while he sipped a spoonful of mush. "He'll feed us for three years."

"You can't eat hope," the woman said.

"You can't eat it, but it sustains you," the colonel replied. "It's something like my friend Sabas's miraculous pills."

He slept poorly that night trying to erase the figures from his mind. The following day at lunch, the woman served two plates of mush, and ate hers with her head lowered, without saying a word. The colonel felt himself catching her dark mood.

"What's the matter?"

"Nothing," the woman said.

He had the impression that this time it had been her turn to lie. He tried to comfort her. But the woman persisted.

"It's nothing unusual," she said. "I was thinking that the man has been dead for two months, and I still haven't been to see the family."

So she went to see them that night. The colonel accompanied her to the dead man's house, and then headed for the movie theater, drawn by the music coming over the loudspeakers. Seated at the door of his office, Father Angel was watching the entrance to find out who was attending the show despite his twelve warnings. The flood of light, the strident music, and the shouts of the children erected a physical resistance in the area. One of the children threatened the colonel with a wooden rifle.

"What's new with the rooster, Colonel?" he said in an authoritative voice.

The colonel put his hands up.

"He's still around."

A four-color poster covered the entire front of the theater: *Midnight Virgin*. She was a woman in an evening gown, with one leg bared up to the thigh. The colonel continued wandering around the neighborhood until distant thunder and lightning began. Then he went back for his wife.

She wasn't at the dead man's house. Nor at home. The colonel reckoned that there was little time left before curfew, but the clock had stopped. He waited, feeling the storm advance on the town. He was getting ready to go out again when his wife arrived.

He took the rooster into the bedroom. She changed her clothes and went to take a drink of water in the living room just as the colonel finished winding the clock, and was waiting for curfew to blow in order to set it.

"Where were you?" the colonel asked.

"Roundabout," the woman answered. She put the glass on the washstand without looking at her husband and returned to the bedroom. "No one thought it was going to rain so soon." The colonel made no comment. When curfew blew, he set the clock at eleven, closed the case, and put the chair back in its place. He found his wife saying her rosary.

"You haven't answered my question," the colonel said.

"What?"

"Where were you?"

"I stayed around there talking," she said. "It had been so long since I'd been out of the house."

The colonel hung up his hammock. He locked the house and fumigated the room. Then he put the lamp on the floor and lay down.

"I understand," he said sadly. "The worst of a bad situation is that it makes us tell lies."

She let out a long sigh.

"I was with Father Angel," she said. "I went to ask him for a loan on our wedding rings."

"And what did he tell you?"

"That it's a sin to barter with sacred things."

She went on talking under her mosquito netting. "Two days ago I tried to sell the clock," she said. "No one is interested because they're selling modern clocks with luminous numbers on the installment plan. You can see the time in the dark." The colonel acknowledged that forty years of shared living, of shared hunger, of shared suffering, had not been enough for him to come to know his wife. He felt that something had also grown old in their love.

"They don't want the picture, either," she said. "Almost everybody has the same one. I even went to the Turk's."

The colonel felt bitter.

"So now everyone knows we're starving."

"I'm tired," the woman said. "Men don't understand problems of the household. Several times I've had to put stones on to boil so the neighbors wouldn't know that we often go for many days without putting on the pot."

The colonel felt offended.

"That's really a humiliation," he said.

The woman got out from under the mosquito netting and went to the hammock. "I'm ready to give up affectation and pretense in this house," she said. Her voice began to darken with rage. "I'm fed up with resignation and dignity."

The colonel didn't move a muscle.

"Twenty years of waiting for the little colored birds which they promised you after every election, and all we've got out of it is a dead son," she went on. "Nothing but a dead son."

The colonel was used to that sort of recrimination.

"We did our duty."

"And they did theirs by making a thousand pesos a month in the Senate for twenty years," the woman answered. "There's my friend Sabas with a two-story house that isn't big enough to keep all his money in, a man who came to this town selling medicines with a snake curled around his neck."

"But he's dying of diabetes," the colonel said.

"And you're dying of hunger," the woman said. "You should realize that you can't eat dignity."

The lightning interrupted her. The thunder exploded in the street, entered the bedroom, and went rolling under the bed like a heap of stones. The woman jumped toward the mosquito netting for her rosary.

The colonel smiled.

"That's what happens to you for not holding your tongue," he said. "I've always said that God is on my side."

But in reality he felt embittered. A moment later he put out the light and sank into thought in a darkness rent by the lightning. He remembered Macondo. The colonel had waited ten years for the promises of Neerlandia to be fulfilled. In the drowsiness of the siesta he saw a yellow, dusty train pull in, with men and women and animals suffocating from the heat, piled up even on the roofs of the cars. It was the banana fever.

In twenty-four hours they had transformed the town. "I'm leaving," the colonel said then. "The odor of the banana is eating at my insides." And he left Macondo on the return train, Wednesday, June 27, 1906, at 2:18 P.M. It took him nearly half a century to realize that he hadn't had a moment's peace since the surrender at Neerlandia.

He opened his eyes.

"Then there's no need to think about it any more," he said.

"What?"

"The problem of the rooster," the colonel said. "Tomorrow I'll sell it to my friend Sabas for nine hundred pesos."

The howls of the castrated animals, fused with Sabas's shouting, came through the office window. If he doesn't come in ten minutes I'll leave, the colonel promised himself after two hours of waiting. But he waited twenty minutes more. He was getting set to leave when Sabas entered the office followed by a group of workers. He passed back and forth in front of the colonel without looking at him.

"Are you waiting for me, friend?"

"Yes, friend," the colonel said. "But if you're very busy, I can come back later."

Sabas didn't hear him from the other side of the door.

"I'll be right back," he said.

Noon was stifling. The office shone with the shimmering of the street. Dulled by the heat, the colonel involuntarily closed his eyes and at once began to dream of his wife. Sabas's wife came in on tiptoe.

"Don't wake up, friend," she said. "I'm going to draw the blinds because this office is an inferno."

The colonel followed her with a blank look. She spoke in the shadow when she closed the window.

"Do you dream often?"

"Sometimes," replied the colonel, ashamed of having fallen asleep. "Almost always I dream that I'm getting tangled up in spider webs."

"I have nightmares every night," the woman said. "Now I've got it in my head to find out who those unknown people are whom one meets in one's dreams."

She plugged in the fan. "Last week a woman appeared at the head of my bed," she said, "I managed to ask her who she was and she replied, 'I am the woman who died in this room twelve years ago.' "

"But the house was built barely two years ago," the colonel said.

"That's right," the woman said. "That means that even the dead make mistakes."

The hum of the fan solidified the shadow. The colonel felt impatient, tormented by sleepiness and by the rambling woman who went directly from dreams to the mystery of the reincarnation. He was waiting for a pause to say goodbye when Sabas entered the office with his foreman.

"I've warmed up your soup four times," the woman said.

"Warm it up ten times if you like," said Sabas. "But stop nagging me now."

He opened the safe and gave his foreman a roll of bills together with a list of instructions. The foreman opened the blinds to count the money. Sabas saw the colonel at the back of the office but didn't show any reaction. He kept talking with the foreman. The colonel straightened up at the point when the two men were getting ready to leave the office again. Sabas stopped before opening the door.

"What can I do for you, friend?"

The colonel saw that the foreman was looking at him.

"Nothing, friend," he said. "I just wanted to talk to you."

"Make it fast, whatever it is," said Sabas. "I don't have a minute to spare."

He hesitated with his hand resting on the doorknob. The colonel felt the five longest seconds of his life passing. He clenched his teeth.

"It's about the rooster," he murmured.

Then Sabas finished opening the door. "The question of the rooster," he repeated, smiling and pushed the foreman toward the hall. "The sky is falling in and my friend is worrying about that rooster." And then, addressing the colonel:

"Very well, friend. I'll be right back."

The colonel stood motionless in the middle of the office until he could no longer hear the footsteps of the two men at the end of the hall. Then he went out out to walk around the town which was paralyzed in its Sunday siesta. There was no one at the tailor's. The doctor's office was closed. No one was watching the goods set out at the Syrians' stalls. The river was a sheet of steel. A man at the waterfront was sleeping across four oil drums, his face protected from the sun by a hat. The colonel went home, certain that he was the only thing moving in town.

His wife was waiting for him with a complete lunch.

"I bought it on credit; promised to pay first thing tomorrow," she explained.

During lunch, the colonel told her the events of the last three hours. She listened to him impatiently.

"The trouble is you lack character," she said finally. "You present yourself as if you were begging alms when you ought to go there with you head high and take our friend aside and say, 'Friend, I've decided to sell you the rooster.' "

"Life is a breeze the way you tell it," the colonel said.

She assumed an energetic attitude. That morning she had put the house in order and was dressed very strangely, in her husband's old shoes, and oilcloth apron, and a rag tied around her head with two knots at the ears. "You haven't the slightest sense for business," she said. "When you go to sell something, you have to put on the same face as when you go to buy."

The colonel found something amusing in her figure.

"Stay just the way you are," he interrupted her, smiling. "You're identical to the little Quaker Oats man."

She took the rag off her head.

"I'm speaking seriously," she said. "I'm going to take the rooster to our friend right now, and I'll bet whatever you want that I come back inside of half an hour with the nine hundred pesos."

"You've got zeros on the brain," the colonel said. "You're already betting with the money from the rooster."

It took a lot of trouble for him to dissuade her. She had spent the morning mentally organizing the budget for the next three years without their Friday agony. She had made a list of the essentials they needed, without forgetting a pair of new shoes for the colonel. She set aside a place in the bedroom for the mirror. The momentary frustration of her plans left her with a confused sensation of shame and resentment.

She took a short siesta. When she got up, the colonel was sitting in the patio.

"Now what are you doing?" she asked.

"I'm thinking," the colonel said.

"Then the problem is solved. We will be able to count on that money fifty years from now."

But in reality the colonel had decided to sell the rooster that very afternoon. He thought of Sabas, alone in his office, preparing himself for his daily injection in front of the electric fan. He had his answer ready.

"Take the rooster," his wife advised him as he went out. "Seeing him in the flesh will work a miracle."

The colonel objected. She followed him to the front door with desperate anxiety.

"It doesn't matter if the whole army is in the office," she said. "You grab him by the arm and don't let him move until he gives you the nine hundred pesos."

"They'll think we're planning a hold-up."

She paid no attention.

"Remember that you are the owner of the rooster," she insisted. Remember that you are the one who's going to do him the favor."

"All right."

Sabas was in the bedroom with the doctor. "Now's your chance, friend," his wife said to the colonel. "The doctor is getting him ready to travel to the ranch, and he's not coming back until Thursday." The colonel struggled with two opposing forces: in spite of his determination to sell the rooster, he wished he had arrived an hour later and missed Sabas.

"I can wait," he said.

But the woman insisted. She led him to the bedroom where her husband was seated on the throne-like bed, in his underwear, his colorless eyes fixed on the doctor. The colonel waited until the doctor had heated the glass tube with the patient's urine, sniffed the odor, and made an approving gesture to Sabas.

"We'll have to shoot him," the doctor said, turning to the colonel. "Diabetes is too slow for finishing off the wealthy."

"You've already done your best with your damned insulin injections," said Sabas, and he gave a jump on his flaccid buttocks. "But I'm a hard nut to crack." And then, to the colonel:

"Come in, friend. When I went out to look for you this afternoon, I couldn't even see your hat."

"I don't wear one, so I won't have to take it off for anyone."

Sabas began to get dressed. The doctor put a glass tube with a blood sample in his jacket pocket. Then he straightened out the things in his bag. The colonel thought he was getting ready to leave.

"If I were in your shoes, I'd send my friend a bill for a hundred thousand pesos, Doctor," the colonel said. "That way he wouldn't be so worried."

"I've already suggested that to him, but for a million," the doctor said. "Poverty is the best cure for diabetes."

"Thanks for the prescription," said Sabas, trying to stuff his voluminous belly into his riding breeches. "But I won't accept it, to save you from the catastrophe of becoming rich." The doctor saw his own teeth reflected in the little chromed lock of his bag. He looked at the clock without showing impatience. Sabas, putting on his boots, suddenly turned to the colonel:

"Well, friend, what's happening with the rooster?"

The colonel realized that the doctor was also waiting for his answer. He clenched his teeth.

"Nothing, friend," he murmured. "I've come to sell him to you."

Sabas finished putting on his boots.

"Fine, my friend," he said without emotion. "It's the most sensible thing that could have occurred to you."

"I'm too old now for these complications," the colonel said to justify himself before the doctor's impenetrable expression. "If I were twenty years younger it would be different."

"You'll always be twenty years younger," the doctor replied.

The colonel regained his breath. He waited for Sabas to say something more, but he didn't. Sabas put on a leather zippered jacket and got ready to leave the bedroom.

"If you like, we'll talk about it next week, friend," the colonel said.

"That's what I was going to say," said Sabas. "I have a customer who might give you four hundred pesos. But we have to wait till Thursday."

"How much?" the doctor asked.

"Four hundred pesos."

"I had heard someone say that he was worth a lot more," the doctor said.

"You were talking in terms of nine hundred pesos," the colonel said, backed by the doctor's perplexity. "He's the best rooster in the whole province."

Sabas answered the doctor.

"At some other time, anyone would have paid a thousand," he explained. "But now no one dares pit a good rooster. There's always the danger he'll come out of the pit shot to death." He turned to the colonel, feigning disappointment:

"That's what I wanted to tell you, friend."

The colonel nodded.

"Fine," he said.

He followed him down the hall. The doctor stayed in the living room, detained by Sabas's wife, who asked him for a remedy "for those things which come over one suddenly and which one doesn't know what they are." The colonel waited for him in the office. Sabas opened the safe, stuffed money into all his pockets, and held out four bills to the colonel.

"There's sixty pesos, friend," he said. "When the rooster is sold we'll settle up."

The colonel walked with the doctor past the stalls at the waterfront, which were beginning to revive in the cool of the afternoon. A barge loaded with sugar cane was moving down the thread of current. The colonel found the doctor strangely impervious.

"And you, how are you, Doctor?"

The doctor shrugged.

"As usual," he said. "I think I need a doctor."

"It's the winter," the colonel said. "It eats away my insides."

The doctor examined him with a look absolutely devoid of any professional interest. In succession he greeted the Syrians seated at the doors of their shops. At the door of the doctor's office, the colonel expressed his opinion of the sale of the rooster.

"I couldn't do anything else," he explained. "That animal feeds on human flesh."

"The only animal who feeds on human flesh is Sabas," the doctor said. "I'm sure he'd resell the rooster for the nine hundred pesos."

"You think so?"

"I'm sure of it," the doctor said. "It's as sweet a deal as his famous patriotic pact with the Mayor."

The colonel refused to believe it. "My friend made that pact to save his skin," he said. "That's how he could stay in town."

"And that's how he could buy the property of his fellow-partisans whom the Mayor kicked out at half their price," the doctor replied. He knocked on the door, since he didn't find his keys in his pockets. Then he faced the colonel's disbelief.

"Don't be so naïve," he said. "Sabas is much more interested in money than in his own skin."

The colonel's wife went shopping that night. He accompanied her to the Syrians' stalls, pondering the doctor's revelations.

"Find the boys immediately and tell them that the rooster is sold," she told him. "We mustn't leave them with any hopes."

"The rooster won't be sold until my friend Sabas comes back," the colonel answered.

He found Alvaro playing roulette in the pool hall. The place was sweltering on Sunday night. The heat seemed more intense because of the vibrations of the radio turned up full blast. The colonel amused himself with the brightly colored numbers painted on a large black oilcloth cover and lit by an oil lantern placed on a box in the center of the table. Alvaro insisted on losing on twenty-three. Following the game over his shoulder, the colonel observed that the eleven turned up four times in nine spins.

"Bet on eleven," he whispered into Alvaro's ear. "It's the one coming up most."

Alvaro examined the table. He didn't bet on the next spin. He took some money out of his pants pocket, and with it a sheet of paper. He gave the paper to the colonel under the table.

"It's from Agustín," he said.

The colonel put the clandestine note in his pocket. Alvaro bet heavily on the eleven.

"Start with just a little," the colonel said.

"It may be a good hunch," Alvaro replied. A group of neighboring players took their bets off the other numbers and bet on eleven after the enormous colored wheel had already begun to turn. The colonel felt oppressed. For the first time he felt the fascination, agitation, and bitterness of gambling.

The five won.

"I'm sorry," the colonel said, ashamed, and, with an irresistible feeling of guilt, followed the little wooden rake which pulled in Alvaro's money. "That's what I get for butting into what doesn't concern me."

Alvaro smiled without looking at him.

"Don't worry, Colonel. Trust to love."

The trumpets playing a mambo were suddenly interrupted. The gamblers scattered with their hands in the air. The colonel felt the dry snap, articulate and cold, of a rifle being cocked behind his back. He realized that he had been caught fatally in a police raid with the clandestine paper in his pocket. He turned halfway around without raising his hands. And then he saw, close up, for the first time in his life, the man who had shot his son. The man was directly in front of him, with his rifle barrel aimed at the colonel's belly. He was small, Indian-looking, with weather-beaten skin, and his breath smelled like a child's. The colonel gritted his teeth and gently pushed the rifle barrel away with the tips of his fingers.

"Excuse me," he said.

He confronted two round little bat eyes. In an instant, he felt himself being swallowed up by those eyes, crushed, digested, and expelled immediately.

"You may go, Colonel."

He didn't need to open the window to tell it was December. He knew it in his bones when he was cutting up the fruit for the rooster's breakfast in the kitchen. Then he opened the door and the sight of the patio confirmed his feeling. It was a marvelous patio, with the grass and the trees, and the cubicle with the privy floating in the clear air, one millimeter above the ground.

His wife stayed in bed until nine. When she appeared in the kitchen, the colonel had already straightened up the house and was talking to the children in a circle around the rooster. She had to make a detour to get to the stove.

"Get out of the way!" she shouted. She glowered in the animal's direction. "I don't know when I'll ever get rid of that evil-omened bird."

The colonel regarded his wife's mood over the rooster. Nothing about the rooster deserved resentment. He was ready for training. His neck and his feathered purple thighs, his saw-toothed crest: the animal had taken on a slender figure, a defenseless air.

"Lean out the window and forget the rooster," the colonel said when the children left. "On mornings like this, one feels like having a picture taken."

She leaned out the window but her face betrayed no emotion. "I would like to plant the roses," she said, returning to the stove. The colonel hung the mirror on the hook to shave.

"If you want to plant the roses, go ahead," he said.

He tried to make his movements match those in the mirror.

"The pigs eat them up," she said.

"All the better," the colonel said. "Pigs fattened on roses ought to taste very good."

He looked for his wife in the mirror and noticed that she still had the same expression. By the light of the fire her face seemed to be formed of the same material as the stove. Without noticing, his eyes fixed on her, the colonel continued shaving himself by touch as he had done for many years. The woman thought, in a long silence.

"But I don't want to plant them," she said.

"Fine," said the colonel. "Then don't plant them."

He felt well. December had shriveled the flora in his gut. He suffered a disappointment that morning trying to put on his new shoes. But after trying several times he realized that it was a wasted effort, and put on his patent-leather ones. His wife noticed the change.

"If you don't put on the new ones you'll never break them in," she said.

"They're shoes for a cripple," the colonel protested. "They ought to sell shoes that have already been worn for a month."

He went into the street stimulated by the presentiment that the letter would arrive that afternoon. Since it still was not time for the launches, he waited for Sabas in his office. But they informed him that he wouldn't be back until Monday. He didn't lose his patience despite not having foreseen this setback. "Sooner or later he has to come back," he told himself, and he headed for the harbor; it was a marvelous moment, a moment of still-unblemished clarity.

"The whole year ought to be December," he murmured, seated in the store of Moses the Syrian. "One feels as if he were made of glass."

Moses the Syrian had to make an effort to translate the idea into his almost forgotten Arabic. He was a placid Oriental, encased up to his ears in smooth, stretched skin, and he had the clumsy movements of a drowned man. In fact, he seemed as if he had just been rescued from the water.

"That's the way it was before," he said. "If it were the same now, I would be eight hundred and ninety-seven years old. And you?"

"Seventy-five," said the colonel, his eyes pursuing the postmaster.

Only then did he discover the circus. He recognized the patched tent on the roof of the mail boat amid a pile of colored objects. For a second he lost the postmaster while he looked for the wild animals among the crates piled up on the other launches. He didn't find them.

"It's a circus," he said. "It's the first one that's come in ten years."

Moses the Syrian verified his report. He spoke to his wife in a pidgin of Arabic and Spanish. She replied from the back of the store. He made a comment to himself, and then translated his worry for the colonel.

"Hide your cat, Colonel. The boys will steal it to sell it to the circus."

The colonel was getting ready to follow the postmaster.

"It's not a wild-animal show," he said.

"It doesn't matter," the Syrian replied. "The tightrope walkers eat cats so they won't break their bones."

He followed the postmaster through the stalls at the waterfront to the plaza. There the loud clamor from the cockfight took him by surprise. A passer-by said something to him about his rooster. Only then did he remember that this was the day set for the trials.

He passed the post office. A moment later he had sunk into the turbulent atmosphere of the pit. He saw his rooster in the middle of the pit, alone, defenseless, his spurs wrapped in rags, with something like fear visible in the trembling of his feet. His adversary was a sad ashen rooster.

The colonel felt no emotion. There was a succession of identical attacks. A momentary engagement of feathers and feet and necks in the middle of an enthusiastic ovation. Knocked against the planks of the barrier, the adversary did a somersault and returned to the attack. His rooster didn't attack. He rebuffed every attack, and landed again in exactly the same spot. But now his feet weren't trembling.

Hernán jumped the barrier, picked him up with both hands, and showed him to the crowd in the stands. There was a frenetic explosion of applause and shouting. The colonel noticed the disproportion between the enthusiasm of the applause and the intensity of the fight. It seemed to him a farce to which—voluntarily and consciously—the roosters had also lent themselves.

Impelled by a slightly disdainful curiosity, he examined the circular pit. An excited crowd was hurtling down the stands toward the pit. The colonel observed the confusion of hot, anxious, terribly alive faces. They were new people. All the new people in town. He relived—with foreboding—an instant which had been erased on the edge of his memory. Then he leaped the barrier, made his way through the packed crowd in the pit, and confronted Hernán's calm eyes. They looked at each other without blinking.

"Good afternoon, Colonel."

The colonel took the rooster away from him. "Good afternoon," he muttered. And he said nothing more because the warm deep throbbing of the animal made him shudder. He thought that he had never had such an alive thing in his hands before.

"You weren't at home," Hernán said, confused.

A new ovation interrupted him. The colonel felt intimidated. He made his way again, without looking at anybody, stunned by the applause and the shouts, and went into the street with his rooster under his arm.

The whole town—the lower-class people—came out to watch him go by followed by the school children. A gigantic Negro standing on a table with a snake wrapped around his neck was selling medicine without a license at a corner of the plaza. A large group returning from the harbor had stopped to listen to his spiel. But when the colonel passed with the rooster, their attention shifted to him. The way had never been so long.

He had no regrets. For a long time the town had lain in a sort of stupor, ravaged by ten years of history. That afternoon—another Friday without a letter—the people had awakened. The colonel remembered another era. He saw himself with his wife and his son watching under an umbrella a show which was not interrupted despite the rain. He remembered the party's leaders, scrupulously groomed, fanning themselves to the beat of the music in the patio of his house. He almost relived the painful resonance of the bass drum in his intestines.

He walked along the street parallel to the harbor and there, too, found the tumultuous Election Sunday crowd of long ago. They were watching the circus unloading. From inside a tent, a woman shouted something about the rooster. He continued home, self-absorbed, still hearing scattered voices, as if the remnants of the ovation in the pit were pursuing him.

At the door he addressed the children:

"Everyone go home," he said. "Anyone who comes in will leave with a hiding."

He barred the door and went straight into the kitchen. His wife came out of the bedroom choking.

"They took it by force," she said, sobbing. "I told them that the rooster would not leave this house while I was alive." The colonel tied the rooster to the leg of the stove. He changed the water in the can, pursued by his wife's frantic voice.

"They said they would take it over our dead bodies," she said. "They said the rooster didn't belong to us but to the whole town."

Only when he finished with the rooster did the colonel turn to the contorted face of his wife. He discovered, without surprise, that it produced neither remorse nor compassion in him.

"They did the right thing," he said quietly. And then, looking through his pockets, he added with a sort of bottomless sweetness:

"The rooster's not for sale."

She followed him to the bedroom. She felt him to be completely human, but untouchable, as if she were seeing him on a movie screen. The colonel took a roll of bills out of the closet, added what he had in his pockets to it, counted the total, and put it back in the closet.

"There are twenty-nine pesos to return to my friend Sabas," he said. "He'll get the rest when the pension arrives."

"And if it doesn't arrive?" the woman asked.

"It will."

"But if it doesn't?"

"Well, then, he won't get paid."

He found his new shoes under the bed. He went back to the closet for the box, cleaned the soles with a rag, and put the shoes in the box, just as his wife had bought them Sunday night. She didn't move.

"The shoes go back," the colonel said. "That's thirteen pesos more for my friend."

"They won't take them back," she said.

"They have to take them back," the colonel replied. "I've only put them on twice."

"The Turks don't understand such things," the woman said.

"They have to understand."

"And if they don't?"

"Well, then, they don't."

They went to bed without eating. The colonel waited for his wife to finish her rosary to turn out the lamp. But he couldn't sleep. He heard the bells for the movie classifications, and almost at once—three hours later—the curfew. The gravelly breathing of his wife became anguished with the chilly night air. The colonel still had his eyes open when she spoke to him in a calm, conciliatory voice:

"You're awake."

"Yes."

"Try to listen to reason," the woman said. "Talk to my friend Sabas tomorrow."

"He's not coming back until Monday."

"Better," said the woman. "That way you'll have three days to think about what you're going to say."

"There's nothing to think about," the colonel said.

A pleasant coolness had taken the place of the viscous air of October. The colonel recognized December again in the timetable of the plovers. When it struck two, he still hadn't been able to fall asleep. But he knew that his wife was also awake. He tried to change his position in the hammock.

"You can't sleep," the woman said.

"No."

She thought for a moment.

"We're in no condition to do that," she said. "Just think how much four hundred pesos in one lump sum is."

"It won't be long now till the pension comes," the colonel said.

"You've been saying the same thing for fifteen years."

"That's why," the colonel said. "It can't be much longer now."

She was silent. But when she spoke again, it didn't seem to the colonel as if any time had passed at all.

"I have the impression the money will never arrive," the woman said.

"It will."

"And if it doesn't?"

He couldn't find his voice to answer. At the first crowing of the rooster he was struck by reality, but he sank back again into a dense, safe, remorseless sleep. When he awoke, the sun was already high in the sky. His wife was sleeping. The colonel methodically repeated his morning activities, two hours behind schedule, and waited for his wife to eat breakfast.

She was uncommunicative when she awoke. They said good morning, and they sat down to eat in silence. The colonel sipped a cup of black coffee and had a piece of cheese and a sweet roll. He spent the whole morning in the tailor shop. At one o'clock he returned home and found his wife mending clothes among the begonias.

"It's lunchtime," he said.

"There is no lunch."

He shrugged. He tried to block up the holes in the patio wall to prevent the children from coming into the kitchen. When he came back into the hall, lunch was on the table.

During the course of lunch, the colonel realized that his wife was making an effort not to cry. This certainty alarmed him. He knew his wife's character, naturally hard, and hardened even more by forty years of bitterness. The death of her son had not wrung a single tear out of her.

He fixed a reproving look directly on her eyes. She bit her lips, dried her eyelids on her sleeve, and continued eating lunch.

"You have no consideration," she said.

The colonel didn't speak.

"You're willful, stubborn, and inconsiderate," she repeated. She crossed her knife and fork on the plate, but immediately rectified their positions superstitiously. "An entire lifetime eating dirt just so that now it turns out that I deserve less consideration than a rooster."

"That's different," the colonel said.

"It's the same thing," the woman replied. "You ought to realize that I'm dying; this thing I have is not a sickness but a slow death."

The colonel didn't speak until he finished eating his lunch.

"If the doctor guarantees me that by selling the rooster you'll get rid of your asthma, I'll sell him immediately," he said. "But if not, not."

That afternoon he took the rooster to the pit. On his return he found his wife on the verge of an attack. She was walking up and down the hall, her hair down her back, her arms spread wide apart, trying to catch her breath above the whistling in her lungs. She was there until early evening. Then she went to bed without speaking to her husband.

She mouthed prayers until a little after curfew. Then the colonel got ready to put out the lamp. But she objected.

"I don't want to die in the dark," she said.

The colonel left the lamp on the floor. He began to feel exhausted. He wished he could forget everything, sleep forty-four days in one stretch, and wake up on January 20th at three in the afternoon, in the pit, and at the exact moment to let the rooster loose. But he felt himself threatened by the sleeplessness of his wife.

"It's the same story as always," she began a moment later. "We put up with hunger so others can eat. It's been the same story for forty years."

The colonel kept silent until his wife paused to ask him if he was awake. He answered that he was. The woman continued in a smooth, fluent, implacable tone.

"Everybody will win with the rooster except us. We're the only ones who don't have a cent to bet."

"The owner of the rooster is entitled to twenty per cent."

"You were also entitled to get a position when they made you break your back for them in the elections," the woman replied. "You were also entitled to the veteran's pension after risking your neck in the civil war. Now everyone has his future assured and you're dying of hunger, completely alone."

"I'm not alone," the colonel said.

He tried to explain, but sleep overtook him. She kept talking dully until she realized that her husband was sleeping. Then she got out of the mosquito net and walked up and down the living room in the darkness. There she continued talking. The colonel called her at dawn.

She appeared at the door, ghostlike, illuminated from below by the lamp which was almost out. She put it out before getting into the mosquito netting. But she kept talking.

"We're going to do one thing," the colonel interrupted her.

"The only thing we can do is sell the rooster," said the woman.

"We can also sell the clock."

"They won't buy it."

"Tomorrow I'll try to see if Alvaro will give me the forty pesos."

"He won't give them to you."

"Then we'll sell the picture."

When the woman spoke again, she was outside the mosquito net again. The colonel smelled her breath impregnated with medicinal herbs.

"They won't buy it," she said.

"We'll see," the colonel said gently, without a trace of change in his voice. "Now, go to sleep. If we can't sell anything tomorrow, we'll think of something else."

He tried to keep his eyes open but sleep broke his resolve. He fell to the bottom of a substance without time and without space, where the words of his wife had a different significance. But a moment later he felt himself being shaken by the shoulder.

"Answer me."

The colonel didn't know if he had heard those words before or after he had slept. Dawn was breaking. The window stood out in Sunday's green clarity. He thought he had a fever. His eyes burned and he had to make a great effort to clear his head.

"What will we do if we can't sell anything?" the woman repeated.

"By then it will be January 20th," the colonel said, completely awake. "They'll pay the twenty per cent that very afternoon."

"If the rooster wins," the woman said. "But if he loses. It hasn't occurred to you that the rooster might lose."

"He's one rooster that can't lose."

"But suppose he loses."

"There are still forty-four days left to begin to think about that," the colonel said.

The woman lost her patience.

"And meanwhile what do we eat?" she asked, and seized the colonel by the collar of his flannel night shirt. She shook him hard.

It had taken the colonel seventy-five years—the seventy-five years of his life, minute by minute—to reach this moment. He felt pure, explicit, invincible at the moment when he replied:

"Shit."

MA CHIA

unfading flowers

1

It was the end of the month of May on the Mongolian steppe and as far as the eye could see the grasslands were dotted with perennially blooming flowers. Not a single streak or so much as a wisp of cloud was to be seen in the limpid blue dome of sky overhead. Swallows skimmed through the air; orioles trilled their dulcet melodies.

The earth was everywhere green with lush grass and the whole expanse garlanded with cerulean asters, white morning glories, the many-petalled "cat's eyes" and pastel-hued wild chrysanthemums. A breeze rolled over the grasslands, stirring the clumps of multi-tinted blossoms and the reeds into a lively dance. "Cart wheels," sporting leaves pointed like swords, lined the way, and plumes of the reedy wolftail waved like so many diminutive flags.

Four rubber-tyred carts had just set out from the town of Tungliao in the East Khorcin Middle Banner. The drivers brandished their whips and the horses trotted ahead spiritedly, the rubber-tyres leaving their tread on the carpet of grass.

There were altogether more than thirty persons in the carts; military cadres, cadres engaged in work among the masses, workers from women's organizations, and literary and art workers. Besides these there were about a dozen guards travelling along as escort. The group had left Changchiakou at the end of April and was bound for the Northeast, where they would work for the development of newly liberated areas.

Peking. Foreign Language Press, 1961.
A copy of this material has been filed with the Foreign Agents Registration Section, Department of Justice, Washington, D.C., where the registration statement of China Books & Periodicals, 334 W. Schiller St., Chicago 10, Ill., as an agent of Guozi Shudian and China Reconstructs, both of Peking, China, is available for inspection. The fact of registration does not indicate approval or disapproval of this material by the Government of the United States.

From the end of April to the end of May, however, the military situation had materially changed, and when they reached Tungliao they had got news that their fighters had withdrawn from Szeping and the railway line from Tungliao to Kaitung was cut. Thus this passage through the steppe-land of the East Khorcin Middle Banner was the only route open to Harbin where the Northeast Bureau of the Party's Central Committee was located.

Between Tungliao and Chanyu, another town on the way to Harbin, was a two-hundred-*li*[1] expanse of steppe. The travellers' knowledge of the geography and people of the area was all too meagre; neither were they familiar with the prevailing conditions. It was said that only a few days before Chiang Kai-shek had despatched one of his henchmen named Pai Yun-ti to stir up subversive activities in Inner Mongolia and, specifically, to plot a revolt of the armed bands of local landlords infesting the area against the forces of liberation. There was no one in the party who was not fully aware of the hazards besetting them on their journey under such circumstances, but all had set their minds to their task and no one would remain behind at Tungliao.

The leader of the group was Regimental Commander Tsao, a man who had been in the thick of the agrarian revolution in northern Shensi, later at the front fighting the Japanese, and from then on had engaged in battles against the Kuomintang reactionaries. A man of courage and ingenuity, he was rich in combat experience. In the heat of battle against the enemy he made decisions in the twinkling of an eye, but when the engagement was over he would sling his binoculars aside, tilt his radiant face to the comrades about him and joke genially with them. No one could be around him without having his confidence and spirits braced.

At the moment he was thinking about the situation facing his men: the Inner Mongolian Autonomous Federation had already convened and Chairman Ulanfu had made his political report. East and west Mongolia had joined forces and, in order to crush any counter-revolutionary plots, Asgen had concentrated Mongolian cavalrymen around Tungliao. With a small detachment of armed Mongolian horsemen as guides for the cadres' team, and with the weapons brought by the cadres themselves, six rifles and twenty to thirty pistols, the problem at hand did not seem to the regimental commander to be too serious. He was certain he would succeed in leading the group to the Northeast Bureau.

The carts rolled lightly over the steppe, neither their wheels nor the horses' hoofs picking up any mud but the vehicles advancing quite a piece with each forceful pull. The four of them, forging ahead, kept a certain distance between nose and wheel, so that verdant patches of

---

[1] A *li* is equal to about one-third of a mile.

steppe appeared constantly between them. The Mongolian pony at the lead whinnied now and then, and when he did the sound reverberated far and wide over the prairie. Here was the East Khorcin Middle Banner! Ahead was endless horizon, behind limitless space, while all around was a sea of grass.

Regimental Commander Tsao had participated in the War of Resistance Against Japan at the northern China front. From the Luliang Mountains he had marched off to the Taihang Mountains and later to northern Shensi, the area to the west of Peking, and to Jehol. In those seven or eight years he had never left the mountain fastnesses in his game of hide-and-seek with the enemy till he felt he had indeed had quite enough of the mountains. That was why now the sight of the vast flat grassland made his eyes so bright and his whole being buoyant and happy. How good the mild fragrance of the grass was in his nostrils as he breathed deeply of it! He put down his map-case and nudged a man beside him whose face was darkly stubbled. "Look, Old Wang," Tsao said in merry mood, "what a vast prairie this is!"

Wang Yao-tung was in a grey, well-worn army tunic with the hook on its collar undone, revealing the collar of a coarse home-spun shirt, while clamped to the peak of his cap was a pair of fur-edged goggles. With its narrow jaw and high cheek-bones, his face bore every trace of the care-worn traveller on a long journey. He was gazing enrapt at the plains—these grassy plains so dear to him! Recollections from his childhood flitted through his mind: how as a boy he had pastured horses on the plain, cut the lush grass, enjoyed pouncing on grasshoppers and crushing locusts. He felt for all the world like turning a somersault and rolling on that grass! At the regimental commander's nudge, he woke from his reminiscences as if suddenly bitten by a mosquito.

"Oh, yes, Old Tsao, there's no end to it!" he said. "From western Manchuria south, and from south to north, it's nothing but vast prairie."

"How about the lay of the land around Harbin? Is it flat there too?" Tsao asked.

"You'll never see a mountain all the way," replied Wang, gesturing sweepingly with his arms and smiling with pride. "Nothing in our way. Railway communication is quite well developed here too. We can take a train at Kaitung and reach the Northeast Bureau inside of two days."

"It's a marvellous spot here," Tsao remarked.

"Yes indeed, the Northeast is a treasure-trove of our revolution!"

"Old Wang," Tsao then suddenly asked him, "when we have reached the Northeast Bureau, what kind of work do you think you would like to take up?"

"I'll take up whatever post I'm assigned by the Party," Wang replied without a moment's hesitation.

Tsao knew that Wang had always worked at the Military Zone Command, so he began to consider the matter in that light.

"I believe the Party will give you the kind of work you're accustomed to. So long as Chiang Kai-shek doesn't let up his attacks on us, we who've taken up military work certainly won't be idle." Tsao laughed heartily, his sun-tanned face glistening now with beads of sweat. The narrow leather strap hanging at his neck, to which his binoculars were fastened, swung rhythmically at every lurch of the cart. The convoy was now entering a territory overgrown with artemisia up to the horses' knees and blades of the grass slapped noisily against the cart wheels. Wang Yao-tung turned his gaze from the regimental commander and, slapping the good-natured Liu Chun, who was sitting beside him, on the shoulder, said "Old Liu will be the one most needed! Until the masses are organized, it'll be impossible for us armymen to chalk up any victories."

Liu Chun had been chief of organizational department of a district Party committee and had all along been doing work among the masses. He was the simple, sociable type and never lost his temper even when someone made cutting remarks to his face. Likewise, no one could feel hurt by any direct remarks he made.

"But a good half of our mass agitational work has to be done by our women comrades. Lin Hsiu, you wouldn't have any objection to my saying that, I suppose?"

Lin Hsiu, who was sitting at the rear of the cart, turned her head at the mention of her name. She had cheeks like rosy apples, a round chin and a high, pointed nose. Her big round eyes had been resting on one cluster of blossoms after another as her cart sped over the plains. Then she appeared to be lost in thought. Regimental Commander Tsao, seeing her so quiet, said jokingly, "Lin Hsiu must be contemplating work among the women folk."

Lin Hsiu blinked her big eyes and asked placidly, "But why should I be?"

"Why? Because you're a woman!"

The girl shook her head, undaunted. "Why, can't women cadres do any other job than organizing women?" she protested.

The carts were headed northwest, the carters urging the ponies on with their whips, which they kept flourishing in the air, and the rubber-tyred wheels rolled smoothly over the turf. Regimental Commander Tsao wanted to know something about the geography of Mongolia and turned to Wang Yao-tung to ask, "Are we heading towards Prince Darhan's Palace?"

"No," Wang replied with assurance, "we don't go that way. Soon we'll make a turn northeast and head towards Chiachiayingtse."

"Old Wang, you are pretty familiar with this part of the country, aren't you?"

"I should be. This road runs right by the front door of my old home. I can tell you the name of every flower that grows here!"

"Ha, ha, Old Wang, then you're a Northeasterner through and through!"

A youth with a gun strapped to his back reined in and brought his black pony abreast of Wang's cart. The exchange of a few words with Wang Yao-tung confirmed that in Wang he had found a fellow-provincial.

"Deputy Regimental Commander Wang," exclaimed the youth, "so you too are a Northeasterner. Glad to meet you!"

2

This youth was a squad leader from the West Manchurian Military Zone Command. His surname was Chao and everyone called him simply Squad Leader Chao. He had been to Tungliao on a mission and was now on his way back to his unit in the company of the group of cadres. It was beyond his expectations that he would meet a fellow-Northeasterner on the way, a veteran cadre straight from the interior at that! A feeling of warmth rose within him and he found he had a great deal in common to talk about with this man, who was quite a few years older than himself.

"Deputy Regimental Commander, how many years have you been away from home?"

Stroking his stubbly chin, Wang Yao-tung glanced at the deeply tanned face of the squad leader and replied thoughtfully, "I've been away since the September 18th Incident[2]—let's see, fifteen years now. Quite a spell to be away!"

Then Chao lifted his face and began to tell his story. "I'm twenty now. At the time of the September 18th Incident I was just a kid of five, completely ignorant of what was going on. When I heard that Japanese troops had occupied the Peitaying Camp, I ran out into the streets to see the ointment plaster flag.[3] That was how I came to be a slave without a country without knowing the whys and wherefores."

"At that time I was a platoon commander at the Peitaying Camp," Wang Yao-tung's recollections of the Incident both moved and enraged him. "The Japanese lobbed shells upon our heads," he went on, "and

[2] On September 18, 1931 the Japanese imperialist forces began their surprise attack on Shenyang and later seized the entire northeastern provinces of China.
[3] A deprecatory remark about the Japanese flag because of its resemblance to a Chinese medicinal plaster.

many in our ranks were either killed or wounded. Those of us who survived were so enraged that we kicked at the ground in our fury, longing to charge the enemy in a bayonet fight on the spot. But that hateful bastard Chiang Kai-shek cabled Chang Hsueh-liang[4] again and again not to resist. When we were all too fed up with disgust we left the place by a spur for the Eastern Hills and later joined the Anti-Japanese Volunteers."

Squad Leader Chao blinked his eyes as he listened to the story. He seemed to be reminded of something and interrupted, "I remember hearing the old folks say that the Volunteers engaged the enemy at a point eighty *li* from Shenyang. The Japanese were so scared they cut the kaoliang in June when it was still green and cleared all the trees from along the railway lines. The old folks called that 'the wretched fate of Manchukuo.' "[5]

The sun was scorching hot and there was not a stir in the still expanse while the pungent odour of grass hung heavy in the air. Orioles flitted hither and yon through the skies, and scarlet-winged butterflies dipped for a breath of fragrance among the flowers.

Chao gave his snaffle a quick jerk then loosened the reins, sending his pony forward in chase of Wang Yao-tung's cart, then riding beside it, he resumed the conversation with his fellow-provincial.

"So you've never been home since then," the youth said.

Wang Yao-tung, who was watching the sparks fly about in the bowl of his pipe as he smoked, knitted his brows.

Chao was too busy spurring his pony in order to keep pace with the cart to notice the expression on Wang's face, and he went on to exclaim:

"What changes have taken place in these years!"

"How many factories are there in Shenyang now?" Wang asked him.

"How many there are I really can't say, but smokestacks, tall or squat, look like the trees in a forest."

Regimental Commander Tsao then joined in. "They're all ours," he said smiling. "Who knows, when the entire Northeast has been liberated perhaps we'll pick up some other work. It'll likely be in factories."

The others in the cart who had heard the conversation felt excited by it, but remained silent. To Liu Chun's eyes everything in the Northeast was novel and fresh. Especially when its factories were mentioned, he could not help regarding them with envy. Lin Hsiu, too, was in very high spirits. Even before she had started out for the Northeast her mind was already teeming with the "soy-beans and kaoliang, forests and coal

---

[4] Then commander of the Northeastern Army of the Kuomintang.

[5] "Manchukuo" was the puppet state set up by the Japanese imperialists in the Northeast between 1931 and 1945.

mines," immortalized in song—these and visions of a railway network, and smokestacks that should look like trees in a wood. Indeed such visions further developed her already rich imaginative powers. She would like to see the driver urge the horse on faster, the sooner to reach her new post!

Wang went on smoking his pipe as he chatted with the lad. From all appearances he was enjoying the pleasure of meeting with a fellow-provincial and found many questions to ask him.

"Is the Hsiaohoyen area in Shenyang still as busy and crowded as in the old days?"

"Yes, it's crowded all right," the youth replied, then added, "say, right behind Hsiaohoyen is Darhan's Palace, isn't it?"

"Isn't Darhan's Palace somewhere out on the grassland?" Regimental Commander Tsao interrupted. "Who's moved it up there?"

"Darhan had two palaces," Wang explained, "one at the East Khorcin Central Banner, the other at Hsiaohoyen in Shenyang."

"Do you still remember the warlord Chang Tso-lin's mansion inside the Hsiaonanmen Gate?" the lad again asked Wang.

"Oh, yes. By the way, Chang Tso-lin and Darhan were relatives by marriage, or so I've heard."

After saying this, Wang Yao-tung smoked another pipe to dispel his fatigue. Squad Leader Chao gave his pony free rein and sometimes it cantered along at a good clip, sometimes slowed down to a walk. Even when the beast stopped to nibble the grass he did not mind. For all the others in the cart it was their first experience in the Northeast and, feeling their new surroundings exciting and strange, they were delighted to hear the anecdotes. Regimental Commander Tsao time and again tried to snatch away Wang's pipe, asking him to go on with his story.

"Come on now," he urged, "tell us some more. What sort was this Prince Darhan anyway?"

Wang Yao-tung finally laid aside his pipe entirely and told his companion-travellers, "Well, there were forty-eight princes in Inner Mongolia, and Darhan was the chief of the lot."

"Then he was a big feudal ringleader!" Liu Chun remarked, inserting some political nomenclature into the story.

"You're right there, Old Liu!"

"Being a big feudal ringleader he must have known how to enjoy himself."

Wang Yao-tung thrust out his lower lip in a wry smile. "That's no lie!" he exclaimed. "Darhan lived in the lap of luxury all right. His favourite dishes were the rarest species of mushrooms—monkey's skull—swallow's nest broth, rare delicacies from mountain and sea; he drank wine from Peking steeped with tiger bones and smoked only the most refined opium from Jehol. And that spouse of his—glittering from head to foot with pearls and emeralds! And that's not a tenth of their extravagance. Besides, they kept a whole bevy of lamas to chant sutras and pray over them and anybody who didn't do that was liable for duty grazing his horses or cultivating his lands for him. The prince set up collecting stations at various spots on the grassland where his men saw to it that whoever reaped a crop paid his tithes."

"I have heard of those who living on the mountain, draw their sustenance from the mountain," Regimental Commander Tsao said with a chuckle, "but here are some who still squeeze glut and drink out of the steppe."

"The Mongolians depend on the pasture lands for their living," put in Squad Leader Chao.

"Yes," Wang continued, "but then Darhan lived too high, wide and handsome too long, and when he reached the bottom of his coffers he sold the grasslands around Tungliao to Chang Tso-lin, who decided to cultivate them as his own. Chang Tso-lin set up an 'Army of Colonists' and resorted to whips to drive the Mongolians from their homes there. Thus the people had their cattle and sheep robbed from them and were deprived of their land."

Liu Chun pounded his clenched fist against the board siding of the cart to give vent to his indignation. "A proper big Han chauvinist, that's what Chang Tso-lin was!" he exclaimed.

"One of the same stripe as Chiang Kai-shek," Regimental Commander Tsao commented.

"Reared by the same bitch," the others agreed.

"In his book, *China's Destiny*, Chiang Kai-shek himself claims that he has long since liquidated the Mongolians as a nationality."

The rubber-tyred carts jolted and bumped over a patch of sand-dune and soon arrived at the Shar-muren River where the drivers "whoa-ed" their beasts to a halt. The travellers jumped down from the carts and glanced back over the plains. Squad Leader Chao, who had been left quite a distance behind, drew up slowly on his black pony.

3

It was after the spring thaw had swelled the Shar-muren River, cutting a narrow but swift channel through its sandy beach. White flakes of foam, chips of wood, grass and clumps of manure floated in its current, which took its load to the far ends of the steppe-land. A few twittering, white-feathered water-fowls were perched on the sandy bank, but at the commotion of the approaching carts they took fright and flew off across the river.

While fording the stream one of the carters got off the road, sending the cart lurching into a pool. The horses were in up to their bellies and water swept the floor-boards, wetting the baggage in the cart. Wang Yao-tung wasted no time jumping into the current and shouting to the guards to help him haul the cart out onto the bank. When he climbed out he was soaked to the skin, with water pouring from his trouser legs.

They proceeded on their way a bit damp, the mounter Mongolian guides riding out in front and the carts following in a line behind.

The convoy was penetrating deep into the heart of the grassland.

Wang Yao-tung, who had straddled a pile of luggage to let his trouser legs dry, was peering into the vastness of the steppe. What he saw was indeed profoundly beautiful. Emerald green were the sturdy leaves of grass and crimson the blossoms, while the tendrils were of paler green and the rootlets purplish, the plants raising their heads to different heights over the prairie. After the fifteen years that he had not had a chance to return to his native Northeast Wang felt this steppe-land most dear to him. But what an abominable blot had been the story of Prince Darhan!

The sun was high and there was not a stir of breeze on the prairie. The carts rolled over the flat ground so lightly that their wheels appeared not to touch the road at all. Regimental Commander Tsao, sweeping the distance with his binoculars, nudged Wang Yao-tung and asked him to go on with the story.

"Old Wang, tell us what happened next! The prince sold the grass-plains to Chang Tso-lin; but didn't the Mongolian people ever rise up against him?"

"Of course they did. The Mongolians are a very brave people. At that time there arose a hero by the name of Gada Meren who fought together with his followers against Chang Tso-lin and Prince Darhan on the plains. But unfortunately he was drowned in the Shar-muren River."

Regimental Commander Tsao raised his eyes and asked, "Wasn't that the Shar-muren River we just crossed?"

"So it was," Wang replied.

"We forded it without the least awareness of what happened there!"

"But people around here all know about it. The legends of heroes will for ever be told and retold."

"Old Wang, tell us of this hero's feats till the very end then."

Animation filled the group as they anticipated the treat in store for them. Their interest in the heroic episode had been so piqued that they forgot both fatigue and hunger, nor did they think any more about the long, weary miles behind them. Wang Yao-tung's spirits rose also, deeply moved as he was by the recollection of Gada Meren's story. Straightening his back he took up the thread of the legend.

"Well, let me start from the beginning then. Gada Meren's home was at Shebert in the East Khorcin Middle Banner, about fifty *li* from here. His name was simply Gada, while Meren was his title since he had been a low-ranking military officer at Darhan's Palace. At home he had a wife called Peony and the daughter of one of his relatives, by the name of Tienjiliang. Gada Meren was a very generous man, straightforward, daring and courageous; he was fond of riding horses and sharp shooting. Besides, he possessed a keen sense of justice and had made friends with many of those who tilled the soil and at the same time herded animals."

"He was close to the masses, and surely his leading the uprising sprang from that fact," observed Liu Chun, interposing. When Liu analysed a situation he always linked it up with the mass line, and thus now he seemed to have drawn his own conclusions in the matter.

"Yes, I think it had something to do with it," Wang Yao-tung assented with a knowledgeable nod. "At that time Chang Tso-lin's terrible gang, his 'Army of Colonists,' was riding roughshod over the Mongolian people. They gobbled up any land that suited them and grabbed all livestock that caught their fancy, which so enraged Gada Meren that he led the people of the Darhan Banner to Fengtien (now Shenyang) to voice their grievances. Of course they found the prince and Chang Tso-lin birds of a feather. The pair of them drove away the people who had come peaceably with their petition; the prince removed Gada Meren from his military post and clapped him into the Darhan Banner gaol to boot. They were all set to shoot him and tried their best to prevent their plot from leaking out. But there was a little boy in the prince's palace who had become very attached to Gada Meren, and he secretly got word out to Peony. Now Peony was such a woman that upon receiving the message she set fire to her cottage without a moment's hesitation, arranged for Tienjiliang to stay with others and, pocketing a pistol, jumped on her pony and galloped off. She mustered the men who had gone to petition the prince and Chang and together they went to release her husband from gaol. The gaoler, one Basarata, was not only taken aback by the great number of men Peony had with her but his conscience was also pricked. He therefore unlocked the gaol door and set Gada Meren free without further a-do. The Mongolians of the Banner were overjoyed and forthwith elected Gada Meren as the leader of their planned uprising. At his call the people rushed to contribute what munitions, grain and fodder they had to their cause. There were also those who sent their sons to join him. Armed with foreign guns and automatic rifles they galloped in a long and stirring cavalcade across the grass-lands of Mongolia and succeeded in routing Chang's 'Army of Colonists' and giving Prince Darhan a good beating."

As the story reached its climax the listeners' emotions were roused to high pitch. They would at once jump down from the cart and help fight Gada's guerrilla warfare! Some of them were unable to contain themselves and clamoured for Wang to tell them immediately the upshot of the revolt.

"Old Wang, don't leave us to die of our suspense; hurry up and get on with the story!"

Wang Yao-tung thrust his stubbled chin forward, looking very serious as he gazed into the eager faces of his audience. Then, heaving a deep and agonized sigh, he continued: "As time went on Gada Meren's army was faced with more and greater difficulties—ammunition ran out, grain and fodder got low, discipline slackened. After all, without the leadership of the Communist Party no revolution can succeed. Seeing Gada as the thorn in their sides which must be extracted at all costs, Chang Tso-lin and Darhan threw a whole army into the campaign, the troops of Tang Yu-lin, "Big Horse Stick" Yang and Li Shou-hsing, Li Shou-hsing being the vilest and most insidious of the lot. That villain ordered cartridges boiled in water and had them delivered to Gada by well-wishers in disguise so that in his next battle all his cartridges fizzled out. With his cavalry-men Li Shou-hsing pursued the partisans across the plains till all were either killed or put to flight. Peony was among the defeated in the battle. The catastrophe filled Gada's heart with anxiety and hatred but failed to dampen his determination. He would die rather than surrender. So, spurring his charger, he dashed forth, picking his way over the dead bodies of men and horses. Alone, on horseback, this Gada crossed the Shar-muren, which was beginning to thaw after deep winter, with ice-floes drifting in the raging current and the water biting cold. Clenching his teeth Gada directed his mount across to the southern bank where the crust of ice had not yet melted. He spurred his steed and the beast responded with two successful lunges, but then its hoofs lost their hold on the frozen bank and it came plunging down headlong into the swirling, icy waters. . . ."

4

Anguish filled Wang Yao-tung's heart as he reached this interlude in the story. He could not bear to go on, but, turning his head, filled the silence by glancing briefly at the receding Shar-muren. The river, hazy now in the distance, looked serene enough, beautiful and wide, but it appeared too to be capable of hiding unfathomable hazards in its depths. The comrades knew the story had ended but they found it hard to compose their thoughts again. Ill at ease they kept asking, "And what happened to Gada Meren after that?"

Wang Yao-tung heaved a sigh as he said, "The ending is tragic."

"What do you mean tragic?" one of the guards asked in a voice deep with concern. "Was he drowned then?"

"That he was drowned was sad enough," Wang replied, "but the most grievous part of all was that his ideals failed to materialize."

"Yes, every man lives for his ideals," put in Lin Hsiu, a lively, straightforward girl always ready to speak out whatever was in her mind. "I remember at the time of the December 9th Incident[1] some of our schoolmates from the Northeast were ones with the loftiest ideals and deepest feelings. Whenever we sang *On the Sungari River* or *Fresh Blossoms of May*, they would think of home."

"Do you think of home when you sing?" Regimental Commander Tsao asked her in a light mood.

"I don't even sing now," Lin Hsiu said, tossing her head to one side and smiling open-heartedly. She did not blush, nor was there any trace of superciliousness in her tone. Momentarily she recalled how her thoughts and feelings had undergone a great change, becoming much healthier now that she had completed the course of study in Yenan for ideological remoulding and the rectification of working style and had later worked for some time in the local organizations.

"Comrade Lin Hsiu, sing *Fresh Blossoms of May* for us! It's May now," Wang Yao-tung and Liu Chun urged her. The others in the cart responded and some clapped their hands as encouragement. Lin Hsiu found herself in a very awkward position: she was in no mood to sing, but neither could she very well refuse. Then, seeing everyone so eager and earnest in his request, she consented and began softly:

> Fresh blossoms of May,
> Blooming o'er the fields,
> Shroud the blood of patriots
> Who, to save their country from danger,
> Fought unflinchingly in the War of Resistance.
> And yet the Northeast today,
> . . . .

Wang Yao-tung's face showed deep emotion as he drank in every word of Lin Hsiu's song. At her opening line, Wang's eyes happened to be on the flowers in the fields. Exquisite, lovely blossoms they were, the vivid hues of live coals. At the second line, a moment of gloom

[6] The patriotic demonstration of the students in Peking against civil war and Japanese aggression on December 9, 1935 under the leadership of the Chinese Communist Party. It won nationwide support.

passed over him. The word "patriot" certainly fit Gada Meren! This hero who laid down his life on the grasslands was worthy of deep respect. Then he heard *"Who, to save their country from danger, fought unflinchingly in the War of Resistance."* Wang pondered over these lines. They seemed to tell the story of Gada Meren, but they seemed also to tell his own story. As an Anti-Japanese Volunteer he had fought doggedly in many battles. Then he had gone to northern China to join the Eighth Route Army and there too he had unflinchingly resisted the enemy to the very end. After V-J Day he had gone back to his native Northeast. But how were things there upon his return? As Lin Hsiu had sung *"And yet the Northeast today . . ."* a lump had risen in her throat and she had stopped abruptly, like a fiddle whose string had snapped in the middle of a performance. Wang felt very ill at ease.

"Why don't you continue?" he asked.

Lin Hsiu lifted a sober face to mark the disappointed expression on Wang's. She knew he had been thinking of past experiences.

"I don't want to sing any more," she said slowly. "The song's so out of tune with our mood now. It makes one feel bitter."

"Better to feel bitter. It'll awaken the hatred within us, rouse our fighting spirit. The people of the Northeast have been suffering for fourteen long years; that's why we're back here now. We must liberate all the Northeast so that people will never again have to live in suffering."

Wang's words stirred the minds of the comrades profoundly. Almost as one man they looked up at him and then turned to Regimental Commander Tsao, after which they exchanged spontaneous glances with one another. Everyone sensed his own responsibility, as though a heavy load had been shifted onto each one's shoulders, so heavy a load that no one uttered a word. The carter turned his head and put down his whip to listen to their conversation.

Soon Wang Yao-tung saw Squad Leader Chao approaching on his pony. The lad looked carefree and light-hearted with his chest thrown out and his rifle strapped jauntily across his back.

"Hey, my lad," Wang hailed him, "how did you get along under the puppet regime?"

Chao shook his head, and with his lips distorted in a grim smile replied, "Those fourteen years were really tough. Throughout the whole time they pressganged recruits into the puppet army, arrested people at random for 'violating economic controls,' took the people's grain as taxes, seized people and forced them to do hard labour for them. . . . The people were so hard pressed that they often longed for the earth to split before them so that they would have a crack to hide themselves in."

"Did you ever get kaoliang to eat?"

"There would be no grain left for us to eat after the taxes had been collected at harvest. Some people tried to hide a few grains in their pillows, but even those would be ferreted out and confiscated. If a single grain of rice was found on a stove, the householder would be subject to arrest as an 'economic law-breaker.'"

The company were stunned at Chao's account. Lin Hsiu had for years lived in Yenan and found that though the material conditions there were inadequate, at any rate she had more than enough to eat and wear. She could never have imagined such bitter hardship and suffering as people under the puppet regime had had to put up with. The knowledge made her feel both sorry and indignant.

"How dreadful that the people didn't even have the right to eat!" she exclaimed.

The carter could not hold his tongue any longer, and putting down his whip again he turned to Lin Hsiu and said, "I've a cousin who was conscripted for hard labour in a mine. He left a family at home and they couldn't afford even acorn meal to eat."

"Couldn't he have refused to go?" asked Lin Hsiu.

The driver heaved a sigh as he replied, "The police were hand in glove with the local landlords, so when your name was called, with the police glaring into your face and dangling their sabres at you, who dared to disobey?"

"I was told the police and former special agents in Shenyang have joined up with the Kuomintang now," Chao put in.

"No sooner had those devils gone than the King of Hell himself came in. It seemed predestined that the people should live such tortured lives," grunted the driver.

Regimental Commander Tsao gazed at the vast plains ahead from atop the pile of luggage. Anxious to get along, he urged the man, "Come on now, let's put on a little speed!"

The sun was hanging low over the western horizon. The men were weary and the horses too were tired. Even the cart seemed reluctant to move. Having traversed a good piece of the monotonous steppe, they finally came upon a low, sprawling Mongolian village the dwellings of which were dark and rounded with low adobe walls. Drying hayricks stood here and there in the yards while the smoke from horse-dung fires issued from the chimneys, curling about the eaves and tree branches and ultimately vanishing into space.

The Mongolian horsemen who were their guides stopped to water their horses at the village, which, from their hailing and gesturing back to the occupants of the carts, the company knew was Chiachiayingtse and went about making preparations for spending the night.

5

The group forthwith encamped at Chiachiayingtse and were settling in for the night.

Now Wang Yao-tung had a young orderly named Yang Teh-ching with him, a naughty and careless fellow whom people had dubbed "Dunderhead" Yang. The very first evening, carrying Wang Yao-tung's saddle-bag over one shoulder, he burst right into a villager's courtyard and ran into the head of the house, an old Mongolian just back from his day's work in the pasture lands. The old man had a dead hare slung over his shoulder and a staff in his hand. At his heels were a pair of fox-terriers which kept yapping at the sight of Yang. The boy mistook the terriers for strays and picked up a clod and heaved it at them, making the old man very cross so that the two began enchanging angry words.

When Regimental Commander Asao and Wang Yao-tung came upon the scene the dogs were still barking and there stood the blundering Yang glaring at the old man, his eyes bulging, while he, staff in hand, just stood his ground with his brows knit over a face furrowed with age. He was obviously very annoyed but was not saying a word. Tsao and Wang sized up the situation at a glance, criticized Yang Teh-ching, then approached the old man to talk things over.

When the old Mongolian saw the impish lad slink meekly away under Wang's censuring glance, he thought it very strange. Indicating the retreating figure of the boy he said to Wang Yao-tung, "Is that your son?"

"No, he isn't," Wang replied, shaking his head. Then, stepping ahead of the regimental commander, he strode past the hayrick in the yard. At a little distance from the door he stopped and turned to his host to ask, "Have you any children?"

The old Mongolian was wearing a long, split robe with the four corners turned up and nipped in at the waist with a long blue sash the loose ends of which swept the ground like a broom when he walked.

"Have you any children?" Wang repeated his question.

The old man looked him over briefly and, finding him quite friendly, broke through his reserve and replied in a draw, "I have a son."

"Is he at home?"

"No, he is in the Public Security Corps in Chanyu Country."

Regimental Commander Tsao stepped forward and, turning to the old man, said warmly, "We're going to Chanyu. We'll be sure to look up your son."

The Mongolian parted his lips in an open, frank smile as though he had sensed that something pleasant was in store. His eyebrows relaxed as he nodded in gratitude to the regimental commander. Following up this favourable turn of events, Tsao took the old man's hand and asked, "What's your name, Uncle?"

"Nasan Ulji," the man replied, using the Mongolian pronunciation.

Wondering if there was some meaning in the name, Tsao nodded and smiled. "Fine, Nasan Ulji," he said, "but what does it mean?"

"Longevity," the old man replied, smiling now too.

"Nasan Ulji," Wang pursued, "how old are you?"

"Sixty-two."

"Sixty-two, ha, ha!" the regimental commander echoed in ringing laughter. "No wonder you're called Nasan Ulji. You've certainly got many years to live yet."

"You'll have no trouble seeing seventy-two," Wang Yao-tung offered.

"Eighty-two wouldn't be too old for you, I should say," Tsao added.

Nasan Ulji regarded the two with a warm, friendly grin, while the regimental commander, after stroking the fur of the hare still on Nasan Ulji's shoulder, patted the old man on the back.

"Since your son is in the Eighth Route Army we're all members of one family," he said, and with that observation the three entered the cottage amid hearty laughter.

The room was low-ceilinged, the door lintel barely high enough to admit a man of ordinary height without bumping his head, while grimy cobwebs formed an untidy lacework overhead. The furnishings were of the simplest. A round iron stove was placed on the elevated earthen bed and on the fire a pot of buttered tea was boiling, giving off the heavy smell of mutton. By the light of occasional sparks from the stove the visitors could make out hanging on the wall several lassos fastened to long poles, a pile of cow bones in one corner, and beside that a shrine to Buddha. The other objects in the room were too obscured to allow identification.

The trio chatted together for some time, growing more congenial as they talked. Regimental Commander Tsao opened his rucksack and drew out of it some hard-boiled eggs and fruit which he offered to Nasan Ulji. The old man reciprocated by inviting them to try a cup of his buttered tea and some parched rice. Thus, in this happy frame of mind, Nasan Ulji began to tell them his life story.

6

For many long years Nasan Ulji had been a herdsman.

Now, every morning the sun rose over the steppe, giving it the sheen of a golden velvet carpet, and pearly beads of dew shimmered on the green grass leaves. Orioles sang and swallows flitted like arrows through the sky. The lush green plain of the East Khorcin Middle Banner was steadily moving into its ever fresh future.

Nasan Ulji, who was the brisk type, would rise early in the morning, snatch a hasty breakfast of buttered tea and parched rice, and ride off on his pony. With a pole and lasso in his hand he would drive his horses to pasture, his pair of terriers at their hoofs. Throughout the day he tended the horses and hunted a bit of game. In the evenings, when the moon cast its glimmering light upon the prairie, Nasan Ulji would return to his yurt. There would be the breeze from the faraway desert to cool him and the bleating of sheep to break the silence of the night which was complete but for the whisper of stirring grass. Nasan Ulji would then get out his horse-head fiddle and sing to his own accompaniment together with his Mongolian neighbours.

Wang Yao-tung listened to the old man's account of himself with such interest that he seemed to be under a spell, then suddenly he asked, "Do you like to make friends?"

Nasan Ulji straightened his back and, staring at the sparks dancing from the stove, he recalled friendships from the carefree days of his youth.

"When I struck up a friendship with someone," he said with utter frankness, "we would pitch our yurts together, drink our wine together, hunt together, and together we'd roam the plains on horseback and sing our songs. When people get along well, everything's easy. But after some time my children and his children would come to blows; our horses would begin to kick each other, and our dogs would snarl and bite one another. Then we would roll up our yurts and move off in opposite directions?"

"Nasan Ulji, where would you go then?"

"Well, wherever I went, it couldn't be outside the East Khorcin Middle Banner, the grassland of the Darhan Banner. My horses ate Darhan's grass, my sheep were tended at his pasture, I set up my yurt on his grassland. When I died my bones would lie buried in his soil. I was no more than a lamb of his! Since it was his grass that nourished me I had to let him milk me till I went dry. Then he sold the grassland to Military Governor Chang Tso-lin, who opened it up as his own preserve. When his 'Army of Colonists' came, they rode my horses away, grabbed my sheep and took my land. We were so pushed to the wall for our livelihood that my son went to join the troops of Gada Meren."

Recalling his past life Nasan Ulji was pricked with grief, and tears began to trickle down his cheeks. His face turned ashen and he heaved a deep sigh through slightly trembling lips.

Wang Yao-tung moved closer to the old man and asked him warmly, "Was it the troops of Gada Meren that participated in the uprising?"

"Oh yes, they fought Darhan's troops and the 'Army of Colonists,' " he replied.

"Wasn't it a good thing then?"

"They were drowned in the river."

"True, they were, but their heroic deeds live for ever; their cause is immortal."

The legend of Gada Meren's uprising was told over and over up and down the plains of Mongolia where it later was sung in ballad form. Grown-ups and children alike knew how it went. Whenever Nasan Ulji thought of his son, he would like as not sing out some of the verses.

Nasan Ulji cleared his throat after singing the song and then the room was again silent. The tissue paper at the windows showed translucent while the cottage eaves were dimly revealed in the pale light of twinkling stars. The old man blinked thoughtfully at the sparks from the stove and was once more lost in his reverie.

Neither the regimental commander nor Wang Yao-tung understood Mongolian and, not knowing the meaning of the words to the song, they asked for a translation. "Nasan Ulji," they said, "what about telling us in Chinese what it says?"

Nasan Ulji nodded his head and, rubbing his eyes, interpreted two verses of the song:

Wild geese from the south
Will ne'er take flight ere they've paused by the Yangtse:
The uprising Gada Meren fought
For the sake of our native soil, Mongolia!

Wild geese from the north
Will ne'er take flight ere they've paused by the Heiho River;
The uprising Gada Meren laid down his life
For the sake of our native land, Mongolia!

After the puppet "Manchukuo" regime was set up, Nasan Ulji's life had become even more dismal. Everything was taxed—horses, cows, sheep—till all his livestock was gone. Finally the Japanese invaders set fire to the old man's yurt, forcing him to move to Chiachiayingtse where he took up the life of a peasant-herdsman. Then in the middle of August 1945, the Communist forces arrived at Chanyu County. Having heard from people that the Communists would distribute land to the poor, Nasan Ulji sent his younger son to join the Public Security Corps, and upon his departure the old man encouraged him, saying, "Go now, Sonny! Your brother went before you to fight for the sake of our Mongolian soil."

Regimental Commander Tsao looked at Nasan Ulji intently, then with utmost sincerity told him, "The Communists will surely distribute land to the poor."

"They'll have a plot for me too?" Nasan Ulji queried.

"Yes, there will certainly be a plot for you."

"Are you sure?"

"Sure. Since China has Chairman Mao and the Communist Party in the leadership, the common folks will surely have a bright future."

Nasan Ulji took a sip of his buttered tea, then his lips parted in an irrepressible smile at what the regimental commander had said.

"Urge your son to work well at the Chanyu Public Security Corps," Commander Tsao told him.

Nasan Ulji nodded. "Yes," he replied, "when you see him tell him to do his job well, to follow the Communist Party and he will be sure to have a good life."

"When I meet your son I'll certainly tell him what you've said. By the way, what's his name?"

"His name is Bajab."

"Good! I'll remember that."

"Don't forget, eh; his name is Bajab, Bajab," Nasan Ulji told Tsao again and again.

"I'll remember all right," repeated the regimental commander nodding to the old man.

7

When the party resumed their journey on the second day Nasan Ulji became their guide.

The old man was most willing indeed to take the job. Dressed in his long robe secured at the waist by a blue cloth sash, he drew himself erect on a grey pony and trotted off at the head of the convoy of carts at an even pace, neither fast nor slow. Sometimes he would give his mount his head and let him trot or canter ahead into the plains; sometimes he would rein him in and ride alongside the carts. He would then bring up his old question in a hushed voice, "Will the Communist Party really distribute land to the poor?"

The regimental commander gave his cap a shove that moved it onto the back of his head. Gazing first at the great stretch of plain lying ahead and then turning to survey Nasan Ulji, he said with a smile, "Certainly you'll have a plot. You'll have a plot of good land!"

"But will Prince Darhan agree?" the old Mongolian pursued in concern.

Tsao replied with a counter query, "Did he agree when your son went to join Gada Meren's troops; did the prince give his consent either?"

Nasan Ulji shook his head. "We'll never be bullied by any prince any more then!" he concluded.

A sudden gust of wind blew in, sending the grasses and flowers swaying like billows in an ocean.

Wang Yao-tung unbuttoned his tunic to allow the breeze to cool his neck.

"Ah, how marvellous this grassland is!" he exclaimed over and over, charmed by the beauty of the lush green prairie.

"So you've come to like it, eh?" the regimental commander said laughing.

"Yes, I love it," Wang replied, "I believe that if Chairman Mao comes here he too will like the place. When we've set up collective farms here, tractors will roll over the plains; and when industrial construction is in full swing, smoke will swirl from factory chimneys. Ah! how good that will be!"

"Old Wang, you'll see your collective farms all right."

"I hope so."

"That's not an idle dream; you will surely see those things," the regimental commander said with conviction. "All of us will see collective farms established here," he continued, indicating the group with his outstretched arms and laughing heartily. "But without us, Old Wang, there wouldn't be any industrial construction; neither would there be any collective farms."

Stretching to get the kinks out of his back, Liu Chun expressed his agreement with the regimental commander, who then went on speaking. "After the war," he said, "people our age will still have a couple of years or so we can put in driving tractors on the collective farms."

"No doubt you will," put in Lin Hsiu, "if only people don't consider you too old for such work."

Tsao stroked his chin. Since they had started out on their trek he had not once shaved and now he had a growth of bristly stubble over his chin that pricked his fingers. Glancing at Lin Hsieu he said grinning, "Oh, I'm good for another ten or fifteen years at least."

Wang Yao-tung was prompted too to rub the shaggy brush of whiskers on his jaw and remark, "Oh definitely; the war years turned me into an old man, even changed my nature. When we were in northern China turning back the enemy's 'mopping-up campaign,' the devils laid down a network of traps all over the hills and dales. Their planes strafed us from above, while their machineguns barked at us below. Often we had nothing to eat, even no water to drink. At those times I used to say to myself, 'I don't mind dying in battle but if I can't return to the Northeast victorious to see the grass-plains of my native land, that would indeed be a pity.' "

"Old Wang, but aren't you back now?"

"Yes, I've come back all right."

The day was gloomy, the sun having no sooner risen than it hid itself behind clouds. The dank smell of wet earth and grass pervaded the steppe. Then suddenly a gale arose and swept over the plains with nothing whatsoever to break it. Wolftail grass, pigweed and bluebells shook and danced wildly in the wind while the dewdrops clinging to the grass blades were blown rolling to the ground.

The cavalcade was with the wind for the next thirty *li*.

As the party penetrated deeper into the plains they found the grass much denser, the leaves more lusciously green and the artemisia growing to greater heights. Except for green moss, the earth along the way had been an endless yellowish-brown with neither traces of animal hoofs nor cakes of cow-dung to mark it; not even the small round balls of sheep-dung were to be seen. The cart wheels rolled on and on through the grass, laying low flowers and grass blades which rose again and then were laid flat once again by the next cart. The drivers' whips cracked resoundingly in the air; in the twinkling of an eye Nasan Ulji would have dashed to the head of the convoy.

The sky, which was already streaked with ominous grey, darkened noticeably as patches of cloud overlapped one another in thick layers, these in turn gathering gradually like the pouring of molten lead. In the far distance this "lead plate" dipped so low that it nearly met the horizon.

Suddenly a dzeren leaped out of a dense bush, and soon after that a drove of wild horses, some two hundred perhaps, came into view, dispersing into smaller herds. They nibbled at the grass, capered about and tossed their heads and whinnied. In one tumultuous parade they trotted out of a ravine densely overgrown with grass. In the lead was a snow-white horse which stretched its neck, turned to the drove and neighed. The drove then followed the white horse, charging in the direction of the low-hanging grey clouds.

Indeed the Mongolian grassland abounded in wonders! The men watching the horses clapped their hands and shouted enthusiastically. The orderly, Yang Teh-ching, was ready to take a pot shot at the animals but thought better of it and lowered his rifle. Regimental Commander Tsao peered through his binoculars till he had had his fill of the spectacle; then, turning to Nasan Ulji, he asked, "Why does the drove follow the white horse?"

"The white horse is their leader. As you know, without a leader birds don't take flight, neither do horses run," the old man replied.

Dark clouds continued to gather and the skies would soon be completely overcast. The lead driver scanned the firmament and knew the rain would not be long in coming. The convoy was nearing a Mongolian village: should they enter it or should they continue on their way? The driver, unable to decide, turned to the regimental commander and asked, "Tell us, Commander, what shall we do now?"

"Go ahead! There no question of stopping now."

The regimental commander's reply was terse. Though some of the comrades had thoughts of taking shelter from the rain they did not voice them. Instead, the drivers flourished their whips and the carts rolled on past the village. Tsao glanced at his watch—exactly 2 p.m. The journey would be completed on schedule. They were strangers in this Mongolian territory and must not tarry where they were unfamiliar with the situation.

The wind redoubled its force, the forerunner of rain.

Lashed by the gale, the sea of grass rose in great billows, the leaves of plants fluttering and slapping in mad frenzy, while the blossoms were stripped of their petals. A cold current swept the fields. The horses pricked up their ears and the men felt their foreheads growing numb with the chill. The clouds dipped lower as they grew darker and looked ever more threatening. From the far end of the plains a pounding roar was nearing and everyone knew that the rain would soon be upon them.

8

The first shower of rain soaked the travellers to the skin. Liu Chun, who was wearing a green army tunic, found his clothes mottled in light and dark shades and his green leggings shrunk so that his legs looked like two giant worms. Wang Yao-tung's grey uniform was drenched and clinging to his chest, while water dripped from his sleeves and the furry edging of his goggles. The regimental commander was no less wet than the others, but all wished to get on as quickly as possible and urged the driver to hurry along.

The heavy downpour swept the plains with a continuous torrential roar.

The ruts made by the cart wheels and the hoof-prints of the horses rapidly filled with water. All the low-lying spots were transformed into so many little pools which soon linked up into wide expanses of water. Here and there, washed from their soil-beds, grass roots peeped out while frogs emerged from their hiding places and started up an endless croaking.

The carts continued another seven or eight *li* without leaving the rolling steppe. There was not a village in sight nor so much as a tree big enough to shelter them from the rain. The farther they travelled the more they tasted the boundlessness of the Mongolian plains. Further-more, with every *li* they found their carts more cumbersome. The rubber-tyred wheels bogged down in the mire and the black mule harnessed between the shafts of one of the vehicles struggled hope-lessly with its burden. Straining its white forehead and muzzle forward, it gasped raucously for air.

The driver too was feeling the strain of the journey. His wet clothes clinging to him made him shiver and chilled him to the marrow. Yet he dared not linger on the way. So, cracking his whip, he urged the black mule on with shouts. The beast flinched under the whip and, recoiling from the water ahead, it backed up into the mud and buckled to the ground.

"Ah! The mule's done for! Get out of the cart!" the driver whimpered to the occupants in his despair.

Wang Yao-tung was the first to jump down from the vehicle, followed by Liu Chun, Regimental Commander Tsao, and last of all Lin Hsiu. She was bare-headed, her face ashen, and she was shivering from the cold for she wore only a thin army tunic. Everyone was splashing about in the mud, bustling around the cart. Ahead they could see nothing but the rolling steppe, hazy and shrouded in the downpour.

The carter put aside his whip and yanked at the mule but it refused to get to its feet and just lay there in the mud, its eyes widely open. He pulled at it again, and this time the beast made an effort to get up, splat-tering mud into the faces of everyone nearby. The chestnut trace-pony at the side was also soaked, its soft downy coat plastered to its belly and dark lines of veins standing out sharply on its legs. Time and again the driver cracked his whip to spur it on, but it too refused to budge an inch.

The other three carts, which had been behind, had already drawn up and the men stood there facing each other, their vehicles side by side in mute silence. Sloshing through the mire in the rain the carters all joined in helping drag the beast to its feet.

"The mule is really a goner," they clamoured, "how shall we make it without the mule!"

Yang Teh-ching, lolling in the back of the cart, was trembling with cold. Feeling down-hearted, he began to grumble:

"A man hasn't got but two legs, do you expect him to sprout four to get along on?"

"What did you say?" the regimental commander snapped. "Even if we have to crawl on all fours, we've got to reach our destination! That's an order!"

Having given Yang Teh-ching a piece of his mind, Tsao turned to the other comrades standing around wet and cold.

"Comrades," he addressed them, "what was it we all vowed as we were leaving Tungliao?"

Though all were soaked from head to foot, none of the group wavered in his resolution.

"We will surely cross the Mongolian steppe," they repeated with determination. "A hail of daggers may greet us, but we will not be deterred!"

The comrades peered into the distance and thought they saw hazily through the rain a small black dot faraway on the horizon. They couldn't be quite sure, for the torrential rains beaten by the wind upon the sea of grass made even the various features of the landscape almost indistinguishable.

Bare-footed and with his trouser-legs rolled up, Yang Teh-ching slithered around in the mud trying to make out what the small black object was.

"Hey, isn't it a village?" he cried out in joy.

"You dunderhead," another orderly countered him, "what makes you think it's a village?"

"If it isn't a village what is it then, that black thing there?"

"It must be some objective."

"Now you just tell me, what objective is it? If it's not the enemy, it's surely a village."

"All right, you daft, let's bet on it."

"You don't have to bet with me, just ask that old codger Nasan Ulji."

Nasan Ulji was riding on the muddy road up front, feeling his way along. The rain was coming down heavier and the old man's robe and trousers were drenched. He had tucked his chin into his collar making his face look haggard and long, and a chill ran down his spine. He dismounted and pressed his shoulders against the horse's mane, waiting beside a dense reed bush for the carts to catch up with him. Now all the men were trudging along behind the carts in a slow line like a snake crawling.

Catching up with the old man the regimental commander asked him, "How far is it to the nearest village?"

"You mean to Small Chuho Village?"

"Another thirty li," Nasan Ulji replied, addressing the group.

Yang Teh-ching was reluctant to walk another step. Grumbling to himself he tugged at the old man's sleeve.

"Now tell us," he said, pointing to the little black dot, "isn't that the village?"

"It's a wood," Nasan Ulji replied.

"What the devil, whatever you say goes!"

The carts lumbered on for another three li before reaching the small dark speck. Nasan Ulji was not mistaken—it was in fact an elm grove. Under the elms grew artemisia and wild raspberry, their tendrils reaching up into the tree branches to form a diminutive arbour.

They were still a long way from anywhere they could stop for a rest, there was no sign of the skies clearing and the rain pounded steadily.

When the party arrived at Small Chuho Village, they found the cottages already lamplit.

9

Wang Yao-tung slept soundly that night and when he woke the following morning he stretched himself luxuriously on his bed, sensing his whole being fit and refreshed. His drowsiness had vanished, his fatigue gone. He touched his grey tunic; it was dry. He arose, asked his host for a basin of water to wash himself, and had his breakfast. He called for his orderly, Yang Teh-ching, but the fellow had already slipped out of the room.

It was the third day of their journey. People in the neighborhood told Wang that the road ahead was smooth and easily passable. Another thirty *li* and they would be in the county seat of Chanyu. That was encouraging. It was as though the news had removed a heavy stone from his heart, and he felt light-hearted and happy.

He walked out into the yard and found the rain had long since stopped. Though the skies had not altogether cleared, the clouds had drifted away to a great height. The budding leaves on the trees in the compound looked fresh and green. The drivers had already harnessed the horses to the carts, had the luggage ready, and were now watering the animals from barrels woven from willow twigs. They would soon be on their way! But what was that! Under the feed-trough a fire was burning, its flames licking fiercely, while beside the fire, with a pistol strapped onto his bare back, was Yang Teh-ching, hunched over, his feet planted wide apart and his behind pointing upward. Why, he was there drying his shirt! And as he worked over it he kept arguing with Nasan Ulji.

"So what if I am drying my shirt; what business is it of yours anyway?"

"But you're burning my hay," Nasan Ulji retorted.

"Where did you put your hay?"

"In the feed-trough."

The old man walked to the trough, shoved his grey horse aside, clutched a handful of the hay and threw it beside the stack by the fire. It was exactly like what Yang had taken for his fire.

"You see," the old man stormed, "if it isn't mine, whose is it then?"

But Yang Teh-ching refused to give in. "So it's yours, eh?" he mocked tauntingly. "Well, call it then and see whether it'll go to you."

The night before Yang Teh-ching had stripped off his wet shirt and gone to bed. But he had overslept and only that morning, when the group was ready to start, had he thought of drying his shirt. In haste he had looked around for firewood and finding none he had used the hay in the trough. Furthermore, having done so, he tried to justify his act by fabricating absurd excuses.

"If not for the Communists liberating the Northeast nothing would belong to you," Yang went on.

At that point Wang Yao-tung appeared on the scene and, turning angry eyes on the boy, gave him a good dressing down. "Fine talk indeed! The Communist Party is liberating the Northeast all right; but is it for you to bully people?"

Yang Teh-ching knew he was in the wrong and did not dare argue with Wang, so, hanging his head, he stamped out the fire, took his half-dry shirt and slunk away. When Nasan Ulji heard Wang censure the orderly his anger soon subsided and he blushed and felt a little awkward. Leaving the trough, he approached Wang warmly waving his hand at him.

"Are you leaving now?" he asked.

"Yes, we're going. Goodbye, Nasan Ulji!"

"Goodbye!"

The old man's voice broke as he spoke to Wang. He knew they were leaving, but having just met them he felt loath to part and half hid his eyes behind his hand. Just then Regimental Commander Tsao, his face radiant, emerged from his room. The old man knew that he too was leaving.

"Goodbye, Regimental Commander Tsao!"

Tsao turned to the old man and called with a warm smile, "Goodbye, Nasan Ulji! But we're sure to meet again!"

"Will you come to my home then?" Nasan Ulji asked.

"All right, and when I call on you next time, shall I feed my horse on your hay?" said the regimental commander laughing. He then bade the old man goodbye.

The drivers took their places on the carts and the company left Small Chuho Village. They would soon reach Chanyu, and as the distance was short they did not need a guide.

The sky was still overcast with clouds drifting overhead. Leaves of grass, still wet from the rain, appeared blue-green, and grass roots showed reddish above the wet earth. Here and there were the miniature mounds of mole-crickets.

Since the road was smooth it was no time at all till the cart train had covered five *li* and was on a knoll from where the travellers saw a village lying ahead. Dark cottage roofs, brown adobe walls, some gun-emplacements, and a few tall, sturdy trees—the whole layout of the village could be seen very distinctly, even to the luxuriant green grass around it. The regimental commander was viewing the scene as he said to Wang Yao-tung:

"The carts have made good time, eh? Only another *li* and a half and we'll be in that village."

"We've made good time all right," Wang agreed, "before we know it we'll be there."

Tsao scanned the skies; clouds still lurked overhead. Having lost all track of time in the greyness of the day he glanced at his watch, then he said, "I think we'll reach Chanyu before noon."

"And tomorrow we'll be in Kaitung."

"From Kaitung we can go on by train."

"Look," Wang said, pointing, "somebody's coming. Let's ask him."

From his straw hat and the hoe he had over his shoulder they saw it was a peasant approaching. He was climbing the knoll but from the opposite direction. As he neared the cart the driver stopped his horses and called out, "Hiya fella, let me ask you. . . . Is this the way to Chanyu?"

The man halted and put his hoe on the ground. Noting that the men in the carts were armed with pistols he hesitated a while before replying.

"There's a band of Mongolians ahead—you mustn't go there," he warned.

The men exchanged glances, for the news was contrary to their expectations.

10

The four carts came to a simultaneous halt. Lin Hsiu, Liu Chun, Wang Yao-tung, Regimental Commander Tsao and the other cadres and guards all jumped down and gathered round the peasant, asking for more information.

"Tell us, where's the Mongolian band now?"

The peasant looked at the group and, pointing to the village below, said, "There, at Sanchiatse Village. They're resting and having a meal there, but they'll soon be along this way."

"How many legs do they grow that they're able to get about so fast?" Yang Teh-ching chided the peasant.

"Well, every one of them rides a four-legged horse," the man replied in good humour. He wanted to laugh, but then it was no joke and he checked himself. He looked at the party earnestly then, knitting his brows, added, "When they gallop past here on horseback, you won't be able to catch them."

The regimental commander began to realize what this band might be and asked, "Do you know which unit the Mongolian band belongs to?"

"They're the Third Platoon of the Public Security Corps."

"How many men are there?"

"Over thirty mounted men."

"What's the name of the platoon leader?"

"Han Pao-yu."

Tsao had never heard this name before and he shook his head. "Once on the Mongolian steppe everything is unfamiliar," he mused to himself.

"Where is the Public Security Corps stationed?" he pursued.

"In town."

"The Chanyu County seat?"

"That's right. Strange as it may seem those fellows were part of the Public Security Corps stationed in Chanyu."

The regimental commander bit his lip and was thinking hard as he talked to the peasant.

"But there's Magistrate Sun of our Eighth Route Army in Chanyu County. Do you know him?"

"I've run errands for him," the man replied, "how could I not know him?"

The regimental commander lighted a cigarette, still pondering over the enigma as he continued putting his questions to the peasant. "Isn't the Public Security Corps under the control of Magistrate Sun?" he asked.

"Huh, that lot follows the smell of money. I heard that Nanking offered Han Pao-yu a certain official post and he went scrambling over to the Kuomintang!"

Finding the peasant was in all seriousness Tsao realized that there was an ominous turn in the situation. On leaving Tungliao had they not been told that the Kuomintang agent Pai Yun-ti was instigating a revolt of armed Mongolian landlords? But he never imagined that the armed landlord rebels would turn out to be among the forces in Chanyu where he and his group were headed! Now they were face to face with them. This was indeed an unforeseen state of affairs!

On hearing this news from the peasant the men spontaneously tensed. The carter drew up his cart and took his whip into his hand. Squad Leader Chao and the other guards gripped their rifles tighter. Wang Yao-tung stood with his feet planted apart as he trained his binoculars on Sanchiatse Village to size things up. Liu Chun was watching for commotion to start up in the fields at any moment, while Lin Hsiu was busy gathering up the wet clothes which had been spread out in the cart to dry. After stuffing them into her satchel she climbed down, and stood for a moment wondering if there were any she had forgotten.

His rifle strapped to his back, Yang Teh-ching stamped up to the regimental commander in his still damp tunic. Now this lad was an odd one. At each mention of the enemy's approach the more jubilant he became. With a broad grin on his face he clamoured boisterously, "Let's make hash out of the reactionary sons-of-bitches!"

Wang Yao-tung eyed him dimly and asked him, "What did I criticize you for just a little while ago?"

"I've been serving the people," Yang protested, "can't I burn a little hay to dry out my shirt?"

"Is hay for feeding horses or for you to dry your clothes with?" Wang asked in reply.

"Deputy Regimental Commander Wang, I'm wrong."

As Tsao was smoking his cigarette he tried to figure out the position of the enemy: were they in flight? Or were they trying to effect a link-up? Either was likely, he thought. If they were fleeing they would show evidence of panic and would soon be gone. In either case he must get a clearer picture of the situation before the enemy should discover their presence there, for only then could he make any decisions. He threw his cigarette butt on the ground and stamped it out with his boot.

"I've got to see what the devil they're up to," the regimental commander determined.

Putting aside his field-glasses, Wang Yao-tung strode over to Tsao to report what he had learned.

"Those Mongolian bandits are a savage lot. It'll be rough going if we get into a scrap with them."

"We'd better find out," the regimental commander said curtly.

"Reconnoitre? Let me go!" Wang offered.

Lest the others should feel anxious for his safety, Wang Yao-tung took four of the guards, including Yang Teh-ching with him and, armed with rifles, they went out along the road. Coming upon a mound, the four guards hid themselves, while Wang Yao-tung went down on one knee in some bush to observe the situation ahead through his glasses.

The regimental commander did not shift position but, keeping one eye on Wang's every move, at the same time took special note of the sand-dune to the left front. It was overgrown with elm saplings and in general the terrain was ideal for defence—the soil loose and the area not too extended. In case a battle should ensue they could very well keep the open foreground under fire and prevent the enemy from approaching the dune. He surveyed the grassy fields. The dank odour of wet earth hung over the plains though the air was still cold from the rain. The grass blades were set with pearls of dew, while frogs croaked insistently in the pools.

Regimental Commander Tsao scanned the fore-front and saw Wang Yao-tung duck his head and signal to his men with his hand. One of the guards peeped out from the bush and a curl of gun smoke immediately rose from it. A rifle shot had rung out and the spears of grass nearby quivered momentarily. Wang Yao- tung emerged from cover and waved his hand at the guards.

Liu Chun, who had been standing by the carts, moved over and, darting a glance at the regimental commander, remarked with astonishment, "The shooting's begun!"

11

After a little while Wang Yao-tung led his men back. His field-glasses hung from the strap around his neck and he still grasped his pistol in his hand. His face wore a serious expression, deep furrows lining his brow, as though he had done something that went against his grain. He looked angry.

Seeing Wang return in anger, the regimental commander asked him, "Old Wang, how goes it?"

"Didn't you hear the shot?" Wang asked him in reply.

"Yes. Who fired it?"

"Regimental Commander Tsao," Yang Teh-ching piped up, stepping before the commander with his rifle in his hand, "it was I firing at those damned reactionaries." Then, eyeing the regimental commander, he giggled with self-satisfaction, gaping and gesticulating with his free arm. "I hid in the bush for a long time," he elaborated, "then when I raised my head I saw five or six Mongolian reactionaries on horseback with guns on 'em. They almost brushed us so I challenged 'em. 'Who goes there?' I yelled, but they said nothin', just swaggered past, so I loaded my gun, pulled the trigger, and 'bang!' a bastard bit the dust."

The regimental commander glared at him and asked, "And what happened then?"

"Commander Tsao, those Mongolian reactionaries turned tail and ran, scare to death."

"You're talking rot, my man," Tsao roundly rebuked Yang Teh-ching. "Why did you fire? Were your fingers too itchy to hold on any longer?" He knew it would not help the situation to criticize the lad on the spot; it was too late. "It's true they were frightened and fled, but they'll be back," he said in the confident tone of a veteran commander.

"They'll be back for sure," Wang Yao-tung confirmed. His face was drawn, his stubbled chin seeming to have grown darker. When the men saw this, they at once sensed the tenseness of the situation.

"Old Wang is right," Liu Chun said to Tsao.

The cadres, the guards, the carters, all gathered round looking at one another without exchanging a word. Deep down in their hearts they all knew what was brewing.

As the men waited thus in tense quandary the regimental commander took the matter in hand, having resolved that the next move must be theirs. Pointing to the sand-dune, he gave his order, "Comrades, advance on the dune and assemble there! Set out at once!"

The drivers got the carts moving, paying no heed to pot-holes or bumps in the road but rumbling on in their haste. The cracking of whips resounded in the air and the horses' hoofs seemed scarcely to touch the ground. They had dashed off in such a hurry that even Lin Hsiu had no time to climb into her cart and was running to catch up. The whole group rushed through the grassy field as though on a cross-country race, no one wishing to lag behind.

After running some four hundred metres they looked up at the dune and calculated it was still about three hundred metres off. The way was flat and presented no obstacle whatsoever. Lin Hsiu, who was running alongside the regimental commander, could hardly keep up the pace and was gasping for breath, but she forced herself forward lest she should become a hindrance to her comrades.

"Commander Tsao, go on ahead!" she gasped.

"No, run! We must occupy the dune at once!"

Bringing up the rear together with Lin Hsiu, the regimental commander was perfectly calm and steady. But as he ran he kept raising his field-glasses to peer through them and suddenly spotted the bandit troops emerging from Sanchiatse Village, galloping with a great commotion over the steppe in his direction. Presently the driver of the cart at the head of the onrushing convoy also caught sight of the enemy. In his agitation he laid his whip with all his might upon the horse's back.

"Well, this is it!" he shouted. "The bandits are coming!"

In the twinkling of an eye the mounted band had passed the fringe of cottages and ascended a ridge forming a solid dark silhouette against the sky. Then they tugged at their reins and swept down the ridge in open formation, firing as they spurred their horses so that bullets whizzed past the ears of the charging party.

Kharr. . . .

Without a rise of any kind on the stretch of prairie between them and the dune every one of the party knew what an easy target he was and put all his energy into the dash for their objective, not once stopping for breath.

A sturdy chap with long, wiry legs, Wang Yao-tung was the first to reach the dune, whence he directed the guards to open fire at the bandits to give protection to the comrades behind. Encountered by the fire, the enemy did not venture to approach the dune but withdrew to take positions on a sandy hillock opposite, from where they fired intermittent shots at random.

12

The company of cadres finally occupied the sand-dune and Regimental Commander Tsao immediately ordered his men to dig in. Though they had no spades the loose sandy earth readily gave way under the men's bare hands and within a short space of time improvised defences were set up and Squad Leader Chao and the party of guards took up their positions in the dugouts. Nearby was their temporary command post, where the regimental commander and Wang Yao-tung lay in their foxholes. An elm grove in front of the command post provided a strategic spot for reconnaissance and directing of operations. Liu Chun, a six-chamber revolver in hand, crouched behind the command post, his tunic stiff with wet sand, while Lin Hsiu clutched a Browning, her head down so that her luxuriant hair concealed almost half of her face. Her gaze was riveted upon a cluster of artemisia beyond, beads of perspiration standing out on her brow for she could not get at her handkerchief to wipe them away with. The cartmen made a poor showing; all lay huddled together shielding themselves from the flying bullets behind the wheels of the carts in a ditch near the dune, not daring so much as to raise their heads.

Bullets continued to pound the slope of the dune, wriggling madly on the surface of the sand like little snakes, while some whizzed high overhead like a flight of chattering sparrows and crashed into the elm grove.

Rifle shots cracked for some time before the regimental commander put his head out of his foxhole, raised his binoculars and, having adjusted the range, scanned the area of the dune opposite. It was not large, of white sand, with a gentle slope in front but a steep wall behind. Though they could not be seen there must be about thirty bandits lurking in lee of that wall! The neighing of their Mongolian ponies could be heard clearly. Further to the right were the cottages of Sanchiatse Village with green foliage shading the roof-tops and smoke still curling from chimneys. Yellowish adobe walls, greying hayricks and towering gun-emplacements made up the scene. Commander Tsao trained his binoculars on the slope. About a dozen men with rifles emerging on horseback from behind the hillock cut his range of vision. The bandits were moving in on them!

Tsao studied the terrain, analysed the situation and drew his conclusions: under present conditions they would have to take up the defensive for they lacked fighting men and arms, in particular the heavier pieces. They had neither machine-guns, mortars, grenade-throwers, not even any hand-grenades. Among them they had only six rifles and a couple of dozen pistols. The most annoying thing of all was that they were engaging in a skirmish at a moment they should not be engaging in one. If they should try to make a breakthrough now they would certainly be spotted. Besides, the carts were slow-moving; they would be sure to be surrounded and harassed. They would have to hold out, either till the situation had changed for the better, or else they would have to wait for darkness to cover their breakthrough—in either case victory would be theirs.

"There's no alternative," he said to Wang Yao-tung calmly. "We must hold this dune. If the bandits make a try for it, we'll wring their goddamned turtle necks for them!"

"We're likely to see a change in the enemy's position soon," Wang responded.

"Old Wang, you mean our men in town may come out in pursuit? But we don't know how things stand over there either."

"We should contact Magistrate Sun in town and ask him to send us reinforcements."

"But we can't very well pass through Sanchiatse Village and we don't know any other route to Chanyu. How are we to get our messenger through?"

"Let's wait then."

With a wave of his hand the regimental commander concluded confidently, "Like all thieves with a guilty conscience, those brigands will lose their nerve and sooner or later run for their lives."

Just now though the enemy kept up a continuous firing at the dune. His bullets hissed into the sand and crackled through the bush, some landing among the baggage in the carts. Two that were aimed low bit into the ground right beside Lin Hsiu, throwing a spurt of sand and dust at her and then disappearing. Lin Hsiu pricked up her ears to listen. There was another burst in the rove near the dune and dust, mingled with the acrid smell of powder, assailed her nostrils.

The regimental commander knew the girl had no battle experience and fearing she might be nervous asked her as casually as possible, "Well, how's it going?"

Seeing Tsao so calm and composed, exchanging words and laughing with the other comrades, Lin Hsiu patted her sweat-sodden hair and lifted her grimy face as she replied in an effort to show her own calmness, "Nothing to worry about."

"Crawl a little forward! That spot is no good, too vulnerable to stray bullets!"

"I'm not afraid, Commander," Lin Hsiu replied, creeping forward, however, as he advised.

"Cover yourself well. We must hold our position to the end and victory will be ours."

Lin Hsiu was not the only one of the group to be inspirited by their commander. From his instructions to the girl comrade, the others also took advice. Some dug deeper into their foxholes, some made improvements in their dugouts, while one of the men pulled the clip and loaded more bullets into his pistol. All were getting better prepared to shoot it out with the enemy at the next engagement. Meanwhile the regimental commander was thinking to himself how he could get the cadres safely to the Northeast Bureau at Harbin—that was the task the Party had entrusted to him!

Suddenly Wang Yao-tung pointed at the foot of the hillock opposite them and said to Tsao, "Look there, isn't that the enemy approaching?"

The commander turned his glasses on the hillock and saw distinctly some dozen mounted bandits sweeping down the lower slope in a sidewise thrust on the open field. By the looks of things the enemy was set to wrest the position from the little group by storming the dune in one mad rush. They lashed their charges furiously, and, as the horses' hoofs pounded the plain, dry dust rose in the air and trailed along behind them.

Apprised of the impending attack, two of the guards raised their heads and aimed their rifles over the parapet of their foxholes. Then they followed the madly galloping bandits closely with their aim.

"Now my itching trigger finger will have its chance!" one whispered to the other.

"Get down and don't talk nonsense," the regimental commander admonished them to lie low in their foxholes. But just then he noticed a grey cap pop out from the underbrush. It was Yang Teh-ching's.

"Hey, you dunderhead, cross over from the right and lie flat. Keep your eye on the target in front of you."

Everyone now obeyed the commander's orders and there was not a stir on the dune.

Mistaking the quiet on the dune for fear, the bandits lashed their mounts, firing as they dashed over the plains. The horses sped on in an unbroken column, their legs whipping the tall grass with a continuous whir.

The enemy had now come within firing range and the regimental commander threw up his hand as signal to the guards and shouted, "Fire! Get that one nearest there!"

There were four or five shots and the Mongolian galloping in the lead toppled from his horse while the others scattered in alarm. Then two men on black mounts dashed up from behind, one a tall Mongolian, the other a thickset fellow. They had rushed up to silence the fire from the dune with their guns, and, gripping their carbines at the ready, they charged on towards the dune. Suddenly the tall fellow gave a jerk on his horse and laid his gun on his saddle. Then, hanging on by his steed's mane, he wheeled and beat a retreat, scurrying away for all he was worth.

"That buck must've got one in the shoulder!" Yang Teh-ching cheered from his shelter.

"Who asked him to be such a good target," another guard quipped.

Seeing the situation not in his favour, the stocky fellow also wheeled about on his horse and, together with the other brigands, retreated back to their hillock.

The regimental commander raised his binoculars to his eyes and watched the Mongolians galloping off. Then he turned to Wang Yao-tung and said, "The bandits have turned tail."

The firing ceased and all was again quiet on the sand-dune.

13

There was a lull in the firing, then suddenly from the knoll opposite a pennant appeared and was seen waving for some time before the Mongolian holding it made his way down the slope. When he reached the foot of the knoll he shouted towards the dune, "Don't shoot! Let's not have any misunderstanding here!"

The regimental commander put down his binoculars and said to himself, "Let's see now what the devil's up to!"

Liu Chun crept out of his foxhole slipping his revolver back into its holster then brushed the dust from his clothes and walked up to the command post. The other cadres meanwhile stretched their legs by walking around the dune. The guards then returned to their dugouts to keep watch. Wang Yao-tung took a seat on the ground and took out his long-stemmed pipe for a smoke. Then, looking at the Mongolian on the slope who was still waving his hands, he said to the commander, "By the looks of that the enemy wants to talk things over with us."

But the regimental commander felt he had not yet got to the bottom of things. Why was the enemy wishing to talk things over? Tsao's analysis led him to three possible conclusions: first, the rebels were being pursued by the troops from town and, afraid of being caught between two fires, planned a quick getaway. Or, since the enemy had suffered some losses, he was seeking a respite to recoup for the next attack. A third possibility was that the pennant waving was a ruse, an intrigue of some sort. Regarding this analysis, each of the comrades had his own particular view.

"The enemy has received an unexpected blow," Liu Chun said, "so their morale is shaken. We should make good use of this opportunity to win them over to our side."

Wang Yao-tung did not agree with Liu's view and said, "Though the enemy has suffered some losses he has not yet been dealt a crushing blow. The bandits here in the Northeast are a crafty and unpredictable lot. They often cheat you into the bargain."

But Liu Chun was adamant. "If you look at the matter that way, we'll lose our chance of winning them over," he averred.

"They're our enemy," Wang Yao-tung said sternly, "it's the enemy we're dealing with, not the broad masses we're working among."

The two argued on and on until in the end the regimental commander voiced his opinion. "We must know first what the enemy is up to," he said. "If there's a possibility of winning them over we should do so. It's all right even if it's only a matter of temporarily neutralizing them; we can then go our own way. We may negotiate with them, but we must by no means harbour any illusions about them."

Thus Regimental Commander Tsao made his decision and called Squad Leader Chao to him. The youth called out a response and jumped out of his foxhole. Drawing himself up to his full height he asked, "Regimental Commander, what do you want me for?"

"We're going to conduct talks with the brigands," Tsao explained. "Now you go to see them; since you're a Northeasterner you're better acquainted with things here than most of us."

"I'll go. I was once a courier in the West Manchurian Military Zone and I know the country around here pretty well."

Chao's response was forthright and he followed it up by immediately laying down his rifle and untying his bandoleer, placing the weapons on the ground one after another and waiting for the order of departure.

The regimental commander was deeply moved as he watched Chao and, patting the youth on the shoulder, he said to him affectionately, "You're a new comrade, but you've already been educated by the Party. . . ."

Chao understood what the regimental commander meant and nodded his head. Blood rushed to his cheeks, infusing his already ruddy countenance with new radiance.

"Regimental Commander Tsao," he replied in a ringing voice, "please don't worry. I'm an Eighth Route Army man and I'll never bring disgrace on our Army."

Noting the resolution in Chao's attitude, Wang Yao-tung gave him a word of encouragement. "Chao, you are right to treasure the glorious traditions of our Eighth Route Army," he said.

"Yes, I know," the squad leader replied looking into the faces of the regimental commander and the deputy in turn. "Our veteran comrades endured every hardship imaginable during the Long March, and I'm just a raw recruit. It's not much for me to go once to the bandits's lair. If I return, you may know I have accomplished my task; if not, you may just consider me as one who has done his part in the revolution."

"Go now; we'll cover you from here."

The regimental commander gave him a few other instructions, every word of which the youth took into his heart. Then, saluting the commander, he left the dune for the sandy hillock.

The day was stifling hot and the air enveloping the dune suffocating. Having finished his pipeful of tobacco, Wang Yao-tung emptied the bowl on the ground and stamped out the remaining sparks before rising to follow with his eyes the receding figure of the squad leader until he was out of sight.

"There's a young comrade we should learn from," he thought to himself. "At the time of the September 18th Incident he was just a kid. But he's a grown-up now, and he's doing a man's job. . . ."

The hillock opposite rose about fifteen feet higher than the positions held by our men and the lad had thus to make a gradual ascent from the dune. There on the hill the Mongolian was standing absolutely motionless while all around was a dead silence broken only by the occasional distant whinnying of Mongolian ponies.

From the moment the squad leader took his departure the regimental commander knew not one moment free from anxiety. Again and again he raised his binoculars to his eyes to follow the progress of the lad up the slope. Then at last he reported to the group, "Ah, Squad Leader Chao has reached the spot. A Mongolian in a tall felt hat has come to meet him."

"Old Tsao," the comrades asked to satisfy their curiosity, "take another look, see how he's dressed."

Tsao again peered through his binoculars. The Mongolian was no more than 300 metres from the dune and even the lapels of his suit could be made out.

"Why, it's a Western suit he's wearing!"

"A Western suit? Well, well, that's no joke. Can it by any chance be Han Pao-yu then?"

"Only the devil knows."

After the tension of the battle the men gradually relaxed; they were like hot gun-barrels cooling down in a breeze. The cadres now gathered together, some chatting, others smoking or resting. Even the carters, who had been hugging the ground each in his favourite hiding place, got up and unharnessed the horses to let them graze.

The regimental commander observed the scene on the slope all very clearly. The fellow in the tall hat was face to face with the squad leader making a great to-do and gesticulating wildly. The men at the dune grew restless and started repeating, "Squad Leader Chao should be back by now."

"Chao must be trying to persuade them," Liu Chun offered. "We shouldn't be too hasty."

However, everyone felt extremely anxious for Chao and kept urging the regimental commander to take another look. "Can you tell how he's getting on?" they asked.

The next time Tsao set his glasses to his eyes the focus immediately caught the slope and in it he saw the squad leader coming back. He was in fact running back! Tsao raised his binoculars to the hillock but the fellow with the tall felt hat was not there.

"Funny, why should Chao be in such a hurry to get back?"

"How is it? . . ." the others pressed.

Just then bullets started whizzing overhead and elm leaves fluttered from the grove. The bandits had opened fire and everyone knew the "negotiations" had gone to pieces. The squad leader was racing back, with 200 metres yet between him and the dune. The cadres rushed to their trenches and, shaking his fist, the regimental commander shouted his order, "Guards, cover Squad Leader Chao—fire!"

Receiving the command the men felt their hearts kindled as with a flame. At their touch their guns went off with loud reports—rifles, carbines, pistols. One volley, then another, like a string of giant crackers popping. The bullets whistled over the plains and kicked up a cloud of dust on the hillock opposite.

The squad leader arrived panting and drenched with perspiration. Bounding into a foxhole he began cursing with rage.

"That son-of-a-bitch!" he gasped. "The enemy's cheated us this time!"

14

Seeing that Chao had taken cover the brigands stopped their firing after a brief exchange of shots and instead sent patrols to watch the movements on the dune from a distance. The regimental commander put aside his glasses and turned to the squad leader, saying:

"Sit down and rest first, then tell us all about it."

The squad leader drew in a deep breath, threw off his cap, wiped the sweat from his forehead with the back of his hand and plunked down beside the commander. Wang Yao-tung, Liu Chun, Lin Hsiu and some of the other cadres gathered round, all straining to hear the account of his venture.

"When I'd reached the hillock and was just starting up the slope," Chao related, "a hulk of a Mongolian accosted me. By the looks of him he was a bandit all right. And that grin of his—like a horse's—the hypocrite."

"There's venom behind such a smile," Wang Yao-tung remarked.

"Indeed," Chao affirmed, "Deputy Commander Wang is right there. There was certainly venom behind his grin."

"What did the Mongolian do then?" Wang led him on.

"Well, after grinning and grimacing some more he tried to sound me out. 'What detachment are you with?' he asked. I told him we're the Eighth Route Army, troops of Chairman Mao. But he pretended not to understand and put on that imbecile grin again as he asked, 'And what do the troops of Chairman Mao do?' I answered him that the troops of Chairman Mao are precisely the troops that liberate all people of China. Then he asked me, 'Are you figuring on liberating our Inner Mongolia too?' To which I replied, 'Since Inner Mongolia is a part of China certainly the Mongolian people will enjoy their freedom along with all other peoples once the whole country has been liberated.' "

Chao's expression was natural throughout the telling. It betrayed no sign of nervousness or impetuousness, neither was there any indication of weakness in it. His tone was firm and steady, imparting to his audience a share in his inner fortitude. Wang Yao-tung's heart was perhaps the most deeply touched of all. Patting the youth on the shoulder he commended him again and again. "You spoke well, my lad. And what else did he ask you?"

"He also asked me how many men there are in our group," Chao continued, "and I told him there were seven to eight hundred all told. Well, he just refused to believe it and shook his head. 'You have only four carts,' he countered, and I explained to him that the first few of us had arrived in those carts and that the main forces were still coming."

As the squad leader got into the story he rose from his sitting position, and, mimicking the Mongolian's gait, fingered his hat and gazed into the distance in his adversary's stupid fashion. "Craning his neck and popping out his eyes, he gaped at the carts behind the dune, licking his lips," continued Chao, still miming. 'Your carts look well laden,' said he, 'would you be carrying opium by any chance?' I told him that we Eighth Route Army men don't smoke opium. Then the bastard seemed to lapse into a spell of pondering over something and his bandit face contorted into a smirk in an effort to conceal his anger. 'So you guys don't smoke opium. . . .' he hissed. 'You're on the square? No opium, eh?' By the way he carried on I knew the bastard was trying to probe further and I was put on my guard. I moved back a step and fixed my eyes on him. Then he started off on another tack. 'I don't think you've got the authority to make any decisions,' he said, 'what's your rank anyway?' When I told him I was a squad leader he looked me up and down with condescension and no little surprise. 'So you're not an officer, just a measly sergeant.' Well, I reminded him that this 'measly sergeant' was there representing his superior officers and told him that if he was willing to be placed under the leadership of the Eighth Route Army I could then have a talk with him. His entire expression changed and he hissed crossly, 'You Eighth Route Army men are unreasonable. You shot our men and crippled our horses.' Then I told him we Eighth Route Army men are most reasonable. 'We look upon the ordinary people and our national minority groups as our own brothers and friends,' I said. 'We neither beat nor curse them. But we'll surely go after those enemies that go about bullying people. Now I ask you, do you want to be a friend or an enemy?' He said nothing but gave me another of his horsy grins. Then, at his signal towards the hill, a Mongolian with a head like a pumpkin popped out. He took a pot shot at me and I didn't waste any more time getting back here."

15

It was not long before the bandits launched another attack, creeping stealthily from behind the hillock in a long file. White, grey and chestnut-brown ponies trotted nose to tail out into the broad expanse of the steppe. Holding the reins loose and pressing their bodies close against their chargers' backs, the Mongolians rode into the wind, the muzzles of their guns flashing dully between the steeds' ear-tips.

Presently the mounted bandits, fanning out in open formation, crossed the intervening strip of grassland and rushed down in a left flanking attack.

The regimental commander had the situation well in hand. He had foreseen the enemy's manoeuvre and made his plan accordingly. The men were redeployed and told to lie in wait for the enemy to draw up within effective firing range and then give him a good trouncing. First the commander transferred five of the rifles to the left flank, leaving but one to cover the right; second, he concentrated his ammunition for more rational use; third, he inspected all foxholes and ordered the guards to take good cover. Besides this, he organized the cadres into reserve units, and all comrades, both men and women, prepared for combat. All guns were loaded, their barrels gaping and mute, ready for decisive battle. In strict obedience to the regimental commander's orders, no one spoke an unnecessary word, nobody moved about or fired but the eyes of all were fixed on the commander to catch his every movement.

"We must stick to our positions—hold out to the end, victory will surely be ours."

The regimental commander raised his fist, which was clenched hard as a sledge hammer, and struck an elm tree with a resounding blow which seemed to find response in the men's hearts.

"Comrades, ready. Listen for my commands!"

Squad Leader Chao was all for a retaliatory attack. He felt agitated and could hardly keep down in his foxhole, every once in a while being tempted to stick his head out to take a look. The bandits were rushing towards the left flank of the dune, led in their charge, incidentally, by the pumpkin-headed Mongolian. He was riding a white pony with a brown saddle, the copper stirrups gleaming in the sun. With his shoulders hunched forward and one hand pressing the carbine under his arm, he was fast approaching. Chao sized up the situation immediately. He lifted his gun and aimed at his target, his heart thumping with excitement.

"Commander Tsao," he said in a loud whisper, "that pumpkin-head's the brute that fired at me just now."

"Take good cover," the commander warned, "and listen for my orders!"

Lest his position be exposed, Chao drew his head in.

The bandits were coming ever nearer. The pumpkin-headed Mongolian loosened his reins and, gripping his gun, spurred his white horse through a patch of brush a foot high. With its ears pricked up and its tail swishing, the beast galloped towards the dune with a loud clatter of hoofs. Following behind was a long procession of mounted bandits—over twenty. The sight of them roused the squad leader to a high pitch of excitement.

"Commander Tsao," he shouted, unable to staunch his agitation, "shan't we fire now?"

"Await orders!" was the reply.

But no sooner had he said this than he saw that the Mongolian in the lead had come into effective firing range. The pumpkin-headed one could now be seen to have hefty shoulders and long arms as well. Slowly he raised a sallow face from behind his pony's mane; then, noticing the defences thrown up on the dune, he jerked at his reins, setting his horse back on its haunches. Should he rush the dune or turn back? The Mongolian seemed unable to decide. He looked around and saw his fellow bandits at his heels, and one gave him a wave of his hand. But just then the regimental commander gave his order, "Fire! Get 'em! Shoot! . . ."

"Kharr, kharr. . . ."

Five simultaneous volleys burst forth from the five rifles, bullets whistling through the grass like snakes of fire. At the very first report of the rifles the pumpkin-head's steed, which was in the van of the rebel column, immediately rose up on its forelegs and bucked twice successively, unseating the Mongolian from his saddle. Having freed itself of saddle and bridle, the horse capered out of sight in the grassland. Finding the tables turned, the cavalcade of Mongolians wheeled their horses about and fled. The fellow who had been waving signals at the pumpkin-head kept up his gestures for a time, then he too took to his heels.

"Well, so the bandits have beat a retreat!"

Squad Leader Chao and the guards were so elated that they started to shout but did not relax their firing at the retreating enemy. Chao was the most exultant of all. At the sight of the fleeing brigands he got clear up out of his foxhole.

"Get down, Chao!" the regimental commander shouted to him, "you'll expose our positions!"

The squad leader was turning to obey but already a motley crowd, an old Mongolian among them, was scrambling up the dune from behind, nearing the rubber-tyred carts. The squad leader ducked into his foxhole, shouting at the top of his voice, "Commander Tsao, too bad; the Mongolians are coming up from behind, from behind the carts there!"

At Chao's sounding the alarm, everybody turned his head, not knowing what was in store.

16

It was furthest from anyone's expectations that the old Mongolian in the crowd was their old friend, Nasan Ulji. When the group of cadres had left Small Chuho Village he had stayed on there feeding his horse, smoking and resting, before he must return home across the steppe. He had heard the shots of their skirmish with the bandits and guessed what had happened. Fearing lest the regimental commander and his men might be hungry, the old man had discussed the question of food with the villagers and here they were—come to deliver it!

Nasan Ulji had bowls and chopsticks in his wicker baskets, while the villagers behind him had tubs of steaming rice suspending from the carrying-poles on their shoulders, the men tottering and swaying under their burden as they ascended the dune. By that time the firing had subsided. A gust of wind arose from the south, not high enough to disperse the cloud-drifts, however, and a deathly stillness hung over the plains. After the tension of the battle the men were indeed hungry. Some had sat down for a smoke, some were cleaning their guns and some had just plunked themselves down to rest. Only the regimental commander remained at the alert. He was down on one knee peering through his binoculars to reconnoitre enemy positions.

If man may be compared with iron, then food can make steel of him. At sight of the eatables the spirits of the whole group rose. In two's and three's they gathered round the villagers, vying with them for their shoulder-poles to help carry the rice and rushing to distribute the bowls and chopsticks. They ate the meal making preparations for the next battle.

"Thank you very, very much, folks," they all repeated.

The regimental commander was reminded of the events of two days before when he saw Nasan Ulji: how he and Wang Yao-tung had sat on the *kang* munching parched rice with a cup of buttered tea, how Nasan Ulji, sitting by his round iron stove had regaled them with tales of the grassland and sung the song of Gada Meren. He also remembered the low adobe walls, dark hayricks and wisps of cow-dung smoke curling over the steppe. Now, seeing the old man again was like meeting an old friend and he greeted him very warmly. "So you've come, Nasan Ulji!"

"Yes, I've come, Commander Tsao," the old man replied with a smile, bowing slightly to express his solicitude and sympathy.

"How did you happen to come, Nasan Ulji?" asked the regimental commander.

"Well, I heard shots here, so I thought I'd bring you some food."

The regimental commander nodded in silent gratitude as he said, "Thank you, all of you. After hours of fighting our comrades did for a fact feel hungry."

"Who were those fellows you fighting against?" Nasan Ulji asked with concern.

"Reactionaries," Tsao replied placidly.

"What are reactionaries?" pursued the old Mongolian.

"Well, a reactionary is an inveterate enemy of the common people of Mongolia. Such blackguards as Prince Darhan, Chang Tso-lin, Chiang Kai-shek, Li Shou-hsing, Pai Yun-ti . . . all of their stripe are reactionaries. Do you understand now?"

The old man at once recalled how Darhan had sold the grasslands to Chang Tso-lin whose "Army of Colonists" had forcibly converted it into his own grazing ground and robbed him of his sheep. He felt heavy at heart as, knitting his brows, he said, "Yes, Commander Tsao, I understand. They're all of the same stripe and they're all reactionaries."

"Then aren't you glad we're fighting them?" questioned Tsao.

"Yes, very glad indeed," came Nasan Ulji's ready reply.

Seeing the earnest expression on the old man's face, Tsao patted him on the shoulder as he announced loudly with a smile, "As the father of one of Gada Meren's fighting men, surely you stand on our side!"

"Yes, we're friends," Nasan Ulji affirmed.

Deep emotion stirred the old man and he spoke with a slight tremor in his voice. His eyes shone as he took the commander's hand in his, and Tsao gripped Nasan Ulji's hand till the blood swelled his finger-tips and flooded the old man's being with a warmth such as he had never experienced with anyone of different nationality. Their feelings intertwined in mutual trust while between their hearts was a frankness which dispelled any misapprehension that might have existed between them before.

"Commander Tsao, you must be hungry. Have a bowl of rice please," Nasan Ulji offered.

"Nasan Ulji, you too must be tired. Have one yourself."

The old man had just turned to walk away when the orderly Yang Teh-ching came up from behind him and without saying a word grabbed Nasan Ulji by both sleeves, then in his usual foolhardy way questioned the old man, "Where's your son now?"

"Why, he's with the Public Security Corps in Chanyu," the old man replied.

"Which outfit does he belong to anyway?" Yang pursued, his eyes popping in anger.

"It's the Eighth Route Army," the old man answered.

"You lie! Only we are the Eighth Route Army!" retorted Dunderhead Yang.

Nasan Ulji glanced at Yang's grip on his arms. At first it rather dumbfounded him. Probably the youth did not understand him, so he repeated, "My son is in the Eighth Route Army."

Yang Teh-ching turned livid with anger. Trembling with rage he threw all reason to the winds and accused the old man, "Your son has turned reactionary!"

Nasan Ulji shook his head in resolute denial. "No, it cannot be!" he said.

"Why can't it be? It's the Public Security Corps from Chanyu that's been fighting us just now. They've defected to Chiang Kai-shek's side," the boy stormed.

In the beginning Nasan Ulji had thought the orderly was chiding him for fun, but gradually he came to realize the implications of the youth's accusations and was nonplussed by them. How could the Public Security Corps have turned over to Chiang Kai-shek? Could his younger son have become a turncoat? A sword of the prairie grass seemed to have pierced his heart; he simply could not reconcile himself to what he heard. What should he do now?

"Your son is a reactionary, and you're his father," Yang persisted, his anger rising as his accusations mounted. Without waiting for the old man to get the problem straightened out in his mind, he grabbed him by the shoulders and started dragging him over the ground. The old man was helpless in the boy's grip and, as he reeled over the baskets and food, he stepped on a bowl and broke it. Liu Chun and Squad Leader Chao were sitting on the ground having their lunch and were thoroughly astonished to see the old man and the boy grappling with each other. Yang Teh-ching's eyes bulged to the size of wineglasses as he ranted and dragged the old man about. "You needn't even think of going back home now!" he yelled.

The regimental commander found Yang Teh-ching indeed far too quarrelsome for anyone's good.

"Yang Teh-ching, what are you doing?" he said threateningly. "Do you want to break the discipline of our relations with the masses?"

Seeing the regimental commander's stern countenance, the lad loosened his grip but, still looking daggers at the old man, refused to yield his point.

"Regimental Commander Tsao, his son is a reactionary, and he and that son are birds of a feather for sure."

"How do you know his son is a reactionary?" the commander asked, suppressing the smile on his lips.

"Why, he's mixed up with those bandit troops there."

"But how do you know he's with them? Did he phone you to that effect?"

The longer the argument went on, the more Yang Teh-ching found himself without a leg to stand on in his accusations, and only then did he quiet down. Though Nasan Ulji felt keenly embittered at Yang, when he saw what a childish prankster the orderly was, he was reminded of his own younger son and his animosity gradually vanished. Besides, the regimental commander's big-heartedness and easy manners made the old man feel somehow inexpressibly grateful. One of the villagers who had come carrying the food stepped up and, facing Tsao, gave his testimony regarding Nasan Ulji.

"This old Mongolian grandpa is really a very good-hearted person. When he heard you were engaged in a fight he made every effort to bring you this food."

"Yes, I know," Tsao nodded. Then, taking Nasan Ulji in one hand and the villager in the other, he led them into the elm grove and said to them:

"Let's take a look around here."

17

Dead silence reigned over the steppe. The firing had ceased and the wind too had subsided. Nothing could be seen on any side but the rolling sea of grass no matter how the cadres strained their eyes to gaze into the distance. The dune looked like a lonely island in an ocean of green while the hillock opposite was also desolate. Except for a few patches of green grass the rest was a barren sand hill. Beyond the slope Sanchiatse Village hove in sight—cottages, adobe walls, hayricks, chimneys jutting from the roofs, gun-emplacements—everything as it had been an hour before, everything in its former place, nothing having undergone any change. Only the green of the tree foliage seemed to have deepened in shade.

After surveying all these aspects of the scene back and forth the regimental commander asked the villager, "Must we pass Sanchiatse to get to the Chanyu County seat?"

"You can't pass that way now," the man replied with a shake of his head, "it was infested with bandits."

"How far is it from Sanchiatse to the country seat?" Tsao then asked.

"Twenty-five *li*."

"Isn't there another road leading there?"

"There's the one through Chaotung Village, but the bandits have got in there too."

Then the man pointed to the left to a village far in the distance; it was where the brigands had beat their retreat after their chief had tumbled from his mount. The village stood hazy on the horizon, altogether too faraway for them. Cottage roofs and trees could not be distinguished one from the other. The regimental commander gazed at the scene for a while and then further questioned the villager, "Do you know Magistrate Sun?"

"Yes, I know him."

"Does he live in the Chanyu County seat?"

"Yes."

"Is the Public Security Corps under his control?"

"The corps was in town yesterday. Who knows today. . . ."

The man paused and glanced at the regimental commander's face and then at Nasan Ulji's in turn. He did not know what he should best say under the circumstances. The mutiny of that corps had flared up so suddenly he had not had an inkling of it.

After midday the heat grew fiercer. Tsao unbuttoned his collar and shoved his cap onto the back of his head to scratch his head while he talked with the villager.

"But isn't there any other way to get to the town?" pursued Tsao.

The man stared with wide-open eyes as he thought, but no matter how he racked his brains he could not think of any other road. Nasan Ulji approached the commander, and, indicating with his right hand the plains below, told him that was the way to Chanyu.

"This plain here," he said.

"Which plain do you mean?" Tsao asked.

"Commander Tsao, just look here, it's across this very plain."

Nasan Ulji shook his hand to free it from his big sleeve and pointed to the plains but still the commander could not follow him to his satisfaction. Just then Wang Yao-tung stepped up followed by his guard and Squad Leader Chao.

"Old Tsao," Wang addressed the regimental commander, "aren't you going to eat? Everybody's finished."

"I've left a mess-tinful for you, Commander," the guard offered.

"I don't feel like eating," Tsao replied.

"Now what's going on here?" Wang interposed.

"Old Wang, you've turned up just in time," responded the regimental commander. "Let's put our heads together and see what we're going to do."

Regimental Commander Tsao took Wang by the arm and made him sit down beside him. Squad Leader Chao and the guard squatted on their haunches under the elms, silent, but following with their eyes the route Nasan Ulji had pointed out. It led to the right of the dune and over the plains where, across a level stretch of grassy ground, the bare earth could be seen and the tracks of the carts that had blazed a trail. Farther on there was a rise in the plain with low-sprawling bushes skirting the rise. Beyond that all they could see was a vast expanse of green grassland stretching into the horizon.

Nasan Ulji pointed with his hand for everyone to see. "Proceed from this point of the grassland along the cartroad, rounding that crest till you reach those low bushes. From there turn left and you'll reach Chanyu," he delineated.

The regimental commander reflected for a while and then asked the old man seriously, "Have you ever been there?"

"Yes, I've been there. I used to go there rounding up horses."

The squad leader searched his thoughts too then lifting his brows said with a nod to the regimental commander:

"That's the way all right. It's a roundabout route to the country seat of Chanyu."

"Do you know the place too?" the regimental commander asked Chao.

"While I was on courier duty at the West Manchurian Military Zone Command I sometimes used that route delivering messages to Chanyu. I think I'm not mistaken in the direction."

"Is it that you wish to contact Magistrate Sun?" Wang Yao-tung asked, grasping Tsao's idea.

The regimental commander smiled and nodded, "Yes, I want him to send us reinforcements."

"I wonder what's going on in town. Why haven't they sent out men in pursuit of the enemy before this?"

"That's just it. We must make contact. We know nothing about them," replied Tsao.

"But if we dispatch a messenger the enemy will track him down," interposed Wang.

"They'll track him down.... Ha, ha, ha! That's precisely what we want, and they'll have to dissipate their forces doing it. As soon as we have the opportunity we should strike out and occupy the height now controlled by the enemy in preparation of a breakthrough at night," concluded the regimental commander.

Tsao had his eyes fixed on Squad Leader Chao as he spoke to Wang Yao-tung and the lad understood at once what the commander had in mind. His face beamed and his eyes opened wide with excitement as he asked pointblank, "Regimental Commander Tsao, is it someone to deliver the message you're looking for?"

The commander regarded the lad for a while and, reading the ardour in his face, said to him, "You're just back and here you are wanting to go again! Aren't you too tired?"

"That doesn't matter. I'll go right away," answered the lad.

The squad leader took a letter from the commander, slung a carbine over his shoulder, mounted his black pony and, saluting the regimental commander, set off.

Chao had gone but three or four hundred metres when the enemy spotted him and the next instant mounted bandits appeared from behind the hillock, skirting the rise of ground and emerging onto the plain. They lashed about with their whips as they pursued the squad leader like a pack of maddened hounds. Thirteen or fourteen horses of them raced after him in an unbroken column.

The group watched in breathless excitement, the cadres, the guards, Nasan Ulji and the villager all filled with anxiety for Chao. If they could only give him a pair of wings to fly across the steppe! Yang Teh-ching was consumed with agitation in his concern for the squad leader. Standing on tiptoe he waved his arms wildly into the distance. But who knows whether the squad leader saw him or not? Chao was spurring his steed onto the crest. He turned his head back once to glance at the bandits; then giving his charger another touch of the crop, he shot forward like a finch in a storm, leaving the bunch of them far in the rear.

Once again the regimental commander deployed the men for battle, concentrating the rifles to form a screen of fire between them and the enemy. The cadres too had their pistols at the ready as they watched for the situation to change and waited in full preparation for their chance to attack.

"Keep well covered; don't expose yourselves."

"Commander Tsao, look on that hill!" Yang Teh-ching said, pointing. "There are bandits big as life!"

The bandits were indeed again venturing out from their hiding places on the hillock. Some were crouching, some standing to their full height, and one was even walking his horse about.

There were seven in all watching their fellow bandits galloping over the plain in pursuit of Chao, and they too showed signs of excitement and concern for their men. The squad leader had just passed the low bush area. He made a turn and then his figure receded till it was no larger than a bean darting over the steppe. The long cavalcade of bandits fanned out on the plains, and, in order to avoid the firing from the dune, they made a detour and were thus left far behind. At this the bandits on the hill got nervous and some put their hands to their eyes to shade them as they squinted into the distance while others looked up and down the plain in high excitement. The fellow with the tall hat again appeared on the scene, waving both arms and pointing at the mounted Mongolians lagging behind the object of their pursuit.

Having concentrated his rifle fire, the regimental commander shouted his order, "Shoot!" And the guns sounded with one loud report. Bullets cut through the air felling two of the Mongolians on the spot. The tall topper was sent rolling on the ground and the bandits were stricken with panic. Without returning a single shot they slid back down the hillock. Later some of them ventured out to pick up their wounded, not daring to straighten their backs however.

The regimental commander saw the whole operation clearly through his binoculars. The enemy had taken fright; their chance had come!

18

While Tsao was making his observation of the enemy Wang Yao-tung too raised his glasses to his eyes. He saw the barren hillock opposite covered with crusts of naked earth between clumps of grass, looking like a scalp infested with scabies—indeed no pleasant sight! On the slope at the left were two patrolmen sitting on their mounts and not firing a shot posted obviously only to watch the movements on the dune, while on the road skirting the hillock two small groups of the Mongolians were moving in the direction of Sanchiatse Village, apparently removing their wounded. The enemy had suffered a severe blow, with three or four casualties inflicted upon them. The regimental commander figured there were no more and likely less than ten Mongolians left on the hillock after subtracting their stretcher-bearers and the thirteen or fourteen in pursuit of Squad Leader Chao. The time was ripe now to take the sandy hill while it was so poorly defended and the enemy was scattered and in panic. He glanced at his watch and said to Wang Yao-tung, "It's now 11 hours; we've been engaged with the enemy for quite some time and still no response from town."

Wang Yao-tung pointed to the enemy patrolmen on the slope and said angrily, "From such a height the enemy's got us right under his eye; his position on that hill is a thorn in our sides."

"Then we'll pull the thorn out," said the regimental commander with decision. "We must go into action at once and occupy that hill! In case reinforcements from town fail to arrive, we shall prepare for a break-through tonight. We must organize a shock unit. I wonder who will lead it."

Wang Yao-tung knew that none of the other cadres had any battle experience and immediately volunteered to go.

The commander hesitated, saying nothing. He felt that for the deputy commander to lead the shock unit, whether viewed from the aspect of the overall deployment or the composition of the unit, was unfit. But for the present he could think of no other person suitable for the task; thus he pondered the question.

When Wang saw the commander's eyelashes quivering in indecision, he felt ill at ease and questioned him, "Old Tsao, I really think you should let me go. Are you considering the matter in the interest of one person or of all?"

"Old Wang," the regimental commander replied with a smile, "all right, you've talked me into it and I'll let you go." Wang noted the mixed feeling of admiration, trust and deep comradely love in the regimental commander's voice.

Five guards and five rifles—that comprised the hastily knocked together shock brigade. Wang Yao-tung spoke to his little band of fighters of their task and showed them the route they would take in the attack. Wang took a red flag and a pistol, and after the men had determined their signals they prepared to set out.

Just then Lin Hsiu came up from under the elm grove and, lifting her serene face, saw Wang Yao-tung with the red flag and pistol. "Deputy Commander Wang," she asked, "are you leaving?"

Lin Hsiu had made a deep impression on Wang by singing *Fresh Blossoms of May* on the very first day of their journey. He remembered the light and flowing melody touched with just a note of sadness that was altogether delightful: the grass leaves so green; blossoms so red. . . .

Living on this soil were indeed many heroes and miserable people who, like the blossoms of May, flourished in spring and withered in autumn, only to bloom again with the burgeoning of spring the following year. New forces were constantly growing and coming to the fore. The more he turned these things over in his mind the greater he felt his own faith.

Seeing that Wang had something on his mind, the regimental commander asked him with deep concern, "Old Wang, what is it you're thinking about so hard?"

Wang Yao-tung raised his head to gaze upon the radiant countenance of Lin Hsiu—a girl healthy and plump, simple, sincere and glowing with the ardent aspirations of youth. He then surveyed the other comrades on the dune talking and laughing cheerfully, and said in a voice tremulous with emotion, "Well, what I was thinking was that all of you comrades will succeed in reaching the Northeast Bureau; the whole Northeast will certainly be liberated!"

The regimental commander felt Wang's remark not totally apt and added a complement to it. "All our comrades, including you, Old Wang. Don't you figure on participating in the victory too?"

"I've thought about it of course," Wang said with a smile, "how could I not have thought of it! Even when I was south of the Great Wall fighting against Japan, I never doubted for a moment but that we would triumph. And now what a fulfilment it is to have returned to the Northeast and seen the boundless grassland of my native country again!"

As he said this, Wang spontaneously lifted his gaze to the expanse beyond the dune. All around was flat rolling steppe, and green of it succulent after the rain. The dense grasses, their sword-like tips and spreading blades seeming to have clasped hands, held the red, yellow and blue flowers above their own verdure. Oh, how dearly he loved these flowers! He gazed farther into the distance but could see nothing but one vast stretch of green steppeland.

Suddenly Wang heard the guards bolt their rifles, then there were the voices of Lin Hsiu and Liu Chun conversing and he heard the whinnying of Mongolian ponies faraway. His heart was stirred with agitation and he rose and said to the regimental commander, "It's time I got going!"

"All right, Old Wang, then go now," Tsao said, his voice solicitous. "Watch out for enemy fire."

Wang Yao-tung led his advance party of five guards down the dune; then when they had advanced about 150 metres they began to ascend the slope of the hillock and at the same time the exchange of fire with the enemy commenced. Six or seven Mongolian bandits stuck their heads out above the crest and began firing downward, wisps of smoke curling from their guns. Meanwhile clouds of dust were raised on the mound by the bullets fired from below. The *crack, crack* of shots in the exchange was incessant.

Wang Yao-tung deployed his men into two groups, one on each side of him, forming a skirmish line and pressing forward like a pair of knives posed to cut into the enemy's heart. Thus advancing, they gave him no centralized target and kept his firing scattered. The enemy guns would fire off and on as though gasping for breath at intervals. Wang Yao-tung took one of the guards and with him rushed up the hill, making an advance each time a few shots were fired and then flattening out on the ground to fire the next round. The enemy, who were already feverishly busy, were further engaged with the two guards rushing up the slope from the right side, hunched over for action. The brigands fired at them but they paid them no heed.

The cadres on the dune were in perfect readiness to attack. When they saw Wang Yao-tung and his men ascending the hillock they became tense, wishing they could at once rush forward from their positions.

The regimental commander was following very carefully the course of events, training his binoculars now on the left, now on the right.

The men attacking the enemy from the right made a second push forward, advancing another 50 metres and leaving only 150 metres between them and the crest.

Seeing that the guards on the right had already made a dash up the slope, Wang Yao-tung directed those on the left to charge. Yang Teh-ching and another lad, one behind the other, fired at the crest while watching carefully for Wang's signals. A few quick strides and they were over a patch of grass on the steep slope leading to the crest, then they crawled and fired again. But the bandits' attention had been drawn by Wang's signalling and they directed their firing on him. A few bullets cut into the sandy earth beside him without, however, slowing him down in his upward charge. He swung his arm forward into firing position and his pistol sounded off, exhausting one clip after another.

The regimental commander saw that Wang and his men had all charged up the hillock and were now separated from the crest by less than 120 metres. The enemy began to appear panicky, firing aimlessly. Tsao judged that the hillock would be taken in a matter of minutes now and, in order to co-ordinate with the shock unit in the assault, he led his group of cadres out of their foxholes and rushed forward. Except for Nasan Ulji and the villagers who had delivered food for the men, everyone joined the attack.

"Comrades, charge forward! We must take this enemy position!"

As Wang Yao-tung saw the regimental commander leading the cadres in storming up the knoll like a tempest he felt agitated and resolved to occupy the crest within two minutes so that they might rout the enemy completely and break through the encirclement in their victorious march to the Northeast Bureau! At once he unfurled the red flag as signal for Yang Teh-ching's assault. Then, seeing that Yang had almost reached the crest, he was waving the flag for the men on the right flank when he was struck by a bullet. He continued giving his signal, but his vision suddenly blurred and his strength gave out. "Why haven't the men occupied the crest positions?" he gasped, anxious, but before he had found his answer he fell to the ground.

In an instant the guards occupied the hillock, the bandits fleeing on their ponies. The red flag was planted on the crest but beneath it lay the lifeless body of Comrade Wang Yao-tung.

19

By now the group of cadres led by Regimental Commander Tsao had all reached the top of the hillock. Cigarette wrappers, empty cartridges, shreds of cloth, horse-dung and a grey tophat pierced through by a bullet lay scattered on the slope while everywhere were the hoofprints of horses that had trampled the patches of grass into the earth. The knoll was connected with the dune by a ridge which resembled the spine of some giant fish. All around was the boundless steppe-land, lone and deserted, while hanging over the grass was the choking mixed smell of gunpowder and blood.

The regimental commander walked up the steep slope to where the body of Wang Yao-tung lay. Another 20 metres and he would have been on the crest! He lay with his head pointing southeast and his feet northwest; in his breast was a ragged hole from which blood had poured onto his army tunic. His face was ashen and his teeth were set as though even in death his hatred for the enemy had not abated. He would never reach the Northeast Bureau together with his comrades!

The entire group drew up in a close circle around the body of Wang Yao-tung, and standing with heads bowed in silence, each felt keenly the pain in his heart. Of all the comrades, however, the regimental commander was the one with whom Wang had had the closest relationship. Hadn't it been but a few brief moments before that Wang Yao-tung had volunteered for the assignment of spearheading the attack? He had led the shock unit in the charge up the hill and now had given his life in order that the group of cadres could make a breakthrough, in order that they could all succeed in reaching the Northeast Bureau! Overwhelmed with respect and admiration for the greatness of character of his dead comrade, the regimental commander bent down and took the cold, bloodless face of Wang in his hands to have a good last look at it. Wang's bristle of dark beard gave his face an aspect of seriousness that reminded Tsao of the man's unyielding spirit in battle against the enemy.

The regimental commander straightened up and, still looking upon the fallen Wang Yao-tung, bared his head and stood in silence. Liu Chun too removed his cap, followed by the rest of the cadres, the guards and Lin Hsiu, all of whom stood over the body in silent respect for several minutes.

A deep stillness pervaded the hill at sunset, the fired having long since ceased. Even the whinnying of the Mongolian ponies sounded hushed. A gust of wind blew in from the plains turning up the corners of the men's tunics and rustling the blood-stained leaves of grass. The men reluctantly took up their task of digging the loose soil to bury their dead comrade. All shared in the work and in a little while the small grave mound was completed. Then with slow, heavy steps the regimental commander walked round the mound, after which he stopped and, gazing out over the vast plains of grass, said with deep feeling, "Old Wang grew up on the steppe of the Northeast; let him now rest in peace on the same steppe!"

Liu Chun, recollecting Wang Yao-tung's simple way of life, turned to the group and said reverently, "Old Wang always led a thrifty and simple life. Others smoked ready-rolled cigarettes; he preferred his home-grown tobacco. And he would choose an old home-spun cloth tunic to a new tailored jacket. Now that he is dead he has no other shroud than the old coarse cloth shirt he was wearing."

Yang Teh-ching showed deep reverence and respect for Wang as he recalled incidents in his life. "You could hardly get him to put on a new shirt even when he had one," the lad said. "He had a couple of good shirts but if it wasn't the grooms then it was some sick comrades he gave them to."

How were these people to hold a memorial service for Deputy Commander Wang? There was no wine to be had, and neither were there fruits for offerings, no funeral scrolls and wreaths. Lin Hsiu was the first to pick a bunch of wild flowers and place it tenderly on the little grave mound. As she did so an indescribable pang of grief stabbed her heart and she dropped her head. It had been such a short space of time since the comrade was wielding a flag and had talked to her. And now? He was lying there in that little grave, parted from his comrades for ever! Thoughts flitted through her mind of that first day out when she had sung for him "Fresh blossoms . . . shroud the blood of patriots." How deeply moved she was now by the personality of this patriot! Her feeling of respect for him had increased a thousandfold since the day she sang that song!

The sun had already dropped behind the crimson clouds gathering on the western horizon. The steppe was tinted violet, gradually darkening to purple.

There was not one of the comrades but had a sensation of extreme heaviness in his heart. Words came to their lips but no one said anything. It was Yang Teh-ching who bore Wang Yao-tung's binoculars, map-case and pistol. The boy's eyes reddened and his voice broke as he told how Wang had bought him exercise books out of his own allowance, how he had helped him with his studies and how he had tucked his quilt about him at night when he had kicked it off. The more he talked of these things the more tearful he became.

The regimental commander turned away from the grave in sorrow. "If I hadn't let him go, this would never have happened," he reproached himself, taking upon himself the loss of the comrade as a mistake in carrying out his duties as commander. It was a lesson written in blood that had further deepened his sense of responsibility. Realizing this inspirited him, and finally, addressing the group, he said, "Deputy Regimental Commander Wang was a faithful fighter of the proletariat. He needed nothing—nothing but the glorious name of Communist. For the cause of the people's liberation he was willing to give the last precious drop of his own blood. Comrades, we should learn from Comrade Wang Yao-tung."

It was nearing twilight. Smoke of hearth fires curled from the chimneys at Sanchiatse Village, while the clouds overhead had not yet dispersed. Patches of light and dark overlapped one another and covered the greater part of the sky. Yang Teh-ching stood watch by the grave mopping at his eyes as he wept bitterly.

The regimental commander approached him and gave him a pat on the head.

"What are you crying about?" he asked.

"I . . . I'm thinking of Deputy Commander Wang . . ." the lad whimpered through his tears.

"But didn't he criticize you just this morning?"

"If he criticized me it was for my own good. I regret now I didn't listen to him before."

"Well, have you made up your mind to listen to him from now on?"

"Oh, I want to but it's too late. I'll never have the chance to be criticized by him any more!" the boy bawled.

"If you really want to improve there are other comrades who will be able to help you," the commander comforted him.

The regimental commander left the grave mound and, taking his binoculars, made an observation of the situation to prepare for the breakthrough. He turned to the group and said to them in a calm, even voice, "Comrades, Deputy Regimental Commander Wang is dead, but we should keep firmly in mind what he has told us. All of us comrades will succeed in reaching the Northeast Bureau and the whole Northeast shall be liberated!"

20

It was almost dark when the group of cadres left the sandy hillock and headed for the grass-plains.

The regimental commander took the first cart, while the other cadres occupied the three following behind. Each cart was charged to look after itself and also to look out for one another. Descending the hill in their breakthrough operation and entering the grass-plains, the group was excited and tense at the same time—a mixed feeling too complicated for description. The drivers, bent on speed, kept flourishing their whips. Seeming to understand what the men had in mind, the beasts strained in their harness and pulled the rubber-tyred carts like a flight of arrows over the steppe, the rumbling of the four vehicles lightening the hearts of the comrades aboard.

The skies gradually darkened, casting a blur over the steppe. Neither the rubber-tyred wheels, nor the body of the carts, nor the horses' hoofs could be seen but the laden vehicles looked like four big rolling trellises of plants one after the other plunging into the deep bush where they were swallowed up in the darkness of the night. The pitch blackness wrapping itself around the steppe evoked two kinds of feeling in the group: one was apprehension; the other was joy. No object was visible, and the roads and human beings too were blotted out. There was nothing but the inky expanse of the steppe.

The grassland was indeed infinite. The farther the group penetrated it, the less they could fathom. The plant smells became stronger too—the aromatic artemisia, fragrant blossoms and the earthy smell of washed out grass roots filled the comradese' nostrils alternately.

After rumbling on thus for more than an hour the horses began to tire and a cart got bogged down in a tangle of bush. The regimental commander asked the driver to stop so they could get their bearings. He put down his whip and, grasping the thill for support, let himself down from the cart. But, when he glanced around into the pitch black void of the plains he realized that he had lost his sense of direction.

"Commander Tsao, aren't we going south?" he queried.

"Chanyu lies due east of the place where we had the fight," the regimental commander told him. "Don't you remember? Squad Leader Chao went in that direction."

"After we came down the hillock I made a turn," the carter said, "and after that I didn't have the slightest idea which way I was going, not the slightest."

"Oh! How could you get so befuddled as to take the wrong route?"

Filled with anxiety Tsao jumped down from the cart and took a few steps through the bush. The grass was dense with no path visible through it. He paced around reconnoitring for quite some time and then returned to the cart. He consulted with the others, but they too were all at sea. Leaving the hillock they had thought only of making the breakthrough and nobody stopped to think in what direction they were speeding along. The carter squatted down and groped around as though looking for something in the trampled grass, then turned around and continued his search. The patch was thickly covered with a growth of erect stalks—artemisia perhaps—anyway too thick for him to probe very far. He stood up and gazed around at the grassland. He had forgotten the direction he had taken to get to the present spot! He scratched his head in his anxiety as he said, "Oh my, this one day of fighting's got me all muddled up."

"How fine it'd be to have Squad Leader Chao with us now," the regimental commander said to himself, thinking of the lad. "I wonder whether he's got to the town by now."

As the night deepened a thin veil of fog drifted in like a smokescreen over the steppe, enveloping the vegetation in a haze, while through the mist a crescent moon gave out its dim light Clouds drifted towards the horizon like waves in an ocean but gradually gave way to an azure sky with the North Star twinkling brightly. The star pointed directly to the tail of the cart.

When the carter saw the star he cried for joy, "Commander Tsao, look! We're heading due south!"

"But it's not south we want to go!" reminded the commander.

"That's just it. This day's battle has mixed everything up in my mind. Let's turn east then!" So the carts made a ninety-degree turn and the party continued on their way.

Now everyone felt better. Surely after another two or three hours they would be in Chanyu. But then suddenly thick clouds began to gather in the skies which soon became blacker than the bottom of a frying pan, blotting out both the crescent moon and the North Star. The convoy slowed down in caution, the lead driver not daring to give play to his whip as though afraid he should strike something unseen with it. It wasn't long till rain was pouring down and water flooded that entire stretch of steppe. As the carts sank deep into the mire they made a *splash splash* sound which was punctuated by the croaking of frogs that had appeared in the shallow pools, while wild ducks, hidden in the reed bush, quacked eerily.

Hungry, thirsty and tired after the day's battle, the party was not in its usual high spirits, and getting lost on the way and drenched by the rain into the bargain made them almost peevish. The cry of the wild ducks and the croaking of the frogs disgusted them now. Indeed they wished to move along without anything in the world detecting their movement.

After jogging along for seven or eight *li* they came to a place where the flood water seemed less. In fact the grassy sound was dry in spots and the tall growth was plumed at the tip, marking it as a rush field. Then they came to a sand-dune, and after that ground overgrown with low grass and elm shrubs which cast a dark wall of shadows. They were just thinking of passing through the grove when suddenly they heard the barking of dogs ahead. The driver pulled in his reins with a start, bringing the cart to a gradual standstill.

On the other side of the shrubs there seemed to be a village, for there was a light to be seen flickering there.

"Commander Tsao," the driver called, pointing with his whip, "look, there's a light ahead."

The light he pointed out was no bigger than a soy-bean and glimmered unsteadily in the dark—now brighter, now dimmer.

Dogs set up a fuss not far off, for the cadres heard their barking distinctly and lapsed into apprehensive silence.

The regimental commander peered at the light very much disgruntled. "A devil of a place!" he cursed.

Haven't we gotten into Sanchiatse Village?" Liu Chun warned.

The four carts drew up to one spot, the horses side by side, foam dripping from their bits as they sneezed noisily as if exchanging the latest news. The cadres sat facing one another, yawning in mute expectation of something happening that night.

The regimental commander rapped the shaft with his hand and called impatiently to the driver, "Find out the way then!"

Taking his whip, the driver waded through the bush, sweeping the grass aside with the whip handle to make way. He was groping with one foot and then the other over the undulating grassy ground when he stopped short in his tracks, for he caught the smell of damp upturned earth and horse-dung. Bending down to feel the grass with his fingers he came upon a shallow indentation in the ground just like the rut made by a cart wheel. He looked around for some time and then returned to the group.

"Well, if that wouldn't beat all!" he exclaimed to the commander, "we're right back to exactly where we started from!"

This was the very thing the regimental commander had been afraid would happen. Very much exasperated, he looked the driver in the eye and asked him seriously, "Are you sure you're not mistaken again?"

"Yes, I saw it all clearly," the driver replied.

"You're sure?"

"Commander Tsao, I saw it for a fact. There's horse-dung and ruts made by our own cart wheels. Farther up will be the sand-dune where we had the scrap with the bandits."

Liu Chun edged closer to the regimental commander and, patting him on the shoulder, pointed to his left with his finger. "This is the cart road we took down from Small Chuho Village. Ahead is the sand-dune, and the place where the dogs were barking is Sanchiatse Village. Have you figured out the lay of the land now?"

Commander Tsao glanced around. A dark thicket loomed ahead all right, bulky and big, exactly like the elm grove on the dune. Above the grove a couple of stars could be seen twinkling faintly through the light mist. The lamps at the place where the dogs had been barking glowed brightly for a while only to die out again, sending the place for the second time into pitch darkness. It was as though somebody was playing a trick on the little party—having sport not letting them see where they were!

"A devil of a place," the regimental commander repeated vehemently. "Let's hurry with the carts and get the hell out of here."

The carters started up the cart train, flourishing their whips, and again the party moved on into the steppe.

For a long time the drivers kept up their lashing of the animals, whose hoofs pounded against the ground, turning the cart wheels furiously. The carts plunged into deep seas of grass, bumped over mounds, crashed through brush, splashed through pools of rain water and rumbled over vast stretches of wasteland. It seemed to the cadres that they had covered the whole of the Mongolian steppe! But where were they headed? How far had they gone? Had they or had they not passed the enemy lines? All these questions remained unanswered in their minds.

It was growing light. The cloud slowly began to disperse and the stars to set beyond the horizon. A white fog came floating over the steppe, engulfing everything in a mist and, like a mammoth pane of opaque glass, barring the way ahead with its hazily hanging bulk. It was impenetrable to the eye, untouchable to the hand—altogether inscrutable. The carters were like blind men groping about. And yet the carts rolled on for quite a stretch of steppe before leaving it and turning onto the village road. Soon they were greeted by a huge dark shadow and suddenly heard *cock-a-doodle-doo . . . cock-a-doodle-doo . . .* joined in by several other cocks in chorus. They were nearing a village! Now they felt the night had been altogether too short; time had slipped by and daybreak was upon them, which meant that their whereabouts would be disclosed.

The driver was at a loss whether to proceed or stop.

"Commander Tsao," he asked in a whisper, "what shall we do now?"

At the regimental commander's order Yang Teh-ching entered the village to reconnoitre. Before long Yang returned, but he had gone for nothing since he had not learned anything regarding the situation. Tsao decided they should enter the village, so he turned and passed the word on to the comrades in the other carts.

"Everybody must be on the alert, no noise, and listen for my orders!"

It had rained there too during the night and the village streets were inundated, while water covered a large surrounding area. The cart wheels went *squelch squelch* in the mire as the horses plodded *pit-a-pat* with their hoofs on the rain-soaked paths, creating a resounding noise. The more anxious the party were not to raise the alarms the louder the noise seemed. When the horses' hoofs sank into the mire it seemed to take ages to pull them out again. The party had in fact been discovered at the first street corner by a lone dog which had barked at them naggingly. Now the villagers too discovered them and climbed the walls the better to hear the rumble of the vehicles and to cough into the darkness.

"Who goes there?" came several voices.

"Who are you on the wall there?" the cadres in the carts asked in reply.

"I'm one of the folk from the village," came a voice from over the wall.

The village was wrapped in darkness, its cottages, trees, chimneys all blended into a single black, almost square mass. At one corner was a tall earthen structure which very much resembled a gun-emplacement. Though no one could be seen manning it, there were people there talking in undertones as if in secret consultation. In the street the dogs set up their confounded barking again—three or four of them now taking part in the rumpus. Their barking was loud and sharp, sometimes drawn out into a cacophonous howl.

None of the group uttered a word but, with bated breath, gripped their weapons tighter in their hands. They kept their eyes glued to the adobe-walled battlement above while listening for any stir in the village, ready to fire at any moment.

A shadow moved over the ground and neared the first cart. The shadow was gesturing with its hands instead of speaking, but the regimental commander recognized it as one of the guards coming up with news.

"Let the carts behind draw up even with us," Tsao told him.

"The fourth vehicle has fallen into a ditch," the man said.

"Then you go and ask what village this is so that we may ask the villagers for help."

"Hey there, what village is this?" the man shouted.

Somebody immediately answered from the wall, "This is Sanchiatse Village."

At the mention of Sanchiatse the party instantly grew tense.

21

The very day before and at the very hour the regimental commander was engaged in battle with the bandits at the dune, Magistrate Sun was fighting it out with the brigands in town. As it happened the operations worked out as a co-ordinated attack of the forces of the two fraternal revolutionary detachments. By their simultaneous attack on the enemy from front and back they had kept him hopping like so many jumping-beans. Mutineers as they were and, furthermore, with the blood of several revolutionary cadres on their hands, the bandits in Sanchiatse Village were all on edge, knowing that their time was running out. So before the cart train entered the village the blackguards had taken to their heels without waiting for the day to dawn. Fortunately the cadres had not fired any shots but had raised a mock alarm instead.

Thus in broad daylight the four carts entered the town of Chanyu unopposed.

Magistrate Sun warmly greeted the group of cadres who had succeeded in making the breakthrough. The joy of meeting so unexpectedly with comrades from the rear after battle was too great for any of them to express adequately. Magistrate Sun prepared a meal for them and asked them to refresh themselves with cigarettes and baths all around. He also saw to it that their provisions and other necessities were replenished. It was a great comfort for the comrades to meet together, and heart-to-heart talks followed unconstrained.

The regimental commander recounted for Magistrate Sun all that had happened: when the group of cadres had set out from Changchiakou, how they had passed through Tungliao, about the trek over the Mongolian grassland, and how they had been engaged by bandit troops. He told him how Wang Yao-tung had been killed and suggested that they give him proper burial. Magistrate Sun approved his suggestion and then went on to tell him that the bandit troops he had engaged were in fact the landlord armed forces. Han Pao-yu, the ringleader, was by social status a reactionary; besides that he was a thoroughly depraved character morally, being an opium fiend, a gambler and an opportunist of the first water. After the reorganization of Han's followers into the Third Company of the Public Security Corps of Chanyu County, much energy had been spent in an effort to win them over and reeducate them but Han Pao-yu showed not the slightest intention of turning over a new leaf. He mouthed a lot of fine words for the Communist Party while dealing with the Kuomintang behind the scenes. After the people's forces had withdrawn from Szeping, Han showed himself in his true colours. He murdered three cadres of the region, fled the town of Chanyu and turned an out-and-out renegade. Most of the Mongolian army men were fine, loyal people, however, Sun added. Though for the time being some had allowed themselves to be hoodwinked by the enemy, once they realized their mistake they would come back. There were other Mongolians at the Public Security Corps who had never lost their heads and gotten tricked by Han Pao-yu, for their attitude was resolute.

"Where are they now, these resolute Mongolians who have stood firm?" asked Regimental Commander Tsao.

"Tomorrow we'll ask some of them to escort you to Kaitung and you'll see them then," Sun replied.

"Yesterday we knew nothing about the situation," Tsao said. "We sent somebody to contact you but he didn't get through."

"We did make contact," Sun told him.

"And who was it sent you the news?"

"Early this morning Squad Leader Chao phoned me from Kaitung," Sun explained, "he told me your group had met with some incident."

The regimental commander nodded again and again as he said confidently," Chao is a good lad all right. Must've been pretty tired. Any other news from the West Manchurian Military Zone?"

"The Zone Command called me by phone," Sun said. "There's a Mongolian Work Team coming here. They've been sent by Chairman Ulanfu. The team has had some short-term training courses and, in accordance with the May Fourth Directive of the Central Committee of the Party, they're to work among the masses at the East Khorcin Middel Banner."

"Well," the regimental commander concluded with a smile, "since that's the case our problem is solved."

22

The group rested the night at Chanyu and the next day again set off on their journey. They planned to reach Kaitung that afternoon, whence they would entrain and, passing through Tsitsihar, arrive at the Northeast Bureau in Harbin. Magistrate Sun, in his great concern for the group of cadres, sent the Public Security Corps along to escort and protect them on the way. Most of the corps men were Hans, but there were also the Mongolian cavalry men of the Third Company who had remained firm against the rebels. All were in a light-hearted, almost gay mood, as the group resumed its trek. After a good meal and plenty of water to drink, and what with a night's sound sleep, the travellers' fatigue had vanished. They had put out of their heads practically all thought of the battle two days before. Dawn found the carters busy watering the horses and readying the carts, pumping air into the tyres till, when they started rolling, they bounced along as on big balloons.

The day was bright. The sun rising crimson in the east bathed the East Khorcin Middle Banner in its glow. After its long absence during the long rainy spell the sun appeared especially fresh and bright, its crystal-clear rays dazzling to the eyes. Everyone greeted the sunshine as a long lost friend. Blazing upon the steppe, it showed up the grassland in all its verdure; and as it cast its fresh rays upon the blossoms, they too appeared more lovely than before. Morning glories lushed with pink, stately asters, dainty-petalled shining buttercups, off-white daisies, wild fennel flowers, "cat's-eyes." . . . Oh, how manifold were the flowers of the steppe! At the bidding of the sun they all seemed to awake from their slumber.

Bountiful indeed were the flowers of the grassland! They turned their smiling faces to the travellers and gave off their sweet fragrance and danced in the warm breeze for them!

After the rain all the vegetation of the steppe flourished. Thistles sprouted, young shoots of reeds shot up and rushes showed their heads, red like fiery wands.

An azure sky covered all from end to end without a single cloud. Steppe and sky were clean, spotlessly clean. How calm the serene steppe-land sky! How lovely and charming the blossoms of the grass-plains! Skylarks that the day before had been buffeted about in the rain-storm reappeared from the recesses of the reed-bushes, soaring into the air unchallenged, singing their songs and spreading their wings at will. The boundless East Khorcin Middle Banner grassland had become their free and happy land!

Regimental Commander Tsao too was in a particularly happy frame of mind. He had put away the old rain-soaked army tunic he had been wearing and doned a new green uniform and put on a pair of brand-new leather shoes and brand-new leggings. Trim from head to foot, he packed his map-case away in the cart; nor were his field-glasses around his neck. Spick and span, he looked as if he had nothing in the world to worry about and would strike up conversations with Lin Hsiu or Liu Chun every now and then as they travelled. They talked about the Northeast Bureau of the Central Committee, of their future work, about the liberation of the northeastern provinces. Their conversation led naturally to Wang Yao-tung, for in their minds the cause of liberating the Northeast was inseparably bound up with the memory of their fallen comrade-in-arms.

With the advent of bright weather not only were the people in high spirits but the horses too became animated. As the driver, his head bare, gave play to his whip, the trace-pony hurried along, swishing its tail as it swung its legs in a trot. The wheels rolled over the smooth road without a hitch and the occupants of the carts sat comfortably back in their seats. Travelling thus no one any longer found the journey tedious. Some sat enjoying the view, some relaxed with a smoke, and some, having arranged the luggage in the middle of the cart as an improvised table, started up a game of poker. After a few hands, how-ever, they resumed their conversation.

Lin Hsiu asked the regimental commander several times for information as to how they should proceed on their journey. "Does the train we take at Kaitung go straight through to Harbin?" she asked. "We needn't change trains?"

"I've heard that Harbin is a much grander place than Changchiakou," Liu Chun interrupted. "I wonder what it's like!"

"Harbin is a great city all right," the regimental commander said, "but I think the Northeast Bureau is likely to be situated in a rather quieter sector."

The cadres discussed their future work, pictured how it would be staying at the guest-house and visiting friends. Some of the guards speculated with interest on seeing motion pictures, taking baths and finding grease for their guns. Each had his own ideas; each his own visions. But beyond all the entire group had a common outlook, the great cause, which Wang Yao-tung had failed to see realized—the cause of communism that was sure to take root and blossom on the soil of the Northeast!

Now they were in all probability nearing the edge of the Mongolian steppe. Villages came into view more frequently and trees became more luxuriant. On both sides of the road large stretches of cultivated land could be seen while piles of earth and thatched cottages dotted the landscape. The grass was emerald, fresh and tender, looking more like wheat seedlings bobbing gently in the breeze.

The road was smooth, the air no longer cut by the cracking of whips, while the hoofs of the beasts seemed never to touch ground and the cart wheels fairly flew over the patches of grass, leaving the escorts behind in clouds of dust. To prevent losing contact with the comrades in the rear, Regimental Commander Tsao cried to the driver, "Slow down a bit; we've left the Public Security Corps behind!"

Turning to reply, the driver laughed and said, "Regimental Commander Tsao, we can buzz right along now, eh? And we won't be driving back to Sanchiatse Village either, getting our heads all muddled up!"

Tsao too bantered back with the driver. "Well, you are a fine one," he said, "taking a whole day from dawn to dark just to get us back where we started from!"

The carts slowed down till the escorts had caught up with them. There were 20 to 30 of these mounted corps men in all, most of them young lads in khaki army tunics with guns strapped onto their backs and flicking their crops as they followed in the wake of the carts. Abreast of the left thill of the lead cart was a youth with a broad face, high forehead, bushy eyebrows and high-bridged nose. He was gazing intently at the regimental commander and the commander too was observing him. His face, figure and bearing all told Tsao that he was a Mongolian.

"You're a local boy, my lad?" Tsao asked.

"Yes, I am," he replied with a nod of his head.

"To which company of the Public Security Corps do you belong?"

"Third Company."

The regimental commander at once placed the company and pursued, "Isn't that the company of Han Pao-yu?"

"Oh, Han Pao-yu is a trickster!" The lad cocked his head to one side and at the mention of Han Pao-yu his voice became a snort. Shaking his head he said, "Han Pao-yu has gone over to the Central Army of the Kuomintang, while I remain with the Eighth Route Army. Each takes his own path."

Commander Tsao lauded the lad by giving him a "thumbs up" and said to him, "You're an example of the resolute Mongolians. What's your name?"

"Bajab."

The commander seemed to find the name somehow familiar but the impression was not deep, and for a time he could not place it.

"Bajab, where's your home?" he pursued.

The youth raised his crop and pointed into the distance over the rolling steppe. "Over there," he said, "at the East Khorcin Middle Banner grassland."

"We've come from that Banner," Tsao told him.

"Did you pass through Chiachiayingtse?"

"We stayed in Chiachiayingtse at Nasan Ulji's house."

"Nasan Ulji is my father," Bajab said, bursting into a grin.

"Oho, this poor head of mine; now I remember. Your father mentioned you, Bajab."

The commander rapped his head as he laughed together with the young man. He thought of saying something but then, with quiver of his chin, sneezed instead, and a fresh rosy glow infused his face. He remembered the story Nasan Ulji had told by the round iron stove, how the old man had led the life of a shepherd, how he had suffered under Prince Darhan and the "Army of Colonists," and how finally he had sent his younger son to join the Eighth Route Army. Now he had actually met the old man's son!

"Your father's a fine old man," he said to the lad, "and you're a good son. You haven't failed to live up to your father's expectations."

The commander's praise stirred the lad and made him blush. He tugged lightly at his reins and hastened to ask other questions, "Whom else did my father mention?"

"Besides you he mentioned your brother."

Bajab's face changed and, lifting his brows, he said to himself, "So he also mentioned my brother."

"Your brother joined Gada Meren in the uprising," the regimental commander said to him, "and fell in battle on the steppe. Whenever your father thought of that his countenance would become very sad. Do you still remember *The Song of Gada Meren?*"

The lad's face darkened and wrinkles lined his broad forehead. He gazed into the distance of the rolling steppe for some time, then collecting his thoughts, softly sang the song:

> Wild geese from the south
> Will ne'er take flight ere they've paused by the Yangtse;
> The uprising Gada Meren fought
> For the sake of our native soil, Mongolia!
>
> Wild geese from the north
> Will ne'er take flight ere they've paused by the Heihc River;
> The uprising Gada Meren laid down his life
> For the sake of our native land, Mongolia!

As Bajab ended his song Regimental Commander Tsao pondered over the lines and seemed to see vaguely two giant geese flying from the south, one was Gada Meren, the other Wang Yao-tung. But when they reached the Mongolian steppe they seemed to have got lost from the flock and to be flying alone. Finally they came down to earth to rest in peace. But millions had heard their voices and were heartened in their march forward on the steppe.

Bajab sat his horse very erect, his face lifted to gaze into the infinity of the grassland, his eyes ablaze under the rays of the sun. Then, as though suddenly remembering something, he asked the regimental commander, "How is my father faring?"

"When I went there that day," Tsao replied, "there was a pot of buttered tea boiling on his round iron stove."

"Does he have enough parched rice to eat?"

"I don't think he has any too much."

"Does he still go hunting with his terriers every day?"

For a time the commander was at a loss to say anything. He knitted his brows and hesitated. How was Nasan Ulji's life to become really prosperous? He remembered the round iron stove and the lasso tied to a pole. And there was the limitless grassland. Then he thought of the impending arrival of the Mongolian Work Team. That would be the solution, he knew, and silently smiled to himself. At the commander's silence Bajab again asked him with concern, "Has my father been getting on well lately?"

The commander turned his face to the lad and said, "What did you ask just now? Oh, yes, your father will have a good life from now on."

"You're telling me the facts?" the lad pressed for confirmation.

"Yes, it's true. How many heroes have there been among us who have laid down their lives for the liberation of the people! If we weren't to realize their ideals we should surely feel beholden to them."

The regimental commander looked at him seriously and nodded his head. The lad's bearing was very much like his father's. Using Nasan Ulji's own words Commander Tsao told him, "When I was at Chia-chiayingtse your father asked me to tell you that he wanted you to work well here. Prospects for the future are bright."

The cart train continued on its way to Kaitung. It was the best season of the year on the Mongolian grassland, the weather being neither cold nor hot and the grass was deep green while the flowers were at their best. Bloom after bloom, cluster after cluster, red corfu lilies and gay little yellow buttercups carpeted whole strips of ground, all full blown.

The wind did not sting the face today; neither did it raise clouds of dust. Skylarks sang their songs while swallows from the south skimmed to and fro over the grassland.

The party would soon be at the fringes of the Mongolian steppe, for the county town of Kaitung had come into view though hazy still in the distance. Suddenly a train whistled shrilly from afar, stirring the group with animation till they bubbled over like water boiling in a pot. But they had nothing to say, only that the carts were so slow, and wouldn't the drivers double their speed?

Today was the beginning of June. It was the last day of the long trek undertaken by the group of cadres. There were many things along the way and they would always remember the unfading display of flowers of many kinds over the vast expanse of the steppe.

PAULE MARSHALL

british guiana

"Bowl him out, man!

Bowl him out!"
The week-long, unseasonable rain had only just ended but the village
boys had already planted their wicket (three parallel sticks with a flat
stone teetering on top) like a sign of conquest in the muddy road and
were intent at a cricket game, their shouts of "Bowl him out" defying
the ruin and desolation of the drenched land and their own hunger, their
bodies—so Gerald Motley thought as he saw them through the last of
the rain stippling his windshield—mere stick figures draped in dun-
colored rags. At the sound of his horn they scattered, the rags flapping
like wings, and stood on either side of the road with the mud sucking
between their bare toes and their eyes white with worry in their dark
faces as the battered Jaguar sedan bore recklessly down on their
abandoned wicket. But as it swerved past in a spume of mud and
Gerald Motley waved and shouted, "Get him on the outside next time,
boys," their shrill, deferent cry of "Morning, Mr. Motts" pierced the
morning pall and their laughter promised that the sun would soon heave
into sight above the scudding clouds.

Oddly, their familiar shouts this morning reminded him of sounds
he sometimes heard during sleep. At the beginning of sleep when he
hovered—feeling small despite his bulk, and somehow vulnerable—
between consciousness and a welling dream. As these two wrestled to
win him—consciousness calling him back for another rum at Ling's,
sleep beckoning him with a fabulous form of some dream—he would
struggle on the bed and call for his old nurse, who had died decades
ago. Now the boys' cries seemed to call him away from a dangerous
dream he was pursuing unawares, to urge him toward life again, and

as their warning was snatched by a damp gust, Gerald Motley became suddenly wary of the day.

This small caution sounding faintly beneath the irreverent laugh which summed up all that Gerald Motley felt about himself woke him fully and even sobered him, so that last night's drinking was no more now than a taste like that of his own decay in his mouth and a dull gnawing in his stomach as an old ulcer stirred vaguely into life. But the slight pain would cease, the taste would vanish once he had had his first drink for the morning.

To assure himself of this, he glanced at his reflection in the rear-view mirror and, as always, smilingly lifted his Panama hat in apology. For the reflection could have been a stranger's face, someone with whom he had collided on a busy street in Georgetown, some Englishman, perhaps, who had remained in B.G.—British Guiana—too long and whose aging face revealed the damage done by the rum, the pitiless Guianese sun and his own lost purpose. The reflection had nothing to do with the only image Gerald Motley held of himself, the only one he permitted to consciousness: this was of a young man in a photograph taken forty years ago on the eve of his return to B.G. from school in England.

He had been handsome then, with a taut athlete's body astride a pair of muscular legs, powerful arms which gauged the fullness of his young strength as they hung at his side, a fine head set at an assured angle and a gaze which reached beyond the frame of the photograph to probe the future with confidence.

He could have been white then (and he had often been taken for an Italian or Spaniard in England), for early in his long complex history a British Army officer sent out to B.G. had bequeathed him the thin features, the fair skin and hair; or black, since the slave woman the officer had used once and forgotten had passed her dark hand tightly over his paleness and claimed him with a full expressive mouth; or East Indian, for some Hindu brought to the colony along with the Chinese when the slave trade was over had added a marked passion and tension to his thin nose and touched his eyes with an abstract and mystical fire.

He was all these strains, yet no one singly, and because of this he was called in B.G. creole or colored—*high-colored*, since his family had once been modestly wealthy and very proud. But Gerald Motley had dissipated that wealth and he had even begun to betray that pride, for occasionally now when he had had enough to drink so that his vision of himself was clear and his voice so slurred he could not be understood, he would call out in a bar or at a crowded party, "The name, gentlemen? Gerald Ramsdeen Motley. My title, sirs? B.S.W.C.; Bastard

Spawned of the Worlds Commingling!" the words raveling on the sharp edge of his laughter.

This sense of being many things and yet none, this confusion, had set the mold of his life. He wanted to be, to know, everything. So that, as a student in England, he had read law at the Inns of Court for a time, begun medicine at Edinburgh, studied economics at the London School for a short period and the classics at Oxford. His stay at each school had been brilliant but brief, and at thirty-four he had left England well-educated but without a career.

Once home, he had again taken his place among the high-coloreds of Georgetown, enjoying his privileged life in the large colonial house on Dodds Road (and he still lived there, alone, the last of his line), sharing his class's indifference to the colony's troubles, moving through the round of jobs his father and uncles had secured for him before they died and, at the appropriate time, he had married the fair-complexioned daughter of a highly respected Georgetown family and had had a child.

But even then he had managed to contradict all this by frequenting the notorious sailor bars along Water Street to drink rum and shout politics with the stevedores there—he had even once, they say, attempted to lead them in a strike against Orly Shipping Ltd. And, worse, a year after his marriage, he had met Sybil Jeffries, a part-Chinese Negro girl from a village outside Georgetown and begun the long, bold affair that was to send his wife and child to America (where they passed for white and forgot him) and, inadvertently, make him a successful man.

Gerald Motley pressed the accelerator (he might have been fleeing the thought of Sybil Jeffries) and the big car seemed to pause and assess his mood and then surged forward like an animal gathering speed as it ran. The land on both sides of the narrow road stretched like a vast, empty stage waiting for the props and players to visit it with life, and as Gerald Motley entered a Hindu village, the props appeared—the sun-bleached wooden houses raised on stilts above the flooded ground, the frayed prayer flags on tall poles outside each house, the mosques angled toward Mecca and the swarms of Hindu children digging for shrimp in the mud of the drainage trenches which lined the road, while their mothers swathed in saris squatted under the gnarled, leafless forms of the saman trees.

A small rice field ended the village. It had been ruined by the unseasonable rain and the Hindu family who owned it stood in the flooded field surveying their loss, small bowed shapes beneath an indifferent sky. The rice field yielded to an interminable wall of sugar cane and, as he sped by, the black men cutting the cane paused and held their machetes at a quivering height for a moment, and he waved back. These were the forms and rituals of the land and each morning on his long, sobering drives into the country outside Georgetown Gerald Motley sought their meanings. . . .

He had reached the sea wall which guarded the land from a brown and sluggish sea when the sun which the boys' laughter had promised rose like a tarnished coin above the immense bush surrounding Georgetown. It was as if the sun had come from out of the bush, as if it had been spawned within its dark vitals—so Gerald Motley thought as he saw it rise each morning and remembered the one time he had been in the bush. It had been almost thirty years ago, just after he had been offered his present position as program director for B.G. Broadcasting and just before he had decided to accept the job. Thinking back now, he could no longer recall what Cyril Orly, who had not only owned the broadcasting station but the large sugar estates in B.G., the big shops in Georgetown and most of the colony's shipping interests, had said. It had been something like:

"I hear you're bright, Motley, and something of an organizer down on Water Street at nights. If you could perhaps transfer those talents to our camp, you might prove just the sort of chap we need to get the new broadcasting station under way. We'd send you to England for a few courses with the B.B.C. Of course, I don't have to tell you what this would mean. You'd be the first colored man in the West Indies to hold this high a position in broadcasting. . . ."

But he remembered clearly Cyril Orly's face, although he had been dead many years now and his son, Frank, ruled. Veins had fingered the white parchment skin. The eyes had still been shrewd beneath their thick rheum. Gerald Motley remembered the paneled walls and heavy maroon drapes in the office, the portrait of George V amid the shadows, which somehow denied that this was B.G. and that there was a torpid sun outside.

Orly had given him a week in which to decide and it was then that he had taken the trip into the bush. It was to have been an overland trek to Kaieteur Falls deep in the interior and he had taken two friends, a guide and Sybil—since his wife had already left for America. Early in the trip, when they had stopped because of the heat, he had wandered alone into the bush surrounding their camp, curious to know what it would be like away from the marked trail they were following. Slowly, as he had moved over the thick underbrush, parting the tangled branches and looped vines which hung like a portiere before him, he had sensed it. The bush had reared around him like the landscape of a dream, grand and gloomy, profuse and impenetrable, hoarding, he knew, gold and fecund soils and yet, somehow, still ravenous. So that the branches clawed at him, the vines wound his arms, roots sprang like traps around his feet and the silence—dark from the vast shadows, brooding upon the centuries lost—wolfed down the sound of his breathing. He had felt a terror that had been the most exquisite of pleasures and at his awed cry the bush had closed around him, becoming another dimension of himself, the self he had long sought. For the first time this self was within his grasp. If he pursued this dark way long enough he would find it hanging like a jeweled pendant on the trees—and it would either shape his life by giving him the right answer to Orly's offer or destroy him.

But then he had heard Sybil—and she might have been the sane and cautious part of himself coming to save him; indeed, he had come to believe this over the years—a twig snapping under her step and her puzzled voice in the stillness. "Gerald . . . ?"

He had turned to drive her away, but her expression had stopped his angry gesture and her eyes, which she had inherited from her part-Chinese father—swift, prescient, set at a slant in her dark face—gazed past him to the bush ahead. She clearly saw what he had only glimpsed and understood better than he ever would its danger, and with a protective cry she had rushed forward and placed herself between him and what could have been a vision of himself.

"Come, man," she had said, her hand insistent on his sleeve. "Let's get out this damn jungle." And he had followed her back to the camp, hating her for the first time.

That night Sybil had complained of feeling ill and had asked to be taken home. The next morning they had started back to Georgetown. The following week Gerald Motley had accepted the job with B.G. Broadcasting, assuring his success. Shortly after he had begun stopping at the King George Bar across from his office for a drink each morning and spending his evenings at Ling's on Water Street.

He was in Kitty Village now, an old suburb that was really part of Georgetown. The houses huddled on their stilts above the eddying mud would be filled, he knew, with the smell of mold and mildew, damp bodies and water-soaked wood and smoke from the kitchen fires. But this no longer mattered, for the rain had given way to the advancing sun and a small girl, her skirt tucked between her legs, was laughing as she fished a drowned hen from the flood, and a black woman sang as she washed clothes under a house. Everywhere the shutters were propped open to welcome the first dry wind.

Gerald Motley stopped the car in front of a house where a tall coconut palm still dripped in the front yard, and straightening the trousers of his expensive cream-colored linen suit, tightening the belt over the thick flesh at his waist, he settled down to wait. He watched the child pursuing the drowned hen, sharing her tension and excitement.

He had finished two cigarettes, the child had gone off triumphantly with her hen, when a young man of about twenty-five appeared on the steep flight of sagging steps which led from the house to the yard. At first glance he looked no different from a minor clerk in the government service. A part cleaved his rough hair down the middle like a narrow track through a jungle. He wore a white shirt and a tie, but no jacket, and a watch, a harsh, cheap gold against his black wrist. He was ready, it seemed, for a day sifting papers in an airless office.

But his manner denied this. He stood, a slender, dark hand at his waist, scowling down at the flooded yard and ignoring Gerald Motley, who waited below. Frowning, he finally descended, tall and slim-hipped, his shoulders drawn in slightly as if he disliked being touched. There was a subtle contempt in each small gesture and a disdain in his lidded eyes which, since he was so young, only betrayed his helplessness. He leaped across the drainage trench to the car and, as he almost slipped in the mud, his hand reached up in a gesture of anger and disgust which would have hauled down the sky if possible.

Five years ago the young man, Sidney Parrish, had won a scholarship to study in England; then his father, a stevedore, had been killed in an accident on the docks and, as the oldest of many children, he had had to remain in B.G. and work. He had come to B.G. Broadcasting for a job and, as he got into the car now, Gerald Motley remembered him standing at his desk that first day, his anxiety showing beneath a thin armor of arrogance. Gerald Motley had hired him because he had glimpsed something about himself in the boy's cold stare, and he had kept him on since, in a way he could not know, the boy became the part of him which refused to spare him the truth, which remained always critical and unforgiving.

Gerald Motley had been grateful for this, and to prove it he had promoted Sidney frequently. With each promotion Sidney had become more distant and contemptuous, and then openly insolent. And Gerald Motley encouraged this disrespect. Two years ago, he had started buying Sidney's drinks and lunch, and more recently he had started driving him to work and taking him along to Ling's in the evening and to the elite Georgetown parties. He had even taken him once to a reception at Government House. Sidney, for his part, repaid this generosity, fed it, with his scorn and abuse.

"Oh, Christ, man, see if you can't drive without trying to wreck the car for a change. My head feels like the drum that chap at Ling's was beating last night," Sidney said, and rested his head against the back of the seat.

"Be glad it's your head, boy, and not your gut. That's when you can start worrying." And then as Sidney closed his eyes, he added quickly, "How was the little craft you had in tow when you left Ling's last night?"

"Don't ask," Sidney said with weariness and disgust. "The craft drank more Russian Bear rum than you and me put together and stayed sober the whole bloody night. So that every time my hand would reach for the goods she was pushing it away. I finally had to get out the pacifier." With his eyes closed he reached in his pocket and held up a small white pill, which he dropped deftly into his other hand as if into a glass. "This in a Black Velvet finally did it."

Gerald Motley glanced at the pill and then at the slim, perfect line of Sidney's throat, his taut flesh, and thought of his own flesh, which was heavily creased and hanging in great folds over his frame. He sat up and held in his stomach. "How was she?" he asked.

"The bitch had skin like cold fat."

Their laughter floated across the traffic and was lost, and Gerald Motley had to press the brake as one of his long, curved fenders nudged a donkey cart loaded with sugar cane. The driver of the cart had been asleep at his whip, but he awoke now and turned angrily; then as he saw the Jaguar and glimpsed Gerald Motley's pale face through the windshield, he hastily lifted his cap, gave the pained smile of deference and turning back began flailing his donkey.

Gerald Motley swept by with an apologetic wave and, pressing a way through the slow-moving pack of lorries, cars and bicycles, reached downtown Georgetown, the part of the city which had been rebuilt after the great fire of 1945. The unsightly drainage trenches had been hidden under an island of grass and flamboyant trees in the middle of the wide main road, the government buildings, large shops and offices set well back from the sidewalks and painted a flat, unnatural white, so that at noon, when the sun was a single hot eye within the empty face of the sky, Georgetown became a city of chalk, without shadows.

Sidney was asleep by the time they reached the offices of B.G. Broadcasting, and after he parked Gerald Motley also rested his head against the back of the seat. He thought he saw the dampness and heat rising in a thick steam from the concrete road. He felt the perspiration secreting itself in the cracks of his dried skin, under the sweatband of his Panama hat. His linen suit would be wilted within the hour.

He looked up at the air conditioner in his office window and muttered with an amused and despairing smile, "A blasted air conditioner which hasn't worked in over four months, because the only person in the whole of the colony who can fix it is sick in hospital. That's what we call progress in B.G." He turned to Sidney. "Up and out, boy, and, oh, Christ, don't forget the Tide commercial again today."

He left Sidney in the car and, pitching slightly as if he had already had the drink, crossed the road to the King George Hotel. The bar was to the back and it had been built of woven palm fronds lashed to a bamboo frame, so that it always held, as if it were a reservoir, the cool, dry solemnity of nights in the dry season. Gerald Motley stood in the middle of the room, breathing the coolness and smiling at the sunlight which had edged in through the palm leaves and lay in golden scales across the floor. Standing there, swaying slightly, he somehow resembled the houses he had passed on his morning drive into the country. Like them his legs seemed too weak to sustain his weight. At any moment they might buckle and he would come crashing down.

He clapped and the old Hindu waiter emerged from behind the bar, as swift and silent as the shadows there. "Is you, Mr. Motts," he said, and began pouring the drink.

He brought it to Gerald Motley between trembling hands and stood beside him while he drank, his white hair flaring around an ancient face that had been sucked in around the bones so that he resembled a fakir. His clotted eyes gazed up at Gerald Motley with a strange sorrow and reproof.

"It's true, sir, everything is changing up," he said, taking the empty glass, and he might have been resuming a conversation they had had yesterday or a year ago. "It's raining now when it ought be dry. And come time for the rain we'll have drought instead. People don't know when to plant little rice any more."

"Ah, Singh . . ." Gerald Motley said softly, remembering the Hindu family standing in their ruined rice field that morning.

"The paper says it's the bombs the Yankees are dropping in the sea for practice that's got things so turned around. Well, I guess we ought to be glad they ain't practicing on us yet. . . ." His laugh, a thin, toneless wheeze, blew the flecked sunlight across the floor.

"Ah, Singh." Gerald Motley touched his shoulder and was glad to find it so warm, so charged with life under the fragile bone. Singh's agelessness was the small part of Gerald Motley which would remain ageless.

"Don't worry, old man," he said, and patted the shoulder. "You don't know it, but you're living in the safest place on God's earth. The Yankees won't be dropping any bombs here because they've never even heard of a place called B.G. In fact, nobody is quite certain of our existence except a few chaps in the Colonial Office and they don't count. . . ."

Gerald Motley remained a little longer, listening to Singh's fears and nodding while the rum eased the gnawing in his stomach and seeped his blood; then he left, taking the coolness of the bar with him into the surging heat outside. He was halfway across the road when he paused suddenly under a flamboyant tree on the island of grass over the trench and, staring across at his office window and the useless air conditioner there, he was reluctant to begin the morning's work. He would have liked to hold back the day, to gain time. He wanted suddenly to return to the bar, which excluded time, and to Singh, who had escaped it. He would be safe there, he sensed. From what? He did not know. Whatever it was had been contained in the boys' shouted warning that morning.

He had turned back toward the bar when a large white Open Kapitan stopped him at the curb and the driver, a dark, heavy woman with graying hair and wearing a rumpled doctor's coat, called out to him, "Get out the road, Motts, and know you're obstructing traffic."

"Ah, Murie-mine," he said, laughing, and leaning down kissed the puffy arm propped on the window. "Let the patient die and come have a grog with me."

"I can't stop."

"Only one, Murie, it'll make your hand steadier on the knife."

"Yes, just as yours is steady," she said, and glanced piercingly at his hands as though she could see the twitching of each fine nerve within the thick flesh.

"One."

"You hear, I can't stop!" she cried, laughing. "I've got to pick up the children from school, get out to the airport and be back at the hospital all in an hour's time."

"Who're you meeting out at the airport?"

"Sybil," she said, and the pause was imperceptible before she added, "She's coming down on holiday."

Beneath the surprised laugh he quickly summoned, the uneasiness of a moment ago returned, stronger this time, and the wariness crouched behind his eyes.

"Sybil, eh?" he said. "So the old girl finally decided to give us a shout."

"Almost twenty years," Murie said.

It seemed longer, for he had forgotten that this stout, successful matron was Sybil's sister and that they had once even looked alike, with the same fine bones set at a slight tilt under the dark skin and eyes like two swiftly moving crescents of light. They had both been slender and quick, although Sybil had also been capable of a lovely stillness that had been like a dancer pausing after a leap. He had met them just after their return from the university in England (like most of the Chinese in B.G., their father had owned a large shop and had died indulging them). Gerald Motley had been almost forty then, Murie thirty and Sybil somewhat younger. As black women who had been to university they were rarities in B.G. and they had used this. Murie, shrewd and tireless, had built a successful practice and then married into a leading high-colored family which had lost its money and whom she now ruled, ruthlessly, with her money, while Sybil had been the first colored reporter for the *Georgetown Herald*, but unlike Murie she had never settled in, but had remained somehow remote, restless and lonely.

Thinking of her now as he chatted about her with Murie and tried to shape her face out of the shifting memories, Gerald Motley could only really remember the quality of her loneliness. It had been as much a part of her smell as the cologne she had used; it had often lent a fierce and excessive note to her laughter, and it had always brought on her rages during the long rain. It had been his loneliness, and the loneliness and despair of the land. Even now, on nights when he had not had enough to drink and Sidney had gone off early with a woman, he would feel it—like an alien wind hiding in the acacia trees around his house. . . .

"How do you think the old girl looks after all this time?" he asked, and smiled as Murie scrutinized him from behind her sunglasses.

"Old," she said flatly. "Just as you're old, and me, for that matter."

"I mean . . ."

"I know what you mean," she said with a sudden roughness and impatience. "She's probably the same damn Sybil. Look how I didn't get the cable that she was coming until last night. Well, thank God, the rain stopped. You know how she hated this place when it rained. Want to ride out to the airport with me?"

He felt a tremor jar his heart and hid his reluctance behind a laugh. "There's nothing I'd like more than to be part of the welcoming committee, dear Murie, but I haven't even been to the office yet."

"But I'm sure you've been over to your other office already." She waved toward the hotel bar. "All right," she said, and started the motor. "Just make sure you come over to the house tonight. I'm having in what's left of the old crowd to give her a real Guianese welcome. She'll probably curse me good and proper for doing it. As for you, I suppose you'll be bringing along your bodyguard."

"Ah, Murie, I'm a man beset by enemies and must be heavily guarded at all times. . . ."

"Beset by your own damn self, you mean. Well, just tell Sidney Parrish not to come in my house looking as if he smells something bad." The car lurched into motion and she was gone.

She would be exhausted by the time she reached the airport and irritable, he thought, and felt his own sudden exhaustion and irritability at the thought of Sybil's coming as he climbed the stairs to his office. The main office through which he had to pass held the dampness of every rainy season, the oppressive heat and dust of a drought and the mingled odors of the clerks who worked there. A toneless fugue of "Morning, Mr. Motley" trailed him to his private office and the guarded glances above the rattling typewriters told him that they knew he had stopped for the drink and that they both envied him and disapproved.

He opened his office door and his secretary looked up from her idle typewriter, her face ghostly with the whitish powder she used to make her dark skin lighter, her eyes moist with the thought of the flowered yard goods she had seen in Woolworth's window on her way to work.

"Morning, Mr. Motley. Mr. Orly called."

"What in the bloody hell did he want?" He carefully hung up his jacket and absently shuffled the papers on his desk, feeling the grit of weeks on his fingers.

"He wanted to know if you were making arrangements to tape the governor's speech on the Queen's birthday."

"And did you tell Frank Orly, O.B.E., S.O.B., that we don't need him to remind us of something we've been doing for the past twenty years?"

"No, I didn't tell him all that, sir, I just said we had arranged for it."

"Well, if he calls again, Miss Davis, you tell him what I just said."

"Yes, sir, Mr. Motley."

"Is there anything else of equal urgency?"

"No, sir, Mr. Motley."

"Then come, girl, let's hear who died last night."

"Oh, dear, I almost forgot the time," she cried, excitement edging her voice as she turned on the radio.

A hymn emerged from the static: "Abide with me/Fast falls the eventide . . ."

" 'The darkness deepens,' " Gerald Motley sang, and Miss Davis clasped her hands over her chest pressing back her shock and laughter. The music receded and Sidney's voice loomed—grave, sonorous, deeper than it was ordinarily, coming, it seemed, not from the speaker but through the slats of the closed shutters and creating shadows which stood like mourners around the room.

He would be slouched in front of the microphone in the studio up-stairs, refusing to touch the sheet of paper which listed the names of the dead, Gerald Motley knew. He listened to the subtle anger beneath Sidney's soothing voice and watched Miss Davis, who sat with her head bowed as though she was at devotions. He heard her small gasp each time Sidney paused dramatically before giving the next name and then her breath rushing out as he spoke it—and Gerald Motley knew that like himself Miss Davis was only certain of being alive in the midst of the dead.

". . . We regret to announce the demise of Millicent Dembo of Sala-mander Road, Kitty Village, the beloved mother of fifteen and the revered grandmother of sixty and great-grandmother of well over a hundred, who passed peacefully in her sleep last night at the age of ninety-five. . . ."

It was the last name. The music rose, then faded, and Sidney began the commercial for Tide in his normal voice. Miss Davis stirred; her shoulders flickered with annoyance. "Nobody interesting today, sir," she said, half turning to Gerald Motley. "But at least Mr. Parrish didn't forget Tide again."

Gerald Motley started to nod, but instead his head gave a slight shudder and dropped, and the cigarette he was smoking fell from his hand. It was not Miss Davis or her remark which jarred him. He always forgave her because he considered her no more than the part of himself which had remained callous and mean-spirited and filled with an abstract resentment. Rather, it was the thought of the old woman who had died last night. He might have passed her many times on the road through Kitty Village. Suddenly he was sure that he had. He remembered her— an old woman with shriveled flesh and eyes thick with cataracts leading a gaunt cow to pasture.

He rose, pushing aside the papers. "Telephone across to the hotel if anything comes up."

"Yes, sir, Mr. Motley."

This time he sat on the patio which opened off the King George bar, his sodden bulk in the wilted linen suit sprawled in a low chair. He listened to a shrike in the palm trees which walled the patio and waited for Singh to bring him the drink, but before Singh could come he had nodded off, a dream stumbling across the troubled surface of his mind. In the dream the shrike's piercing-sweet cry became a siren's call which urged him through the deserted streets of Georgetown at night, through a swirling yellow fog of heat to the empty house where his wife had once lived. He ran through rooms which no longer had walls between them, searching for her, until he came to the servants' quarters in the back yard. There he found, not his wife, but Sybil, her face covered with a whitish powder and a flamboyant blossom growing from her mouth. Beneath the shroud she wore, her body above the waist was that of an old woman with shriveled flesh and dry flapping dugs and, below, the lithe, pleasing form of a young boy.

"Did you hear your blasted Tide?"

He was instantly awake, the dream forgotten. "Yes, my boy, and you gave your usual moving performance. Have a grog." He clapped for Singh. "There was only one thing wrong with today's announcements according to my secretary. There wasn't anybody really interesting, she said."

"What about the old woman in Kitty Village ninety-five years old?

Think of the funeral, man! The weeping and wailing of the fifteen head of children and the hundred-and-sixty-odd grands and great-grands. Think of the women at the funeral dressed up in white like the Foolish Virgins. And the cars lined up from here to Kitty Village. The rum flowing . . ." Sidney broke off.

"Yes, that one impressed me too, but I think Miss Davis wants big names."

"That ghoul. She sucks blood, you know. You can tell from her eyes."

Gerald Motley's laugh drowned out the shrike and as he fell back in the chair, his body rigid in the paroxysm of the laugh, Sidney hunched forward, unsmiling, and drank the rum which Singh had placed before him and then very carefully set the glass into the wet ring it had formed on the table.

"Blast her in hell," he said quietly and then, with his eyes closed, "and blast me for sitting there each and every day taking the name of the dead in vain to the tune of 'Tide's In.' You think they'd have this rotten business on a station in New York or London?"

"They've got worse there," Gerald Motley said, suddenly sobering. "But at least the chaps there are making big money and can afford a decent grog to wash the bad taste out their mouths and a time with a good-looking craft to help them forget. But what is our reward in this God-forsaken patch of Her Majesty's Empire—yours for singing the praises of the dear departed, mine for kissing Frank Orly's pink ass all these years and his father's before him? Nothing but Russian Bear rum giving us cirrhosis of the liver, a few syphilitic sailor hags down on Water Street giving us paresis to the brain and an equatorial heat." He downed the last of his drink. "But you know what the real trouble is with B.G.?"

"No, what is it today?"

"Ah, Sidney," Gerald Motley chuckled, pleased. "There's no pity in you, boy, and no respect, and that's a good thing. It makes me feel young, since only the old are to be pitied and respected."

"What is it?"

"The bush."

The word uttered with a lingering sibilance seemed to bring that immense and brooding tract suddenly close, so that both Sidney and Gerald Motley glanced at the wall of palm trees, Sidney frowning and strangely irritated, Gerald Motley smiling ruefully and thinking that with Sybil's return that day in the bush had also returned. He sat back in his chair now and said quietly, "That's the real B.G. and until something is done with it nothing else about the colony will matter."

"Oh, Christ, what's this about the bush all of a sudden?" Sidney said, and snatched up Gerald Motley's cigarettes. "Last night at Ling's you were getting on about the same thing."

"Was I?" he said, and strained in his mind to separate last night from all the other nights. "I don't remember."

"You were too damn salt to remember."

Gerald Motley's laugh reached into the bar, to Singh, who peered at him through the dimness with the same sad reproof.

"The bush!" Sidney stabbed out with the cigarette. "What bush? Tell me, you ever went near the blasted place?"

"Yes."

"And?"

But Gerald Motley had answered too quickly and could find no way of telling him what had happened, too eagerly, for Sidney was suddenly suspicious. They waited in a silence loud with the battling of two flies around the mouth of Gerald Motley's glass, until finally he said lightly, "It was years ago on a trip to Kaieteur. We didn't get very far though before we had to turn back because the rains started up. . . ."

He wished that the cigarette Sidney held was a whip Sidney would use to scourge him for the lie. He added casually, "Before I forget, we're going to a spree at Murie Collins' tonight. She's giving it for her sister, who's flying in from Jamaica today. The sister, by the way, was one of the people on this trip to Kaieteur years ago. You might have heard her name. Sybil Jeffries. She used to be with me at the station when I first started. She's assistant to the program director for Radio Jamaica now and doing damn well, I hear."

"I know all about her," Sidney said. "I also know that you went around with her for years but you wouldn't marry her, even when you could, because she was black and her father was only a shopkeeper—and that's why she finally left B.G."

The thrust was well aimed and deep and the pain perfect. Gerald Motley smiled gratefully and said, "I see you've been talking to my enemies. Yes, that was partly it. You can put up your knife. Regrettably, Sidney, I come from a bastard breed that once considered itself highborn. But there were other, more important reasons . . ." and could not confess that whenever he had slept with Sybil she had not only brought her body and laid that beside him, but her loneliness also, stretching it out like a pale ghost between them, and her intense, almost mystical suffering, asking him silently to assuage it. But she had asked too much. He would have had to offer up himself to do so, and he refused. Nor could he admit to Sidney the most important reason: that he had never forgiven her for having denied him that vision of himself that day in the bush.

"Come, let's have some lunch." He rose heavily.

Upstairs in the hotel dining room the closed shutters did not succeed in barring the noon heat, and the fans droning louder than the flies, the potted ferns and white walls and tablecloths failed in the illusion of coolness. As soon as the waiter finished serving them, Sidney said, "Was I invited tonight or am I just being taken along for effect?"

Gerald Motley put down his fork and waited, a smile forming.

"I just want to know whether I should thank you or Murie Collins," Sidney said, and pushed aside his untouched plate.

Gerald Motley glanced at the food he would pay for, at the dark hand poised on the white tablecloth as if to strike him and his smile broadened. He drank half of his gin and tonic before he said, "Don't thank anybody. Just come. The grogs'll be flowing and that's all that matters. There might even be one or two crafts your age about the place ..."

Sidney nodded. "You've told me. Thanks. I didn't think it was Murie Collins, who doesn't speak to me unless I'm with you. And why should she speak; after all, I'm not in the league of the great." His sarcastic gesture took in Gerald Motley and the others in the dining room. Aside from a few English planters and businessmen and Portuguese merchants perspiring over the heaped rice and overfried steak on their plates, and an occasional wealthy East Indian and Chinese, the majority were the colored and black professionals, politicians and highly placed civil servants of Georgetown, most of them as dark as Sidney; there were now only a few left as fair as Gerald Motley.

"After all," Sidney was saying quietly, "I don't live in a big house on Dodds Road, nor do I drive a long expensive car, nor do I wear white linen suits. And I don't look white. My father and his father were like so." He raised a dark, angry hand. "And he worked on the docks, man, and died there in some bloody, senseless accident. And my house?" He gave a sudden wild laugh which was like a lament. "But then you've seen my house. As for me, I'm just a two-shilling-a-week announcer and that only by the grace of my benefactor and for his amusement."

He sat back, distraught beneath his calm, cruel and somehow old, staring coldly at Gerald Motley and through him at the others in the room. Then, although his eyes didn't change, he laughed again, a loud, boyish burst this time, which flung back his head to reveal the perfect line of his throat.

"Oh, Motts, I'm going to the damn spree," he said. "I just wanted to make my position clear."

Gerald Motley closed his eyes for a moment to shut out Sidney's pain. The perspiration was like guilty tears on his face and he bowed his head. Finally, when he was certain that his hand was steady again, he picked up his fork and when he was sure of his voice, he gave the old laugh and said, "Well, then, let's eat, boy. I'm hungry from your talking."

After lunch Sidney returned to the station and Gerald Motley remained at the hotel, in hiding from the sun which had usurped the sky by now. Each noon it was as if Singh's fear was made flesh: the Yankees had dropped the bomb. For the heat then, searing white on the chalk-white buildings, must have been similar to that which comes at the moment of a massive explosion. The glare offered even the blind of Georgetown a vision of the apocalypse and the weighted stillness mushrooming over the city was the same which must follow a bombing, final and filled with the broken voices of the dying. Georgetown at noon was another Hiroshima at the moment of the bombing, and the minor clerks in the government offices on Main Street wound their cheap watches to spur the afternoon; over at B.G. Local Broadcasting, Miss Davis rested her powdered forehead on the cool hump of her typewriter; upstairs in the studio Sidney read the praises of hot Ovaltine into the microphone and across the street Gerald Motley accompanied a few of the older colored professional men like himself down to the bar.

As always, their eyes offered him the image of his public self. For them, and for most of B.G., he was as Sidney had described him at lunch, a Motley—with his Panama hat and linen suits, his car—one of the few elite left. It did not matter that he had contradicted this image over the years by his long affair with Sybil Jeffries and the others after her, by his nightly visits to Ling's on Water Street and now, in his old age, by his attachment to Sidney. They forgave him all this and jokingly called Sidney his Aide-de-Camp. They insisted that he, Gerald Motley, was still one of them, indeed, better than them, and confirmed this whenever he joined them for an afternoon drink by a subtle show of deference. (Now one of them hurried over to Singh for a drink for him.) To them he was a success. It did not matter that he had done nothing outstanding at B.G. Broadcasting. What was important was that he had been the first colored man in the West Indies to hold such a position.

Seeing that image in their eyes, Gerald Motley closed his own eyes for a moment and wished that Sidney was hovering somewhere on the edge of the group so that he might look up and see the truth in his cold stare. Then, with an ironic laugh, Gerald Motley ordered drinks for them all, and to amuse them he talked—his voice drowning out the thought of the fleeting day and of Sybil, who awaited him at its end.

". . . an army, gentlemen," he shouted at one point. "That's another thing this colony needs. And some guns. And once we get the army and the guns, we must do one of three things. Either invade Surinam to the east, declare war on Venezuela to the west or provoke Brazil to the south. That's the only way the world will ever know there's a place called B.G. Or better yet, call on the Russians. And then watch, gentlemen. Overnight we will have arrived! Uncle Sam will toss a few million our way and the Queen herself will be hotfooting it down here with some pounds. . . ."

Later, when the sunlight scattered along the floor had softened, he was still talking, but now the linen suit sagging from his shoulders defined his sadness and his laugh was a ragged snatch between the words. "There's no hope, gentlemen," he was saying, but he was aware only of the cool, moist surface of the glass Singh slipped into his hand and the rum stinging his throat as he swallowed. "The only solution to what ails B.G. is a bomb at the heart of Georgetown. And *mirabile visu*, our problems solved! An end to the P.P.P., the unholy triumvirate of poverty, politics (he bowed to a member of the House of Assembly) and prejudice which rules B.G. still. An end to a sun which burns our brains to an ash and a rain that drives us all to drink and delirium tremens. One bomb, gentlemen, and oblivion!" He finished his drink and clapped for Singh.

"And guess who'll come crawling out of the ashes," someone called.

"Motts, holding tight to a bottle of Russian Bear."

"You're damn right," Gerald Motley cried, and his laugh joined theirs. "And do you know why I'll survive, gentlemen? Because I'm the only one out of the lot of you who really loves the old place. I am B.G." And his extravagant gesture did seem to embrace the vast sweep of the land. "We're one and the same." He paused, thinking of his morning drives into the country and knowing suddenly that what he had sought all along had been the reflection of himself in each feature of the land. And he had been there, although he had not been able to see himself. The listing Hindu houses this morning had in some way reflected him, as had the family standing in their ruined field and the black men wielding their machetes among the gliding canes, the boys at their cricket.

"We're the same," he said, with an awed laugh.

A silence touched the room and he laughed again, a loud, echoing sound that scarcely resembled laughter and, bending over the bar, he stretched out his arms in the prostrate pose of a penitent before Singh, who waited on the other side with a drink for him. While he rested there and Singh held the rum over his head as if it were a holy oil he would use to anoint him in some final rite, the first breeze of the approaching evening came off the patio and sifted through the plaited walls. Gerald Motley felt its beneficence on his moist flesh and knew that there would be thin shadows slanting along the streets of Georgetown now and that the sun was groping, blinded by its own brilliance, down the western passage of the sky.

"Lemme leave you rum-heads," he said, straightening up. "Singh," he tossed some bills on the bar, "for the gentlemen's drinks."

"Old Motts," one of the men said affectionately. "We'll see you over to Murie's tonight."

"Hey, that's right," someone else said. "Motts's old craft is back. No wonder he's getting a little excited."

"Man, you best get in shape."

"Prime the instrument, Motts."

"All you do, go easy, because many an old man has breathed his last trying to run that race."

"Remember our reputation, Motts: studs second to none, and don't disgrace us."

He was borne across the room on their banter. He turned at the doorway and gazed at them with an affection ringed about with contempt. All of them except Singh were caught within this ring, including himself, for he was no different from them after all. He raised his hand, halting their amiable laughter, and said almost solemnly, "Hail, gentlemen, and farewell."

The thought of Sybil which had been muted inside the bar awaited him outside and followed him across the road and up the stairs to his office. She had been in the colony some hours now and he felt the pull of her presence as if he were joined to her by an invisible rope which she controlled. Each time she breathed or moved, he felt the slight pressure on the rope. Some fragment of the dream he had had on the patio nudged his mind—Sybil with withered breasts—and as he hurried through the empty main office (it was past four o'clock and the clerks and his secretary were gone, leaving only the studio upstairs open), he tried to drive out that image with the memory of her as a young woman. But even this was distasteful and he had to admit what he had long denied: that he had always been secretly offended by the lack of purity in her woman's form, the slight fullness to her breasts and hips. How would it be now that she was middle-aged? He closed the door to his office and spat into his handkerchief.

Sidney opened the door an hour later and paused, startled, at the sight of Gerald Motley at work on the papers piled on his desk. "How is it you're not cat napping as usual?" he asked, and did not wait for an answer. "Ready for a grog?" He held up the bottle of rum.

"No. Telephone across to the hotel for some tea."

"Tea?"

"Tea," he said sharply, and continued working.

Sidney stared closely at him for a moment and then left. He returned after some time with a waiter from the hotel who brought in the tea on a tray. But the teapot remained under its cozy and the cup stayed empty as Gerald Motley worked on. Sidney sat on the window ledge, drinking from the bottle of rum, which was a blaze of amber in the abrupt tropic sunset, and staring gloomily down at the deserted streets.

As dusk invaded the room, he turned toward Gerald Motley with an inexplicably sad and angry motion. It was as if the silence between them and Gerald Motley's absorption in the work on his desk, as well as the night burgeoning above the distant bush, had brought on his despair. He stared at Gerald Motley with a profound and abstract bitterness. His eyes became mere slivers in his dark face, his look that of a man watching another die with utter dispassion.

"Well, let's hear it," Gerald Motley said, and put aside the last of the finished papers before he looked up.

"Hear what?"

"The announcement you're busy composing. Mine, isn't it?"

"You and your damn secretary have the same ghoulish turn of mind." Sidney turned back to the window.

"Let's hear it. 'We regret . . .' "

"I'm through work for the day." Sidney rose quickly. "You'll have to wait until tomorrow."

Chuckling, Gerald Motley followed him from the office down into the street, past the shuttered buildings and shops into the wind which bore the night through the city. They were headed, as on every evening at this time, to Water Street and Ling's.

Ling's was one of the sailor clubs which cluttered Water Street. Like all the others it was always filled with the idle of Georgetown, the cheap thieves and cozeners, the petty gamblers and toughts of the race track, the panderers for the sailors who might wander in, the brawlers and sots—the veins of their eyes gorged with blood and radiating in amber spokes from the dark centers. Curses flouted the hushed and sacred night outside, and the laughter, thick as the heat, was a hosanna to the pin-up goddesses from America hanging on the walls.

Ling herself presided from a high stool near the cashbox behind the bar, her one good eye resting maternally on her customers, her head cocked toward the breeze of a sluggish fan and nodding to the noise—an old bawd she was, with a gelid glass eye and a stomach swollen with tumors, whom Gerald Motley loved, for in a way which he could never know, she had become the part of him which had gazed upon the darkness within and found it pleasing. . . .

"But, Ling, my love, when are you going to drop that child, eh?" he leaned across the bar and tapped the huge belly.

"Soon, God willing, Mr. Motts. It's an immaculate conception, you know. A damn Chinee Jesus." The stomach shuddered with her laugh and pouring them a drink she began the familiar recital of her ailments: "But it's not the stomach so much any more; the blasted arthritis is the thing that's got me going nowadays. . . ."

Usually they would stay only long enough for this single drink with Ling and then leave, returning later on in the night for the last rum with her before going home. But tonight Gerald Motley left Sidney behind at the bar with Ling and wandered around the crowded room, greeting the familiar faces there and pouring drinks from a bottle of expensive whisky he had bought from Ling.

As he penetrated into the violent center of the crowd and felt the intimate press of their bodies against his and the hands clawing at his arm for the bottle, as the warm yeast smell of their sweated, unwashed bodies overwhelmed him and the noise roared like a rough sea in his ears, he felt rid of himself: of his old man's body, that sodden, slow-moving hulk he hid in expensive linen suits, of his face which had come to remind him of a reflection seen in a trick mirror where all the features appear to thicken and dissolve, of his mind which had grown barren waiting for the seed.

Freed of this single self, he became those around him. He was the thief whose hand glanced his pocket as he passed, the panderer whispering as he did every night, "A nice coolie girl just up from the country, Mr. Motts, a guaranteed virgin," the tout muttering a hunch on the next day's race as Gerald Motley poured him the drink, the beggar counting the day's spoils in a corner. . . .

"Are you still going to the spree or what?" Sidney's voice was a cold prod which roused him from where he sat, half-asleep, among a group of gamblers.

"And have you ever known me to miss a spree?" he said, groping up, his hand reaching for Sidney, who quickly moved away. A laugh rattled like phlegm in Gerald Motley's throat. "What did I say about pity," he said, wagging a finger. "Come, let's be off and change. After all, we can't go to Murie Collins' smelling under the arms. I'll drive to my place; then you take the car and go home and dress, and come back for me."

On the way out he leaned over to kiss Ling and as he did, her glass eye seemed curiously alive and filled with a yellow light which probed him deep; slowly the light changed, becoming somber and gray with concern. In that fragile moment, while the light altered, a chill struck Gerald Motley's muscles so that he could not move; then, as quickly, he laughed and kissed her again.

"Ling, my love, we'll be back for our nightcap."

"God willing, Mr. Motts," she said, and the glass eye went blank.

With Sidney strangely tense and silent beside him, Gerald Motley walked back to B.G. Broadcasting for the car and, once settled behind the steering wheel, he sped through Georgetown, chasing the night, which seemed to be racing now toward midnight, eluding him, just as the day which he had hoped to hold back had eluded him.

When they reached his house on Dodds Road, Sidney took over the wheel as Gerald Motley got out of the car and drove off without breaking his silence.

The Motley house reared like a high, white, stilted monument in the darkness, its closed shutters hiding room where the last echoes had long been stilled. As usual, the servant had left a light within and Gerald Motley followed its faint glow down the long stale passages, through the close cavernous rooms of silent clocks and faded anti-macassars, calling her.

"Medford!" He pulled off his limp jacket for her to take. "Medford."

She usually appeared almost immediately, a thin, black, severe form, as ageless as Singh was ageless, her head wound in a silk kerchief printed with the Statue of Liberty which her daughter had sent her from America. But tonight he had to call several times before he heard her slurred tread and, when she emerged around the corner of a dim passage, he saw that she was dressed in white with a white straw hat instead of the kerchief. As she hobbled toward him—her face, arms and ancient legs lost in the shadows—she might have been an apparition.

"Where're you going this time of night?" He impatiently flung her the jacket and his hat.

"I'm not going, I'm just now coming, but I was gone for the whole day," she said with measured defiance. "My friend from years back died and I was to the funeral . . ." He abruptly walked away and she followed him, still talking. "Did you hear Mr. Parrish give the announcement this morning about a Millicent Dembo in Kitty Village? That was my friend. She had a hard life but a sweet funeral. You never saw so many cars, Mr. Motts. And Millie made such a pretty dead. I helped dress her the morning. But you know something, Mr. Motts"—she was standing in the doorway of his bedroom now, the linen jacket trailing down from her lax hand—"her limbs was still loose when I was washing her and she was still warm, even though she had passed early the night before. And they say when you see a dead come like that, the limbs soft and limber so and warm, you can always look for somebody else to dead soon."

"Oh, Christ, woman!" He turned irritably and then paused. Behind her innocent and murky gaze he thought he suddenly glimpsed himself as a boy. It was as if Medford had kept, and would always keep, the memory of his boyhood safe—and, thus, somehow alive. Humble suddenly, again the boy begging her forgiveness for some misdeed, he said gently, "Ah, Medford, mark my words, you're going to turn into a *bacoo* yet. Come, get out some clean clothes for me and stop with your foolishness. Come!" He clapped, startling her. "I was due at a spree hours ago. I'm keeping a lady waiting."

By the time he had bathed and dressed and drunk the small glass of rum which Medford brought him, Sidney returned. He had not changed his clothes and, as Gerald Motley walked toward the car, Sidney got out and handed him the keys.

"I'm not going to the spree," he said. "I've called up a craft and arranged to meet her in town instead."

"Oh," Gerald Motley said, and waited.

"To hell with Murie Collins' spree! And to hell with your damn Lady Sybil from Jamaica. It's your bloody funeral, not mine."

There was a moment's disbelief and then Gerald Motley laughed, "Ah, Sidney, did I ever accuse you of having no pity? I was wrong, boy. You are the soul of pity. And that almost disappoints me. Not only that, you're wise, boy. Come, I'll drive you to meet the craft. Which is it? Not the one from last night with skin like cold fat."

They remained silent on the way to town, Sidney staring out the window and Gerald Motley watching the black road streak past the car as if it were a reel of film depicting his life—the events, the scenes, so blurred that nothing emerged and, thus, nothing mattered.

He opened the glove compartment and handed Sidney a flask of rum. "One for the road, boy."

Sidney took the flask and held it for some time before taking a drink. When he finally drank and passed it over, Gerald Motley felt the warm place where Sidney's hand had rested; as he fitted the mouth of the bottle to his he tasted Sidney there—and that taste and touch, so intimate somehow in the darkness, along with the rum searing his throat, restored him. The limp muscles across his back stiffened, the faint gnawing within his stomach ceased and he was ready suddenly for Murie's party and for Sybil.

By the time they reached the place where Sidney was to meet the girl Gerald Motley was almost gay. He brought the car to a jolting stop and as Sidney got out with a mumbled parting word, he called after him, "I'll make quick work of this spree and meet you at Ling's, so don't waste too much time with the craft."

Sidney turned, his movement full of a surprise he could not contain. Bending down he peered across the short distance into the car, his hand lifting in a tenuous gesture and his eyes, caught by the light of a street lamp, revealing a sudden solicitude and devotion beneath their cruelty. He started toward the car as though he had changed his mind and would accompany Gerald Motley but he paused before completing the first step —an invisible hand might have jerked him back—and his own hand slowly dropped.

"At Ling's then," he said, and turned away.

Gerald Motley drove back the way he had come, thinking of Sidney. He had felt just then the terrible weight of his youth, and the bitterness which would waste him. He thought of him scowling down at the flooded yard that morning, and of his outburst at lunch, of the cheap watch he wore and the girl he would not enjoy tonight, and was suddenly glad that he was old and almost finished and would never know pain again.

Murie's house was on Dodds Road, near his, and like his it was a white, towering relic raised on stilts and secured behind a high stone wall with bits of broken glass cemented into the top. Ferns grew in baskets hung from the veranda roof, and the hibiscus and bougainvillaea clustered round the house mulled the air until it was like wine. Tonight the lighted windows were briliants richly displayed against the black sky, and the gay voices and laughter rushing from the open windows seemed to ward off the night, keeping the world safe till the morning.

Gerald Motley swung the car into the driveway, its tires skidding as her made the turn without slowing down, and sent it hurtling down the narrow aisle between the row of parked cars, past the veranda where the overflow crowd from inside was gathered under loops of yellow lights.

"There's Motts," someone called above the loud pelleting of the loose gravel under the car and Gerald Motley gunned the motor in a salute.

The only parking space was some distance from the house, at the end of the driveway beyond the reach of the veranda lights, under a saman tree which was thick with the night as if with leaves. The loose gravel settled under the car as he parked it. The motor died. With his hand on the door, Gerald Motley paused. The lights beyond and the laughter suddenly wearied him. The thought of the people there—Murie, who would chide him for being late, Sybil, who would forgive him again and again with her smile, all the others whose eyes would offer him the false image of himself—oppressed him suddenly. He would have preferred Ling's. His hand started toward the steering wheel.

But it was too late for him to leave. He saw Sybil—a dark figure in a pale diaphanous dress who moved away from the crowd on the veranda to stand at the railing with her arms folded quietly and her face turned toward the darkness which hid him. He saw her turn once to call something to the others, saw her laugh with an easy lifting of her head. Then she slowly came down the veranda steps, across the yard and down the driveway between the parked cars. The hem of her dress flickered in the rush of light from a window and her heels raised little flurries of dust as they struck the ground.

It was the same step, but firmer and more resolute now—as if she came with a plan and would not be dissuaded—the same graceful form, but a little heavier and less fluid than he remembered it, and her shoulders, which had always been somewhat loose and sad, were set now, assured. Gerald Motley was certain, although he could not see her face, that this was not the Sybil of his dream on the patio, no old woman with dried breasts and blurred eyes. (He was relieved. This would make it less painful to look at her once they went into the light—his smile would be less false.) Rather, she seemed more the Sybil of his remembrance. Time was reversed suddenly. The years telescoped. The past, which had trailed and nettled him like a dog's tail, had been caught finally in the teeth of the present.

"But, Gerald, man, you drove in here as if you had a woman about to deliver on the seat next to you." She called while still a little distance away, her voice light and amiable, signaling him, it seemed, that she would be discreet and not restore the past or accuse him of old sins.

And grateful, he called back, "Is that Sybil loose in the land again?"

"Yes, man," she said, leaning down at the open window and pressing her face briefly against his. "Like the elephant I've come home to die."

Her skin was like stone that had been cooled and worn smooth by water passing over it, her fragrance the familiar one he had once carried home on his clothes and body every night. Her voice was the same. She had always unconsciously pitched it to the time of day. At night it would be hushed and driven deep in her throat as it was now, tense in the noon heat and listless during the rainy season. It was still young.

"You know that Murie is a lying brute. She told me Sybil was old," he said, slipping into the old bantering, indirect form of addressing her.

"She is," she said blithely, and stood up. "And tired. So open the car door and let her sit quietly for a minute before we go inside. Dear God!" she said, when she was settled on the seat beside him, her head resting on the back and a wide space between them. "This is the first rest I've known for the day. This morning it was the damn noisy plane, then Murie's rude children all afternoon and now this spree. . . ."

"It looks like we both need a grog then," he said and, finding a paper cup in the glove compartment, poured her a drink from the flask he and Sidney had used. As he sought her hand stretched toward him for the cup, he avoided looking at it or her face—even though they were both obscured by the darkness. He was afraid, absurdly so, that by some alchemy she had assumed her former self and was young again.

"You know," she said, taking the rum, "there's nothing worse than a welcome-home spree when you've been away as long as I have. It's like a bloody wake. You see all the old pack—or what's left of them—and you realize how old you are. Take Sylvan Hanes, for instance. Gerald, I scarcely knew Sylvan when he came up and spoke to me just now. And he's younger than I am, I know. And Dora. Look at Dora!"

"Didn't Murie write and tell you what happened to Dora?"

"No, man."

He told her and for a long time they spoke of Dora and the others they had known together, and of the dead, their voices easy and intimate in the night, their faces veiled. Both of them, as if by a silent pact, carefully avoided the question of themselves.

Finally, when there were no more names but theirs, she said, filling the silence, "Well, at least the old place hasn't changed. Orly and Company still own everything, I hear. The heat's the same. And the roads, especially that one from the airport, are still an abomination of mud. And the bush is still out there. We flew over it for miles and miles this morning. I never knew there was so much of it." Then, with a light, guilty laugh—as if she knew she was breaking their pact not to talk of each other—she said, "Tell me, did you ever try reaching Kaieteur Falls again?"

He felt a tightening across his chest and the need for a drink, for her question suddenly swept aside the intervening years and brought them both back to that time. He suspected, with a wariness which made his hand grope for the steering wheel, that she had never really moved beyond that time. Her years in Jamaica and her success there might have been nothing more than an attempt to forget those moments with him in the bush. And he had to admit, as he sat there trying to dismiss her question with a laugh as light as hers and a casual "No," that those moments were still vivid and urgent to him also. Perhaps neither of them had moved beyond that time and place. They might have left their selves behind among the trees and wandered in whose forms down the years. He felt like cursing her, like shouting as he pushed her from the car and drove off that it was unjust for her to return bringing the old pain. He wished that he was at Ling's having a rum and waiting for Sidney to come from the woman.

"B.G. is the only place on God's earth you could leave for a century and come back to find nothing's changed," she was saying, trying to restore the pleasant tone, but as she continued talking her voice slowly failed—and finally she broke off and said, asking his forgiveness for the question with a gesture hidden by the dark, "And what of you, Gerald, man?"

He would have liked to have been able to recount a long list of successes, thus proving to her that despite her leaving he had been able to take hold. And yet, on the other hand, he knew that he owed her his failure. It would give her perhaps the comforting illusion that she had been crucial to any success he might have had and that by refusing to marry her he had brought on his ruin. His failure was the only way to make amends for having refused her, the only way, perhaps, for him to make amends for all his life: his privileged place, his name, the wife and child he had driven away. . . .

"Yes, what of me?" he said, with the laugh he used to deny himself.

"Well, you could say that my life since Sybil left has been one slow decline into rum and inertia. In the mornings and for most of the day there's Singh over at the King George Bar who ministers to my needs (he still asks for Sybil when he can remember that far back, by the way) and a lady named Ling at night who runs a bar on Water Street. It's not of a very high order, but then it's the only place in Georgetown that stays open all night.

"But don't mistake me, I work when I can spare the time. I'm still the puppet director at B.G. Broadcasting. But then, thank God, there's not much to direct since the program hasn't really changed since Sybil worked there and she and I had such grand schemes of making B.G. Broadcasting the voice of the West Indies. It's still cricket, news from the B.B.C. three times a day, the governor's speeches on the Queen's birthday and funeral announcements. That's the way Frank Orly and Company want it. But I can't say anything against Frank, you know. After all, he saves me the trouble of exerting myself in all this heat. The old boy has even installed an air conditioner in my office. It's yet to work properly, but it's there at least. No, Frank has been good."

He drank from the flask and remained silent for some time before he said, "Yes, and I still have the old place on Dodds Road and Medford still airs out the rooms once a week as though expecting company. What else, now? Oh, yes, about ten years ago I went up to England on my long leave, but I couldn't take the cold and fog. I still go over to Barbados once a year though and stretch out like a dead fish on the beach for a week or so. . . ." He turned to her, giving the little laugh, knowing its cruelty. "You mean to say Murie hasn't told Sybil all this in her letters? That doesn't sound like your sister."

The darkness had cleared a little so that he could make out her arm as it raised the cup to her lips.

She said quietly, "Yes, she's told me."

"Ah, I didn't think a Murie would miss the opportunity. Well, she's been busy because she's also kept me up to date on Sybil. I get full reports. I was informed of every step of Sybil's ascendency to power at Radio Jamaica, every detail of the big house with glass walls she built on a hill—what was it, five years ago?"

"Seven."

"And of course Murie told me about Sybil's getting married, but that was years ago now, and about the divorce. She said Sybil never told her what had happened though."

"Nothing happened. I got married too soon after I left here, that's all. After that I decided not to inflict myself on anyone again. No more marriage. I would just ask them to return my keys when I had had enough or tell the servant that I wouldn't be home to Mr. So-and-So any more and that was the end of it. But I've gotten too old for that." She gave a taut laugh. "You might say I don't go out in society any more."

Her voice had wandered listlessly over the words, refusing them all feeling and color, and now her sudden silence was so final she might have fallen asleep. As the moments passed and her breathing became inaudible, Gerald Motley had the curious feeling that she had vanished and it was Sidney asleep beside him as he had been that morning on the way to the office. She and Sidney seemed one and the same suddenly. And in an odd way they were. For although Sidney watched and waited for Gerald Motley's destruction to be complete and Sybil in her limitless compassion would have saved him if he had permitted her, the two things, his salvation and his end, were the same to him.

He glanced across at the still profile etched against the lesser blackness of the night, almost expecting to see Sidney there. But instead of that flawless line which Sidney's chin formed with his throat, he saw, dimly, the small sac of flesh, like a tremulous globule of water, beneath Sybil's chin.

He felt kindly toward her suddenly and sad about the husband she had lost and the score of lovers she had abandoned, for her body which had once pleased and impassioned him and now only filled him with distaste, for her memories which seemed drained of feeling (how well he knew about that!), above all, for whatever it was that had brought her back to B.G. Curious to know what this was, he said, "And so Sybil finally deigned to look up the old pack again."

"No, not the old pack, not even Murie so much. I came to see you," she said quietly, and he stiffened, offended, afraid that she would reach out and touch him, wanting to move further away from her. But, surprisingly, she was the one who moved deeper into her corner of the seat and folded her arms protectively over her breasts as if she was afraid he would touch her.

"It's about Radio Jamaica," she said, her voice stirring into life now. "Our program director is leaving. In fact, he's left by now. He was the usual white incompetent England dumps on her colonies and he couldn't half do the job. So I'm to be the new program director—Sybil's ascendency to power as you put it—but there's also been a new position created for someone above me who will coordinate the entire project. Of course, there was the usual talk about getting down someone from England, but I prevailed on them to look around the West Indies first. I suggested you and since they respect my judgment and knew your name, they asked me to come down and talk to you personally. . . ."

She was still talking when he started to laugh, and the sound, building into a small whirlwind, sucked up her words into its eye and spun with them from the car, through the trees and across the yard to the veranda. A few people on the edge of the crowd turned and peered toward the sound; someone called inquiringly. But even when a stout figure—Murie probably—came halfway down the veranda steps and stared toward them, Gerald Motley did not stop laughing. He could not. The absurdity of her offer, its irony, convulsed him: life offering itself when there was hardly any life left. It was a rare, grotesque touch which appealed to his taste, the fitting coda to his long day, and he wished that Sidney was present to enjoy the moment with him.

"This calls for a drink," he said, reaching for her cup and, as she waved aside the flask, he added, "Oh come, Sybil mustn't mind my laughing."

"It's all right," she said stiffly. "You always laughed and said, 'This calls for a drink,' when anything came up."

"Only when it wasn't anything serious, if you remember."

"This is quite serious."

"Of course it is. It only becomes ridiculous, indeed ludicrous, when Sybil brings me into it. Perhaps she's forgotten the matter of my age."

"I know how old you are," she said quietly.

"And knowing that she would send me to do a young man's job, have me leave a nice little air-conditioned sinecure here to work like a coolie for Radio Jamaica? She would have me spend what little time is left to me in a heathen place where they don't even sell Russian Bear rum? Sybil isn't kind. Why how in the hell would I hold together without Russian Bear and the King George every morning and Ling's each night, without the old place, as hopeless as it is with the heat and the blasted rain, without the old packinside." He motioned toward the house.

"Another thing"—and his voice had reached a savage pitch now—"who told Sybil I could coordinate anything? Not Murie certainly. She knows better. In all the years Sybil worked for me, did she ever see me do any co-ordinating, or any directing for that matter—any work? So where then do I get all this experience she's claiming for me . . . ?"

"Oh, Gerald, stop going on, you could do the job." And her impatience was suddenly familiar. She had, how often in the past, urged him to something in just this way, not knowing as he had secretly known that it was not hesitancy or a lack of confidence on his part, but, simply, the terrifying awareness of his deficiencies.

His laughter was like the final agony, and he held out his hands in the dimness. "Sybil must let Murie tell her sometime how my hands shake these days," he said. Then: "No, I could not do the job. And even if I could I wouldn't. I'm afraid Sybil has put herself to all this trouble for nothing."

He was silent, his hands still raised between them. She was watching them, he knew, and then as if their tremor was contagious she began to tremble and her head slowly dropped in an eloquent gesture of defeat.

To seal that defeat, he said, "Sybil always had something of the missionary in her. She was always looking for souls to save."

"Oh, Christ, Gerald, but why have you always put me off so?" Her cry, full of rage and bewilderment, burdened the darkness and he knew suddenly—and his hands dropped—that she had waited all these years to ask the question.

He could have answered it but he didn't. He could have told her that he had never forgiven her for intruding between him and the discovery of himself that day in the bush. He could have said—if there had been words for it—that he had resented and feared the part of her love which had wanted to pool their suffering; above all, he could have confessed that although he had not known it then, he had found her woman's form distasteful.

But instead he said, "I'm sorry. I didn't mean to put Sybil off. In fact, I'm going to see to it that she doesn't go away altogether empty-handed. I can't find her a co-ordinator, but perhaps if Radio Jamaica needs an additional announcer I can be of some help. You see, I have a young chap by the name of Parrish on the staff who's really first-rate. There's no scope for him here though and no future. He does the funeral announcements and most of the commercials. We know where that will lead him in a few years. To the King George Bar and Ling's at night. I'd really like to see him get the chance to work for a big station like Radio Jamaica. Perhaps if Sybil is downtown tomorrow she will be kind enough to stop by the office and meet him. He was supposed to come tonight but was so overwhelmed, I think, by the prospect of meeting Lady Sybil—that's what he calls you—that he changed his mind at the last moment."

She turned slowly, her dress whispering at the movement, her voice as she spoke touched by an unnatural calm. "Wait, is this the boy Murie mentioned in her letter?"

His laugh exploded like a flare in the darkness. "Oh, God, that Murie! I should have known I could have depended on her. What did she write?"

"Something about a boy you're always walking about with as if he's a son or close friend or something so . . ."

"Or something so, eh? That sounds like Murie."

"She said that if people didn't know you they'd think something foolish was going on." She paused, waiting for his outrage and denial, for the laugh which would have cancelled all that Murie had implied.

When the laugh did not come, when he said nothing and his silence became an admission, she suddenly stiffened—and the air grew stiff—and, darting forward, she snatched up a book of matches which lay on top of the dashboard. She struck one, but it did not light—the sulfur was damp from the week's rain—and she flung it down. And another, her arm tracing a desperate arc in the dimness. Finally one caught and, cupping the small flame as though there was a wind, she leaned close and held it to his face.

He merely glanced at her through the flame and, finding what he had suspected—the worn flesh around the eyes, the subtle collapse of the tiny muscles beneath the skin which had drawn the skin down with them, the loneliness which had wasted her more than any disease and aged her faster than the years—he closed his eyes almost all the way and watched her from under his lowered eyelids.

Her mouth was tight with concentration, her eyes almost eclipsed by the heavy fold of flesh which gave them their Oriental cast; yet the same time they seemed infinitely large, like huge elliptical mirrors which magnified his image so that he saw the old man who had once been her lover as clearly as she saw him, with his flesh arranged in slack folds which fluttered each time he breathed, his features so thickened they had lost their original forms, the skin discolored by his excesses. He could no longer be mistaken for white, or black for that matter, or East Indian. Over the years the various strains had cancelled out each other, it seemed, until he was a neuter.

She leaned closer, bringing the match so near he could hear the determined sputter of the flame as it edged down the damp stick and could feel its meager heat, and her eyes now probed within each crevice of his lined face and within the depth of his lidded eyes, finding there the confusion which had begun with his heritage, spread over the whole of his life and found its final expression in Sidney. The evidence was all there. And she saw something else which made her suddenly start and draw back and give a muted cry of fear and pity which made the small flame waver. It was, simply, the unmistakable form of his death lurking there—a death so imminent Gerald Motley would not be permitted to finish out the night, but would die in an accident on the road through Kitty Village into town.

All this was no more than the fraction of a moment, for the match quickly died, and in the silence a woman on the veranda laughed, a long, hysterical burst, the fitting response, it seemed, to some monstrous and eternal jest.

"Remember what the old people used to say?" Gerald Motley said, and his voice was light, gay. "That if you grant a man his last wish he dies easy and has a chance at heaven."

When she finally answered, her whisper was a thin quaver which betrayed her age. "All right, Gerald, I'll come down to the office tomorrow and meet the boy. If he's really good I'll see what I can do. . . ."

"That does it then. Let's have one for the road."

"You're not stopping?"

"No, man, we've had our little chat. I'm sure Sybil can find some excuse to give Murie."

She allowed him to pour her a drink and then, with it poised near her lips, she said, her voice suddenly strong again, "This damn place. This damn, bloody place."

She got out of the car, leaving the door open behind her, and walked toward the veranda, where they were dancing now under the strung lights. She was still holding the paper cup of rum, bearing it gently between her hands as if the ash of his life was dissolved there.

"Remember me to Murie," he shouted after her, and gave the old irreverent laugh.

AHARON MEGGED

the white city

1

Everything was moving southwards. Like armored stallions thirsting for
battle galloped trucks, jeeps, buses, bulldozers, cranes, tanks, stamped
impatiently in their places, panting and neighing, and galloped again,
biting one another's tails, separating and clashing, trotting onwards,
breaking at crossroads like a river into tributaries. Sharp as an arrow
glittering in the sun, racing forward towards its target, the noise of the
vehicles cut through the once-quiet space now startled by the din. Far
off in the fields white settlements lay peacefully, like flocks of white
doves which landed to pick up seeds after the ploughing.

As the convoy stopped for a while, checked and deterred by headlong pace, an army of heads rose above the vehicles' sides and calls were
thrown, from one group to the next: hands and caps waved in greeting, and hullos flew like swallows in swift volley from one end of the
line to the other.

Then came the high and low hills and after them the broad flat plain,
whose silence quivered like a string in the soft wind coming from the
end of the world.

I ran to the sergeant's tent, and from there to the sergeant-major's
tent, and from there to the quarter-master, falling into the ranks, swallowed up in them, like a coil in a snake, leaving them like an ant its
colony, hurrying to the open square swarming with ants running and
meeting one another and separating and returning to their rows and
separating again in the quiet rustle which etched countless lines in all
directions, and from there with my equipment and my belt and my arms
to the pup tent.

I was one of a battalion, one of ten thousand, one of a nation. I shook people's hands, laughed, greeted people I didn't know. All of them were my friends.

Then I was alone on the hard, dry earth, and the muscles of my back, which were stuck to it, listened to the currents moving through its bowels, moving the muscles of its loins powerfully, reinforcing its bones like iron bars.

Then the earth was a large sea and I moved slowly over its broad waves, floating on my back from horizon to horizon.

I fell asleep. And when I awoke, I saw the first stars glistening in the sky and the sound of men singing far away. I got up and went outside. The camp was empty. Below, on the slope of the hill, a dense mass of men blackened the grey field. There the battalion was sitting, on the ground, and the voice of its singing, which grew louder and louder in a single choir, sounded like the beating of iron wings in the clouds.

O, Almightly God, what a miracle it was that war came along to save me from death!

I went down and seated myself at the edge of the large mass and pressed my body against its body. A soldier came up and put the palm of his hand against my shoulder so that he could sit down. At the touch of his hands a wave of warmth passed through my flesh. I wanted to shake his hand and thank him. Oh good people, I said to myself: an army of brothers who march together to conquer life!

"Officers, soldiers," the O.C. of the battalion said in his quiet voice, standing in the center of the mass, with his hands behind his back, "in another day and a night we shall face the great trial. We are already in the midst of the war, and at this very moment our army's advance troops are already deep in the enemy's territory, on the other side of his strongholds. Our task is to shatter his offensive positions, which threaten the integrity of our land and its very existence and to foil once and for all the enemy's aggressive plans. I will not dwell on the importance of this operation. All of you know this as well as I do. I will only say one thing: no country can put up with a state of permanent threat to its borders and unceasing attacks on its settlements. War is an unpleasant business, which involves suffering and sacrifice. But it is more unpleasant to live in constant fear, when at any moment the enemy is liable to flourish his naked sword and cut off your hand. Our orders are to attack the most strongly fortified sector of the enemy's front lines. On the border of this front is a dense chain of positions, separated by minefields and barbed wire fences. The enemy's forces include companies of infantry and tanks, and heavy artillery, mortar, anti-tank and armored car units. The General Staff has seen to it that for this attack sufficient manpower, tanks, light and heavy weapons have been concentrated at this point to overcome all the resistance the other side will show. I have no doubt about our victory, but it's up to you whether this victory will be gained with the lowest possible number of casualties. When I say that it's up to you, I mean that this depends on the bravery of each and every one of you, on the exhaustive use of all your battle skill, on the display of the right degree of daring, on the precise co-operation between the commander and his fellow soldiers in theu nit, on the spirit of brotherhood which is the powerful force at our disposal, and with which the enemy can never compete . . ."

The enemy front was shrouded in darkness, and a dome of sky clustered with thousands of glittering diamonds hung over the whole earth. I knew no fear. I was proud of the trust the O.C. had placed in me. In me and in each of the hundreds of people who were sitting with me, whose faces I had never seen but whose voices I had heard when they sang together. I saw myself storming the enemy's lines with a drawn bayonet. Bursting into the lines, felling warriors all around me. I knew that no bullet would strike me and that I would enter, live and upright, into the conquered city, and my chest swelled with the joy of victory.

In the center of the camp, next to the headquarters tent, the radio brought good tidings from the distant desert, from the mountains of iron and copper, from the shores of an ancient sea. In the darkness, I could feel how the hundreds of bodies standing around me were bolt upright like drawn bayonets, and how the shudder of the electric current went from body to body until they became a single body yearning to thrust forward, to wherever their orders would take them. Then the racket made by the people, gay, laughing, greeting one another, patting one another on the back, slapping one another's palms, whistling, whispering, looking for their mates, hurrying to their tents, falling into line for food, eating from their mess tins, their arms making a clanking sound—which mingled with the noise of armored cars, gun-carriers, tanks, which ploughed the earth and the night with their roar, moving like a mighty steel beast southwards, somewhere. Everything was bound with a sound which injected fearless strength. Left-right, left-right, like one man marched groups beside the armored column in the darkness on other side of the camp, left-right, and the dust of their step turned to gold in the lights of moving vehicles. To march with them. To reach the battle-field. To run into the wall of fire, to fall and rise. To storm enemy positions. Face to face. To jump into them. To yell like an animal. Oh, another day and a night!

Suddenly the palm of someone's hand was placed on my shoulder again. This time it was the sergeant. "Come, let's go to the O.C.'s tent" he said.

Around the table, which was covered with a large sketched map, in the yellow light of three field lamps, sat the O.C. and five other officers. A strong heartbeat throbbed in my chest when my eyes fell on Debbele, who sat at the edge of the table. "You didn't think we would meet here," he said in his quiet, almost inaudible voice, and smiled a faint smile at me. The memory of my wife, the nightmares, the pistol, rose up in my heart like someone rising from the dead, but was immediately suppressed. Next to him sat Gabi and Yoram Nash. They hadn't aged at all. White khefiyas covered their necks, and their faces were dusty. Like then. Good God! As if it had been exactly at this place, exactly at this hour, around the table in a tent yellowed by field lamps. How everything repeated itself. And I as well. The hoarse, quiet voices, rasping from smoke and burning dust.

Yoram Nash shook my hands from his seat, and Gabi called out the name of my old company, as if uttering a slogan. We hadn't seen one another for eight years.

"We wanted to ask you if you are ready to go out on a patrol," the O.C. said.

"Yes, commander," I said, and a blush of pride came to my face.

"Tonight."

"Yes, commander."

"Do you know the terrain at all?"

"No."

"Go to the quartermaster with this slip, get your equipment, and come back here."

"Yes, sir."

About an hour later we went out in to the silence, with submachine guns, pistols and hand grenades. There were four of us, apart from Debbele, who led the way. We were swallowed up by the darkness, and only the slither of our steps in the soft sand was heard. The terrain was flat, and we saw nothing in front of us, only Debbele, who set the pace with a rapid stride. No obstacles stood in our path, and it seemed that we could just go on walking like that until we reached the sea. An enormous land and we were its only rulers. If a bullet were fired, it would fly above us, to our right, to our left, but would not hit us. The war was a sport. The war was freedom. All man's power. I felt the power in my legs which would never grow weary, in my waist, braced by the weight of the belt, in my hands, strengthened by the iron of the arms, in my chest, which challenged the chill air, the darkness, the hidden anticipated fire. I was twice my height. A giant bestriding the earth. If a bullet hit Debbele, I would carry him on my shoulders as one carries a child. I would be the last to remain on my feet. I would be a whole peole, whose love swelled within it until it choked in its throat.

Oh, my many friends, thousands of them, who had gathered again into a single mass rooted to the earth. Oh, my name of which I was so proud. My father of whom I was so proud. My youth, of which I was so proud. Oh, the great night, on which I conquered my life anew.

Debbele got down on his haunches, and the rest of us did likewise. We crouched down like frogs, and listened to the night, so far and so close. Only silent nibblings could be heard among the thorns, the rustle of insects in the dry grass. The feeling of sawing legs in the stalks of straw. The quiet slither of a beetle over the soft earth. And from afar there was a surprised silence, like a calm before the storm. Before we left we had seen the two enemy positions on a sand table: like two giant tortoises sending out horny limbs in front and behind through their openings. Barbed wire fences, hidden cannon positions. A mine-field sketched in crosses like the tracks of a beetle in the sand. A pock-marked, blocked road. Now everything was dark. We could easily fall on the fence before we came to it. Or fly up in the air from a mine exploding under our feet. Were we still far away?

Behind me Debbele hissed in a whisper, rose to his feet and marched. Again the plain was blind, without any obstacles. Oh, if only all of life was like that! Not in closed rooms. Groups of friends moving in the valleys or on the hills. Bearing a burden without growing tired. Each man for the other. And only a whisper going from man to man like a slogan, without any need to ask questions, because everybody understood. And no dark plots which called for duels. And everyone did what he was called upon to do, under the law of the single fate. If only all of life—

We stopped still. Two huge searchlights, far away in the West, sent long sickles to reap the broad darkness of the night. "Down!" Debbele ordered, when the light reached us, and we got down to the ground. The light was blinding, and the plain in front of us became hills and valleys for one sharp moment and then went dark again, even more so than before, and the sickle moved on and slipped away. We rose and marched, and from now on we froze in our places and knelt down every time the long sword of light was brandished. We felt our way in the darkness, unknowingly. Debbele slackened his pace, hesitating. He tried to examine what was in front of him in the ray of light, but this only revealed a mirage. Now he ordered us to sit and wait, and he himself went forward to the north, diagonally, until he disappeared from our view. We had strayed away, it seemed. No path crossed our way, and no sign indicating a paved road, as marked on the map and shown on the stand table. No sound of a dog barking, no clank of metal, no human voice. We put our ears close to the ground, straining ourselves to hear the sound of Debbele's footsteps. But there was no sound. Could he have lost his way and be unable to find his way back to us? The whistle of a distant bullet suddenly pierced the silence. Then came the rattle of a machine gun, with an explosive burst. A red star shone and grew in size, hanging in the air and opening out like a fan, splintering and dying out. The sound of an explosion on the ground, and a sheaf of light upwards. Far away in the south. Had the battle already begun without us? Or had the orders been confused? To go back? To wait? To run forward? To run towards the firing area? Where were we needed? Where was Debbele? Was this the battle already? But suddenly everything stopped, and became silent again.

Debbele returned and stood over us, without us noticing it. "Those are the sappers of the southern wing, blowing up the minefield," he said calmly. We looked to the south and waited for the resumption of the fire, but there was none. Again the broad, sharp stripe of the searchlight slid over us. "Follow me," Debbele said. "Have you found something?" "Yes. A long fold in the earth, a mound. A good place for an alignment of forces. Behind it are their positions, I think." Now, we walked straight, and Debbele was our eyes. The sound of our steps grew louder in our ears, and we held the guns tightly. Why isn't he careful at all, when we are getting close to the enemy lines? Suddenly a black patrol will appear out of the ground, and we will fall before it like chaff before the reaper.

After ten minutes, we came to the mound. It was lower than we had supposed, but it was an event in the blank plain. We lay down on the ground and listened. Yes, now we could hear voices. A dull murmur from afar, the murmur of the sea beating against the breast of the land and the sound of muffled bangs from close up. They were digging in. The enemy. Soon a volley of shots will burst out. We'll be a single corpse, on which the sun will rise in the morning, and a swarm of flies will hover round its mouth open to the heavens and the dry blood on its lips.

We lay down reclining and warm against one another, with Debbele next to me. I wanted to say something to him which perhaps I would never have a chance to say. To ask his forgiveness for the duel I had fought with him. To whisper to him that what had happened was no longer important to me, compared with the great war and the great, tremendous life, the power of which we now felt together. That really it was of no importance, that I had been a fool and had imagined things. That I loved him. That he was the country which I loved. That I was ready at that moment to get up and cross the track in order to throw a grenade at the enemy's sappers. And not to return. If he would just give the order.

Debbele ordered us to spread out along the length of the track, two to the south, two to the north, about five hundred paces to each side, and one of us to remain. To find the sand track leading between two positions. To mark the route of the attacking force to its objective. I walked along with Debbele and spoke to him in my heart. I told him that I could not go on living as I had until then. That after the war I would not return to my previous place of work under any conditions. That the smell of papers and the ink and the banknotes nauseated me. That I had to feel people around me, warm souls all bent on a single cause. Working together I told him that if we remained alive—and we would certainly remain alive!—we would organize, the five of us here and people from all different companies, and set up a new settlement in the south of the country. We would live in wooden huts. We would raise cattle. At night we would ride horses. We would be thirsty unto death in the burning sun. We would start everything again. We would form a pact. Like now . . . Suddenly he stopped, rubbed his shoe in the dust and said: "That's it." I felt it with my foot. Yes, it was a hard road, covered with sand. "That's it," he repeated, pressing my arm firmly. "This is the road we've been looking for. Let's go back."

The two men who had turned southwards also came back. We lay down on the ground again and crawled up on the low mound of earth. When we came to its peak, and the rays of light swung again in a broad bow over the open space, we saw the enemy's position. We saw it when it was shrouded again, in blind darkness. Fence poles. A hill of dust. Black openings. Gaping holes. Moving figures.

2

A night of splendor. A night of sparks and light. A night of a fiery river.

At 01.10 after midnight, on the second night the force began to move eastwards, company after company, platoon after platoon, armed from head to foot, loaded on shoulders and back, marching in the darkness, stumbling through soft sand, carried on the crest of a rising wave, and we, the scouts, at the head of the column piloting its way to the objective.

We led the way, light footed, floating, knowing all the long way by heart, in the dark plain, halting every few moments until one platoon would take hold of the next one's tail, pulling again impatiently, westwards, westwards, thousands of feet behind us, as a dark forest of guns, a long beast whose inside was iron and whose scales clinked as it moved, pulling and hastening to get there in good time before dawn broke.

Far away in the south the fireworks in the air flew up and died, rushing on high as if on a festive night and falling into the tracks of the fire, sent up with shrill whistles, like thousands of slashing whips, with a quick, hunted rattle, snakes after snakes, the head of one in the next's tail, with the tinkle of stones falling and rolling down into the black abyss, splitting holes in the surface of the earth, with yells which cleft the heavens. There, far away in the south, the battle was already in full swing.

We stumbled on, getting heavier and heavier, and our steps pulling at one another's heels, and the hiss of short breathing like a bellows from row to row, and the sound of curt sentences coming from the telephones, strained like wire, torn and tied, and the wheels of light vehicles, somewhere behind us, moving and making a noise and churning up dust, and moving again, and from the north we already heard the sound of tanks' chains.

I was a warlike knight. Happiness choked my throat like an anthem. It flowed through me like a river from the beginning of the column to its end. Sparks flashed between me and my comrades whenever my shoulders touched theirs. An incessant shudder rooted me to all the rows in the front and behind me. All the chests shielded me, and my own chest was about to burst with pride. What a mighty mass of people, whose entire history marches with it when it goes out to fight back!

And when we reached the border, and the walkie-talkies sent forth staccato syllables and the row halted like a train of wagons, with a jangling of chains, creaking and sighing, and the force spread out to its breadth, platoons following brief commands, running bent-up under the weight of full kit and belt, the clink of parcels and metal, a flock of little foxes going out to hunt—I was like a bush squashed down, its roots stuck to its earth, and a soft wind passed hurriedly through my branches and passed on its rustles like a whispered slogan to all the long line of bushes extending to the end of the night from north to south. Spades were taken out and a brisk, diligent, panic-stricken clatter of dust passed along the entire length of the line, digging and throwing out, burrowing and deepening, like the patter of rain, or the noise made by full sacks when one sack is thrown on top of another.

We waited for a signal, for the hail of fire from the heavens which would fall on the enemy's head and would set his fortresses and land on fire as in the destruction of Sodom and Gemorrah. On the southern horizon lightning flashed, and the din of battle flared up and died down there alternately. But in front of us was the ambush of silence in the plain, in which the rays of the searchlights roamed nervously, feeling along its length, stopping, hesitating, continuing to prowl around up and down, passing over our heads and going on to the dead areas, wandering purposelessly, feeling around without feeling. "Another twelve minutes," Debbele whispered beside me, looking at the hands of his watch. We looked up at the sky. Only a host of stars glistened there, thousands of light years away.

Suddenly, the entire camp grabbed at its arms, at the sound of planes' buzzing and before the ear had caught it, three dull explosions split the womb of the earth, far apart from one another, north and south, and a third one in the midst of us, and the searchlights went out at once.

Oh, Great God! A buzz scratched the face of the sky, and immediately afterwards heavy thunder exploded and shattered in a din from one horizon to the next, scorching the whole earth. Twelve, twenty, twenty-eight, forty-two, sixty, one hundred! One hundred and fifty-eight!

Like a veteran war horse, my body as one with the whole army, I plunged forward with the rows of infantry, and with the armored animal which rolled over on its stomach and came up to us, with the track cars which travelled beside us, stopping, retreating, moving again kicking up a rocket, rumbling on an empty stomach gathering strength and advancing, and greetings and hasty orders cutting through the air as if there was no enemy . . .

And suddenly—from all sides, at one go, in front of us on both the right and the left, a sparking fire cut through the open space, fed by whistling bullets, vomited out of jaws in a hail of hoarse missiles, flaming and scorching, falling in shrapnel, and the whole enemy front suddenly took fire in an instant.

Oh, that was the battle already. And I felt no fear! As if my chest was made of armor and no fire could destroy it! The commands came out one after the other, companies collected together, putting machine guns, bazookas, mortars in position, and the whole earth was licked by fire, bullets hitting one another, passing with a screeching whirr to my right, to my left, above my head and bombs tore up the earth and a heavy banging, and the buzz of swarms of bullets, piercing and pointing in a thick net—and I knew no fear!

A burst from a light machine-gun passed on my left, a cry was heard, and a boy turned over on his stomach and doubled up. Cries of "Orderly! Orderly!" from all sides, and at once two people came running and put a stretcher down, and while I was still stunned, Debbele called out: "Forward!"

And I ran after him, bending down with a row of shadows intermingling in turn with the flashes of fire and firing in front of the row and falling in front of a high barbed wire fence. "Sappers!" came a call amid the constant rattling noise from both sides, and passing high above, and four or five or six men ran towards the fence and placed bangalores and called out warnings and retreated towards us, falling on their faces and a powerful explosion tore the wires with a screech and turned the poles upside down and forced a large breach, into which we ran, countless ones, pushing against one another and falling down and digging in again.

Oh, a night of fiery river, a night of festive fireworks! Among the whirl of flashes and shadows I ran, attacking, falling and rising, as if in a dream. As if in a dream, Death had no dominion over me, and there was no Time. My being was an electric flash in the night, unthinking, unknowing. The bullets shot out of my body, emerged in front of me, I know not where. Had an hour gone by? Or three? Or a moment like a light-year?

As in a dream the noise suddenly died down. The enemy's jaws on the right were suddenly dead, and only one position still rattled away incessantly, with the music of mingled voices, making the earth shake around it, and it became an open target for our fire, which was directed towards it from all sides, continuous, insistent, vigorous, scorching the earth and puncturing walls.

And after hundreds of explosions, when the armored divisions turned to outflank the enemy in another direction, and the first seemed to stop for a moment, came the order to spring forward, and again all the shadows rose up and began running forward, and at the sound of a loud explosion under my feet, I called out: "Debbele! Debbele!" running forward frantically. But I saw only a toppling fence and people running through it, and next to the bending pole a man's body was thrown up into the air and fell to the ground doubled-up. "Debbele!" I called once more and froze in my place.

But amid the commotion of the rush towards the enemy position, in order to capture it by throwing grenades which exploded somewhere and the whistling of bursts of bullets, no one heard my cries. I knelt down beside the body and bent over it. I wanted to cry out again to the people running past me, to tell them that he was dead. Killed. Finished. No more. Everything stopped. But the cry froze on my lips. I shook his shoulders with all my strength and whispered: "Debbele, Debbele, listen, Debbele, Debbele, listen to me." But the body was stiff, lifeless. His chest was riddled with bullets, and the warm blood wet his whole shirt. His eyes were open, and in the darkness I could see them staring without any expression. His face was as hard as stone, and the palm of his one hand was clenched round the butt of his gun. Platoons of men ran past us towards the enemy positions.

I bent my head on to his forehead and closed my eyes. Around me the fire seemed to have slackened, or receded, and only stray bursts of fire passed with a sharp, desperate hiss, rushing and dying away when buried somewhere. Then my ears started buzzing. I heard nothing apart from the long, monotonous humming.

When I opened my eyes again, there was a pale dawn light. Everything was different and unbelievably strange. Unrecognizable. And impossible to grasp. And unlike anything that had been before. There were still stray bursts of fire, sounding like last sighs. Faint fire still hissed here and there, next to the opening of the enemy positions. People jumped into the communication trenchs with dying cries. From afar I could see figures scurrying away as quickly as rabbits from the bullets whistling after them. Bodies lay on the grey, cloddy earth, which was just freeing itself of darkness. White smoke rose up here and there from the dust. Massive armored cars moved off, slowly, as if in a nightmare. Opaque buildings, grey and brown, were scattered far off on the sand, and strips of road shone blackly between them. Lonely, sad trees with sagging branches. Fences of prickly pears. Upturned and shattered fences. A tank sunk and lying on its side. A big land, burnt, naked, scarred. And more groups of people running. Where to?

A shiver ran through my flesh. The night had died, and the morning lay like a corpse. Like sadness, going from one end of the world to the other, without a sound.

3

When I had left Debbele alone, I ran after the last of the men towards the position whose fire had died down and, jumping into the communication trench, I sprained my ankle. The pain was so strong that it forced from my mind all the horrors of the night, and all the dangers of death were as nothing beside it. I stood pressed between walls of earth, and wanted to cry with humiliation and helplessness. Soldiers passed on the run in front of me, with their guns held in front of them and I didn't know what to do. I knew that it would be silly to call for a medical orderly at a time like this, when all the available orderlies were taking care of those wounded by bullets or mines. As I had lost my platoon, I also had no one to whom I could turn. I began stumbling after the running soldiers and pulling my one foot after me, and the pain grew stronger with every step. Eventually I became slightly used to it, feeling only that the ankle was fat and swollen, and like a heavy weight hanging on my foot. When I got inside the post, which was full of people, and in some miraculous way was already filled with the hustle and bustle of a command room, with communications facilities, maps and plans on the table, I threw myself on to one of the benches and lay down. The whole commotion around me, the running of the people going out and coming in in such a hurry, the sound of the commands being given to the messengers, the sound of jubilation, the whistling of bullets far above, outside, the chugging of the armored cars, the look of tinned cans lying about among the men's feet, the torn copies of illustrated weeklies, cartridge cases—all this now seemed a different, unreal world, like the hallucinations of a fever-ridden man. Everything was on the other side of an opaque wall, unattainable, inconceivable.

Fear seized me lest I be sent home, before I had seen the victory with my own eyes. I would reach home with a sprained ankle, limping, wretched and downcast. This thought brought me to my feet. I began walking up and down, placing the weight of my body on my aching foot in order to accustom it to carrying me. Slowly, the pain spread to the length of the leg, and seemed to become duller.

An hour before noon we entered the white city, in a column clanking in its armor, marching briskly, striking the stones of the long street rhythmically. On both sides of the column, standing with their backs pressed against the houses of earth and stone, the fenced walls, the bolted doors, stood the people of the town: slender youngsters, broad-waisted men, old men leaning on their canes, women with babies in their arms, bare-footed children with torn shirts clutching at their parents' clothes—long lines of angry eyes, torn with fear, stricken by shock. On all the roofs, on poles, broken branches, thin bars of iron, hung the white flags of surrender, rags, pieces of torn cloth, infants' diapers.

I kept in the lane, walking and limping as quickly as I could, dragging my sprained foot behind me in order to keep up with the marchers. But the pain grew and increased and pricked through unbearably. My strides slowed down more and more, and I began falling back row after row, trying to march together with every row and separating from it despite myself, until after a little while I found myself at the end of the column. I still tried to catch up with the last row, running and walking, walking and running, but I couldn't catch it up. My two feet were very tired by now, and straggled along with a heavy gait. The distance between me and the advancing line increased, until I formed a sort of line on my own, because from now on the eyes of the large crowd on both sides of the street were turned on me, and the glances of anger or amazement turned to looks of contempt. I saw the column advancing and drawing away from me, and the distance between it and me was like the distance between a drowning man and the ship receding and going on its way.

A low, white city. A great mass of people in tattered clothes, afraid, shaken. A line of soldiers drawing away from me. And I marching, walking and limping on my own.

Suddenly, I saw that all the people at the sides of the houses were drawing close to one another and pouring into the street, and in another minute the crowd closed around me and swallowed me up in it. The broad stream flowed after the column of soldiers, hurried after it to catch it up as if to watch some show or other, and I was drawn along with it, pushed here and there, shoved against, trying to hurry my steps, and to reach the head of the stream, but the crowd pushed more and more until it became a single pressed mass, which moved a little bit forward and then stood quite still, and I was squeezed inside it from all sides, with all of it a wall between me and my battalion.

I drew myself up on the toes of my sound foot, and beyond the crowd's shoulder I saw a small square, a white house with a dome and arched windows. A lawn, with a fountain in the middle. Two palm trees, and a high pole between them. The column fell in line on three sides of the square. I made another effort to push myself forward and to reach my comrades, elbowing the people standing round me and asking them in a halting language to let me pass, but no one paid any attention and it was impossible to force my way through the dense crowd. I heard brief, brisk commands, the clicking of heels and guns, and then there was a hushed silence. An officer came up to the flagpole, stood with his hands behind his back, and made a quiet speech. At the side of the house with the dome stood a group of old men, broad-shouldered, with khefiyas on their heads and girdles around their waists, blinking because of the sun. The officer finished what he was saying, and a soldier came up to the group and whispered something into the ear of the oldest among them, a man with the bony face of a camel, a long chin and a narrow, prominent forehead lined with wrinkles. His eyes were sunken deep under the bone of his forehead and could hardly be seen. He nodded his head as if he understood, then went up to the flag-pole twirled one end of his mustache and said a few words. His voice was hoarse and shattered. The first two or three sentences came out frantic from his mouth, as if he had learned them by heart. Then, he paused a while, blinked his eyes, and his lips and the ends of his mus-tache quivered. Again, he uttered a few hasty sentences, and then whis-pered something to himself. At last he plucked up courage, said one long sentence, clear and plain, like a sort of blessing, and, when he had finished, looked around him, as if asking whether he should add any-thing. The sound of a command was heard, and a concerted click of heels. Two drums shook the air with quick beats like an alarm, and then a flag was raised up on a string; it climbed up to the top of the flag pole, opened and unfurled, and when it came to rest, waved slightly in the midday breeze.

I looked up at the flag, as did the crowd around me, without pride, without joy. I felt only the paid in my ankle and humiliation at the thought that at a time like this fate had separated me from the victori-ous column.

Again curt commands were heard, which were answered by brisk clicks of heels, and then the crowd began to disperse.

I hurried to limp towards the square in order to find the men from my platoon, but none of them came my way. "Where's everyone going to? Where to?" I asked the soldiers, who had also dispersed in groups and went past me in various directions. They replied that they had been given leave for an hour, to stroll round the streets of the town, and the meeting place afterwards was the school at the end of the main street. They hurried on their way, but because of my limp I could not catch up with any of the group and remained walking by myself.

I entered a narrow street, and before taking many steps in it, some of the city's inhabitants gathered around me. At first some boys fell upon me and held out packets of cigarettes. I took two of the packets and put money in the boys' hands. Then several youngsters came along and began plying me with questions. As I stood and spoke to them in their own language, more people clustered around me, young and old, until there was a large crowd with me in the center. They asked me about the value of our money, the prices of various commodities, what was happening on other fronts of the battle, and I could only answer a few of their questions. Not far from me stood a shaven-pated man with a squashed nose and a split upper lip. He wore broad black pantaloons, and his large soles were encased in coarse, heavy shoes. He stood at the side all the time with legs astraddle, hands folded on his chest, and looking at me with a smile which, because of his deformity, seemed bitter, almost a sneer. When there was a moment of silence, he took two steps towards me and, standing in front of me with his hands folded, he asked me where I came from. I gave the name of my former kibbutz. He blinked a little, as if chasing a fly away, and grimaced, pursing up his thick lips. He asked me if I knew the village of A. "Yes," I smiled, seeing in front of me group of huts the color of red earth, hugging the shoulder of a hill like a nest of wasps, surrounded by crude fences of prickly pear bushes. He asked me if I knew Bergmann's orange grove. For a moment I was speechless. Within me rose the strong intoxicating perfume of the orange blossoms, the sight of the dense dark-green foliage, the cool pools of shade around the tree trunks, the dampness of the earth during the hoeing, the irrigation canals with their ends blocked with wet, rotting sacks, the flies above the dump of rotten fruit, the well house marked with spots of lichen and containing empty boxes, rugs, packing material with a smell of resin, a hill of sandstone on which blue beehives stood tilted on their sides in a field of wild yellow daisies with bees humming around them, the sound of the well being pumped in the great stillness of the afternoon. "Did you work there?" I asked. He didn't answer my question, but mentioned names—Rappaport, Zelkin, Schechtman, Abramski. This was a row of densely-located orange groves lying next to one another along the side of the road. "How is Mr. Yakub?" he asked in my own language. Then he said: "Weeds, right? A lot of weeds there." The people around us stood open-mouthed, as if watching a conjuring show, and waited for me to say something. I was stunned and couldn't say anything in reply, and after my silence became prolonged, they began throwing cries at me from all sides, like stones: "Zeligman!" "Marmorek;" "Tannenbaum!" "Yavne!" "Moskowitz!" Now the close-shaven man smiled a smile of victory. He unfolded his hands and showed me one of the fingers of his left hand, whose upper joint was missing. "That's from a hoe," he said, looking at me as if waiting for my reaction.

I wanted to shake his right hand as a sign that we were friends but at that moment the noise of a jeep was heard dashing in a great hurry from the end of the street. Inside it were men from the military police, and at once the crowd scattered in all directions, like a flock of chickens among which a stone has been thrown. The jeep stopped with a screech of brakes, and one of the soldiers asked me if I hadn't heard the order forbidding fraternization with local inhabitants. I said that I hadn't been at the parade because of my sprained ankle, and that I knew nothing about the order. The other policeman laughed at this in ridicule, and he warned me that I would be liable to arrest if I was seen talking to the people of the city again. I promised that it would not happen any more, and the jeep hurried on its ways, sweeping the people standing in the street to both sides until they were forced against the walls of the houses and stood silent.

I limped to the end of the street, and turned into another one, a broad street of sand and low stone houses. The street was desolated and burning from the afternoon sun, and there was no one in it. My eyes hurt from the white light. There was a smell of salt in the air. I repeated to myself that I was the conqueror, the ruler of the city, but I felt no joy about it. There was a hot vapor over the sky, and this was like an ominous portent, like an eclipse of the sun. When I was halfway along the street, I saw a little girl, about eight or ten, carrying on her back a torn mattress twice as big as herself, which was slipping all over her body in all directions and covering her head. Her bare legs were sunk in the sand, and her back was bent like a bow, until it seemed that her head was touching the ground. I stood still for a moment. There was no one around. A burning silence possessed the street. I lowered the gun on my shoulder and limped towards her. I knew that she was returning from the sand dunes, like many of the city's inhabitants, who had run away there at night. Perhaps she was the only one left in her family, and was going alone to her empty home. She was so small compared to the mattress that bent-up way she was walking, she didn't notice me. I came up to her and said quietly: "Little girl." She lifted her head up slightly, and then her eyes opened in a deathly panic and the mattress slipped off her back, and she began running with all her strength to where she had come from. "Little girl!" I called again, and began stumbling after her, but she increased her speed, like a rabbit fleeing from a hunter, and disappeared in one of the courtyards. I retraced my steps, lifted the mattress on to my shoulders and began walking towards that courtyard. I went in through a wooden gate to a place strewn with donkey dung, where two red-feathered chickens were scratching in the dust with their feet. The chickens fled from me with a frightened cackling, overturning a tin in their flight. I couldn't see the girl. While wondering what I should do with the mattress, I heard from afar an approaching loudspeaker, announcing a curfew from ten until the following morning at ten; everyone found outside his house would be shot at. Four or five times the voice repeated this announcement, each time in a different direction, until it vanished like an echo. The loudspeaker struck terror through the town.

I put my mattress on the ground and stood next to it, not knowing what to do. If I remained in the courtyard, the girl wouldn't find the mattress any more, and if I returned it to its place in the street, someone else would take it, or a car would run over it and ruin it. If I took it with me, I would only be laughed at. I knocked on the door of the house facing the courtyard. No one answered. A shutter of the window was lifted slightly, and immediately shut down loudly. I peered into the street. There was no one in its entire length. It occurred to me that the curfew might be meant for soldiers as well. I left the mattress standing against the wall facing the street. I placed a dry branch next to it, like a policeman guarding it against those who might want to steal it.

I turned back towards the square I had started from, moving along the sides of the houses. But I couldn't find my way. Everything was strange because there were no people around, and the city was shut and silent. The swollen carcasses of yellow dogs lay in the middle of the street, and when I went past them the swarms of flies which hovered over took fright and flew around my head. Here and there lay about, as if after a storm, filthy rags, crushed tins, abandoned pots and pans, limbs of chairs, shreds of wool, scraps of clothing. Pouches of bullets. I went past the shops locked with heavy bolts, past red and green signs, square courtyards surrounded by walls, low dens, houses. The later it got, the more panicky I become. A cold sweat covered my brow and my back, and trickled like ants between my armpits and my calves. My steps were the only sound heard in the street, scraping the stones because of my limp.

At three I reached the school, a whitewashed building two stories high, which stood in a large sandy courtyard, surrounded by a brick wall. Inside there was a great commotion, as if during an assembly parade in the camp. Everyone ran up and down in the corridors, with their knapsacks and equipment, and squeezed into the classrooms, grabbing places to rest and sleep. On the floor lay exercise books, textbooks, crushed pieces of chalk and scraps of food. In the room the pupil's chairs and desks were piled up in the corners, making way for green blankets, sleeping bags, boxes of ammunition, sacks of bread and tins of food. In the room at the end of the corridor, which was the head-quarters, sat now, behind a table covered with green paper, on a high-backed chair, the O.C. of the platoon. On his right exercise books were piled high on top of one another: on his left were three thick books, and in the middle was an inkpot made of horn, a jotting pad, and a tray with paper clips and pins. On the wall behind him hung the picture of a man with a magnificent grey beard, with wavy hair surrounding his bald pate, a short nose and tightly-clenched lips; underneath was the word DARWIN.

I explained to the O.C. the reason for my being so late and showed him my swollen ankle. After he had reprimanded me, as was his duty, he sent for a medical orderly. The orderly came, and led me behind him to a small room, in the corner of which stood a pile of books. I removed my shoe, and after he had examined my foot, which was swollen as if from a bee-sting, he brought a bucket, poured a kettle of hot water into it, and told me to bathe my foot in it. Among the unintelligible lines were strewn chemical formulas and sketches of bottles, test tubes and joined instruments. A hand cut off at the root held a candle over the mouth of a test tube, and over it was written: CO_2. A glass bowl gave off vapors from its neck. A small bottle hung above a spirit lamp. Smoke issued from the end of a wooden stick. A pestle and mortar stood on a narrow shelf. A woman in a chemist's apron held a flame in front of her. Through the door, in the corridor, soldiers carrying guns hurried up and down.

The medical orderly returned, felt my ankle, buried his fingers in the soft, white flesh, rubbed the bone at the joint, took hold of the heel and moved the whole leg backwards and forwards, and then said: "There's nothing wrong with you. But to make you happy, I'll put a splint on you. Lie down for a few hours, and then you'll get up a new man." He bandaged my foot, and told me to go into the next room. This had been the teacher's common room, and contained two high black tables. I placed the tables next to one another, took my sleeping-bag out of my knapsack, climbed up, squeezed myself inside and lay down.

The night of the battle now seemed something very remote, which had taken place a long time ago, half real, half a dream. A night of lightning and storm which had passed and calmed suddenly. A night without fear. Like a fireworks display in the sky. And the night was clean, and its showers purifying, leaving behind them a fresh smell in the air. A short but eventful holiday night, in the hot, hazy, endless desert of sameness.

But this was far away, a long, long time ago. And now the city was white, besieged, and I was trapped within it. And the burning, heavy skies, over which a sort of white fog had spread. And the awe of the hostile eyes along the houses. And the deep sand. And the filth of the corpses and the flies and the rags. And the sight of the people whose faces were like nightmares. And the feathers hanging on the barbs of the wire fences, as if after riots. And the scream of the little girl who had thrown the mattress away and run . . .

And the heavy skies, which boded ill, as if locusts were coming from the desert in enormous, countles swarms, covering the face of the sun and laying everything waste . . .

I wanted an earthquake to come suddenly and destroy all the houses and leave nothing alive—and one wouldn't be able to run away . . .

And now there was this school, with dust on its floors and exercise books lying strewn about the corridors and in the class-rooms. And the idle books in their piles. And the pieces of white chalk, crushed underneath the hobnailed boots. And the inkwell at rest.

The plaster of the ceiling was peeling in various wide-bayed islands. On the wall opposite hung a map of the country, with arrows pointing towards it from all sides. In Jerusalem was struck a pole on which flew a green flag with a star and crescent; it blew over the whole country. I felt no pain in my ankle. I sank into slumber.

I woke up to the sound of a cry. A man's cry, stunned, wild, broad, far away. And two shots cutting into it, one after the other, and the sound of voices receding outside. It was dark. "Who's there?" came a loud voice, angry and scolding, from nearby. I raised myself on my elbow. Beside me lay two other men, in their sleeping bags. "What happened?" I asked. The two of them also raised themselves. "An attack?" one of them asked. "They must have fired on the patrol," the other one said. The steps of four or five men hurried through the court-yard and receded. And then voices speaking, quickly and briefly, as if giving orders. "They can wipe us out as easy as anything," the one furthest away from me whispered. "One really big bomb in this building and we're finished." Then there was silence, and I heard only the hum of the sea.

The steps came close again, but were slower and quieter. Someone inside asked what had happened. And a voice answered him from out-side: "Go back to sleep. Some nut thought they were aiming a gun at him from one of the houses. What an idiot!" A rustle of laughter went through the rooms. There was silence again, and the steps of two men walking in the courtyard calmly. "What's the time?" I asked. "About half past one. Go to sleep."

I tried to fall asleep, but couldn't. On the previous night, in the noise of the battle and the quake of the fire, I had not known fear. But now there was this silence. A great black silence which covered the whole city, blanketing it from all sides, tense as a bowstring, strangling cries, hiding eyes that looked out of their sockets. A hostile silence, which would soon tumble down like a high wall and bury us under it. If it wasn't for the silence, I said to myself, my courage would come back to me. But the fear of silence. Deep and black like an abyss.

And perhaps in the morning the whole mass would rise up against us in order to avenge its violated honor. Young and old, women and children would attack us, and we would retreat, one step after the other, until there would be nowhere to retreat to, and their pitchforks would be sunk in our flesh. A dog's death.

And the night of the fire would be like a shooting star flashing by in the darkness for an instant and melting and fading in eternity and nothing would be left of it.

Again there were measured strides in the sand. A watchman's steps. If the crowd did not attack us the next day, it would do it the day after, or the day after that. Or a week later. It had to happen. Some time, and not far off. A great mass of people. Thousands, tens of thousands, like locusts from the desert. Thirsting for blood, shouting for murder, drawing knives for the slaughter, the rod of their anger. No mercy.

And if the miracle should take place, and I returned alive? Where would I return to? From after, from beyond the mountain, I would always hear the sound of the crowd, like the flutter of locusts coming from the desert. Soon they would cover the face of the sun, and there would be darkness at noon . . .

I covered my head with the fold of the sack against these thoughts, but they crawled inside, like ants, like beetles, making my flesh creep.

When the first ray of dawn filtered in through the window, I got up. The soldiers were sleeping a tired sleep, and their faces were pale. The young men were children, and the old men were fathers. The young men did not know evil, and the older ones only knew worry. They lay in rows, rib to rib, wrapped in black and green blankets, up to the shoulders, up to the neck, up to the eyes, over their heads. Eyelashes pale as dawn. A hand covering an unshaven cheek. Hands crossed on a chest. Hands folded on a chest. A mustache quivering with breathing. An open, swollen mouth. A pinched mouth. A beard glistening like dewdrops. A worried, unrested brow. An innocent, peaceful brow. The breath of dreams. And there, somewhere, women were getting up in the house to kindle the first fire, to make food for the child. Babies waking up crying in their beds. Milkmen cycling from house to house. Women hugging their pillows. The steps of an early-rising worker, walking alone in the street.

The soldiers lay sleeping in long lines, and there was no war in their faces: children and fathers, and husbands and the vapors of their breath as if they were at home. The breathing of the morning like the spirit of a dream, hovering over the tired men.

I walked alone in the empty school, along the deserted corridor. In the second wing of the building were the empty classrooms. Rows of small tables and chairs, all facing the blackboard, on which was written in chalk:

$$28 : 4 = 7$$
$$32 : 4 = 8$$
$$36 : 4 = 9$$
$$40 : 4 = 10$$

I stopped at the threshold and could not take my eyes off the blackboard. All the sums were correct. The numbers were so innocent that they were the complete opposition of war. Abandoned and ignored, the blackboard gazed at the empty room and at the moment it seemed as if nothing in the world was sadder than an empty classroom.

In the next room two pictures of the human body, one flesh and blood, and one a skeleton, hung on the walls. One all muscle, muscles which were pink and tense, thick, tied to one another tightly by sinews, one above the other, and one below the other. A mighty man, proud of his strength. And the second one was the Angel of Death. A bald skull, with two gaping holes, a squat nose, clenched teeth laughing cruelly, a chin pointing forwards, and underneath this, the neck bones like a spring, the collarbone like an iron axle, hollow ribs like a camel's skeleton, things like the flat stones by the seashore, and very long hands, with heavy fingers, tied together with screws, held out towards someone unseen. On the one side was hung the diagrams of the heart, with its various chambers and its several arteries, as in a butcher's shop, the insides with their intestines writhing like earthworms, the kidneys and the spleen swollen, the lungs, the eyes, the ear drums, the brain, placed like a folded embryo, half plant, half swollen sponge.

In the pale morning light, in the desolation of the empty classroom, in which slivers of white dust covered the small tables and the black inkwells in them—the two people on the wall looked lonely and bewildered. The muscular man stood with his back to the room, with only half his face showing. His one foot was forward, touching the ground with the tips of his toes, and the other foot rested on its heel, like an athlete maintaining his balance. His face looked as if it was afraid to look inside, and the hands, which were held outstretched, at the sides of the body, seemed helpless. The skeleton man was filled with dread, not like a man carrying death but like a man who has a terrible fear of death. And the eye sockets, the cheekbones, the rows of teeth, which chattered against one another, as if from cold, wanted to cry out in a cry which was frozen in the bones, fossilized. The hollows of the ribs and the holes of the thighs were shocked by their emptiness. And the very long hands, like pitchforks, asked a question—like the burghers of Calais, when they handed over the keys of the city.

In a third room the chairs and tables were thrown about as if after a wild fight, and the teacher's chair was overthrown. But in an eternal peace, like the peace of grey morning skies, a map of the world looked down from the wall. This was the map in which two ellipses kiss one another, the eastern hemisphere and the western hemisphere. The map from Grade Four, when the world is still a mist-wrapped mystery and life the discovery of latent wonders. The great oceans, so clear and blue, endlessly broad, so that their horizons cannot be seen. The Pacific Ocean, so tranquil and foggy on both sides of the continents. The Atlantic Ocean, in the centre of the world, was cut in half by the two spheres, and the lines of latitude and longitude in it seemed to indicate the paths of the many ships. Columbus, Magellan. Twenty thousand leagues under the sea. The warm Indian Ocean, whose waves washed the shore of the jungles. The South Pole. The huge continent of white ice. Captain Scott. Snow blizzards. Starvation. Pages of a diary lying about on the snow. The narrow North Pole, squeezed against the axis. Captain Byrd. Eskimos. Sharks. Whales. The equator and the sun traveling above it, around the earth, above dense primeval forests swarming with monkeys and snakes, above deserts of golden sand in which lions walked with quiet and terrifying tread. The Tropic of Cancer, along which the crabs ran on the land and in the sea, surrounding the whole earth. The Tropic of Capricorn, along which the goats leaped on the surface of the water. America, a large country of trains and herds of cattle and large cities. America of Charlie Chaplin and Shirley Temple. And of a girl called Suzie who spoke English and chewed gum during lessons and had a red bicycle at home and a yo-yo which jumped up and down at the end of a string, and the largest collection of stamps in the world. America, the country in which they rake in gold and lifts go up and down the buildings and the people wear checked trousers, puffed up below the knees, sing Valencia, Valencia, and bang with their suede shoes on the smooth tiles. The great, much-desired America, stretching from ocean to ocean. And the many numbers at the edge of the semi-circles, outside the world, in the ether which surrounded it. Oh, for a morning like this, and a large map on the wall. And children dreaming of the strange, peaceful world, open as the heavens, enveloped in mystery.

The teacher's stool had fallen over, and the inkwell rolled among the upturned benches. On the floor, next to the blackboard, on which traces of a damp rag had made zigzag and blurred streets of chalk, lay two pieces of chalk, one white and one red. I picked up the white piece and wrote on the blackboard, in Latin characters:

MOON

and put the chalk down on the side of the board.

Then I went up to the roof. From there I could see the whole city. Flat roofs, narrow, mysterious streets. Courtyards. A chill ran through my body, and my shoulders shook. The white flags were still hanging loose at the heads of the poles and bars. The sky was cloudy, and a silent, quivering air from a cool breeze hung over the city and the sand dunes all around it. The town's shutters were pulled down and there was not a soul to be seen inside or outside. Among the red fences a dog padded slowly, walking along and sniffing. Inside the fences, in the courtyards, the sand had been swept by the night wind, and out of it projected pitted stones, dry, leafless stalks, ill-clad scarecrows, faded patches of cabbage, rusty tin hovels. On the far side were square land holdings, checkerboard fashion, surrounded by prickly pear hedges. In the streets, here and there, were tall, dark, palm trees. From afar, the salty sea air was wafted. There wasn't a person around. Only in the sealed houses did men, women and children, clad in rags, breathe the breath of a pale hour, the last before the morning rose.

As I went down to the corridor, I picked up an exercise book which had fallen creased and trampled, on the floor. I opened it and read. In a round, shaky child's hand was written:

$$11 \times 5 = 55$$
$$11 \times 6 = 66$$
$$11 \times 7 = 77$$

4

In the middle of the day when the sun was already high in the sky stoking up the white houses and the yellow sand, the officer commanding the platoon called me to the headquarters tent and asked me if I still felt pain in my foot. I said that the ankle had returned to position, and everything was all right. He asked if I was ready to go to the refugee camp and relieve one of the guards. "Yes, officer," I said. I took my gun and went off.

The curfew was in force, and the white city was empty, apart from the patrols of soldiers, which marched up and down the streets in twos or threes, looking like lonely trees in the desert in their green uniforms. I went past the same courtyard which I had entered the previous day. The mattress lay there in its place, as I had left it. When I came to the end of the unpaved street, and went up on to the sand hill, the camp appeared in front of me. It was an enormous block of dense tin dwellings, piled up on top of one another and touching, like tabernacles in the desert. In front of it, between the huts and a long barbed wire concertina fence, a great congregation of men, women and children squatted on the sand. Next to the fence stood five soldiers, with their guns aimed at the feet of the squatting people. Behind them was a small house, surrounded by a fence. A burning silence hung in the air, cut every two or three minutes by the short sharp whistles of bullets.

I wondered what they were shooting at, and only after standing there for some time did I understand. The crowd was hungry, and in the small building they were handing out rations of flour and oil. Every now and then someone in the yard called out the name of a clan and the name of the village from which the clan had come. When they heard this, all the people of the village in question rose together, old and young alike, holding one another's clothes, with sacks and bags in their hands, hurrying impatiently to burst through to the other side of the barbed wire. The din of women's cries and babies' screams arose for a moment, and the collapse of people stumbling and being stampeded on. Then the shots threw the crowd back to its place, until the silence was restored.

Again I heard the whistle of bullets, but only in order to frighten. Now the roll-call of clans and villages could clearly be heard in the midday silence. Family after family passed the narrow strip between the barbed wire barrier and the yard, flurried, bent and shirking, as if running on hot coals, holding one another, children hiding behind their fathers' backs as they passed under the butts of the guns, and the babies hiding their heads in their mothers' bosoms. When they reached the courtyard, they breathed in relief, as if grasping the horns of the altar at last.

When the names of the villages were heard, the villages of the coastal plain, one sight after another passed in front of me. The sight of thick, dark orange groves with the damp, hoed earth luxuriant with long-stalked creepers, twisting around age-old trunks spotted with lichen. The sight of fields of millet, shining in the sun, rustling in the afternoon wind. The sight of threshing floors and camels turning with panniers laden with stones. The sight of a market with its booths laden with slabs of juicy dates, loaves of sun-dried figs, jars of lemonade and honey water, surgary sweets, roasted chestnuts, dried apricot rolls. The sight of broad-waisted men wearing girdles, walking slowly, heavy with possessions. The sight of women in green dresses walking from the wells, upright like stalks and carrying jars on their heads.

Then I felt in my nostrils the smell of fine chaff, thrown with a wooden pitchfork, flying in the hot khamsin, and the smell of smoke and dung coming from afar, from the huts of sun-baked mud.

For a long time I stood like this, and the crowd of people squatting on the sand, so densely-packed, now looked very tired, like sheep fainting in the midday heat. The babies' heads hung on their mothers' shoulders, and the congregation was dozing. Only a very faint humming in the air, like the rustle of leaves in an olive grove in the heat of the day. The soldiers were also too lazy to shoot.

From the top of the hill on which I stood the sight of the crowd squatting shoulder to shoulder, in its rags and white dresses, looked like a very ancient sight, from the time of the great desert. And dread hovered over it, as a falcon hovers in the sky, seeking its prey. For a moment, it seemed to me that the commanding officer had told me: "Come now therefore, curse me this people and extinguish it." And I stood at the head of the abyss, looking towards the desert, and saw the people lying there according to their tribes. I answered him: "Let my last end be like this." I was afraid to approach, and stood silent on the top of the hill, with the great noon around me.

But suddenly, I don't know how (perhaps something had been announced without me hearing it), the whole crowd rose and moved forward with a great cry and burst towards the barbed wire barrier, and the soldiers ran hither and thither to stop them, hitting with the butts of their guns to left and right, shouting loudly, and amidst this shots were heard and the crowd retreated like a herd of cattle, falling back to its place, and when all the voices died down I saw a little girl fluttering in the sand like a slaughtered chicken weltering in its own blood.

Everything was silent now, and only a faint wailing could be heard from somewhere, like the chirp of a wounded bird, and in the air of the blazing noon the wailing circled round the heads of the squatting people, flying among the sand dunes, coming closer and then receding again, until it died away.

Then I saw a man climbing towards me through the sand. He walked barefoot, had long black hair, and wore a cloth robe, like a villager. He was young, about my age, only slightly taller and slimmer in build. When he reached me he stood calmly and gazed together with me at the large city of tabernacles, stretched out in the wilderness, and at the crowd squatting in it in dreadful silence.

In a whisper, so as not to disturb the silence, he asked me why I did not proceed to carry out what I had been ordered to do. I told him I was afraid. Without looking at me he said that he had seen me on the night of the battle, and I had been as brave as a tiger. I said that then it had been dark, and in the sparks of fire it was impossible to see human faces. "Aren't you happy that you are the conqueror?" he asked me. "No" I answered, "there is no happiness in my heart." Then he asked me whether I loved my enemies. "They are hungry," I said, gesturing towards the crowd. He asked if I would like to be in their place. I thought a long moment about it, and then replied that I would not want to be among those guarding them with guns in their hands. "Are they so bad?" he asked, motioning with his head towards the line of soldiers. "No," I hastened to reply, "no, they are only doing their rightful duty." "Aren't you better than them?" he asked. "No," I replied, "certainly not. It's just that I haven't enough courage to see people suffer." Now, for the first time, he turned his head to me with a smile, put his hand on my shoulder and said: "Are you ashamed of that?" "Yes," I nodded my head, and a shudder ran through my body. "That's not good" he said. And after a short pause he added quietly: "Go and do your duty."

Now I was more afraid to move my place. I repeated in a whisper and with quivering lips, as if pleading for my life, that I was afraid of the crying of a hungry or frightened child. That I couldn't stand it. "Aren't all the little children equal?" I asked. "Yes, they are," he said quietly, "but now go and do your duty."

The two of us stood and observed the silent crowd.

Suddenly he disappeared. There was only the burning sand around me, and the city of tabernacles hugged by the dunes.

5

Tht next day, at three in the afternoon, I was summoned to the Military Governor. When I entered the house with the dome in the central square, and went into the room, which was shrouded in semidarkness, I was taken aback to see B. sitting in the arm-chair behind the table. Apparently he didn't recognize me, because without looking at me he gestured to me to sit down on one of the chairs, next to four other men who had apparently come for the same purpose. I tried to catch his eye and to hint to him with a smile that we were old acquaintances and that it was a happy occasion when old friends met under these circumstances, so different from those we had known previously, and so binding in comradeship. But he was busy giving orders to the people coming in and going out, some of them soldiers and others inhabitants of the city, and paid no attention to those who were sitting and waiting for him. On his table stood a copper tray, on which was a coffee pot and six blue china cups, a polished shell casing, a large sea-shell ashtray and a pile of official forms. To the people of the city he spoke in their own language, and these coming to him one after the other, heard his orders with great submission, bowing slightly, straining themselves not to miss a single word that left his mouth and uttering only a few short sentences indicating agreement or confirmation, or posing some practical question or other. On leaving the room they put their hands on their hearts and bowed a little, with a smile on their lips, or touched their foreheads lightly with their open palms. He spoke to them in a fluent and business-like way, without any formalities, as a man would speak to a colleague of his, and without emphasizing his superior office. Like the manager of a company, he gave instructions about operating the water pump, the electric power station, the bakery, and other things which affect the vital needs of a city. This simple, almost friendly, way of talking to the men of the conquered city, which gave him a charm I had not noticed in him before, aroused great affection in me and increased my desire to attract his attention. If I can only find the right opportunity I said to myself, I will express to him feelings of appreciation for behaving in such a humane manner towards the inhabitants of the city, who are now his subjects. I thought in addition that I would draw his attention to the question of the refugees who should be treated with more sympathy so as to avoid unnecessary suffering. In his army uniform, with two fig leaves glistening on his shoulders, one on each, he looked sturdy and strong, and at the same time not like a regular military man, perhaps because of his shirt, which was not tightly clasped to his body, but hung rather carelessly, and perhaps because of his short grey hair and the look on his face, which displayed no tension, but a sort of alertness to everyday civilian affairs.

Eventually he sent all the supplicants away, ordered his aide to close the door and to remove everybody from the vicinity of the building, and, putting his arms on the table, he turned to us. "The inhabitants are cooperating in general, isn't that so?" he said with a smile, passing his gaze from one to another, as if seeking our confirmation of something we had just witnessed. He still didn't seem to realize who I was, because although I returned to him a smile full of agreement, and more than that, even filled with admiration, he didn't let his gaze linger on me. The others uttered a few words of agreement, both expressive of contempt for the local inhabitants and praise for military strength. "Will you have some coffee?" he asked, clasping the neck of the coffee pot. All of us smiled with pleasure, because hot Turkish coffee was a real luxury after the foul and lukewarm drinks we had been given the last few days. He poured coffee into the porcelain cups, and handed one cup to each of us with his own hands. "The stocks of food that we found in their army stores are enough for the whole country for a few months," he said, as we sipped the coffee. We laughed with him, and two of us added some descriptions drawn from their own experience. When we had finished drinking his face took on a serious expression, and he said: "This is about a rather unpleasant job. We have obtained a detailed list of the gangs in the city. I don't need to explain to you who they are and what their activities have been during the last few years: infiltrating, sabotaging, spying, killing, pillaging and so on. This list contains 32 people at present. Well . . ."

The rest of his words reached me like a distant hum. He said that we had to go from house to house, according to the list of addresses, to arrest the people and to take them in lorries to a place outside the city where they would be kept. When night fell we would have to finish them off. He added that the operation was secret and no one apart from us was supposed to know anything about it. We would receive more detailed orders during the course of the operation.

"Any questions?"

There was a long silence, which blended with the silence of the city, sunk in curfew, on the other side of the barbed window. Outside the stifling afternoon heat lay on the pavements like a tired dog in the doorway of a house. I felt that my face had gone very pale; my knees shook and my insides quivered. With all my heart I hoped for something, some miracle, which would avert the operation or release me from it. At first, when I entered the room, I had a feeling of pride that I had been chosen for the job, about which I hadn't known yet, and that I was one of a small group of five, which included a sergeant-major, two captains and lieutenant. When I saw B. I had been happy that in one operation we would be working together, bound by a link which could be everlasting, even in days to come as well. He was a man of duty, and when he spoke I knew that was only doing the right thing, which could not be avoided. But now I was caught up in a trap. The choice was not in my hands. I had to do a thing more terrible than I had ever done; but this was my rightful duty.

"What will happen if someone displays resistance" the sergeant-major asked.

"I hope this won't happen. I really hope not," B. Said. "But that's what guns are for, isn't that so?"

The two captains sniggered.

"How will we find the addresses?" the sergeant-major asked.

"That's a good question," B. said. "You will be accompanied by one of the inhabitants. You can trust him."

"He's probably the person who gave you the list," one of the captains said.

"Allow me not to answer that question," he said. "Anything else?"

The four of them looked at one another and then at me. As if it was my turn to ask something. A shudder ran through my shoulders, I saw clearly that I could not escape the inevitable and couldn't stop at the edge of the abyss. That no miracle was going to happen. I was a soldier, and my duty was to carry out orders. Fear was not to taken into account, and to reveal it meant surrendering one's honor. A badge of shame for all my life. Were there any moral considerations? The gangs had to be wiped out, that was plain. Not only as a punishment, but in order to prevent disasters, clashes, murder.

My lips quivered.

"You said that we had to finish them off," I stammered in a faint voice. "Do you mean to kill them?"

B. sneered. It seemed to me that only then had he recognized me, and identified me with the man who had told him that he could not commit evil because he was afraid of the pangs of his conscience. As he didn't reply to my question, and the silence grew longer, I understood that I had uttered a hopeless slip of the tongue which had only aroused contempt or pity. I felt that the others, like him, thought me to be a fool for this reason, and were sure that it was a mistake to have chosen me as one of the five for this operation, which required men who knew what they were in for and understood much more than was said to them explicitly, and who were ready to carry out commands without hesitation and weakness. In addition to my previous fear, although it seemed opposed to it, I was now seized by fear that they would remove me from the operation.

"Any more questions?" B. threw a glance at all of us.

The others straightened up in their seats, as if indicating that they were ready to go off to action and everything was clear.

B. leaned backwards, and throwing a glance at the sergeant-major, he said:

"As I said before, this isn't the pleasantest of jobs. If any of you feels that it's not for him, because of a soft heart or moral inhibitions (he said these words with a contemptuous sneer, from which I realized that he was referring to me), or anything else, he has the choice of getting out of it, of simply saying, 'leave me out'. That's all. There will be no complaints. Of course, the order of secrecy will fall upon him afterwards as well."

Again there was silence, and although none of those present turned his head to me, I felt that they were waiting for me to reply. This was the fateful moment. The choice lay in my hands, and this was harder to bear than the state of no choice which preceded it. I had to decide. If I were to announce that I was withdrawing, I would forfeit my honor in B.'s eyes and the eyes of the four other men, whom I didn't even know. Perhaps this would never become known to more than this small number of people, although it could be supposed that one day the veil of secrecy over the operation would be lifted and my shame would become public knowledge. In any event, in B.'s eyes I would always remain a coward and a fool who would not succeed in any man's job. And B. was not only one man, but most of the society in which I lived. How would I be able to hold my head up afterwards? On the other hand if I did not withdraw, I would have to do something whose horror would haunt me all the rest of my life. I didn't know which of the two evils was worse . . .

"Well, then, everything is quite clear now," B. said, and leaning his fist on the table, he rose from his place.

All of us rose after him. Everything was plain, as the choice had been taken out of my hands.

When we stood in the square, the empty streets of the city glittered in front of us, white and still. After a few minutes the truck came and stopped next to us. Beside the driver sat one of the townspeople, his face covered by a filthy khefiya which hid his head to the forehead, throat and mouth. Only his nose could be seen and his black, hooded, frightened eyes.

At first the operation proceeded quietly. So quietly that the fear which had seized me when in B.'s presence was almost wiped from my heart. We would knock on the door of the house, go inside, call the name of the man we were looking for, inform him that he was wanted for questioning, tie his hands behind his back with a handkerchief or a piece of cloth, throw him into the truck, which was covered with a tarpaulin, and continue on our way. In the house there would be only shock, a silent shock, without any cry of protest or weeping, and the arrested people, all young men, accepted their fate without any opposition, silently, although with the silence of resistance, in which there was a sort of threat of revenge, which would come. Slowly I took heart, saying to myself that this was only a routine action, part of the reality of the first days of any conquest. I even avoided thinking about the last stage of the operation, which I would have to go through at the end. The knock on the door, the entry into the dark room, the firm but dry announcement by the sergeant-major about the arrest, the man's presenting himself, the silence of the relatives, who received it as the decree of fate, the click of our hob-nailed boots on the floor of the courtyard, then on the pavement, the lifting of the prisoner into the truck, throwing him on to the floor—all this was done with such polished efficiency and speed that it seemed more like a military exercise in the training camp than an act which had latent in it certain cruelty. The feeling of routine was augmented by the behavior of the sergeant-major, who sat next to me in the lorry: a short, fat fellow, with a bright face sprinkled with large freckles. For him it was a form of amusement, and during our journey he cracked jokes with the prisoners, spoke to them in

Hebrew, made fun of them in Yiddish, asked stupid questions about their wives, promised them all the delights of life in the next world, and enjoyed the fact that they didn't understand a single word of what he was saying. In the semi-darkness inside the lorry we couldn't make out their faces.

Only when we came to the sixth house did the feeling of terror grip me again. The door was opened by an old man, short in stature, most of whose face was covered by the bristles of a white beard; his blue eyes were round and open like two lakes. Behind him, on the bed, lay a heap of rags, out of which peeped a little face, creased like sun-dried figs. An old woman lay there wrapped up in her tatters. A smell of chaff and of chicken droppings befouled the air. When the sergeant-major called the name of the person we wanted, the old man's face began shaking nervously as if saying no. The man was apparently deaf and perhaps aslo dumb, because no matter how loud the sergenat-major shouted he didn't answer, but only went on shaking his head. We were ordered to search the house, and overturned everything in it, including the bed, out of which the old woman rolled with a faint squeak. Only after searching the courtyard did we find the person we were looking for, hiding in the dog's kennel. The sergeant-major aimed his gun at him and threatened to shoot him if he wouldn't emerge, but he didn't budge. He was crouched on his belly, and when he looked at us, as we stood on the threshold of the kennel, he shrank still further, holding on with his fingers to the rear wall. The sergeant-major fired a burst of bullets into the ground in front of the kennel. The body inside shuddered slightly, but did not move. Then two of us crawled inside and dragged him away from the wall, by force. He was as heavy as a sack full of stones. When we stood him on his feet, we saw before us a boy of fourteen or fifteen. Black, smooth hair hung over his forehead, and his face was elongated and soft, like a plum. His eyes were red, and when they looked at us they glittered with stubborn resistance. I was taken aback by the look on his young face, and, holding his arm tightly, I said quietly to the sergeant-major, who stood on my left:

"Must be a mistake."

"No mistake. Take him away," he said impatiently, making a gesture as if chasing away a chicken.

"He's only a child," I repeated, nodding my head in his direction.

"Not a child. They're all the same," he continued, repeating the same gesture with his hand.

"Perhaps it's worth while checking," I whispered.

"I said take him away," he shouted. "All of a sudden he's taking pity on them!"

"Not taking pity," I said, still holding my ground, "but a mistake in name can take place . . ."

"Then why did he hide there?" he shouted.

"Perhaps he saw us coming and was afraid," I said.

"And why was he afraid? Why?"

"Seeing soldiers, he became frightened."

"Whom are you taking pity on? On whom?" He lost his patience with me. "And if there's been a mistake, so what? So another one will go? In war you don't examine identity cards. Do what you're told, that's all. Take him away."

The boy stuck to the ground like a stubborn root, and we had to hit him with the butts of our guns in order to drag him out of the courtyard. When we carried him away from there in our arms we could still see the old man, standing in the door of the house shaking his head nervously all the time, as if saying no, no, no.

Apparently, despite the curfew, word of the arrests had gone from house to house, in some mysterious way, because from now on the people were not given up of their own accord, but hid in holes, in attics, in outhouses. From time to time the whistle of bullets flew overhead in the silent city. I felt a terrible weakness, so much so that my hands would not answer me, and I felt sick in my stomach, as I had felt once when a boy, after I had tried to kill a chicken in the courtyard and the knife had been very blunt. The thought of the young boy who had been caught didn't leave me for a moment. It was clear that this was a mistake, on our part or on the part of the informer, but, whatever the reason, this mistake would cost the boy his life. When we sat in the lorry I didn't take my eyes off him, and I felt that I was personally responsible for him, in charge of him, as it were. But he didn't look at me. He sat hunched up, retired into himself, his head between his knees. Only his narrow back could be seen, the back of an adolescent boy, rounding over the curves of the shoulders, the spine protruding prominently with its joint continuing towards the narrow, smooth and swarthy neck. The thought that I wasn't doing anything to save him, that I didn't have the courage of doing this, to rebel against by commanding officer or at least to demand firmly an examination of the question in the first place, made me hate myself, and then filled me with a single desire to sleep. To forget. To throw myself down somewhere and to sink into a deep sleep. I carried out the commands without thinking, my limbs moving like those of a puppet.

When we came to the last house, the ninth, there stood in front of us a young, clear-faced woman, with two pigtails, thick as ropes, hanging down her back. At first she tried to smile at us and charm us with her beauty, but when she saw the sergeant-major aiming a gun at her father, she fell at his feet, embraced his ankles and swore to God that they didn't know where her brother was. He kicked her, and she rolled on to the floor, and when he saw a grimace of pain in my face, he cried: "She's breaking your heart, isn't she? See if she isn't lying, the bitch." And he was right, because after a few minutes we found the man, hiding in the hay in the attic. When we returned to the lorry, hot and breathing heavily from exhaustion and excitement, he burst out at me: "They're all like that, the bastards! Go and believe them when they swear by God. Do they have a god, those carrion?"

Now we went off to dump the load of prisoners at the concentration site. The road lay past the entire length of the silent city, left it and ran between the sand dunes, stopping before a long, yellow, oblong building with a rounded tin roof. On the other side of the building was the compound, surrounded by petrol drums and a barbed wire block. When we arrived there with our nine prisoners, fifteen or twenty others already sat on the ground together. All of them had their hands tied behind their backs, and their bodies were bent forward. Three soldiers stood next to the fence, holding guns.

We pushed the nine men inside the enclosure, and then the sergeant-major ordered me to stay with the guards. He and the three other men climbed into the lorry again and went off towards the city.

The sun was already sloping towards the horizon, and its rays gave a purple tinge to the silken waves of sand and the faces of the people squatting in the enclosure. Some of them were as black as Negroes, with ball-shaped heads and hair as curled as rings of iron wire, with slant eyes and mousy pupils. Some had smooth boylike faces, with tender mustaches soft with down and swarthy arms like rolls of copper, with round elbows. Others were stalwart, broad-shouldered, muscular, strong-faced, with feet as large as spades. Some were squat-nosed, harelipped, pockmarked, their faces gnawed by the climate and disease. Others had thin noses and sloping hairy cheeks, set in long faces, and their heads on their chests; others whispered prayers to themselves, and others never took their eyes off us, with a harsh, rebellious look. There was the boy whom we had caught in the kennel, his hair falling over his forehead, as if he was returning from a wild game in the street; his eyes were small now, looking in front of them, like the eyes of a child who has been injured and is plotting to take revenge against his enemies.

The sun set, and a soft silence settled down over the curves of the dunes, with only a passing rustle of sand being heard from time to time. It was a calm twilight hour, and those people crouching down in the compound, who did not know of their impending doom, were like a community of worshippers. The pink light illuminated their faces, and when they looked towards the horizon whose light had died away, they were like dreamers. Sadness descended upon the stretches of sand, and I seemed to hear a distant tune shivering in the still space. It was their last hour, and again the same man appeared before me, wearing the white robe of a villager and barefoot, approached them and whispered something. I heard words whispered like the rustling of the stand: "Our Father which art in heaven, Hallowed by Thy name. Thy kingdom come Thy will be done in earth, as it is in heaven."

After about an hour, when the last light died upon the hills, and the evening shadows lay in the hollows, the lorry returned, followed by a jeep. Three soldiers jumped out of it, and marching briskly towards us, observed the prisoners—who tensed in foreboding, as if wondering what was coming—strode to and fro, consulted one another in a whisper, asked something, went back to the sergeant-major, who took his five prisoners off the truck and ordered something curtly, and at this the sound of a loud shout was heard, and all the sitting men rose to their feet at once, and while they were pushed against one another, the soldiers urged them on in order to force them into the building.

Three of us were called into the building, and I remained outside. The door was slammed to, and a few minutes later, after what seemed like a very long time. I heard a rapid burst of fire and the sound of shattered groans.

But only for a minute, because at once everything became silent again.

6

In the third watch of the following night I went out on patrol, together with an old private named Rivkin. It was completely dark in the city, and cold ruled the streets. We walked side by side, hugging the walls of the buildings, tightening the scarves round our necks and drawing our heads in between our shoulders. Our measured strides thudded on the pavement, and their dull echo followed us, spread to the alleyways and died away among the houses.

"There'll be rain tomorrow," I said.

"It's about time," said Rivkin. "The fields need it badly."

"Did you manage to sow?" I said.

"Yes, I did."

In my imagination I saw him tramping down water-soaked furrows with his rubber boots, striding with broad steps from one furrow to another. He was about fifty, short, broad-shouldered and energetic. He had a squarish face, in the center of which was a dense, colorless mustache, half grey, half white. His eyes were narrow and alert, always peering around inquisitively, hurrying to catch everything around them, in case they missed something, and when they smiled creases gathered at their corners, in the corners of his full lips, and then even his mustache shrank up and laughed. His hands and feet were always busy, walking, fetching, handing, doing something. During the three days we were together, there wasn't a single person we met who didn't call him by his name, if only to show their affection for him or to win some humorous remark from his lips. They called him an old warhorse, since there wasn't a war for which he hadn't volunteered or that he hadn't forced his way into, like this war, for which he had left his farm and his wife and two daughters. But the image one had of Rivkin was more that of a work mule than of a warlike horse. The officers treated him with a certain amount of affectionate ridicule; but instead of minding this he used to ignore them, pointing out, half angrily and half jokingly, that they were novices and he was a veteran at the game. The privates never missed an opportunity of making friends with him, because he was always cheerful.

"There is good soil around here," he said. "But these people don't know how to make use of it."

"I've seen some well-cultivated plots," I said.

"Yes, next to the houses, but farther away they are fallow. They sow barley where they could have grown vegetables."

"There's probably a scarcity of water."

"There is water in the ground, but they don't pump it up. They should be taught some things."

"Meanwhile the vegetable gardens are dying," I said, "because of the curfew."

"It won't last much longer," he said. "Just a few days more. A week at the most. War is war."

We walked to the end of the street, and from there we turned into another street, whose two narrow pavements almost touched one another. Among the low houses, with their flat roofs, stood a broad house with a dome, on the side of which was a narrow, high tower. Behind it was an empty plot of ground, on which stood black shapes. We stopped and looked around us. The shapes did not move: apparently they were poles and barrels. Complete silence reigned as our steps died away.

"It's cold," said Rivkin, rubbing his nose. Then he stamped on the pavement to warm his legs.

We were silent. Then I said:

"I heard that they fired at people returning from the sand dunes."

"Who told you that?" he asked angrily, standing in front of me with legs astride.

"They said so this morning. Some of the inhabitants came from the seashore with raised hands and when they came close, some soldiers aimed their guns at them and finished them off."

Rivkin gave me a long, hostile look, and then said in a decisive voice: "Don't you believe it. Just fairy tales."

And, turning away from me, he took several heavy steps in front of him. Then he turned round again and said:

"Don't you believe it. I tell you. They're just boasting. They like boasting. They think it's a sign of bravery. Let them pull someone else's leg. They killed people who came towards them with their hands raised? Just like that, eh? For the fun of it! I know our boys. Pure gold, that's what they are. No army in the world would have treated the inhabitants as we have at a time of occupation."

I walked a few steps behind him. We passed the plot, and then a row of shops close to one another, whose doors were shut with iron bolts and locks. He must still have been thinking about what he had just heard, for he stopped again and turned to me with an open stance, the butt of his gun peeping out behind his broad shoulder:

"Listen, you're a young man, aren't you? Thirty years old? Thirty-five? I've been through several wars already. Do you know how a victorious army behaves when it takes a strange city? Stealing, looting, raping, murdering. Never mind the Nazis. The English, the Russians, all of them. How can you compare it at all? Did you see anything of that here? Did they rape a single woman? Or rob a single shop? And here you have to deal with enemies who, if they only had a chance . . ."

He looked at me, blinked his eyes as if thinking with great speed, and then added, taking hold of the lapel of my jacket:

"Listen to what I'm telling you. If they had come into one of our cities, they would have slaughtered all of us. Do you hear me? All of us. Me and you and the women and the children. Keep this in mind!"

He was quiet for a while, and still holding my lapel and with his eyes fixed on me, his face beamed in a broad smile and he said:

"They fired on people returning to their homes, just like that, eh? You don't know them. They're boasting. That's all!"

And he pushed me away from him with force.

We continued to walk, until we heard the sound of steps from the other side of the street. We stopped and listened. The steps were measured, confident, one and one, one and one, iron on silent stone. "They're ours," Rivkin whispered. We gave the password and were answered. Two youngsters came up to us, strolling along shoulder to shoulder, with their hands in the pockets of their coats. When they reached us, they stopped.

"What's new?" Rivkin asked.

"Everything quiet," said the swarthier of the two.

"It's cold," said the other one.

"Tomorrow one platoon is going south, isn't it?" Rivkin said.

"We're staying here. Too bad," the swarthy one said.

"Don't you like it here?"

"Nothing to do. Curfew all the time."

"You want to fight, eh?"

"We came here to fight, didn't we? We want a bit of fun. Something to happen."

"Or else to go home," the light-colored one said.

"So soon?"

"I got a wife and child. Got to be back at work," he smiled.

"You've just conquered a city," Rivkin said. "Now take it easy for a while."

"Call this taking it easy? It's getting on my nerves!"

"It's quiet in the city, isn't it?"

"The quiet makes me more nervous than the fighting. Like a cemetery. Especially with all these white houses."

"Last night there was some firing," the swarthy one said. "I heard that they finished off two of them."

"They fired on a patrol?" Rivkin asked.

"Before dawn. From a house not far from the square. Today our boys blew up the house."

"Really?"

"There are still a few terrorists in the city. Armed. Looks like they're trying to start something."

"No wonder. They're being treated with kid gloves," the light-complexioned one said. "We should have finished off a few dozen of them."

"Of women," Rivkin interrupted him.

"Just like that, a few dozen of them. To scare them a little. They don't seem afraid at all."

"You should really be going home already," Rivkin reprimanded him, and turned to go. "We'll be seeing you."

"Good night."

The sound of their footsteps receded, and again we heard only the click of our shoes. Rivkin walked a little ahead of me, and his broad shoulders, the shoulders of a man used to carrying loads, looked at me as if he could have put the gates of the city upon them and carried them up to the top of the hill. Now and then I squinted at the houses on both sides of the street and at the alleyways between them. When we reached the square, we stopped and looked at it. It was the nerve center of the city, which was so nervous under its calm skin. During the day there was constant movement here of military men, vehicles, representatives of the inhabitants who were allowed to move about freely during the curfew. From here the orders went out. Here came the reports from the other battle fronts and from the world beyond the war. Jeeps which dashed through the city and stopped here with a screech of brakes brought with them the dust of the desert or the silence of the corpses. Here shining cars spewed out people wearing civilian clothes, whose faces were silent, and whose stealthy movement presaged fateful decisions. Army lorries stopped here, loaded with frightened people wrapped in filthy scarves, no one knowing where they were going to. High-ranking officers came and went from the house with the white dome. Under the surface of the open happenings, flickered the fear of a conquered city, arrested in its silent houses. Fear of the unknown. A blank waiting for what might happen suddenly, sudden thunder or an earthquake.

The square now was lying under the night, small, shrunk in upon itself, relaxed, sunk in a quiet sleep, after the troubles of the day. On the other side the tops of the black palms moved a little, and next to the entrance to the green lawn of the courtyard stood a guard who did not trouble to ask who we were.

We circled the square and continued to stroll in a street of low white-washed houses. From the alleyways blew now a light breeze, which shifted fine sand on to the pavement. Blind alleys led from the street to dark quarters pregnant with evil. Rivkin slackened his stride. Then we stopped near the ruins of a house. Two beheaded walls leaned against one another, with a great heap of broken bricks between them. Between the sloping walls stood out a crooked iron bow. The frame of a bed. The lintel of a door remained standing by a miracle, upright, like the gateway of an ancient ruin.

"This must be the house they were talking about," said Rivkin.

I looked at the ruins, whose broken and shattered forms were like a vision seen in a nightmare, and said:

"A lousy business, war. Even when you're the winner."

Rivkin thought for a while, his gaze fixed on the heap of bricks in front of us. Then he turned his head to me and said:

"Look, my boy. What are we anyway? A small plot of earth surrounded by a desert. All the time hot winds, sandstorms, armies of locusts, foxes and jackals come to destroy us. What should we do in order to continue working? Put up fences around us, build shelters, windbreaks. Sometimes this doesn't work. Then one goes outside and bangs on tins to chase the locusts away. Or one fires a gun to frighten the jackals. We want to live, don't we? We're entitled to live, aren't we? If so, then we shouldn't complain about the need for what has to be done. Necessity comes from God."

Necessity comes from God, I repeated to myself as we continued walking, necessity comes from God. I have to understand its laws and to surrender to them. If I don't understand them, then I am behaving like a fool. I have to understand its laws, in order to stay alive. Otherwise, I will again have need of the revolver hidden beneath the mattress of my bed. Is it still there? The choice does not lie between being good or bad, but between being strong or weak. The strong one becomes a necessity. He is able to fight all other necessities. The world is nothing but an incessant war between one necessity and the others. Oh, what darkness. How strange that one thinking about the pistol hidden in my distant room, when I am holding a gun in my hands.

An early morning breeze pased by. The houses began shedding their darkness; they looked like phantoms wearing shrouds. In the sky could now be seen blocks of heavy clouds, travelling eastwards. In the courtyards were revealed barrels, poles, squashed bushes, dry, grey sand. Shutters and doors shone in their nakedness. Bubbles of dew covered the iron bolts. A frozen silence hung in the air.

Oh, if only everything was like this early morning, I thought to myself, silent and wrapped in grey mist, breathing a quiet breath, not plotting any evil, and in another hour the air would grow paler, and within the house, so warm from the breath of children, women would get out of their beds, pattering across the floor in their bare feet, silently, so as not to wake anybody, to put a kettle on the stove, amidst the shadows of the kitchen, and the men would pull the heavy work boots out from under the beds, tying their laces slowly, feeling with a blind hand for the holes, trying to patch together the tatters of a vanished dream, and there would be no necessity to kill in order to live, or to tear a man away from his home suddenly in the afternoon or to stand on guard between the women and the flour, and it would be possible to go out to the courtyard and examine a cauliflower, to see whether the white head was hard already, and to say good morning to the neighbor on the other side of the fence, and the clouds would be clearer and perhaps there would be rain. . .

The shots froze my thoughts, and at the third a glint of fire flashed from the depths of the alleyway. "There!" Rivkin called out, running bent up along the sides of the houses, holding his gun. For a moment I stood there, stunned. Where from? Where to? How? And then a sharp pain cut through my chest, and I fell down on my face. I felt a warm wetness spreading over my whole chest, and the pain also spread and grew blunter, like a stone. Hard. Hardening. Stone. That's it, that's it already, a voice mumbled inside me. It had to happen. Like a glass being shattered to pieces. The luck of a good man. Many people with goblets in their hands. What laughter. Moving and rolling all around. Round and round with the goblets. Where is my wife? The porch is falling. The pitol. That's it, the pistol. It's fallen into the jukebox, and is firing at a spinning wheel of elephants and monkeys, elephants and monkeys, moving at a great speed until nothing can be seen, only a crowd of white-clad people surrounding me with arms raised to hit and calling out. Necessity comes from God Necessity comes from God There is no God Rivkin There is no God Rivkin where . . .

Then everything went white and I sank into it as if in cottonwool, sank and sank in a wet pleasantness, sinking, only white and white, above me and around me, sinking into endless depths.

7

A little bell, rather like a school bell, tinkled, and then the old man with the bushy mustache and the uniform took my arm and said that we had to go in. I got up from the bench and let him lead me to wherever we were going. Before entering I stopped and asked him what I was charged with. He shrugged his shoulders as if to say that he didn't know. Was I being tried because I had been killed? I asked again. "Perhaps," he said, taking my arm and pulling me inside.

It was a long and broad hall in an unfurnished building. The walls were unplastered and one could notice the cross-lines made by the bricks. On the floor there were many blobs of plaster. Above me I could see the tiles and the wooden beams which formed the under-pinnings of the roof. The glass of the large windows, one on each side, was spotted with dabs of whitewash, and the light that came through them was grey as on a rainy winter day. At the far end of the hall was a long black table, with only one man sitting behind it. He wore a uniform, but as he was bent over his papers, I couldn't make out his face. On his right was the small copper bell. Two very long benches without back rests, facing one another, took up almost the whole length of the room, close to the walls behind them. The right-hand bench was empty, and there were some people on the left-hand bench. At once I made out Argaman, who was sitting hunched-up, supporting his chin with one hand. When I entered he looked at me intently through his large glasses, as if he was afraid he would lose a single flicker of expression on my face. On both sides of him sat the account-ants, who exchanged whispers when they saw me, and a few other people, whom I did not know.

The old man led me to the center of the hall, a long distance from the judge's table, let go of my arm, and, walking slowly towards the empty bench, sat down on it, holding its edge with his fingertips. His feet did not reach the ground, and they waggled slightly. Standing in the center of the hall was torture, because I had nothing to lean against, neither behind me nor in front, and I didn't know how to stand or what to do with my hands. At first I let them hang down at my sides; then I folded them on my chest, but I was afraid this might be contempt of court and so I let them drop in front of me again, with my palms together and my fingers playing with one another. But then I was afraid of appearing nervous, and so I stopped playing with my fingers. Once the movement of the fingers stopped, it was worse than before, because I felt as if ants were crawling under my left foot, creeping to my leg and my thigh and reaching as far as my groin. I shuffled my feet a little and the grains of sand on the floor made a creaking noise, which seemed to me to arouse the immediate attention of the spectators. Again I saw Argaman's high forehead with its two bays of receding hair on the sides of his head. He didn't take his eyes off me, piercing me right through and turning me inside out. The way he looked at me made me think that he had come here in order to confirm his beliefs, and that I was a sort of a guinea-pig for him. I met Ben-Hen's eyes, but they didn't betray for a second that he knew me. When I managed to summon a faint smile, as if to say hullo, he immediately turned to his neighbor and whispered something to him.

The way all those people were sitting on the bench struck me as highly uncomfortable and increased my nervousness, because they also had nothing to lean against and their backs were either too straight or too bent, so that they looked quite unnatural. I looked around for Johnny, but he wasn't there. On the other hand, I noticed my neighbor from the first floor of our building: her broad face was flushed and she looked at me with wide-open eyes, eagerly awaiting whatever I would do or say. I became very embarrassed when I recalled that she knew a great deal about me, especially as I had borrowed the ladder from her. I wanted to ask her how my wife was, but of course that was quite impossible. Or perhaps I could get to her? I had an idea which seemed promising. Just whispering didn't constitute contempt of court and maybe I could whisper: "Is she at home?" Then she could answer with a movement of her head.

I had already motioned in her direction when the judge cleared his throat loudly, and when he raised his head from his paper I was stunned to see that it was B. His blue eyes were very cold, and then I knew what was in store for me.

"I hope you know why you were killed," his voice reached me from the other end of the hall.

I lowered my hands to my sides. Now it was obvious what they were accusing me of.

"It was an accident," I said in a weak voice.

"What's that?" he called out.

"It happened by accident," I repeated.

"No," B. said. Then, as if he was speaking from a long way off (I made out his words from the movement of his lips): "You didn't carry out the commandment: make haste to kill him who seeks to kill you."

When I understood this, I felt a sort of relief. The charge wasn't such a grave one. After all, my death was my own private affair.

As if he had heard what I was thinking he said: "Obviously, as a soldier your life is the property of the state."

Automatically I sprang to attention and saluted. I heard a rustle on the bench and noticed that some of the spectators had straightened up and turned to one another to whisper something. B. made a movement with his hand to indicate that I could stand at ease.

"Well, what do you have to say to that?" he asked.

"To what?" I said. Now the rustle on the bench was louder than before. I could even hear the sound of faint laughter.

B. leaned his head forward and looked at me from under the cliff of his forehead. He waited for my answer. Perhaps I was wrong, I thought to myself. Perhaps it wasn't just chance that I was killed. I tried to remember the details of what had happened in the last few minutes before the sharp pain pierced my chest. The silence seemed to last very long, and I could see that all those present were losing patince with me.

"I couldn't shoot," I said. "My hands froze."

"Why?" B. fired the question at me as if he had been waiting for exactly this answer.

"Because it was morning already," I said.

"What difference did that make?"

"Well, it was light," I said, "and I can't kill a man when I see his face."

Ripples of laughter came from the bench. Only in Argaman's face could I detect any eagerness to listen: his face tauntened with the effort. In the silence the rustle of papers from the table sounded like the rattle of sheets of irons. B. looked at some documents in front of him.

"You were sent to replace one of the guards in the refugee camp," he said, "and you kept at a distance."

"That's right," I said.

He removed a piece of paper from one heap and put it on another. The rustling sounded like the echo of thunder in a cloud.

"You guarded the gangsmen," he said, "and then, when they were taken inside you remained outside."

My silence was tantamount to a confession.

"Why?" he asked.

"It wasn't fair," I said, "they couldn't defend themselves."

"Who, those murderers?" he fixed his blue eyes on me.

"They didn't look like murderers to me," I said, "perhaps because the rays of the setting sun shed a purplish light on their faces."

Again there came a laugh from the bench, and Argaman straightened his back and placed his palms on his knees. B. sniggered.

"In other words, you wanted to keep your hands clean," he said. As I didn't reply, he went on: "You felt relieved that the job was being done by others."

I could see heads nodding in agreement on the bench. Only my first floor neighbor continued to look at me with wide-open eyes, full of worry and concern. Her cheeks were flushed.

"Pure soul!" B. sneered. He bent his head down over the papers, turned a few of them over, then turned to me again, looked at me with his bright, glittering eyes, and said in a loud voice: "You saint! You were ready to sacrifice your brothers' lives in order to save murderers! If we had to rely on you, we'd be done for! What do you have to say in your defence? What?"

The echoes reverberated all over the hall.

I felt my legs trembling. I would never have thought that this moderate man could become so heated. The more I tried to move my lips, the less they responded. The glances thrown at me by the people sitting on the bench pierced me like arrows; they looked at me accusingly as if eager for revenge.

"Speak up!" B. shouted at me.

And as I still remained silent, as if paralyzed, he picked up the little copper bell and rang it angrily.

The old man got up from the bench and gripped my arm. I turned my head to the left and saw the spectators were getting to their feet and stretching themselves. It seemed strange that the court session had been so short, particularly as nothing had really been cleared up. Was the trial over, I wondered, with a sudden burst of fear? "Intermission," said the old man, leading me to the bench on which he was sitting.

I sat down. Next to the window which faced me sat the accountants, arguing among themselves. My neighbor continued sitting, her cheeks even redder than before and her eyes wide open. Argaman strolled up and down the hall, with his hands in his pockets.

I thought over what I had said and what I hadn't said. I was angry with myself. Why did I have to be tried? After all, my life and my death were my own private affair. Even if I was a soldier. A soldier who was killed in battle couldn't be tried. The state had lost nothing through my death, especially as in any case I had intended to commit suicide. Why didn't I have the courage to say what I had felt in the last few days, and what I really thought?

My eyes met those of my neighbor. "May I leave my seat for a moment?" I asked the old man who sat next to me. "Only for a minute," he said, wagging his finger in front of my face. I rose and walked over to the opposite bench. It seemed to be a very long distance, because everyone standing around noticed me, stopped talking, and looked at me with undisguised curiosity. I finally reached the place where my neighbor was sitting, and asked her in whisper: "Perhaps you know if my wife is at home?"

She shrugged her shoulders and smiled sadly.

"Hasn't she been there since I left? I asked.

She placed a finger on her lips as a hint that I should be silent, and, turning round, I saw the old man coming up behind me. He took my arm, saying: "The minute is over!" and led me back to the bench.

Now I began worrying about what had happened to my wife. Perhaps she didn't know that I had gone off to war. Certainly she didn't know about my unfortunate accident. This supposition depressed me still more. As if I didn't exist at all. As if my life and death were worth nothing and nothing would remain of them, not even sorrow. And whatever I would say at the trial was also of no importance. Can one die twice?

A man in a shabby grey suit, with a black hat, was walking up and down near me, with his hands behind his back. From the way he squinted at me when he passed, I realized that he wanted to say something. He had a long, pale face, with a thin pointed nose and sad, watery eyes. Eventually he plucked up courage and sat down next to me, lifting the hem of his jacket.

"Excuse me," he said, "but how old are you?"

"Thirty-five," I said.

"Older than me," he said, "although I look older than you. Born in this country?"

"Yes."

"I thought so. You know very little."

He said this with a sad smile and sympathetically, but although I was so anxious for any of the spectators to come up to me and to offer me a word or two of encouragement, or even to ask me something, the few words he spoke had such a chilling effect that inwardly I wished he would go away and leave me alone.

"I can tell you a lot, but I will only tell you very little," he said. "I died three times." Here he held up three fingers. "But I shall only tell you about my first death."

I looked towards my neighbor and tried to catch some hint in her face. I was worried about my wife. Hadn't she been home for all those long days?

"Well, imagine yourself," I heard the monotonous voice, like the drone of distant prayer. "Imagine me walking in the snow, in a long black procession. I was twelve then. A boy. On my right was my mother, with a large parcel under her arm. She walked and limped and walked, and I had to help her, otherwise she would have fallen in the snow. We came to a gate in a barbed wire fence, and they told us to stop. I was shivering with cold, and my mother wrapped me in a large scarf. Suddenly we heard screaming. People were being taken through the door. A soldier came up to us and took my mother away. She struggled with him and called to me. I ran toward her and tried to take hold of her. But they pulled me away. I shouted, without a voice coming out. I see her going away from me, into the large, open space surrounded by barbed wire fence. I want to cry, but can't. And endless night. I have no one in the world . . . That was my first death."

"That's terrible," I whispered, "terrible."

"You understand?" He fixed his eyes on me.

"It's unbearable. Impossible. The human heart is too weak."

The little bell rang again. The audience hurried back to their places. The old man took my arm and led me to the same place where I had stood previously. There was complete silence in the room. I crossed my hands behind my back.

B. sat hunched up over his papers, writing something. The creaking of his pen sounded like the scraping of a piece of pottery, and could be heard all over the hall. Two swallows flew swiftly after one another under the roof, and all the spectators looked upwards.

"Well, then, I understand that your intention was to avoid doing evil," B. said, turning his head in my direction. "Of course, something which you consider evil."

I moved my lips without uttering a sound. He looked at me closely, and then said:

"You probably remember your visit to my house. At the time you wanted to prove that you could also be wicked. Is that correct?"

"Yes," I whispered. "I was wrong."

"It's good that you admit it. Then you wanted to kill someone because you were under the impression that he thought you were a good man, so to speak."

"I was wrong in this too," I said.

"Wouldn't it be correct to say that at hime, too, you behaved not like a good man but like a man who perhaps seeks the good but is not at all proud of it?"

The spectators on the bench straightened up and looked at me expectantly. For the first time Argaman turned to his neighbor and whispered something in his ear.

"Is that true?" B. raised his voice again.

At that moment I turned and was struck dumb to see my wife enter the hall. She walked in the direction of the right bench, bent over slightly and walking on the tips of her toes, as if afraid to be noticed or disturb the proceedings. She didn't look at anybody, but sat down next to the old man. She was holding a handkerchief to her nose, and her eyes were red.

"Naturally you caused your wife untold suffering by your foolish conduct," B. continued in a loud voice. "Conduct which was ostensibly good, but which led to evil, as you forced her to deny her real feelings. Were you wrong in this too?"

Tears choked me. I turned my head towards my wife, but she didn't see me. Her eyes were fixed on B. When I turned my gaze to the judge's table again, I saw that my neighbor from the first floor was whispering something in great excitement to those sitting beside her, who leaned forward to hear what she was saying.

Argaman nodded to his friends several times, as if in complete agreement with what B. had just said.

"Is that true?" B. asked again.

I swallowed the lump in my throat, and said: "Yes, commander!"

"And only here, in the midst of the war, you found the courage to refrain from hurting your enemies in order not to cause them suffering!"

"Yes, commander," I said.

"And to put an end to your life."

Here my wife broke into tears, and pressing the handkerchief against her mouth in order to check her outburst, she ran out of the hall.

The neighbor from the first floor also rose, bowed slightly towards the judge's bench, threw a reproachful look at me and went out, following my wife. Argaman gave me a contemptuous glance through his glasses, holding his chin in the palm of his hand. I felt very lonely.

B. took hold of the handle of the bell and lifted it a little from the table. I was seized by a terrible fear that that was the end of the trial.

"One moment . . ." I stepped forward.

He put the bell back in its place. The old man, who had already got up from the bench, sat down again.

"Well?" B. asked.

"I . . ." I began, but I couldn't continue. With great effort I managed to get the following words out: "I can't go on like this."

"Meaning what?" B. asked in surprise.

"Meaning . . ." I turned my head to the people sitting on the bench, hoping for some sign of help or encouragement. But they looked at me in indifference as if they no longer expected anything from me.

"Meaning that there's no end to it," I said. "Evil breeds evil and there's no end to it."

"What do you mean by that?" asked B.

"I mean," I said in a low voice, "that this has to be stopped once and for all. Someone has to stop it. At a certain moment. Because otherwise one murder will lead to another and one humiliation will lead to another and there'll never be an end to it. Who'll gain by this?"

"The strongest," said B.

"If that is the case, then there still won't be any end to it, because sometimes certain people are strong and then others."

'Well, so what should be done about it, in your opinion?" asked B., bending towards me impatiently.

"Perhaps simply to refrain from doing evil," I said.

"In other words, you would rather be killed than kill," he chuckled.

"After all, if I am dead or someone else is dead," I whispered, "the amount of suffering caused is the same. I'm not better than anyone else. At least I will know I haven't committed any evil. Perhaps in this way the amount of evil in the world will be reduced."

"Oh, that's going too far!" The voice came from the left bench. It was Argaman. He was saying it to himself, but his words could be heard clearly all over the hall. "It contradicts all logic!" he added, stretching his hands out to his fellow spectators.

"You want all of us to be saints," B. chuckled.

"As far as possible . . ." I said.

"To love our enemies and forgive them."

"We are not better than them," I said. "They want to live. Exactly as we do."

There was a commotion on the bench and a great deal of movement. I heard people saying that this business had to stop. B. gave them a look and waited until they had quietened down.

"That means you don't think that you are in the right," he said.

"To do what is right—that is my whole life," I whispered.

"Then defend your life! Defend it with all your might!" his voice echoed in the hall.

"When I kill others, my life loses its justice," my lips trembled.

"So you sought justice beyond life on this earth," B. scoffed. "I am sure you have found it. There, where all are equal, because they are all disembodied souls! Isn't that true?"

I was bewildered by his words and gaze, and could not answer.

"Justice is bought with force," he called out loudly. "Only a fool believes that justice and weakness go hand in hand! Do you understand this? Do you?"

He didn't wait for my reply any more. A sigh of relief came from the spectators' bench, and the hall seemed to sink in it. He lowered his head once more to the papers in front of him, took the pen and quickly wrote something on a piece of paper. While doing this he muttered, as if talking to himself:

"You wanted us to commit suicide and thus to bring salvation to the world. Fortunately our desire to live is greater than yours. You realize, by now, of course, that your death wasn't an accident."

My throat was choked. There was complete silence in the hall; the only sound that could be heard was the scratching of the pen. The spectators' gaze was now rooted to the slip of paper, as if waiting for the verdict to be given. I saw his sleeve move from line to line. Then he affixed his signature with a flourish, folded the sheet of paper twice, placed it in an envelope, pasted it down, wrote something on it, and summoned the old man to him with a motion of his finger. The old man came up to the table step by step, tiptoeing and took the envelope from B. Then he walked towards me, his back very straight. When he reached me, the bell rang. Everyone stood up. The old man handed me the envelope and said: "That's all."

"No verdict?" I asked fearfully.

"Here there are no verdicts," the old man said. "This is the routine procedure of registration of deaths."

I didn't know what to do. B. rose and walked past me on his way out of the hall, without giving me a glance. The accountants moved towards the door in a group, arguing heatedly among themselves. The moment I turned round to go, I was stunned to see Johnny come towards me, with a broad smile on his face. Was it possible that he had been there the whole time, without me seeing him? I wondered, blushing. He came up to me, shook my hand and said: "Thank you. You were wonderful. Fantastic. Exactly what I would have said if I were you."

"Were you here all the time?" I asked.

At that moment he disappeared.

I remained standing alone in the hall. The old man had also gone. Only then did I remember the envelope in my hand: I held it up and saw the words on it: "To deliver to Rivkin."

When I left the hall, it was bright light outside, and it blinded my eyes. From the look of the house on the other side of the sandy street I knew that I was in the village in which I was born. It was an old house, painted a faded brown, with a red-tiled roof and green shutters. A high avenue of cypresses led to its door, and inside the rusty, bent iron fence were dusty myrtle bushes. Clumps of weed dotted the farm-yard, and a low tap dripped, one drop at a time. A midday silence cast its spell around, and the sand burnt in the sun. From the door of the house a grey-haired man emerged, he stopped and scrutinized me closely. I wanted to call out: "Father!" But I was dumb. Apparently he didn't recognize me, because he turned on to the wooden pavement and went on his way.

JOSE DONOSO

hell hath no limits

FAUSTUS
First will I question thee about hell:
Tell me, where is the place that men call hell?
MEPHOSTOPHILIS
Under the heavens.
FAUSTUS
Ay, so are all things else; but whereabouts?
MEPHOSTOPHILIS
Within the bowels of these elements,
Where we are tortured, and remain for ever.
Hell hath no limits, nor is circumscribed
In one self place; but where we are is hell,
And where hell is, there must ever be . . .
—Marlowe, *Doctor Faustus*

1

La Manuela forced open her bleary eyes, stretched briefly and, twisting away from the sleeping Japonesita, reached for the clock. Five to ten. Eleven o'clock mass. Sticky films again sealed her eyes as she put the clock back on the box by the bed. Half an hour at least before her daughter would ask for breakfast. She ran her tongue over her toothless gums: hot sawdust, and breath like rotten eggs. From drinking so much new wine to hurry the men out and close early. She felt a shiver —of course!—she opened her eyes and sat up in bed: Pancho Vega was in town. She covered her shoulders with the rumpled pink shawl from her daughter's side of the bed. Yes. Last night they came to tell her. Be careful, the truck had been seen around, his snub-nosed red truck, with the double tires on the back wheels. At first La Manuela didn't believe it because she knew that, thank God, Pancho Vega had other interests now, near Pelarco, where he was hauling grape-skins. But later, when she had almost forgotten what they said about the truck, she heard the horn by the post office on the next street. He must have honked it for almost five minutes, that hoarse, persistent horn, enough to drive any woman crazy. He always honked like that when he was drunk. The idiot thought it was funny. Then La Manuela went to tell her daughter they better close early, why take chances, what happened last time might happen again. Japonesita warned the girls to finish up quickly with the customers or send them away: remember last year, when Pancho Vega came to town for harvest and invited himself in with a bunch of roughnecks, all of them full of wine . . . there might have been bloodshed if Alejandro Cruz hadn't arrived in the nick of time. He made them behave in a civil way, so they got bored and left. But they said that afterward Pancho Vega was real mad and went around swearing: "I'll screw the two of them, Japonesita and her fag of a father . . ."

La Manuela got up and started to put on her trousers. Pancho might still be in town . . . Those hands, hard and heavy like stone, like iron, she remembered them all right. Last year the beast got it into his head that she had to dance flamenco. He heard that when the party warmed up with the new wine, and when all the customers were like pals, La Manuela would put on a pretty red dress with white polka dots, and dance flamenco. You bet! Big brute! Think I'd dance for you, just look at you! I do that for gentlemen, for my friends, not for stinking bums like you, stuck-up peasants who think they're big shots because they have a week's pay in their pockets . . . their poor wives in the shanties, breaking their backs over laundry so the kids won't starve to death, while the sports are out drinking wine and punch and even hard liquor . . . no sir. And since she had one too many, that's exactly what she told them. Then Pancho and his pals got angry. They started by barricading the place and smashing bottles and smearing the bread and cold cuts and wine on the floor. Then while one of them twisted her arm, the others pulled off her clothes, and trying to force her into the famous flamenco dress they ripped it in two. They had begun to molest Japonesita when don Alejo arrived, like in a miracle, as if they had invoked him. Such a good man. Why he even looked like the Good Lord, with his China-blue eyes and his snowy mustache and eyebrows.

She bent down to fish her shoes out from under the bed and sat on the edge to put them on. She had slept badly. It wasn't just the wine, which made her feel bloated. But also, God knows why, don Alejo's dogs had been howling all night long in the vineyard . . . She would be yawning all day long, with no strength for anything, and pains in her legs and back. She tied the laces slowly with double bows . . . if you got down on your knees, there, way back under the bed, was the suitcase. A cardboard job, with peeling paint and white mouldy edges, held together with rope: in it was everything she owned. And her dress, or rather what was left of her lovely dress. Today, when she opened her eyes, no, wrong, last night, when they told her Pancho Vega was in town, God knows why, she was tempted to take the dress out again. She hadn't touched it for a year. Who does she think she's kidding with her sour wine, dogs, rib pains? She had insomnia! Quietly, so she wouldn't upset her daughter, she bent down again, pulled out the suitcase and opened it. A total loss. No use touching it even. But she did touch it. She examined the bodice . . . hey, it's not so bad, the neckline, armpit . . . it can be fixed. I'll sew the whole afternoon in the kitchen so I won't get stiff. Fiddle with the skirt and train, try it on so the girls can tell me where it has to be taken in since I lost six pounds last year. But I don't have thread. Tearing a strip from the end of the train she put it in her pocket. As soon as she served her daughter breakfast she'd drag herself to Ludovinia's to see if she could find the same color red thread among her odds and ends. Or something like it. You can't be choosy in a town like Estación El Olivo. She pushed the suitcase back under the bed. Yes, Ludo's, but before going out she better make sure Pancho was gone, and if he really had been in town last night. After all, the honking might just be a dream, like for the past year when she sometimes thought she heard his rough voice or felt his brutal hands, or it could be that she only imagined last night's honking, remembering the horn from last year. Who knows. Shivering, she put on her shirt. She wrapped the shawl around her, put the dentures in and walked out into the patio with the dress on her arm. Raising her little, wrinkled raisin face, her black and hairy old mare's nostrils flared as she detected the unmistakable aroma of the new harvest in the cloudy morning air.

Half-naked, carrying a sheet of newspaper in her hand, Lucy came out of her room like a sleepwalker.

"Lucy!"

Lucy's in a hurry: new wines are so treacherous.

She locked herself in the outhouse that straddled the sewer at the end of the patio, next to the chicken coop. No, I won't send Lucy. Clotilde's better.

"Hey, Cloty!"

. . . with her stupid face and skinny arms deep in the soapy water of the wash tub, surrounded by the reflections of ivy leaves.

"Listen, Cloty . . ."

"Good morning."

"Where's Nelly?"

"In the street, playing with the neighbor's kids. That woman is so good to her, knowing what she is and all . . ."

Poor, unlucky whore. That's what she said to Japonesita when they took Clotilde in a little over a month ago. And so old. Who would want to go upstairs with her? But drunk, at night, flesh starving for other flesh, for any flesh that's hot and can be bitten and squeezed and licked, they don't know or care what they go to bed with—dog, hag, anything will do. And Clotilde would work like a dog, never complaining, not even when they made her haul the Coca Cola crates from one place to another. Last night she had it bad. The fat yokel was eager enough, but when Japonesita announced that she was closing up, instead of going with Cloty to her room he said he was going out to vomit and he never came back. Fortunately he had already paid for his drinks.

"I want her to do an errand. Don't you realize that if Pancho's around I can't go to mass? Tell Nelly to check every single street and to tell me if she sees the truck. She knows which, the red one. I can't miss Sunday mass!"

Clotilde dried her hands on her apron.

"I'll go right now."

"Did you start the fire in the kitchen?"

"Not yet."

"Then treat me to a few coals so I can make the kid's breakfast."

Squatting over Clotilde's stove to scoop some coals onto a flattened tin can, la Manuela felt her spine creak. It's going to rain. I'm too old for these things. She was even afraid of the morning air now, afraid of the morning most of all, afraid of so many things, the way she coughed, the bile in her mouth and the cramps in her gums, the early morning when everything is so different than at night when she's cradled in the sooty brightness of the carbon lamp and wine and dancing eyes, the conversations of friends and strangers at the tables, and the silver that falls dollar after dollar into her daughter's purse, which by now must be good and full. She opened the door to the big room, set the coals on the ashes in the stove and put on the kettle. She cut a loaf of bread in half, buttered it, and while she got the saucer, spoon, and cup ready she sang soft and slowly:

> . . . then dawn brought the day
> your boat left the bay . . .
> And now I dream
> Aaaaaaaahhh me . . .

She might be old but she would die singing, and with her feathers on. In the suitcase under the bed, besides her flamenco dress she had an old moth-eaten feather boa. Ludo had given it to her years ago as a consolation because some man had ignored her . . . just which man it was I don't remember now (one of the many who made me suffer when I was young). If the party got lively, and if they pleaded with her a little, it was no sweat off her back to put on the feathers even though they made her look like a scarecrow and didn't have anything to do with the flamenco number. Just to make people laugh, that's all, the laughter all around me and caressing me and the applause and compliments and lights, come have a drink with us honey, whatever you want, anything you want, just so you'll dance for us again. Why be so afraid of Pancho Vega! Those thick-browed, rough-voiced brutes are all alike: the minute it gets dark they start pawing you. And they leave everything smelling of engine oil and garages and cheap cigarettes and sweat . . . and at dawn the wine dregs souring in the bottom of the glasses on the seven dirty tables, the lopsided, scratched tables, everything too clear, too glaring this morning and every morning. And there's a puddle by the chair where Clotilde's fat man had been sitting because the lout spit all night long—an abscessed tooth, he said.

The kettle started to boil. Today without fail she would talk to Japonesita. She was too old to be fixing breakfast every morning after working all night, with gusts of wind blowing into the parlor through the cracks in the loose siding and where the shingles had fallen from the earthquake. Clotilde was having such poor luck in the parlor that they might as well use her for a servant. And Nelly for the errands, and when she grows up . . . Yes, let Clotilde bring them breakfast in bed. What other work could she expect at her age? At least she wasn't lazy like the other whores. Lucy returned to her room. Now she'll get back into bed, the slut, and spend all afternoon between the filthy sheets, eating bread, sleeping, getting fat. Of course, that's why she has so many clients. Because she's fat. Sometimes a real fancy gentleman comes all the way from Duao to spend the night with her. He says that he likes to hear the swishing of her soft, white thighs rubbing together when she dances. That that's what he pays for. Not like Japonesita who even if she wanted to be a whore, poor thing, she's so skinny she'd never make it. But as a manager, Japonesita is tops. There's no denying it. So efficient and thrifty. And every Monday morning she takes the train to Talca to deposit the profits in the bank. Heaven only knows how much she's hoarded. She never tells me, even though it's as much mine as Japonesita's. And what good did it do them, Japonesita is such a miser that no one gets any good out of it. She never buys herself a dress. A dress! Why, she wouldn't even buy another bed so that we can each have our own. Like last night. La Manuela didn't sleep a wink. Probably because of don Alejandro's dogs barking in the vineyard. Or was she dreaming? And the honking. In any case, at her age, sleeping with a pubescent female was no fun.

She put the saucer and bread on top of the steaming cup and walked outside again. Clotilde, scrubbing away, yelled to her that Nelly had gone to look. La Manuela didn't answer or thank her. Instead, coming over to see if Clotilde was doing the other whores' laundry too, she raised those thread-thin eyebrows, leered in mock passion, and warbled:

Havanaaaaaa for a
Niiiiiiiiiiiiiight

2

The house was sinking. One day they realized that the sidewalk was no longer even with the dirt floor, but higher, so they tried to check it by installing a stone slab, with two wedges, in the doorway. It was no use. As the years passed, the sidewalk, God knows how, rose almost imperceptibly, while the floor kept sinking. Maybe it was from wetting and flattening it so much for dancing, or from the yokels grinding the floor into a dirt pit with their stomping feet. The stone slab, which was slowly wearing away, had never been level and now its cracks collected burnt matches, mint wrappers, scraps of paper, toothpicks, lint, and buttons. Sometimes grass sprang up around the edges.

La Manuela stooped in the doorway to pick up some scraps. She was in no hurry. It was still a half-hour before mass. A harmless half-hour, not a care in the world according to Nelly's report: not one truck, not even a car in the whole town. It was a dream, that's all. She couldn't even remember who told her about the truck. And the dogs. Why would they be running loose in the vineyard now, when there's not so much as one bunch of grapes left to steal? Okay. Five minutes to Ludovinia's, a quarter of an hour to find the thread, and five minutes for nothing special, to drink some tea or to stop and gossip with someone on the corner. And then, her mass.

Just to make sure, she looked up the street toward the poplar grove that marked the edge of town, three blocks away. Not a soul in sight. Of course. Sunday. Even the kids, who are always screaming their heads off, playing ball in the road, are probably waiting for handouts at the chapel door just in case some rich man's car drives up. The poplars trembled. If the wind blew any harder the town would be invaded by yellow leaves for at least a week and the women would be sweeping them all day out from everywhere, the street, the alleyways, doors and even from under the beds, to gather them in heaps and burn them . . . the blue smoke hovering in putrid clarity, creeping catlike against the adobe houses, coiling into the cavities of crumbling, weed-infested walls, the blackberry thickets devouring them and devouring the rooms and the sidewalks of the abandoned houses; blue smoke in eyes that smart and tear with the street's dying warmth. In her jacket pocket la Manuela's hand grasped the piece of dress like someone who rubs a charm to urge it to perform its magic.

Only a block more to the station, the end of this side of town, and then Ludo's house just around the corner, always cozy and warm with the stove lit since early morning. She hurried past the houses in that neighborhood, the worst in town. Very few were occupied because the coopers moved their businesses to Talca long ago; now, with the good roads, you could get from the country to Talca in no time. It wasn't that the other side of town, where you have the chapel and post office, had better houses or more people, but after all, it is downtown. Of course, in better days this was downtown because of the railroad station. Now it's nothing more than a pasture divided by a line, a dead traffic light, a cracked concrete platform, collapsed among the fennels under a pair of crazy-looking eucalyptus trees, an antediluvian threshing machine on whose rusty orange iron the children played, as if with a tame dinosaur. Further on, behind the mouldy wooden shed, more brambles and a canal separated the town from don Alejandro's vineyards. La Manuela stopped on the corner to look at them for a moment. Vineyards, vineyards, and more vineyards, as far as the eye could see, all the way to the mountains. Perhaps they weren't all don Alejandro's. If not, they were sure to belong to his relatives, his brothers and brothers-in-law, or at least his cousins. All of them Cruzes. The network of vineyards converged around the houses bordering the town, surrounded by a small park, but a park nonetheless, and a conglomeration of iron works, dairies, coopers' shops, sheds and wine cellars, all belonging to don Alejo. La Manuela sighed. So much money. And so much power: don Alejo, when he came into his inheritance over a half-century ago, built Estación El Olivo so that the train would stop right there and pick up his produce. And such a good man, don Alejo. What would become of the townspeople without him? Word has it that the gentleman is now going to see to it for sure that we get electric light in town. So cheerful and not at all pompous, considering he's a senator and all. Not like the others, who think a harsh voice and a hairy chest give them the right to insult a person. But who can match a man like don Alejandro? It's true that in the summer, when he'd come to town to hear mass with Misia Blanca and they'd meet by chance on the street, he'd pretend not to see them. Although sometimes, when Misia Blanca wasn't looking, he winked at her.

Ludo served her tea and pastry. La Manuela settled into a chair next to the stove and began rummaging around in the boxes filled with pieces of ribbon and buttons and silk and wool and buckles. Ludovina couldn't see the contents anymore because she was so near-sighted. Almost blind. And la Manuela had told her so many times not to be a dope and to go buy a new pair of glasses. But she never did. When Acevedo died, the moment before they sealed the coffin, Ludo almost went crazy and wanted to throw something in that would accompany her husband through all eternity. The only thing she could think of were her eyeglasses. Naturally. She had been Misia Blanca's servant when Moniquita died of typhus: the missis, desperate, cut off her blond braid that was down to her knees and threw it into the coffin. All of Misia Blanca's hair grew back. But for imitating her, stupid old Ludo lost her eyesight. For Acevedo's sake, she said, he was always so jealous. So that she'd never look at another man. When he was alive, he wouldn't let her have friends of either sex. Just la Manuela. And when they kidded him by reminding him that no matter how things seemed, la Manuela was still Japonesita's father, the cooper just laughed in disbelief. But Japonesita grew up and there was no doubt about it: skinny, dark, bucktoothed, with stiff hair just like la Manuela's.

With the passing years Ludo had become forgetful and repetitive. Yesterday, Ludo told her that when Misia Blanca came to see her she brought a message from don Alejo saying that he wanted to buy her house, funny isn't it don Alejo mentioning that he's interested in my property again but I don't see why and I don't want to leave, I want to die here. And on and on. It's no fun gossiping with her anymore. She didn't even remember what stuff she stashed away in all those boxes, packages, bundles, tubes that she hid in her drawers or under the bad or in corners, covered with dust behind the dresser, stuck between the wardrobe and the wall. Why, she's forgotten everything, everything except don Alejo's family, she knows all their names right down to his great grandchildren. And now she can't even remember who Pancho is.

"What do you mean, you don't remember. I talk about him all the time."

"You talk about so many men all the time."

"You know, that big hunk with the mustache and the red truck who came to town so much last year. He used to live outside of town but he went away and got married. Then he came back. The one with the coal-black eyebrows and the bull's neck that I thought was so nice when I was younger, until he came to the house that time with his drunk friends and was such a pest. That time they tore up my flamenco dress."

No use. For Ludo, Pancho Vega didn't exist. La Manuela felt like leaving, like throwing the tea and boxes of thread on the floor and going home. Stupid old woman. All she had left in her head was a soft lump. Why talk to Ludo if she didn't remember who Pancho Vega was? She poked around in the box so that she could find her thread and leave. Ludo remained silent while la Manuela searched. Then she began to talk.

"He owes don Alejo some money."

La Manuela looked at her.

"Who?"

"The one you were talking about."

"Pancho Vega?"

"Yeah, that one."

La Manuela wrapped the red thread around her little finger.

"How do you know?"

"Did you find some? Don't take it all."

"All right. How do you know?"

"Misia Blanca told me the other day when she came to see me. He's the son of the Vega that passed away who was don Alejo's head cooper when I worked for them. I don't remember the boy. Misia Blanca says that this what's-his-name wanted to be independent of the Cruz family and when don Alejo found out that he was looking to buy a truck, even though it had been a long time since the boy had been in town and his late father had passed away and Berta too, he told him to come around, this kid, and he lent him some money, just like that, without a signature or anything, so that the boy could pay the first installment for his truck . . ."

"So he bought the truck with don Alejo's money?"

"And he hasn't paid him back."

"Not a cent?"

"I don't know."

"He hasn't been around for a year."

"That's why."

"Scoundrel!"

Scoundrel. Scoundrel. If he came around to bother her again, she could say: Scoundrel, you swindled don Alejo, who's been like a father to you. Then, telling him that, she wouldn't be afraid. Or at least, as afraid. It was as if the word would help her break open a hard and sinister scab of Pancho's, that would still be hard and sinister, but in a different way. What a pity all that honking was just a dream . . . then why fix her red dress? She uncoiled the thread on her finger. What was she going to do all afternoon? Rain. Her bones told her so. Go see Ludo? Why? If she spoke to her about Pancho Vega again she was sure to say:

"You're too old to be thinking about men and traipsing around. Stay home and relax, woman, and wrap your feet up, don't you know that at our age the only thing a girl can do is to wait for death to carry her away?"

But death is a woman like herself and Ludo, and among women things can always be arranged. At least with some women, like Ludo, who had always treated her that way, without ambiguities, the way it should be. Japonesita, on the other hand, was all ambiguity. All of a sudden, especially in winter, when the poor thing got so cold that she'd shiver from vintage time until the pruning season, she would start saying that she'd like to get married. And have children. Children! And yet here she is, over eighteen years old and she hasn't gotten her period yet. Amazing. And then Japonesita would say no. She didn't want to be pushed around. And since she owned a whorehouse she might as well be a whore too. But let a man touch her and she'd run like mad. Of course, with that face she didn't have much choice. La Manuela had begged her so many times to make up her mind. Ludo said that she'd be better off getting married, because if nothing else, Japonesita was a hard worker. She should marry a real stud who would get her glands worked up and make love to her. But Pancho was so rough and so drunk that he couldn't excite anyone. Nor could don Alejandro's grandsons. Sometimes, in the summer, they'd get bored with their country homes and with doing nothing and they'd come in for a few drinks: unshaven, four-eyed, quiet, but very young and so busy thinking about their exams that they'd leave after barely drinking anything and without getting involved with anybody. If Japonesita were to get pregnant by one of them . . . no, of course she wouldn't get married, but after all, the child . . . Why not. That was one destiny.

They didn't understand her, la Manuela told herself on the way to chapel, the red thread wrapped around her little finger again. She was going to take the dress in here, at the waist, and there, in the back. And if she lived in a big city, you know, where they say they have carnivals, and all the fags go out dancing in the street all dressed in their finery and having a great time and no one says anything, she would dress up fit to kill. But the men here are all stupid, like Pancho and his friends. Ignorant. Someone told her that Pancho carried a knife. But it wasn't true. When Pancho tried to hit her last year she had the presence of mind to feel the brute over: he wasn't carrying anything. Idiot. They talk against poor fags so much and we havn't done a thing to them . . . but when he grabbed me with the other men and squeezed me hard, with good intentions of course, who's going to stop and think how ugly or how old a woman is. And him so mad because a girl's a fag, heaven knows what he said he'd do to me. Well let's see, scoundrel, swindler. It makes me want to put the dress on right in front of him, just to see what he'd do. Like if he were in town right now. I'd put on my dress and go out with flowers behind my ear, with makeup and all, and everybody in the street saying hello, Manuela, my, you're looking swell today sweetheart, want me to come along . . . Triumphant. And then Pancho, real angry, runs into me on a corner and says you make me sick, go take that off, you're a disgrace to the town. And just when he's about to hit me with those paws of his, I faint . . . into the arms of don Alejo, who's passing by. And don Alejo tells him to leave me alone, not to bother me, that I'm decent folk and after all he's just a tenant's son while I'm the great Manuela, famous throughout the province, and he throws Pancho out of town for good. Then don Alejo lifts me into his car and takes me to the country and puts me in Misia Blanca's bed, Ludo says it's all smooth and pink, simply lovely, and they go get the best doctor in Talca while Misia Blanca puts compresses on my forehead and gives me smelling salts and tells me look, Manuella, I want us to be friends, stay here in my house until you get well and don't worry, I'll lend you my room and anything you want, just ask, and don't you worry because Alejo is going to throw all the bad people out of town, just wait and see.

"Manuela."

A crossing. Her feet in a mud puddle in the middle of the street. A white mustache, vicuña cape, China-blue eyes under the hat brim, and behind, four black dogs in single file. La Manuela drew back.

"Heavens, don Alejo, how can you come out on the street with those beasts. Hang on to them. I'm getting out of here. Hang on to them."

"They won't hurt you unless I tell them. Easy, Moor . . ."

"They ought to lock you up for walking around with them."

La Manuela was backing off to the other sidewalk.

"Where are you off to? You just stepped into a puddle."

"I'll bet I catch cold. I was on my way to mass, to obey the commandments. I'm no heathen like you, don Alejo. Look at your face, you look half-dead. I'll bet you've been out on a spree, at your age, haven't I told you . . ."

"And you, you must be going to beg forgiveness for your sins, you shameless . . ."

"Sins! Wishful thinking! The spirit's willing, but look how skinny I am. A Saint: Virgin and Martyr . . ."

"Haven't they been saying that you've got Pancho Vega under your spell?"

"Who said that?"

"He did. You better watch out."

The dogs stirred behind don Alejo.

"Down, Othello, Moor . . ."

Water soaking her socks, cold pant-legs stuck to her shins. She hadn't felt so near collapse in years. As she walked up the slope toward the next sidewalk she kicked at a pig to make him move away, but she slipped and had to lean on him to keep from falling. From the other side she called to don Alejo:

"Watch out for whom?"

"For Pancho. They say you're all he ever talks about."

"But he never comes to El Olivo anymore. Didn't I hear that he owes you money?"

Don Alejo chuckled.

"You know everything, you old gossip. Do you know, too, that yesterday I went to Talca to see the doctor? And do you know what he told me?"

"The doctor, don Alejo? But you've never looked better . . ."

"You just finished telling me I looked half-dead. And you're going to be half-dead too if Pancho catches up with you."

"But he's not around."

"Oh yes he is."

The honking then, last night. No, she wouldn't go to mass. And she wasn't in the mood for smart alecks on the street. It was too cold. God would forgive her this time. She might catch cold. At her age, the most sensible thing was to get into bed. Yes. Get into bed. Forget about the flamenco dress. Get into bed, if Japonesita didn't have something for her to do, God knows she's always yelling at her to do something or other. Last year Pancho twisted her arm so hard he almost broke it. Now it was hurting her. She didn't want to have anything to do with Pancho Vega. Not a thing.

"Don't go yet, woman . . ."

"Sure. You're not the one he's going to hit."

"Wait."

"Then tell me what you want, don Alejo. Can't you see I'm in a hurry? My feet are wet. If I die you'll have to pay for my funeral because it'll be all your fault. And nothing but the best, ah . . ."

Don Alejo, followed by his dogs, was walking a little ahead of la Manuela on the other side of the street and talking. The last call for eleven o'clock mass. He had to shout to make himself heard because he was near the Guerreros' wagon, full of kids singing:

It's raining,
it's pouring,
the old man is snoring . . .

"Well, don Alejo. What do you want?"

"Ah, yes. Tell Japonesita that I have to talk to her. I'll come by this afternoon. And I want to talk to you, too."

La Manuela stopped before turning the corner.

"Will you come in your car?"

"I don't know. Why?"

"So that you can park it in front of the door. That way Pancho will see that you're with us and won't dare come in."

"If I don't bring the car, I'll leave the dogs outside. Pancho's afraid of them."

"Naturally, since he's a coward."

3

Miss Lila looked at Pancho Vega through the window grille, but in spite of the things he was saying she didn't lower her eyes; she had known him too long to be shocked. Besides, it's good to see this big clown again.

"Why you're just like a sailor now, Pancho, only on land, what with your truck and your freight trips: a woman in every port. I'll bet poor Emita never sees hide nor hair of you. Being married to you must be torture."

"She's not complaining."

This time Miss Lila blushed.

"And you, Lilita?"

He tried to take her hand through the grille.

"Cut it out, silly."

Miss Lila motioned toward Octavio who was smoking in the doorway, gazing at the street. Pancho turned to see the object of Lila's fear but seeing only his brother-in-law he shrugged his shoulders. The inside of the shed, whose far end functioned as the post office, was empty except for don Céspedes sitting on one of the bales of clover stacked at the other end. The old man got off his bale and leaned on the doorpost opposite Octavio, to watch the street. Across the road, a few people were hanging around the other shed, the one that was a chapel on Sundays and a party meeting place during the week. It, too, belonged to don Alejo and was even smaller than the post office shed, but this didn't upset the religious ceremonies: the present chapel space was more than enough for the parishioners, especially after harvest when the outsiders and the owners' families would leave. Pancho turned around and lit a cigarette.

"Did the priest from San Alfonso arrive?"

Don Céspedes shook his head.

"They probably had car trouble."

Octavio slapped the old man's shoulder.

"Don Céspedes, you old fool. That priest was probably sleepy this morning and stayed glued between the sheets. They say he danced all night long at old Wooden Heart's house in Talca . . ."

Miss Lila stuck her head out.

"Atheists! You'll go to hell for that."

Pancho laughed while don Céspedes took his hand out of his cape and crossed himself. Octavio went and sat on a bale. Don Céspedes looked at the sky.

"It's going to rain."

He followed Octavio and sat higher up on the pyramid of bales, dangling his dark, dwarfed feet, deformed by scars and dirt in their muddy sandals.

Through the grille the conversation continued.

"Didn't you sleep with Japonesita last night?"

"Me? Not me. I haven't been there for a long time. I'm not wanted there."

"Well, you do overdo it . . ."

"The worst part is that I'm in love."

Miss Lila said sure, Japonesita was a good girl and all, but is she ugly, and no taste at all in clothes. She looks as if she came from an orphanage, with those baggy pants down to her ankles that she wears under her apron. Of course, it's strange that she does that kind of work, since everyone knows she's a decent girl. Yes, yes, she inherited the house from her mother, but she could sell it. When she was a kid, Big Japonesa sent her to school. It was right here, in the shed, before don Alejo bought it. Anyway, my little sister told me that, even though the other girls and the teacher, too, were nice to her, she'd run and hide in the station until school was over and Big Japonesa never found out, and Japonesita never went out to play or anything and wouldn't even talk to anybody . . . All the decent folk feel sorry for Japonesita, such a queer little thing. And for the time being, Miss Lila keeps an eye out for Japonesita so that she can greet her as nicely as possible whenever she sees her on the street. It's only fair, isn't it?

"Yes, but I'm not in love with her . . ."

Miss Lila looked confused.

"Who is it then?"

"It's la Manuela . . ."

Everyone laughed, even Lila.

"Pigs, bums. You ought to be ashamed . . ."

"It's just that she's so cute . . ."

The couple began to whisper again through the bronze bars. Don Céspedes got down from the bales again and stationed himself in the doorway, looking at the sky.

"Christ! Here comes the rain . . ."

The people waiting near the chapel door took shelter under the eaves, plastered to the wall with their hands in their pockets, behind the curtain of rain that fell from the tile roof. The Guerreros' horse was soaked in a second; the Valenzuelas, who had just arrived, waited for mass in their Ford. Don Alejo came running into the post office, his four black dogs behind him. He brushed the water off his cape and hat. The dogs shook themselves violently and Octavio climbed further up to avoid being soaked too. Then they pranced around the shed, making it seem too small for the four of them.

"Good morning, Céspedes."

"Good morning, boss."

Don Alejo glanced at Octavio but didn't greet him. He saw Pancho from behind: the conversation had come to a halt, but he still had his back turned.

"It's good to see you, Pancho . . ."

When Pancho didn't move, don Alejandro motioned to his dogs, who got up from the floor.

"Othello, Sultan . . ."

Pancho turned around. He raised his hands as if he expected to be shot. Don Alejo called his dogs before they could attack.

"Here, Moor . . ."

"Some joke, don' Alejo . . ."

"You could at least answer when someone speaks to you."

"People shouldn't make jokes like that."

Octavio looked at them from the top of the bales, near the crossbeam that supported the roof. Don Alejo walked through the storeroom toward Pancho, surrounded by the leaping dogs. The only things alive in the whole place, where even the lime on the walls was brownish, were the blue of don Alejo's eyes and the red flames of his dogs' slavering tongues.

"And how about your little jokes? Do they seem so trivial to you, you ungrateful bum? Do you think I don't know why you came? I got you a job hauling grapes, but a few days ago, I personally called Augusto to tell him to take it away from you."

"We'd better talk somewhere else . . ."

"Why? Don't you want people to know that you're an ungrateful scoundrel? Besides, it's raining and I don't want to get any wetter, the doctor told me to take care of myself. Don Céspedes, could you do me a favor and run to the butcher, the one just down a ways, and tell Melchor to send me a few good scraps so these dogs will quiet down. And who's that?"

Octavio quickly jumped down from the bales. He cleared his throat while he dusted his dark suit and adjusted the tie that had slipped inside his shirt. Pancho answered.

"Octavio, my brother-in-law."

"The one who works at the gas station?"

"Yes, sir. At your service. Me and Pancho are buddies, you can talk in front of me . . ."

The restlessness of the four black dogs, their magnificent tails, and pulsating throats, filled the shed. Don Alejo's deft eyes withstood Pancho's black look, forcing it to stay fixed under the shadowy eyelashes. He read those eyes like a book: Pancho didn't want Octavio to know about his debt. The wind rustled through the shreds of old letters tacked to the wall.

"So you don't care if I call you an ungrateful scoundrel just as long as we're alone? In that case, you're a filthy coward as well."

"That's enough, don Alejo."

"Your father, God rest his soul, wouldn't let me talk to him like that. Now there was a man. The son who was going to take after him! I lent you that money for him and he's the only reason I haven't had you put away. Get it?"

"I didn't sign anything."

The dogs, sensing don Alejo's fury, stood up, teeth bared, growling at Pancho.

"You lying bastard."

"Here, I've brought you the five overdue payments."

"And do you think that will satisfy me? Don't you think I know why you came? I can see under that layer of grease, I know you as if you were my own. It's obvious, they canceled your freight contracts. So you've come with your tail between your legs to pay me, so that I'll get them back for you. Give me the money, you ungrateful bum . . . give it to me, I said . . ."

"I'm not ungrateful."

"What are you, then, a thief?"

"All right, don Alejo, cut it out, that's enough . . ."

"Give me the money."

Pancho handed him the wad of bills, warm because he had been clutching them in his hand in the bottom of his pocket, and don Alejo slowly counted them. Then he put them under his cape. Negus licked the toe of his shoe.

"All right. You still owe me six installments, and I want them on time, you understand. And listen, I want you to understand something anyone less stupid would already know: I pull a lot of strings, so be careful. You're not getting away with anything just because you didn't sign a piece of paper; if I gave you some freedom it was to see how you'd act, although knowing you like I do, I should have known better and let you sweat it out by yourself. Now you know. Next time tell me you can't pay me on time, act like a man, and then we'll see what I can do for you."

"It's just that I didn't have the time . . ."

"That's a lie."

"It's because I haven't been in the neighborhood, don Alejo."

"Another lie. When are you going to break that damn habit? They told me you were seen several times in your brother-in-law's gas station on the north-south road. Would it have done you any harm to drive the mile and a half here or to the outskirts of town? Or don't you know the way to the house where you were born?"

No. He didn't want to have anything to do with that house or with this lousy town. It pained him to give his money to don Alejo. It meant recognizing the old link, and being chained again to everything he had managed to forget for a while, like a person who whistles to forget his fear of the dark; for five months he had the strength to not pay him, to resist him and save the money, to dream about using it for other things as if he had the right to spend it. It was a little extra money for the house that Ema wanted to buy in that new district in Talca, the one with the houses that looked alike, only painted different colors so that they don't look alike, and when Ema wants something there's no stopping her. Fortunately, Pancho didn't spend much time at home now with all his jobs, sometimes he even preferred to park the truck on the side of the road and sleep there. That's why, she was always saying, that's why I need the house, I almost never see you and how do I know what you're up to, the child and I should have some compensation. . . . And when I take to bed with my ulcer, a fire that burns me here, an animal that roots and gnaws and tears and sucks me, here, inside, and I can't sleep or talk or move or drink or eat, or hardly even breathe; sometimes when everything is hard and cramped and I'm afraid the animal will bite me and I'll burst, then Ema takes care of me, and I look to her because without her I would die and she knows it. So she takes care of him as if he were a moaning, repentant child, but she knows he'll still do the same things the same old way. That's why Pancho needs the house. Sometimes he drives by the neighborhood in his truck to see how fast the "For Sale" signs are disappearing. Now there are no more pink ones left, just blue and yellow, and Ema wanted a pink one. What are a few hundred dollars to don Alejo?

"So why don't you call don Augusto back so I can have those good freight routes again?"

"What was so hard about settling your accounts with me, if the freights were so good?"

Pancho didn't answer. The rain was running the puddles together in the road: impossible to cross. The priest arrived and the people went into the chapel. Pancho didn't answer because he didn't want to. He didn't have to make excuses to anybody, much less to this pompous ass who thought that just because Pancho had been born on his land . . . They said he was don Alejo's son. But then they'd say that about everybody, Miss Lila, Japonesita, and God knows who else, every blue-eyed peon for miles around, but not me. I'd stake my life on my old lady's virtue, and my eyes, they're black and so are my eyebrows, sometimes they take me for a Turk. I don't owe him anything. As a boy his work was driving a tractor and later he learned, on the sly, to drive the car, stealing it from don Alejo with the help of the gentleman's grandsons who were the same age . . . That's all. Learning to drive was all that he owed don Alejo. Plus the last payments for the truck. Until his debt was settled, keep it quiet. Let Ema wait. Maybe another neighborhood like that one, and then everything he wanted, freedom, being on his own, not having to make accounts to anyone . . . that'll be the last of this lousy town for me. But the old man had to say I was behind in my payments in front of Octavio. So that later Octavio might mention it and Ema's stuck-up brothers . . . no, not Octavio, he's my friend . . . the rest of them, yeah, they'll gossip about me all over the place.

"So? What was so hard about it?"

Don Céspedes came back with the scraps. The dogs whined eagerly, licking his feet, his hands, jumping on him, all but knocking him down.

"Throw them a scrap, don Céspedes . . ."

The gory hunk flew and the dogs leaped after it, the four of them falling together in a clot on the floor, fighting over the piece of meat that was still warm, almost alive. They clawed at it, trampling it into the floor and howling at it, bloody snouts drooling, pimply palates, yellow eyes flashing in narrow faces. The men stuck to the walls. The meat devoured, the dogs began to dance, not around don Céspedes who had fed them, but don Alejo, as if they knew that the man with the cape owned the meat they ate and the vineyards they guarded. He caressed them—his four dogs, black as wolf shadows with their bloody fangs and heavy ferocious paws of the purest blood line.

"No. Not until you pay me the remaining installments. I don't have any reason to trust you. I'm old and I'm going to die and I don't want to leave any loose ends . . ."

"All right, whatever you want, don Alejo . . ."

The floor was a crimson swamp. The dogs sniffed, snorting in search of something to lick. Pancho Vega clenched his teeth. He looked at Octavio, who winked at him, don't be upset, pal, just wait, we'll straighten this thing out between ourselves. But boy, this old rooster was tough. They heard the church bells.

"Aren't you going to mass, Pancho?"

He didn't answer.

"When you were little you used to help during the services. It made

poor Blanca very happy to see you so pious, such a pretty little boy.
And those long confessions, we almost died laughing . . . How about
you, don Céspedes?"

"Of course, boss . . ."

"See? Don Céspedes goes to mass."

Pancho looked at Octavio, who shook his head.

"Don Céspedes is your tenant."

And he swallowed hard so that he could add:

"I'm not."

"But you owe me money and he doesn't."

True. Better not start anything now. Better go to mass without arguing. Can't do me any harm. When I'm home on Sunday, Ema dresses
Normita in her sky-blue coat with the white fur and tells me to come
with them to the eleven-thirty mass, which is the best one, and I go
because it makes no difference to me and I like to greet the neighbors,
sometimes I enjoy it and even look forward to it, other times I don't, but
I always go because we look so elegant. I'll go with don Alejo, he's
watching me from the door, ordering me to go. But Pancho couldn't help
saying:

"No. I'm not going."

Octavio smiled, satisfied at last. But before leaving, don Alejo turned.

"Ah. I almost forgot. They told me you've been talking about la
Manuela, saying you're going to get her or something. Don't let me find
out that you've gone to Japonesita's to bother them, they're good people.
You've been warned."

He walked out followed by his dogs, who splashed across the muddy
road and waited under the eaves behind the sheet of water. Don
Céspedes, hat in hand, held the chapel door open: the dogs entered with
the ringing of the bells, and behind them, don Alejo.

4

Japonesita couldn't guess at first why don Alejo wanted to speak to her
so urgently. When la Manuela gave her the message, she was surprised,
the senator would always drop in without warning like a man in his
own home. But soon she realized that so much protocol could mean only
one thing: he was finally going to tell her the result of his efforts to
bring electricity to town. He had been promising to get it done for a long
time. But the answer to the request was always put off from year to year,
who knows how many now, and it was never the right moment to
approach the authorities. The Commissioner was always away on a trip
or we're already spending too much on another area or the secretary of the
Commission belongs to the enemy party and it would be better to wait.

But last Monday, as she crossed the Place of Arms in Talca on her way to the bank, Japonesita met don Alejandro on his way to the Commission. They stopped on the corner. He bought her a bag of roasted peanuts, a present he said, but while they talked he ate almost all of them himself, crushing the shells which stuck to the hair of his vicuña cape as they fell, there where his belly protruded a little. He said this time for sure: everything was ready. He had an interview with the Commissioner in half an hour and he was going to throw the Commissioner's neglect of Estación El Olivo back in his face. Japonesita had wandered around the square waiting for don Alejo to return with the results of the momentous interview. Then, since she had other things to do and it was time to catch the train, she had to leave without seeing him. All week she had waited for him to come into town, but he didn't even pass through, not once. She resigned herself to wondering, and more waiting.

But today's the day. Finally. Japonesita stayed in the kitchen after lunch, while all the whores crawled back into their caves and la Manuela took Lucy to her room. Instead of adding another log to revive the remaining cinders in the stove, she kept creeping closer and closer to the fading fire, burrowing deeper and deeper into her shawl: my bones are blue from cold. It was already getting dark out. The rain kept coming and the water slowly covered the brick stepping stones that Cloty had placed across the patio. On the other side, facing the kitchen, Lucy's door was open and Japonesita watched her light a candle. From time to time she looked over to see what they were laughing about. The last outburst, the loudest yet, was because la Manuela, with his mouth full of hairpins from the modern hairdo he was giving Lucy, couldn't help laughing and scattered the pins on the floor, which kept the two of them on their knees quite awhile.

There was still some light outside. But it was reluctant, and too feeble to defeat the kitchen's darkness. Japonesita reached out to touch one of the burners: a trace of heat. All this was going to change with electricity. This awful weather. The water invaded the kitchen through the adobe wall, forming a mud that struck to everything. Maybe then she could stand the aggressive cold that seized her body with the first winds, cramping and squeezing it. Maybe the humidity would stop mounting from May to June to July, until by August the scummy mildew seemed to completely cover her body, her face, her clothing, her food, everything. Electricity would bring the town back to life as in the days of her mother's youth. Last Monday, while she waited for don Alejo, she wandered through a store where they sold Wurlitzers. She had often stopped at the window to look at them, separated from their colors and music by her own reflection in the glass. She had never gone in. This time she did. A salesman with colorless eyelashes and translucent ears waited on her, demonstrating, wooing her with pamphlets, assuring her of long-term guarantees. Japonesita realized that she was going through the motions without really believing that she could ever buy one of those wonderful machines. But she could. As soon as the town got electricity she was going to buy a Wurlitzer. No, sooner. Because if don Alejo was bringing her the news today that he had receive permission to install the electricity or that he had succeeded in signing an agreement or document, she would buy the Wurlitzer tomorrow, Monday morning, the one with the most colors, with the painting of a turquoise sea and palm trees, the biggest one of all. Tomorrow morning she would talk to the boy with the colorless lashes and ask him to have it delivered. Then, the first day the electricity went on in town, the Wurlitzer would go on in her house.

Better not say anything to la Manuela. She would only have to mention the project and he'd go crazy with excitement, jabbering, anticipating, not a moment's peace, until she'd end up deciding not to buy anything at all. He was undressing in the room across the way, to try on the red dress by candlelight. At his age he was no longer afraid of the cold. Just like my mother, may she rest in peace. Even on the worst days, like this one for instance, she'd always wear a low-cut dress, big and fat, her heavy breasts like bulging sacks of grapes. At the neckline's V where he breasts began to swell she always carried a tiny handkerchief, and while she was chatting or drinking from her enormous wine bottle or making the best pastry in the world, she would take out her handkerchief and dry the almost imperceptible drops of perspiration that always broke out on her forehead and nose, and especially around the low neckline. They said that Big Japonesa died because of some liver thing, from drinking so much wine. But that's not true. She didn't drink that much. My mother died of grief. Grief because Estación El Olivo was going downhill, because it was no longer what it used to be. All the talking she'd do to don Alejo about the electricity. Nothing doing. Then they said the paved road, the north-south, was going to go right through El Olivo, and that would make it an important town. As long as she had hope my mother thrived. But then they told her the truth, I think it was don Alejo, that the road would only come within a mile and a half of the town, and then she began to lose hope. The north-south is silver-plated, straight as a knife: with one slash it cut the life out of Estación El Olivo, nestled in a cozy bend of the old road. They didn't ship the freight by rail anymore, but by truck, on the road. Now the train came through only a couple of times a week. Scarcely a handful of townspeople were left. Big Japonesa remembered, toward the end, how in the old days the midday summer mass would attract the most sumptuous wagons and carriages in the area, and the elegant young men from the country would meet at sunset in front of the post office, on purebred horses, to pick up the mail that came by train. The boys, so proper during the day when they escorted their sisters, cousins, or sweethearts, let their hair down at night at Japonesa's house, which never closed. And then just the road construction men came, traveling the mile and a half on foot, and then not even them, only the common laborers from nearby, the tenants, the peons, the outsiders who came for harvest. Another class entirely. And later on, not even them. Now the trip to Talca was so short that Sunday was the slowest day—you could be in the city in no time, and it was useless to try and compete with houses like Wooden Heart's. Not even electricity, she used to say, not even that, she was always complaining about so many things, about the fire in her stomach, monotonously, softly complaining, bloated and hollow-eyed toward the end. But no, never, nothing, in spite of don Alejo's telling her to wait just a bit more but one fine day she couldn't wait anymore and she started to die. And when she died we buried her in the cemetery at San Alfonso because El Olivo doesn't even have a cemetery. El Olivo is nothing but a few run-down houses scattered by the geometry of vineyards which seem on the verge of swallowing them up. And what's he laughing about? What right does he have to ignore the cold that's shredding my bones?

"Father!"

She shouted it from the kitchen door. La Manuela stopped in the lighted frame of Lucy's doorway. Thin, small, she looked like a teenager, standing there in the doorway with one hip gracefully turned out and his face outlined in the dark. But she knew that body. It didn't give off heat. It didn't warm the sheets. It wasn't her mother's body: that almost material heat that she had crawled into as if it were a cauldron, sinking into it, drying her moldy clothing and her bones and everything . . .

"What?"

"Come here."

"What do you want?"

"Just come here."

"I'm busy with Lucy."

"I'm telling you I need you."

La Manuela, covering himself with the flamenco dress, crossed the lake in the patio as well as he could, paddling among the fallen leaves from the grape arbor. Japonesita sat down again by the dying fire.

"So dark here, child. Is this a wake?"

Japonesita didn't answer.

"I'm throwing another log on the fire."

He didn't wait for it to catch fire.

"Shall I light a candle?"

What for? She could spend the whole afternoon, the whole day in the dark, like now, without the slightest nostalgia for light, although she would long for a little heat.

"All right."

La Manuela lit the candle and after putting it on the table near the potatoes, put on his glasses and sat down to sew by its light. Lucy's room was dark. She would sleep till dinner. It was easy to kill time that way. Five o'clock. Still three hours till dinner. Three hours and it was already dark. Three hours before night, before work.

"I'll bet no one comes tonight."

La Manuela stopped. He held the dress up against his body, the neck with his chin, the waist with his hands.

"How does it look?"

"Okay."

The rain stopped. In the henhouse they heard Lucy's turkey ruffle his feathers arrogantly: the payment of one lover who didn't have anything else to give. The dress fit perfectly.

"I'll bet no one comes tonight."

"You know that Pancho Vega will come."

La Manuela pricked her finger with the needle and sucked it.

"Me? That Pancho Vega's coming?"

"Of course. Why else are you fixing your dress?"

"But he's not in town."

"You told me last night you heard the horn . . ."

"Yes, but I don't . . ."

"You know he's coming."

Why deny it. The girl's right. Pancho will come tonight come hell or high water. She picked up her dress, the ancient percale, warm from the fire. The whole damn day raining like the devil and she fixing her dress, and herself. Let's see if he's the man he says he is. He'll regret it. If anything happens tonight, the whole town will know, everyone, even the dead, we'll see how much he likes saying things about poor fags. La Manuela laid the dress down and put the candle on the wash basin, below the piece of mirror. She began to comb her hair. So little left. Barely four strands to slick across my skull. I can't do any hairdo with it. Those days are gone.

"Listen."

Japonesita raised her head.

"What?"

"Come over here."

She moved to a wicker chair in front of the mirror. La Manuela took hold of Japonesita's lank hair, squinted both eyes and looked at her, you have to try to look pretty, and began to untangle it—what good is it being a woman if you're not a flirt, that's what men like, silly, that's what they come here for, to forget the scarecrows they're married to, and with your hair this way, look, this is how you do it, now it looks nice, with a bit falling over your forehead and the rest up in what they call a beehive; and la Manuela untangles it for her and here they put a ribbon, don't you have a pretty ribbon? I think I have one stuck away in my suitcase, I'll lend it to you if you want, I'll put it right here. Last summer I saw one of don Alejo's granddaughters with her hair like that, see how nice you look with it this way, don't be silly, take advantage of it . . . look, this way . . .

Japonesita calmly gave in. Yes. He was sure to come. She knew it as well as la Manuela did. Last year, when he tried to take advantage of her, she felt his sour breath on her cheek, in her nostrils. Under her father's thin hands, which occasionally grazed her face, the memory pressed on Japonesita. He had seized her with his brick-rough hands, his square thumb, the corroded, oil-stained, wide, flat nail imbedded in her arm, hurting, a bruise that lasted over a month . . .

"Father."

La Manuela didn't answer.

"What do we do if he comes?"

La Manuela put the comb down. In front of the mirror Japonesita's hair was as smooth as an African's skin.

"You have to protect me if Pancho comes."

La Manuela threw the hairpins on the floor. That was the limit. Why did she keep playing the fool? Did she expect her, la Manuela, to stand up to a hulking brute like Pancho? She's got to realize it once and for all and stop telling herself lies . . . you damn well know I'm just a hopeless fag, no one ever tried to hide it from you. And you're asking me for protection: when Pancho comes I'll run and hide like a nervous hen. It isn't my fault I'm your father. He didn't make the famous bet and he didn't want anything to do with the whole affair. What could he do. I've asked you I don't know how many times since Big Japonesa died to give me my share so that I can go, where I don't know, there'll always be some whorehouse where I can work . . . but you never wanted me to go. And neither did I. It was all Big Japonesa's fault, she had convinced him—that they would make a fortune with the house, what did the girl matter, and when Big Japonesa was alive the girl didn't count because la Manuela liked her mother . . . but it's been four years since they buried her in the cemetery at San Alfonso because this lousy town doesn't even have its own cemetery, and they'll bury me there too, and in the meantime, here sits la Manuela. Not even a floor in the kitchen: plain mud. So why should Japonesita bother her? If she wanted someone to protect her, she should get married, or get a man. Why he wasn't even good for dancing anymore. Last year, after that Pancho thing, his daughter bawled him out saying she was ashamed of being the daughter of an old fairy like him. That of course she'd like to go somewhere else to live and start a new business. But that she wouldn't because Estación El Olivo was small and everyone knew them and were so used to them that they didn't even notice. Not even the children asked questions because they were born knowing it. There's no need for explaining, that's what Japonesita said, and one of these days the town is going to go up in smoke and you and me with it, this shitpile of a town that never asks questions and that nothing ever surprises. A store in Talca. No sir. No restaurant, no cigar stand, no laundromat, no warehouse, nothing. For us El Olivo, to hide in. . . . Okay, okay, you crappy girl, then don't call me father. Because when Japonesita called him father, the flamenco dress over the washstand looked older, the percale threadbare, the red faded, the stitches showing, horrible, inane, and the long, cold, dark night reaching through the vineyards, clutching, choking this spark that had been cultivated in the deserted town, don't call me father, empty-headed bitch. Call me la Manuela, like everybody else. And you want me to protect you! That's all I need. And what about me, who's going to protect me? No, one of these fine days I'm packing my wares and leaving for a big town like Talca. I'm sure Wooden Heart will give me a job. But he had said that once too often and he was sixty years old. He went on smoothing his daughter's hair.

"What am I supposed to protect you from? Don't be a fool, go to bed with him. He's splendid. The best stud around and he has a truck and everything and he could take us for rides. And since you'll have to be a whore someday . . ."

. . . let him have her. Tonight's the night, even if there will be bleeding. With Pancho Vega or anyone else, she knew that. But today it's Pancho. For a whole year she'd been dreaming of him. Dreaming that he beat her and raped her, but in that violence, beneath it or within it, she found something that beat the winter's cold. Last winter, because Pancho was cruel and brutal and had twisted her arm, had been the warmest winter since Big Japonesa died. And la Manuela's fingers, touching her head, patting her cheek near the ear while fabricating a flirtatious curl, they weren't so cold . . . he was a child, la Manuela. She could hate him, like a minute ago. And not hate him. A child, a little bird. Anything but a man. He himself said he was very much the woman. But that wasn't true either. Anyway, he's right. If I'm going to be a whore I may as well start with Pancho.

La Manuela finished doing Japonesita's hair up in a beehive. A woman. She was a woman. She would get Pancho. He was a man. A poor old queer. A fag who was mad for parties and wine and rags and men. It was easy to forget, sheltered here in town—yes, she's right, we better stay here. But then Japonesita would suddenly call him that and his own image would blur as if a drop of water had fallen on it and then he'd lose sight of herself, himself, myself, I don't know, he doesn't know, he can't see la Manuela anymore and there's nothing, this anguish, this helplessness, nothing else, this enormous blot of water in which he's shipwrecked.

As he gave the finishing touches to the hairdo la Manuela sensed through her hair that his daughter was warming up to him. As if she had really surrendered her head so that he could make it beautiful. This kind of help he could and wanted to give her. Japonesita was smiling.

"Light another candle so I can see myself better . . ."

He lit it and set it on the other side of the mirror. Japonesita softly touched her own reflection in the piece of mirror. She turned around: "Do I look all right?"

Yes, if Pancho wasn't such a beast Japonesita might fall in love with him and they'd be lovers for a while until he left her and went away with someone else because that's the way men are and then she'd be different. And maybe not so stingy, thought la Manuela, not so tight with my money, after all, I work hard enough to get it. And maybe she won't be so cold. A little pain or bitterness when the brute leaves, but what did that matter, if she, and la Manuela too, would feel easier.

It was one of those nights when la Manuela felt like going to bed: bundle up, take a pill, and, another day. She didn't want to see anybody because she had given all her warmth to Japonesita, leaving herself with none. Outside the clouds chased around the vast sky that was beginning to clear, and in the patio the kneading trough, chicken coop, outhouse, everything, even the most insignificant object acquired volume, flinging precise shadows over the water wasting away under the speckled sky. Maybe Pancho wouldn't come after all . . . it was probably one of don Alejo's jokes, him being so fond of jokes. Maybe not even don Alejo would come in this cold—he himself said he was sick and that the doctors were pestering him with examinations and diets and treatments. She touched her dress, wilted over the dirty potatoes, and in the silence she heard Lucy's snores from the other side of the patio. She saw herself in the mirror, over her daughter's face which gazed at itself ecstatically . . . the candles, on either side, were like those of a wake. Her own wake would have light like that, in the parlor where she used to dance when the party's warmth had melted the harshness of everything. She was going to remain in Estación El Olivo forever. Die here, a long, long time before this daughter of hers who couldn't dance but was young and a woman whose hope, as she looked at herself in the broken mirror, wasn't a grotesque lie.

"Do I really look good?"

"Not bad . . . for an ugly thing like you . . ."

5

They put a jar of wine, the very best, in front of him, but he didn't even taste it. While he was talking, Japonesita removed one of the pins that held her hair and scratched her head with it. The dogs were lying on the mud sidewalk, growling near the door from time to time or scratching at it so hard that they almost knocked it down.

"Easy, Negus . . . easy, Moor . . ."

La Manuela also sat at the table. She poured herself a glass of wine, the kind her daughter reserved for special occasions and never let her drink. Cloty, Lucy, Elvira, and another whore were drinking tea in a corner where the wind, blowing in through the cracks in the doors and roof, wouldn't get them. Pour me some more. No one's coming tonight. They were yawning. She'll probably close up as soon as the gentleman leaves and then we can go to sleep. Elvira, change the record, put on "Bésame Mucho," no no, something better, a happier one. Elvira wound the Victrola on top of the counter, but before putting on another record she started to clean it with a rag, straightening the pile of records next to it.

Don Alejo brought bad news: they weren't going to install electricity in town. Until who knows when. Maybe never. The Commissioner said he didn't have time to bother with anything so insignificant, that it was El Olivo's destiny to disappear. Not even all of don Alejo's influence combined with that of the whole Cruz clan could convince the Commissioner. Maybe in a couple of years, but he wasn't making any promises. Come back then and we'll see if things have cleared up any. It was the same as a flat no. And that's what don Alejo told Japonesita, in no uncertain terms. He tried to convince her that it was logical the Commissioner would think that way, he gave her reasons and explanations even though Japonesita didn't utter a single word of protest—yes, well you see, child, there are so few coopers left, a couple, I think, and so old now, and the rest of the people, as you can see, are so few and so poor, and the train hardly even stops here anymore, just on Mondays, so you can get on in the morning and come back in the afternoon when you go to Talca. Even the wine cellar at the station is falling down and it's been so long since I've used it that not even the smell of wine is left.

"Even Ludo told me this morning when I went to ask for red thread, before I met you, don Alejandro, that she was thinking about moving to

Talca. It's only natural, what with her Acevedo buried there, and mass every day, and her sister and all . . ."

"Ludo? I didn't know that. How strange that Blanca didn't say anything and I saw her just a while ago. How is Ludo? Is the house hers . . . ?"

"Of course, Acevedo bought it for her when . . ."

Then la Manuela remembered that Ludo had told her that don Alejo wanted to buy it from her, so he know very well who the property belonged to. She looked at him, but when her eyes met the senator's she looked away, and glancing at the whores she motioned them to come over by the stove. Lucy settled herself between Japonesita and don Alejo and she offered him the wine again.

"Don't you dare turn me down, don Alejo. It's from the vintage you like so well. Why even you don't have any of this left . . ."

"No thank you, dear. I'm on my way. It's getting late."

He picked up his hat, but before getting up he lingered a moment and covered Japonesita's hand with his huge one. She dropped the hairpin in a pool of wine on the table.

"You ought to get out of here too. Why do you stay?"

La Manuela was burning to take part.

"That's what I keep telling her, don Alejo. Why are we staying here?"

The whores stopped murmuring in the corner and, as if expecting a verdict, looked at Japonesita. Huddled in her pink shawl, making the slow steady motion of negation with her head that la Manuela knew.

"Don't be silly. Go to Talca and set up business with la Manuela. You have plenty of money in the bank. I know because the other day I asked the manager, my cousin, about the state of your account. I wish it were mine . . . that's what he told me, a lot of holdings and a lot of debts, but Japonesita has it all cleared up. Buy a restaurant, for example. If you don't have enough I'll ask the bank for a loan and I'll endorse it for you. You'll have the money in a couple of days, everything arranged among friends, people you know. Cheer up, girl, can't you see, this isn't living. Right, Manuela?"

"Certainly, don Alejo, help me convince her . . ."

"Why ask him when all he wants is to fool around?"

"The money belongs to both of you, in equal shares, that's how I see it. Isn't that how Big Japonesa left it?"

"Yes. We would have to sell the house . . ."

Don Alejo let scarcely a minute elapse.

"I'll buy it from you . . ."

His eyes were turned down, staring at the hairpin floating in the wine. And on the back of the generous hand that sheltered Japonesita's golden hairs flamed. But she, la Manuela, was very sharp, and he wasn't going to fool her. She had known him too long not to realize he was plotting something. She had always wanted to catch him at one of those shady deals his political enemies accused him of. Of course, when they elected him deputy almost twenty years ago, he sold the voters a lot of cheap land, on long terms, here in Estación, because this town is on its way up, there's a big future here, in these parts, and the people started painting and fixing their houses, because naturally, values were going up around here ... yessiree, not even a sewer, and barely a couple of streets of flattened ground. What do you want to do to us now? Don't you think you've done enough already? What's gotten into your head now, want to buy the few houses in town that aren't already yours. Don't come around telling her, la Manuela, stories. Don Alejo didn't come to tell them the bad news about the electricity, he came to offer to buy the house. His blue eyes had sparkled at the mention of Ludo's house. And now this house ... he wanted to take it away from them, hers and Japonesita's house. What did it matter if don Alejo made them jump through hoops and lose all their money, as long as they went to live in Talca!

"You don't like this business, you never liked it, not the way your mother did. I'll get you the money tomorrow if you want, and we can draw up the sales contract at the notary's, if you decide. Give her a little push, Manuela. I can help you find a convenient locale in Talca, a good one, a really good one. Are you taking the train tomorrow?"

"Yes. I have to make a deposit."

"Well then ..."

She didn't answer.

This time don Alejo stood up: the kernel of light in the neck of the carbon lamp fluttered with the cape's motion. The dogs began to pace around outside, thirstily smelling the air of the room through the door hinge. La Manuela and Japonesita followed him to the door. He reached for the latch. With his other hand he put on his hat; it shadowed his face. He spent a few moments talking to them, repeating that they should think it over, if they wanted they could talk about it again another day, he was at their service, they knew how fond he was of them, if they wanted the house appraised, he knew an honest authority and was prepared to pay the appraiser's estimate ...

When he finally opened the door, went out into the air and the stars, and closed it again, the Wurlitzer behind Japonesita's frowning eyes shattered into a million pieces. She and the town faded into darkness. What did it matter if everything went downhill, it made no difference as long as she didn't have to move or change. No. She'd stay here, surrounded by the things she knew, surrounded by this obscurity in which nothing happened that wasn't a degree of slow, invisible death. No. The electricity and the Wurlitzer were nothing more than mirages which for an instant, a blessedly short one, made her believe that something else was possible. But not now. Not a hope remained to grieve her, even fear was eliminated. Nothing would ever change, it never had, it would be the same forever. She went back to the table and sat in the chair warm from don Alejo's cape. She leaned over the stove.

"Lock the door, Cloty . . ."

La Manuela, who was walking toward the Victrola, stopped short and turned abruptly.

"Are we going to close up?"

"Yes. No one's coming now."

"But it's not going to rain anymore."

"The roads are probably filled with mud."

"But . . ."

". . . and there's a frost coming."

La Manuela went to sit on the other side of the stove, and also leaned over it. Cloty put "Black Flowers" on the Victrola and the record began to shriek. The other whores disappeared.

"Why don't we think about what don Alejo said?" she said.

Because suddenly she saw that don Alejo, just as he had created the town, had other plans now, and to carry them out he needed to get rid of Estación El Olivo. He would tear down all the houses, he would wipe away the crude mud streets and cow dung, he would reunite the adobe of the thick walls with the land it came from and he would plow that land, all for some incomprehensible purpose. She saw it all. Clearly. The electricity would have meant salvation. Now . . .

"Let's leave, daughter."

Japonesita began talking without looking at la Manuela, scrutinizing the gray-headed coals. At first it seemed as if she were only singing softly, or praying, but then la Manuela realized she was talking to him.

"Stop the record, Cloty, I can't hear."

"Will you need me?"

"No."

"Well, goodnight."

"Goodnight. I'll close up later."

They were alone in the parlor huddled over the stove.

". . . let well enough alone. What would we do in a big town? People laughing at us . . . no friends, living in another house. Here there'll always be peasants who are horny or who feel like getting drunk . . . We won't die of hunger or shame. Every Monday when I go to Talca I get back to the station early to wait for the train so people won't look at me—sometimes I wait for over an hour, sometimes two, and there's almost no one at the station . . ."

When Japonesita started talking like that la Manuela felt like screaming, it was as if his daughter were drowning him in words, slowly encircling him with her flat voice, that monotonous singsong. Damn the town! Damn the girl! Believing things were going to change and his life would improve because Big Japonesa made him her partner and house proprietor after the bet that, thanks to him, she won from don Alejo. Of course things were better then. Even the carbon lamps gave off more light, not like now with the rains starting and oh, my God, four months of feeling ugly and old, when I could have been a princess. And now don Alejo offering to help us so that we can go to Talca and start a business, the two of us happy, no troubles, she'd like dry goods since rags was something she knew about, but no, the girl would start in talking and never stop, like now, slowly building a wall around la Manuela. Japonesita turned the screw to put out the lamp.

"Leave it alone."

She stopped for a moment but then continued turning the screw.

"Fuck you, I said leave it alone. . . ."

La Manuela's scream startled Japonesita, but she kept turning down the light, as if she hadn't heard. Even if I yell I don't exist. Until one fine day she, who could have been the princess of the whorehouses from Chanco to Constitución, from Villa Alegre to San Clemente, princess of all the whorehouses in the province, she would kick the bucket and the old woman of death would come to carry her off forever. Then no trick or lie would convince the stinking old witch to let her be for a little while longer, why do you want to stay, for God's sake, Manuela, let's go, business is much better on the other side, and they would bury her in a niche in the San Alfonso cemetery under a stone that would say, "Manuel González Astica" and then, for a while, Japonesita and the girls from the house would bring her flowers but then Japonesita was sure to go somewhere else, and of course, Ludo would die too and no more flowers and no one in the whole area, just a few spitting old men, would remember that the great Manuela was lying there.

She went to the Victrola to put on another record.

Black flowers
of destiny
in my loneliness
your soul will tell me
I love yoooooouuuu . . .

La Manuela stopped the record. She put her hand on the black turntable. Japonesita had stood up too. In the center of the night, far away, on the road that led into town from the north-south highway, a horn swelled, a hot, insistent, red flame that got closer and closer. A horn. Again. Playing the fool, the idiot, waking everyone up at this hour. It was coming into town. The truck with the double tires on the back wheels. Honking all the time, now in front of the chapel, yes, honking and honking because he's probably drunk. La Manuela smiled, the fragments of·her face neatly arranged.

"Turn off the lamp, you fool."

Before it went out, la Manuela made out a smile on her daughter's face—fool, she's not afraid of Pancho, she wants him to come, she's waiting for him, the fool is eager for him to come, and I'm waiting too, dirty old woman . . . but it was important for Pancho to think that no one was up. And important that he not come in, that he think everyone in the house was asleep. That he knew they weren't waiting for him and that he couldn't come in even if he wanted to.

"He's coming."

"What are we going to do . . ."

"Don't move."

The horn came closer in the night, undeniably closer, as if in the whole vineyard-striped land there was nothing that could stop it. In the dark la Manuela went to the door. She opened the latch. Scoundrel, waking up the whole town at this hour! She remained by the door while the horn summoned and aroused every muscle, every nerve and left them alive and suspended, ready to receive wounds or blows—that horn wouldn't stop. Here he comes, yes, in front of the house . . . her ears ached and Japonesita closed her eyes and covered her ears. But like la Manuela, she was smiling.

"Pancho . . ."

"What are we going to do?"

6

The women of the town agreed not to complain for having to stay home that night, even though they knew perfectly well that the men were going to Japonesa's. The mayor's wife, the police sergeant's wife, the postmaster's wife, the schoolmaster's wife: they all knew their men were going to celebrate don Alejandro Cruz's victory, and they knew exactly where and how they'd celebrate it. But because the party was in don Alejandro's honor and anything that had to do with him must be good, they didn't say a word.

That morning they had seen the three Farías sisters step off the train from Talca: Fat and squat like barrels, their flowered silk dresses girdling their beefy flesh like steel bands; they were sweating from the effort of carrying the harp and guitars. Two younger women also got off, and a man, if you could call him that. The women, watching from a careful distance, discussed what he might be: skinny as a broomstick, with long hair, his eyes were made up almost as much as the Farías sisters'. Standing near the platform, knitting to not waste time, surrounded by kids whom they had to keep scolding so they wouldn't beg from the strangers, they had something to talk about for days to come.

"He must be the queer who plays the piano."

"But Japonesa doesn't have a piano."

"That's true."

"They said she was going to buy one."

"He's an actor, look at that case he's carrying."

"He's a queer, that's what he is . . ."

And the kids trailed after them on the dusty road to Japonesa's house.

The ladies, back home for lunch, chided their husbands to not forget a single detail of what went on that night at Japonesa's house, and if there were any delicacies, could they possibly save some tidbits for them in their pockets when no one was looking, after all, they had to stay home alone and bored while the men would be doing God knows what at the party. Of course, it was all right if they got drunk today. This time it was for a good cause. But it was important that they stay close to don Alejandro so he'd see them at his celebration, and they could remind him offhand as if they really didn't want to, about the land deal, and the barrels of wine he had promised to sell them at a discount, yes, let them sing together, dance, and paint the town red, today it didn't matter as long as they were with don Alejandro.

For months the town was wreathed in green, sepia, blue posters of don Alejandro's face. Barefoot boys ran everywhere hurling flyers or kept handing them out to the same people on the street, while the rest of the children, the ones who hadn't been trusted with the political propaganda, collected them and made paper boats or burned them or sat on the corner and counted them to see who had the most. The campaign headquarters operated out of the post office shed, where the citizens of Estación El Olivo met nightly to revive their faith in don Alejo and to spread that faith by arranging interviews and campaign trips to the neighboring towns and districts. But the real heart of the campaign was Japonesa's house. It was there that the ringleaders met, from there came the orders, the projects, the assignments. Now no one went to the house who wasn't a member of don Alejo's party, and the women, drowsing in the corners with nothing to do, heard the voices that schemed untiringly at the tables in the parlor, buzzing around the wine and Japonesa. Especially during the last month; when approaching victory inflamed the proprietress' gift for speeches and made her forget everything but her political passion, she would serve her wine generously to any visitor whose political leanings were precarious or ambiguous, and in the course of a few hours she'd either resolve his doubts or clear up the ambiguities, leaving him with a keen sense of duty.

The election took place ten days ago but don Alejo had only recently returned to town. Japonesa's salon and patio were plastered with pictures of the new congressman. Only the select few in the district received invitations, the chosen citizens of El Olivo, administrators, majordomos, and vineyard keepers from the nearby estates. And from Talca Japonesa commissioned her friend Wooden Heart to send a reinforcement of two whores, the Farías sisters, so there'd be music, and la Manuela, that funny queer who does flamenco dances.

"It's going to cost me plenty. But why shouldn't I please myself too. This is for the bright future that the pride of our county, that brilliant congressman don Alejandro Cruz, here with us, has promised us . . ."

Naturally Japonesa was pleased with it all. She wasn't a kid anymore, no doubt about that, and the last years had fattened her so that the accumulation of fat around her cheeks stretched her mouth perpetually into what seemed to be—and almost always was—a smile. Her myopic eyes, which had earned her the nickname "Japonesa," were nothing more than two oblique slits under the brows that she stenciled in high arches. In her youth she had had an affair with don Alejo. It was whispered that he had brought her to this house years ago, to a former proprietress now long dead. But their affair was a thing of the past, a legend that gave root to the present reality of a friendship that united them like a couple of conspirators. Don Alejo used to spend long periods of time working either in his country vineyards, not returning to his city home until after harvest, or on the pruning or spraying. So he was often away from his wife and family, which was very boring for him. But at night, after dinner, he'd escape to Estación for a few drinks and laughs with Big Japonesa. In those days she took it upon herself to have a special girl for don Alejo, a girl that only he could touch. He was generous. The house that Japonesa lived in was an ancient holding of the Cruz family and he gave it to her for an insignificant annual rent. And every night, winter or spring, the people from the neighboring area, the administrators and the vineyard keepers, the chief mechanics and sometimes even the smaller landowners, and their sons who had to be kicked out when their fathers appeared, all would come to Japonesa's house. Not so much to climb into bed with the women, although they were always young and fresh, but to amuse themselves for a while talking with Japonesa or downing a bottle or playing a hand of cards in a cheerful but safe atmosphere, because Japonesa didn't open her doors to just anybody. Only refined people. Only people with money in their pockets. That's why she belonged to don Alejo's political party, the historical, traditional, organized party, the party of decent people who paid their debts and stayed out of trouble, the people who went to her house for amusement and whose belief that don Alejo would do great things for the region was as unshakable as Japonesa's.

"I have a right to do what pleases me."

The great pleasure of her life was giving the party that night. And she took over la Manuela almost the moment he arrived. She had thought the dancer they told her about was younger: this one was pushing forty, like herself. But it was better this way because young ones tried to compete with the women when the clients got drunk: a big mess. Since la Manuela came early in the morning and didn't have anything to do until late that night, at first he just wandered around and watched, until Japonesa motioned him over to her.

"Help me put these boughs on the platform."

La Manuela took the decorating into his own hands: not so many branches, he said, the Farías sisters are too fat and with harps and guitars and boughs to boot, you won't see them. If you just put branches up there it's better, yellow willow branches with colored paper that looks like green rain, and at the foot of the platform the biggest picture of don Alejo you can find, framed in weeping willow branches too. Japonesa was thrilled with the results. Manuela, help me hang the paper wreaths, Manuela, where's the best place to put the grill for roasting the pigs, Manuela, peek at the salad dressing, Manuela this, Manuela that, Manuela, check that over there. All afternoon and with Japonesa's every order or request, la Manuela would suggest something that would make things prettier or the barbecue sauce tastier. By late afternoon Japonesa, half-drunk, fell into a chair in the middle of the patio, still shouting orders but relaxed because la Manuela was doing everything so well.

"Manuela, did they bring the strawberries for the burgundy?"

"Manuela, let's put more flowers there."

La Manuela ran, obeyed, corrected, suggested.

"I'm having a marvelous time."

Wooden Heart had told him that Japonesa was nice, but not this nice. So unpretentious, being a proprietress and all. When Japonesa went to her room to dress, la Manuela went with her to help: soon after she came out looking elegant for sure with her black silk dress coming to a low point in front, and all her hair gathered in a discreet but coquettish chignon. The wine flowed as soon as the first guests arrived, while the aroma of the pigs, starting to brown, and of the oregano, hot garlic, onions, and cucumbers soaking in the salads' juices, floated into the patio and salon.

Don Alejo arrived, quite bombed, at eight. During the applause he hugged and kissed Japonesa, whose eyeliner had run either from perspiration or from sentimental tears. Then the Farías sisters climbed up to the platform and the music and dancing began. Many of the men took off their jackets and danced in suspenders. The women's flowered dresses darkened under the arms with sweat. The Farías sisters seemed inexhaustible, as if they rewound themselves after every tune, and heat and fatigue didn't exist.

"Bring out another bottle . . ."

Japonesa and don Alejo had quickly finished the first bottle and now they ordered a second. But before starting it the new congressman carried the hostess off to dance while the others formed a circle around them. Then they went to sit down again. Japonesa called to Rosita, who had been brought from Talca especially for don Alejo.

"See, don Alejo? Look at that rump, feel it, go on, just what you like, soft, pure affection. I brought her down just for you, I knew you'd like her, shouldn't I know your tastes by now . . . Come on, let me be, I'm too old for that sort of thing. Yes, look, and Rosita isn't too young because I know you can't stand them when they're like kids . . ."

The congressman squeezed the proffered buttocks and then sat her beside him so he could put his hand under her skirt. The mayor of Estación wanted to dance with Japonesa, but she told him no, that tonight she was at the exclusive service of the guest of honor. She herself chose the golden slices of pig, watching over don Alejo to see that he ate well, until he got up to dance with Rosita, his mustache stained with sauce and oregano and his chin and fingers smeared with grease. La Manuela walked over to Japonesa.

"How're things?"

"Have a seat."

"And don Alejo?"

"All right. He hasn't said a word."

"Good."

"Did you help yourself to everything?"

"It was delicious. All I need is a small glass of wine."

"Drink some of this."

"What time do I dance?"

"Wait until the party warms up a bit."

"Yes, that's better. The other day I danced in Constitución. I had a lovely time and stayed to spend the weekend at the beach. Don't you ever go to Constitución? So pretty, the river and everything, and such good sea food. The owner of the house where I stayed knows you. Her name is Olga and they say she's half German. Which isn't surprising since she's full of freckles, here on her arms. No, I'm from around here, I was born in the country near Maule, that's right, ah, so you've been there too. Hah . . . we're countrywomen. No. I moved into town and later worked with a girl and traveled all the towns in the south, yes, she did well, but don't think it went too badly for me either, just between you and me. But I was young then, now I'm not. I don't know what's become of her, we even worked in a circus once. But that didn't work out at all. I prefer this kind of work. Of course, a girl gets tired of moving around so much, all the towns are alike. No. Wooden Heart is getting senile. Over sixty, way over, almost seventy. Haven't you noticed her varicose veins? And they say she used to have such lovely legs. I brought the dress in my suitcase. Yes. One of the prettiest I've seen. Red. A girl who worked in the circus sold it to me. I guard it like a saint's bone, it's real class and since I'm so dark the red looks magnificent on me. Hey . . . Now?"

"Wait."

"How much longer?"

"About an hour."

"But shall I change?"

"No. It's better to surprise them."

"All right."

"God you're in a hurry."

"Of course. I like to be the belle of the ball."

Two men who overheard the conversation started to laugh at la Manuela, trying to touch her to see if she had breasts. Hey honey . . . what have you got here? Let's have a feel, get out of here you drunk bastard, don't come around here trying to feel me. Then they said it was too much having queers like this around, it was a disgrace, they were going to talk to the policeman sitting in the corner with a whore on his lap, and he'd put la Manuela in jail for being immoral, for being a degenerate. Then la Manuela scratched one of them. Leave her alone. She could have the policeman thrown out of office for being half-drunk. He'd better watch his step, because la Manuela was well known in Talca and on good terms with the police force. I'm a professional, they paid me to put on my show . . .

Japonesa went to get don Alejo and hurried him over so that he'd intervene.

"What are they doing to you, Manuela?"

"This man is bothering me."

"What's he doing to you?"

"He's calling me names."

"Like what?"

"Degenerate . . . and queer . . ."

Everyone laughed.

"Well aren't you?"

"I might be queer but I'm not a degenerate. I'm a professional. No one has the right to treat me like that. What's this ignoramus bothering me for? Who's he to call a girl names, huh? They brought me here because they wanted to see me, so . . . If they don't want the show, fine, pay me for tonight and I'll go, who wants to dance in this shitpile of a town full of starving beggars . . ."

"Okay, Manuela, okay . . . drink this . . ."

And Japonesa made him drink another glass of wine.

Don Alejo broke up the group. He sat down at the table, called to Japonesa, sent away someone who wanted to sit with them, and sat Rosita on one side of him and la Manuela on the other: they toasted with the newly imported burgundy.

"May you be ever triumphant, Manuela . . ."

"The same to you, don Alejo."

When don Alejo got up to dance with Rosita, Japonesa moved her chair next to la Manuela's.

"The man's taken a liking to you, honey, that's easy enough to see. Nope, there's no one like don Alejo, he's one of a kind. He's like God here in town. He does whatever he wants. They're all afraid of him. Don't you know he owns all the vineyards, all of them, as far as the eye can see? And he's so good that when someone offends him, like the guy who was bothering you, he immediately forgives and forgets. He's either a very good man or else he doesn't have time to worry about people like us. He has other worries. Projects, always projects. Now he's selling us land here in Estación, but I know him and I haven't fallen for it yet. According to him, everything's on its way up. Next year he's going to parcel out a block of his land and he's going to make a town out of it, he's going to sell model homes, he says, with easy payments, and when he's sold all the lots he's going to have electricity brought to town and then we'll be riding high for sure. They'll come from all over, my house, you know, already has quite a reputation, they'll come from Duao, from Pelarco . . . We'll expand and my house will be more famous than Wooden Heart's. Ah, Manuela, what a man he is, I was so in love with him. But he doesn't let himself get tied down. He has a wife, of course, a pretty blond, very ladylike, distinguished I'd say, and another woman in Talca and who knows how many more in the capital. And all of them working like dogs for him during election. You should have seen Misia Blanca, she didn't even buy stockings, and the other woman too, the one from Talca, working for him so he could win. Naturally, we all profit by it. And on election day he even came with a truck and anyone who didn't want to vote was thrown in by force and let's go my friend, to San Alfonso to vote for me, and he gave them money and they were so happy with the whole thing that later on they went around asking when there were going to be more elections. Of course they would have voted for him anyway. He's the only candidate they know. The others just from the propaganda posters while don Alejo, him they really know. Who hasn't seen him on that gray horse of his, on his way to the bazaar in San Alfonso every Monday? And besides the money, he gave the ones who voted for him a good supply of wine and he killed a calf, they said, so they could have an all-day barbecue, and he brought them all back to San Alfonso in the truck again, they all said he was such a nice man, but later on he disappeared because he had to go back to the capital to see how things were going . . . Look how the mayor is dancing with that blond . . ."

Japonesa squinted her eyes so she could see the far end of the patio: when she couldn't see something, she'd tell la Manuela to check and see if the blond was still dancing with the same man, and who was Sergeant Buendía with and were the cooks putting more pigs over the coals, look they might not be hungry now but in a little while they'll want to eat again.

Don 'Alejo came over to the table. With his delft blue doll's eyes, the earnest eyes of a saint's statue, he looked at la Manuela who trembled as if all her will power had been absorbed by the gaze that surrounded and dissolved her. How could she help feeling ashamed of meeting those marvelous orbs with her grizzly little eyes and skimpy lashes? She lowered them.

"What's the matter, sweetheart?"

La Manuel looked at him again and smiled.

"Shall we go, Manuela?"

He said it so softly. Was it possible, then . . . ?

"Whenever you want, don Alejo . . ."

Her shivering grew more intense, or multiplied into chills that circled her legs and her whole body, while those eyes remained fastened to hers . . . until they dissolved into a laugh. And la Manuela's chills subsided with don Alejo's friendly slap on the shoulder.

"No, woman. It was just a joke. I don't go in for that . . ."

And they drank together, la Manuela and don Alejo, laughing. La Manuela, still swaddled in a blanket of sensations, took short sips, she smiled a bit, gently. She couldn't remember ever having loved a man as much as at that moment she loved Congressman don Alejandro Cruz. Such a gentleman. So suave, when he wanted to be. Even when he made jokes the others made, with their thick, gross lips, he made them another way, with an artlessness that didn't wound, with a smile far removed from the guffaws of the other men. La Manuela laughed, drinking what was left of her burgundy, as if trying to hide the flush that climbed to her plucked eyebrows behind the greenish wine glass: right then, as she raised the glass, she forced herself to admit that anything besides this platonic cordiality was impossible with don Alejo. She had to break this feeling if she didn't want to die. And she did not want to die. And when she set the glass down on the table again she no longer loved him. What for. Better not to think about it.

Don Alejo was kissing Rosita, his hand under her skirt. He removed it to smooth his hair when a group of men moved their chairs over to the table. Of course he had promised to make the sheds near the station bigger if he was elected, certainly, and of course, remember the electricity as soon as possible and the business about enlarging the police force, especially during harvest, because of the outsiders who wandered around the vineyards looking for work and sometimes stealing, of course he'd remember, this victory isn't going to give me a swelled head, don't forget about us don Alejo, we helped you when you needed us, after all, you're the town's mainstay, its support, without you it would die, yes sir, pour yourself a little more don Alejo, I'd be hurt if you didn't, and pour your girl a little more too, look how thirsty she is, why if you don't take good care of her, she's liable to go off with someone else, but as I was saying, sir, all the sheds leak and they're so small, you can't say no after we've helped you, you said you would. He answered stroking his mustache from time to time. La Manuela winked at him because she saw he was trying not to yawn. She was the only one who realized he was bored, humming along with the singing Farías sisters: that isn't any kind of talk for a party. Men are so tiring with their business talk, isn't that right don Alejo, la Manuela said to him with her eyes, until don Alejo couldn't hold back a monstrous wet yawn that displayed his epiglottis and the whole of his pink palate ending in the tunnel of his trachea, and the men, while don Alejo yawned in their faces, shut up. Then, when he managed to close his mouth, his eyes watering, he searched for la Manuela's face.

"Hey, Manuela . . ."

"What, don Alejo?"

"Weren't you going to dance? This is getting dull."

7

La Manuela whirled in the center of the platform raising a cloud of dust with her red train. The moment the music stopped she plucked the flower she wore behind her ear and tossed it to don Alejo, who rose and caught it in the air. The crowd broke into applause as la Manuela dropped panting in the chair next to don Alejo.

"Let's dance, sweetie . . ."

The sharp twanging voices of the Farías sisters took command of the patio again. La Manuela, head thrown back and body arched, pinned herself to don Alejo and together they danced a few steps surrounded by the cheering men forming a circle around them. The postmaster came forward and snatched la Manuela from don Alejo. They managed one turn around the floor before the mayor took her away from him and more and more came from the circle that closed in on la Manuela. Someone stroked her while she was dancing, another rubbed her leg. The vineyard boss of a neighboring estate tucked up her skirt, and when they saw that, the men grouped around her, trying to carry her off, helped raise the skirt over her head, binding her arms as if in a strait jacket. Embarrassed and choking with laughter, they felt her skinny, hairy legs and lank backside.

"She's hot."

"She's steaming."

"Let's throw her in the canal."

Don Alejo stood up.

"Let's go."

"We've got to cool her off."

Several of them lifted her up. Squawking trills, and flapping her arms, la Manuela let them carry her off. In the street's light they marched toward Estación's eucalyptus grove. Don Alejo gave orders to cut the wire fences, which after all were his, and forcing their way through the brambles they reached the canal that bounded his vineyards and separated them from Estación.

"One . . . two . . . three . . . heeeeeave . . ."

And they pitched la Manuela into the water. The men who were watching her from above, standing between the blackberries and the canal, doubled over with laughter, pointing at the figure that struck poses and danced waist deep in water with her dress floating around her like a wide stain singing "El Relicario." She shouted to them as she took off her dress and threw it on the bank, she dared them, taunted them, insisting she liked them all each for himself, don't be cowards in front of a poor woman like herself. One of the men tried to piss on her, but she managed to dodge the stream's arc. Don Alejo gave him a shove and the man, cursing, fell into the water, where for an instant he merged into la Manuela's dance. When they finally gave them a hand so they both could climb onto the bank, la Manuela's anatomy startled them all.

"What a stud!"

"Hey, this guy's well-hung . . ."

"Wow, that doesn't look like a fag to me."

"Don't let the women see that or they'll all fall in love with you."

La Manuela, teeth chattering, answered with a laugh.

"I only use this thing to pee."

Some of them went back with don Alejo to Japonesa's house. Some went home without being missed by the party. Others, their bodies heavy with wine, fell among the weeds on the bank or the street or in the station to sleep it off. But don Alejo still felt like celebrating. He ordered the Farías sisters back to the platform to sing, and sat with some cronies at a table littered with leftovers, some cold bones and a greasy knife. Japonesa joined them to listen to the details of la Manuela's bath.

"And he says he only uses it to piss."

Japonesa raised her tired head and looked at them.

"That might be what he says, but I don't believe it."

"Why?"

"I don't know, just because . . ."

They argued about it for a while.

Japonesa became excited. Her swollen breast rose and fell with the passion of her conviction: yes, la Manuela could do it, if she were handled in bed in a special way, you know, with a little care, delicately, so she wouldn't be afraid, yes, Big Japonesa was sure that la Manuela could. The men felt the wave of heat that emanated from her body, sure of its technique and its charms, not quite as fresh as before but hotter and more insistent . . . yes, yes . . . I know . . . and of all the men who listened to her saying yes, I can excite la Manuela no matter how queer he is, there wasn't one who wouldn't have given anything to be in la Manuela's place. Japonesa dried her forehead. She ran the tip of her pink tongue over her lips, which were shiny for a minute. Don Alejo was laughing at her.

"But you're old now, what could you . . ."

"Bah, the older the wiser . . ."

"But la Manuela! No, no, I'll bet you can't."

"All right. I'll bet you I can."

Don Alejo cut short his laughter.

"It's a deal. Since you think you're so good, you've got a bet. Just try and get that queer hot for you. If you manage to excite him and he performs like a man, fine, I'll give you whatever you ask for. But it has to be with us watching, and put some action into it."

Everyone was silent waiting for Japonesa's answer. She motioned to the Farías sisters to keep singing and ordered another bottle of wine.

"All right. But what will you give me?"

"I told you, whatever you want."

"And if I asked you to give me El Olivo?"

"You wouldn't. You're an intelligent woman and you know very well I wouldn't give it to you. Ask for something that I can give you."

"Or that you would want to give me."

"No, that I can . . ."

There was no way of breaking him down. Forget it.

"All right then . . ."

"What?"

"This house."

When the bet was first mentioned she had thought of just asking for a few barrels of wine, the good kind that she knew don Alejo would send her without having to ask for it. But then he made her mad and she asked for the house. She had wanted it for a long time. She wanted to be a proprietress. How would it feel to be a proprietress, me the owner of this house where I started working as a girl. She had never dreamed of owning it. Only now, because it angered her that don Alejo should count on what he called her "intelligence" to take advantage of her. If he wanted to laugh at la Manuela, and at everybody, and at her, fine, then he would pay for it, don't count on her to be reasonable. Let him pay for it. Let him give her the house if he was so almighty that he could push them around like that.

"But the house is worthless, Japonesa."

"Didn't you say that property values are going up here in Estación?"

"Yes, of course, but . . ."

"I want it. Don't try to get out of it, don Alejo. I have witnesses here, and they'll say you don't keep your promises. You build up a lot of hope and then, nothing . . ."

"You're on, then."

While the onlookers applauded, don Alejo and Japonesa touched glasses and emptied them. Don Alejo got up to dance with Rosita. After that they went inside to spend some time together. Then Japonesa wiped her mouth with the back of her hand and closing her eyes yelled:

"Manuela . . ."

The few couples who were dancing stopped.

"Where's la Manuela?"

Most of the women had already paired off with the men they'd stay with for the rest of the night. Japonesa crossed under the grape arbor, whose leaves had begun to shiver in the wind, and walked into the kitchen. It was dark. But she knew he was there next to the black, but still hot stove.

"Manuela . . . Manuela?"

She sensed him shivering near the coals. The poor thing was wet and tired from so much revelry. Feeling that la Manuela was there, Japonesa drew near the corner and touched him. He said nothing. Then she leaned her body against la Manuela's. She lit a candle. Thin, wet, diminished, revealing the truth of his miserable structure, his feeble bones, as a bird is revealed to someone who plucks it to throw into the pot. Shivering by the stove, wrapped in a blanket someone had lent him.

"Are you cold?"

"They're such boors. . . ."

"Like animals."

"It doesn't matter to me. I'm used to it. I don't know why they always do this or something like it to me when I dance, it's as if they were afraid of me. I don't know why if they know I'm just a fag. At least they only threw me in the water, usually it's worse, you should see . . ."

And laughing he added:

"Don't worry. It's included in the entertainment fee."

Japonesa couldn't keep from touching him, as if she were searching for the wound so she could cover it with her hand. They both had sobered up. Japonesa sat on the floor and told him about the bet.

"Are you crazy, Japonesa, for God's sake? Can't you see I'm hopeless? I don't get it. How could you think of such a dirty thing?"

But Japonesa kept talking to him. She casually took his hand. He withdrew it, but while she talked she took it again and this time he didn't object. No, he didn't have to do anything if he didn't want to, she wasn't going to force him, it was just a matter of playacting. After all, no one would be watching close to them, just from the window and it would be easy to fool them. It was just a matter of undressing and getting into bed together, she would tell him what to do, everything, and by candlelight they couldn't see much, no, no, no. Not even if they didn't do anything. He couldn't stand women's bodies. Flabby breasts, excess fat, fat that things sink into and disappear in forever, those hips, those thighs like two huge mountains that fuse together in the middle, no. Yes, Manuela, hush, I'll pay you, don't say no, it's worth it because I'll pay you whatever you want. Now I know that I must have this house, that I want it more than anything else, because the town's expanding and the house and me along with it, and I can do it, this house that used to be the Cruzes can be mine. I'll fix it up. Don Alejo wasn't at all happy when I asked for it. I know why, they say the north-south highway will come right through here, right by the door. He knows what the house will be worth and he doesn't want to lose it, but he was scared that the others heard the bet and he had to put up or shut up . . . and then he said okay, it can be mine. I would bring in performers, you, for example, Manuela, I'd always bring you in. Yes. I'll pay you. For just being naked in bed with me for a while. Just a little while, a quarter of an hour, no, ten minutes, no, five . . . and we'll have a good laugh, Manuela, you and I, I'm tired of those big studs I liked before when I was young, they stole my money and two-timed me with the first woman who came along, I'm tired of them, and the two of us can be friends, as long as it's mine, my house, mine, if not, I'll always be clinging to don Alejo, doing whatever he wants, because this house is his, you know that. But it scares me, even that scares me, Japonesa, the playacting, it doesn't matter, it doesn't matter. Do you want me to pour you some tea, you're shivering, I'll drink some with you, no, I don't like tea, I'll just have some now to keep you company: damn you Japonesa, you're feeding me propaganda, confusing me, you'll see how warm the tea will make you feel don't be afraid, don't be afraid of me, the rest of the women yes but not me, see how good the tea is, in a few minutes you won't be cold. But la Manuela kept saying no, no, no, no . . .

Japonesa put the tea kettle back on the fire.

"And if you were my partner?"

La Manuela didn't answer.

"As my partner?"

Japonesa saw that la Manuela was thinking.

"We'll split everything. I'll sign you as a partner, you too as owner of this house when don Alejo transfers it to me before the notary. You and me, partners. Half of everything. The house, the furniture, the business and everything we'll have . . ."

. . . and that way, as a proprietress, no one could throw her out, because the house would be hers. She could give orders. So many whorehouses they'd thrown her out of because she always went wild when the party got going and her mug hot from the wine, the music and everything, and sometimes the men started fighting because of her. From one whorehouse to another. Ever since she could remember. One month, six months, a year at the most . . . it always had to end because the owner got mad, because, she would say, la Manuela added fuel to the fire by being so scandalous . . . to have my own room, mine forever, with cute pin-ups on the wall, but no: always from one house to another, ever since they threw him out of school when they found him with another boy and he didn't dare go home again because his father had an enormous riding crop that drew blood when he beat the horses, and then he went to the woman's house who taught him flamenco dancing. And then she threw him out, then others, always from house to house, not a nickel in his pocket, nowhere to rest when his gums hurt, those pains he always had, ever since he could remember, and he'd never tell anyone about it and now at forty my teeth are falling out and I'm afraid of spitting them out when I sneeze. Big deal. It was just for a few minutes. I don't like beans but when there's nothing else to eat . . . big deal. Me a proprietress. No one can throw me out, and if it's true this town's on its way up, maybe life won't be so bad, and there's hope even for an ugly fag like me, and then my misfortune wouldn't be a misfortune but would turn into a miracle thanks to don Alejo, and things could be wonderful, singing, laughing, dancing in the spotlight every night forever.

"Okay."

"Is it a deal?"

"But you better not do anything to me or I'll scream."

"Is it a deal, Manuela?"

"It's a deal."

"We'll put one over on don Alejo."

"And then we'll sign at the notary's?"

"At the notary's. In Talca."

He wasn't trembling now. His heart was beating fast.

"And when are we going to put on the show?"

Japonesa looked out the door.

"Don Alejo hasn't come yet, wait a bit . . ."

They sat by the stove in silence. La Manuela took his hand away from Japonesa's, who let go because now it didn't matter, that person was all hers now. La Manuela in her house forever. Tied to her. Why not? She was a good worker, that was obvious, and cheerful, and she knew so much about decorating and clothes and meals, yes, she wasn't bad, better to be partners with La Manuela than with some other man who would make her suffer. La Manuela would never make her suffer, a friend, just a friend, the two of them together. Easy to love him. Maybe some day she would suffer for him, but in a different way, not with that scream of pain when a man stops loving her, being torn in pieces because a man goes off with another woman or deceives her, or takes her money, or takes advantage of her and she, so he won't leave her, pretends that she doesn't know anything, scarcely daring to breathe at night next to that body that suddenly, suddenly could say no, never again, this is as far as it goes . . . she can excite him, she's positive, almost without trying, because inside, without knowing it, the poor thing was already responding to her warmth. If he hadn't she never would have decided to try him.

Exciting him is going to be easy. And making him fall in love with her. But no. That would ruin it. Complicate things. It was preferable that la Manuela never forget his place in the house—the queer of the whorehouse, the partner. But business aside, it would be easy to make him fall in love with her, just as easy as, at this moment, it was for her to love him.

"Listen, Manuela, don't you fall in love with me . . ."

8

"That's all that counts, buddy, don't be a jerk: money. Don't you think you'd be as good as him if you had it? Or do you think don Alejo is something special? No, no two ways about it. You're afraid of the old man because you owe him money, period. No, of course I won't tell anybody. You think I want people to know how he treated my sister's husband? In the envelope I gave you there's enough money to pay him what you owe . . . no, pay me whenever you can, there's no hurry, you're one of the family. I'm not a two-faced heel, I won't treat you like he does. The things he calls you, my God! I told you not to worry about it, I'm loaded. People like him make me furious . . . Why should you do what he says and not go to Japonesita's house if you feel like it and pay your bill? Does Japonesita belong to him? Of course, that ass thinks everything belongs to him, but no sir. He can't order you around, or me either, and we'll go wherever we feel like going. Right? Pay him his money and good-bye . . . Come on, Pancho, cheer up, it's no big deal . . ."

The truck went by Japonesita's house without stopping. It turned the narrow corner slowly and went back around the block past Japonesita's house, not honking this time, Octavio persuading him, going around and around the block.

"And what will I do about the freight jobs?"

"Don't worry. Don't you know that all the trucks from around here go by my gas station and I know where the best jobs are in the area? Don't worry. I'm telling you you're not the old man's slave . . . Okay. I'm sick of the whole thing. Let's pay him right now, yes, now . . ."

"It's late . . ."

Octavio thought it over.

"So what, what do I care if they're eating. Let's go."

Pancho spun the truck around in the narrow street and headed the other way, toward the El Olivo estate, past the station. He knew his truck, and on the road past the blackberries and canal that bordered the station he dodged ruts and holes, maneuvering the enormous machine that seemed lighter now that he was going to don Alejo's to wrest from him the part of the truck that still belonged to him.

"We're going to get stuck in the mud."

Octavio opened the window and threw his cigarette out.

"No . . ."

Pancho stopped talking because he was going through a narrow passage of blackberries. He had to move very slowly, squinting his eyes, his head bent over the windshield. To see the rocks and potholes. He knew the road well, but better to be careful anyway. He even knew the noises: there behind the thickets, the Palos canal split into two and the branch that flowed toward Los Lagos pasture gushed through a wooden spout for a stretch. Now you couldn't hear it. But if you went on foot, like he did as a boy, you'd start hearing the noise of the water in the wooden spout right here, passing the crooked willow. This was the road on which he used to run barefoot to school every day in Estación El Olivo, when there was a school. A waste of time. Misia Blanca had taught him reading and writing and simple arithmetic along with Moniquita, who learned so quickly that she always beat him at everything. Until don Alejo said that Pancho had to go to school. And after studying, who knows, the university maybe. You bet. I was the dunce of all times and I never went to the next grade because I didn't feel like it, until don Alejo, who's no fool, realized it and fine, why bother with this kid if he's no good at studying, just let him learn the numbers and reading so they can tell him from the animals and then let him help out in the fields, let's see what we can do with him, why waste time in school if he's so stubborn. Every rock. And further on, the concrete landmark that's always been broken. Who knows how it got broken. It must be hard to break a concrete landmark, but it's broken all right. Every hole, every rock: don Alejo made him learn them by heart, back and forth every day from the estate to the school and back to the estate until they said enough, what good was it doing. But Ema wants Normita to go to nuns' school, I don't want her to be another nobody, like me, who had to marry the first man who looked at me so I wouldn't be an old maid forever—think what I'd be if you had studied a little, why do you say that, you know you liked me the first time you saw me and you walked out on the kid who owned the butcher shop because you fell in love with me, but it would have been different if you'd studied what does studying mean, Mamma, and what are nuns? I want the girl to study something quick like obstetrics, what's obstetrics, Mamma? And he didn't like her to ask, she's too young and what can you tell her, better wait until she grows up. If I want to, if I feel like it, I'll make my daughter study. Don Alejo has nothing to say about it, nothing to do with me. I'm my own boss. Except, of course, the family, like Octavio, who's my buddy so I don't mind owing him and he won't do anything if I'm a little behind on my payments . . . he'll be happy that I'm going to buy a house for Ema. Now I'll pay the old man and leave for good.

The truck wheeled between two plane trees and turned into an avenue of palm trees. Warehouses on either side. And piles of fetid grape pulp beside the dark closed sheds. At the far end, the park, the gigantic holm oak where he used to watch them lying in hammocks and multicolored canvas chairs—watching them from the other side, but not when he was little because he and Moniquita would play together among the giant hydrangea, the two of them alone, and the grownups would laugh at him asking if he was Moniquita's boyfriend and he'd say yes, and then they'd let him in, but not later, when he was bigger: they'd read magazines in strange languages, napping in the faded canvas chairs.

The dogs lunged toward the truck, which was approaching through the palms, and attacked its shiny body, scratching and muddying it as soon as it stopped at the gatehouse.

"Let's get out."

"How, with those mongrels?"

The dogs' leaping and growling kept them inside. Then Pancho, because they made him angry, because they frightened him, because he hated dogs, started to honk the horn like a madman and the dogs leapt higher scratching the red paint that he polished so often, but now it didn't matter, now nothing mattered except honking the horn, honking enough to knock down the palm trees and the oak, to pierce the night from one end to the other until nothing is left, honk that horn, and the dogs howl while a light goes on in the hall and figures come to life among the shadows and in doorways, yelling at the dogs, running toward the truck but Pancho keeps on, he has to, the furious dogs ignoring the peons who are calling them. Until don Alejo appears at the top of the porch and Pancho stops honking. Then the dogs quiet down and run to him.

"Othello . . . Sultan. Here Negus, Moor . . ."

The dogs fell in behind don Alejo.

"Who is it?"

Pancho remained mute, anemic, as if he had used up all his strength. Octavio nudged him, but Pancho remained mute.

"Bah. Coward."

Pancho opened the door and leaped to the ground. The dogs lunged at him but don Alejo managed to call them off while Pancho scrambled back into the truck. Octavio had turned off the lights and the landscape of darkness loomed, the black oak, the palm leaves, the mass of walls, the roof tiles were all suddenly etched against the deep empty sky.

"Who is it?"

"Pancho, don Alejo. Why don't you take care of your mutts?"

"What's this damn racket you're making? You must be drunk to think you can come to my house at all hours making noise like that, you good-for-nothing. You—put the dogs away, go on Moor, Sultan, over there, Othello, Negus . . . and you, Pancho, wait on the porch while I look for my cape, it's getting cold . . ."

Cautiously Pancho and Octavio climbed down from the truck, and trying not to fall into puddles, they worked their way to the porch. At the base of the driveway that circled the estate they saw some lighted windows. They looked in. The dining room. The family gathered around the lamp. A boy with glasses—grandson, don Jorge's son, what's he doing here when he ought to be away at school? And Misia Blanca at the head. White-haired now. She used to be blond, with a long braid she wrapped around her head and cut off when he gave Moniquita typhus. He saw Misia Blanca do it in the stuffy chapel—she raised her arms, her hands grasped her heavy braid and she cut it straight off, at the nap of her neck. He saw her: through the tears that came only then, only when Misia Blanca cut off her braid and threw it into the box, he watched her swimming in his tears, as he saw her now, swimming in the dining room's tarnished glass. Let me have Pancho for a while: she came to ask his mother so he could play with Moniquita because they were almost the same age and the house servants laughed at him because he said he was the boyfriend of the boss's daughter. Now she was like an old lady. She ate in silence. And when don Alejo finally joined them on the porch, wearing his hat and vicuña cape, Pancho thought he looked so tall, as tall as when he used to look up at him, a boy barely up to his knees.

"What a surprise, Pancho!"

"Good evening, don Alejo . . ."

"Who's with you?"

"It's Octavio . . ."

"Good evening."

"What can I do for you?"

He dropped into a rattan chair and the two men remained standing in front of him. He looked small now. And sick.

"What brings you around at this hour?"

"I came to pay you, don Alejo."

He stood up.

"But you paid me this morning. You don't owe me a thing until next month. What's gotten into you all of a sudden?"

They paced around the U of the porch. From time to time the image of Misia Blanca presiding at the long and almost empty table reappeared, once, stirring her medicine, another time closing the cheese crock, another, crumbling a piece of bread against the snowy tablecloth, all within the framed light of the window. Octavio was explaining something to don Alejo . . . who knows what, I don't want to hear it, he does it better than I do. Yes, let him do it, he won't let don Alejo run all over him like he does me. From a plate Misia Blanca selects a lump of toasted sugar for her medicine. One for her, one for Moniquita and one for you, Panchito, there's a piece of juniper leaf on it, that gives it a special flavor, Misia Blanca likes it that way, well, go play in the garden, and don't lose sight of her Pancho, you're bigger and you have to take care of her. And the colossal hydrangea there in the shade, next to the drain with its dusk-colored velvety bricks, he was the doll's father and she the mother, until the kids caught us playing with the little crib, me singing a lullaby to the doll in my arms because Moniquita says that's what fathers do and the kids laugh—sissy, sissy, playing with dolls like a girl and I don't want to ever come back but I have to because they feed me and dress me but I prefer going hungry and I spy from the flower hedge because I'd like to go back but I don't want them to call me the boss's daughter's sweetheart and sissy, sissy because of the dolls. Until one day don Alejo sees me spying behind the flowers. I've caught you, you little bastard. And his hand grabs me here, at the neck, and I hang from his cape kicking, him so big and me so small looking up at him, like looking up a cliff. His cape a little slippery and very hot because it's made of vicuña. And he drags me through the bushes and I hang onto his cape because it's so soft and so hot and he drags me along and I tell him they didn't give me permission to come, liar, he knows everything, you're a liar Pancho, don't pull away, who's going to take care of her except you, and he pushes me toward the big park and I have to look for her in the briar bushes, and I run and my feet get tangled in the periwinkles but what's the reason for running so hard, she's where she always is, in the hydrangea, in the shade by the wall embedded with shiny pieces of broken bottles, and I find her and touch her and from the tip of my body, after running and breaking through the underbrush, the tip of my body drips something and wets me and then I get typhus and she does too and she dies and I don't, and I'm left watching Misia Blanca and only when her hands lift her braid to cut it off do the tears start because I got well and because Misia Blanca's cutting off her braid. The dining room light has been turned off. This time around she's not there. Octavio's voice keeps explaining: yes, don Alejo, of course, it doesn't matter if they don't give him the cargo, I've already found him some others, yes, very good ones, some brick shipments, that they're making on the other side of . . ."

"Whose bricks are they?"

Octavio didn't answer.

Don Alejo stopped, surprised by the silence, and they did too, Octavio meeting the senator's eyes for an instant.

Was it possible? Pancho realized that Octavio wasn't answering don Alejo's question because if he found out whose bricks they were he could make a telephone call, that was enough to stop them from giving him shipments. He knew everyone. Everyone respected him. He had them all eating out of his hand. But his brother-in-law Octavio, his buddy, Normita's godfather, was standing up to him: Octavio was new in the district and not afraid of the old man. And because he didn't want to answer he didn't. They made a complete turn around the porch without speaking. The park was quiet but alive, and the silence in the wake of their voices was heavy with almost imperceptible noises, the drop that fell from the edge of the roof, the keys clinking in Octavio's pocket, the rustle of the nearly bare jasmine spikes piercing raindrops, the slow footsteps that halted at the house door.

"It's cold . . ."

"Of course. There's a lot of fresh air here."

Pancho trembled at his brother-in-law's words: don Alejo looked at him on the verge of asking what he meant by that, but he didn't, and he started to count the bills Octavio handed him.

"Tons of it . . ."

"What did you say?"

"Tons . . . of fresh air . . ."

Pancho cut his brother-in-law off before he could continue, inspired by his victory. Or was it a victory? Don Alejo seemed too calm. Maybe he hadn't heard.

"No, nothing, don Alejo. Well, if it's all right with you we'll go now and stop bothering you. We're taking up your time. And in this cold. Please give my regards to Misia Blanca. She's well, I hope."

Don Alejo walked to the end of the porch to see them off. Crossing the mud on their way to the truck they turned and saw the four dogs beside him.

"Easy with the dogs . . ."

Don Alejo laughed out loud.

"Get 'em Sultan . . ."

The four dogs shot after them. They barely had time to leap into the truck before they started clawing the doors. As they turned toward the exit the headlights lit up don Alejo's figure at the top of the steps for a moment and then the advancing lights gradually swallowed the palm trees along the lane. Pancho took a deep breath.

"That's that."

"You didn't let me call him a bastard to his face."

"Aw, the old goat isn't so bad."

But he's an operator. Octavio had been telling him that on their way into town and he believed him then, but now it was harder to believe. He said even the stones on the road to Estación knew it. Don't be an idiot the old man never intended to bring electricity to town, it was all lies, on the contrary, now it suited him better that the town never had electricity. Don't be naive, that old man's a shyster. The times he went to talk to the Commissioner were just to irritate him, so he'd never give the town electricity, I know what I'm talking about, the Commissioner's chauffeur is a friend of mine and he told me, wake up, buddy. It's obvious. Think about it. He wants everybody to move out of town. And since he owns most of the houses, if not all of them, what can he lose by having another chat with the Commissioner so that he'll grant him the land the streets are on, it was his to begin with, and then he'll tear down the houses and plow the town, rich, fallow land, and plant vineyards as if the town had never existed, hell, that's what he's after. Now that his plans for making Estación El Olivo an important town have fallen through, because he thought the highway would come right by his door . . .

Leaning over the wheel Pancho studies the darkness because he has to if he doesn't want to topple into a canal or be grafted into a thicket. You have to watch every stone in the road, every hole, every one of those trees that I'm abandoning forever. I thought all this would keep some trace of me, so that later I could think about these streets I'm driving along, but now they won't exist and I won't be able to remember them, because already they don't exist and I can't return. I don't want to return. I want to go on to other things, go forward. The house in Talca for Ema and school for Normita. I'd like to have a place to come back to, not really to come back to, but to have it there in case, that's all, and now I won't. Because don Alejo's going to die. The certainty of don Alejo's death drained the night and Pancho had to clutch the steering wheel to keep from falling into the abyss.

"Octavio."

"What's the matter?"

He didn't know what to say. It was just to hear his friend's voice. To see if he really wanted to be like Octavio, who didn't have a place to go back to and didn't care. He was the best man in the world because he made his own way and now he owned a service station and a little café on the north-south highway where hundreds of trucks passed. He did what he wanted and his wife gave him spending money, not like Ema who took all the money as if he owed it to her. Octavio was a great man, really great. It was a stroke of luck that he married his sister. It was good to have someone to back you up.

"We settled the score. Better not to have anything to do with him. They're a bad lot, pal, I'm telling you, you don't know the trouble I've had with those sons of bitches."

They were coming into town.

"Where are we going?"

"To celebrate."

"But where?"

"Where do you think, old buddy?"

"To Japonesita's."

"To Japonesita's it is."

9

Japonesita put out the lamp.

"It's him."

"Again?"

After they slammed the truck doors, a dense moment of waiting passed, so long that it seemed the men had gotten lost in the night. When they finally pounded on the door, la Manuela clutched her flamenco dress.

"I'm going to hide."

"Papa, wait . . ."

"He's going to kill me."

"And what about me?"

"Who cares. He swore he'd get me. What happens to you is no concern of mine."

She ran to the patio. If she made it through this she was sure to die of bronchial pneumonia like all the other old women. Why should Japonesita be any affair of hers? If she wanted protection, let her protect herself, if she wanted to give in to him, let her give in to him, she, la Manuela, wasn't in the mood to save anybody, barely her own skin and much less Japonesita, who called her "papa," papa when la Manuela was afraid Pancho would kill her for being a fag. The best thing was to sneak away and spend the night with Ludovinia, warm in her bed, a nice double bed, no, none of that getting into bed with a woman, now that she knew what could happen to her. But maybe Ludo had some leftover pastries from lunch and could heat them over the coals and serve some tea and they could talk about nice things, Misia Blanca's hats when they used to wear hats, and forget all this, because she certainly wasn't going to tell Ludo about it, she didn't want her to ask questions she'd have to answer. Until this thing let up and faded into the darkness, until she could say to Ludo how do you like that, maybe she could tell her about it tomorrow, how do you like that, the girl finally made up her mind and took him to her room, she's finally come down off her high horse, everything's going to be okay now, and darkness would surround everything until it would be time to go to sleep and she could fall drop by drop by drop into the puddle of sleep that would spread until it completely filled Ludo's warm room.

The light in the parlor went on again. A man appeared in its rectangle. The Victrola needle began to rasp against a record. Octavio leaned against the door frame. La Manuela stepped back, opened the henhouse grid and hid under the water dispenser next to the perch bleached white by chicken shit, and Lucy's turkey began to strut and bristle its feathers, all swelled up and angry. La Manuela tried to warm one of her hands under her shirt but every crease in her musty skin seemed like frosted cardboard, so she took it back out.

Japonesita crossed the rectangle of light, clinging to Pancho Vega.

La Manuela knew they'd soon begin to search the house for her. If only Japonesita were woman enough to keep them busy to divert their virility toward herself, she who needed it so much! But no. They were going to search. La Manuela knew it, they were going to make the whores come out of their rooms, take the kitchen apart, look for her in the outhouse, maybe in the henhouse, wreck everything, dishes, glasses, their clothes, the women, and her too if they found her. That's why they came. They can't fool me. Those men didn't just appear out of the night to rush into the house, go to bed with just any woman and drink a few bottles of just any wine, no, they came for her, to sacrifice her, to make her dance. They knew she had made it plain that she didn't want to dance for them, no more than she did last year when Pancho kept insisting that she had to dance for him, warped bastard, he's coming for me, la Manuela knows it. For the present he settled for dancing with Japonesita. But he'd come looking for her. Yes, I should have gone to Ludo's. But no. Japonesita was dancing, strange, because she never danced, even when they begged her. She didn't like it. She seemed to now. She saw her whirl in front of the wide-open door, glued to him, as if melted and dripping over Pancho, his black mustache hidden in Japonesita's neck. His dirty mustache, the bottom hairs tinged with wine and nicotine. And clutching the bottom of her buttocks, his hands stained with nicotine and car grease. And Octavio standing in the open door, smoking, waiting: then he tossed his cigarette into the night and went in. The record stopped. Laughter. Japonesita screams. A chair falls. They're doing something to her. La Manuela's hand, back between her skin and her shirt, right where her heart beats, clenches until it hurts, as if she'd like to transfer the pain to Pancho Vega's body, because Japonesita screams again, ay, ay, papa, don't call me, don't call me that again, I don't have fists to protect you, I only know how to dance and to shiver here in the henhouse.

. . . But one time I didn't shiver. Big Japonesa's naked body, oh, if I had that warmth now, if Japonesita had it so she wouldn't need other heat, Big Japonesa's naked, repellent, but warm body surrounding me, her hands on my neck and me staring at those things that burgeoned from her chest, as if I didn't know they existed, heavy and red tipped by the lamp light that we didn't put out so they could see us from the window. They insisted on at least that much proof. And the house would be ours. Mine. And me smothered in that flesh, that drunken woman's mouth searching for mine the way a pig roots in a swamp though we agreed we wouldn't kiss because it nauseated me, but she was searching for my mouth, I don't know, even now I don't know why Japonesa had such a hunger for my mouth and she searched for it and I didn't want to and refused, shriveling it tight, biting her greedy lips, hiding my face in the pillow, anything, because I was terrified to see Japonesa violating our agreement, something was beginning to stir and I didn't . . . I didn't want to be sickened by the flesh of this woman who was reminding me that the house was going to be mine for just this simple and ghastly act, that there was no harm done but . . . and don Alejo watching us. Could we fool him? I trembled. Could we? Wouldn't we die, somehow, if we managed to do it? And Japonesa made me drink another glass of wine so I wouldn't be afraid and drinking it I spilled half the glass on the pillow next to Japonesa's head whose flesh was wooing me, and then another glass. After that she hardly said anything else. Her eyes were closed and her mascara was running and her face was sweaty and her whole body, especially her wet belly, stuck to mine and me realizing that all this is monstrous, unnecessary, they're betraying me, oh how clearly I saw it was a betrayal to capture me and lock me up in jail forever because Big Japonesa was utterly reckless with that odor, as if she were preparing a witches brew in the fire that burned in the triangular vegetation between her legs, and that odor took root in my body and clung to me, the odor of that body with its unimaginable incomprehensible channels and caverns, stained with other liquids, inhabited by other cries and beast, and that boiling so different from mine, my foolish doll's body, depthless, everything on the surface, useless hanging, while she caresses me with her mouth and sweaty palms, her eyes closed terribly so I won't know what's happening inside, everything open inside, passages and channels and caverns and me there, dead in her arms, in her hand that's urging me to live, yes, you can, and me nothing, and on the box next to the bed the lamp hissing lightly near my ear in a long meaningless whisper. And her soft hands explore me, and she tells me you excite me, she tells me I want this, and she begins to murmur again, like the lamp, in my ear, and I hear laughter in the window: don Alejo watching me, watching us writhe, knotted together and sweating to humor him because he ordered it and this is the only way he'll give us this adobe house, with its rat-gnawed beams, and those watching, don Alejo and the others who are laughing at us, don't hear what Big Japonesa is slowly saying in my ear, this is so sweet, honey boy, don't be afraid, we won't do anything, it's just an act to make them believe it, don't worry honey and her voice is warm like an embrace and her wine-stained breath all over me, but now I'm not so worried because no matter how much her hand touches me I don't have to do anything, nothing, it's just an act, nothing's going to happen, it's for our house, that's all, for our house. Her smile stuck on the pillow, etched in the linen. She likes to do what she's doing here on the sheets with me. She's pleased that I can't: not with anybody, tell me, pretty Manuela, tell me not with any other woman before me; tell me I'm the first, the only, so I can have you all to myself my pretty little girl, my love, Manuelita I'm going to have you, I like your terrified body and all your fears and I want to destroy your fear, no, don't be afraid Manuela, no, not destroy them but gently smooth them away to reach a part of me that she, poor Big Japonesa, thought existed but doesn't exist and never has, it never has existed despite your touching and caressing me and murmuring ... it doesn't exist, stupid Japonesa, don't you understand, it doesn't exist. No honey, Manuela as if we were two women, look, see, our legs wound together, sex in sex, two identical sexes, Manuela, don't be afraid of my thighs moving, my hips, my mouth in yours, like two women when the gentlemen in Wooden Heart's house pay the whores to let them watch ... no, no, you're the woman, Manuela, I'm the man, look how I'm taking off your panties and loosening your brassiere so your breasts will be bare and I can play with them, yes you have them Manuela, don't cry, you do have breasts, tiny like a little girl's, but you have them and that's why I love you. You talk and caress me and suddenly you tell me, now darling Manuela, now you can ... I dreamed about my breasts being caressed and something happened while she was saying, yes little girl, I'm making you like it because I'm the man and you're the woman, I love you because you're everything, and I feel her heat devouring me, me, a me that doesn't exist, and she helps me, laughing with me because I'm laughing too, the two of us choked with laughted to cover the shame of our waves of emotion, and my tongue in her mouth and what does it matter that they're watching us from the window, that makes it better, sweeter, until I shudder and am mutilated, bleeding inside of her while she screams and clutches me and then falls, my precious little boy, what a sweet thing, it's been so long, so long, and the words dissolve and the odors evaporate and the hardnesses shrivel, I stay, sleeping over her, and she says into my ear, as if in a dream: my sweet girl, my sweet boy, her words muffled in the pillow. We can't tell anybody, I'm ashamed of what happened, don't be silly, Manuela, you won the house royally, you won the house for me, for the two of us. But swear never again, Japonesa, oh God how disgusting, swear to me, partners yes, but this no, never again because what I'm needing so much now no longer exists, that you and that me I'd like so desperately to call to from this corner of the henhouse, while I watch them dance, there in the parlor ...

... the fists he doesn't have are useless for everything curling themselves up in the faded percale of his dress. Kill Pancho with the dress. Hang him with it. Lucy went out to the patio as if she had been waiting for the moment.

"Ssssttt."

She looked around.

"Lucy, over here ..."

In the parlor the record keeps repeating.

"What are you doing in there like a brooding hen?"

"Go on into the parlor."

"I'm going. Is anyone there?"

"Pancho and Octavio."

Japonesita and Pancho dance past the doorway, waking up Lucy's face.

"Is she alone?"

"Go on, I said."

What right does that damn whore Lucy have to criticize her because she's hiding in the henhouse? Tomorrow she'll make her pay the money she owes her for a dress, she's been pretending she forgot about it. Since men prefer her, she thinks we have to put up with her. She's here on charity like all the rest. And Japonesita too. So what right do they have? Right to what? Papa. What do you mean papa. Please, it only hurts when I laugh ... papa. Leave me alone. Nobody's papa. I'm just plain Manuela, the one who can dance until dawn and make a roomful of drunks laugh until they forget their sniveling wives while she, the artist, receives applause, and the light bursts into an infinity of stars. Why think about the scorn in the laughter that she knows so well, it's all part of the men's fun, that's why they come, to scorn her, but on the stage, with a flower behind her ear, as old and knock-kneed as she is, she's still more woman than all the Lucys and Clotys and Japonesitas on the face of the earth . . . arching her back and pursing her lips and tapping furiously, they'd laugh harder and their wave of laughter would carry her up, up into the lights.

Let Japonesita scream in there. Let them make her learn to be a woman, as they had made her. Lucy is dancing with Octavio, but she's the only one capable of turning the party into something thrilling, because she's la Manuela. Even though she might be trembling here in the dark surrounded by chicken shit that's so old it doesn't even smell anymore. They aren't women. She's going to show them what a woman is and how to be a woman. He takes off his shirt and folds it on the stairs. And his shoes . . . yes, bare feet like a real gypsy. He removes his pants and he's naked in the henhouse, his arms folded across his chest and that foreign thing hanging from him. He puts the Spanish dress over his head and the skirts fall around her like a warm shower because nothing can warm her like those yards and yards of tired red percale. She adjusts the bodice. She smooths the folds around the low neck . . . a little padding here where I don't have anything. Naturally it's because I'm so tiny, a dainty little gypsy girl, a mere child about to dance, that's why she doesn't have breasts, almost like a little boy, but she's not, she's feminine, with her curved figure and all . . . la Manuela smiles in the darkness of the henhouse while she puts the gauze poppy, that Lucy lent her, behind her ear. Do whatever you want with Japonesita. What does she have to do with it. She's just the great artist who's come to Japonesita's house to do her number, she's a fag, she wants to amuse herself, she feels Pancho's heavy hands exploring her that night, like someone who won't explore unless everyone is watching, holding her, yes indeed, holding her and doing it in style. Let them, let thirty men do whatever they want to her. If only I were younger and could take it. But no. My gums hurt. And my joints, oh how my joints hurt and my bones and my knees in the morning, how I feel like staying in bed forever, forever, with them taking care of me. If only Japonesita would make up her mind tonight. If only Pancho would take her away. If only he could make her pale blood circulate through that plucked chicken's body, not even hair where she ought to have it because she's a big girl now, poor thing, she doesn't know what she's missing, Pancho's hands squeezing my pretty girl, don't be silly, don't waste your life, I'm your friend, I, la Manuela, I'm going to dance so that everything will be lively as it should be and not sad like you because you count every dollar and don't spend any of it . . . and the flower in my hair. La Manuela walks across the patio smoothing her dress against her body. So skinny, dear God, no one's going to like me, especially with my stained dress and muddy feet and she removes a vine leaf clinging to the muck on her heel and goes toward the light and before she goes in she hides behind the door, listening, while she makes the sign of the cross as all great artists do before walking into the light.

10

Don Alejo would give don Céspedes all the wine he could drink, drink, don Céspedes, he'd say again and again, that's what it's for, but don Céspedes was a moderate man. Sometimes a small glass before going to bed on the pile of sacks among the wooden barrels cured by harvests and harvests of wine. It was the same wine that don Alejo would sell to Japonesita wholesale, simply because of their friendship and so the poor girl could make a little profit, but not to anyone else, not even if they begged him. Sometimes, late at night, when don Céspedes couldn't get to sleep because of the pains that were always bothering some part of his body, he'd put on his sandals, throw a blanket over his shoulder, walk through the vineyard, cross the Palos canal on a fallen willow trunk, and poking through the barbed-wired blackberry thicket laced with gaps known only to himself, he'd reach Japonesita's house where he'd silently install himself at one of the tables near the wall to drink a bottle of red wine, the same kind that was within easy reach at the gatehouse.

Octavio saw him come in. Japonesita didn't want to dance with him, so while Octavio waited for Lucy and Pancho to finish their dance he called to don Céspedes, who moved to their table. Octavio was going to ask the old man something, but he didn't because he saw that he was sitting rigidly in his chair, staring at one fixed point in the darkness, as if it contained a detailed blueprint of the night.

"The dogs . . ."

"What did you say, don Céspedes?"

"They turned the dogs loose in the vineyard."

They listened.

"I don't hear a thing."

"Me neither."

"But they're out there. I can feel them. Now they're running north, to the Lagos pasture where the cattle are . . . and now . . ."

A flock of geese flew over the town.

". . . and now they're running this way, toward Estación."

Japonesita and Octavio tried to listen to the night, but they couldn't penetrate its obstreperous music, nor glean the country's atoms of noise and faraway gusts of information. Octavio poured himself a glass of wine.

"And who let the dogs loose?"

"Don Alejandro. He's the only one who can turn them loose."

"Why does he?"

"When he's in a strange mood . . . and tonight he was. Tonight, when he came to the gatehouse, he told me he was going to die, a doctor told him so. He said strange things . . . that he seemed to be leaving nothing behind because all his projects had failed . . ."

"Greedy bastard . . . if a millionaire like him is a failure, where does that leave us poor people?"

"I'll bet anything he's in the vineyard with them."

"And why does he turn them loose if there wasn't a grape left after harvest and there's no reason to break in?"

"Who knows. Sometimes people come for other reasons."

"Like what?"

"You've got to be careful with the dogs. They're vicious. But they don't bite me . . . why should they bother when there's no meat left on my bones."

Japonesita watched him from the other side of the carbon lamp, gray, remote, like someone to whom nothing can happen anymore; she envied his immunity. Even the dogs didn't bite him. Probably not even the fleas in his mangy straw mattress. Once someone told her that don Céspedes didn't even eat anymore, that sometimes don Alejo's house servants would remember his existence and look all over for him, in the warehouses and sheds, and they'd take him some bread or cheese or a hot plate of food. But then they'd forget him again and who knows how the old man would feed himself, sleeping on sacks in the warehouses, lost among the plows and machinery and bales of straw and clover, on top of a pile of potatoes.

Pancho and Lucy sat down at the table.

"What is this, a funeral . . ."

No one answered.

"Cheer up, pal, if you don't, I'll run off with Lucy . . ."

And he looked at Japonesita to see how she reacted: she was looking at the same point in the dark as don Céspedes. Pancho touched one of her breasts, too small, like a wizened pear, the kind with no perfume, inedible, fallen under the trees. But her eyes. He took his hand away and looked at them. Two orbs lit from within. Each eye flared brightly swallowed up by the translucent iris and Pancho felt that if he leaned over them he would see, like an aquarium, the underwater gardens of

Japonesita's soul. It wasn't pleasant. It was weird. If it were up to him he'd let her alone right then and there. But why should he? Because the old man told him to, because don Alejo warned him not to go near her? We're not outlaws, don Alejo, we're as good as you, so don't look down on us. don't think that . . .

"Let's dance, honey."

Lucy closed her eyes and opened them again. But when she opened them she didn't know how much time had passed since she closed them, nor into which fragment of vast, stretched time she was looking. A band of geese passed over. Again? Or was this another part of the same time when she thought she heard them a while ago? The howling of the dogs, some near, others faraway, traced the country distances in the night. A horseman galloped along the road, and suddenly Lucy, who was trying to hear only the bolero on the Victrola, was tangled up in the anguish of not knowing who the rider was or where he came from or where he was going and how long this gallop would last, faint now, very faint, but always galloping further into the interior of her ears until he remained fixed there. She smiled at Octavio because she saw he was annoyed.

"God it's boring . . ."

Don Céspedes yawned and listened.

"That's Sultan . . ."

"How do you know which dog?"

"I trained them for don Alejo, I've known them since they were pups. Since they were born, really. When don Alejo sees that one of his black dogs isn't doing well, that he's getting lazy or tame or has injured his paw, we shut ourselves up, don Alejo and I, with the dog, and he shoots him . . . I told him so the bullet will hit the right spot and then I bury him. And when the bitch we keep locked up at the far end of the orchard is in heat, we give the dogs a stimulant, and don Alejo and I, we shut ourselves up again with the dogs in the shed, and the beasts fight over the bitch, they go mad, sometimes they're wounded, until they mount her and that's it. He keeps the best pups for himself, but if he's killed only one of the big ones he just takes one pup and I put the rest in a bag and throw them in the Palos canal. Four, he always likes to have four. It makes doña Blanca furious, she says it's not right, but he laughs and tells her not to interfere with men's affairs. And the dogs, even though they change, always have the same names, Negus, Sultan, Moor, Othello, always the same ever since don Alejo was a boy just this high, the same names as if the dogs he kills kept on living, don Alejo's four dogs, always perfect, he likes them savage, if they're not he kills them. And now he's turned them loose in the vineyard. Of course, he was very depressed . . ."

While don Céspedes was talking, Pancho and Japonesita sat down and listened.

"What's that got to do with his being so sad?"

"He's going to die . . ."

"Enough with don Alejo!"

Enough. Let him die. Don Alejo and his charming wife could go to hell as far as he was concerned. Couldn't he and his friend have some fun without having to hear about don Alejo this, don Alejo that. Misia Blanca can go to hell, Misia Blanca who had taught him to read and sometimes gave him sweets that she kept in a tea jar in the pantry. That pantry. Row after row of marmalade jars with white labels written in the angular nun script that he, Pancho Vega, was forever writing—Plum—Peach—Apricot—Raspberry—Chokeberry—and the jars of preserved pears and cherries in brandy and plums floating in yellow syrup. And further on, the rows of white earthenware molds in the shape of castles: apple or quince marzipan, and they always gave Moniquita a castle tower where the candy was clear and sparkling. They can go to hell. Pancho's hand climbed up Japonesita's leg and no one said a word while Lucy's ears scanned the night for another rider to revive her fear. He had paid off the whole debt and the truck was his. His red truck. Caress his red truck instead of Japonesita who smelled of clothing, and the harsh-voiced horn, just like Daddy's voice Normita always said. His. More his than his wife. Or daughter. If he wanted, he could race it down the knife-straight highway, tonight, for instance, he could race it like a wild man, blowing his horn at anything he felt like, slowly pressing the accelerator to invade the depths of the night and suddenly, just because, because don Alejo doesn't have any control over me now, I could turn the wheel a little more, barely flexing my wrists, but enough to make the truck go off the road, bounce and overturn and become a smear of silent, smoking iron on the edge of the road. If I feel like it. And I don't have to explain anything to anybody. Under his hand Japonesita's leg began to relax.

Japonesita was drinking a glass of wine. She wished Lucy would go dance with Octavio so that she could drink it all on the sly. Wine. All the men who ever came to her house smelled of wine and everything tasted like wine. During harvest the wine odor invaded the entire town, and the rest of the year, heaps of grape pressings rotting bv the warehouse doors. Disgusting. She had the same wine smell, like the men, like the whores, like the town. What else was there to do except drink wine. Like Cloty, who when she didn't have customers would say, listen Japonesita write me down for another bottle of the cheapest wine you have and then she'd get into bed and drink until she was a total wreck the next day, working like a mule from the crack of dawn, her nose red and her stomach queasy. But I never noticed the smell of wine on my mother. And Big Japonesa was a great one for drinking, everybody knew that. She always smelled of Flores de Pravia soap even though she had drunk quarts of wine in the parlor, and then my mother would light up like a torch and there was no stopping her from talking and laughing and dancing. How did she do it? Her warmth would fill the bed when she'd fall into it and Japonesita would have to undress her, she or la Manuela. Even the tomb in which they laid her in San Alfonso was probably hot and she would never feel that warmth again. Only Pancho's hand, abandoned on her thigh because he was dozing while Lucy danced glued to Octavio. But Pancho was drunk. Like every man she had seen in the house since she was born. And she played among trouser legs under the tables while they drank, hearing their obscenities and smelling their vomit in the patio, playing in the dirty sheets piled next to the wash tub, those sheets on which those men had slept with those women. But if Pancho's hand could excite her the way her mother could be excited, then she could get away from it all, her father told her. Who was that shadow who counted dollars uselessly? The hand moving along her thigh was saying that, because now she wasn't afraid of it and la Manuela had told her, had asked her who are you, and the hand that assaulted her thigh, while the man it belonged to yawned, could give her the answer, this hand that was like the hands of all the men who had come to this house, it wanted to excite her, that blunt thumb with its eroded nail, yes, I saw it, those fingers covered with hair, the square nail advancing and she didn't want it to but now yes, yes, to find out who you are Japonesita, now you'll know, that hand and that warmth from his heavy body and afterward, even if he goes away, at least something will remain from this night . . .

"God this is boring . . ."

Then he looked the old man in the face.

"Right, don Céspedes?"

He smiled.

"Hey, Octavio, let's go somewhere else . . ."

Don Céspedes asked him:

"Why?"

"This place has no atmosphere."

It was only then that he realized Octavio was no longer there.

"What happened to Octavio?"

"He went inside with Lucy a little while ago."

He sat Japonesita on his knee.

"Well, I guess it beats eating mice."

She remained stiff. Pancho gave her a shove that almost knocked her to the floor.

"I'm fed up."

He started to walk around the tables.

"Shitpile of a whorehouse! Don't even have whores. Where are the other girls? And that beat-up Victrola. Nothing to stuff your gut with even. Let's see . . . Bread: stale. Cold cuts . . . huh, half rotten. And what's this? Candy crusted with flies from the year one. Japonesita, dance at least. Do a striptease. Dance? How the hell can you if you're as stiff as a broom. Not like your mother, she was built like a barn but she was graceful. Like la Manuela, they say . . ."

The same eyes. He remembered from last year la Manuela's eyes looking at him and he looked back at those terrified eyes, shining between his hands that squeezed her neck and her eyes looking at him like glowing orbs with the certainty that he was going to drown that shore of terror in the tides within him. He remained standing.

"And la Manuela?"

Japonesita didn't answer.

"And la Manuela, I said?"

"My father has gone to bed."

"Send for her."

"He can't. He's sick."

He grabbed her by the shoulder and shook her.

"Don't tell me the old whore is sick! Do you think I came to look at your frigid little rabbit's face? No, I came to see la Manuela, that's what I came for. Now, I said. Go call her. I want her to dance for me."

"Let go of me."

Pancho's eyes were scowling, his matted, confused, bloodshot eyes almost blind with rage. Tell her to come. I want to laugh. It can't be all so damn sad in this town don Alejo's going to tear down and plow under, surrounded by vineyards that are going to swallow it up, and tonight I'll have to go home and sleep with my wife and I don't want to, I want to have fun, that nutty Manuela has to come out and save us, there must be something better than this, she has to come out.

"La Manuela . . ."

"You brute. Leave me alone."

"Tell her to come out, I said."

"And I said that my father can't."

"Don Alejo is your father. And mine."

But he looked at her eyes.

"You're right. Madame Manuela is your father."

"Don't call him that."

Pancho burst out laughing.

"At this late date, honey?"

"Don't call him that."

11

"And why not?"

La Manuela stopped in the center of the parlor.

"Put on 'El Relicario' for me."

Back arched, arm raised, snapping her fingers, she circled around the empty space in the center, pursued by her muddy, shredded red train. Applauding, Pancho tried to kiss her and hold her, laughing his head off at this crazy old harridan, this dried prune of a queer, shouting yessir, darling, now the party really starts . . . but la Manuela slipped away from him, snapping her fingers, weaving proudly among the tables before delivering herself up to her dance. Japonesita went over to stop her. Before Pancho slapped her away she managed to murmur:

"Go inside . . ."

"You dumb girl, how much longer do I have to put up with you? You go inside if you want. Right, Pancho? You're spoiling all the fun."

"Yeah, go away . . ."

He dropped into a chair. From there he shouted that now things were moving, why weren't there more people, bring wine, pastry, a roast pig, everything they had, he was paying, to celebrate . . . Lucy honey, sit here and you pal where have you been you left me stranded at this funeral come on over don Céspedes don't be afraid you'll catch cold if you stay so far away and a whore came out to the noise and revived the lamp's flame and Cloty stationed herself beside the Victrola to change the records, staring popeyed at la Manuela. . . .

"Good God, look at this old pro . . ."

In Talco they had told Cloty about la Manuela's dances, but how was she to believe it, the crazy thing was so old. She wanted to watch. They lit two lamps on the table near the platform and then Pancho saw la Manuela's eyes glow, like flames, he remembered them between his hands, and Japonesita's eyes glowed and he took a long drink because he didn't want to see and he poured more wine for Pancho, and for Lucy, drink up everybody, it's on me. He held la Manuela's head and forced her to take a long drink like him and la Manuela wiped her mouth with the back of her hand. Lucy was asleep. Don Céspedes was watching la Manuela but as if he didn't see her.

"Go to it, Manuela my love, go to it . . . Let's make my farewell party a good one. And anyway you're all going to be wiped out, whoosh . . . blown away by you know who. Don Céspedes, you know don Alejo is going to wipe out every one of these ball-busters, just for the hell of it . . ."

In the fields surrounding the town, the vineyards and night were perfectly sketched under the moon: don Céspedes saw it with wideopen eyes. The methodical stripes, the orderly pattern that contained the village of demolished walls, the confusion of this place that the vineyards were going to erase—and this house, this small point where they, together, barely bruised the inflexible night: la Manuela on the platform in her glowing dress must amuse them and kill dangerous, mercurial time that wants to devour them, demented Manuela on the platform: they applaud. They tap their heels on the dirt floor, they slap the lame table where the lamps quiver. Cloty changes the record.

Pancho suddenly becomes quiet watching la Manuela. Watching that thing dancing in the center of the room, all eye sockets, hollows, spasmodic shadows, that thing which is going to die despite its cries, that incredibly repulsive thing that, incredibly, is the party, and dances for him, he knows he aches to touch it and caress it, he doesn't want that writhing thing to be alone there in the center but against his skin, and Pancho lets himself watch and caress from a distance that old queer who is dancing for him and he surrenders to her dance, and now it isn't funny anymore because it's as if he too were gasping for breath. Octavio mustn't know. He can't know. No one must know. They mustn't see him being touched and fondled by la Manuela's contortions and frantic hands that don't touch him at all, letting himself go, but from here, from the chair where he's sitting no one can see what's happening under the table, but it can't be it, can't be and he takes one of Lucy's sleeping hands and puts it there, where it burns. La Manuela's dance handles him and he would like to grab her like this, till she breaks, that corrupt body fluttering in his arms and me with a quivering Manuela, pressing her against me so she doesn't move so much, so she stays still, holding her, till she looks at me with those terrified flames and sinking my hands into her hot slimy viscera, clawing, leaving her flattened, harmless, dead: a thing.

Then Pancho roared. After all, he was a man, he was supposed to feel everything, even this, and no one, not Octavio or any of his friends would think him a freak. This was a party! A fling. He had met too many whorehouse fags in his life to be frightened by this ridiculous old woman, and they always fell in love with him—they felt his biceps, they felt the rough hair that grew to where his shirt opened at the neck. He relaxed under Lucy's hand.

The music stopped.

"The Victrola's broken."

Octavio got up to try and fix it. He quickly took it apart on the counter while Lucy and Japonesita watched. It didn't look as if it would work again. La Manuela, sitting on Pancho's lap, gave him a glass of wine. She begged him to go away from here, no, no, the three of them should continue the party somewhere else. What were they doing here. Wasting time, getting bored, eating and drinking badly. Even the Victrola was broken and who knows if anyone would ever be able to fix it. They don't even make those prehistoric machines anymore, let's go, please let's go. With the truck they could go anywhere to continue the party, in a few minutes they could be in Talca and there, in Wooden Heart's house . . . no, let's go, take me away, honey, I can't stand this any longer. I'm dying of boredom in this town and I don't want to die under a sagging adobe wall, I have a right to see a bit of light, I've never left this hole, because they tricked me into staying telling me that Japonesita is my daughter, I ask you, how could I have a daughter when Japonesita is almost as old as I am, we're just girls. Take me away from here. They say that at Wooden Heart's house they have a spread about this time and there's always something good to eat, even ducks if the customers ask for them, and there are singers, I don't know if the Farías sisters are there, I don't think so because they'd be older than me, it's all the same, somebody else who's as good with the harp and guitar as the Farías sisters used to be, may they rest in peace. Let's go now, take me away, look how that cruel girl tells everyone she's my daughter to make me stay, you saw how she treats me, like a servant, her own mother, and she never lets me go out except for mass and to see Ludo. I want to go away with you and have a party somewhere that's fun, where we can laugh for a while . . .

"It's a mess."

"What's wrong with it?"

"The spring broke."

"Listen pal, just leave it and we'll go somewhere else."

"Where?"

"Look at don Céspedes, he looks like a mummy. Wake up, old man . . ."

"Let's go to Wooden Heart's . . ."

They talked for a while and paid Japonesita.

"Where are you going?"

"What's it to you, you mackerel?"

"Where are you going, papa?"

"To whom are you speaking?"

"Don't play dumb."

"Who are you to give me orders?"

"Your daughter."

La Manuela saw that Japonesita said it spitefully, to ruin everything and make them remember. But la Manuela looked at Pancho and the two of them laughed so hard that they almost blew out the lamps.

"Sure, I'm your mother."

"No. My father."

But they were already leaving, la Manuela, Pancho, and Octavio, arm in arm and stumbling. La Manuela was singing "El Relicario," the others singing the chorus. The night was so clear that the walls cast sharp clear shadows over the puddles. The underbrush grew along the path and the blackberry's eternally renewed leaves covered that mass of things with their precise, obsessive, detailed graphic lines. They made their way to the truck parked on the corner. They walked on either side of la Manuela, holding her waist. La Manuela swayed toward Pancho and tried to kiss his mouth while he laughed. Octavio saw it and let go of la Manuela.

"Come on, pal, don't you be a fag too . . ."

Pancho also let go of la Manuela.

"I didn't do a thing . . ."

"No excuses, I saw . . ."

Pancho was afraid.

"You think I'd let this cruddy fag kiss me, are you out of your mind, pal, would I do something like that? Let's ask Manuela, hey, did you kiss me?"

La Manuela didn't answer. It always happened with men like Octavio, why the hell did he have to snoop and why doesn't he clear out of here. He's going to ruin everything.

"Come on, fag, answer."

Pancho loomed threateningly over la Manuela.

"Let's find out."

His fist was clenched.

"Don't be silly, boys, let's get on with the party."

"Did you or did you not kiss him?"

"It was just a joke . . ."

Pancho hit her in the face while Octavio held her down. The blow wasn't well aimed because Pancho was drunk. La Manuela looked around frantically, for the right moment to run.

"It's one thing to celebrate and live it up, but slobbering on my face is something else . . ."

"Stop. You're hurting me."

Standing in the mud, paralyzed by Octavio who was twisting her arm, la Manuela woke up. He wasn't la Manuela. He was señor Manuel González Astica. He. And because he was he they were going to hurt him and Manuel González Astica tasted terror.

Pancho gave him a shove that staggered him. Octavio, letting go, slipped and fell in the mud while Pancho bent over to help him up. And la Manuela, gathering his skirts up around his waist, fled toward the station. Familiar with the street, he avoided the ruts and stones while his pursuers stumbled at every step. Maybe they would lose sight of him. He had to run this way, toward the station, toward the outskirts of El Olivo because there on the other side of the town's limits don Alejo was waiting for him, and he was the only one who could save him. His face ached, his frail ankles, his bare feet cut by the rocks or a piece of glass or a tin can, but he had to keep running because don Alejo promised he would be all right, that he would take care of him, that he needn't be afraid anymore if he stayed near him, it was a promise, almost an oath, and he had stayed and now they were coming to kill him. Don Alejo, don Alejo. He can help me. To the other side of El Olivo. Cross the vineyard like don Céspedes and tell him that first these wicked men try to take advantage of a girl and then . . . Tell him please protect me from the fear you told me nothing would ever happen to me that you would always protect me and that's why I stayed in this town and now you have to keep your word and protect me and take care of me and comfort me, I've never asked you before, I've never forced your word but now I do, you're the only one, you're the only one . . . don't ignore me don Alejo now that they're trying to kill me, I've come running to ask you to keep your promise . . . this way, through the thicket behind the shed like a fox so that don Alejo will defend me with his shotgun. You can kill these sick bastards and no one will say a thing, after all you're a great man, you can do anything and fix it up later with the police.

He crosses the blackberry-covered fence without realizing that the barbed wire is tearing his dress. He crouches beside the canal. Further on is the vineyard: the dirty water separates him from the symmetrical safety of the vineyards. He has to cross it. Don Alejo is waiting for him. The houses of El Olivo surrounded by oaks and a tall pine like a belfry there where the vineyards meet, waiting for him, don Alejo waiting for him with his sky-blue eyes. He has to rest a little. He listens. They aren't coming. He can't go any further. He drops on the grass. Nothing, silence: even the natural sounds of the night have stopped. La Manuela is panting, Ludovinia would say you're too old to be trotting around like this and it's true, true because his whole body aches—oh, his shoulder, how it hurts, and his legs and suddenly the cold of the entire night, of the leaves and grass and water at his feet, if he could only cross this river, but how, how if he can barely move, sprawled on the ground.

"My little darling . . ."

"Now you're really going to get it . . ."

"No . . . no . . ."

Before he could move, the men burst through the bushes and fell upon him like hungry animals. Octavio, or maybe Pancho first, started lashing at him with fists . . . perhaps it wasn't them, but other men who had pierced the thicket and found him and thrown themselves upon him, their hot bodies writhing, gasping over la Manuela who could no longer scream, their heavy, stiff bodies, the three of them one sticky mass squirming like some fantastic, three-headed animal with multiple limbs, wounded and seething, the three fused there in the grass by vomit and heat and pain, looking for the one to blame, punishing him, her, them, shuddering gratifications, excruciating confusion, la Manuela's frail body resists no more, breaks under the strain, can't even moan from the pain, hot mouths, hot hands, slavering, hard bodies wounding his, bodies that howl and insult and grope, that monster of three tortuous bodies, breaking and tearing and raking and probing, until nothing is left and now la Manuela scarcely sees, scarcely hears, scarcely feels, sees, no, doesn't see, and they escape through the blackberry bushs and she is left alone by the river that separates her from the vineyards where don Alejo waits, benevolent.

12

"That's Sultan."

Another bark, further away.

"That's Moor. He likes to lie beside the wall of the blacksmith's shop at night because it gets hot in the sun and retains the heat . . . but there was no sun today. I wonder why he's roaming around there now."

Japonesita had sat down facing don Céspedes on the other side of the lamp's dwindling flame. She turned it down till it was barely a point inside the lamp. She, too, listened to the dogs. She and la Manuela heard them so often last night that they could hardly sleep, but this was different. Because the sky had cleared up around the moon after the rain and the dogs were howling steadily at it, as if they were talking to it or begging it for something or serenading it, and since the moon was too faraway to hear them, don Alejo's dogs kept on howling.

"That's Sultan again."

Everyone had gone to bed. Cloty had left the Victrola on the table in front of don Céspedes, who kept unscrewing, opening, cutting with a kitchen knife that had a greasy wooden handle. They don't make parts for this kind of machine anymore. May as well throw it in the canal. It's no good for anything.

"But we can't get along without a Victrola."

"It won't be long before they put in the electricity."

"They're never going to. Don Alejo came to tell me today."

Don Céspedes sank into his chair, smaller than ever. He pushed the mess of worn cogs, screws, nuts, and wires aside, and slid his glass nearer. Almost empty. Barely a couple of red fingers at the bottom where the flame multiplied its reflections.

"It looks like one of those things churches have."

"What things, child?"

"Those red things with light inside."

Better be getting back. Don Céspedes drank what was left. It was late. Or maybe it wasn't; time had an eerie way of stretching itself, today seemed short, tomorrow endless, and you never knew in what part of the night you were.

"I'm going to Talca tomorrow to buy another one."

"Another what?"

"Another Victrola. From one of those places that sells things second-hand, in the stores here I'll never find one like this that you have to crank. This was my mother's. I know a place where they sell used ones, they don't charge much at all. The gentleman who owns it, I think someone brought him here one night. I'll see if he can make me a good price."

"Negus . . . no, Othello . . ."

They listened. It was easy for Japonesita to sketch the whole country-side in her imagination now, as if, like don Céspedes, she had suddenly acquired the power to roll out the country like a carpet so that it filled her whole head.

"They're restless tonight."

Because the moon's out Japonesita said to herself, or maybe said out loud, or maybe don Céspedes, bent over the stove, said it, or maybe he just thought it and she sensed it.

"Why does he turn them loose?"

"He's in a funny mood. Last night he didn't go to bed. He roamed all night around the walks and under the oak. I watched him from the gate-house in case something happened, you know how bad people are, so many have sworn to get him. I stayed there without his seeing me, and he kept walking around and around, looking at everything as if he wanted to fix it all in his mind, hungrily, I'd say, until when it was almost dawn Misia Blanca came out and said why don't you come to bed and then before he followed her in he turned the dogs loose in the vineyard."

"Yes. It was dawn when they started barking."

"God knows what's wrong with him."

"He's probably worrying about people like Pancho . . ."

"No, this was yesterday."

"It's the same thing. You can't trust anybody these days."

The old man yawned. Japonesita yawned. Tomorrow she was going to Talca. Like every Monday. Now she couldn't daydream about the Wurlitzer. So much the better. Try and be like don Céspedes who never daydreamed about anything, just watching to see if anything happened, alert, hiding in the shadows. Alert, that's all, no Wurlitzers. Just a sec-ondhand Victrola to replace the one Pancho Vega broke. No, Pancho didn't break it. He had left. He was never coming back. Just as well: he left tranquillity behind, no expectations whatsoever, which was better than tranquillity here in Estación El Olivo, until they finally plowed the whole town under. Except her house. No matter what don Alejo said she wasn't going to sell it. No sir. He can do whatever he wants with the rest of the town but I'm staying here, right where I am. Even if less and less people come and everything comes to an end. Endings are peaceful, and if things don't change they end, they always do. The terrible thing is hope. I'm going to Talca just like I do every Monday to make a deposit in the bank. And I'm going to come back after lunch with the week's groceries, the same things I always get, sugar, tea, noodles, red chili, the same things I always get.

Don Céspedes stood up, listening. Japonesita picked up the screws, cogs, the broken spring, and tied them all in her handkerchief to save. You never know when you might need them.

"I have to go."

"Why?"

"I have to go see. They're barking a lot."

Japonesita smiled at him.

"How much?"

"Ten cents."

Don Céspedes paid. She put the money away. She knew everything, she saw everything, everything she needed to see and know. This house. In the dusky adobe walls the spiders nestled in small holes filled with tapestries of pale slime.

"And la Manuela?"

Japonesita shrugged.

"Can't something happen to him?"

"What could happen?"

"He's old."

"He might be old but every day he gets fonder of chasing around. Didn't you see him leave with Pancho and Octavio? He clutched at the party like a dying man. He was burning up inside. I know him. He's done this to me before. The men buy him drinks, he dances, goes crazy, and leaves with them . . . the wine excites him and they go to Talco and sometimes even further. One of these days something's going to happen to him, I tell myself that every time, but he always comes back. After three or four days. Sometimes after a week of wandering around whorehouses in other towns where they know him, triumphing as he says, and he comes back here with a black eye or a pair of broken ribs because when the men get drunk they hit him for being a queer. Why should I worry! He has nine lives like a cat. I'm tired of the whole thing. And with Pancho's talent for celebrating they'll be roaming around for at least a week. The police know him and don't say anything, they bring him back without telling anyone about it, I give them a few drinks, and it's like nothing happened. But there might be a new policeman, one of those who gets an idea and doesn't let go. And then, a couple of weeks in bed and I have to take care of him. Crying the whole time, saying he's going to die, that he's too old for these things, forgive him, he won't do it again, and he says he's going to throw his flamenco dress away, you saw it, it's a rag, but he doesn't throw it away, he puts it in his suitcase. And then it's the same old story about the men here, the men there, they're all bad because they hit him and laugh at him and then father cries and says what a horrible fate and says what would become of me without my beloved daughter, his only support, and don't ever leave him. My God, don Céspedes! If you could see how he cries! It breaks your heart! And then, of course, after a few months he goes off and I lose him again. It's been over a year now since he did it. I thought he wasn't going to leave again because the poor thing is such a wreck, but you saw what happened . . ."

Don Céspedes was listening to something else.

"What?"

Japonesita studies him, trying to guess what he hears.

"No, nothing, don Céspedes . . ."

She walked him to the door. She opened it just a bit, barely a crack for don Céspedes to slide through. A little wind and some stars filtered in and she huddled in her pink shawl. Then she bolted the door. Rubbing her hands she walked among the tables, putting out the lamps one by one.

". . . three, and four . . ."

She's told them she doesn't like them to light so many lamps when there are so few people, they can't make a profit. The air is full of reeking carbon. Of course, the dance . . . oh well. She went out to the patio. She doesn't know what time it is, but those devils keep howling out there in the vineyard. It must be around five because she hears Nelly cry and Nelly always whimpers a little before dawn. She went to her room and got into bed without even lighting a candle.

MOHAMMED MRABET

love with a few hairs

1

Mohammed lived with Mr David, an Englishman who owned a small hotel near the beach. His mother had been dead for many years, but he went often to the house where his father and brothers and sisters lived. The only thing about Mohammed's life which made his father sad was that during the four years he had been living with Mr David he had learned to drink.

You're seventeen now, his father would say. It's time you stopped acting like a boy. One day soon you'll be getting married. Do you want your wife and children to see you drunk?

Once in a while when Mohammed arrived at his father's house he would have Mr David with him. Then his father's wife and his sisters would work hard and make a big meal to serve them. At these times Mohammed was careful not to show that he had been drinking. Mr David's fear was that some day the old man might insist Mohammed stop living at the hotel with him and return home. He did not intend to let this happen if he could help it. Usually he brought with him a gift or two which he would hand to Mohammed's father at the beginning of the meal. He could not understand why he never saw any of these objects again, once he had given them to him. Mohammed knew that his father generally sold them the following day, but he could not tell this to Mr David.

You should be like the Englishman, his father would tell him. He doesn't go out into the street drunk.

Mohammed did not want any other life than the one he had with Mr David, and so he said nothing.

During these summer months Mohammed suddenly began to come every day to visit his family. He would go up onto the roof and sit for

George Braziller, Inc. Love With A Few Hairs by Mohammed Mrabet, translated from the Moghrebi by Paul Bowles. Reprinted with the permission of the publisher. Copyright © 1968 by Mohammed Mrabet and Paul Bowles.

an hour or more in the hot sun. A few doors beyond, across the street, lived a girl called Mina. Long ago, when they had been very small children, they had played together. Then he had forgotten her. This summer he had seen her grown-up for the first time. She was beautiful. Several times she had appeared in the window, but this was not enough. He wanted to talk to her. Each afternoon he sat in a chair on the roof waiting. The sun burned his skin and the flies bit him, but he went on sitting until the moment came when her face would appear in the window, and she would look out into the street as if nothing were on her mind. Then she would squint up at the roof to see if he were there. At this he would smile and bow his head once. She would laugh and vanish from the window, and he would not see her again until the next day.

When he passed Mina's house he walked more slowly, in the hope that some time she might be standing in the doorway. And one day she was there. She turned quickly to go inside, but he called to her.

2

Mina, please! I want to talk to you.

All right, she said. Talk.

He was not sure what to say. Do you remember a long time ago when we were both little, and you used to come to our house and play? You don't come any more, do you?

To your house? Are you crazy? What would your family think?

They'd be glad to see you.

She laughed. Then as if she were thinking of something else she said: Tomorrow I'm going into the city.

What time?

Around nine in the morning.

I'll be waiting for you in the garden at Sidi Boukhari, by the statue of the frog.

It was very early, but he made himself be there by the fountain the next morning when she walked up the steps. She was dressed in European clothes: a grey sweater and black trousers.

Did you sleep well? he asked her.

Yes, she said. I slept well.

What did you dream?

She looked down at the ground. I dreamed I was in Heaven. And you were there too.

That's a very sweet dream, he said happily. I dreamed I was sitting on a throne, and you were sitting beside me.

Allah! The King and Queen!

They walked side by side into the city. She had to buy fish and vegetables. And he bought her some bananas and apples, and two bars of chocolate. In the bus on the way back to her house he said to her: Can't I see you this afternoon? We could go to the cinema. Or a café. Or up to the mountain if you like.

She shook her head. I don't want people saying things about me.

Before they got to her house, he stopped under a tree and said to her: I want to see you later, Mina.

Yes, she said. What time?

I'll be here under this palm tree waiting for you at five this afternoon.

Ouakha, said Mina, and she walked on to her house. He stood and watched her open the door, go in, and shut it behind her. Finally he went to his father's house. He said down and rested his elbows on the table, his head in his hands. Soon his older sister came in and looked at him.

What's wrong with you?

Nothing.

I know you! she said. There's something the matter.

I'm not sick. I'm fine.

Then why have you got your head in your hands like that, with your eyes looking at nothing? Do you want some lunch?

I'm not hungry. I don't want anything.

You can't do this to me! she cried. I'll be sick unless you tell me what's wrong with you. Have you been in a fight?

No! Not even in an argument. Nothing.

He was merely sitting, waiting for five o'clock.

A little before five he went out and found Mina already there in the narrow street, standing under the same palm tree.

3

They sat in the cinema, waiting to see Abd el Wahab in *El Ouarda Beida*. Mohammed stood up. Excuse me a minute, he said. I'll be right back. I want to buy something.

At the tobacco shop next door he bought two bars of chocolate. When he went back into the theatre the lights were off. He found Mina and sat down. He unwrapped one of the bars, broke off a square, and put it into her mouth. She laughed and crunched on it.

The film began. In a little while he moved his arm around her shoulder and rubbed his lips across her cheek. She sat up straighter.

Mohammed, she said.

What?

Mohammed, I've never been out with a boy before. I've never even talked to one alone before. And this is the first time I've ever been to the cinema.

And you don't like it?

I'm afraid. People can see us.

Afraid! Do you want to drive me crazy? He hugged her to him. I'm going to marry you, he whispered.

Mina had risen quickly and was hurrying to the back of the theatre. He jumped up and ran after her, saying: What's happening? I don't understand.

Outside in the street, people were going past. Mina stopped. You're impossible, she told him. You don't know how to behave with a girl. I've always heard that, but I didn't believe it. Besides, you drink. From now on I'd rather you didn't speak to me when you go by my house. Just leave me alone.

Whatever you say, he told her. Thank you for coming with me. I'm sorry if I bothered you. I didn't know anything like this was going to happen. I'll take you home in a taxi.

I'm going by myself, she said, and walked away.

4

He met Mr David in the entrance-hall of the hotel.

Come and sit down with us, said Mr David. I want you to meet my friends.

They went into the bar. There were five Americans there, making a great deal of noise.

Yes, I'll have a whisky, said Mohammed.

He had another, and another. Mr David was looking at him. What's the matter with you tonight, Mohammed? he said. You look sad. And why so much whisky?

I don't feel so well.

What's the matter with you?

Nothing.

Mr David kept looking at him. Finally he leaned towards him and whispered: Do you need money?

Mohammed had not been thinking of money. Yes, he said.

Come out into the hall, Mr David said.

There he gave Mohammed fifteen thousand francs. Mohammed thanked him and Mr David patted him on the back. With the bills in his pocket he went out into the street, and along the seafront to the Bar Jamaica. He had another drink. As he sat looking around the bar, a friend named Mustafa came in. After they had talked a minute, Mustafa said: Mohammed, you look worried.

I don't feel much like talking. I think I'd better sit by myself.

What's the matter? Tell me about it.

I can't.

Begin, that's all.

There's a girl.

Mustafa laughed.

We were in the cinema, and when I put my arm around her she began telling me how she'd never talked to a man before. She'd never even been to see a film before. She told me I was no good. Then she went home.

Mustafa laughed again. Is that all?

For me it's something. I'm not twenty-seven like you. I've got to get her back.

I know a woman, Mustafa said. A witch who lives in Beni Makada.

You think she could do something?

I know she can. I've used her. We can go out there now.

They paid the barman and walked down into the Avenida de España. It was nearly evening. A cab came past, and they stopped it and climbed in.

5

They drove all the way through Beni Makada, to the other end of the town where the radio towers stood. There were rows of small shacks stretching across the fields. Mustafa stopped the taxi and Mohammed paid the driver. Then Mustafa knocked on a door made of oil tins pressed flat. An old woman wrapped in rags opened it and stepped out.

What is it?

Can we talk to you? asked Mustafa.

She looked at him closely and let them in. Sit down, she said, pointing to an old mattress in the corner. There was a torn reed mat on the floor, and a blanket that had been folded and pushed between the mattress and the wall. Everything was grey with dirt. The smell in the room made Mohammed feel sick.

The woman sat on the floor. What do you want, son? she said, looking at Mohammed.

Lalla, I'm in love with a girl. I want to marry her. I don't want to do her any harm.

I see, she said.

The trouble is, she doesn't love me.

I can do it, she told him. But it's a little expensive.

How much would it be, Lalla? More or less?

It would cost ten thousand francs.

I'll pay you ten thousand, Lalla.

One thing, she said, pointing her finger at him.

What's that?

You'll have to bring me a piece of something she's worn, or a few of her hairs. One or the other.

How am I going to get her hair? Or her clothes, either? It's impossible.

There must be somebody who goes into her house now and then. You can manage it, she told him.

Then he thought of a twelve-year-old boy who was a cousin of Mina's. The boy was always going in and out of the house.

Yes, Lalla, he said. I'll bring you something. If I don't come tomorrow I'll be here the day after.

Yes. She got up and opened the door. Good-bye.

They went down the road.

I'm going to talk to little Larbi, said Mohammed. He'll do anything for money. I'll see you in the morning at the café.

6

At the crossroads they said good-bye, and Mohammed started walking up the hill towards Mstakhoche, where his father lived. On the way he saw a small boy standing in the street. He sent him to the house of Larbi's parents, telling him to bring Larbi right away. Then he stood in the street waiting. When Larbi arrived he asked him if it were not true that he went nearly every day to Mina's house.

Yes, said Larbi. Almost every day.

Here it is, said Mohammed. You're going to do something for me, and I'm going to pay you.

What do I have to do?

You have to cut off a little piece of one of Mina's dresses or something. Or you look in her comb and see if there are any hairs in it. If there are, I want them.

Good, said the boy. I'll bring it.

Larbi went off. In Mina's house he waited until he saw her combing her hair. When she went into the other room he seized the comb and pulled out several long silky hairs. Then he folded them in his hand and carried them back to Mohammed, who was waiting at his father's house.

Mohammed took out five hundred francs. Here, he told him.

The next morning he went down to the café.

Good morning, said Mustafa. Did you get it?

Larbi brought me some hairs. I paid him enough so he'll be quiet. Here they are. Let's go and see the witch.

They found a taxi and went to Beni Makada. The old woman let them in. They sat down on the mattress and Mohammed gave her the hairs. She pulled out a cloth sack and began to search through it for things:

packets of herbs and envelopes full of fingernails and teeth and bits of dried skin. She shook things out onto a sheet of paper, along with Mina's hairs. Then over it all she poured a powder that looked like dirt. She folded everything inside the paper and put it into a tin. A long string of words kept coming out of her mouth. She threw benzoin on to the hot coals of the brazier and put the tin in the centre of the fire, stirring it for a long time until it all had become a black powder. When it had cooled off she poured it into a paper and folded the paper into a packet.

She handed the packet to Mohammed. Take this. Pour the powder outside the door of her house. When you've left it there, don't look down at it. Walk away.

But when? Said Mohammed. At night or in the daytime?

You can do it whenever you like.

He put the folded paper into his pocket and handed her five thousand francs.

Here's five thousand, he said. As soon as it's worked, I'll bring you the other five.

I see, she said.

And if it doesn't work I'm coming back here to get my five thousand.

The old woman laughed.

7

By two o'clock in the morning Mohammed was drunk. He had stayed in the Bar Jamaica the whole evening. Now he left it, and walked along the avenues on his way out to Mstakhoche. When he got to his street there was no one in sight. At Mina's door he pulled the paper out of his pocket. The street light did not shine on the front of the house. He knelt down and sprinkled the powder on the ground by the door. Then he stood up and walked on to his father's house.

In the morning when Mina got up she did her work, washing dishes and glasses and scrubbing the floor. Finally she started to make her mother's lunch. She opened the door and went out with a pail to get water from the fountain. And she had to step over the powder.

When he saw her standing in the doorway for a minute, Mohammed went out and walked slowly past her house. Good morning, he said. But she pretended not to have heard, and he walked on.

At the end of the day, when he had changed his clothes, he went back to Mstakhoche and strolled in the street, back and forth in front of her house. Soon he caught sight of her in the window. When she saw that he had noticed her she began to laugh.

He stood still near the window. What are you laughing at? he asked her.

You!

Why? What's funny about me?

Nothing. But this morning you said hello to me and I didn't answer. And I was afraid you'd gone away angry.

Angry? I went away feeling fine. I said good morning and you didn't. I was thinking all afternoon of how happy I was.

I'm glad you were happy all afternoon, at least, she said.

And now, if I say good evening, can you say it back to me?

Yes, I can, now, she told him.

Mohammed decided then that the spell was beginning to work. Can you come out for a walk? he asked her.

There's nobody in the house. I have to stay here until my mother and father come back.

How about next Friday at five? Can you come out?

Pass by the park at Sidi Boukhari, she said. I bight be sitting on a bench there.

Good.

There were some flower pots in the window. Mina disappeared inside. A moment later she was in the window again with a pair of scissors in her hand. She cut a white carnation from one of the plants, kissed it, and tossed it to him.

He caught it, and raised it to his lips. Good-bye.

Good-bye, she said.

Sitting in a café, Mohammed held the flower in his hand, thinking of how far away Friday afternoon was.

8

On Friday afternoon Mohammed went and knocked on the door of Mr David's office. Mr David was typing at his desk.

What are you writing?

A letter to my father in England. Did you want something?

I need some money, Mohammed said. He knew that Mr David liked him to ask outright rather than give him hints.

How much?

Fifteen thousand.

Fine. He took out the bills and gave them to him.

And I wonder if you could do me a favour? Mohammed went on.

What's that?

I wonder if I could take the car?

I suppose so. But don't get drunk.

Of course not, said Mohammed.

When he drew up at the park Mina saw him coming. She got up and walked towards him. They drove off by way of the mountain. It was midsummer and the air smelled sweet when they went through the pine forest.

We had fun when we were little, didn't we? said Mohammed. Remember how we used to play in the mud? And go to the park and hide behind the trees, and run out and splash in the fountain there? We'd pull up the plants and chase each other and have fights with them. Do you remember?

Yes, she said. And the time you hit me in the head with a stone?

You haven't forgotten that?

They began to laugh.

He parked in front of the café there at the top of the cliff at El Achaqal, and they went inside and sat down. He ordered a Coca-Cola for Mina and a beer for himself.

Presently she said: Mohammed, why do you drink?

I have to, he said. I live with a Nazarene in a place that's always full of Nazarenes, Americans, Englishmen, Frenchmen. They come in and order drinks at the bar, and then they ask me if I want a drink. I can't tell them I'd rather have a coffee or a tea or a Coca-Cola. If an American offers me a whisky I can't take anything but a whisky. Isn't that right?

Yes. That's true.

But some day, he went on, I'm going to stop. I can live without drinking. That's what I really want.

You're right, she told him.

Mina, if I wanted to marry you, would you marry me?

She was laughing. Mohammed, I like you a lot, she said. But I'm afraid.

Of what?

Of you.

Of me? But why? We wouldn't do anything together until we'd been to the notaries and the qadi and had the papers all made out.

I think we ought to go, said Mina.

He got up and paid. They drove back to the city along the airport road.

Mohammed, she was saying. I don't feel like going back to my house. I don't want the day to end.

I don't want it to end either, he said. But you've got to go home now, or your family will be wondering what's happened. Can I see you next week? I could meet you early, and we could go wherever you like.

Perhaps we could eat at El Achaqal, she said. I love to eat on the beach, the way the Nazarenes do.

All right.

I'll meet you at two o'clock in the park, she told him.

9

Early the next Sunday morning while it was still cool Mohammed was buying bread from the breadsellers in the street. Then he went to the market and bought tuna fish, olives, hard-boiled eggs and bananas. He put everything into the car and drove home to put on his bathing suit, and get a towel and some sun lotion.

She was waiting on the same bench. This time he drove all the way down to the shore at El Achaqal, and they sat on the sand near the big rocks. It was a fine day. The beach was covered with English and American tourists. The sun was very hot and the sea was as flat and smooth as a highway. He spread a big towel at the foot of the rocks while Mina took off her slacks and her skirt. Underneath she was wearing a bikini. He undressed and took out the jar of sun cream.

Mina stretched out face down on the towel, and he began to rub the cream over her back and legs. Then she turned over so he could spread it on the rest of her. When he got to her ribs she laughed and sat up.

They lay side by side on the towel in the sun.

Mohammed, she said.

What, Mina?

What would it be like if one of us should die, I wonder?

Die! He rolled his head towards her. If you died I'd be lost. And if I should die I suppose you'd be sad, too. Let's not die. Let's stay alive.

He sat up and lit a cigarette. She looked at him. Mohammed, she said.

What?

That cigarette you're smoking. What does it do to you?

Oh, nothing. It's only a vice. It doesn't give any pleasure. And it's bad for the body. But a man has to have a vice, or he might as well be dead. Some drink, some smoke kif or tobacco. Some have to be with a different woman every day. Each one has something.

But you've got two, she said. You've got tobacco and alcohol too.

No, that's not true, he told her. I only drink when I'm nervous. Cigarettes are different.

Let me try, she said, sitting up and reaching for the cigarette.

You won't like it.

She took it and puffed on it once. Then she began to choke and cough. You're right, she said.

They got up and started to chase each other along the beach. He let her run far ahead of him so he could watch her. Finally he caught her. For a while they played ball with a group of Spaniards. Then they ran on, into the ocean. They waded out until the water was up to their shoulders, and Mohammed tried to pull her further, but she did not know how to swim. He did his best to show her how, supporting her from beneath on the palms of his hands. The sun glistened like fire on the water all around them. Soon she was tired.

Back by the rocks, they dried themselves.

Wait, he said. I'm going up to the café a minute. He climbed up the side of the cliff and in a few minutes was down again with two bottles of beer and a Coca-Cola. Then they brought out the food.

As they were eating, she suddenly exclaimed: What a vice! Do you have to drink beer every time you sit down to eat?

If I don't I can't eat.

I know, she said, shaking her head. Some people have to have wine with their meals. But most people just drink water.

They finished eating and stretched out on the sand in the sun.

Why don't we get dressed and go up to the café? he said.

In a little while.

If your mother knew you were here with me at El Achaqal, would she make trouble?

You know she would.

He touched her face with his fingers. Then he put his arm around her and pulled her to him, to kiss the spots he had touched with his fingers. When her arms went around him, he kissed her lips. Suddenly she was saying: Mohammed, I love you. I want to be with you always. Every minute.

The spell is working, thought Mohammed.

They climbed the path that went back and forth between the rocks, up the side of the cliff. He went first, holding her arm to keep her from falling. In the café they drank black coffee.

I'm going to take you home now, he said. I've got something to do in town.

She sighed.

As they drove past the cows and camels in the fields beside the road, it occurred to him that he would like to know more about how the spell had worked. You've got to tell me something, he said.

What's that?

Tell me. When did you first know you liked me? A while ago you wouldn't even speak to me. Isn't that true?

Yes, Mohammed. But there are thousands like us. They argue and quarrel, and in the end they fall in love. If two people haven't fought they don't know each other. It's better to fight at the beginning than later. It's true I didn't like you at the cinema. And whatever I said then, I'm sorry I said it.

That's all finished. You didn't say anything so bad. You were angry, so you went out of the theatre. I couldn't force you to stay there. Besides, I thought you might change your mind some day.

He stopped the car in a side street not far from Mina's house. People walking by stared at them. He kissed her cheek, and then her hand, and she got out.

Next Sunday, can I meet you? he said.
I have to go somewhere with my family.
And the week after?
Yes.
At half past four, or five?
Half past four.

10

Mohammed was standing in a bar on the beach in the city having a beer. Mustafa came in.

So here you are! You've forgotten all about us. What news of the girl-friend?

Beautiful, said Mohammed. He laughed.

Have you been back to pay the witch?

No, but I will.

And the powder really worked?

Worked! I just this minute left her. What are you having?

Beer, said Mustafa. Soon he looked at Mohammed and said: You're not really going to marry her, are you?

Is that what you think? Don't you know what love is? When I was this big I used to take care of her. I've always loved her.

Mohammed went on drinking. After a while he was saying, again and again: She could die or I could die. But there's nobody alive who could pull us apart.

That's the way to talk! said Mustafa. Marry her, get yourself a good house, and fill it with young ones. This is a hard world. You might as well try to be happy.

Mustafa did not really believe this, but they were drinking in a bar.

Incha'Allah, said Mohammed, already feeling happy. He was thinking: There's nothing wrong with a world where you can get love with a few hairs. It's wonderful!

11

Late one afternoon Mohammed and Mr David were sitting in the garden having a drink together. Mohammed was nervous. He was putting off asking if he might take the big car. Mr David had a Mercedes as well as the Volkswagen which Mohammed usually borrowed. When the moment came to say the words, he found himself asking for the Volkswagen. Of course, said Mr David. But remember we're going to a party tonight. And don't forget what we were talking about. Be careful of that girl.

Mohammed hurried out and got into the car. He drove to Sidi Boukhari and picked up Mina. It was a hot midsummer evening, and he felt like being in the country under the sky smelling the plants. He drove on, out to Boubana, and stopped by the river. They got out and sat down, leaning against the trunk of a high eucalyptus. There was a soft light in the sky, and the air under the trees here by the river was cool.

He passed his hands over her hair. It's like silk, he said. He kissed her lips. The kisses ran between them like the waves of the sea.

He drew back and looked at her. Mina, some day I'm going to eat you.

She stared into his eyes. Eat me now, she said. Do whatever you want. Anything. Everything. Whatever you say is all right. Kill me and cut me into pieces if you feel like it.

Mohammed sat straighter. This was surely the spell working, he thought. And he remembered that he had not gone back and paid the witch the other five thousand francs. The words Mina was saying could be the old woman's way of making trouble for him. He resolved to go and pay her in the morning.

Get up, he said to Mina. Let's go.

What for? It's still early.

It's half past six. We should go. Your mother's going to start asking where you've been.

You're right, she said, and got up slowly.

They walked back to the car, and he drove her home.

That night he lay awake thinking. There was something disturbing about Mina's words. For two weeks he kept away from Mstakhoche. In the meantime he told Mr David about the witch, and was astonished to see how delighted Mr David was to hear that he had worked magic on the girl. He wanted to know all about it. At the end he gave him the five thousand francs, and told him to be sure and go to pay the old woman.

At the witch's shack, before giving her the money, he told her about Mina's behaviour, and asked her if she could not reduce the effect of the spell a bit.

The old woman laughed. You asked me to make her fall in love with you, and I did it. Now manage it the way you like. Either you want her or you don't.

He paid her and went away dissatisfied. At least, he thought, the witch would not be working against him now.

12

Finally Mohammed went back to Mina's house at Mstakhoche and arranged to see her the following Sunday evening. When he met her in the park she was wearing a bright green satin evening dress, black shoes with very high heels, and two heavy gold bracelets. Her hair fell down lightly around her shoulders. When he had looked a while at her, he said: Come with me to the hotel. I want you to meet my friend. I think you'll like him.

They got into the car and drove to the centre of the city. He parked on the Boulevard and took Mina into a shop. The Indian came up to him.

What can I do?

I want to see some ladies' wristwatches, he told him.

Yes. We have them. And he began to pour watches on top of the counter.

Mohammed looked and said: Not this sort. I want something good.

Yes. We have them too. He brought out some watches from behind a screen. These are gold.

Mohammed picked up a thin square watch. This is a beauty, he told Mina. How much is this one?

That is seventeen thousand, said the Indian.

That's the one we want. He tried to pay fifteen thousand, but the Indian would not listen. Then he paid him sixteen thousand, and they went out to the car. When they were sitting inside, he handed Mina the parcel.

You shouldn't waste your money this way, Mohammed. I love you anyway, without presents.

No, he said. We have to go to good places, and you have to wear good things. I don't want to see you in old clothes with no shape to them, or look at your legs and see a pair of old worn-out shoes. I want you to look better than anybody else.

Thank you. You're very sweet. She kissed him, and people walking past stared into the car. He started the motor and they drove off.

When they got to the hotel, Mr David stood in the doorway looking into the street.

I want to introduce my fiancée, Mohammed told him. Mina, this is Mr David.

Enchanté, mademoiselle, said Mr David, looking up and down the street. *Je suis content que vous soyez venue. Entrez, entrez.*

Mina did not understand anything but Arabic. Mohammed pushed her ahead of him, and Mr David led them into the bar without looking at them. The room was very smoky and full of Americans. Mohammed presented Mina to the Americans who were friends of his. There was a good deal of laughter among the Nazarenes, but Mr David did not laugh. Then the two sat down at one of the tables. The Americans tried to talk to Mina in Spanish. She smiled.

What are you going to have? Mohammed asked her.

A limonada, she said.

Limonada!

Yes.

You can't get that here. All you can get is things like whisky or cognac. But I'll bring you something that won't leave any smell on your breath. It's sweet.

All right.

Mohammed got up and went over to the bar. He filled a glass with Cinzano and put in a maraschino cherry. Then he took it over to her. Try this, he said.

He got himself a whiskey and brought it back to the table. She was drinking her Cinzano and liking it. When she had finished it he got her another, and then another, until she had drunk five. By this time she was talking very fast.

Mr David came over to the table and bent down to speak into Mohammed's ear. You've got to take that girl home, he told him. She's very drunk.

No, no, Mohammed said. She's not drunk yet. She's just playing.

Mina jumped up and ran in front of Mr David, out into the middle of the floor. She began to sing and dance. Between dances she went on talking in Arabic.

Mohammed watched Mr David and his American friends. When he saw that they were all tired of Mina, he got up. Let's go, he said, taking hold of her arm. I'm going to take you home.

13

Mohammed had Mina say good night to each one of the Americans, and then he led her outside. When they were in the car, she turned to him and said: Mohammed, there's only one person in the world I love.

Me too, he said.

But you don't know who it is, she went on.

Who is it?

You don't know? The one person in the world I love? You don't know who it is?

No.

It's you, Mohammed. She laid her head on his shoulder. You're the first boy I've ever loved.

Mohammed started the motor. And I could never love any other girl the way I love you, he told her. Nobody. Nobody else can make me feel the way you do, Mina. And now we're going to the pharmacy and I'm going to get you some medicine to clear your head. And then we'll stop at a café and have some black coffee with lemon in it, and by the time you get home you'll feel all right.

Mina did not seem to understand what he was saying. She only shook her head back and forth. I'm going to stay with you, she told him. Always. I'm not going home. What am I going to do at home? I want to be with you.

With a pill and some coffee you'll feel better, Mina. You've got to go home. If you stay with me now, what's going to happen? Nothing but trouble. And by the time it's over we won't even love each other any longer.

But she went on shaking her head. It's no use, Mohammed, she told him. From the way she said it, he felt that she was right, that no one could stop her from doing what she had decided to do.

Ouakha, he said, and started the car up the hill with a great noise. He drove beyond Mstakhoche to the very edge of the town, where he had a small room that he kept for nights when he felt like staying up and having a good time with his friends. He unlocked the door.

It was damp inside.

They went in and sat down, he on the chair and she on the bed. There was a bottle of whisky on the table. He poured himself a drink.

Give me some, she said. I want to drink whisky. I've never drunk whisky.

Whisky's no good for you, he told her. If you begin to drink whisky you're going to throw up. You'll feel terrible.

But she insisted. I want to try it, she kept saying.

Mohammed stood up. I'm going out and get you that medicine, and you're going to take it. And then you're going home.

Mina lay back on the bed. I'm going to sleep here. And I'm going to drink whisky.

All right, he said angrily. And he took a glass, poured whisky in and added some water, and handed it to her.

She got up off the bed with the glass in her hand and started to walk across the room. When she had nearly reached the chair where he sat, she began to sway. He jumped up and caught her.

You get into bed and rest, he told her, stroking her hair. I'm going to sleep in the chair.

No, you're not, she said. You're going to sleep in the bed with me.

No, no, no! He was looking away from her, across the room.

Both of us. She held his waist more tightly.

Good! he said so suddenly and so loud that she let go of him and tried to look at his face. He walked to the other side of the room and stood there with his hands in his pockets.

Mina leaned on the chair and began to undress. She took off her green evening gown and her *soutien-gorge*, and stood there in her underpants. Then she got into the bed. He went back and sat in the chair, and slowly drank the whisky, until there was none left. He was wishing that she had not drunk so much. He wanted to feel that it was he who had decided everything, and instead he felt that Mina was doing exactly as she pleased with him. How can she want to sleep here in this dirty bed? he thought.

He got up and took off his jacket, then his shirt, then his trousers. He hesitated, then got into the bed, still wearing his shorts. As soon as he lay down she put her arm over him. He seized her and kissed her. They said I love you, back and forth. Then he said: It was a bad thing you did, coming here.

Don't talk about it, she said.

Soon he ran his hand down her thigh and slipped off her underwear. Then with more kisses he finally went in, and from being a girl Mina became a woman. She hugged him very tight. And that way they stayed until it was morning.

14

When Mina got out of bed she looked down and saw the streaks of blood on the sheet. She sat down again on the edge of the bed and burst into tears. Mohammed opened his eyes.

It's a sin, what you've done, she finally said between sobs. You made me get drunk. If you hadn't given me those drinks I never would have come here. What am I going to do now? I can't go home.

She went on weeping. Mohammed sat up and put his arm around her. Don't cry. We'll get married, he said.

She wiped her eyes. I'm afraid. Sooner or later you'll leave me. It's just a game for you, but everybody's going to be against me. My father'll kill me. I know he'll do something terrible. And if the police hear about it, they'll make trouble for you.

Mina, he said. I swear by the food we've eaten together and the blood on this sheet, you've got nothing to worry about. You're going to live with me. Now lie down and stop thinking about it. I'll be right back. Stay here in bed.

He went out, and shortly he came back with fruit and vegetables and meat. And he had bought a live chicken. Mina was still in bed. He took the chicken out into the street and cut its throat. Then he came in and began to make chicken broth for Mina. It took a long time. When the meal was ready, he carried the table across the room, and they ate sitting side by side on the edge of the bed. As soon as they had finished, Mohammed said: Why don't we go out?

I couldn't. I'm too tired.

478 / INTERNATIONAL SHORT NOVELS

I'll bring the car.

Leave me here, she told him. I'm going to sleep a while. You go wherever you want. She lay down on the bed.

I'll be back, he said.

He walked down to the Boulevard and went into a shop. He bought two nightgowns and three bathrobes and two pairs of bedroom slippers lined with white fur and a large bottle of Eau de Cologne and a box of bath powder and several bars of bath soap. When he got back to the mahal he found her having coffee.

Wouldn't you like some? she asked him.

Good.

She poured it out for him. What's in all those packages? she said.

I brought you some things. I don't know whether you'll like them.

She put one of the packages on the table, opened it, and pulled out the nightgowns.

Mohammed, she said laughing. I'm so happy! Thank you. Nobody else could make me so happy.

It's nothing. Just a few clothes. He took her hand. Later we'll live better than this, and I'll get you better things than these. We have plenty of time ahead of us.

Mina was looking at him and shaking her head. I didn't know you were going to be so nice to me. I thought you didn't care. But now I know you do love me. We really will get married, won't we?

Of course.

But Mohammed, she said, her voice sounding frightened again.

What?

My father and mother must be looking for me. Suppose they find out I'm with you?

Her words made Mohammed feel very uncomfortable, but he said: Leave that to me. Don't think about it.

That evening when it had got dark he managed to make Mina agree that if he could get the car she would take a ride with him.

Mr. David said nothing, but it seemed to Mohammed that his glance was not very friendly.

Yes. Of course, he said after a moment. Take it.

Mohammed parked the car in the street at Mstakoche and walked to the mahal. Mina put on her green evening gown, and they walked together through the alleys until they got to the car. As he was helping Mina to get in, he saw an old woman in a grey djellaba stop and look closely at them. He shut the car door. Then he went round to the other side and got in. The old woman was still standing there, staring at Mina.

Trouble, he thought. But he said nothing, and they took their ride.

15

The old woman went directly to Mina's house. I've just seen your daughter! She was getting into a car in the Souq el Bqar with Mohammed, that boy who lives here across the street, and they drove away together.

What!

A few minutes ago.

Her father's spent all night and all day looking for her. It's a terrible tragedy. These girls today are the worst ever. God help all women with daughters! Bitches and dogs in the street, that's what the young people are today.

When Mina's father came in, Husband, she said to him, Mina's with that Mohammed from across the street.

What are you saying?

Hadija was just here. She saw her getting into his car.

He's taken her to that filthy Christian hotel down there, said Si Ahmed, and he started out at once for the hotel, walking as fast as he could. About forty-five minutes later he arrived, and asked the night watchman for Mohammed.

Mohammed had just left Mina in the mahal at Mstakhoche after their ride, and gone back to the hotel with the car. In a moment he came out of the bar. His heart sank when he saw who had asked to see him.

Salaamou aleikoum.

Aleikoum salaam.

Is your name Mohammed Ouriagli?

Yes, he said, keeping his eyes narrow. He felt that they had opened too wide.

My daughter is with you?

Yes.

And how do you explain that? shouted Si Ahmed, waving his cane.

We're in love with each other. We want to get married.

Garbage. That's what you are, said Mina's father. Where is she?

She's not here, said Mohammed. Tomorrow at twelve o'clock I'll come to your house and take you to see her.

You'll do much more than that, said Si Ahmed. Then he went out, talking to himself.

Mr David tried to keep Mohammed from going out that night. I know what you're doing, he told him, and you're going to ruin your health. Why don't we take a bottle of champagne into the bedroom and play some music?

Mohammed did not answer. His face grew red and he looked at the floor, and Mr David knew that there was no way of keeping him in.

It was late when Mohammed arrived at the mahal in Mstakhoche. He opened the door. Mina was sitting in the chair in the centre of the room, waiting for him. He shut the door behind him, and she jumped up and threw herself into his arms.

There was a strong warm wind that night. Mohammed opened the window and stood leaning out for a moment. Then he got into his pyjamas. Mina was already in bed.

Lying beside her, he stared at her for a long time, thinking of many things. As he looked at her, her face seemed to change shape and take on many different expressions. The one face became many faces. She had large eyes with long lashes, and her eyebrows were high and arched. He glanced down at her body. It was small and plump. He slid his arms around her and began to kiss her eyes, her nose and her cheeks.

Mina. Mina. Without you there'd be nothing, he was saying. You've got to stay with me always. If God would only help us we could get out of this country and go somewhere else. Some place far away, like America or France or London. No people always making trouble. He could not bring himself to tell her that he had seen her father and was going to bring him to the mahal in the morning.

You know, even after we're married, your family's never going to like me, because of what we've done, he said.

Don't talk about it! She began to cover his lips with kisses, so that he could not go on speaking. The warm wind blew in over them, and made a noise in the canes across the alley. Later they fell asleep.

In the morning when Mohammed was dressed and ready to go out, he turned to her and said: What would you do if your father should come here?

Here! He can't!

I just wondered, said Mohammed.

He'd beat me! He'd kill me!

Don't worry. I won't let that happen, he told her. I'll be back around noon.

16

Mohammed walked in the morning sun to his father's house. He had not been there this early in the morning for a long time. His father's wife opened the door. He went inside and found his father sitting with his brothers.

Father, he said.

Yes.

A girl called Mina, the one who lives across the street. You know who I mean?

His father's wife looked at him. Yes, she said.

We've got to get married. Can I have my wedding party here in the house? That's what I wanted to say, to see whether you were willing or not.

His father's wife said nothing. She went on looking at him.

Mohammed! cried his father. Do you know what you're doing?

What am I doing?

His father sat back and was silent for a moment. Then he said: I have only one thing to say to you. If you marry that girl, don't bother to come back to this house again. And don't take the trouble to speak to me if you see me in the street, either, because I won't be your father. Think about it.

Mohammed went out of the house and sat on the grass above the reservoir for an hour or so. It occurred to him that he had often heard his father speak with scorn of Mina's mother as a whore. He may be right, Mohammed thought. He may have good reasons for keeping the families apart. Then he remembered something that Mr David had told him many times: The day you get married you can say good-bye to me. He had never paid the threat any attention because he had never thought of getting married. Now, however, he was convinced that Mr David meant what he said. He could not understand Mr David. Sometimes he complained about Mohammed's girls, and sometimes he did not seem to care. But he always urged him to get rid of whatever girl he had at the moment, and look for a new one.

He got up and walked to Mina's house. Si Ahmed was waiting for him, and Mina's mother was in her veil and haik. The three of them set out on foot for the mahal. They did not speak on the way.

When Mohammed unlocked the door, Mina was standing just inside. Her mother rushed into the room and took her in her arms, and they both burst into tears.

Oh, my baby! My precious! Why did you run away? Why have you made us wait so long?

They both went on crying. Then Mina saw her father, and she ran to him and kissed him. Forgive me! she cried. Forgive me! I know it's a terrible thing. But I love Mohammed and I've got to stay with him. We're going to get married.

As she spoke, Si Ahmed was looking around at the furniture in the mahal. He patted her shoulder. Thank God no one knows about it, he said. It'll come out all right. We'll arrange everything.

Sit down, said Mohammed. He was growing more nervous each moment. Mina, get some coffee for your father. He took out a pack of Olympics and offered one to Si Ahmed.

Si Ahmed lighted the cigarette, sat back, and said: What are we going to do now?

Mohammed took a deep breath. I can't marry her, he said.

Mina's father stood up. You'll marry her or I'll have you in court! he shouted.

You can put me in front of the firing squad if you like, Mohammed cried. I can't marry her.

Without looking at Mina he ran out into the street.

17

That afternoon Mr David was at a cocktail party. There was no one in the hotel but Mohammed and Ali the dishwasher. About four o'clock a jeep drew up in front of the door. Mina's father came into the bar, and there were three policemen with him.

Good afternoon, said the policemen. Then they said to Mohammed: Come with us.

Yes, said Mohammed. He went out with them and got into the jeep. They drove him to the Mendoubia and left him in an office there.

Sit down, the official said.

You've got to marry this girl, he told Mohammed.

Mohammed talked a long while. At the end he said he could not marry Mina because his father would not permit it.

The official wrote down the information about him and his family. He took up the telephone. While he was still talking, a man came in and led Mohammed into another room. He sat here alone for fifteen minutes or so. Then two policemen opened the door and beckoned to him. As he went through the doorway, they said: Put your hands out.

Why? Why are you putting handcuffs on me?

They pushed him into a van with some other prisoners and took him to the jail in the Casbah. There they left him alone in a small room with no light in it.

The sixth day after lunch, a guard came and opened the door. Come out, he told him. Mohammed went out into the corridor.

We can't have you sitting there in the dark all the time, said the guard. We thought you ought to get out into the sun for a while. Come up on the roof.

There was no other prisoner in sight on the roof. Wherever Mohammed walked, the guard walked with him.

You must have a good job, the guard said.

Yes, said Mohammed.

I've seen this girl, you know, said the guard. She's a real beauty! Why don't you want to marry her? I don't understand you. It's the only way of getting out of here, anyway. You'll be here for two months before your trial. And then they can give you two years. At least marriage doesn't take that long.

Mohammed listened to the guard's words, and felt his heart sink. He had thought the entire thing would take a month at the most.

I'm telling you the truth, the guard told him. I have your papers downstairs. It says on them two months until the trial, and after that they send you to Casablanca or Larache. They won't leave you here. The only way you can save yourself is to marry her. That way you get out of here, stay with her a month or two and beat her up every night. She'll be glad to escape. I feel sorry for you, young and strong like this, wasting your life breaking rocks in jail. You'll be in and out of the hospital for the rest of your life. That's what happens if you stay in places like this.

I know, said Mohammed.

He passed most of the night thinking about it.

Every day someone came for him and took him up onto the roof to let him walk around in the sun, but he did not catch sight of the guard who had talked to him.

One day Mr David arrived at the jail, asking to see Mohammed. What is this? he demanded.

I can't tell you, said Mohammed.

Tell me, for God's sake! I can help you. I can get you lawyers.

You can't help me. It's no use. It's the girl I brought to see you that night at the hotel.

I knew it! cried Mr David. I knew she'd get you in trouble! Whatever it is, you can't just stay in jail. I won't let you stay on in this place. You've only been here two weeks, and already you look terrible! Your health will be ruined.

The visit is over, said the guard.

Don't get me any lawyers or anything, Mohammed called after Mr David.

Time passed. He had been in jail a month. One day when they took him up onto the roof, he met the guard who had taken him up the first day. He was standing by the railing, looking down into the courtyard. Then he saw Mohammed.

Good morning, 125. How are you?

Mohammed greeted him. As the guard was about to go downstairs, Mohammed said: Can I speak with you?

Of course. What is it?

I'm sick of this place. Alone in a dark room. Always alone. I can't stand any more of it. I'll explode. I want to marry the girl.

The guard laughed. Tonight you'll sleep at home. I promise you.

Mohammed went downstairs to the office with him while he telephoned to the Mendoubia. Then he went back to his room. Later in the day the guard came and opened the door. Let's go, he said.

They went out and got into a station wagon, and the guard went with him to the Mendoubia. In the office of the oukil ed doula the official asked him: And why did you refuse the other time? You wouldn't have had to spend a whole month sitting up there. Look at you now, sad and dirty.

Mohammed was angry, and he looked at the floor. I wanted to see what jail was like, he said.

Now you know, said the official. The secretary handed Mohammed a pen. Sign here, he told him.

You're free now. Be here in this office tomorrow morning at nine o'clock.

18

Mohammed went out into the street with his filthy clothes and his long hair. He took a taxi at the Zoco de Fuera and went straight to the hotel. Mr David was sitting with some friends. When he saw Mohammed he sprang up and took him in his arms. Then he began to cry.

Give me some money, said Mohammed. I've got to pay the taxi driver.

Mr David excused himself from his friends and took Mohammed out to his bedroom in the garden.

Tell me everything, Mohammed. How did you get out?

If I tell you, you're going to be very upset, said Mohammed.

Why? What is it?

I've got to get married. Then he told him the whole story. At the end, he said: But it won't take long. The way I'm going to treat her, she'll be begging to leave.

Mr David's face brightened a little. There's nothing else to do, he said.

You're going to be very sad, Mohammed told him.

No, I'm not. I'm just happy to see you now. He hugged Mohammed and kissed him. Mohammed was very good to him, and kissed him and made him feel happier. Then he said: Please. I want to take a bath. I've got to shave and go out and get a haircut, too.

He had been alone for so long that he felt like seeing his family. From the barber's he went to Mstakhoche. If his father asked him where he had been, he was going to tell him he had been on a trip with Mr David. He did not intend to mention Mina.

There was no one at home but two of his brothers. He sat and talked with them for a while, and then he went up the street to Mina's house.

Mina herself opened the door. As soon as she had kissed him, she began to weep. Her mother came in, looked at Mohammed angrily, and sat down in the corner. When her father appeared, he said: How was the jail?

Terrible, said Mohammed. I decided I'd rather marry Mina.

Good, said Si Ahmed.

Tomorrow you're supposed to go down to the Mendoubia, Mohammed told him. At nine o'clock in the morning. That's all I came to tell you. I've got to go now.

I'm going with you, said Mina, jumping up.

No, you're not. You stay here with your mother.

Mohammed went back to the hotel. That night he slept with Mr David. Early in the morning he was in the market buying food. At nine o'clock he went to the Mendoubia and met Mina and her parents outside the big gate. The secretary spoke with each one of them, and when they left, he gave them three papers, one for Mohammed, one for Mina and one for her father. Then they all went to the mahal in Mstakhoche. Mohammed had invited them for lunch.

Mina and her mother made tea for Si Ahmed and Mohammed, and then they went into the kitchen to prepare lunch.

How much do you earn where you work? Si Ahmed asked Mohammed.

Mohammed hesitated. I don't know, he said. It depends on the tips. Some days are good. Some days are bad.

The Nazarenes must pay you quite a lot. You live well.

Come and sit down, said Mina, and we'll eat. They got up and went to sit at the taifor. Mina poured water over their hands, and then they began to eat.

When this accident happened with Mina, said her mother, why didn't you let us know? You could have sent somebody to tell us she was alive. at least.

Satan didn't want it that way, said Mohammed. But the wedding will make it exactly as if nothing had happened. As long as nobody talks about it. Mina must have a big party. Tomorrow we'll go and arrange the papers. My father mustn't know anything or he'll make trouble. And Mina must stay with you until after the party.

You're right, said Si Ahmed. Everybody must be very calm and do everything the way it ought to be done.

When they finished eating, Mina carried in the pitcher and the bowl, and poured water over their hands. Then she brought the tea tray and made tea for them.

Mina, said her mother. We've got to go now, and you've got to come with us.

But I haven't seen Mohammed in a month! Mina cried.

And what do you think people are going to say if you stay here?

Si Ahmed got up. You come with us, he said, and all three of them went out.

19

Mohammed was sitting in the Café Central that afternoon, thinking. A deaf and dumb man was going from table to table, waving his arms, asking for money. Mohammed gave him a coin and smiled. He was happy that Mr David had not complained that he was getting married, but he had not yet mentioned the money. It was going to cost a great deal. Mohammed planned to remind Mr David of the money he had been willing to spend for lawyers to get him out of jail.

Soon he caught sight of Mustafa going through the square.

Mustafa! Mustafa! he cried. Come here. I want to talk to you.

Mustafa stopped and sat down at the table.

I need a house. Do you know of one?

A house! What do you want of a house?

Mohammed began to laugh.

You've done it, haven't you? cried Mustafa. Didn't I tell you to be careful or you'd get into trouble?

This is the way it had to be, or it wouidn't have happened this way, Mohammed told him. I've done it, and I've got to keep her.

Mohammed, you're only a boy. Seventeen! You're going to ruin your life with an army of babies. In a little while the only thing you'll be good for is worrying. No more life, no fun, no nights with your friends. From the house to work. From work to house. The babies always sick. Something always wrong. Never any money. By the time you're thirty you'll be an old man, good for nothing. Like me. I'm twenty-seven. But I've got three, and I look sixty.

Just tell me if you know of a house, said Mohammed.

I think I can get one for you by the end of the week.

Where?

In Benider.

Mohammed had decided that during the next few days he would spend all his time with Mr David, eating, drinking and sleeping with him, and going with him wherever he wanted him to go. It was a great pleasure for Mr David when Mohammed would consent to go with him to a party.

The next morning at breakfast he mentioned the money. It's going to be expensive, he said. I should have stayed in jail.

Don't talk that way, said Mr David. We'll manage.

20

The next day Mohammed met Mina's father in the Zoco Chico, and they walked down to the tunnel that led into the courtyard of the notaries. They went through the gate. There was a basin full of goldfish in the centre, under some small orange trees. They sat down on a bench and waited. Mohammed took out a cigarette and began to smoke.

Finally they were taken into the notary's office. What do you want? Si Ahmed said: Sidi, this boy.

Let me talk to him, said Mohammed.

Talk, said Si Ahmed.

Sidi, an accident has happened between me and a girl. She came to my house and spent the night, and I damaged her. What we want is to arrange it so no one will know anything about it. No one but Allah. I want to make out the papers according to the law.

I must talk with the girl, said the notary. We can't do anything unless she's here too.

You can come to the house and see her, said Mohammed.

That will cost you more.

It's all right.

The notary got up and put his books and pens into a briefcase. Then he went out and found two assistants to go with him, and all five of them set out through the Medina to go to Mstakhoche.

When they got to Si Ahmed's house, Mina served them pastries and made them tea. Then she sat down facing the notary.

Mina, do you love this boy? he asked her.

Yes, Sidi, she said.

Not just think it would be fun to marry him, and then after three or four days decide you don't like him?

No, Sidi. I'll never, never leave him until the day I die.

Good, good, said the notary. Then he turned to Si Ahmed. How much are you asking for the girl?

A hundred thousand francs, said Si Ahmed.

You heard that? the notary asked Mohammed.

Yes, said Mohammed. A hundred thousand. It's all right. He was thinking about Mr David. I'll have it here for you tomorrow.

21

Mohammed was sitting in a beach chair in the garden outside Mr David's room. He could hear him typing inside. When he would stop for a moment, Mohammed would cough. Soon Mr David came to the door, and saw Mohammed leaning forward with his head in his hands. Mohammed, he said.

Mohammed did not look up.

488 / INTERNATIONAL SHORT NOVELS

Now what's the matter?

Finally Mohammed stood up. I came to say good-bye, he said. I've got to go back to jail.

Back to jail! cried Mr David. I thought it was all arranged.

How can it be arranged if her father wants a hundred thousand francs for her? He's a criminal! I told him I'd go back to jail before I'd pay that much.

You will not! You'll pay him the money.

I have to pay him tomorrow. How can I?

Mr David sighed. I told you I'd help you, he said. You can't go back to jail.

It's robbery, said Mohammed.

That day he stayed by Mr David's side. He mixed his drinks for him, and had a match ready each time he took out a cigarette. And when evening came, he helped him into his bathrobe, and listened with him to London on the radio, instead of switching the programme to Rabat as he always did. Before they went to sleep Mr David told him that he had never known another boy like him.

The next day Mohammed went back to Mstakhoche with the money in his pocket. The notary and his assistants were sitting in a row on the mattress, and Si Ahmed's face looked worried. It changed when Mohammed came in, walked over to the notary and counted out the money. The notary counted it again and handed it to Si Ahmed. Then Mohammed signed. When the notary himself had written his name on each paper, Mohammed gave him another ten thousand francs.

Keep this paper, the notary said. At the end of the month you have to take it to the qadi. You sign it in front of him, and he'll give you the final paper. Then it will all be in order.

Mohammed folded the paper and put it into his pocket. The notary and his assistants got up. Bslemah, bslemah, they said. May Allah give you happiness, they told Mina. And they went out.

22

So, it's all settled, said Mina's mother. I hope you'll both be very happy. Allah ikimil aleikoum b'kheir.

Mina was not listening to her.

Her mother went on. We've got to begin to think about the wedding party.

Let me tell you something, said Mina. You've just sold me, haven't you? You couldn't have said to the notary: I'll give her away according to the Koran. I don't want any money for her. When you heard the words: How much? you had to say: A hundred thousand francs. And this boy paid the hundred thousand. He bought a girl. He's got the paper in his pocket.

Mina! cried her mother.

Mina turned to her.

He shouldn't have had to pay anything. It's shameful what my father did! Does he think I'm a cow? He sold me for a hundred thousand francs, and now he's got the money. Is that right? So I'm not yours any longer, and I'm not going to live here, and I don't want any wedding party.

We're poor, said Si Ahmed. If we'd given you away for nothing, where would we have got the money for the wedding party? We haven't got enough.

You haven't got enough! I know what you have! Mina cried. You could pay for six weddings! You're just stingy. All you know how to do is get money out of people. You don't know how to let go of it, do you? You think everybody doesn't know what a miser you are? You can't think of anything else, even in your sleep. And I don't want any party.

Mohammed got up. I'm going. You're staying here, he said to Mina.

Mina did not reply. He said good-bye. He had promised to let Mr David know what had happened with the notary.

Mr David was waiting for him. Is it all right? he asked him.

Mohammed handed him the piece of paper the notary had given him.

It's all in Arabic, said Mr David. What does it say?

It says I'm married to Mina.

Is that all they give you?

Why? What more should they give you?

Mr David laughed. The Moslem world always made him laugh, because he knew nothing about it. Mohammed did not tell him that he had to go and see the qadi at the end of the month in order to get the final papers.

23

At the end of the week Mohammed saw Mustafa again, and they went to look at the house in Benider. Mustafa unlocked the door. There were two rooms, a kitchen and a bathroom.

It's not a bad place, said Mohammed.

There's a good terrace on the roof.

How much is it?

Three thousand. The owner gave it to me to rent for him. I could get more from somebody else.

Mohammed pulled out the money and gave it to Mustafa. I'm bringing my things tonight.

You've got two keys to the house, Mustafa told him, and he handed the keys to Mohammed as they went out into the street.

Mohammed hurried down to the Fondaq ech Chijra and hired a truck with two porters. He got in beside the driver and had him go to Mstakhoche. They carried everything out of the mahal and took it into the city, to the house in Benider. When it was all inside, he paid the men and they left.

He spent the whole afternoon arranging the furniture the way he wanted it. Then he went to the hotel. At first he thought he would tell Mr David about the house, and take him to see it, because he was pleased with the way it looked. Then he decided not to say anything about it that day.

Now that the house was ready, he was eager to show it to Mina. The next morning he went to Mstakhoche and knocked on the door of her house. Mina herself came to answer. There's nobody home, she said. You can't come in.

Meet me in the garden at five, he said. I've got something to show you.

And in the afternoon he took her down to the house in Benider. As soon as she saw it she said: I'm moving in tonight.

Before the wedding? You can't. Your family'll make a scandal.

If I wait at home there'll never be any wedding, she said. My father's got the money now. That's all he cares about.

They'll blame me, said Mohammed.

They don't care now, as long as nobody knows about it. But if I come and stay here, it'll worry them and they'll want to get the wedding over with.

Tomorrow's better, he told her.

24

Mohammed slept with Mr David that night. The next morning early he was at the house in Benider, waiting for Mina to arrive. She came about ten o'clock with all her clothes.

What did they say? he wanted to know.

She shrugged. Nothing very much. Only they're going to have the wedding party soon.

Good, said Mohammed. Now let's go out. I want us to have our picture taken, so we'll have a souvenir of today. If anything should happen to either one of us, at least the other would have a souvenir.

Yes, that's true. She put on a woollen skirt and a white blouse and an open sweater. Her hair fell to her shoulders and then curved outwards. He combed it for her until it looked the way he wanted it to look. Then they set out for Emsallah. There was a photographer's studio there with a sign that said: Casa Lux. They went in.

Qué quieren?

Queremos hacer una foto, said Mohammed. We want the largest size, and with the widest frame. How much will it cost?

The proprietor said: I can make it for you for seven thousand francs, with the colouring and the glass.

Yes, said Mohammed. The Spaniard took them inside, into a room where there was a big screen with trees painted across it. He put two chairs side by side. Then he told them to sit down facing him. Mina put one arm around Mohammed, and he put one arm around her. The Spaniard uncovered his machine and took the photograph. Mohammed gave him two thousand francs on account, put the receipt into his pocket, and took Mina out into the street. They walked down through Emsallah and stopped in front of a shop that sold kitchen utensils.

We need all sorts of things, Mohammed said. They bought as many things as they were able to carry between them, and took a taxi back to the Medina.

Mohammed wanted to get a woman to help clean the house, but Mina thought they should do it themselves. They spent the afternoon working there together. When it got dark, he said to her: Let's eat dinner and go to the cinema.

They went into the kitchen. Mina put a pot on the stove and poured some oil into it. Mohammed sat down and began to peel potatoes. They finally got the meal ready. It was not very good and they ate it quickly. Then Mohammed went back into the kitchen and made coffee while Mina was changing.

25

They walked slowly up the Boulevard. When they got to the Ciné Roxy they looked at the photos outside. It was a film of Brigitte Bardot. They went in and sat down.

Mina began to whisper: What a pretty girl she is!

I'm not interested in Brigitte Bardot or any of the others, he told her. I've got something here with me better than a hundred Brigitte Bardots, and that's all I want. There's nobody like you. You're different from all the others. That's what scares me. I'm afraid somebody's going to take you away from me.

Oh, no! she exclaimed. Why do you say that?

They might, he said. He could not give her the true reason: that he knew she could never have real love for him because the false love of the spell had taken its place, and that the effect of the magic could end at any time.

He went on. When I walk with you in the street, people look at us and think: Look at that beautiful girl. Like a rose. And what a perfect body!

Mohammed!

How could anyone compare Brigitte Bardot to you? Next to you she looks like nothing. Nothing at all.

Thank you, Mohammed, she said. When I'm sitting alone at home, I think of you. I can see you right there, standing in front of me. And I say to myself: How can any boy be so handsome? And so strong? And so sweet-natured and good-hearted too? Nobody can make me feel the way he does. He's more beautiful than I am. And then you disappear.

Only girls are beautiful, said Mohammed. Let's watch Brigitte Bardot now.

He put his arm around her and kissed her eyelids and her cheeks and her lips. Then he began to kiss her throat. He unbuttoned her blouse.

There are people behind us, she whispered.

They sat through to the end of Brigitte Bardot, and then they went out.

Let's go and sit in a café, he said.

All right.

They walked over to the Café Pilo and went inside.

He called a waiter. Bring us two orders of chicken with some peas on the side. And a Coca-Cola and a beer.

The food was put on the table, and Mohammed said: Eat.

They ate and drank. He kept ordering more beer. When they went out of the café he had his arm around her, and he rolled from side to side as he walked. He held her hand under his arm as they went down the hill past the Hotel Minzah, and he was singing.

Don't sing! she kept telling him. If a policeman comes along, he's going to take us to the comisaría.

What's the comisaría? he cried. I never heard of it. Keep going, and don't talk so much.

All the way down the hill he stopped every few seconds and took her face between his hands to kiss it. You're the most beautiful girl in the world, he would tell her. Or: You're my whole life. Or: Nobody ever existed that I could love the way I love you.

They got to the house and went in. Then he took her in his arms. He picked her up, carried her to the bed, and laid her carefully down on the soft mattress. She laughed and jumped up.

He took off his jacket and hung it on a chair. He took off his shirt and his shoes and his socks and his trousers. Mina came out of the bathroom wearing one of the nightgowns he had bought her. It was made of very thin material. He turned off the lights, and left only a little lamp on the night table. It gave a very dim green light. They got into bed and began to kiss.

I love you! I love you! Mohammed cried.

One person doesn't love another person, she told him. It's not the person that loves. It's the heart. My heart loves your heart, Mohammed. And I wish I knew why.

Don't think about it, he said. They kissed and held one another very close.

Mohammed turned off the green light, and they went to sleep.

26

Mina stayed on at the house in Benider with Mohammed. Time went by. Her parents did not come to see her, and she began to worry. One morning she said to Mohammed: I've got to go and find out what's happening. Are they getting ready for the wedding or not?

She came back pleased, and said that the wedding would take place soon. Several times during the next few days she went to see her mother, and she became more and more excited.

Thinking about Mina's party was making Mohammad unhappy about not being able to have his own. He decided that if only one party were going to be given, he was going to be there. No man ever goes into a girl's wedding party. However, he thought his plan would work.

One day not long afterwards Si Ahmed went down to the town and bought a young bull and two sacks of flour. He got two men to lead the bull and carry the flour back to Mstakhoche. A great many women had come to the house to help Mina's mother knead the dough for the fqaqas. They had hired a black woman to go around from house to house announcing the wedding and inviting the women to come to it, and Si Ahmed had sent to Tetuan for Andaluz musicians.

The hotel was full of tourists. Mohammed stood behind the bar talking with Mr David. I'm inviting you now to my wedding party, he told him. I'll let you know when it's going to be. You've got to come.

Mr David was delighted. Thank you, Mohammed. A real Arab wedding? I'll certainly be there.

And bring whoever you like, said Mohammed. Bring lots of people. The only thing is that everybody must wear evening clothes, and each one brings a present of some sort with him. As you go through the door you hand the present to Mina's mother. That's the custom.

I understand, said Mr David.

That night and the others that followed, Mr David told several American and English people about the great chance they soon would have of going with him to a native wedding ceremony. When the day was finally set for the party, Mohammed gave him the news, and he began telephoning to tell his friends where he would meet them in order to take them out to Mstakhoche.

Remember, you've got to have some sort of gift with you, he told each one, and they all agreed.

The night of the party came. The house was full of girls and women in their best kaftans, and they were all dancing. Mina sat on cushions without moving, and everyone passed by her to admire her. She was wearing a white European-style wedding gown.

Mohammed and his friends drove out in three cars. There were nine of them, and they all wore dinner jackets. They walked in a group to Mina's house, and Mohammed knocked on the door. When Mina's mother opened it and saw Mohammed, she was very angry. What are you doing here? she cried.

Mohammed bowed. Lalla Khaddouj, these Nazarenes wanted to come with their presents for Mina.

Nazarenes? she said. Then she saw all the Europeans standing there holding their packages wrapped in tissue paper and tied with ribbons. Wait, she told Mohammed. She shut the door and went in to talk with the other women of the family. Mohammed heard them saying: They don't know any better. We can hide them. You'll have to let them in.

After a while Mina's mother came back to the door and threw it open.

They can come in, she said. Their room is in there. She pointed to one end of a room where they had hung sheets. The Europeans handed their gifts to Mina's mother, and went through the room to sit down on the mattresses behind the sheets.

It's like being in a tent. You can't see anything! the Nazarenes kept saying.

This is the way they do it, Mr David explained.

They drank tea and ate couscous and pastries. Some of the Europeans had kif with them, and smoked it, and pounded on the trays in rhythm with the music.

This is a modern wedding, Mohammed told them. Instead of waiting at home for the bride, I've come myself to get her. That's the way it ought to be done.

About midnight the music stopped. Mohammed jumped up. We've got to leave now, he told them.

They all went out into the street. The women and girls were calling: Youyouyouyou! Mina kissed her mother goodbye, and walked with Mohammed to the place where the cars were parked. Everyone else walked behind.

Mr David drove Mohammed and Mina in the Mercedes, and the other cars followed. There were eight taxis full of Moslems. They went directly to the Casa Lux studio, where Mohammed had arranged with the Spaniard to keep the place open until they arrived.

Mohammed and Mina went in and sat for their picture, and as they came out the girls and women began once more to scream: Youyouyouyou! After that they set out for the Boulevard Pasteur to drive up and down and blow their horns for an hour or so. Everyone who could reach was pounding on the sides of the cars. The ones inside clapped their hands and played drums. They sang: Aabaha, aabaha, ouallah makhallaha! When they had finished on the Boulevard they drove down to the waterfront and parked the cars at the bottom of the Ciné Americano stairway. They climbed the stairs and went singing and laughing through the alleys to the house in Benider.

Some of the guests sat on the mattresses drinking Coca-Cola and eating pastries. Mohammed stayed with the Europeans in the other room. Mr David had hidden several bottles of whisky in the car, to drink after they left Mina's house, because Mohammed had told him not to take alcohol to the wedding party. After a long while, they said it was time to go.

Mina and Mohammed stood alone in the doorway looking after them.

27

Mohammed shut the door.

You see? he said. All the things you were afraid of, that people would talk about you, that your father was going to beat you, that I wasn't really going to marry you, all those things were in your head. Everybody's happy. Your family, your friends. And so are we.

They kissed each other. Mohammed went into the kitchen. He lighted the stove and made some coffee. Then he put some pastries on a plate.

Why didn't you let me make the coffee? Mina said.

I don't want those little hands to do anything, he told her. And he cut the pastry into pieces and pushed them into her mouth. Then he held up her cup of coffee to her lips and tried to make her drink it. She could not do it very well. He pulled out his handkerchief and wiped her mouth and chin.

From now on, he said, I'm going to get up in the morning and make breakfast. Then I'll bring it in here to you and you can eat it in bed. And I'll feed you and wash your face.

No, she said. I married you to help you. I'm going to wash your clothes and iron them and mend them. And I'm going to cook for you.

Let's go to bed, said Mohammed. They took off their clothes and got into bed. He held her in his arms.

Now you're really my wife, he told her. Up to now we've had a marriage like the wind, like false money. But now we have a real one. And he kissed her. The day I have a son, he went on, I'm going to invite everybody in Tangier to a party, Moslems and Nazarenes, and I'm going to have an orchestra.

Incha'Allah, murmured Mina.

He looked closely at her. Mina, there's something on your mind. Tell me. What are you worried about?

My mother, she said.

Your mother! Why?

Mohammed, she doesn't like you. She's going to do something. For years she's been planning to have me marry her brother-in-law's nephew. But I'd never have married him.

You didn't tell me.

I know, but it's true.

Mohammed said: Your mother's not going to do anything. After all we've gone through so we could be together, are we going to let her break us up? Stop thinking about your mother. What can she do if we love each other?

I suppose you're right, said Mina.

They went back to kissing and hugging, and played games together for a long time. Finally Mohammed turned out the light and they went to sleep.

28

A loud knocking at the door awoke them in the middle of the morning. Mina got up, put on her bathrobe, and went to open the door. The street was full of women and girls, and they were singing and laughing. Her family and friends had come to pay the visit of the morning after the wedding. They pushed into the house.

Mina frowned. It's too early, she told them. My husband is still asleep.

When they heard this, they all began to scream: Youyouyouyou! and to clap their hands. Many of the girls had brought drums with them. They pulled them out and pounded on them.

With all the noise, Mohammed woke up. He ran into the bathroom and slammed the door. There he washed and dressed quickly. Then he put on his bridegroom's slippers, and without looking towards the women and girls, he hurried to the door and went out into the street. He did not want to lose his new white slippers so soon. If the girls had been able to catch him, they would all have rushed at him and pulled them from his feet. He went down to the Zoco Chico and sat in the sun on the terrace of the Café Central.

Soon he saw some of his friends going past. He called to them.
Sit down, he told them.
I hear you're married, said Ali.
That's right.
Wait until she begins filling up with brats. You won't even be able to
buy yourself a new pair of shoes. You'll be going along in the street
barefoot and you won't even know it.
Mohammed did not want to listen. I've got to get some breakfast, he
said. He got up and went around the corner into the Calle del Comercio.
There was a stall there with tubes of flickering light in the ceiling. He
sat down at a table. When he had eaten he remained sitting there, looking into the street, watching people walk by. Time passed slowly, but
there was no way of going home while the women were still there.

29

In the weeks, and finally the months, that followed, Mr David grew more
and more nervous. It seemed to him that Mohammed was taking a long
time to get rid of Mina. He came to the hotel to see him several times a
week, but it was always in the afternoon, and Mr David preferred to
see him at night.
If you don't leave her soon, she'll be having a baby, he would tell
Mohammed. Then you'll be in a cage.
Mohammed would look at him with an empty face and say: Yes. Mr
David suspected that he did not intend to separate from Mina, and this
made him angry. Sometimes Mohammed was surprised by the unfriend-
liness he saw in Mr David's face.
Often when Mohammed went to the hotel Mina would go to see her
mother. As time passed, she went more and more frequently, until she
was spending some part of nearly every day in Mstakhoche. Mohammed
thought about this and was troubled by it. It seemed to him a bad idea
that she should pass so much time with someone who probably did not
like him. Each time he thought about it he was more certain that Lalla
Khaddouj spoke ill of him to Mina. When she came back from there he
would watch her carefully for some sign that would prove he was right.
It was winter now. The markets were full of flowers and people's
clothes were always wet with rain. Mohammed drank only whisky these
days, but he drank a great deal of it, and many times came home very
drunk.
One evening when he arrived at the house in Benider he opened the
door and stood a moment with his hand on the wall to steady himself.
Mina was looking at him. He shut the door and walked across the room
to kiss her, but she turned her head away.

Why are you doing that? What am I, garbage or something?
No. Did you ever take that paper to the qadi?
He was surprised to see that she remembered it. No, he said. I haven't
had a chance. I've been too busy.
Mina walked away and went into the kitchen.
Another night when he got home she was not there. She came in soon
afterwards, and looked at Mohammed without speaking to him. He
watched her changing her clothes. When she had finished, he said:
Where have you been? To your mother's?
She turned angrily towards him. Where else would I have been?
What's the matter with you? What's happened?
Leave me alone! she shouted. Go out for a walk. Or go and sit with
your friends. Just leave me alone.
What are you so excited about? You don't have to yell.
Don't talk to me.
All right. He went out into the other room and sat down on the couch.
When Mina had prepared supper, she brought in food for him, and
none for herself.
Come here and eat, he told her.
No. I don't want to eat. I'm not hungry.
He got up from the table, put on his jacket, and went out into the
street. At the Café Fuentes he sat down and ordered black coffee. He
look at the floor under his feet, wondering what had happened. It was
possible that Mina's mother had gone to consult a fqih who had discovered the spell. If that were the case, they were already working to
destroy the effect of it. Or it could merely be her mother's talking against
him day after day.
He paid for the coffee and went home. Mina was in bed asleep. He
put on his pyjamas and got into bed beside her. When he tried to play
with her and kiss her, he had the feeling that she had become somebody
else. In the end she kissed him, but not in the way she always had until
now. Something was missing. For the first time, they lay together, and
did not make love, and the night was like a poison to Mohammed.

30

The next day Mohammed said to Mr David: I'd like to sleep here with
you tonight.
It made him feel good to see Mr David happy. That night Mr David
did not mention Mina at all, nor the next night, nor the next night.
Mohammed spent three nights, one after the other, with Mr David,
going back to the house in Benider each day at sunrise, when Mina
returned from her mother's. She would come in and be busy around the
house, but she spoke to him only if he asked her a question.

The fourth night he decided to sleep in the house. As soon as he got into bed she turned over, saying she felt sick. Mohammed slept very badly.

The next morning Mina was up very early.

What's the matter? said Mohammed.

I've got to spend the whole day at my mother's, she said.

At home in Mstakhoche Mina found an old woman sitting with her mother.

Mina! cried her mother. Come and have Lalla Meriam tell your fortune. She throws snails onto the dirt. She's just told mine. Sit down and let her tell yours.

Mina sat down and the woman began to look carefully at her. She had a black cloth spread out, and it was covered with sand. She shook the snails back and forth in her fist, and then tossed them out onto the sand.

My daughter, she told Mina, you're under a spell. And the one who put it on you is a boy. He's not tall, and he's not short either. Medium. And he's still very young. He wants you all for himself. You think you like him, but you don't like him at all. It's just the magic working.

Mina looked at her with wide eyes. The woman nodded her head slowly, up and down.

Can't you help her? cried Mina's mother.

Yes. I can get her out of it. But it's expensive work.

How much?

It comes to around fifteen thousand francs. But I can cure her.

It's worth it, said Mina's mother. I'll pay for it. I can get the money.

Good, said Lalla Meriam.

Do you agree? her mother asked Mina.

Mina was thinking of Mohammed, and how he would come into the house and fall onto the bed, smelling of what he had drunk.

Yes, she said.

31

That evening Mohammed came in and went to kiss Mina, but it was like kissing the wall.

Ouakha, he said to himself. That night they lay in bed listening to the rain. They did not touch one another.

In the morning Mohammed went out without breakfast. Mina was still asleep. He walked to the courtyard of the notaries. He had the paper in his pocket, and he was going to tell the notary that he had changed his mind. I don't want the girl, he said to himself as he walked along. I'm going to get rid of her. Then he thought: That means she'll get everything in the house.

He stopped as he came to the doorway. Why, he asked himself. Why should I lose everything? There's the money hidden there, and all the jewellery I bought her. She'll marry somebody else and he'll get it all. Or when she's stayed her forty days she won't give back the key. No! I'll put up with it and see what happens. If I play a good game I'll win. I'll keep everything, and she'll go out of the house with her hands folded over her heart, without money, without furniture, without clothes.

He turned around and went back into the street.

Now he slept every night with Mr David. Each morning he would get up, take a kouffa and go to the market to buy Mina her food for the day. Then he would carry it to the house in Benider and leave it with her. She never seemed glad to see him. Once in a while, when her face was a little less angry, he would return at night, hoping to stay. But he never did.

One morning when he came in she began to complain. There's nothing to eat in the house! she cried. I want some bananas. And get me some chocolates and some apples.

Mohammed stood still and looked at her. This is bad, he thought. She's got a baby inside her. And then he thought: It's mine, and he felt very happy.

That morning, and the mornings afterwards, he went out and searched in the different markets for chirimoyas, grapes, tangerines, and every other kind of fruit he could find. And he brought her chocolates and biscuits. He did not even mind her bad humour, or care when she found fault with everything he brought her. He would sit and watch her eat it, and then comfort her when she vomited it up.

Mina's mother now forbade her to visit her in Mstakhoche, saying it would be bad for her health to go into the street. She came to the city each day to see her. Mohammed knew that, but he did not know that each day she stopped on the way at Lalla Meriam's house to get a fresh batch of the powder the old woman was making in order to cure Mina.

As soon as she got to the house in Benider, Mina's mother would sprinkle the powder over the coals of the brazier. She always arrived in the afternoon when Mohammed was not there. She had arranged a system of signals with Mina, and if he happened to be in the house, she would wait hidden in a stall or a doorway until she saw him go out. Then quickly she would run to the door and knock. And Mina would have the coals ready in the brazier.

Now Mohammed came more often to sleep. He arranged himself a bed on the mattress that lay along the wall, in the bedroom with Mina. It excited him to think that she was lying over there in the bed with his baby inside her.

One night he awoke and heard her groaning. He got up and went over to her.

I have a headache, she told him. He got her an aspirin. Then she asked for a glass of coffee. When he had got back into bed and turned off the light, she called to him again.

I have a fever!

He brought her a basin of cold water and a cloth, made a compress, and put it on her head. Now and then he wrung it out. He was still sitting there by her at seven in the morning. Then he went out to a pharmacy and told the clerk that his wife had a fever and a headache.

The pharmacist gave him some pills and told him to cover her well and let her sleep. He did as he had been told, and sat down again beside her, thinking of how his life had changed since Mina had stopped loving him. He was certain that her mother had something to do with it. She was determined to bring their love to an end. The thought frightened him. Suddenly he got up. He bent over Mina and kissed her lips.

32

About eleven o'clock Mina stirred and opened her eyes.

How are you? he said.

I feel fine.

She got up. While she was washing he stood in the kitchen having his breakfast. Then he went to the market and bought liver and beefsteak and salad. He took it back to the house and spent an hour or so preparing lunch. When it was ready they sat down. It was the first meal they had had together in half a month.

Tell me the truth, Mohammed said suddenly. Why don't you love me? What's happened?

Why do you say that? That I don't love you. Mina sighed. It's not true.

You're hiding something. You don't want to tell me.

She looked at him. Mohammed, if you did it, it's a sin. My mother says you put a spell on me. You liked me, and just because I didn't like you, you went out and paid somebody to put a spell on me. That's not love.

Mohammed tried to speak, but she would not let him.

A friend of my mother's found out. She says it's magic. And my mother's doing everything she can to break it, if it is. That's all I can tell you.

Your mother's an old bitch, said Mohammed.

I won't let you insult my mother! Mina cried. The fortune teller asked to see me. As soon as she saw me she said I was under a spell. And then she told me the whole thing.

What's finished is finished, said Mohammed. Anyway, he went on bitterly, I can see that whatever magic there was, your mother's already broken it.

It could be, said Mina thoughtfully. Mohammed's heart sank.

But we can stay together anyway, he said after a moment.

I wonder, said Mina. Every day you seem more like a stranger.

He got up and went out, down to the hotel, and into the back garden where Mr David was sitting. Mr David looked up.

What's the matter now?

Nothing.

Have a drink.

No. He sat in the hotel all day, looking sad. When night came he went back to the house. Mina was asleep in her bed. He climbed into his own bed, but he could not sleep. He got up and sat in a chair, smoking one cigarette after another. It's over, he thought. No more kisses and games and laughing, when we did whatever we wanted, and then when we were tired, fell asleep in each other's arms, my face against her face. These days when I come in she's there already asleep. If I climb into the bed with her she turns her back. If I touch her she hits me with her elbow. And when I finally get to her, I might as well be in the Moujahiddine with a corpse. What good is that?

He got up and went over to the bed. He pulled the sheet away from her face, bent over and kissed her. She did not stir. He knew she was awake. He put on his clothes quickly and went out to the Café Pilo to drink vodka. It was five in the morning. When he left the Café Pilo it was noon.

33

Mohammed got back to the house about half past one, very drunk. He opened the door and leaned inside. Mina saw him and came running to push against the door.

You can't come in! she cried. I won't have you in here like that.

He raised his arm to hit her. Then he lowered it.

You say that to me and you're not ashamed? He pushed her and went inside. Mina shut the door. Mohammed turned and tried to kiss her. She hit him in the mouth with the back of her hand, and her ring cut his lip. The blood dripped from his chin. He seized her.

I'd like to kill you now, he told her. And kill the one who's inside you. But I suppose it would be a sin. Since the day I was born, no woman or whore or girl has ever hit me, until you hit me now. You're living here in my house with me, eating my food. I've given you everything I have. You're living better than a sultana. You've got better clothes than you ever had in your life. What are you, anyway? You're just a Djiblia. Your father with his djellaba and his pants a kilometre wide, and the turban down over his ears like somebody in the cinema. I've made you into something civilized. I ought to have knocked you down when I came in, but I was sorry for you. And so you hit me.

Mina said nothing. She was merely looking at him. It made him happy to see that there was fear in her eyes. He walked out into the kitchen. There were some bottles of wine on the table. He took one and opened it. Mina had followed him and was standing by the door.

Mohammed sat down at the table and put his feet up on it. Sit down, he told her.

I'm going to ask you something, Mina. Do you want to go on with me or not? You know when I was supposed to be at the qadi's to sign the papers? Four months ago. More than four months. You understand?

Yes.

I never went back. Because when you cooled off I decided it wasn't worth it. But I'd like to know. Do you want to stay on and be my wife or don't you? I can go and sign the papers any time. If there's somebody else you want to go and live with, and he loves you and you love him, just say: Excuse me, Mohammed, I'm going. I won't stop you.

I'll think about it, she said.

He got up, lurched into the other room, and fell onto the bed. Drunk and dressed in his clothes, he went to sleep.

34

Soon Mina's mother arrived. She pulled out the brazier and poured her packet of powder over the coals, and the smoke filled the house. Mohammed did not stop sleeping. Lalla Khaddouj finished her work quietly, took up her kouffa, kissed Mina, and went out.

Late in the afternoon Mohammed woke up. He called out: Mina!

What is it?

What's that smell?

I put a little bakhour on the brazier.

That's not bakhour, he said. Bakhour never stank like that.

I mixed it, she said. I put in a little djaoui and some fasoukh.

I see. Who's been here?

Nobody.

Nobody came?

No.

Do you want to go to the cinema?

You know I can't go out, she said. Can't you see my belly? Are you making fun of me?

Lots of men take their wives everywhere with their bellies sticking out. Europeans, Moslems. It's nothing.

I'd be too ashamed. I can't go out.

Ouakha, he said.

He went to the kitchen and spread some jam on a piece of bread. While he ate it he made some coffee. Then he went back into the other room and took hold of Mina. She grew stiff. He managed to kiss her in spite of her struggle. Then he went out.

A month or two went by. Most nights Mohammed slept with Mr David at the hotel. But now and then he would begin to think about Mina, and the idea always came to him that someone else might be around. Then he would go and spend a night in the house at Benider.

35

One night when Mohammed was there asleep on his mattress, Mina began to cry out: Ay, yimma! Ay, yimma!

What's the matter? he said.

My belly!

Mohammed got up and dressed. I must find a taxi first, he thought. It may be the baby.

He ran down to the Zoco Chico in the rain. After midnight the police allowed the taxis to line up there. He found one, and told the driver to wait. Then he went back to the house and wrapped Mina in a sheet, lifted her in his arms, and carried her groaning down through the alleys to the Zoco Chico where the taxi was waiting.

They went to the Spanish Hospital at Ain Qtiouat. Mohammed rang the bell. A guard came to the door. Two nurses carried Mina inside. After a while a doctor came and told Mohammed that his wife was fine, and that he could go home and sleep, and come back in the morning.

How can I go home and sleep? cried Mohammed. He took a taxi that was waiting under the pine trees in front of the hospital and went back to the city. The streets were wet and empty. In the house at Benider he sat down in a chair and looked around the room. It was very still. He felt his flesh prickle. There was a sound inside his head as if someone were screaming. The fear came up from inside him. He rose and went into the kitchen.

He lighted the stove and made a glass of strong black coffee. He sat down at the kitchen table and listened to the rain running down the drainpipe. He lit a cigarette and watched his hand tremble. Quickly he finished the coffee and went out into the street. He did not want to see the house or think about it.

In the Zoco Chico the water was running down the middle of the sidewalk. He sat under the awning at the Café Fuentes and ordered a black coffee. At seven in the morning he stood up and paid for the coffees he had drunk. Then he took a taxi to the hospital.

They led him up to the room where Mina was, and he found her lying in bed with the baby beside her. Her eyes were shut. When he touched her she opened them, and he kissed her. They both laughed. He took the baby in his arms. It was a boy. He tried to tickle him, but the baby screamed.

What are we going to call him? said Mina.

Driss, we'll call him.

Ouakha, she said. It's a pretty name.

You won't be in here long, he told her. You'll be home soon. We'll have a big party and invite everybody. We'll have hundreds of pastries.

Incha'Allah.

He kissed her. Get well. Good-bye.

He went down to the hotel and told Mr David about the baby. Then he said: I'm going in to bed.

Now? Why?

I couldn't stay alone in the house, so I sat in the café.

So now she's got the baby, said Mr David. I told you from the beginning if you got married you'd have a terrible life. You can have any girl you want. You didn't have to marry her. I could have got you out of that. But you wanted to marry her, that's the truth. And now look at you. Are you happy?

No matter how much you'd paid for your lawyers you couldn't have done anything for me, said Mohammed. What I did was a crime. There's no way of getting off on that charge. Anyway, it's all happened, and I'm tired. I've got to go and sleep.

Go to the studio, said Mr David. It's quieter in there.

Mohammed went to the room, shut the door behind him, and dropped onto the couch.

A person dressed all in white was coming towards him. It was saying: May you always be in good health, Mohammed. Allah has preserved you from many evil things. Soon you will have a new life.

When he got up it was seven in the evening. He shaved and went into the bar. He made himself a glass of coffee. Mr David was sitting with some Englishmen. Mohammed told him his dream.

It sounds like a good dream, said Mr David. It might have been one of your Moslem saints come to talk with you.

Mr David did not know anything about Moslem saints. Mohammed went on drinking his coffee.

36

When Mina was out of the hospital and back at the house in Benider, she stayed in bed the first day. Mohammed sat in the chair facing her. Now and then he would tell her again how glad he was to see her at home. At last I'll be able to sleep, he said.

Where have you been sleeping these two nights? she asked him.

I couldn't sleep here alone, he said. I had a noise in my head. I had to go and sleep in the hotel.

She laughed. What were you afraid of?

I don't know The night I came back I had gooseflesh.

And now? How do you feel?

Now? I'm happy. The baby's beautiful. And when he gets his name he'll be even more beautiful. And we'll have the party here.

Why don't we have it at my mother's house? said Mina.

He did not answer at first. I don't know what to say, he told her.

What do you mean?

I want it here. I want my friends to come. The baby was born on Saturday. Next Saturday we'll have a party.

On Thursday he went to the souq at Souani and bought two large rams. And he bought oil and white flour and almonds and raisins and onions to go with their flesh. When he got back to the house he found Mina's mother and her older sisters and several women neighbours already starting to make the pastries. They were going to try a special kind called Qadi's Turbans.

On Saturday Mohammed went to see a fqih in the quarter and asked him to go with him back to the house. There he led him up onto the roof where Mina stood with the baby in her arms, along with the other women who were holding the rams.

The fqih seized one of the rams by its horns, and Mohammed took hold of its body. Bismillah! Allah o akbar ala Driss! the fqih cried. He ran the knife once across its neck, and the animal fell. Mohammed had set a glass nearby. Quickly he put it beside the sheep's neck and filled it with the blood that was coming out. While the ram was still living he drank it. The women screamed: Youyouyouyou! as he wiped the blood from his lips. Soon they sacrificed the other ram, so there would be enough meat for all the guests. The Sudanese slave-woman that Mohammed had hired to wait on the party pounded on the door, and they went down and let her in. On the roof the women were stripping the hides from the carcasses and cutting flesh into pieces. Then they soaked the flesh in pots of cold water and put it to cook.

Mohammed went all around the town inviting his American and English friends to the feast. He had arranged the bedroom as the place where the Nazarenes would sit together, and one end of the sala was blanketed off from the rest. The Moslem woman would be behind the blanket. In the Nazarene room he had a bottle of whisky, a bottle of gin, a bottle of vodka, a pail of ice, and soda and tonic water. In the room for the women he put a brazier with a teapot on it, and silver boxes of mint and verbena and orange buds.

Several days earlier he had asked a Djibli musician he knew to bring his orchestra and dancing boys. They arrived before the other guests, and the boys got into their girls' clothing, to be ready to dance. In their velvet kaftans and their gauze tfins and their sashes they looked better than girls. When the guests arrived the boys got up and began to dance. On their heads they carried trays full of tea glasses and lighted candles. The musicians were singing and playing their drums and violins and lutes and tambourines, and the boys were whirling around among the guests. The Americans clapped their hands very loud and began to shout. While they were eating they kept telling Mohammed how much they liked the food. They emptied all the bottles on the taifor and began to dance, trying to do the same steps as the Djibli boys.

When the Moslems saw the Nazarenes having such a good time, they decided it was a fine party, and they too enjoyed themselves.

At three o'clock in the morning the musicians stopped playing and said good night. Then the other people got their coats and wraps and went out. And Mohammed and Mina were left alone.

Everybody had a good time, he said. Hamdoul'lah!

Yes.

Are you happy?

Of course, she said.

Because of the baby. Isn't that why?

No. Not just the baby, she said. You too.

He laughed scornfully. Yes. I know how happy I make you.

They got ready for bed. Mina put the baby into its crib. It had been lying on the couch so everyone could see it.

She got into bed. He kissed her, and went to his bed.

Just before daybreak he awoke. He could hear Mina's soft breathing. He got up, went over to the bed, and slipped in beside her. When he kissed her, she pushed him away and said: Leave me alone. I'm sleepy.

You can sleep whenever you like, he told her. You've got all day and all night.

No! Let me sleep.

But he held her tight and went on kissing her. She was not yet well from the birth seven days before, and she made it difficult for him to have her. He knew he would not be able to sleep again until he had done what he wanted, and he kept on struggling with her until he had won the battle. Then he went back to his bed and quickly fell asleep.

37

At eleven o'clock in the morning Mohammed was up, bathing. When Mina appeared, she was angry. Don't you ever do that again, she said.

Coming and waking me up in the middle of the night and bothering me.

It's not my fault, said Mohammed. I can't help it. I can't sleep. When I feel like doing something, with you or anybody else, I have to do it. It's a habit of mine.

I don't like your habit, she told him.

What are you complaining about? You're still whole. Nothing so awful happened to you. I didn't eat you.

Finally she laughed. Then she said: I'm going out to my mother's.

Ouakha. There's money on the table for the taxi.

Mina took the baby and went off to her mother's house in Mstakhoche. Lalla Meriam was sitting there with Mina's mother.

Very good! Very good! cried Lalla Meriam. Your daughter has come just at the right moment.

I was only now talking to your mother, she said to Mina. I have some new things I want you to take home and try on your brazier. This powder I'm giving to your mother. She'll go with you to your house and put it on the fire for you. Then you must straddle the brazier and let the smoke go up. If the powder explodes under you, you'll know once and for all that Mohammed gave you magic, and that it's broken. Everything will be all right then for you. If it doesn't explode, you'll know the whole thing was nothing anyway, a love as empty as air. And you won't have to worry any more in either case.

Later that day Mina and her mother went back to the house in Benider and did as Lalla Meriam had told them. And while Mina was straddling the brazier and feeling the heat of the coals all the way up to her belly, there was a loud cracking sound below her, and she screamed.

Hamdoul'lah! Allah has saved you! her mother cried. You're safe. The spell is broken. Now at last you're going to be happy.

I hope so, said Mina. Why don't you sit down now? I'll make you a glass of tea.

They sat down and talked, and drank their tea. At last her mother said: I've got to go. I did what I said I'd do. You're free now.

She kissed Mina and went out.

38

Mr David was getting ready to make a trip with some American friends, and he mentioned it at lunch one day.

Would you be able to go with us? he asked Mohammed. He felt certain that Mohammed was going to refuse. We're going to Spain to look around and buy some clothes.

I'll go with you, said Mohammed. I'll have to let Mina know.

We're going tomorrow on the afternoon ferry, said Mr David, looking very happy. It leaves at three-thirty.

Mohammed went home. Mina, he said. I have something to tell you, but don't get angry.

Why should I get angry? What is it?

Mr David has to go to Spain, and I'm going with him. We'll be over there a week or ten days. If you don't want to stay here alone, why don't you sleep at your mother's? Or have her come here.

Ouakha, she said.

He gave her some money, took what clothes he needed, and kissed her good-bye. And he lifted up the baby and kissed it, so that it began to cry.

Allah ihennik.

He went back to the hotel and went on packing his bags, putting in the things that he kept at Mr David's. In the morning he went up to the Spanish Consulate and got his visa. The Americans invited him to have lunch with them in the bar. Then the four of them got into the Mercedes with their luggage and drove to the port.

In Madrid the Americans took Mohammed to bars and dance-halls and nightclubs, but he did not seem to be enjoying himself. He was sad and had nothing to say. Much of the time he was thinking about Mina's mother. She may try to do something now that I'm not there, he thought.

The ten days finally passed, and Mohammed never brightened. He bought a great many presents for Mina and Driss, and when they came back into Tangier he got them all through the customs without paying duty. Mr David let him take the Volkswagen to carry the packages home.

At the house in Benider, carrying his luggage and the bundles, he began to knock on the door.

Ah, Hamdoul'lah! Mina cried when she saw him. How are you, Mohammed?

He kissed her and went into the house.

What did you bring me from Spain?

All these parcels here are for you, he told her.

She unwrapped six or seven dresses and four pairs of shoes and three handbags. There were baby clothes, and several bottles of perfume and jars of powder and tubes of cream.

So many things! she kept saying. Thank you!

It's nothing.

She went into the other room and tried on one of the dresses. How's this one? she wanted to know, walking back and forth.

Beautiful, he said.

She quickly put on another. And this one? she asked him. Do you like this one?

Even better than the other.

She tried all the dresses and bags and shoes. And he said: Yes, yes, to everything, because she looked more beautiful than ever before.

He went over to the crib and lifted the baby out of it. He poked it and kissed it, and asked it when it was going to be big, so it could go out for walks with him and he could take it to the cinema and the beach. And school, he said. You've got to go to school. And maybe you'll be a fqih, or a doctor, or a lawyer, or a minister in the government. Something important. Not like me.

I'm going to my mother's now, Mina said.

But I just got back, and I want to lie down for a little while. You can go later. Or tomorrow.

No, I can't. I have to go now.

I see, said Mohammed. Well, you know the way.

She took the baby and went out, and Mohammed lay down alone.

39

That evening, sitting in the garden, Mohammed said to Mr David: I'm going to sleep in Benider tonight.

You never stay in one place any more, Mr David told him. As soon as you come in you go out again. I never get a chance to talk to you. We never have any fun together. If I didn't love you I wouldn't have you here. But you've got to stay with me now and then.

I know, said Mohammed. It's my fault. You told me if I got married I'd be sorry. And you were right. But I didn't listen to you. I know, you give me money and food and clothes and the car, and I don't sleep with you every night. If you don't want me to stay on with you, just tell me.

No, Mohammed! Mr David exclaimed. I never said that. You've always been good to me and my friends. That's not what I mean. I'd just like to see more of you.

Whatever you say, said Mohammed, standing up. You know what you want.

He went to the Zoco Chico and sat down in the Café Central. In a little while Hussein came by. Ahilán, Mohammed! Where have you been?

Spain.

Listen. I've got something to tell you. You're not going to like it, but don't blame me for it.

Blame you for what? said Mohammed. What is it?

Then Hussein said: I saw Mina with somebody. One day while you were away. I saw her talking with him. And she kissed him.

Never! Mohammed cried. It's not true!

I'm talking seriously, brother to brother. If you don't believe me, you can ask Chaib. He was with me.

It can't be, Mohammed kept saying.

I'm telling you I saw her with a man.

It wasn't Mina.

It was Mina. It was your wife talking to him. And afterwards she kissed him, and they separated. I saw it.

Not Mina.

Mohammed got up, paid the waiter and went to the house. Mina was there. He sat down and began to smoke a cigarette. He was sitting facing her, looking at her, thinking of Hussein's words. As he looked, his face became more fierce, until it seemed as if he might suddenly rise and kill her.

She stared at him. Why are you looking at me like that? What's the matter with you?

Nothing, he told her, turning his head away. I was thinking of something.

It's not true! she said. I saw you looking at me. You looked as if you hated me. I don't like your face. What's happened? Somebody's told you something.

When he heard these words, he said to himself: Hussein's not lying. It's true. He's right. She's been with somebody. In all the time I've known her she's never said such a thing, until now.

Can't you talk? Mina asked.

I'm thinking of something I forgot.

But what is it?

I tell you I wasn't looking at you, he said. I was just thinking, and my eyes got stuck on your eyes, and I stayed that way. And you thought I was looking at you. But I was thinking. I didn't even see you. I was somewhere else.

What was it you forgot? Money?

No. Some things I meant to buy in Spain at the last minute. Things I wanted. I was just thinking how I can't get them here.

What things?

A watch. A lady's watch with diamonds on it.

Allah! It must have been beautiful! she said.

I wanted to bring back two, he told her. One for you and one for your mother. Too bad. The next time I'll bring back two of them. Only who knows when that'll be?

Incha'Allah!

I'm going to sleep now, he said. I'm tired. I didn't sleep very well in Spain.

He put on his pyjamas and got into bed. Mina laid the baby in his crib. Then she got into bed, too. Mohammed kissed her, but her kisses were lifeless and chilly. He grew tired of kissing her, and drew back to look at her. She lay there as though she were thinking of something else. He felt his own heart growing cold, and the inside of his head seemed to come apart and be swimming around. How can this girl do this to me? he thought. I'm young and handsome and strong and clean.

He touched her again to be certain. Her flesh was cold. He got up from the bed and went out into the kitchen. In the closet on the shelf there were several bottles of red wine. He opened one and sat down at the table. He could hear it raining outside in the street. He cut himself some slices of cheese. He poured the wine into a tall glass and drank it off at one draught. Then he ate some cheese. Then he poured another glass of wine, and he went on doing it until both the cheese and the wine were gone. He went back into the other room and turned on the pale green light. He opened the window. The air that came in was cold and damp. He sat down in the chair facing Mina as she slept.

Later he went back to the kitchen and got another bottle of wine, and took it in with him to sit drinking it and watching Mina sleep.

Too bad, he said to his heart as he looked. What a world! In the beginning we were together. We lived another kind of life, with love in it. Whatever she wanted I gave her, and whatever I wanted she gave me. Clothes and money, words and love. And now if I put my lips on her lips, it's like kissing the cliffs at Merkala in January. If I lay my face against her face I get cold all over. There's no way of touching any part of her.

He had the glass of wine in his hand, and tears fell into it. He stared and went on staring at Mina, not moving his eyes from her face, until he saw fires lighted inside his head. He lifted the glass of wine and drank it. Then he set the glass on the table and began to drink from the bottle.

40

In the morning Mohammed was still sitting there with his head on the table. Mina got up.

Without waking him she washed and dressed, took the baby, and quietly went out.

At her mother's house she set the baby down on a mattress. Where's Mohammed? said her mother. Is he back?

I left him asleep in a chair, with his head on the table. Like a dog.

I pray to God the day will come soon when you'll be leaving him, her mother said.

Mother, I'm not going to leave him, Mina told her. The day I leave him, there'll be nothing left of him but his bones. I swear I'll kill him. She thought a moment. Or maybe I'll drive him crazy, so he'll go along the street talking to himself.

That's up to you, said her mother.

Early in the afternoon Mohammed woke up. He looked around for

Mina, but she was not there. He dressed. Then he took a taxi out to Mstakhoche. Mina was still at her mother's house when he arrived.

Why didn't you wake me up? he asked her. You just went out and left me there.

Lalla Khaddouj told him: Mina said she didn't want to wake you up. She thought it was better to let you go on sleeping. She said you were tired.

That's true, Lalla, Mohammed said. Then to Mina he said: Let's go home. He took the baby in his arms, and they left.

At home they were sitting in the sala. Get me a cup of coffee, he told Mina.

I don't feel like it, Mina said.

He went to the kitchen and put the water on to boil. Then he came back and sat down. Mina, he said. We've been together for almost a year, so you can tell me the truth. Why can't you even look at me? What is it that's come between us?

You know what it is, she said. It's my mother. But that doesn't mean I'm going to let you go.

You're wrong, he told her. I can't go on hanging in the air like this forever. I try to kiss you, but I can't. I can't even touch you in bed. You don't want anything. You're dead. You weren't like this before. Don't you understand?

We're tired of it, that's all, she said.

It's not true! he cried. I'm not tired of it! And if two people are together, one of them can't just leave the other one by himself.

It's not that I don't love you, she said. I don't know what it is.

But your mother knows.

Get up! Get up! The water's all boiled away!

There was still water in the pot. He made two glasses of coffee and poured in some milk. After they had drunk the coffee he said: I'm going down to the hotel.

He kissed her hand, mocking her, and went out.

Mr David was sitting at the bar, and Mohammed sat down with him.

I'm thinking of selling the hotel, he said, looking at Mohammed. And going to England.

Mohammed knew that he was saying this because he was annoyed with him.

I'm doing everything I can, he said. I'll be out of it soon.

But when? cried Mr David. If only you could really finish with her! Once I get rid of her I'll be all right.

Some people came into the bar then, and they did not go on talking. At two in the morning they shut the bar and went out to the bedroom in the garden. But Mr David did not mention Mina at that time. The next day he and Mohammed drove to Souq el Had. They had a picnic lunch with them, and spent the day lying in the sun. Mohammed did not get back to the house in Benider until two o'clock the following morning.

41

Mina was sitting in a chair. She looked pale. Didn't you sleep last night? Mohammed asked her.

No, she said. I wasn't sleepy. I've been sleeping a lot lately.

Mina, I'm going to take another trip with Mr David. We're just going to Casablanca for a few days.

I see.

We're leaving tomorrow afternoon at six.

They went to bed. He tried to run his fingers over her body, but it gave him gooseflesh. He got up and went to lie in the sala on the couch. He did not even want to be in the same room with her.

They ate breakfast together, dressed the baby and themselves, and walked down to the beach called Las Palmeras. There they rented chairs and lay in the sun.

Now I know it's impossible for us to stay together, said Mohammed suddenly. But who's going to take the baby? I think I ought to have him. He'd have a better life with me. If you take him it'll be the end of him. You'll marry somebody who won't take care of him. And you can't help him. You're only a woman.

Mohammed, why are you talking about such things?

Because I can see them coming. The time is getting close. I've thought about it, and I know it's going to be soon.

Don't think I'm just going to let you go, whatever you do.

We'll see, said Mohammed. Maybe we can still settle it. Who knows?

On the way home neither one of them spoke. When they were back at the house, he said to her: Why aren't you talking?

All you want to talk about is getting rid of me, and taking my baby away from me. The baby's mine. He's not yours.

Ah! Now you say he's not even mine?

He's not! she cried.

He turned away. Whenever you want to finish, just tell me, he said. I've got to go and help Mr David get ready for the trip.

He filled a valise with clothes and carried it down to the hotel.

42

Some time after midnight that night Mohammed went up to the house in Benider. He took out his key, opened the door, and went in. It was dark inside. Mina's mother lay asleep in the bed. The baby was in his crib, but Mina was not there. He went out and locked the door behind him, and started back to the hotel. As he got to the bottom of the long staircase that led down to the tannery, a taxi came up the ramp from the waterfront and stopped. A girl got out. Mohammed backed into the shadows at the base of the ramparts and watched. It was Mina. A man got out after her and paid the taxi driver. Then the two stood there in the street. They were saying good-bye, and they had their arms around one another, kissing. Finally the man walked back down the ramp, and Mina began to climb the stairs.

Mohammed went on to the hotel. The door was bolted. He rang the bell, and the night watchman came.

What's the matter, Mohammed? I thought you were sleeping at home tonight.

No. I'm going to sleep here.

The patron's gone to bed, said the watchman.

It doesn't matter, said Mohammed. He spent the night with Mr David. The next afternoon he took his valise and went up to the house.

We didn't go anywhere, he said to Mina. Mr David changed his mind. He had too much work to do. We'll probably go next week.

Mina's mother arrived while they were having lunch. Come in, said Mohammed. Sit down and have some lunch with us.

After Lalla Khaddouj had eaten, she said: Mina, can you come out to the house with me now?

Mina began getting ready to go out.

I've lost my key, Mohammed said to her. The key to the house here. Yesterday when I went out I must have put it into my pocket on top of my handkerchief.

While he was saying this he had his fingers around the key in his pocket.

Here's mine, said Mina. When you go out, lock the door.

Suppose you come back first and I'm not here? he said. You'd better take the key, because I might come back late.

All right. She took it back from him. Mina and her mother left. Shortly afterwards Mohammed went out for a walk in the Medina. After about a half hour he turned and walked back to the house. When he was inside, he picked up a small overnight bag that was lying on the floor in the bedroom, and opened the closet where Mina kept her gold bracelets and watches. He took them all out and put them into the plastic bag. Then he opened the box where his money was hidden, and put the money into the bag on top of the jewellery. He zipped the bag shut, pulled a few things off the shelves onto the floor and kicked them around, and went back out into the street. As he stepped through the doorway he hit the wood of the door jamb beside the lock and splintered it. He left the door slightly open and walked down the street.

At the hotel he hid the bag in a closet where Mr David kept a great many things. He piled Mr David's bags on top of it and left it there.

43

At twilight Mohammed went up to the house in Benider.

Mohammed! Mina cried.

What's the matter?

Don't ask what's happened!

What is it?

When I got back I found the door broken open. I went straight to my gold, and it was gone. And your money, too. It's all gone.

Allah! What do you mean? It's impossible.

He ran in to look for his money, saw the empty box, and slapped his thigh. Who's been in here? he cried. You had nearly a million francs' worth of gold here! And I had two hundred thousand francs wrapped in paper in this box. I'm going now to the comisaría. They may be able to catch the thief before he sells anything.

Good, she said.

He went out, walked up to the Café de Paris, sat down and ordered a Flag Pils. He ordered a second bottle, watched the people going by, and went back to the house. On the way he looked in his wallet for a small piece of paper.

He found one, and held it in his hand as he went in.

What'd they say? Mina asked.

I went to the Brigada Criminal and told them everything. They wrote it all down and gave me this. He waved the paper and put it into his pocket. They'll find the man. Give them five or six days. They'll have him. They'll be telephoning to Casablanca or Rabat.

Mina went on thinking about it, and suddenly she began to cry.

There's no use in crying. Please. Don't make me even more unhappy. Every month I'll buy you something, and that way you'll collect a lot of new things.

She was listening.

Then if the police catch the man and you get back your own, you'll have more than ever.

For a moment Mina did not say anything. Then she said: The only person who could have taken that gold is you.

If I wanted to be as mean as you are, I'd say the same thing about your mother, Mohammed told her. I think she took it. Only let's not fight about it. I've had enough arguments with you. Let's try to be happy.

Mina was quiet for a moment. He turned to her and went on: So you thought I'd come and stolen your gold! Why would I have been giving you things all this time if I was going to come and take them away? You know I can get hold of more money than anybody in Tangier. I can charge tourists a thousand francs for a three hundred franc drink, and on top of that they'll tip me. Every day Mr David gives me things to bring home. Food, money, clothes. I bring everything back here. Even if it's an apple, I don't eat it, do I? I bring it to you and watch you eat it. I don't even drink my glass of milk at breakfast time unless I know you have milk in the house. Sometimes at night when Señor David is asleep I get up and go out and sit in the garden. Everything is quiet, and I'm thinking of you. Something may happen to Mina. Somebody may hurt her, or she may get sick. And you! All you think is that I'm going to come and steal your jewellery. And when I was in Spain, you went to Emsallah, and you were standing in front of the Ciné Moghreb talking to a man. Yes or no?

No. It's a lie, she said. What time?

At ten at night.

By ten I was always in bed.

Last night when I was going to Casablanca, I came back here to the house at half past one and found your mother asleep in the bed, and the baby asleep in the crib, but I didn't find you.

Mina stared at him.

And then by the tannery I saw you getting out of a taxi. Yes, and he got out after you, and kissed you twice.

You're all wrong, Mohammed. That was my cousin. My father's brother's son. I went to their house. I've always gone to their house. He has four children now.

Yes. Your cousin.

Ask my mother. She'll tell you.

All right. We'll ask her.

Good.

Not now, said Mohammed. We'll go tomorrow. I thought I could trust you. I didn't believe you'd do that to me. Now why don't you get up and make some food so we can eat? Then I'll go to the hotel and you can sleep.

She got up and made him three fried eggs, and poured some tomato sauce over them. Then she got something for herself and sat down to eat with him. While he ate he talked.

I've spoiled you, he said. And that's why it's going to be hard for you when you leave me. And when you remember the words I'm saying now, you're going to be very sad.

Eat your food and stop talking, she told him. I never went out of the house while you were in Spain. And the man who brought me back in the taxi was my cousin. And he's got four children. And tomorrow my mother's going to be right here so you can ask her.

He finished his supper and went down to the hotel to spend the night with Mr David. Before they went to bed Mr David began again to talk about selling the hotel, and it took Mohammed a long time to make him stop.

44

Early in the morning Mohammed went back to the house in Benider. He tiptoed into the bedroom. Mina lay on her side, asleep. He went into the kitchen and made himself a glass of tea. Mina woke up and called to him to bring her some tea. They sat together having breakfast, and he glanced at her from time to time. She seemed nervous, and he imagined she was thinking: If I let him go, I'll lose him. Perhaps I should be good to him now, make him think I still love him. I'll bury my hatred in my heart for a while. I've got to make him think: She's happy again.

When Mina had finished her tea she got up and went over to him. Then she began to kiss him all over the face, so that the things he had just been imagining seemed to be completely true. He was pleased to think how right he had been, and how well he knew her. Knowing that he understood her game made him feel safe enough to pay attention to her kisses, and he began to feel happy. They went over to the bed, and in a moment they were both naked. She lay down and he bent over her, looking at her.

Mina, he was saying. The best body of all. The best girl. The only one I want, the only one I always want to see. He began to kiss her all over her body. Everywhere he could think of. Then he had his pleasure and was happy.

In the afternoon there was a knock at the door. Mohammed slipped on his trousers and went to open it. Mina's mother was standing there.

Ah, Lalla Khaddouj, said Mohammed.

She came in and he shut the door. Before she had sat down and before Mina could say anything, he started to speak.

I want to talk to you. I saw Mina with a man. And he told her everything he had seen.

Oh, that was her cousin, Lalla Khaddouj said straightway.

How's that? Her cousin! For a short moment he felt shame that he had been so harsh with Mina.

Mina burst out laughing, but Mohammed did not laugh. They've arranged this between them, he thought. I don't trust that old woman. They're both lying.

Lalla Khaddouj, you've got to have supper with us, he told her.

All right, Mohammed. But Si Ahmed's coming too in a little while.

So much the better, said Mohammed. He left Mina with her mother and went out to the market to buy the food. Soon he was back with chopped meat, new potatoes, grapes, raisins, onions and lettuce. He helped Mina prepare the food. Now and then she glanced at him with a question in her eyes, as if she were waiting to find out whether or not he believed her mother's story. When Si Ahmed came, Lalla Khaddouj went into the kitchen to help Mina, and Mohammed sat down in the sala with the old man.

How are you and Mina getting along? asked Si Ahmed.

Fifty per cent, said Mohammed. At least she does what she likes. If she doesn't have her way she gets sick. What can I do? Right now we're in the middle of a terrible mess.

Why? What's the matter?

Does your brother have a grown son?

My brother's boy? He's not so big. He's about twelve. The sisters are older.

I mean a married man with four children.

No, said Si Ahmed. Did they tell you that?

They didn't tell me anything. Only I saw a man yesterday who looked so much like your brother, I thought it must be his son. But he had four young ones.

No, no. My brother has no grown son.

Mina and her mother came in with the taifor. Si Ahmed broke the bread, and they all ate from the same dish. Presently Si Ahmed turned to Mina and said to her: Mina, why aren't you nicer to Mohammed? He's good to you. You always get your way. He gives you whatever you want. You wouldn't find another boy who'd do all this for you. If you'd married anyone else, by this time you'd be having a terrible life, like everybody. You're living in heaven, let me tell you. He even lets you go out when you like and come in when you like.

All right, said Mina. And what am I doing to him? Why are you saying all this? What have I done that's so bad?

She hasn't done anything, said Mohammed. The poor girl's just unhappy.

Mina said nothing. They finished eating, drank a little tea, and then Si Ahmed said they must be going. They all got up. Bslemah. Bslemah. And Mina's mother and father went out.

45

Life went on in the same way for Mohammed. Once in a while Mina would let him make love to her, but not very often. Sometimes he would spend a whole week at the hotel without going near the house in Benider.

Then he would begin to wonder what she was doing, and he would go back and quarrel with her. After this he usually moved in for a few days. One evening when he was staying there in the house he said to her: Why don't we go to the cinema tonight? I feel like taking you out.

Good, she said. Only we'll have to go out to my mother's and leave Driss.

She got the baby ready, and Mohammed and she dressed carefully and went out. After they had taken the baby to Mstakhoche and left it there, Mina said: Let's not go to the cinema. Why don't we go somewhere we can sit and drink and dance if we feel like it?

Mohammed was happy to hear that she felt like drinking. Ouakha, he said. They walked to the hotel and went into the bar. Mr David was there, and the barman, but there were no clients.

Oh, hello, said Mr David when he saw Mina. Sit down and have a drink. Mohammed poured himself a whisky, and gave Mina some Cinzano. Mr David put some records on the machine and turned down the lights. This made Mina want to dance. She asked Mr David to dance with her. The trouble was that she did not know how. They stopped very soon, and had dinner. Then they went on drinking and laughing until three in the morning. A few Nazarenes came in.

I really need the car tonight, Mohammed told Mr David. We have to go to Mstakhoche to get the baby, and Mina's drunk.

So I see, said Mr David. Here are the keys.

Mohammed drove to Mstakhoche, parked the car, and went to knock on the door of Mina's father's house. Her mother got out of bed and handed him the baby, and he carried it back to the car where Mina was waiting.

They went home and put the baby in its crib.

Sit down, said Mina, when they were back in the sala. I want to talk to you.

Ouakha.

Mohammed, I don't like the way we're living.

I told you that first, a long time ago, he said.

I don't love you the way I did at the beginning.

I've told you that, too. Why don't you love me?

You did put a spell on me, Mohammed. You must have. I know you did. That's why it was so easy for my mother to pull us apart. If it had been real love, she couldn't have done anything.

Can't you forget that? he said.

I wish I could forget it. But it keeps coming into my head. You did put a spell on me.

No, Mina. It's Satan working inside you. That's why you go on thinking about these things. You have to try, at least. Try not to think about them.

I pray to Allah that He won't let you leave me. If you do, I'll never forget you.

If we're not together, it won't matter to me whether you're thinking of me or not, he told her. What difference will it make, if I don't even know where you are?

She did not answer.

Are you sleepy? he asked her.

Yes, she said.

Let's go to bed.

She got up and kissed him. They undressed and got into bed. They did everything they were used to doing, but it was not the way it had been. It was hard and cold, and when it was finished it was finished. There was nothing left. It was as if nothing had happened. For a long time Mohammed lay there, turning from side to side. Finally he put on the light and went into the kitchen for a glass of water. He went back to bed, and this time he fell asleep. It was about noon when they got up and dressed.

I've got to go and see my mother, said Mina.

The car was at the foot of the stairs. He drove her to Mstakhoche and then went to the hotel.

Good morning. I'm hungry, he said to Mr David.

It's good afternoon now. Get yourself something in the kitchen.

Mohammed went out and made himself fried eggs, buttered toast and coffee. He carried it out to the bar and sat down with Mr David.

Mohammed, I want to talk to you about that girl of yours. You know she doesn't love you. I can tell you that. I was watching her last night, the way she acted with you. Europeans aren't all idiots, you know. Some of us can see what's going on.

I know Mina, Mohammed said. I can understand anybody. It's nothing new that she doesn't love me. I've know that for a long time. Ever since before the baby was born. Let's talk about something else.

I'm sorry. I'm not trying to upset you by talking about her. I'm warning you. She's no good for you. If you stay on with her, your life's just going to fall to pieces. You'll have nothing left in your bank account, and you know how you like to watch it grow.

Yes, said Mohammed. Long ago he had taken everything out of the bank.

You'll get rid of her, Mr David said as if to comfort him. I know you'll find a way somehow.

46

Mohammed had walked out to Dradeb. Mustafa's house was on the side of the hill, in Derb Sidi Qacem. He pounded on the door. There were many small children playing and running up and down the steps of the street in front of the house. Mustafa opened the door.

Mohammed! How are you?

Fine.

What can I do for you? Come in.

I thought I'd come and see how you were, said Mohammed. He did not step inside.

I know why you came, Mustafa told him. Just tell me what you want me to do.

Mohammed hesitated. I want you to come with me. Out to Beni Makada. I want to see the witch. I want to talk to her.

Which one? I don't remember. The old hag?

Yes.

All right. Let's go now.

They went together and caught the bus. It was very crowded and they did not stand near each other. In Beni Makada they walked to the house in the long street. Mustafa knocked on the door. The old woman opened it and motioned them in.

Do you remember me? Mohammed asked her.

Yes. You came once about a girl, and I did the work for you. And now what do you want?

I want you to do something to make me forget her. I don't want to think of her any more. I don't want to love her.

The old woman scratched her chin, and said: I don't know what to say. That kind of thing is very hard to do. I can try. You'd have to give me five thousand francs now. There are a lot of things to buy. If you want, I'll see what I can do with that much, and later we'll talk more about money.

How long will it take? said Mohammed.

Ten days, two weeks, a month. Who knows? If it works.

I can stand it that long, he said. He gave her five thousand francs. Bslemah.

Mohammed and Mustafa got back on the bus, rode into the city, and went to sit in a café

Why do you want to get away from Mina? said Mustafa.

I can't leave her. I love her too much. But she's no good. If I don't do this I'll never get away from her. He told Mustafa what he had seen her do.

I can't believe Mina would do that, Mustafa said.

Have you finished your coffee? said Mohammed. Come around to-morrow or the next day.

Why don't I come now and have dinner? Mustafa said.

Good. I'll buy the food and be waiting for you.

When Mohammed got to the house Mina was not there. He took a kouffa and went to the market, where he bought lamb and olives. Back at the house he found that Mina had arrived. What's all that food? she said, looking into the kouffa.

I've got a friend coming for dinner.

She took the food into the kitchen and began to prepare it.

I'm going out for a minute, he said.

He ran and bought three bottles of expensive Spanish wine, carried them back and put them in the middle of the table. When Mina saw them she said: Very fine, indeed! And what does this mean?

Once a year it doesn't hurt.

It's all we needed.

You've got nothing to do with it, he told her. This is for us. If you want to eat with us, good. If you don't you can eat in the other room or go to bed.

I see, she said.

There was a knock at the door. Come in! Sit down!

Mustafa came in. This is my wife, said Mohammed. Mustafa is an old friend of mine.

Mustafa took her hand.

They sat down and talked until Mina brought in the food. Mohammed opened one of the bottles and began to pour wine into the glasses. Soon the room was full of laughter.

What are you laughing about? demanded Mina. You've only had one glass each, and you're already drunk?

No, said Mohammed. It's not the wine. What we're laughing at is something we remembered. One time when we were drinking together we saw somebody who made us laugh.

And I'm the person, said Mina, looking at him.

No, Mina! Mustafa cried. We were talking about something else. How can you think that? We were remembering something that happened a long time ago. There was a Spaniard who used to dance in a bar, and whenever he began to dance he would go: Eheh! Eheh! Eheh! and we would always laugh.

I'm sorry, said Mina. And she began to talk and joke with them. They finished the first bottle and the second, and they began on the third.

Why don't we go out for a while and drink somewhere else? said Mustafa.

It depends on Mina, said Mohammed. Ask her.

He's not going out now, she said. He's going to bed.

Mustafa said good night to them and went out. Mohammed bolted the door.

You don't see anything wrong with that? said Mina. Bringing your friends off the street into the house? Getting drunk in the house where your son is sleeping? You could use the money for a lot of better things. And your friend was drinking in front of me.

What do you mean? You were drinking too, weren't you?

Mina did not answer. A minute later she said: If you try to divorce me I'll say no. You're going to pay money.

I see, said Mohammed.

47

The next afternoon Mohammed went to the courtyard of the notaries.

What do you want?

I've been living with a girl now for a year, he said, and I'm going to leave her.

Have you got your marriage certificate with you? The one the qadi gave you?

No, said Mohammed. I never went to get it.

Then the marriage is not official, said the notary. You're only living with the girl. Have you any children?

One.

Why do you want to leave her? Why don't you legalize the marriage?

She's got somebody else.

Wait, said the notary. I'll have to send for the girl.

About an hour later the chaouch came back with Mina. She had the baby in her arms and looked very angry.

The notary told her: This man wants to finish with you.

I won't leave, she cried. I have a baby, and the baby's got to have a father. Even without the baby, I wouldn't leave him.

The notary watched Mina closely. You're being very foolish, the notary said. He's willing to give you everything in the house.

Mina did not reply. The notary turned to Mohammed and shrugged his shoulders. You'll have to try and put up with her. Perhaps you should be kinder to her. You'll come to some sort of understanding between you. You should try to get along together, because now you have a child, and you'll have more. And you should go to the qadi and get your marriage paper.

Mohammed could see it was of no use. Yes, Sidi, he said.

Come on, he told Mina.

When they were back in the house, Mina looked at him and said: Here I am. Where did that get you? Nowhere.

No. Nowhere, said Mohammed. You won. You were always lucky, weren't you?

48

It was eight o'clock, and Mina was not yet at the house in Benider. Even though he knew she was not there, Mohammed looked behind the doors and in each place where she might be hidden. He went out into the street and took a taxi to Mstakhoche. At Mina's house he knocked. Her mother opened the door.

Is Mina here?

No.

He went into town on foot. When he got to the middle of the Boulevard Pasteur, he saw Mina coming towards him, carrying the baby in her arms. She was dressed in a djellaba and her face was covered. This surprised him, for she wore Moslem clothing only at festivals.

Where have you been? he asked her.

Taking a walk.

What kind of hour is this to be taking a walk? It's been dark for a long time.

I didn't think you'd be back, she said. I went out for a walk.

Let's go, he told her.

When they got home, she took off her djellaba and veil, and put the baby to bed.

Tell me where you've been, said Mohammed.

For a walk.

Where did you go and who were you with?

He took off his jacket.

Is it any of your business? she said. I was taking a walk with someone.

He slapped her so hard that the blood began to run out of her nostrils. She burst out crying, and he began to feel sorry for her. He took out his handkerchief and tried to stop the blood. Then he wiped her face. He hugged her tightly. Forgive me, he said. I'm sorry.

He kissed her.

It's all right, she said. Now get away from me.

She went into the kitchen and put cold water on her face. He followed her.

Tell me the truth, Mina. Where were you?

All right, I'll tell you. I went to see a Spanish woman who lives opposite the Ciné Goya. She's a seamstress. I wanted to see her about making me a suit. But I stayed too long.

How much did she want? Does she buy the material?

No. I saw what I want on the Boulevard. It's seven thousand francs a metre. I need three metres, and she wants eight thousand to make it. But she does very good work.

I may be able to get it from the Nazarene, said Mohammed.

Whenever you have the money, she said. There's no hurry.

They went to bed. Suddenly Mina seized Mohammed and began to kiss him very hard, saying many sweet words. But when he tried to take her she slipped away. Immediately he felt a pain like fire in his heart. Soon she was asleep. He could only lie there. And he got up and turned on the light and sat down in a chair beside the bed. He looked at her. She was perfect.

He stayed a long time watching Mina sleep. Then he got up, leaned over and kissed her forehead, saying aloud: Too bad.

He meant: Too bad your mother has ruined everything. He turned out the light, and went into the kitchen, shutting the door behind him. There was a bottle of Coñac Fundador on the shelf. He took it and sat down. And he began to drink, so that he could forget everything. As soon as he crushed out one cigarette he lit another. In an hour he had smoked a pack. He thought of the unhappy life he was living, and it seemed to him that his life would be the way he wanted it only when he got rid of Mina and the baby. He remarked his dream. The figure in white had told him he was about to begin a new life. He wondered if the witch's magic had begun to take effect. I've got to get free, he told himself.

He emptied the last drops of cognac into his glass, drank them, and got up. He opened the kitchen door and went into the bedroom, drunk. He turned on the light again and looked down at Mina. Then he tiptoed over to the crib and looked a long time at Driss. How am I going to leave him? he thought. I'll stay until I catch her talking to someone again, and then I'll kill her.

He left the crib and went back to the bed. As he looked at Mina he thought of how pleasant it would be to strangle her. But he was afraid, and could not move. The fear made him think again: If I hold out I can win. If a man can keep going long enough he can win. She'll get no money from me.

We went back to the kitchen and slept sitting in the chair with his head on the table. At ten in the morning Mina got up. She found him there asleep.

Mohammed, Mohammed, she said, trying to wake him up.

What?

Why don't you lie in the bed?

He went and got into the bed. She began to wash the dishes. Then she sat down in a chair beside the bed, while Mohammed slept and the baby lay on the rug. She was embroidering a piece of cloth.

Finally Mohammed opened his eyes. Have you been sitting here long? he asked her.

I'm making something. She showed him the handkerchief she was embroidering. I'm finishing it, she told him.

He got up and washed. After lunch he said: Shall we go out? Do you want to take a walk?

Tomorrow.

I'll see you later, he told her.

49

Mr David was in the bar. When he saw Mohammed come in he called to him. Listen, he said. Some friends of mine from England have come. I used to go to school with them. They want me to take them down to Marrakesh and maybe to the Sahara. Can you take charge of the hotel while I'm away? You'll have to keep your eyes open. I don't want any fights or noise. Everything's got to go on the way it always does. The bar's the hardest part.

Don't even think about it. I'll take care of everything, said Mohammed.

I know. You're careful.

After he shut the bar that night, Mr David gave Mohammed the cash box and the accounts. I've got no idea how long I'll be gone, he told him. It may be two weeks or it may be two days. It depends on how it all turns out. Whenever they want to come back they'll come back.

He and Mohammed went in to sleep. When Mohammed awoke the bed was empty. He sat around the hotel all day, drinking. When evening came he went into the bar and washed all the glasses and shined up the bottles. Around nine o'clock a few people came in, but they did not stay very long. He felt sleepy and he closed the bar early. Then instead of going home he went in and slept in Mr David's bed.

At one the next afternoon Mina arrived with the baby. Mohammed was having his breakfast. Hello, Mina, he said. What's the matter?

Why didn't you come home last night? she demanded.

I was too tired. I slept here.

You brought some girl in. The Christian isn't here now.

You haven't got the right to say that! You know I've got no girls. You're lying.

That's all right, he said. You can think whatever you want to think, señora.

Aren't you ever coming home? she said.

I'm coming now if you'll wait a minute. He counted the money in the cash box and handed the box to Abdelkrim the barman. Let's go, he said.

Take the baby, Mina told him. He took the baby and carried him in his arms through the streets.

That evening, sitting in the house at Benider, Mina said: This time I'll forgive you. But the next time you sleep away from the house you'll see. Unless the Christian is there too.

Listen, he said. I'm not your slave. I'm free. I can sleep here or where I like. It's all the same anyway. There was nobody in the hotel, and there's nobody here. If you had a heart that was still alive, even though you don't love me you could at least do me a favour in bed, and move a little when I'm with you, instead of pretending you're not there. Any other man would have left you the first time you did that to him. Even animals know how to make love.

As he talked his voice grew more bitter.

My cousin, he mimicked. My father's brother's son. I swear he has four children. What sort of girl would do a thing like that? With a piece of garbage! He may have syphilis or yaws. Maybe he doesn't wash himself. And you go to bed with him and then come into your husband's house. Your handsome husband that you'll never leave! He laughed. But your handsome husband knows what women are like. You're treacherous, and I'm too tired to go on trying to watch you. There are plenty of girls waiting. Half a word and I'm married. I wanted to have a real marriage with papers, so we could have some sort of life and live in the real world. But you saw everything backwards. You did everything without thinking first. That's why you'll always lose.

She looked at him. You understand, she began.

What?

If you run away from me I'll find you and kill you. You understand?

I'll die the way I'm meant to die, he said. Not until then. You don't exist. I'm going to leave you. He pounded his palm with his fist. And forget you. And never see your face or hear your voice again. You won't know the difference. When I come in, you look as if you'd never seen me before. Who's that? Just somebody who comes in and goes out. Just a shadow. When he comes and wants a clean shirt there aren't any clean shirts, and when he wants his trousers pressed they stay wrinkled. All my clothes are dirty! Everything! If I didn't pack them up myself and take them down to the hotel with me and give them to the black woman they'd always be dirty. I've had enough of it.

He stood up.

Is that all? she said.

That's all.

50

Mohammed went down to the hotel. It was a cold rainy night, and practically no one came into the bar. Soon he shut it and went in to bed.

The next morning early he got up and went to the courtyard of the notaries.

The notary looked up. What is it? he said frowning.

I'd like to speak with you, but alone, said Mohammed.

Ouakha. He took Mohammed into another room. It was small and empty.

I'm leaving that girl, said Mohammed. I can't live with her any longer. She's going with other men. I can't stay with a girl like that.

You told me the whole story, said the notary. And you've got to try to make things better between you.

Mohammed took out his wallet and handed a ten thousand franc note to him. This is your propina, he said. And I'd like to know how much I've got to pay her.

Let me see. There would be one month at fifteen thousand. And four months for the baby would be twenty thousand. That's thirty-five thousand.

I'll give her forty to get out right away. She can take anything in the house she wants. She can have it all.

The notary sent for Mina's father while Mohammed waited in his office. Two or three hours afterwards the old man came in. The notary told him that the marriage had been cancelled, and he said: Yes. It's all right.

Then Mohammed and Si Ahmed went together to the house in Benider, and Si Ahmed told Mina what had happened. She jumped up and quickly began to gather together all the best things in the house.

Mohammed was watching her. Why don't you take the other things, too? he said. Take everything.

He went out and got a large taxi. Then he came back to the house and helped Mina pack the things she wanted. When all the suitcases and boxes and baskets were full he carried them down to the waterfront where the taxi was waiting. He had to make four round trips. Mina and her father sat in the taxi.

I'm sorry, Mohammed told Si Ahmed. He kissed the baby, and the taxi drove away.

He went back to the house and packed his clothes into his valises, and carried it all in a taxi to the hotel. Then he went up to the Joteya and spoke with an auctioneer. He took the man back with him to Benider and showed him the furniture.

I'll buy it, said the auctioneer. He looked at the radio and the phonograph and the tables and chairs and rugs. I'll give you a hundred thousand.

If that's all you can pay, let's forget it, said Mohammed. I can sell the things.

What's your last price? the man asked him. Go on. Tell me.
A hundred and forty thousand buys it all.
No! the man said. Then he turned and said: All right. I'll take it. He pulled out a hundred and forty thousand francs and gave them to him. Mohammed tucked the bills into his wallet. The auctioneer went and got some men, and they carried everything out of the house. Then Mohammed locked the door from the outside. He went to Dradeb and said to Mustafa: Take your keys. I'm not going back there. Mustafa tried to find out from him what had happened, but he waved and walked away.

51

That night after Mohammed had opened the bar, two Americans came in and sat down. What will you have? he asked them.
Whisky with soda and ice, they said. What will you drink?
Thank you. I'll take whisky too. He drank it, and then offered them another whisky. They invited him, he invited them, back and forth. They went on drinking until it was very late. When the Americans had gone and he was alone in the bar, he sat down and poured himself a large glass of straight whisky. As he drank it he listened to the clock ticking behind the bar. He still had not heard from Mr David. He got up and put on a record. It was Farid el Atrache singing Hekayats Gharrami. He listened to the words and grew sad. The music filled the room. He had the glass in his hand, and his head was spinning. And in a little while he found his hand gripping the glass with such force that it broke. He went into Mr David's room and fell onto the bed. The blood was coming out of his hand. At two o'clock the next afternoon he opened his eyes and saw the sheets covered with blood. His hand ached. It was cut in three places. He took a taxi out to the Spanish Hospital and had them clean and bandage his hand. When he got back to the hotel he washed the sheets and hung them in the garden to dry.
During the early part of the evening Mohammed sat in the bar alone, waiting for customers to come in. Instead, two Moslem boys whom he knew slightly arrived, sat down at the bar and began to talk with him.
We're having a little party Saturday night, they told him. And you've got to come.
Neither Brahim nor Mokhtar had ever invited him before, and he thought it was strange that they should invite him now.
I won't be able to stay very late, that's all, he said. I have to be back here to take care of the hotel. The only thing the night watchman knows how to do is turn off the light over the front door. I have to do everything else myself.
That's all right, they said. Just be sure and come.

He poured three whiskies, one for each of them and one for him. Two Frenchmen came in. Mohammed served them. Brahim stood up saying: I've got something to do, and went out. Mokhtar stayed behind. Soon he leaned across the bar towards Mohammed. Listen, he said. There's a girl out looking for you to kill you. She's sworn to do it. She's got three or four other girls working for her, all whores, but you don't know any of them. Each one has the tsoukil ready to give you. Wherever they find you, they'll wait till you're drunk. Once it's inside you you're dead, so be careful.

Thanks for telling me, said Mohammed. He looked at Mokhtar suspiciously, wondering why he had stayed behind to tell him this.

I heard the story. I wanted to tell you because you're a friend of mine, said Mokhtar. Be very careful.

I will

Allah ihennik.

Bslemah.

52

Several days passed. On Saturday afternoon while Mohammed was having his breakfast he looked up. Mr David was standing in front of him.

How are you, Mohammed? He sat down beside him. How did everything go?

Everything went well. Nothing happened. Everybody's happy.

That's what I wanted to hear! said Mr David, patting his shoulder. But you don't know why I'm happy.

No. Why?

You can't guess?

The girl's gone?

I'm free!

Mr David hugged him. I can't believe it, he said, shaking his head.

I told you I'd get rid of her, said Mohammed, laughing. He went to the bar, and a moment later he called to Mr David: Here are the accounts. Mr David said they could wait until later, but Mohammed insisted, and so he went and examined them then, and found everything in order. He counted the money and turned to Mohammed.

Mil gracias, Mohammed. Everything is perfect. You always do everything right. He took out thirty thousand francs and handed them to Mohammed. A little present for you, he said.

Shortly afterwards Mohammed went out. As he was walking through the Zoco de Fuera he head someone call his name. It was Mokhtar, and Brahim was with him. He stopped to talk with them.

Don't forget to come to Dradeb tonight, they said.

A girl came up and greeted them. Where's the party tonight? she asked them.

We're having it at the house in Dradeb, they told her.

I'll be there, she said.

Mohammed was looking at her. I'm going to spend the night with this one, he thought. What's your name? he asked her.

Melika.

You've got to sit beside me tonight, he said. I'm asking you now. Don't sit with anybody else.

She smiled. Ouakha.

Would you like to take a walk? he asked her.

All right.

They said good-bye to Mohktar and Brahim and started up the street. My name is Mohammed, he said.

Yes.

Don't you have any other clothes? He was looking at her old European sweater and skirt. Those things aren't right for you.

Yes, of course, she said. I have other things.

I'll go with you and wait while you change, and then we'll go somewhere good.

He waited in a street of Emsallah while she disappeared down an alley to her house and changed her clothes. Finally she came back, looking much better, except that she was still wearing the same worn and dirty shoes.

Are those the only shoes you've got? he said.

Yes.

Haven't you got a handbag?

No.

Come on, he said. He had hidden the money he had got for the furniture with the gold and the two hundred thousand francs in Mr David's closet, but in his pocket he had what Mr David had just given him. They went into the Bata store opposite the Hotel Minzah, and she bought a pair of shoes. Then they went to an Italian in the Boulevard Mohammed Khamiss and got a handbag and a big square silk handkerchief. Melika was delighted.

Now come with me, he said. He took her into the Café de Paris and sat down. But the place was crowded with Europeans, and Mohammed did not feel like talking. They drank their coffee and ate their pastries quickly.

Let's go up to Sidi Amar, he told her.

All right.

They got into a taxi and drove up to the top of the mountain, where there was a bar that belonged to a Negro from America. He was a friend of Mohammed's. They sat in a booth and ordered drinks. Then the

American saw Mohammed and called to him. Mohammed left his drink on the table and went over to the bar. Now and then he looked into the mirror behind the bar and watched Melika sitting alone at the table. If she had something to put into his drink, this was the time when she would do it. But she merely sat there. After a while he went back to the table. They had another drink and joked a while, and then Mohammed telephoned for a taxi.

53

They drove down to a house in the Calle Canarias at Dradeb. A great many young men and girls were inside drinking. There was a bar with bottles of wine set out. A row of braziers lined one end of the room, and the steam came up from the pots of food cooking on the coals.

Mohammed and Melika went around greeting people, and then they sat down side by side on the cushions. Everyone drank and everyone ate, and there was dancing and laughter. At two o'clock Mohammed got up. I've got to go, he said.

Melika and Mohammed said good-bye to their friends. When they were in the street, he said to her: I'll take you home.

After a time they found a taxi and went to Emsallah. They got out and walked through the alleys. The moon was very bright and the shadows very dark.

Take me to the door, she said.

They went into a long narrow alley, and she stopped in front of a door and took out her keys. She opened it, stepped inside, and said: Come in.

He found himself in a comfortable room with a thick rug on the floor. Through an archway he could see a huge bed with gauze curtains around it and a light inside. There was a sewing machine by the bed. The walls were covered with big framed photographs, and there were two long mirrors.

This is a fine place, said Mohammed.

Come in here, she said, and she led him into her bedroom. There he sat in a chair and smoked a cigarette while she undressed. She took off everything but her pink underpants. And as she did this she kept her eyes on his face.

He looked back at her. She came over to him and sat down in his lap. He put his arms around her, but did not move.

He could not do anything with her, he told himself. The same thing would happen again. He would find himself loving her and then lose her to someone else. But I've got to do it, he thought. If I don't, she'll say I'm not a man. He took her head between his hands and stroked her hair. Then he kissed her. She bit his lips. He cried out and she laughed. He got up and undressed, leaving on only his shorts. She stared at him and ran her hands over his chest. You've got a beautiful body, she told him. I love it! Muscles everywhere.

Let's talk about your body, he said.

She pulled back the curtain around the bed, and they climbed in. Then she shut the curtain. He helped her take off her underpants. As soon as she lay back naked, he seized her and pulled her on to him. She kissed him and played such serious games with him that his thoughts went back to Mina, and it seemed to him that Melika was like Mina, that she was doing everything the way Mina had done it. He climbed on top of her and pushed into her flesh, imagining that she was really Mina. When he was finished they lay together, kissing, and each kiss lasted a long time. At the end he went to sleep still lying on her flesh.

He was asleep, and Melika was saying: Mohammed, Mohammed.

I want to sleep, he murmured. Then he raised his head. What's the matter?

Nothing. Are you angry?

What do you mean? I'm happy! How could I be angry with you? I've got something new in my life now. I feel as if something might happen at last.

I'm going to tell you the truth, she said. Listen to me.

What?

Mina gave me tsoukil to give you. Here it is.

She picked up a small cloth bundle that lay on the night table, laid it on the pillow, and unwrapped it. He stared at the powder inside.

I couldn't make myself do it, she said. I was going to put it in your drink in the bar up at Sidi Amar, but it just stayed in my hand. She folded the cloth again and laid it on the table.

Mina has a lot of friends, she went on. She called us all in to hear her make a vow. And she swore in front of us that she was going to kill you, and made us promise to help her. Her girls all know you by sight. You've got to look out for yourself.

Mohammed kissed her cheek. There's no way to repay such a favour! he said. You're a wonderful girl!

The important thing is that you've got to watch everybody every minute, she told him.

He put his arms around her and kissed her again, and they went to sleep. In the morning they awoke and began to kiss again. When they had finished doing everything, Mohammed got up and washed. Then he put on his clothes.

Are you going? she said.

Yes.

When can I see you?

I can come by tonight. But not early. I might come at three. Or it might be two or four. I don't know.

Here's the key, she said.

You live here alone?

Yes. I live alone.

Haven't you got anybody? A boy-friend, or a husband?

Look. I'm not going to pretend with you. I work in the street. If I give you the key it's because I want you to have it. I want you to be with me. But you'll do as you like.

He put his hand into his pocket and brought out five thousand francs. Here, he said. Buy some food. I'll be back later.

Ouakha. Incha'Allah.

He went down to the hotel and had lunch with Mr David. Why don't we take a drive? Mr David asked him.

All right.

He handed Mohammed the car keys. You drive, he said.

They went out into the country and took the airport road to El Achaqal. There they sat in the bar on top of the cliff and ordered two cognacs. They looked out at the sea. The wind that blew in through the windows smelled good.

Think of it, Mohammed! said Mr David. We've been together more than five years! And you still mean more to me than anybody in my family.

You mean a lot to me too, Mohammed told him. You're something very important in my life. Not even my father has ever done so much for me. I have everything I want, go where I like, do as I please. How could anybody not love a man who gave him all that?

Yes, I suppose that's true, said Mr David. They drank their cognacs and had others, and began to feel very well. When they left the café, they went out with their arms around each other, singing. As Mohammed drove he went on with the song. They sped around the curves near Cape Spartel on two wheels. At the hotel they surprised people walking past by going in together singing. They opened the bar and had some more cognac. The customers began to arrive. It was a noisy night, but by half past two everyone had left. They shut the bar. Then Mohammed said: Excuse me. I've got to go somewhere.

What, again? said Mr David.

Yes, Mohammed said. Goodnight.

54

Mohammed walked to the alley in Emsallah, unlocked the door, and went in. Melika was sitting on the couch.

Haven't you gone to bed yet? said Mohammed.

I was waiting for you to come. Do you want some supper?

No. I'm not hungry. I'm just sleepy. He hoped she would not see that he was drunk.

They got into bed. This time he lay face upward, and she was stretched out on top of him. They kissed a while, and then he rolled her over and made her happy. Then they slept.

The next afternoon at one o'clock they got up. Mohammed gave her a little money and said he would be back later.

When he went into the hotel Mr David told him that a Moslem woman had come that morning and given him a letter she said was for Mohammed.

Where is it?

He opened it. It was a very polite letter written in Arabic. It said that the friends who had invited him to their mahal in Dradeb the night before last would like him to come again tonight, and that they hoped he would not disappoint them. They counted on his coming.

I won't be here tonight, he told Mr David. I've got to go somewhere.

I see. Tell Abdallah he'll have to stay.

At seven in the evening he took the car and drove out to Dradeb. He knocked and was let in. Again there were many people in the mahal. A few of them were friends of his, but most of them he did not know. He took a glass of wine, and looked at the girl who was pouring it. When Moslem boys and girls get drunk together, it is not polite for anyone to have his own glass. Everyone must drink out of the same glass. First one drinks, and then another, in turn. One glass for everybody, and only one girl pouring the wine. It is done this way so there is less chance of being poisoned. Still Mohammed watched the girl who was pouring. And she must have taken a bottle that had only a little wine left in it, and dropped the powder into the bottle, and then left the bottle nearby with the other empty bottles. By this time Mohammed had stopped watching her. He was singing with his friends. And the next time it was his turn to drink from the glass, he let her fill it without paying attention. And she must have filled it from the bottle that had only a little wine in it. He was hot. He reached out for the glass and took it from her hand. He drank it and gave her back the glass.

It was about two o'clock in the morning. I've got to leave, he said.

When he had thanked Brahim and Mokhtar and said goodbye, he went out and got into the car. He drove as far into Emsallah as he could, parked the car, and walked along the alleys. He was cold. By the time he got to the house he was colder, so cold that he could not get the key out of his pocket. He pounded on the door.

Melika was inside. Who is it? she said.

Me.

She opened the door. Ah! she cried. What's the matter with you?
I'm sick, he said. I've never felt so cold.

She helped him undress and got him into bed. Cover me up, he kept
saying, and she piled many blankets on top of him.

She was sitting beside him, saying: What's the matter with you?
What is it? And he was falling asleep in the cold. And as he slept he
groaned.

The next morning about nine o'clock, in spite of all Melika said, he
got up and went out to a café that was nearby in the quarter. He went
inside and sat in a chair. Suddenly he began to vomit. When he looked
down, he saw that what he had vomited was blood. Blood was running
from his nose. He fell forward onto the floor.

An ambulance finally arrived, and they took him to the Kortobi
Hospital.

55

Just after the ambulance had left, Melika went out of her house to go to
the market. When she got to the café she saw the crowd of people, and
then she looked inside and saw all the blood.

Who was it? she said. Poor thing!

A boy who knew that Mohammed was living with her came over
and told her what had happened.

What? she cried.

She got into a taxi and went to the hospital. Mohammed was in a
very bad state. We don't know now, they told her.

She kept looking at Mohammed. He can't talk, she thought. That's it.
Mina's managed to do it.

She took another taxi down to Emsallah to see a Djibli who sold charcoal in a side street.

What can you give somebody who's taken tsoukil? she said. How
can you save him?

I have a very old oil, he said. And some fifty-year-old sminn.

In the hospital the doctors pumped Mohammed's stomach and did
many things to him. After a few hours he woke up. I want to go home,
he told them.

A little later Melika arrived in her taxi, and they let him go out with
her. She took him home to her house and put him into bed. Then she
went out and got the Djibli charcoal seller and brought him back to the
house with her.

The Djibli sat down beside the bed and took out his oil. Mohammed
drank it and ate the sminn. The Djibli sat waiting. Soon Mohammed
got up and went into the bathroom. He began to vomit, and he went

on vomiting. When he came out they made him eat. Then he vomited
again. He ate, rose, vomited, came back and ate again, rose and vomited,
several times. Then the Djibli said: Now drink a large glass of cold
water. Mohammed drank the water and lay down.

We'll leave him like that, said the Djibli.

In the morning when Mohammed woke up, he had no more pain,
and he felt warm and alive. Melika saw that he was awake and looked
at him closely. How are you? she asked him.

I feel fine now, only I'm a little dizzy, he said. A lot better than yesterday! I had a bad time.

I told you to be careful! I was so worried!

He hugged her and kissed her. Let's go out for a walk, he said.

Not today. You're not well enough.

I've got to go to the hotel anyway, he said. I'll only stay a little while,
and then I'll be back.

When Mr David saw Mohammed, he began straightway to ask him
questions. Where have you been? What's the matter with you? You're
so pale!

Mohammed sat down and told him the story. Sometimes he seemed
to forget it. He would stop and repeat the last sentence before going on.
When he had finished, Mr David said: It was Mina who did that?

Yes.

I told you to look out for that little bitch. She's no good. From now
on you've got to be careful every minute. You're too young to die or
have your health ruined. You think you're a man, but you're not. You're
just a boy. You're lucky not to be dead.

It was a girl. She saved my life. She did everything for me.

Who's this one?

Mina gave her the tsoukil to give me. But at the last minute she was
afraid and didn't do it. She told me about it, and showed it to me.

She sounds very dangerous to me, said Mr David. Don't trust her.
Don't trust any woman. Why don't you save your money? One girl
after another, and no rest in between. How do you expect to stay strong
and healthy? Sitting up all night in filthy rooms drinking. Take care of
yourself. You'll never be anything this way.

Mohammed sighed. I know, he said.

After a time, he said he was tired. I'm going back to Emsallah and go
to bed, he told Mr David.

56

Mohammed was living with Melika, but he was not happy. He kept
telling himself that he did not want to fall in love with her. He would
walk along the street talking out loud to himself, saying: I don't want

any more trouble. I'll never fall in love again with any girl or woman. Never. Here's a girl who makes her living in the street. She saw I was with an Englishman who gives me everything. She sees that I give her money. She knows how I spoiled Mina when she was with me. And she wants me to fall in love with her so she can be another Mina. And before it's over she'll have me on the end of a string. I've got to finish with her! I've got to finish it!

He began to plan ways of getting rid of Melika. The more he thought about it, the more eager he was to get it over with. It seemed to him that once he had freed himself from her he could begin once more to live.

One night when Mohammed was being barman, serving drinks to the Nazarenes, Mr David came into the bar and stood watching him for a while. Then he went behind the bar and spoke with him.

Mohammed, he said. I don't like the way things are going.

Why? What have I done? said Mohammed.

You're acting crazy. I don't know what's wrong with you. When you get drunk your language is terrible. I don't want to hear such things in the bar.

If you don't want me to drink here, I won't, said Mohammed.

I think it would be better if you didn't.

That's all right.

After this whenever a Nazarene invited Mohammed to have a drink with him at the bar, he said: I'm sorry. It's forbidden. During the weeks that followed many Nazarenes offered him drinks, and he always gave the same reply. When they heard this, some of them were indignant and spoke to Mr David about it. It's a shame, they would say. He's so amusing when he's had a few drinks. And the women would cry: Oh, let the poor boy have a drink! Some of them said the bar was not the same now that Mohammed always had such a sad face.

One night a group of drunken Englishmen announced that if Mohammed were not given a drink right away, they would go to another bar down the street where there was a barman who was able to smile.

But Mohammed's impossible when he drinks! Mr David cried. He gets insolent and starts fights. You don't have to put up with him afterwards, but I do.

Then he shrugged and went over to the bar. You can have a drink if you want, he told Mohammed. I don't mind.

That's all right, said Mohammed. He poured himself a straight whisky and drank it. The Englishmen stayed on at the bar and everyone was happy.

After they had closed for the night, Mr David went out to the Bar Parade to keep an appointment. Mohammed stayed behind and drank some more. Then he decided to go out. He shut the front door behind him and walked down to the Avenida de España. The wind was making a great noise in the palm trees there.

He found a taxi and told the driver to go to Emsallah.

He got out and went into the alleys. As he walked along he began to say to himself: No, I won't go in. I don't want to see her. I'm afraid of her.

Before he got to the house he turned and walked the other way.

57

One morning not long afterwards while Mohammed was having his breakfast in the bar he heard the bell ring. He went out and found Melika in the doorway.

There was no one else around at that moment, and so he said: Come in. He led her into the bar and she sat down with him. He gave her a glass of coffee and went on with his breakfast.

How are you? he asked her.

It's so long since I've seen you, she said. I was afraid something had happened to you, or that you were sick again.

I'm all right. Only it's the tourist season and the hotel is full of Nazarenes every night, and I've been too busy to go anywhere.

You could always have taken a taxi to Emsallah and kept it waiting, and come to see me just for a minute. So I'd have known you were alive, at least. I've been waiting and waiting. She kept looking at him. Are you sure you're all right?

He knew she was talking about the tsoukil, which can leave a man with many things wrong. And he knew that since he had come out of the hospital he had often been dizzy and found himself talking aloud when there was no one there to hear him. He lighted a cigarette.

A taxi to Emsallah? he said. I didn't think of it. Why don't we go out?

They took a long walk, along the beach to the Monopolio and then up to the Boulevard Pasteur. When they came to the park above the harbour they sat down on a bench there and looked out at the water.

You don't seem happy, Mohammed, she said at last.

Melika, I've got something to say to you, and you're going to be upset.

No, no, Mohammed. Tell me.

This is something very serious. I can't see you any more. I keep thinking of Mina. You've been good to me and I love you. But we can't see each other. If you meet me in the street, a glance is enough. If you ever need anything, come and tell me, and I'll always be ready to help if I can. I hope you understand.

She had begun to cry. He touched her arm. It's all right, she said. It's nothing.

They got up. She was still crying.

Don't cry, he said. He wanted to go quickly. Allah ihennik.

He walked away. She sat down again on the bench. When he got up onto the pavement under the trees he stood still a moment and looked back. It made him ill to see her sitting there alone with her hand over her eyes, but he walked on.

58

Mohammed sat in the bar at the hotel, regretting what he had just done. I could have lived with her, he told himself, and I sent her away. That was a terrible thing to say to her. He remembered her tears, and how she had slowly sat down again on the bench.

And I came back to the hotel, he said aloud. And here I am sitting alone, thinking of her.

He got up and went into the kitchen. It was the middle of the afternoon and no one was there. Everyone was asleep. There was a small room beyond, in the garden, where he sometimes went, and where he kept most of his clothes. He opened the door and went in. There were two litres of wine on the table. He shut the door and sat down. He wanted to drink and pretend that the world did not exist.

Instead, he drank and thought about his life, and he began to sob as he remembered that he had a wife and a child, and that he had left her and she had taken the child away. And he saw her married again, with the father not loving the boy, and the boy unhappy. He might not even be sent to school, so that when he grew up he would never have any work, and then he would become a criminal. Mina won't care what happens to him, he thought. Her heart is dead.

He had finished the two bottles of wine. Now he got up and went to the kitchen to get two more. He came back through the garden, sobbing, thinking that he did not know whether he was alive in the world, or only remembering being alive after he had died. He was not sure whether he was a man or a shadow. He went on swallowing wine, thinking and weeping. Until now he had never thought of what the boy's life might be like. He might be hungry and cold. His mother would not put any good ideas into his head or good feelings into his heart.

She's bound to ruin him, he thought. I can't let her! I've got to get him away from her! He emptied the third bottle, and began on the fourth. If only I'd thrown her out and taken him right after he was born.

There was a knock at the door of the little room. Mohammed opened it. Mr David stood there.

What's the matter? he wanted to know. Why are you crying?

I'm not, said Mohammed. I was thinking.

Thinking? What about?

Mohammed did not answer. Mr David was quiet for a moment. Then he said: I've got to go in and open the bar. It's late.

Mohammed wandered out through the kitchen and into the bar, very drunk. It was hot that night, and there were a great many people wanting drinks. They bought him more drinks, and this went on until almost daylight. The people went home, and Mr David said he was going in to bed. But Mohammed stayed on by himself in the bar, still drinking.

Mr David got up at noon, went out into the garden, and did some exercises. Then he walked into the bar. Mohammed was sitting at a table with a bottle of Marqués de Riscal. What's going on? he said. Haven't you slept yet?

No, said Mohammed.

Why not? And you're still drinking?

Yes.

But why?

I've got nothing left, Mohammed told him. It was hard for him to speak. I'm tired of being in the world. I feel as if I were going to die.

What do you expect? cried Mr David. With that mixture of drinks and no sleep? Of course you feel awful.

Alcohol has no effect on me, said Mohammed.

Mr David laughed.

I'm different from other people. When I feel, I feel from my heart. Other people just feel. When I love, I love from my heart.

And who do you love now? said Mr David.

She's gone and I'll never find her. I've lost everything. I don't exist. I won't live much longer.

Mohammed, stop all this! said Mr David. You'll go to other places, meet other people, have a whole different life. Everything will be new and you'll forget about it.

I'll never forget. How could anyone forget? When you've had a girl like the one I had? You didn't know Mina. I was crazy ever to let her go.

You had to, said Mr David. And remember how you got her. For a few hairs. You were lucky. Lucky to get her and lucky to get rid of her. Come on. Get up, and go in to bed. I'm going to give you a pill that will make you sleep.

Ouakha.

Mr David went into the bathroom and brought out a red capsule. Mohammed took it with a swallow of water, and went into Mr David's bedroom. Mr David helped him undress, and Mohammed got into bed. The light that came through the blinds was very dim. Mr David stood looking down at him for a moment, and went out. He shut the door softly.

59

Mohammed slept for twenty-four hours. When he got up the next afternoon he opened the door and stepped out into the garden. The sun seemed very bright. He heard voices in the bar and went to the door. Mr David was sitting with some Americans. When he saw Mohammed in his pyjamas with his hair rumpled and his eyes almost shut, he stood up.

Mohammed!

What's happened? cried Mohammed.

Nothing.

Something's happened. Hasn't somebody come to ask for me?

No, nobody. And Mr David began to look worried.

Mohammed went out into the garden, and Mr David turned to his friends. That boy's losing his mind, he said. There's something wrong with him. He's been very strange lately.

Mohammed went back into the bedroom and sat down on the edge of the bed. He held his head between his hands and looked down at the fur rug under his feet. What's happened? he thought. What have I been doing? What was I saying just now? Where have I been? Who have I been with? Who was it?

Mr David came into the bedroom. How do you feel, Mohammed? What's the matter?

Where have I been? said Mohammed, looking up at him. Who have I been with? Who was I just talking to?

You were talking to me, said Mr David. You haven't been anywhere. And he told him everything he had done the day before. That's right, said Mohammed. I remember. He stood up and put on his clothes. Then he had a glass of coffee and went out into the street. He wanted to go to his father's house in Mstakhoche. It was a long time since he had been to see his family. He walked up to the Zoco de Fuera and waited for the bus.

His little brother opened the door when he knocked. He kissed all his brothers and sisters. And his father's wife came in and greeted him. He sat with them, and they said: Why don't you come and see us any more? Where have you been?

At the hotel. There are a lot of tourists. There's been no time at all.

It's not right, what you do to your father, said his father's wife. Staying away so long.

I know, said Mohammed. But remember what he did to me.

He was right! she told him. That girl's worthless. She's no good for you. Are you still with her?

Mohammed looked down. I haven't seen her in a long time. A long, long time.

Your father's going to be very glad to hear that.

Then Mohammed called to each of his brothers and sisters, and gave each one a little money. And he handed some to his father's wife, and went out.

Almost as soon as he had shut the door he met Mina's father.

Well, Mohammed! How are you? How have you been?

As they talked, Si Ahmed suddenly said: It would have been better if you'd taken the baby. We ought to have helped you. If we'd talked with Mina she might have let you have him. But her mother wouldn't do it. Now she's gone off somewhere with a soldier. We don't know where she is.

Mohammed did not answer for a moment. Then he said: And she took the baby.

Yes, son, said Si Ahmed. It's too bad. I'm glad to see you looking so well.

She wanted to go, said Mohammed.

They said good-bye, and he went on his way down the street, leaving Si Ahmed standing at the door of his house.

60

One day Mohammed and Mr David were sitting alone in the bar drinking whisky together. Mr David drank more these days. He thought it was a way of keeping Mohammed in the hotel with him.

I've got to get out of this town, Mohammed was saying. I can't stay here any longer. Every time I go out I see something that reminds me of Mina. It's driving me crazy.

Did you ever go back and pay the witch in Beni Makada, when she got rid of Mina for you? Mr David asked him.

I'm not rid of her! cried Mohammed. She's all I can think of. It didn't work. I want to think of something else.

There's nothing you can do about it, then, said Mr David.

I can go to some other country and work. I could have a whole different life.

You can do that without leaving Tangier, Mr David told him.

How?

You Moslems have holy men, don't you? They can change your ideas for you. There are all kinds of things they can do to keep you from thinking of her.

Mohammed was not listening. It was her mother who did it, he said. She got hold of something very strong.

You can stay here perfectly well, Mr David went on. You're here in the hotel with me. You just stay on, and when I sell it we'll go to England. I can take you along with me. You can live there with me and work if you like, and you'll forget about all this.

He saw that Mohammed was paying no attention. He was muttering to himself as he poured another glass of whisky.

You could be having a good time, Mr David told him. But you'd rather lie around and feel sorry for yourself. What happened between you and Mina is finished. It's all over. But you're still young! Eighteen isn't old.

I'm nineteen, said Mohammed. He tried to fill Mr David's glass. Mr David put his hand over it and shook his head.

You're not, he said. Not yet. You haven't seen the world. And you're wasting your life sitting here thinking about something that's been finished a long time. You say you have no friends, and nobody wants to see you. Look at you! Who wants to see anybody that looks the way you do, with your face half white and half black, and your hair that hasn't been cut for months, and those clothes!

Mohammed said nothing. He drank his whisky slowly and looked at the other side of the room. Mr David poured himself a little whisky. He was thinking that perhaps he had said too much. He spoke now more gently.

You're such a fine, good boy. Everyone loves you. When people come into the bar, if you're not there, they always want to know where you are. At least, they did until you got this way, until you forgot how to joke and laugh and be happy. But who wants to look at somebody who's dirty and drunk and angry? You come into the hotel without speaking to anybody and go into that little room. Then you come out drunk and wander out again into the street. You stay all night in some bar or café. You get no sleep. You feel sick. If you go on like this another year or two, you're going to end either in the hospital or the cemetery. Look at Englishmen! When they love a girl and something happens and they lose her, they go right on with their lives. They forget about her. Later they may even meet her in the street and not know who she is. They find one better than the one they lost.

Englishmen are cold, said Mohammed. They don't feel anything.

You could get up, went on Mr David, and go in and take a bath and shave, and go and get your hair cut, and put on some clean clothes. And then you could go out and find a better girl than you've ever had in your life. And she could give you something new. Then if you should see Mina you wouldn't even look at her.

Mohammed started to pour himself more whisky. Mr David frowned at him and he stopped.

You've got a hard head, Mohammed. Most Moroccans have. They say: I'll do it, but they don't do it. You tell them: Do this. And they do something different. A man's got to use his head. He's got to listen to words and try to understand them. He's got to be able to look at the other person and know what he's telling him, and say: Yes, that's true. And if he doesn't agree, he's got to say: No. That's not true. Am I right or wrong?

You're right, said Mohammed. But what do I do?

You look into the mirror.

Mohammed got up and walked slowly into the bathroom. He ran the hot water and took a long bath. Then he shaved and dressed in a clean shirt and a pair of well-pressed trousers, and went out to the barber's shop.

He was pleased with the way he looked when he came back to the hotel. Mr David sat with an American in the bar. Look at that! he cried as Mohammed came in. He followed Mohammed with his eyes as he walked around the room watching himself in the mirror.

It makes me feel so good to see you looking like this again, said Mr David. Now it's a pleasure to look at you. He turned to the American and said: Do you see Mohammed? He's a boy again. More handsome than ever.

Thank you, said Mohammed. He was tidying up the bar. His body felt very light, and he was happy everywhere in it. And he laughed and drank all evening with the Nazarenes who came in.

Late at night he shut the bar. Mr David was waiting for him in the garden. How do you feel now? he asked Mohammed as he came out.

Better.

What did I tell you?

Yes. You were right. I've thought about what you said. I feel better. Not well yet, but better.

In a few days you'll be fine.

Yes.

Mr David put a pile of records on the phonograph and they went to bed.

61

Mohammed went on living with Mr David at the hotel and helping him in the bar, and they were both happy. In different ways Mr David often told him that everything he had predicted for him had come true. The memory of Mina had gone out of his head. Because he was happy he drank less and grew healthy again. He had other girls, but he did not let himself love any of them. When he thought about it he would say to himself: I'm lucky to have a friend who understands the world. He pulled me back when I was at the edge.

The years went by.

One rainy morning Mohammed stood in the bus shelter in the Zoco de Fuera waiting for a bus to Mstakhoche. He had bought some fruit to take to his family. As he stood there, he noticed a country woman in a dirty haik staring at him. She had two small children with her, and a baby strapped on her back. He looked at her for a long moment, but she did not lower her eyes. It was he who looked away first. An instant later he turned back. She was still looking at him. The bus drove up and the people pushed in. The woman got in ahead of him with the children clinging to her haik.

Everything in the bus was wet. The woman sat down, and Mohammed sat opposite her, because the seat was still vacant. People were running through the aisle to find places to sit. As the bus climbed the hill by the French Consulate, he glanced again at the woman, and saw that she was crying behind her veil.

Maybe I look like someone in her family, he thought. Someone who's dead, perhaps.

She leaned towards him and spoke in a low voice.

Don't you know me, Mohammed?

No.

Then he said: Are you Mina?

Yes.

Allah! Is it really you? I can't believe it. Her face was bony and the skin on it was yellow.

Then he turned around to the seat behind him where she had put the two children. Are they yours?

Yes.

The big one is Driss?

She nodded.

Mohammed turned around further. Do you go to school, Driss? he asked the little boy.

I go to the mcid.

Good! And they teach you the Koran. I like boys who know the Koran.

When the bus arrived at the end of the line they got out. Let's go over there under the trees and talk a minute, said Mohammed.

They walked under the eucalyptus trees and sat down. The ground was wet.

Mina, what's happened? I don't understand how you can look like this.

She burst into tears, and Mohammed did not want to see it. He got to his feet. Mina and the children followed him back to the street.

Mohammed stooped down and put his arms around the small boy. He took out a five thousand franc note and handed it to him.

Go and get something nice, he told him. Good-bye, Mina.

He kissed the child and went on quickly to his father's house.

BHARATI MUKHERJEE

the tiger's daughter

PART ONE
1

The Catelli-Continental Hotel on Chowringhee Avenue, Calcutta, is the navel of the universe. Gray and imposing, with many bay windows and fake turrets, the hotel occupies half a block, then spills untidily into an intersection. There are no spacious grounds or circular driveways, only a small square courtyard and a dry fountain. The entrance is small, almost shabby, marked by a sun-bleached awning and two potted hibiscus shrubs. The walls and woodwork are patterned with mold and rust around vertical drains. The sidewalks along the hotel front are painted with obscenities and political slogans that have been partially erased.

A first-floor balcony where Europeans drank tea in earlier decades cuts off the sunlight from the sidewalk. In the daytime this is a gloomy place; only a colony of beggars take advantage of the shade, to roll out their torn mats or rearrange their portable ovens and cardboard boxes. The area directly in front of the Catelli's doorway is littered with vendors' trays, British mystery novels and old magazines laid out on burlap sacks, and fly-blackened banana slices sold by shriveled women. At night neon tubes from tiny storefronts flicker over sleeping bodies outside the hotel, then die before the breaking of the violent Calcutta dawn.

The Catelli is guarded by a turbaned young man, who sits on a stool all day and stares at three paintings by local expressionists on permanent display by the hibiscus shrubs. He is unusual for a doorman of any hotel; he is given to sullen quietness rather than simple arrogance, as though he detects horror in the lives of the anonymous businessmen who pass through his doors each day. A doorman is an angel, he seems to say. He is not without love, however, this guardian of the Catelli-Continental Hotel. He loves the few guests who come every day but do not stay. He sees flurries of exquisite young women in pale cottons and silks and elegant old men carrying puppies and canes, and he worships them. While small riots break out in the city, while buses burn and workers surround the warehouses, these few come to the Catelli for their daily ritual of espresso or tea. And the doorman gathers them in with an emotional salute.

There is, of course, no escape from Calcutta. Even an angel concedes that when pressed. Family after family moves from the provinces to its brutish center, and the center quivers a little, absorbs the bodies, digests them, and waits.

2

In the year 1879 by the English calendar, on a Monday in Sravan, the month of heaviest rains, Hari Lal Banerjee of Pachapara was standing under a wedding canopy on the roof of his house, once a happy rajah's palace.

Hari Lal stood by the parapet, head unprotected by the red and yellow canopy, legs slightly apart under a fine white *dhoti*, as he watched tenants and workers gather in the covered courtyard below to celebrate the wedding of his children. It was a lonely watch, and his mind kept straying beyond the compound walls to the night beaten by rains.

On other nights Hari Lal might have ridden into that darkness. He knew the territory well, the greenish-black soil, the sudden creeks and canals and treacherous rivers. He claimed no virtue in retreat, he had no desire to exaggerate the safety of ancestral houses. But on this auspicious Monday, chilled and shuddering in spite of astrologers' assurances, he was glad to return to the shelter of canvas awnings on bamboo stakes.

The rain fell steadily in his compound. Small drops trickled down the red and yellow tassels of canopies and dampened the heads of little boys and servants. Some children, wearing leaf hats, floated paper boats in open drains. The barber's son, almost a grown man, dashed out of the canvas shelter and danced clumsily to amuse his friends. They did not hear the straining and imprisoned ghost of change.

Hari Lal's friends, men in their thirties carrying gold-headed canes, detected nothing unusual either. They had patterned their lives around kerosene lamps; now the hissing strings of wedding lights on the roof gave them a sense of mastery over the wet blackness.

"It's a happy night," they said. "It's an auspicious night." They did not expect their lives to be spoiled by astrological errors or fatal paradoxes. A loud sentimentality preyed on these guests. They talked about the stability of Hindu marriages, they came back again and again to the bounty of the Bengali soil and to the orderliness of their little villages. They told their servants to bring out more lights, the *shanai*-players to play with more feeling, and their wives to serve them more vegetable chops and shrimp cutlets. They twirled their gold-headed canes and gossiped and behaved like perfect wedding guests.

But the host stood his lonely watch on the roof, listening to the anguished music of the *shanai*-players. There were no lessons or insights for Hari Lal that night, only a premonition of small violences. He saw little cracks and holes appear in the soil that he thought he knew well, and the rain poured steadily, expanding the openings rather than filling them. His first impulse was to protect his friends, though he knew the night beyond the canopies was more savage, more permanent than the enemies fought by other Banerjee men from Pachapara.

While Hari Lal stood ready, and the musicians played fiercely, the guests from the courtyard were brought to the roof for the wedding feast. Young men busied themselves with brass pails of rice, ran up and down staircases with pitchers of drinking water. Hari Lal's nephews walked between rows of diners, slopping out *pilau* and saffron rice, fried eggplant and pumpkin, potatoes, peas, curried fish and curried mutton, lemon wedges, yoghurt, tamarind, seven kinds of chutneys and ten kinds of sweetmeats. They deposited all this extravagantly on banana leaves to be eaten, digested or carried away by two thousand relatives and guests. The village beggars, no longer ill at ease in the bejeweled gathering, sat in their assigned rows and joked with vegetarian Brahmin apprentices. They watched the elegant Banerjee nephews in silk shirts and gold buttons, and they yielded to the small, secret appeals of aristocratic dress.

In the exact center of the roof burned a sacrificial fire. The wedding ceremonies had suddenly quickened their pace. The moment of indissoluble ties was at hand. The crowd tensed. Virgins dreamed of fulfillment; married women of joys that had been promised them. Hari Lal moved toward the fire to take his part in the wedding rites. He moved past lines of beautiful golden women, past mango leaves in copper pots, a baggy-eyed priest and his earnest assistant, two young men in nuptial crowns, till he reached his weeping little girls in adult bridal ornaments.

Did Hari Lal, his arms around his daughters, guess then the shape and intentions of the dark night? As he grasped the final stunted issue of the Pachapara Banerjees perhaps he only foresaw his own death. The shadows of suicide or exile, of Bengali soil sectioned and ceded, of workers rising against their bosses could not have been divined by even a wise man in those days.

3

Changes in the anatomies of nations or continents are easy to perceive. But changes wrought by gods or titans are too subtle for measurement. At first the human mind suffers premonitions, then it learns to submit.

Life in Pachapara continued to be pleasant enough. There were many more marriages, and of course many deaths. The death of Hari Lal Banerjee was loudly mourned by villagers. He had been a good man, a strong man; he had never protested his fate. Two summers after his daughters' wedding he had ridden out of his compound to stop a feud, and someone with a knife had leaped on him from flowering bushes.

With Hari Lal's death the Banerjee family lost its hold on Pachapara. The Banerjees were replaced by the Jute Mill Roy Chowdhurys, and they too produced good and virile men. But the Roy Chowdhurys thought it prudent to lock the gates of their estate and to replace each brick pried loose by violence. Outside their compond, sometimes on the bathing-steps of rivers, or in red dirt alleys that led to the marketplace, they saw angry, fanatical faces. There were more unreasonable murders, suspicious drownings, bloody and mutilated bodies discovered in paddy fields. There were also more communal riots. Eventually Pachapara was appor-tioned on the map as foreign soil and Hari Lal's marble study became the parlor of a Moslem butcher. By then it was too late for the villagers to remark on the anatomy of change.

But long before that, Santana, Hari Lal's eldest daughter, left Pachapara with her husband. Santana's husband, a barrister, was not a man of vision; prospects of change excited him. After Hari Lal's sudden death, he sold the moldy Banerjee house he had inherited by marriage and moved to Calcutta. The village, he thought, would only exhaust his strength. Certainly the big city developed talents and emotions that the barrister hardly suspected in himself.

Though Santana's husband was successful in Calcutta he remained humble, at least on the surface. He made his points in court so decently that he was often invited to British clubs by liberal young Englishmen, though never of course to the Calcutta Sunbathing Association, where flabby Englishwomen surrendered their charms to the gratified stares of pukka Englishmen.

The barrister's success led to one fateful act. In a year of colonial unrest, in spite of warnings from friendly British colleagues and anxious Bengali gentlemen, he defended two teenage Brahmin nationalists. This action was unfortunately construed not as the necessity of conscience but as deliberate imprudence, and the barrister was unofficially reprimanded.

In aristocratic anger Santana's husband withdrew from the Bar, bought a lumberyard in Assam and a tobacco factory in Calcutta and insulated himself still further from the British, the insults, the dread.

Arupa, Hari Lal's younger daughter, who had from infancy shown signs of chronic nervousness, was abandoned by her husband in the first weeks of marriage. In time the young woman lost her beauty and her strength. In time she became a legend in Pachapara, an eerie shape beneath the red cotton quilt of her bridal four-poster, her hair cropped close as a gesture of defiance, her limbs bare of all ornaments, her eyes cold and accusing. Occasionally driven by some memory or anger, she would steal from under her quilt, unlock from a drawer her bridal photograph yellowing in its silver frame, and stare at the man who was still her husband.

· · ·

So slight were the initial changes among the families of Bengali *zamindars*. An imprisoned and gigantic spirit had begun to move, and all things on its body—towns, buildings, men—were slowly altering their shapes. The alterations were not yet impressive; none suspected they might be fatal. Years later a young woman who had never been to Pachapara would grieve for the Banerjee family and try to analyze the reasons for its change. She would sit by a window in America to dream of Hari Lal, her great-grandfather, and she would wonder at the gulf that separated him from herself. But her dreams and her straining would yield a knowledge that was visionless.

4

Now in these times of disorder Calcutta had to admit that Bengal Tiger Banerjee was not like other men. A strong man is a mediator between divine and mortal fates. While the restive city forced weak men to fanatical defiance or dishonesty, the Bengal Tiger remained powerful, just and fearless.

Calcutta was losing its memories in a bonfire of effigies, buses and trams. But the Bengal Tiger continued to inoculate himself against the city, improving and expanding the tobacco firm he had received as his dowry, working out medical and disability insurances for his workers, night classes in the factory for those who could not write or read. Outside his house on Camac Street and his Barrackpore factory, men were responding with threats or heroism to the sullenness of Calcutta; but the Bengal Tiger remained jovial and impartial, absorbed in his duties, his business, and his charities.

Beneath that stern affability, however, there must have run a deep suspicion or pain, which had urged the Bengal Tiger to send his only child, a girl of fifteen, out of India for college. The motives for that decision remained his secret, but its consequences were terrifying. It had put a rather fragile young woman on a jet for Poughkeepsie, and left out of account the limits of her courage and common sense.

For Tara Vassar had been an almost unsalvageable mistake. If she had not been a Banerjee, a Bengali Brahmin, the great-granddaughter of Hari Lal Banerjee, or perhaps if she had not been trained by the good nuns at St. Blaise's to remain composed and ladylike in all emergencies, she would have rushed home to India at the end of her first week.

"Dearest Mummy and Daddy," she began a hundred times. But there was no way she could confide to her parents the exquisite new pains, no way she dared explain that in Poughkeepsie her love of Johnny Mathis was deep and sincere. As each atom of newness bombarded her she longed for Camac Street, where she had grown up. Tara's Camac Street friends did not forget her. They wrote her long and beautiful letters, meticulously addressed with periods and commas. In their letters they complained wittily of boredom in Calcutta, the movies at the Metro, the foul temper of the whiskered nun from Mauritius, the weather's beastliness, but not once did they detect Tara's fears. These friends who had never left home envied her freedom; they asked for records and transparent nighties; they were ecstatic when she told them she had seen Johnny Mathis in person.

Tara saw herself being pushed to the periphery of her old world, and to save herself she clung to the loyalties of the Camac Street girls. For them she stood in line at the post office, hugging poorly wrapped parcels of shampoos and lipsticks, trying to understand the jokes of the ill-tempered Negro clerk.

The girls in the residence hall tried to draw her out. They lent her books and records and hand lotions unasked. But how could Tara share her Camac Street thoughts with the pale, dry-skinned girls the same way they shared their Alberto VO^5 in the shower? At first she was polite, and anxious to make her contribution.

"My great-grandfather's name was Hari Lal Banerjee. He was a very plucky man." But such remarks she found made a bad impression and soon she gave up.

Little things pained her. If her roommate did not share her bottle of mango chutney she sensed discrimination. Three weeks in Poughkeepsie and I am undone, thought Tara. Three weeks and I must defend my family, my country, my Johnny Mathis. No previous test, not the overseas Cambridge School Leaving Certificate Examination, not even the labor unrest at her father's factory had prepared her for this. She prayed to Kali for strength so she would not break down before these polite Americans. And Kali, who was a mother nursing her infant, serene, black, exquisite, and Kali, who was a mother devouring her infant, furious, black and exquisite, who sat under silk saris in a suitcase at Vassar, smiled out at her mischievously.

Later Tara was fond of saying that she had first started to think for herself in the dormitory at Vassar. That may not be quite accurate. But she did stay up till two in the morning discussing birth control with her dormitory neighbors. At St. Blaise's she had not been permitted to think about sex; love was all right if it could be linked to the poetry of Francis Thompson or Alice Meynell. But now, realizing the girls identified her with the population explosion, the loop, vasectomy in railway stations, she blossomed into a bedside intellectual.

The topic of urban development was quite another matter. Tara had never been farther than Shambazar. She could not fully visualize tenements and beggars. Nor did she wish to talk about it. Dark skinny buildings, devious alleys, rotting garbage, idle men leaning against barred windows, child-beggars in front of food stalls: all this made her physically sick. She was a sensitive person, sensitive especially to places. She remembered in Calcutta the chauffeur had always carried smelling salts for her in the glove compartment. Her memory, elastic, warm and gentle, showed her families asleep on sidewalks, children curled in wooden crates, and this undermined her remarks.

In December of her first year abroad at a gathering of the Indian Students' Association in New York, Tara met a young man from Calcutta. His name was Manik (Mota) Mukherjee and he was studying political science at Columbia. Tara's imagination, in the custody of St. Blaise's nuns since the age of three, while not willingly touching on sex, quite often centered on love. She fancied herself in love with Mota. Though she did not confide in anyone, not even in the Camac Street girls who had seemed ghostly by December, her father was quick to detect her concealed emotion.

"I met one Mr. Chakravorty [wrote the Bengal Tiger] at yesterday's meeting of chamber of commerce. He is brother-in-law of one Mr. Mukherjee who has one son, Manik (Mota), who has been aforementioned. We had whiskey together (prices have gone up), and frank chat. He told me this boy is very, very brilliant, and everyone loves him ..."

When Tara read this letter from her father she could no longer concentrate on her term papers. The Bengal Tiger knew that she had fallen in love, but he had not lost his temper. Three days later she received another urgent letter.

"We have had further talks with the same Mr. Chakravorty, brother-in-

law of same Mr. Mukherjee. We have also made thorough independent inquiries at our end. His family is very much like ours, honest and happy-go-lucky. Remember love is nine-tenths prudence, one-tenth physical attraction. Don't do anything foolish or rash. It is your happiness that I demand. Caste, class and province are more valuable in marriage than giddiness. We do not disapprove of this young man, but we're not there to guide you, Taramoni. It may be only fair to indicate to the young chap that we are modernized people, and do not believe in dowry system. We will give from the bottom of our hearts as you well know, but do not on any account tell him that . . ."

This advice brought tears to Tara's eyes. Her father was treating her as an adult. He who had been embarrassed when Rajah the cocker spaniel had mated was now frankly discussing dating and marriage with her. But the advice was never put to practical application. Before Tara could pursue her fancies about being in love, Manik (Mota) Mukherjee went to Sweden for a vacation, and on his return did not once call her.

Toward the end of May that first year abroad, as the girls around her prepared to go home, Tara was seized by a vision of terror. She saw herself sleeping in a large carton on a sidewalk while hatted men made impious remarks to her. Headless monsters winked at her from eyes embedded in pudgy shoulders. The sounds of classrooms and dorms were cut off by the cardboard sides of her carton. Not a strain of weather reports from someone's radio, no one scoring an emphatic point in a seminar, not even the smell of instant coffee in the corridor. She suffered fainting spells, headaches and nightmares. Her face took on the pinched and almost beautiful look of tragic heroines in Bengali dramas. She complained of homesickness in letters to her mother, who promptly prayed to Kali to save Tara's conscience, chastity and complexion.

The terror seethed in a lonely room at Vassar. It rushed out of borrowed drapes and pictures; it bounced off desktops and lumpy armchairs. Tara's academic adviser, who did not believe in emotion, watched with distaste the sudden defoliation of Tara, and made it her business to keep the young woman occupied all summer.

"Let's see now," began the adviser. She had called Tara to her office, which was close, book-lined and rectangular. "Do you type?"

Tara thought a table lamp could throw cruel shadows on the face of a middle-aged spinster. "No," she answered, tracing the blotches of light and dark with an imaginary finger. "My father's secretary goes out of his way to help us. When Rajah, our cocker spaniel, died and we were so heartbroken, he even arranged a secret night burial for him without waiting for our permission. He's always done everything, all our typing et cetera. That's why I've never had to learn, you see."

The adviser, used to revealing herself only as a liberal missionary, failed to understand the import of Tara's remarks.

"I think you better go to summer school," she said with authority before a new complication could arise.

And so, after two semesters of reading primly in the library, of cycling blithely from class to class, of rubbing Nivea cream on her face to protect it from the hostile weather, Tara left obediently for summer school in Madison. Within fifteen minutes of her arrival at the Greyhound bus station there, in her anxiety to find a cab, she almost knocked down a young man. She did not know then that she eventually would marry that young man. But at that moment she merely said "Excuse me," and continued to drag her offensive luggage toward the taxi stand.

PART TWO
1

Tara's Bombay relatives were all at the airport to welcome her. They had brought garlands and sweetmeats to put her at ease, but after the long flight, the awkward stops in transit lounges, and the clearing of customs she was groggy and nervous about meeting them. Little nephews whose names she did not catch were told to touch her feet in *pronam* when she was introduced to them as "the America auntie." The Bombay relatives hugged her and spoke to her in Bengali, the first she had heard since a Durga Pujah gathering in New York.

"Our poor Tultul!" they screamed at her. "How thin you have become!"

"And so much darker!"

"Tultul, we thought America would—"

She had not remembered the Bombay relatives' nickname for her. No one had called her Tultul in years; her parents called her Taramoni when they wanted to show special affection. It was difficult to listen to these strangers.

"My goodness, Tultul, I cannot tell you how bony you have become!"

"Where is your husband? How dare he not come!"

"We wanted to show off the American *jamai*."

"Then the *Indian Ladies Weekly* would have taken our pictures!"

While the Bombay relatives exaggerated their disappointment that David had not accompanied her, Tara suspected they were relieved that he had not. The relatives lived in a large city but did not know many foreigners; David would have taxed their English too much.

"I'm very tired," said Tara. "Are we ready to go?"

"We are ready, we are ready. Where is the car?"

"You must promise not to look at the bad parts of India."

"Promise to keep your eyes shut! Some parts are horrible."

"What about the smell? She ought to cover her nose."

They drove her from the airport to their apartment on Marine Drive, which seemed to Tara run-down and crowded. Seven years earlier on her way to Vassar, she had admired the houses on Marine Drive, had thought them fashionable, but now their shabbiness appalled her. The relatives must have sensed her disappointment.

"Bombay flats are impossible. We pay nine hundred rupees!"

"To say nothing of the bribes and *pugris* to landlords!"

All the Bombay relatives begged her to spend at least a week on Marine Drive before going on to Calcutta. They agreed it was a shame that her father (whom they called the Bengal Tiger) had been held up at home by an unexpected general strike. Otherwise, they indicated, her reception at the airport would have been ten times more spectacular.

"What a tragedy Bengal Tiger couldn't be here! But what can he do with hooligans bothering Calcutta?"

"He always stays with us when he's here. Why do you fuss so much?"

"Such a hearty man our Bengal Tiger that even neighbors love to hear him laugh in the flat!"

They showed her the train tickets they had already bought for her and her father. But now that Tara had to travel alone to Calcutta the Bombay uncle was hesitant to hand over the tickets. A two-day journey in a compartment full of strangers he considered a dangerous experience for any Banerjee girl. He advised her to fly instead. On the joints of his fingers he enumerated his "very fine connections with the airplane people," and promised to get her plane reservations within the hour.

"Thank goodness things haven't degenerated Bombay-side so far. I myself will fly with you. Two days' leave of absence from office. What is that?"

"She's our responsibility till she gets to Calcutta. Please let Uncle decide what is the best solution here."

But Tara would make no concession to their kindness. She was anxious to rest by herself, she explained; the train journey would be perfect as long as her compartment was air-conditioned. Though she saw the Bombay relatives pale at her stubbornness, she insisted she preferred to be alone so she could prepare for her vacation in Calcutta.

"Vacation!" cried the Bombay aunt. "How can I tell you how terrible Calcutta has become? *Arré baba!*"

"What nonsense you speak!" objected the uncle. "The papers Bombay-side are full of lies. Bombay is always jealous of Calcutta."

"But how will I explain to the Bengal Tiger we're sending you alone?"

asked the Bombay aunt. "How dare you try to cause a misunderstanding, Tultul?"

Defeated and embarrassed, the relatives attributed Tara's improprieties to her seven years in America.

The next evening all the Bombay relatives and their servants came to the railway station to see her off. The uncle rushed ahead, keeping track of the coolie who had Tara's light bags. Tara, lagging behind with several nephews, thought the station was more like a hospital; there were so many sick and deformed men sitting listlessly on bundles and trunks. When she caught up with the uncle she found him very angry. Tara and the Bengal Tiger, if he had come, had been put in a four-berth compartment with two others. He read the names of the passengers on the reservation slip above the compartment's door. "They are both men!" he exploded. "I can't allow you to travel under such conditions."

"What nonsense this is!" added the aunt. "Not only are they men, but on top of that, they're non-Bengalis! *Arré baba!*"

The uncle tried to arrange more proper traveling accommodations, but the air-conditioned coach that night seemed filled with businessmen and one recently married couple who wanted to be together. Tara, anxious to get started on the last lap of her journey home, assured the nervous uncle that he really should not worry, that she would spend both nights on the train sitting up.

The Bombay aunt and the nephews began to cry as they waited for her train to leave. The Bombay uncle became very emotional. He bought her two bars of Cadbury's chocolate, then paid a large tip to the air-conditioned-class attendant so he might give Tara extra care. His entire family entrusted last-minute messages for the relatives in Calcutta. Then the two other occupants appeared, the train began to move slowly, and the aunt, uncle and nephews had to quickly jump off.

She did not wish to study her traveling companions. Her Bombay aunt would have said all Marwaris are ugly, frugal and vulgar, and all Nepalis are lecherous. Tara hoped she had a greater sense of justice toward non-Bengalis. But the gentlemen in the compartment simply did interest her. The Marwari was indeed very ugly and tiny and insolent. He reminded her of a circus animal who had gotten the better of his master. The Nepali was a fidgety older man with coarse hair. He kept crossing and recrossing his legs and pinching the creases of his pants. Both men, Tara decided, could effortlessly ruin her journey to Calcutta.

Before the train had made its first stop the Marwari and the Nepali were starting to bait each other. It began with a quarrel over luggage space, but Tara feared they were responding to other irritations. She sat surrounded by bedrolls, trunks, old leather suitcases, baskets of fruits, while the Nepali tried to push her Samsonite bag out into the corridor.

"This is too large, lady," he objected. "How you think there'll be room here for that monster?"

"It is small, excuse me," answered the Marwari. "The lady's suitcase is the smallest here. I'll call the attendant this minute if you don't move *your* bags and baggage."

Tara's feelings did not appear to matter at all. Her suitcase had become part of a general irritability. In the end the question of luggage was resolved without the aid of the attendant. The two men piled the pieces in the middle of the floor, making the compartment's washbasin totally inaccessible.

She was frightened by the capacity for anger over trivial encounters. She stared out of the window to avoid watching the night ablutions of her companions. I have returned to dry holes by the sides of railway tracks, she thought, to brown fields like excavations for a thousand homes. I have returned to India.

At Jamnagar the aging "boys" in soiled caterers' turbans called out, "Dinner! Dinner!" The Nepali ordered the English menu. Tara, still close to David's worries, feared diarrhea, jaundice and polluted water. She ordered a Coke. The Marwari, true to his nature, ordered nothing.

After years of airplanes and Greyhound buses Tara felt she should be thrilled to travel in an Indian train. Her mother's brother worked with diesel locomotives and so she had been trained since childhood to think well of the Indian railways. But this time the train ride depressed her. She fretted about David as she sat in the hostile compartment. Perhaps I was stupid to come without him, she thought, even with him rewriting his novel during the vacation. Perhaps I was too impulsive, confusing my fear of New York with homesickness. Or perhaps I was going mad.

The dinner tray arrived at a station where there were monkeys on the train tracks, white monkeys calmly eating by the side of freight cars. The "boy" placed the tray before the Nepali passenger. Mulligatawny soup in a stainless steel bowl, poached eggs, toast, boiled okra and carrots, bread pudding. Then a feckless Coke without a straw for Tara. She pursed her lips around the wet, warm bottle, then suddenly panicked. How long had it lain about, opened? Old worries flooded her, warnings from her mother about VD contracted in public toilets, sinister sexual germs lurking in railway stations.

"I don't want it after all," she said, paying for the Coke. The attendant took the bottle away and drank it in the corridor.

The Nepali traveler looked rather embarrassed to be the only one eating. He smiled vaguely, rubbed his hands on the limp napkin, and started on his soup.

"The Indian menu is hopeless," he commented, sucking in a spoonful of rice floating in yellow liquid. "Madam, are you new here?"

"Yes and no," said Tara, preparing to hide behind a *Time* magazine. The Marwari stirred in his corner. Now he reminded her of a spider, impassive and calculating. He stood up, and Tara noted dry, goose-pimpled flesh hanging loosely from his bony arms. He reached under his seat for a tiffin carrier propped between bedroll and suitcase. The tiffin carrier consisted of four round brass cans stacked between two brass stems and held together by a wooden handle. She had not seen a tiffin carrier, not even thought of one, in seven years. She wondered if David had ever heard the word.

The Marwari dismantled the carrier and laid the cans side by side on the white leather seat. Around the bottoms of the cans pale yellow rings of moisture began to spread on the leather. There were wilted *chapatis* and four lemon wedges in one container, fried pumpkin and eggplant slices in another, cabbage curry in a third, and homemade yoghurt in the fourth. The spidery little man pointed to his cans like a roadside vendor and tried to tempt Tara to share his "humble and native food, Madam." Again she thought the meal had been turned into a battle by the travelers, that her answer was crucial to both men though her hunger was, to them, quite inconsequential. She accepted a wedge of lemon, sprinkling it with coarse salt, and pleaded fatigue after the long flight from America.

The sharpness of the lemon pulp and the granular taste of salt released in her faint and nostalgic agitations. As a child she had sucked lemon pieces and her mother had worried about her teeth. It'll melt the enamel, she had said, and at thirty you'll be a toothless *buddhi*. Her mother had never been to the dentist. Her grandmother Santana had chewed cane till the night before her death. Cavities they regarded as a white man's disease. Tara herself had been to the dentist only once, at the university clinic in Madison, where she had cried as a team of dental students had peered at, then extracted, her decayed wisdom teeth. The Nepali seemed to have been humiliated by Tara's obvious savoring of the lemon. The caterers' boy had long since gone with the half-eaten tray of English dinner, and he had settled down with a Hindi movie magazine in the center of his bench, careful to remove his shoes before folding his sock-less feet under him.

"Meena Kumari will be making a new picture about Goddess Durga," he announced suddenly, baring uneven yellow teeth as if he were anxious to start another bout. When Tara did not respond to this new appeal or challenge, he continued, "I see from your luggage tag you have been to New York. I too am foreign-returned. I am Ratan, not quite but almost *Prince* Ratan, Madam." Tara wondered why he did not mention his last name. "And who, may I ask, sir, are you?"

"P. K. Tuntunwala," answered the spider.

"You mean *the* Tuntunwala?" asked Ratan.

Though she generally scorned heroes, the first night back in India Tara did not mind that the man who had made room for her Samsonite bag should be a National Personage. She had heard the name Tuntunwala as a young woman in Calcutta. So this was P. K. Tuntunwala, Esq., originally of Rajasthan, but now of Bombay, Delhi and Calcutta, perhaps even of Geneva. She had heard men say that he was a corporate fear and a selfish energy. She had not expected him to remind her of a spider.

It was difficult to determine the Marwari's response to the question. His teeth were buried in a *chapati* as he sat, still and malevolent, in his corner.

"I'm Tara Banerjee Cartwright."

"You are so beautiful and you are married to a European, Madam?" The Nepali's question, or charge, went unanswered.

"We might have never met if it hadn't been for the *goondahs*," said Mr. Tuntunwala. "I only fly. But happily this was not the best of times for such action."

The Nepali ignored the Marwari and opened a small scratchy leather attaché case. Again Tara felt there was an undercurrent of venom to his smallest actions. The attaché case was jammed with snapshots. He rifled through them carelessly, spilling some on the seat near his bare feet, and some on the dusty floor.

"I want to show you something," he said, fingers curling around the black and white photographs. "I too have been to England. I know many Europeans. Bertie Russell is my friend. And Greg Peck." He finally found the picture he wanted. "Here is me in lederhosen, and her ladyship my spouse. We're eating lunch in Venice with Greg Peck. He thinks I'm a very interesting man."

It was too dark now to make out the photographed faces. If one of them were to turn on the lights, Tara wondered, would something snap? At St. Blaise's she had learned to humiliate people gently. Now on her way back to Calcutta, the gestures, the tones of voice, the deportment and dismissals that she had forgotten in the States suddenly came back with dizzying assurance. She had not thought that seven years in another country, a husband, a new blue passport could be so easily blotted out. She wanted to tell the two men sparring in the dark that she had done more than eat with movie stars, but that nothing she had thought or done could soften her suspicious nature.

The darkness outside the window deepened, giving Tara time for unhappy self-analysis. For years she had dreamed of this return to India.

She had believed that all hesitations, all shadowy fears of the time abroad would be erased quite magically if she could just return home to Calcutta. But so far the return had brought only wounds. First the corrosive hours on Marine Drive, then the deformed beggars in the railway station, and now the inexorable train ride steadily undid what strength she had held in reserve. She was an embittered woman, she now thought, old and cynical at twenty-two and quick to take offense.

Tara could not give shape to the dark scenery outside; to her it seemed merely alien and hostile. Except for vacations in the hills or at seaside resorts, she had rarely been outside Bengal. Now, amid subdued malice in a railway compartment, she thought her father's decision to send her to Vassar had been strangely ruthless, though courageous. There were dry river beds out there in the night, she decided, and dry fields and cracked mud houses on hillocks.

Ratan began to put away his photographs. He looked aggressive but defeated from the start. He was talking very rapidly now as if he believed the logic of malevolence would crush his silent and spidery enemy. He leaned closer to Tara while his faintly regal wife stared dimly out of cellulose eyes from leathered recesses.

"I think you're an especially sensitive person, Madam. I see it in your face, it is so pained and beautiful," he said to Tara, balancing himself on his heels on the white seat. "I am also like that. In fact, I don't mind telling you I have ESP. Bertie and I have talked a lot about ESP. He's interested in my ESP. He has invited me to stay with him whenever I'm in England."

"If I'm not mistaken Bertrand Russell died last year," said Tara.

The man did not seem to hear her. He continued about his extrasensory gift, issuing inarticulate little challenges to the spider in the corner. Tara wondered if she could turn this railway encounter into a story . . . *When I was in Tunla, just before the monsoons* . . . But somehow things were less ironical and manageable than she had expected. These men had desecrated her shrine of nostalgia. David at the airport, stooping and sideburned, seemed far less real than the flat-faced Nepali with extrasensory perception. She watched David's healthy face disappear into the fleshy folds of the Nepali's neck and the spider's body, and she was afraid.

"At the end there will be only a few of us left. You know that, don't you? Just a few of us special people. You will be there. Don't be afraid. I promise. I will see you there. Bertie will be there."

"And Gregory Peck?"

The spider laughed in his corner. Ratan went on and on, his voice, like snowflakes, like applause, concealing the silence of a new intimacy between the National Personage and Tara.

2

Howrah Station took Tara by surprise. The airport in Bombay had at least been clean. The squalor and confusion of Howrah Station outraged her. Coolies in red shirts broke into the compartment and almost knocked her down in an effort to carry her suitcase. The attendant sneezed on her raincoat and offered to wipe up the mess with his dusting rag. A blind beggar who had slipped in and had begun to sing and rattle his cup was thrown bodily out of the train by Tuntunwala.

Then the outrage, the confusion, lifted. She had spotted her parents. "Taramoni, my darling!" her father shouted. Time had not shrunk her parents' bulk. They were fat and authoritative on the platform, soft and sentimental as they rushed to embrace her. They dismissed the coolies and handed her bags to family servants.

The Bengal Tiger was still a handsome man, though long years of dominating relatives and factory hands had blunted the delicacy of his features. His curly black hair was cut very close, exposing two small rolls of fat at the base of the skull.

"You look so tired," pronounced the Bengal Tiger.

"I've been traveling, Daddy," said Tara, though she knew there was no excuse for looking tired in public, not even the fifteen thousand miles she had covered in three sleepless nights.

Her father inspected her, frowning, holding short fingers up to her cheek and chin. "What is this? This is not the same little girl I sent off to Vassar."

"I was only fifteen, Daddy. Have I become old and ugly?"

Tara's mother was embarrassed. "No, no, of course not. How could *you* become ugly?" She herself was a good-looking woman with finely grained skin, and dark brown hair drawn into a gentle knot. Extreme emotion was injurious to beauty, she had taught Tara; but now she was becoming almost emotional.

"But so thin," insisted her father. "Doesn't this fellow feed you?"

"I was fat when I went away, Daddy. It isn't healthy . . ."

"Yes, yes, that's all Mummy and I hear from these new Bengali doctors. I tell them if it was healthy to be thin then Calcutta would be the healthiest city in the world." He shook with sudden, loud laughter. People on the platform turned and smiled.

"Don't just stand around," shouted the Bengal Tiger to his servants. "Get those bags quickly. Where is the driver?"

While the Bengal Tiger turned to shout instructions to the chauffeur, Tara's distant relatives squeezed closer so they could touch her. They had come to the railway station in two small delivery trucks from the tobacco firm. For days they had chattered about welcoming little "Taramoni," whom they claimed to remember vividly. But now that they were actually in front of Tara, they had nothing to say to her. Surrounded by this army of relatives who professed to love her, and by vendors ringing bells, beggars pulling at sleeves, children coughing on tracks, Tara felt completely alone. Only the Bengal Tiger, body half-turned away from her while he shouted instructions, seemed to her real.

The Bengal Tiger had assumed, Tara recalled, a characteristic position. In profile his stomach stuck out extravagantly from the edges of his tropical-weight trousers. Except for the stomach, he was not really a fat man but gave the appearance of being fat.

Tara watched his body turn now left, then right, slicing as it turned through that shy and brutal atmosphere of Howrah Station. For a moment she thought she was going mad. For she felt that the Bengal Tiger, set apart from the smell and noise of the platform, had in her absence moved out of the private world of filial affection. He seemed to have become a symbol for the outside world. He had become a pillar supporting a balcony that had long outlived its beauty and its function.

During those first minutes beside an emptying and hissing train, Tara felt the crowd's reverence for her father draw toward her and then recoil, embarrassed. Awed and vulgar stares scored their triumphs against her. Then the Bengal Tiger was at her side, raising raucous laughs from the crowd, and she felt safer. She caught the sense of occasional sentences he uttered, his explanations of car arrangements, the remarks he had made to her mother at breakfast about the perfect timing of Tara's train, his grave and impersonally tragic revelation that Tara's grandmother had died four years before of a heart attack. All Calcutta, it seemed to her, had been touched by public rages and ideals; and in its ceaseless effort to escape the present, her familiar part of Calcutta had created of the Bengal Tiger its key to a more peaceful world. They leaned on him as naturally as she had. The vacation, she realized, would not be an easy one; every trivial gesture, every tea party or card game would torture her with its suspicions.

"Come along now. Let's not talk of such sad things here. As the lovely lady said, *Que será, será.* What will be, will be. We're all powerless."

So Tara was received by her family on a crowded platform in Howrah Station. The place was too noisy and filthy of course to allow her any insight into the world to which she had returned. In any case she did not excel in insights and intuitions. She did, however, feel the Bengal Tiger was slightly disappointed in her. He had said nothing of course, but then they had never really talked about important things. They had covered up misgivings with loyalty and trust. She could depend on him to protect her now that she was back within his reach; yet the certainty that he would remain loyal to her in spite of deficiencies depressed her. Calcutta had already begun to exert its darkness over her, she thought.

3

After the journey from Bombay, Tara rested for a full forty-eight hours. Her parents' house on Camac Street was designed to be restful. All anxiety and unpleasantness was prevented from entering the premises by two men in khaki suits. These men were the *durwans*, the gate-keepers. On their breast pockets, embroidered in red, they wore her father's initials. The men were proud of the uniform, which they knew would be taken away from them in the event of dismissal or resignation.

When an unfamiliar visitor approach the Banerjees' front gates, he was carefully inspected by the two *durwans*. The *durwans* relied solely on their scrutiny: hard, embarrassing, almost arrogant. For though they were armed with light nightsticks and curved daggers, they were gentle souls, and would have been afraid to use their weapons. The visitor who handled himself competently in this first trial was then escorted by the younger durwan up the semicircular driveway to the carport. On either side of the drive was a large and aggressive lawn, kept green by a full-time *mali* and his six-year-old son. The *mali*'s job was to make sure there were enough flowers for the daily religious rituals, and for the thirty-odd vases and bowls scattered throughout the house.

The lawn was rarely used. It was too hot during the day to sit out-doors, and in any case Tara's mother, who suffered from headaches, preferred the darkness of the air-conditioned interior. The Banerjees would perhaps have liked to sip their cocktails outdoors, but they were inhibted by their good breeding. It was considered impolite to eat in full view of others, and though there were high brick walls studded with spikes and shards of glass, they were afraid someone might spy from an upstairs window.

At the carport the visitor was handed over by the *durwan* to the bearer, who then escorted him to the hall, verandah, or formal drawing room. To enter the hall, one had to pass through gigantic double doors, hung with coir blinds. The blinds were sprayed with rose-scented cold water on the hour. These doors remained open all day, but were chained and padlocked in four separate places at ten every night when the family retired. A few servants who had been with the family for at least eight years, and who had business in the house early in the morning, were allowed to sleep in the main building. The rest of the staff, their wives, children, cousins and occasional friends, lived in the servants' quarters behind the house.

The hall was eclectically furnished. Italian marble tables, and mahogany tables in the shapes of hearts, clubs, diamonds and spades, occupied the dingy corners. On two heart-shaped tables stood enormous ebony elephants. On the high-ceilinged walls hung framed photographs of earlier Banerjees. From legend one knew these Banerjees had noble faces, that some had been photographed in yogic positions, bare chests girdled by Brahminic thread. But the grime on the glass made these facts impossible to verify. As a child Tara had often amused herself, especially in the rainy season, by scratching the grease with her long fingernails. But she could only reach the toes and ankles of the photographed men. In a poorly lit corner hung one headless tiger skin. It had been acquired by Tara's maternal grandfather, a hunter of moderate renown, before he had given up big-game hunting. Tara's father was not a sportsman.

The living room was filled with imported furniture—heavy, dark, incongruous pieces whose foreignness had been only slightly mitigated by brilliantly colored Indian upholstery. In built-in glass cabinets, expecting to be admired, were large, tarnished silver cups that Tara and her father before her had won in annual debating championships.

"I like glass cabinets," Tara's mother had often said. "We're honest people. We have nothing to hide." She obviously had the courage of her convictions, for she did not try to hide the one tiny cup, a fifth prize, that the Bengal Tiger had won in the egg-and-teaspoon race on the Banerjee & Thomas [Tobacco] Co. Sports Day.

On the days the *mali* performed his work, clumps of tropical flowers sprang from the vases. They had been arranged by Tara's mother, who had been trained in the minor decorative arts, to sing well, play the sitar, supervise cooks, and above all to please her husband and her in-laws. There was a great deal of dust everywhere. The sweepers cleaned regularly, morning and late afternoon, but they were not expected to rid the room of dust. There were occasional ants on the floor, large, black and indolent. Insects were not a source of embarrassment.

An old-fashioned wooden door, armed with steel bolts, hooks, and chains, draped with diaphanous pink net curtains, gave access to a spacious verandah. As a child, surprisingly shy in spite of the solidity of her background, Tara had found the verandah the most comfortable place in the house. She had loved the chalky whiteness of its walls, pillars and grilles. Against this whiteness exploded bougainvilleas, purple and vermilion, hibiscus, marigolds, full-bodied dahlias, cascades of golden laburnum. These flowers were not carefully contained in vases or bowls, but grew, almost in spite of the *mali*, in pots lining the wide edges of the balcony railing. They flowered in insolent detachment from the landscaped garden below, sharing nothing with the cut flowers in the living room so pleasantly arranged, nothing with the Banerjee family and their servants who loved flowers. They grew as if they had independent destinies.

Dwarfed by the flowers were two deep canvas easy chairs—reminiscent of the order and ease of the British days without its bitterness or alarms —four green rattan chairs, a table, and a low divan. Pale brown lizards slept on the walls of this verandah, and once Tara had seen a chameleon among the flowers.

The only extraordinary equipment in the verandah was a Sears and Roebuck garden swing, sold to the Banerjees by a departing librarian of the local USIS. The swing had been redone by the family tailor in green and yellow brocade. Even the awning was made from silk brocade. Though the swing was no doubt intended to be hammered into the earth, it had adapted itself to Bengal Tiger Banerjee's wishes, and settled firmly into the marble floors of the verandah. And here was the tableau she suddenly remembered: in the center of the garden swing, with his wife at his side (she suffered his drinking grimly), a servant massaging his tired feet, would sit the Bengal Tiger, confident and sentimental, over his nightly pegs of local Scotch.

After seven years abroad, after extraordinary turns of destiny that had swept her from Calcutta to Poughkeepsie, and Madison, and finally to a two-room apartment within walking distance of Columbia, strange turns that had taught her to worry over a dissertation on Katherine Mansfield, the plight of women and racial minorities, Tara was grateful to call this restful house home.

The house on Camac Street began to exercise its hypnosis on her. New York, she thought now, had been exotic. Not because it had laundromats and subways. But because there were policemen with dogs prowling the underground tunnels. Because girls like her, at least almost like her, were being knifed in elevators in their own apartment buildings. Because students were rioting about campus recruiters and faraway wars rather than the price of rice or the stiffness of final exams. Because people were agitated over pollution. The only pollution she had been warned against in Calcutta had been caste pollution. New York was certainly extraordinary, and it had driven her to despair. On days she had thought she could not possibly survive, she had shaken out all her silk scarves, ironed them and hung them to make the apartment more "Indian." She had curried hamburger desperately till David's stomach had protested.

"I can think of a perfect ad for Alka-Seltzer . . ." he had begun, and she had blushed at her own inconsiderateness.

She had burned incense sent from home (You must be careful about choosing brands when it comes to incense, her mother always said), till the hippie neighbors began to take an undue interest in her.

Now she was home, surrounded by imported furniture, in a house that filtered sunlight and unwelcome guests through an elaborate system of coir blinds, rose-water sprays, *durwans*, bearers, heavy doors, locks, chains and hooks. She was home in a class that lived by Victorian rules, changed decisively by the exuberance of the Hindu imagination. Now she was in a city that took for granted most men were born to suffer, others to fall asleep during committee meetings of the chamber of commerce. She was among the ordinary and she felt rested.

While Tara sat in an easy chair, trying hard to relax and recover, a vision, not necessarily benevolent, hidden by flowers and lizards, smiled at her audacity, then quickly retired.

4

On her third day in Calcutta, Tara's mother took her to visit the relatives.

"They will be so offended if we delay any more."

"But I'm still tired," Tara objected.

"Take us to Southern Avenue first," the mother said to the chauffeur. "Poor Jharna must be given top priority."

"Yes, *memsahib*."

"She's had such a hard life. Why does *Bhagwan* permit such cruelty? Your Uncle Sachin died of cancer, and that child of hers is clubfooted."

"So it *was* cancer, after all?"

"Yes. From Jharna's we'll look at saris at New Market. We'll keep the rest of the relatives for another day."

Aunt Jharna and her children lived on the middle floor of a shabby and malevolent building. There were a cabinetmaker and a palmist's clinic on the ground floor; Aunt Jharna lived on the second; a tenant's consumptive family on the third.

The chauffeur let out the two women, and then ran forward to ring the doorbell. There was really no need to ring. A boy of about fourteen in short *khaki* pants was standing at the front door.

"*Namaste, Didimoni*," the boy said, with folded hands. "*Memsahib* is waiting for you upstairs."

The chauffeur returned to the car, flicking it arrogantly with a yellow feather duster, protecting its luster from the fingerprints of neighborhood beggars, while the women followed the servant boy. They went across a tiny inner courtyard, up an open, steep staircase to a spacious foyer. The foyer, partly enclosed by walls and partly by long canvas hangings, was filled with smoke fumes. In the pungent grayness Tara could barely make out her aunt, who was seated on the floor, fanning a clay incense burner. A little girl in a printed cotton dress sat on a rattan chair, and dangled her bare feet above the smoking incense.

"*Didi*, how good of you to come," Aunt Jharna said. "I'll be through with this very soon." Aunt Jharna was an angular woman with a sallow complexion that passed for fairness in India. She continued to fan with an elaborately decorated hand fan, and when that did not produce results quickly enough she blew into the incense burner till her cheeks looked almost transparent and about to burst.

"Mother," said the little girl, "it hurts."

Tara wondered what hurt, the feet or the smoke. She was revolted. Not so much by the legs, absurdly misshapen, but by the scene, by the arrangement of child, mother and incense burner. The fumes, perfumed, opaque, holy, swirled around the women. Tara knew, from remembered scraps of her mother's letters, those feet had pleaded before London-trained Bengali surgeons, Seventh Day Adventists, dead Moslem saints, and tribal faith healers.

"Have you tried plaster casts and special shoes, Aunt Jharna?" asked Tara, wanting to spare herself the humiliation of the scene.

"You think you are too educated for this, don't you?" Aunt Jharna laughed with a quiet violence. "You have come back to make fun of us, haven't you? What gives you the right? Your American money? Your *mleccha* husband?"

Tara heard the embarrassed jingle of her mother's gold bracelets.

"Jharma, don't work yourself up again. She was trying to be helpful, and you know that."

"They're all alike, these college girls, they think they are too educated for us."

If it had not been for a strange, unexpected little twinge called love, Tara would have screamed and run out of the house to the safety of the car.

"Why do you despise our ways? That's what comes of going to a school like St. Blaise's."

How does the foreignness of the spirit begin? Tara wondered. Does it begin right in the center of Calcutta, with forty ruddy Belgian women, fat foreheads swelling under starched white headdresses, long black habits intensifying the hostility of the Indian sun? The nuns had taught her to inject the right degree of venom into words like "common" and "vulgar." They had taught her *The Pirates of Penzance* in singing class, and "If I should die, think only this of me—" for elocution.

Did the foreignness drift inward with the winter chill at Vassar, as she watched the New York snow settle over new architecture, blonde girls, Protestant matrons, and Johnny Mathis? Or was it not till Madison that she first suspected the faltering of the heart?

Madison had been unbearable that first winter. Then one chilly morning in the spring of 1967 David Cartwright had thrust himself through the closing doors of an elevator. "It's been a violent day," he had said, and Tara had fallen in love with him before the elevator ride was over. It was silly to ask oneself questions of the heart, Tara decided. There were no definite points in time that one could turn to and accuse or feel ashamed of as the start of this dull strangeness.

The smoke had made her drowsy. She wanted to pull apart the canvas hangings, so that thin rays of sunlight could insinuate themselves through the tall, narrow buildings and the incense fumes.

"It's too late anyway," Tara said, trying to apologize.

"Why do you hate us" Aunt Jharna demanded.

If she were more passionate she might have said, I don't hate you, I love you, and the miserable child, the crooked feet, the smoking incense holder, I love you all.

The servant saved the situation. He brought in two plates of sweet-meats, set them on low gate-legged tables, and said, with obvious pride, in English, "Good app'tite, *Didimoni!*"

The sweetmeats, circular, white and stolid, rested on heavy blue-ringed china plates on the dusty, filigreed table tops.

"Eat, eat, *Didimoni,*" encouraged the servant from the doorway. "Don't be shy. Treat this house like your own."

"The eight-*anna* size *rosogolla* becomes smaller and harder every week," sighed Aunt Jharna. "So many sweetmeat-makers have com mitted suicide because of the sugar shortage." She had regained her composure of the repressed, and was quietly putting away the incense.

Fearing another attack from her aunt, Tara ate quickly, digging the light aluminum teaspoon into the heart of the *rosogolla*. As Tara and her mother were being shown out by the servant boy, he said, "She is bad-tempered after each fast, and the fasts get longer and longer for *missybaba's* legs. But she's been a mother to me, no, she has been a goddess."

5

On the roof of the Catelli-Continental, dwarfed by two potted mag-nolias, sat Joyonto Roy Chowdhury, owner of tea estates in Assam. He was dressed in a blazer with shiny buttons, crisp white trousers, and sockless sandals. A can, crooked and gnarled, lay on the table next to the morning newspaper. In his youth Joyonto must have been startlingly handsome. Even now he had the deportment of the handsome young. But a habitual and deep distrust gave his face a slightly malicious sneer. It was a face that had known restlessness or failure, the face of a states-men whose country had let him down.

Joyonto's years of distrust had been preceded by many more years of ignorance. Till recently he had gone about his family's business without any distractions. He had inspected his tea plantations, attended annual trade meetings in London, interviewed young trainees from the management schools, consoled widows, placed the sons of faithful employees, and in short, done all the things expected of him and his class. Like his friends in those peaceful times, he had read the Vedas in translation, executed simple lotus positions, consulted astrologers for auspicious occasions and had even fasted on serious provocation. He had suffered no mysteries, and certainly no revelations.

Then one morning very early in the sixties, late for an appointment with a local tobacco magnate (the astrologer had prophesied failure anyway), he had entered the Catelli for the first time. He had taken the self-service lift up to the open-air café, ordered an espresso, and there on the roof of the hotel, alone among giant flowerpots and undersized waiters, he had been struck by the awesome failure of his love. It was a curious and sudden self-judgment, provoked by no incident at the Catelli, no snub, or threat, unless the stench and cries of Chowringhee Avenue can be taken for accusations by decent men.

After that morning of revelation, Joyonto Roy Chowdhury returned to the Catelli every day to order coffee that he rarely drank and to reflect on the deep consequences of a fate he did not understand. He was neither hurt nor angered by the knowledge of personal failure; it merely directed his attention to public questions. He thought his own destiny was but a faint shadow of what Calcutta could expect. And so, like the city, he watched the ugly decay from his hotel perch.

In time the sidewalks beneath Joyonto grew restless with refugees from East Bengal and Tibet. Rioters became insolent. Powerful landowners were at first tormented, later beheaded. Businessmen padlocked their factories and snuck off like ghosts to richer provinces. Housewives cried at night, or retreated into screaming hate.

6

On a bright Monday morning, bare feet withdrawn from sandals and blazer tightly buttoned, Joyonto sat at his usual corner in the open-air café of the Catelli-Continental and leaned over the sun-warmed edge of the balcony to survey Chowringhee Avenue below. On the grassy *maidan* across the street two small boys were running with a kite. A group of beggar women sat under a tree, drying their long black hair. A dog wearing a garland of marigolds panted in his sleep beside a trident-carrying holy man. Farther off middle-aged men in shorts were playing soccer with a soft ball.

"Coffee, *sahib?*" asked the waiter, but did not wait for the old man's answer. Joyonto looked down at his toes, very fair and cracked around the heels, then was distracted by a swirl of pale cotton saris and dark worsted pants advancing toward his table. The legs, the multicolored sandals and black oxfords came nearer and nearer, and the old man panicked and took refuge in a crazy game of words. He liked to call the game his "short-sighted visionary small talk." *Truth is a head on a stake.* The feet had passed his table. But he persevered with his game. *Nostrils are lined with the sourness of death. The sun this year is evil.* Six men and women had joined two tables close to him, and were settling down now in a flurry of pale colors. *Sleep chars the body.* The newcomers began to distract him with their loud talk and gestures; there was no longer any pleasure or safety for him in words though he tried to return to them again and again. *We are the sum of our cities and houses.* The effort only fatigued him, so he abandoned the game of phrases and eavesdropped instead on the elegant newcomers.

For almost an hour he watched and listened to the young people, having nothing to do or say himself. The city had dried the blood in his body, and now he had lost even his curious phrases. *On the skeletons of cows skyscrapers will rise.* But he knew it was no use, the new guests had disturbed his surface of words, and now he must yield to their terrible presence. He thought they were very much as he had been in his twenties, and the thought frightened him even more than he had expected. The young men and women reminded him of trapped gazelles though they were confident, handsome and brashly opinionated as they joked across the aqua tables. They spoke mainly in English, occasionally changing to Bengali in midsentence, almost always in exclamations, favoring "How dare you!" and "What nonsense!" He heard them list with enthusiasm movies they had seen or parties they had recently attended. As he rubbed his cracked and dirt-grained heels against the aqua legs of the table, Joyonto heard their conversation alight on imported gadgets, on stereos, transistors, blenders and percolators; each foreign word was treated with a holy reverence. When they touched current events he thought it was mainly to show their familiarity with *Time* magazine or *Reader's Digest.* The real Calcutta, the thick laughter of brutal men, open dustbins, warm and dark where carcasses were sometimes discarded, did not exist. He knew Calcutta would not be as kind to them as it had been to him.

He tried to comfort himself again with his game of phrases, scurrying desperately between words, long ones and skinny ones, slow ones and sharp ones, to build his defense. *Hill stations are cavities. Smell. Prick the night and see it swell. Cuts and nicks that house insects. Dogs feed on curried cabbage. Smell, smell.* Then a young woman walked in, a sober or subdued young woman, who was greeted with extraordinary emotion by the six newcomers, and Joyonto turned slowly on his aqua seat to watch her.

Luminous Brahmin children must be saved, Joyonto said.

7

"My! It's so weird to have you back here, Tara!"

"I can't believe you've ever been away. She hasn't changed one bit, isn't that just too much!"

"What nonsense, she wasn't always so glamorous! I mean look at her short hair and all. And that sari! It *has* to be from New York!"

They studied Tara with obsessive attention as if she were not present. They seemed perfectly relaxed as they discussed her hair, the shade of her lipstick, her sunglasses; Tara was startled at their tremendous capacity for surfaces. She sat in their midst, cowed and nervous while her silence drove them to more indelicate, more damaging remarks about her appearance. Then having tired of that, they moved lightly to other favorite topics, leaving Tara miserably acquiescent.

"Tara, don't you think Calcutta's changed unbelievably? I mean can you recognize this place at all?"

"Wait till you've seen a riot here. They're really something!"

"What nonsense! She better not listen to you people. She's an *Americawali* now, she won't know you're joking."

"They raided five schools last week. What do you mean?"

"Stop, stop, *arré baba!* Are you going to fight?"

"Talking of schools, Tara should see how St. Blaise's has changed! Those nuns are taking in Marwaris by the dozens!"

"Really, everything. I mean just everything's gone down horribly. Everything stinks nowadays."

It was hard for Tara to respond to the changes in the city and at St. Blaise's. Her friends had warmed to their subject. They were locked in a private world of what should have been and they relished every twinge of resentment and defeat that time had reserved for them. Tara cut through insulating layers of American experiences till she could visualize again Mother Peter entering a classroom, rosary muffled by her habit, to trap violators of the silence rule. She thought at this moment David was probably sitting in his lumpy green chair, surrounded by quarterlies and radical journals and missing her very much.

"I'm telling you at the first hint of riot. Tara's going to run away to America, no?"

"How dare you suggest she'll run away? At least Calcutta isn't uncultured like Bombay!"

Some instinct or intuition told her to stay away from these people who were her friends, only more, much more, for they were shavings of her personality. She feared their tone, their omissions, their aristocratic oneness. They had asked her about the things she brought back, had admired her velours jumpsuit and electric lady-shaver, but not once had they asked about her husband. (Of course I didn't bring *him* back, she thought.) Seven years ago she had worn a garland of roses and gardenias and a yoghurt spot on her forehead for luck, and had taken a plane to America. Seven years ago she had played with these friends, done her homework with Nilima, briefly fancied herself in love with Pronob, debated with Reena at the British Council.

"Calcutta's going to the dogs. No question about it. It's going to the left-of-leftists. It's going communist."

"Oh, don't even mention that word. It reminds me of Mother Xavier on her knees, trying to save the world."

"You know, I can't bring myself to read any Dostoevski," said Nilima.

"But I don't think he was a—," said Tara.

"So what, he was a Russian, wasn't he?"

"I didn't blame the leaders," said Pronob. "It's the workers that disgust me. We pay medical insurance for them, pension plans, education taxes for their kids, and what do they do? Turn round and *gherao* us."

"*Gherao*," repeated Tara "I read about it in the States."

"You may have read about it, dear girl, but you can't possibly know what it is."

"If these *gheraos* continue, we'll all have to move Bombay-side. What a ghastly prospect!"

"Do you know what they did at Pronob's factory?"

"Please, please. I don't want to talk about it," he said with a worldly flourish. "Certainly not in front of these ladies."

"Come on, Pronob, be a sport," said Tara.

"Well, if you feel you can take it. These *goondahs* surrounded us for eighteen hours. There was no food, no water, no nothing. When we tried to get water, do you know what these comm ——, left-of-leftists did? They sent in a Coke bottle filled with . . ." he hesitated. Conversations about bathrooms were not permitted in Calcutta's westernized society.

"I understand," said Tara.

"A damn lot of cheek I call it, a damn lot of gall." The young man quivered with passion.

What were they to do? Tara wondered. Should they leave for Bombay and let the rich Marwaris fight it out with the *goondahs*? The Marwaris were less vulnerable. They belched in public, they wiped their noses on their shirt-sleeves, they were insensitive. They could stand up to the communists. But what of the poor Bengalis, the descendants of Hari Lal Banerjee who had inherited, not earned, their wealth, their frailties, their conscience? Bombay, she knew, was no answer. It was like Chekhov, she felt, yearning for Moscow but staying.

Tara had, perhaps unfortunately, allowed literature to disturb the placid surface of her life. At Vassar she had heard first of existentialism, followed closely by postexistentialism. That first winter in Poughkeepsie she had been given Sartre and Camus, Rilke and Mann, and the Joyce beyond *Dubliners*, and her closed little heart had been flooded. She had even begun writing stories about Calcutta based on the style and subtleties of Joyce and she had stopped only when they had become too easy, too obvious. How could she tell her friends that Bombay was no answer, that people in Bombay snickered at Tagore, and that the girls there wore skirts and were trained for office work? They would have to learn to endure *gheraos* and Coke bottles filled with urine and vulgar men leering at them. But how could she explain the bitterness of it to David, who would have laughed at her friends and wished them luck as refugees and beggars in Shambazar? What would he care? He'd laughed when she described Rajah's burial in a children's cemetery, been disgusted that a servant had been kept just to feed and walk a dog.

"It's all so very different," Tara said. "And it's going to be a lot more different . . . and tragic."

"Don't be silly!" Pronob retorted. "We've got to beat this nonsense out of the system. Purge our factories of unions and things like that."

Tara was not familiar with unions, labor demands or picket lines. Only once when the Bengal Tiger was young had there been a strike and lockout at Banerjee & Thomas [Tobacco] Co., Ltd. There had been no melodrama then that Tara could remember. No petrol-filled Coke bottles, no vulgar exchanges. Only the Bengal Tiger's moving rhetoric. In the end her father's words, intense, hard and sincere, had set him above the other directors. For her father the strike had been a triumph. He had been challenged and he had brought order to his men. But now the shapes of factories and men were different. An appetite for the grotesque had taken over the city. There was no room for heroic oratory in Calcutta; Tara understood that from Pronob's anecdote.

As if to confirm Tara's fears, Pronob shouted, "Come on, you people. Let's be happy-go-lucky, please. Tara, why are you looking so somber?"

Joyonto Roy Chowdhury, two tables away, observed to himself that these men and women, so tall, so straight and elegant, were the last pillars of his world. They did not know or care that a revolution was on its way. They were content to sit at the Catelli and rage against the vulgarity of small riots. He marveled at their dedication to the trivial. Addicted to phrases and words, he said: *Breathe is demolished like green rust. History is a tramline uprooted in Shambazar.* He thought they deserved to die as they called out comic and angry eulogies for a wretched Calcutta—all except the luminous girl who sat like a grateful outcaste. And Joyonto, the old player of phrases, the man who had felt clutches of hurt in the whitest folds of his brain, vowed to seek out this girl and preserve her from the others.

8

Tara's mother, Arati, was a saintly woman. At least, she was given to religious dreams. Her religious dreams were not holy enough to turn her hair white overnight (as had happened to her grandmother once in Pachapara), but they were adequately religious. She could tell, for instance, through Kali or Mother Durga, which pregnant relative would be blessed with a male child, which niece or nephew would pass the final matriculation examination, or which out-of-town acquaintance would suddently arrive unannounced for a month's visit. Once, in younger days, she had dreamed of Vishnu buried deep in the ground, crying to her for help, and her father's workmen, digging according to her instructions, had disinterred two Vishnu statues.

As a saintly woman, Tara's mother spent a great deal of time in the prayer room. To reach the family's prayer room, she had to pass through a dressing room, a bathroom and Tara's study. She managed to leave behind a considerable religious residue in each of these rooms. In the dressing room Arati stored her precious jewelry and life-insurance policies in three fireproof eight-foot steel cabinets. She called the life-insurance policies "those things," and looked after them with a zealot's fastidiousness. "Those things" had caused her great pain. Her mother-in-law had accused her of trying to kill her son. Widowed in-laws had humiliated her by giving her the boniest piece of curried fish at public feasts. A great-uncle-in-law had forced her to choose between "those things" and the affections of the joint-family system. Arati had chosen allegiance to life-insurance policies and had moved to the house on Camac Street with her steel cabinets and her husband.

Tara, trying to explain and share her background with David (he had so little, just his divorced mother in Boston whom he called infrequently) had found "those things" embarrassing. She had feared a foreigner would not understand such devotion to insurance terms and payments. It was the one detail in her life she had deliberately misrepresented.

"My mother's a very modern woman," she had said to David. "She believes in those things. And wills and all that. She thinks of them as

PROGRESS. I mean things were really bad for Bengali women, it's not funny."

The saintly mother also spent an unreasonable amount of time in the bathroom next to the dressing room. Taking three baths a day was a principle with her. These baths were carefully timed, and on the occasions the Palta Waterworks stopped the water supply for a few hours, Arati was devastated. This bathroom was in the "English style," which meant it was equipped with an erratic commode, bathtub and shower in addition to the many pails, cisterns and drains of the native bathroom. There were three other "Indian style" bathrooms in the house.

Why three baths a day for God's sake?" David had asked.

"Would *you* like to touch God when you're all horribly sweaty and dirty?" Really, there was no end to David's naive questions.

Arati's religiosity had encountered no difficulty in Tara's study; Hari Lal's granddaughter Arati was incapable of defeat. She had merely diversified her religiosity. She had selected with worshipful pride chairs, bookcases and desks (there were two); she had spent hours choosing and cooking carp's brain and spinach so Tara might improve her intelligence. Wooden bookcases filled with titles like *Westward Ho, Kon-Tiki,* and *Seven Years in Tibet,* all prizes won at St. Blaise's, lined three walls of the study. Against the fourth wall stood a tall metal bookshelf that had been requisitioned from the reading room of the Banerjee & Thomas [Tobacco] Co., Ltd. This held the school textbooks Tara had used since the age of three when she had been sent to St. Blaise's in earnest. Tara's mother had read every single book on those shelves.

The study led to the prayer room where Arati was at her best. Long after, on homesick afternoons at Vassar, or after misunderstandings with David, or when things went badly between her and Katherine Mansfield, she thought of Camac Street, especially of her mother on a tiny Mirzapur rug, voluminous hips outspread, praying to rows of gods and goddesses.

"It's hard to explain," she had said to the foreign student adviser at Vassar. "I just can't pray here. It doesn't come. Do you know what I mean?"

And the foreign student adviser, who had not known what she meant, had invited her to worship with her at the nearest Episcopalian church every Sunday.

The prayer room was bright, airy and curtainless. Since there was very little furniture in the room, it looked much larger than it really was. Its floor was of white marble, streaked gently with gray. When the morning sun rushed in through the windows, unimpeded by curtains, the floor seemed to dance like waves. The wall farthest from Tara's study supported a marble platform, a sentimental birthday gift from the Bengal Tiger to his religious wife. The Banerjees were serious about birthdays. On this platform stood five small hand-carved tables, their workmanship almost hidden by silk tablecloths. And on these tables were brass and silver deities wearing fresh garlands.

A fortnight after her return to India Tara sat in this room while her mother dusted the icons with affectionate care. If her mother's mind was mainly on God, Tara's was with David's letter, which arrived earlier that day. David wrote that he had brought two or three books on India and that he would read them if his own writing went badly; that the fifth chapter of his novel was proving tedious; that this summer there weren't too many people he knew around; that Susie Goldberg was now peevish over sexism but still capable of occasional charm. A procession of poorly recalled phrases from David's letter moved about the room and was set on fire by the morning sun, charring the precise order and meaning of his words.

So David had bought books on India. This innocent information enraged Tara. She thought the letter was really trying to tell her that he had not understood her country through her, that probably he had not understood her either. Congenitally suspicious, she turned to David's remarks about Susie Goldberg, who Tara now slowly remembered had her rather charming moments. Tara sensed the beginnings of a long headache that was just fastening itself to her neck and eyeballs. David should have theorized about politics and literature. After all he was always trying to educate her, always telling her the names of obscure congressmen and senators, and buying her paperbacks that she concealed in kitchen drawers. Now that David had confessed his weaknesses, his troubles with his novel, Susie Goldberg's occasional charm, Tara was afraid he no longer wanted to make her over to his ideal image, that he no longer loved her.

Once Tara had admitted this monstrous fear, other suspicions and questions quickly appeared. Perhaps her mother, sitting serenely before God on a tiny rug, no longer loved her either. After all Tara had willfully abandoned her caste by marrying a foreigner. Perhaps her mother was offended that she, no longer a real Brahmin, was constantly in and out of this sacred room, dipping like a crow. She thought her mother had every right to be wary of aliens and outcastes. Once when the local Rotary Club had sent them an Australian religious fanatic for a fortnight, Arati had resorted to mild deceit to keep him out of the prayer room.

"How to explain our God to these Europeans?" Arati had said at the time. To Tara's mother all white men were Europeans and she trusted them only when they were in their proper place. Now Tara saw herself as that unwelcome Australian. Still pained by the odd scraps from David's letter, disturbed by the authentic religious emotions of her mother, she thought it best to go away.

"Don't leave," her mother said, swiveling slightly on her tiny carpet but not breaking the rhythm of her Sanskrit prayers.

For a moment all caution against insults and hurts left Tara. She was moved. She wanted to make some lighthearted rejoinder—"I wouldn't dream of leaving," or something of the sort—but no words would come to her, so she offered with signs to grind the sandalwood paste for the morning's rituals.

"Thank you," whispered her mother, then leaned forward on her knees to offer flowers to a silver icon that Uncle Pomegranate had brought back from a business trip to Gujarat.

When the sandalwood paste had been ground Tara scraped it off the slimy stone tablet with her fingers and poured it into a small silver bowl. But she could not remember the next step of the ritual. It was not a simple loss, Tara feared, this forgetting of prescribed actions; it was a little death, a hardening of the heart, a cracking of axis and center. But her mother came quickly with the relief of words.

"If you've finished making that thing, dear, why don't you just go ahead and bathe Shiva."

"I was just getting ready to do that."

She took down the Shiva-*lingam* from its perch on a tale. It was coal black and five inches high, a stone cylindrical protrusion above a stone flower. She thought it looked quite jaunty. With two fingers she dropped some sandalwood paste on the tip of the protrusion and watched it slide down and splash against the black petals of the flower. She did it again and again, savoring the feel of cold paste and stone, then returned the Shiva-*lingam* to its rightful place on the table.

Tara thought a Hindu was always set apart by his God. The icons before her seemed so exuberant on the silk tablecloths that she wanted to rely on them. In her childhood these icons had worn gold ornaments, tiny 22 karat necklaces and anklets that she had dusted clean with cotton balls. But her mother had donated the ornaments to the Camac Street Ladies' Club Brave Jawan Fund during a border skirmish. It was impossible to explain to a foreigner the extraordinariness of this sacrifice. In Madison, Tara had once read a letter from home to her roommate from Hokkaido, and the girl had giggled loudly. It had been a touching letter, she now recalled.

"We're doing our best for the brave jawans *[her mother had written in Bengali]. We have just started the Camac Street Emergency Ladies' Club and Brave Jawan Fund, and I've been chosen [unanimously] president.*

*We're making bandages from old saris every afternoon (2 P.M.–4 P.M.).
Don't worry. We have Patton tanks and many Bengali captains and generals. We'll be successful. Write me more about your studies. I'm sure
Goddess Saraswati will make you famous and a doctorate soon. I've told
your grandmother (paternal) that I may not have sons like her, but my
one daughter is equal to ten sons. I shall pray to Saraswati for success in
your exams. On Saraswati Pujah day remember to wear something yellow, she has always looked after you before."*

Tara, who remembered all insults, who allowed grudges to ferment
till they were unbearable, had never forgiven the girl from Hokkaido.
She had continued to room with her, tolerating her only for her efficiency
in killing mice.

She wondered how David would react if he could see her that instant.

Her mother clapped her hands, and a line of servants' children entered
the room. They arranged themselves against the far wall, quiet and alert,
like a row of sandalwood monkeys. Tara's mother asked them questions
about their school, their marble games, their sick cousins and brothers
as she sliced bananas and oranges and placed them in neat designs on
tiny silver plates.

"Song time now," Arati said finally.

The children began to sing. Their voices were harsh and unformed.
Tara's first impulse was to clap her hands over her ears; she had not
expected such harshness from children. The rough notes and mispronounced names of God mingled dangerously with the sun and incense
smoke of the prayer room.

> Raghupati Raghava Rajaram
> Patita Pavana Sitaram

Tara wanted to sing too, hoping for words, the repetition would stave
off the madness that curled under the pungent sunlight. She thought the
walls of her mind were caving in like black tenement buildings in Shambazar. The children near Tara were screaming now, making each *Raghupati* and *Raghava* crackle, eyeing the fruits offered to the icons on silver
plates. Their bright animal-eyes darted from little table to table. A liveliness or greed settled on the children and quickened their song. Tara
had not thought that holy names could seem so abrasive.

Then the singing stopped as suddenly as it had begun, leaving Tara
unappeased and irritable. The children were making their *pronams* before
the icons, their little bottoms turned up in the air, foreheads touching
the floor.

"Time for *prasad*," said Tara's mother. "No pushing and shoving
please. You know that there's quite enough for all." Fairly and skillfully

she divided the oranges and bananas till the last drying slice had disappeared. Some of the children exchanged *prasad* with each other, clawing and snatching; others tied their share in dirty handkerchiefs to carry back to their parents.

"Tonight we'll have extra special *bhajan*. Come back tonight. Come and sing again." Then Arati turned to Tara and added softly, "It will really be extra special if you come. Very fine *bhajan*."

Was her mother crying? Tara wondered. Or had her eyelids always been so gray? She was still a very beautiful woman, and reasonably young. If she had tried, Tara might have calculated Arati's age within five years. But it was inauspicious to know exactly. Long waves of brownish-black hair hung down her back and curled on the floor near her hips. The face was perfectly oval. And sad, Tara thought, in spite of the promised *bhajan*. As a child, Tara remembered, she had sung *bhajans* in that house. She had sat on a love seat beside a very holy man with a limp and had sung *Raghupati Raghava Rajaram*. But that had been a very long time ago, before some invisible spirit or darkness had covered her like skin.

"You will try?"

It was a simple request to share piety with her family. But Tara hid behind flippant remarks, dragging up half-forgotten invitations to parties and charity carnivals as defenses against her mother's request. Both mother and daughter grew nervous, their nervousness visible like monsoon mildew. Outside the heaviness of noon heat had lightened, though afternoon and coolness were still hours away. Tara knew that in the end she would not stay. She could hear the servants' children in the garden below, probably helping their fathers or uncles weed and rake. There were occasional barks from a tired dog, no doubt a *pariah* the children had brought in without telling their parents. There were more tired barks, pale screams, the soft sounds of slaps, and finally the customary quiet settled over Camac Street.

"I really wish I could stay," Tara said.

9

There were many parties in honor of Tara's return. Many teas, many dinners hosted by friends to convince her Calcutta could be as much fun as her New York or Madison. Some of these were written up in the *Feminine Weekly* and the *Ladies of Calcutta Journal*. It was quite evident to people who cared about such things that the city's westernized high society had fallen in love with the Bengali young woman from the States.

The celebrations in her honor frightened Tara. These celebrations were very proper, very lavish in fact, involving rented canopies, caterers' men, nasty young ladies whispering in the garden while poets recited their Sassoonesque verse.

At first Tara had looked forward to these parties. She had rushed to Pronob's or Reena's so she could share reminiscences with people who understood her attitudes and mistakes. Her friends had seemed to her a peaceful island in the midst of Calcutta's commotion. She had leaned heavily on their self-confidence.

Then after the first round of parties, the beliefs and omissions of her friends began to unsettle her. She was not an unpatriotic person, but she felt very distant from the passions that quickened or outraged her class in Calcutta. Her friends let slip their disapproval of her, they suggested her marriage had been imprudent, that the seven years abroad had eroded all that was fine and sensitive in her Bengali nature. They felt she deserved chores like washing her own dishes and putting out the garbage. The best that could be said for David, she sensed, was that he was, nominally at least, a Christian and not a Moslem.

Pronob's group irritated Tara with its lack of seriousness. The group often sat on the roof of the Catelli-Continental, imagining itself successful and splendid, smoking and swearing in public to flout conventions, imploring Tara not to smile at strange old men in blazers and sun hats. They longed to listen to stories about America, about television and automobiles and frozen foods and record players. But when she mentioned ghettos or student demonstrations her friends protested. What nonsense! They knew America was lovely, they knew New York was not like Calcutta.

Of course they preferred stories about the Calcutta they had all shared. They came back again and again to the nuns of St. Blaise's and to the Radio Ceylon disc jockeys they had worshiped as schoolchildren.

"Did you know Carefree Kevin wasn't English? He was Polish," said Nilima. She was a beautiful girl, a little too chubby perhaps, but a beautiful girl waiting to be married. Her parents were constantly interviewing relatives of possible bridegrooms. She entertained secret fantasies about movie stars like Uttam Kumar and Tony Perkins, and considered the efforts of her parents vulgar.

"My cousin in Bombay," began Tara, "saw Carefree Kevin once. She said he isn't too magnetic."

"What nonsense! Your cousin must be a liar."

One afternoon at the Catelli-Continental, which seemed to Tara much like all other afternoons at the café there, Pronob was unusually withdrawn and severe. Instead of answering their arguments with his own beliefs on disc jockeys and missionaries, he shouted, "Can you shut up for a sec, folks? I want to listen to the English news."

THE TIGER'S DAUGHTER / 583

"Don't be a dashed bore," objected Nilima. "I don't want to hear about bombings. I want music instead."

Pronob, who was considered by the group to have a certain way with impetuous women, merely ignored Nilima and turned up the volume. "I have to find out if they intend to go through with the general strike," he said. "I'm telling you running a factory is turning me gray. They better not try any monkey tricks till Father gets back from Benares."

"This is All-India Radio Calcutta. Here is the news read by Gopal Kumar Bose."

It was hard for Tara to think of Pronob as a businessman. She remembered his long monologues, delivered with some passion, on Tagore and *Ravindra sangeet* when he had been a student. He had seemed to her sensitive then, he had seemed almost a poet. But he had become fat and ill-tempered in the past seven years. He had acquired an official title: Deputy Chairman of the Board of Directors, Flame Co., Ltd. He spent more and more time, in custom-made raw silk shirts and cottage industries ties, managing his father's match factory while his father, not yet sixty-two, spent more and more money purifying himself by the Ganges.

"There have been isolated skirmishes between the police and the demonstrators on Rashbehari Avenue near Deshaprya Park. Eight men have been taken to hospital."

"How dare they?" Pronob sounded horrified. "They are just trying to provoke the police into violence. How can they get away with it?"

"I'm afraid Pronob's awful once he gets started on these things. He loses all sense. He's no fun to be with," explained Reena.

Tara's first instinct was to tell her friends not to explain. She suspected she was in the presence of history, and their explanations, though well meant, would distract her. She was afraid she might miss the newscaster's words, might not know how many bombs had gone off where or how many people had been killed.

"I'm scared," Tara said. "Things sound awful."

"What nonsense you talk!" consoled Reena. "It's just a routine sort of thing. Actually, it used to be much worse before."

"Things were so bad that my mother wouldn't let me go to the movies, not even to the Metro," said Nilima.

"It's all a political stunt," said Pronob. "Farms are being looted, landlords are being clubbed to death. This is reform?"

An angry fat man, thought Tara, is pathetic. She was afraid of these moods in Pronob. They were hard to match with the moods of a young man who had once written poetry and a one-act play for children. She feared such passion would bring on a stroke or some worse tragedy. The other girls in Pronob's group paid no attention to his anger. They were busy recalling happier times when Carefree Kevin had taken charge of the Hit Parade, when Johnny Mathis had sung to them.

"Oh how lucky you are, Tara!" said the girls. "Tell us more about America. Tell us what you do every day."

There they were again, even Pronob, wanting to know what it was like being a Bengali girl in America, not how she had got there, nor why. She described to them in detail how she spent a typical day in New York, what she ate for breakfast, how much the subway token cost, how she washed and hung her nylons about the bathtub, what her thesis director looked like. Pronob wondered if the American quarter resembled the fifty-*naye-paise* coin, and if petrol was as expensive there as it was in Calcutta. He turned down the radio, so he could listen better to Tara.

"*The marchers,*" said the newscaster softly, "*are proceeding in somewhat disorderly fashion. They have passed Firpo's and the Grand Hotel. The police have cordoned that area of the* maidan . . ."

"I wish Carefree Kevin could come back," sighed Nilima. "We all *loved* Carefree Kevin."

"It seems funny now," said Tara, "a Pole in Colombo turning on hundreds of impeccable St. Blaise's girls."

"Turning on?" asked Pronob.

"That's like, well, like making happy."

"Teach us more phrases, please. The words they are using right now in America."

"I would hate to be an immigrant," said Pronob suddenly. "I wouldn't mind giving up the factory, but I'd hate to be a nobody in America. How do they treat Indians, Tara?"

Tara started guiltily as if something she had hoped to hide had suddenly been forced out into the open. She envied the self-confidence of these people, their passionate conviction that they were always right. She could not imagine her friends as immigrants anywhere, much less looking for jobs and apartments in Chicago or Detroit. But, if the great-granddaughter of Hari Lal of Pachapara, the only daughter of the Bengal Tiger of Banerjee & Thomas [Tobacco] Co., Ltd. had adjusted to such loss, why could not Pronob and his gang?

"You don't have to be a nobody, you know," objected Tara. "I mean, someone like you with your experience in managing your own business could make a very comfortable living." She knew, of course, she had not convinced Pronob, that he thought such anonymity inadequate compensation for the loss of class power and privilege.

"*The first phalanx of the procession is nearing the Catelli-Continental Hotel.*"

"Look!" shouted Nilima. "Look down there! Those fellows are right under us now. Gosh! Aren't they awful? What if they come into the hotel and . . . and do something dreadful to us?"

The sight of the marchers filled Pronob with passionate cynicism. He saw them as the identifiable group behind *gheraos* of Flame Co., Ltd. "Calcutta's finished," he said. "These damn left-of-leftist politicians! They are going to force us to shoot it out with men like that. Calcutta will be a hell."

Nilima nestled closer to Pronob's raw-silk shoulders. She is being coy again, thought Tara, she is taking liberties under promise of danger, she is cultivating a look of helplessness.

"I say, there are women among them! What shameless exhibitionists!"

"I have an Aunt Binita," said Reena, "who took part in the More Milk for Mothers and Babies *gherao* at your uncle's office, Pronob. My mother was so embarrassed when she saw your cousin-sister at the Calcutta Club. But I think it's kind of cool to have a marching aunt." She turned to Tara for reassurance that her use of "cool" had been correct.

The procession jabbed its arms through the dusty air. From Tara's perch (she had climbed on a chair for a better view), at first the procession looked like a giant caterpillar, sluggish and quite harmless, on the busy road. Then she was able to make out banners, picket signs, bricks, soda bottles, bamboo poles. The leaders ran back and forth, coaxing people to shout louder and to get in the way of the traffic. It was strange, thought Tara, to see two cars, one a Morris Minor, the other a Fiat, bearing the only PRESS signs. There were no television cameras, no U.S. marshals. No one to manipulate or interpret the course of Calcutta's history. From the roof of the Catelli, Tara saw Calcutta, squeezed horribly together, men, women, infants, some scratching their crotches, others laughing like tourists in an unfamiliar section of town. And always the heartbeat of the slogans. "Blood bath! Blood bath! Blood bath! Blood bath!"

Tara shaded her eyes to see better. She felt safe on the roof, watching the slogan filter through the marchers, row by row, blending and changing, till the last ragged lines merely said, "Shed blood, blood shed, shed blood, blood shed." Customers darted out of expensive Chowringhee Avenue stores, carrying Swiss confectionary, handmade silks, sterling silver coffee sets, while the store owners tried to lock up their display cases.

"Your first demonstration, Tara. I hope you enjoy it."

Oh no, Tara thought. I saw Chicago on television, and Newark, and Detroit.

"Is that the leader? That chap wearing a red hanky on his head?"

"You mean Deepak Ghose? That bastard? This guy's too short. Ghose always looks so big in the newspaper pictures."

They waited for more, something more exciting, some little twist of violence on the streets. They felt closer than they had before, comforted by the threat below.

A marcher tried to hold up a taxi, and was pushed back into the procession by three policemen in red turbans. Tara was amazed to discover this small incident had genuinely frightened her.

"Why *three* policemen?" she asked the others. She hoped her fear would not force her into coy remarks and gestures like Nilima, who was now clinging to Pronob's hand with affectionate violence.

"*Heavy fighting has broken out in the Hindusthan Road area.*"

"Oh my God," said Tara, listening closely to the radio. "How will we get home, Pronob? I'm really scared."

"Life, my dear Tara, is too short for such seriousness. We are such stuff as dreams are made of and our little life rounded with a sleep."

"Don't worry," said Reena. "Pronob will see us all home. It isn't really as bad as it sounds on the radio. They are famous for exaggerating. Do you want a cigarette? Your folks won't find out if you chew a *pan* afterward."

On Chowringhee some marchers broke rank. But before going home they emptied garbage from the municipal dustbins. They walked into spacious stores. They overturned cars parked at the curb. And they slugged the doorkeeper of the Catelli-Continental Hotel.

10

Though David wrote regularly, the David of aerogrammes was unfamiliar to Tara. He seemed like a figure standing in shadows, or a foreigner with an accent on television.

"*I miss you very much. But I understand you have to work this out. I just hope you get it over with quickly. How are your parents? Tell them they'll have to rustle up tiger hunts and moonlit Taj Mahals when I visit. The Mets are doing badly. I'm still reworking the fifth chapter of the novel, the part when Joseph goes to Sweden to meet Tonia. I think the next section is all right. Who is this businessman riding trains with you? I'm not sure I like it. Look after yourself. Remember the unseen dangers of India. Tell your parents to cable me if you get sick.*"

Tara could no longer visualize his face in its entirety, only bits and pieces in precise detail, and this terrified her. Each aerogramme caused her momentary panic, a sense of trust betrayed, of mistakes never admitted. It was hard to visualize him because she was in India, Tara thought. In India she felt she was not married to a person but to a foreigner, and this foreignness was a burden. It was hard for her to talk about marriage responsibilities in Camac Street; her friends were curious only about the adjustments she had made.

She sat in an uncomfortable chair in the hall, under a framed photograph of her great-grandfather, trying to compose a letter to her husband. It was hard to tell a foreigner that she loved him very much when she was surrounded by the Bengal Tiger's chairs, tables, flowers, and portraits. She made several beginnings, seizing the specific questions he had asked as anchors against her helplessness. Her parents, she said, were very well; of course, they worried about the bombings and recurring strikes, and the attitude of servants these days was not what it once had been, but they were both quite well. Mr. Tuntunwala, she said, was a famous and respectable person, extremely ugly and probably a bit vulgar, but she thought his implied hint about improper activities totally unnecessary and cruel. Her voice in these letters was insipid or shrill, and she tore them up, twinging at the waste of seventy-five *naye paise* for each mistake. She felt there was no way she could describe in an aerogramme the endless conversations at the Catelli-Continental, or the strange old man in a blazer who tried to catch her eye in the café, or the hatred of Aunt Jharna or the bitterness of slogans scrawled on walls of stores and hotels.

It was hard, after the welcome from her parents, after the teas and celebrations of her St. Blaise's friends, to think of the 120th Street apartment as home. She remembered how the first semester at Vassar she had clung to the large leather suitcase bought for her in a hurry by the Bengal Tiger at New Market, how she had refused to unpack.

Tara idly scratched grease from the photograph above her head, and discovered Hari Lal's toes locked in a yogic position. She knew from stories she must have heard her mother tell that in that photograph Hari Lal sat fiercely Brahminical and shirtless, that he had maintained his yogic posture long after the photographer had gone away. *I am sitting under my great-grandfather's picture,* she began again. But that too had to be discarded. David was hostile to genealogies and had often misunderstood her affection for the family as overdependence.

Her mother entered the hall, looking extremely agitated. "Taramoni, haven't you finished yet?"

"I just got started."

"Then the letter must wait for tomorrow. I can't tell you what is going on. *Hai hai!*"

Tara was surprised by her mother's emotion. Her mother was not given to melodrama, only to theories about Moslems. She explained she intended to take her time over the letter, then drive to the post office and pay a late fee so it would go out that night.

"What is this nonsense! The *durwan* says therei s too much fighting everywhere."

"No! Again?"

"Not like before. He says a three-year-old girl was killed."

"Where's Daddy?"

"I can tell you he won't let you go. We can send the *durwan* with your letter. *Hai hai!* Never did I think Bengalis would kill like Moslems!"

Tara declined the offer to send the *durwan* to the post office. She expressed fears the *durwan* would be caught by rioters. But her mother laughed at her naiveté and explained that rioters were not after *durwans*, only after the upper classes. She forbade Tara to worry. Her father would find a way of sending the letter to the post office in spite of street violence. In any case Tara should include her parents' "heartfelt and most joyous blessings" to David and "sincere greetings" to David's mother.

Tara put away her pen and aerogrammes. She wished she had not come to India without her husband.

11

Sanjay Basu, assistant editor of the *Calcutta Observer*, thought of himself as a wild bachelor. His days were dedicated to the pursuit of Truth, his evenings to the pursuit of Beauty. Goodness did not enter into his calculations. On Mondays he attended the weekly British Council debate. On Tuesdays he went to Anuradha's jazz soiree. On Wednesday nights he went to the movies; on Thursday nights to the Literary Circle on Lake Temple Road, Fridays and Saturdays to parties, and Sundays to his ancestral home in Barrackpore to visit his grandmother.

This Monday evening Sanjay was a little more agitated than usual. He was to speak to the British Council debate. The motion on the floor was: *English should be abolished as an official language in India.* Sanjay would speak against the motion. He had worked for days to acquire a desired supercilious tone and gesture.

Sanjay's little Fiat with the PRESS signs on the front and back windows darted around buses, cars, taxis, scooters, lorries, bullock carts, occasional cows and pedestrians on Chittaranjan Avenue, emerged on the wider and still more crowded Chowringhee, turned left on Park Street, made a frivolous right into Havelock Row to look at the classy St. Blaise's girls, and finally turned into Camac Street.

He loved Camac Street. He was writing an article on it for a foreign newspaper.

"When the heart reaches Camac Street it discovers the old Calcutta, the fair Calcutta, the Calcutta that never again will be. It has no quarrel with the English for it is too rich and too sophisticated to be peevish. There are few houses on Camac Street and those that are there are set far back from the sidewalks. The houses are immense and they mystify the poorer Calcations and enrage the nouveau riche. These houses are not houses but veritable compounds. Within the walled compounds are aging gardeners, beautiful women, spoiled dogs, and liveried servants."

Sanjay was pleased with the opening paragraph of his article. It captured his love of Camac Street. He felt warm and safe there. Parents of his friends occupied five homes on this street, though the friends themselves had moved out to New Alipore. He did not like New Alipore; it was brash and showy; it lacked the mystery and calm of Camac Street, he often said.

The British Council occupied a large house with wrought iron window grilles and spacious enclosed verandahs on Theatre Road, off Camac Street. Its gardens were well maintained and its gatekeeper *salaamed* Sanjay as he stepped out of his tiny car. It pleased Sanjay immensely to be greeted by wardens of such public places. He managed a smile in return in spite of his nervousness.

He was greeted at the main door by Mr. Worthington, a pale Londoner with a slight trace of dandruff. Mr. Worthington prided himself in being one of a new breed of British Council directors and sought opportunities to inform the Indians that he had gone to Essex rather than Oxford or Cambridge. He was essentially a kind, if rather innocent young man, who liked to wear Indian dress on Sundays and eat curry with his fingers.

Looking spry in a blue Italian shirt and striped pants, Sanjay cut through the crowd to a knot of British Council regulars. He showered compliments on Miss Dutta, the lone female speaker, who had a reputation for being learned and therefore was not expected to be pretty. The audience, large and docile, elated him. He thought he detected admiring glances from college girls and he responded by looking handsome and confident. In the far left corner of the room he spotted Pronob and his group and nodded slightly to them as he rehearsed his speech. He noted Pronob had brought a stranger. And because he considered himself the custodian of Calcutta's records, he knew the strange girl's name, that her father was the redoubtable Dr. "Bengal Tiger" Banerjee of Banerjee & Thomas [Tobacco] Co., Ltd., and that she had gone to Idaho or Ohio or someplace to study. But there was no time to speculate on the girl's presence nor to wonder if she would discover mistakes in his grammar. Mr. Worthington was coughing to get his attention. Mr. Worthington's fiancée (Sanjay knew Worthington slept with her on weekends and he enjoyed his own tolerance of such lasciviousness) was playing a few bars from the popular song "Oh, Why Can't the English Learn to Speak?" on an old piano. The audience was appreciative of her talent and choice, and amid this knowing hilarity the debate commenced.

"Ladies and gentlemen, charming ladies and witty gentlemen," began the Englishman, leaning awkwardly across a low table where he had placed a pitcher of iced water, a bell and an alarm clock. "Perhaps by the end of the evening, if the motion wins, I shall be saying *Bhai ebong bon* or *bhaio boheno* . . ."

The audience did not recognize the actual Bengali or Hindi phrase covering under the young man's thick London accent, but they recognized the goodness of his intentions and clapped madly.

When it was Sanjay's turn to speak superciliousness deserted him. He told the people that Calcutta was in danger, that he was an assistant editor of a reputable newspaper, that he was exposed more than others to the horrors of the city's changes. He begged everyone to remember their traditions, their conscience, their English if they wished to save themselves from lawless ruin. With passion and intensity he urged them to hold on to a Calcutta that was disappearing like mist.

Miss Dutta, however, sprang to her feet. Calcutta cannot disappear like mist, she scorned, for Calcutta has never had any mists. Mists for Bengalis were linguistic tricks; like buttercups and nightingales, in Calcutta they simply did not exist. And poor Sanjay forgot the words and wit he had intended to exercise. He sought refuge in poetry instead, quoting erratically from Tennyson and Keats and Sassoon to prove points he had abused or missed altogether.

After it was all over and the audience had disappeared down the staircase into the library rooms below, and the select few had stayed back for sherry and biscuits in Worthington's private quarters, Pronob introduced Sanjay to Tara. For Sanjay it was an uncomfortable meeting. He still suffered from the disgrace inflicted by Miss Dutta. Though he talked to Tara of the weather, made much of his brief trip to Boston in 1960 when he had lost his Sholapuri sandals in a tourist room on Brattle Street, he was sure the girl was laughing at him. With Reena he knew he could be witty, with Nilima devastating; but with Tara who knew nothing of his journalistic, poetic and amorous coups, he was utterly lost. He stood there, handsome and helpless in his imported shirt and bell-bottom pants, while Tara asked him silly questions about a protest march he had recently covered.

"Did a three-year-old kid really die?"

"Oh yes. What do you think? We journalists are reliable."

"These demonstrators . . ."

"They're hoodlums! They're *goondahs* trying to crack the Establishment. But they get their heads cracked instead." Sanjay repeated the phrase. He liked the balanced quibbling with the word "crack" and filed it away for use in a future British Council debate. "My best phrases come to me when I'm talking to girls!"

Tara did not seem to hear his compliment. She was too full of questions about the conduct of the police, the tactics of the rioters, editorials he had written.

"Have they ever tried to burn your car?"

"You're kidding!" Sanjay exploded. "Don't you know who's the inspector in charge of these shows?"

"No."

"It's old P.S. We play tennis every Saturday at the South Triangle Club."

Tara told him how much easier she thought it was to live in Calcutta. How much simpler to trust the city's police inspector and play tennis with him on Saturdays. How humane to accompany a friendly editor to watch the riots in town. New York, she confided, was a gruesome nightmare. It wasn't muggings she feared so much as rude little invasions. The thought of a stranger, a bum from Central Park, a Harlem dandy, looking into her pocketbook, laughing at the notes she had made to herself, observations about her life and times, old sales slips accumulated over months for merchandise long lost or broken, credit cards, identification cards with unflattering pictures by which a criminal could identify her. And more than the muggings the waiting to be mugged, fearing the dark that transformed shoddy innocuous side streets into giant fangs crouching, springing to demolish this one last reminder of the Banerjees of Pachapara.

Sanjay was embarrassed by this outburst. Behind Tara, the select few were singing "For He's a Jolly Good Fellow" to Worthington, who smiled back like a man who is content to be decent, intelligent and popular. He was anxious to join in the singing tribute to Worthington.

"I'll keep in touch," Sanjay said as he fled from Tara.

12

At night on Park Street, in a six-room flat leased for him by the company, Joyonto thought of the young women he had pledged to protect one rash afternoon at the Catelli-Continental. The flat, though luxurious and old-fashioned, was stuffed with an astonishing mixture of Moghul swords, Sankhera chairs, Victorian mirrors, Jacobean sofas and Chinese Buddhas. Joyonto was aware of the failure of his taste in decorating his home. But he prided himself in that failure. It was the failure of a vanished Calcutta, of a decade when men carrying ladders had stopped by his house to light gas lamps at nightfall, when there had been few trams and cars to burn. He had loved Calcutta then, its gargoyled houses, its business districts where some men tried valiantly to wear bowler hats, even its courts where justice, he suspected, was not always done. But now, by the window, watching the electric light skim the tops of flower baskets, Joyonto thought again of the sober young woman in the café and his desire to protect her.

It would have been a relief if he had been like other old men, intact though weary. He could have retired and gone on a world cruise, taken up gardening or bird watching or some other hobby. But Joyonto, the owner of foothills in Assam and estates in Tollygunge, felt trapped by his assets. He had had to know too many people, remember too many details, see too many things. Yes, that was it, he had seen too much from his perch at the Catelli. He had witnessed men club each other and he had been moved by their violence.

Joyonto walked to the liquor cabinet in the library, where the walls were soft with street lighting. Glasses, rare and unmatched, were neatly laid out on a silver tray. He had picked up the cabinet and the glasses at an auction just after the fierce communal riots of 1947. That was all the riots were to him, a unique chance for bargain antiques. He had collected Czechoslovakian finger bowls from terrified survivors and not once had he admitted any regret. There was no color, not even from dust, in his glass (his widowed aunt who supervised the servants had seen to that), and the ice cubes were clear though bacteria-ridden, the gin clear and syrupy.

On the far wall a flat sword, too decorative to be efficient, teased him with memories of his mother, whom Joyonto always referred to as "a first-class lady." His mother had given him the sword and told him it once belonged to the Rani of Jhansi. With that sword, his mother liked to say, the Rani had driven Robert Clive, "a delinquent hoodlum," out of her palace. In his mother's stories the Indians always won and their world, ritualistic, aristocratic, always remained secure. Joyonto did not consider himself a winner like his mother or the Rani of Jhansi. He was more like the legendary *nawab* who almost lost his life to the invading British because his valet had flew and there was none left to help him tie his shoelaces.

At school in history class the missionaries had made Robert Clive a hero so brave that he had conquered India *and* put a stop to the odious practice of burning Bengali widows. But I like *sati*, his mother the "first-class lady" always protested. If I survive your father, please burn me on his pyre, I don't want to live without him. She had indeed burned with him, fastened to her seat by a protective belt, burned on the foothills of the Himalayas, the holy mountains, watched by the gods as their tiny Dakota crashed among the evergreens a few miles from their tea estates.

Joyonto was troubled by these memories though he had called them up often, had polished and honed them as if they were prized instruments. He was sure his mother returned to this room, hid herself beneath a Victorian mirror or Chinese Buddha and judged him every day.

If she were still alive, he thought, she would not be crushed by the city's changes. He was sure of that, just as he was sure he himself would always respond wrongly. In earlier crises when his mother had worn handloom saris, when handloom had meant defiance, stirrings of the heart in Christian boarding schools and homemade bombs in gym lockers, Joyonto had quietly suffered the knighting of a great-uncle at Buckingham Palace.

The night was darker now, some neon signs had been switched off, and only the destitute in shapeless huddles remained on Park Street. Rats and roaches slithered from the moisture, gnawed on tattered saris, possessed the streets and alleys. Joyonto was afraid. His hands scurried over his naked torso, his fingers as light as spiders' legs, leaving damp nervous patches on his ribs and spine. He felt that his mother and the city had judged and left him condemned.

Beneath his window refugees and professional beggars grunted in their sleep. Joyonto saw a woman directly below him, ungainly mother of indeterminate age, legs locked together, one nipple exposed where an infant had tugged it. At the Catelli-Continental these destitutes were made acceptable by the hotel's livery. As waiters they brought him sandwiches, tea, and coffee. Their faces bore no rage, no hatred as they served ruminating gentlemen like him. But here in Park Street he sometimes felt he recognized their faces, he thought he saw them urinating in public.

Now he could only wait for some final catastrophe to break over him. He would not listen to his mother, whose presence still curled about the room. He would wait and submit instead. He would wait for the first gray streaks of a false dawn to dim the streetlights of Park Street. The waiting of course wearied him. Finally he admitted it had been a bad night, full of anticlimactic premonitions. No vision or revelation would come to him. In despair he flexed his legs, leaped on the Kashmiri rug in the center of the room, and threw himself into the simplest yoga exercises his body could still command.

But just before the false dawn while Joyonto was standing on his head, eyes popping behind closed lids with unaccustomed strain, the vision he awaited snickered at him through the window grilles, stretched its shadow over the house and all the city. Sleeping bodies stirred as the rodents of the night found their daytime cover. Night had passed and the vision shriveled. It nestled in a million corners, in cups and drawers and folds of saris. Joyonto retired. They found him at noon, drunk in the sixth room as usual, when the servants, led by the widowed aunt, were purifying all the rooms in accordance with holy ritual.

13

There were chains of multicolored electric lights in the gardens of the Ramraj Palace, which since 1952 had become the property of the Asian Tractor Company. The Calcutta Chamber of Commerce had selected the palace grounds for its annual charity carnival. The gates of the palace were decorated with young banana trees in clay pots, and festooned by mango leaves. Urchins stood in large numbers outside the main gates. They gaped at the revelers who arrived by the carful, asked for *baksheesh*, and were turned away. Within the walled palace, rows of attractive food stalls, souvenir boutiques and entertainment platforms had been erected by the prominent legations, consulates, manufacturers, airline companies, the Rotary Club and the Lions Club.

Tara, standing between Sanjay and Pronob, who were sampling Swiss cheeses, spied a small, compact man at the other end of the stall. She recognized him as the National Personage she had met in the train on her way from Bombay to Calcutta, and she slipped out from the center of Pronob's Group, so that she might be seen.

"So we meet again," said P. K. Tuntunwala, and folded his hands in a *namaste*.

If it were not for the fact that she had met Tuntunwala on the train and had been drawn strangely to him, Tara thought, she would have found him a repulsively ugly man.

"How do you like Calcutta now?" the National Personage asked.

"It hasn't changed much," she heard herself answer with a girlish laugh. "They had these carnival things when I was a schoolgirl."

He did not believe her, though she struggled to convince him that all her childhood friends were the same as before, that the old movie houses were still there, the old nightclubs, even the nuns who had taught her. He responded with hostility, and she liked him because he did not believe her.

"I cannot tell you what a weritable hell is Calcutta."

He talked bitterly of licenses, import restrictions, pension plans for workers, shortage of investment capital, *gheraos* as Tara followed from stall to stall. They walked through the noisy, magical darkness of the charity carnival, picking at cold pizzas. She was reminded again of a spider, small, ugly, teasing a Nepali in a railway compartment somewhere between Bombay and Calcutta. They paused briefly at the American pavilion as a tribute to David and bought two hot dogs.

"I am a very modern man," said P. K. Tuntunwala. "I have learned to eat pork."

Tara found the National Personage a fast walker. It was hard for her to keep up with him as he moved from counter to counter, making small purchases. He always checked the clerks' additions, occasionally pointed out a mistake, and left the managers of stalls in ill humor. Soon she began to anticipate his pattern. First the salesgirl's eagerness, then Tuntunwala's request for some trivial merchandise or souvenir, next his dissatisfaction with the stock offered, his request for more merchandise, his small and reluctant purchase, followed by his checking and rechecking of the bill, and finally his calculation of the change to be returned.

"What a lot of nonsense this is! Come, I will show you something ten *lakh* times better," said P. K. Tuntunwala finally.

They hurried past women with baggy midriffs throwing Ping-Pong balls into buckets and beautiful girls from St. Blaise's smoking behind trees. Now and then Tuntunwala was stopped by fat Marwaris in beige suits, carrying plush teddy bears and other small trophies. Tara thought Mr. Tuntunwala treated these men with disdain. She wondered at herself for following him, he was so different from the men she knew or admired, so different from her father for instance. She was sure he did not share her Bengali attitudes, that he was not a businessman like Pronob. He showed too much energy.

As they walked a woman who had held a tea for Tara ran up to them with giggling opinions on a new American Western showing at The Old Paradise Cinema. But the Marwari with the deplorable manners led Tara away before she could confess she had not seen the movie.

"I cannot tell you how upset movies make me. They are unreal and silly. A weritable waste of time," Mr. Tuntunwala said with feeling.

They strolled past a small circular platform where four young men with greasy hair crooned English songs from the fifties into a difficult mike. Past blonde old women in shiny jockeys' outfits standing before the booth of the Tollygunge Turf Association. Past an earnest white man in shirt-sleeves demonstrating typewriters and adding machines. Then finally they saw it; they saw Tuntunwala's carnival exhibit.

It was set apart from everything else in the Ramraj Palace by bamboo barriers and canvas hangings. Strung between two mango trees was a neon sign: THE TUNTUNCO MILLS BOOTIK STALL. The walls and ceiling were hung with mirrors that reflected cascades of cotton thread, textiles, towels, sheets, pillowcases, bedspreads, dusters and saris. Here and there, peeking through loops of merchandise, were thirty young Charulata Home Science College girls, well-bred and almost pretty, masquerading for the evening as nymphs, driads and Hindu angels. It was by far the largest stall on the grounds.

Tara was moved by the Marwari's desire to show her his stall. "It's splendid," she remarked.

Tuntunwala stood silent and worshipful before the display. "Oh come, come. It is a very very small operation," he said with the air of a man who rules kingdoms rather than businesses.

He walked briskly up the shallow steps that led to his stall. Tara saw him surrounded by Tuntunco Mills products. He raised both arms while cunning lights played on his little black face and on his white sharkskin suit. He gave a signal, and the thirty Charulata Home Science College girls left their positions amid drip-dry sheets and soft dusting cloths to group themselves around him. A Tuntunco Mills public-relations officer readied his flash bulb to immortalize the scene.

Though Tara was not given to intuitions, she thought the Marwari's ease and mastery frightening. In the new and powerful light she noted a scar under the man's left eye, a sign perhaps of some difficult victory. She knew he was incapable of defeat.

Then he motioned to Tara to join him for the picture, and though she did not like the peremptoriness of his gestures, she knew she would obey without much questioning. Tuntunwala settled her in an armchair upholstered with Tuntunco Mills fabric, then struck a declaratory pose. He addressed her energetically, attacking communists in Calcutta, general strikes, looting of private homes, predicting murders of rival leaders and "veritable godlessness or ten *lakh* times more worse things."

"I must move to Bombay!" he concluded with a flourish. "Yes, I have decided. Calcutta is too damned for all this!" He waved his frail arms to take in the stall and the thirty virginal models.

A nymph draped in printed voile brought Tara a fresh lemon and soda drink. Appalled by the fervor of the Marwari's speech, she tried to make jokes of his predictions.

"You must be putting me on," she said as a St. Blaise's girl on the other side of the bamboo barrier waved to her in envy.

"I'm very definitely not putting anyone anywhere," said Mr. Tuntunwala. The *goondahs* and other such evil elements are doing all the putting, I tell you."

It was an unseemly moment, thought Tara, for an apocalypse. She could see a heavy woman in a chiffon sari throw rings at plastic ducks. A tightly vested man stumbled and broke six jars of lemon pickle that he had been hugging. A family of eight stood in a circle eating Chinese food from cartons.

"You are teasing me," she insisted, nervously jingling a pearl and ruby bangle that her unfortunate Great-Aunt Arupa had worn at her wedding long ago. Mr. Tuntunwala was a dangerous man. He could create whatever situation, whatever catastrophe he needed. It was no use criticizing him, Tara thought; the only thing to do was to get out of his stall. She felt badly now that she had deserted Pronob and Sanjay. They were her kind of Bengali. They could be trusted to enjoy her jokes and attitudes. And they were charming, even witty. "Excuse me. I've got to join my friends now. They'll be worrying about me."

"Nothing to worry!" exclaimed the National Personage. "We haven't as yet begun our fun. Come, come, we too must throw quoits at ducks like that lovely lady there."

And Tara, looking around in panic at the thirty models for some sign of pity, was given three plastic rings. Outside the gates of the Ramraj Palace the urchins tired, fell asleep or dead, and were replaced by other urchins till they too fell asleep.

14

The May morning was unusually dry. On Chowringhee the puddles left by street cleaners were shriveling in the gutters, and the beggars were hanging out their rags to dry on the municipal trees. At the Catelli-Continental the waiters shook out their limp uniforms, set up brightly colored tables and chairs and umbrellas, and opened for business as usual. At one time not long ago a dry sunny day would have brought out thirty or forty mothers, daughters and aging observers to the umbrellas of the Catelli-Continental. But now the almost daily riots frightened away most customers.

Tara came once a week without her friends so she could read at the Catelli-Continental. In the hotel lobby she could buy foreign newspapers and magazines. She always bought the *Times* of London, and old issues of *The New Yorker* and the *Herald-Tribune*. But these weekly rituals left her more confused than ever. She read of crises in foreign stock markets, ads for villas in Spain, presidential commissions, the Mets, hoping the foreign news would bring her closer to David.

This May morning she worked carefully through "Goings On About Town" in *The New Yorker*. She read of Mormon Art exhibits on Madison Avenue and of sculpture by Archipenko during his Paris period. She had never heard of Archipenko, perhaps no one else in Calcutta had either. She had visions of David taking girls to see Archipenko's work, girls who knew about such things and were committed to Women's Liberation, girls like Susie Goldberg.

Then there was a voice by her shoulder, and an old man in a blazer was smiling at her just as he had smiled at her from a far table for many weeks now at the Catelli-Continental.

"I'm Joyonto Roy Chowdhury, fast friend of your daddy."

Tara thought him an odd little man with a gnome's face, and she recalled Pronob's warnings against talking to strangers in Calcutta. But he had already ordered the waiter to bring his tea and toast to her table.

"Your name is Mrs. Cartwright, no? I've seen your picture in the *Feminine Weekly*."

She looked at him coldly; it bothered her that a strange old man had seen her picture, had perhaps taken the magazine to his room so he could study the smudged details of her face. Mr. Roy Chowdhury pushed his tea aside and began involved and pointless stories about his childhood in Pachapara. Tara kept her eyes on the *Times*; other people's memories had always fatigued her. There were comforting sounds around her, shrill giggles from other tables, cups clanking on waiters' trays, and beyond that traffic noises from Chowringhee Avenue. Some phrases came to her, strange words and combinations that she quickly assumed she had imagined, not heard. *Smoky tea, luminous child, poor scratched crow*, she thought she heard such words and was reassured when the old man suggested they take "a breath of fresh air."

Fresh air of course was impossible in Calcutta; she thought it typical of the old man to invent so simple an excuse to take her out. Perhaps his stories had really been hypnotic or perhaps she had been thinking of David, who accused her of having become utterly passive. She found herself agreeing that it was a gorgeous day for a ride and that she would be delighted to accompany him briefly as long as they drove in *her* car. Old men are stubborn. Mr. Roy Chowdhury insisted they take his car, that he was likely to get sick and would be embarrassed if that happened in hers. Tara was surprised at the quickness of her own decision to accompany a stranger. In Calcutta proprieties were paralyzing. While the old man fretted about cars and chauffeurs, she sensed the start of a small adventure. She thought an adventure would come in handy when she wrote David her biweekly letter. David was growing impatient. He had almost said that he thought her lazy, not doing enough, that inertia was the Indian's curse. In the end they traveled in Mr. Roy Chowdhury's '57 Dodge, followed by Tara's petulant chauffeur in her Rover.

Mr. Roy Chowdhury and Tara were driven south through alleys that curled around tenement slums and sudden parks. They passed the Kali temple in Kalighat, where Tara would have liked to stop. But the old man complained that shrines were always dark and stuffy and ordered his man to drive on. Only when they were by the river did Tara realize the old man's goal. He wanted to show her the funeral pyres.

It was a quiet hour on the funerary banks. Just one corpse was burning, and that too at such a distance that it seemed to occur in a faded snapshot. There were no priests nearby, no bereaved relatives, none of the tightly wired bouquets from Hindu weddings and funerals. Only an upturned string bed which had carried a poor man's dead body, and some garden flowers. Tara thought it was not really frightening, this first look at the banks where death was proper. There were no sounds except a *Hari bol* chant from the burning pyre and the muddy slap of the river against the cement steps of the *ghat.*

Joyonto Roy Chowdhury proposed a walk along the bank as if he were suggesting a constitutional, and she agreed that it was a splendid idea. Pronob might have been right as far as it went—one shouldn't speak to strangers; saying yes to anyone in Calcutta was madness. But the banks were so silent and gentle. The city seemed to have faded on the far shore of the river. The cunning world of slums and beggars, of sunless alleys and barricaded storefronts had disappeared. The only sound as they got out was of the river washing the *ghat* and Tara's chauffeur polishing the car.

Then suddenly they heard a song with many trills. A tall thin man in scarlet loincloth jumped from his hiding place behind Joyonto's Dodge. Tara recognized him as a *tantric* from his dress and matted hair. Her first knowledge of *tantrics* had come to her through a Bombay cousin, who had described them as ghouls living among funeral pyres. Only much later had she learned that the Bombay cousin had lied, that *tantrics* were instead religious men.

The singing *tantric* held out his hand to Tara. She hoped he wanted *baksheesh* and quickly gave him two rupees. But the wild man laughed and flung the money at Joyonto's chauffeur.

"Your palm."

Tara ran. She ran and stopped and ran again, not used to this kind of fear, dodged between the two cars that stood like carcasses, and stopped by the hood of the Rover so the *tantric* would not see her. Then she fumbled in her purse for a likely weapon, some forgotten penknife perhaps or pretty stone, and finding none—her purse was empty of complications in Calcutta—she stretched her neck around the corner, saw first the silvery grid of the car, then a curious tableau: the wild man reading Joyonto's palm. She waited a moment longer, and thinking it safe, dashed into the Rover and banged the door shut.

That noise was her triumph. It was shoddy and mean, she knew, but a triumph nevertheless. Her chauffeur stood ready, awaiting her order. Beyond the shadow of the Dodge the wild man pressed Joyonto's fingers and pointed to what she imagined were lines and stars on the mounds of his palm. Then the *tantric* walked away, baring long black teeth at the old man in blazer. To Tara it looked like a smile.

"If I should die," recited Mr. Roy Chowdhury as he came toward her, *"think only this of me: that there's some corner of a foreign field that is forever . . ."*

So madness was as simple as that, a wild man in loincloth reading palms and an old man in sandals reciting Rupert Brooke. Now her faith in Joyonto Roy Chowdhury was slowly breaking. She had hoped he could guide her through the new Calcutta, but his face seemed sinister as it pushed in through the open window of the Rover. He did not finish the sonnet. He stuck his hand in through the rectangle, unlocked the door and sat in the car beside her. There were little gray spots on his face. He had begun to slump, his breath was shallow and noisy, and with each gasp the loose skin around his neck shivered. Tara thought he was going to be sick. She had always disliked people with minor imperfections, people who fell asleep at public lectures or coughed at the movies. Joyonto had no business to be ill at the funeral pyres. She leaned toward him, planting both elbows on the armrest that divided the back seat. The old man looked much worse. Tara thought that paisley ascots were absurd on a dying savior, that his sandals, his blazer, his hair, all were unsuited to the occasion. She hoped it would be easy to leave him. He was after all a stranger.

"Do something," Tara snapped at Joyonto's chauffeur. "What's the matter with your *sahib?* He's dying or something!"

The chauffeur quickly assumed control, telling her not to worry, that his master was given to spells, that she should return home at once. Then he seized the limp body under the arms and carried it to the Dodge.

She had acted foolishly, she knew that of course. She had not listened to the cautions of her friends and she had abandoned a sick old man by the funeral pyres. She wondered if Joyonto Roy Chowdhury would be all right in the hands of his servant. Or would she, sitting with Pronob and his group over iced coffees at the Catelli, read of his death in a paragraph, and would a corner of Calcutta die with the old man in a blazer?

15

Sometimes for a change of pace Tara and her friends went to Kapoor's Restaurant. Kapoor's was not just a café, there are many smaller and smarter cafés on Park Street; it was (Sanjay often said) the symbol of modern India. The opening of this restaurant had been blessed by two cabinet ministers, one Brahmin priest, the cutting of several ribbons and an editorial by Sanjay in the *Calcutta Observer*. Its opening had marked the end of tea shops like Arioli's and Chandler's, where straw-hatted European ladies discussed the natives and the beastly weather over tea and cakes and mutton patties in shaded rooms cooled by *punkhas.* Kapoor's was long, dark and narrow, sealed off from the street by heavy doors. Its interior, unevenly air-conditioned, was crowded with bright and young Indians who talked in fractured vernaculars. At Kapoor's there was no need to imitate the West or to applaud the songs of shapely Anglo-Indian crooners. No need for Indian men and women to hold each other stiffly and coax the body into foreign dancing postures. *It is a relief,* Sanjay had written in his editorial, *to come to Kapoor's to sit and eat and talk, for there is nothing hostile here in the wallpapers. There are only deep vinyl seats, Formica tables, plants and narcissistic mirrors. Kapoor's Restaurant has calculated the longings of modern India.*

Since Tara's trip to the funeral *ghats* a terrible depression had overcome her. Her friends wanted to help. At first they tried to distract her with movies and concerts and *pakoras* at Kapoor's. But when that proved useless they called her "a silly billy" and "a bloody bore" and scolded her. They diagnosed her melancholy as "love sickness," and offered to cable David to join her in Calcutta. For nice Bengalis, thought Tara, to be depressed was to be stupid. Their sanity depended on their being lighthearted and casual in difficult situations. If allowed to develop, this sillybilliness could soil one's carefully bathed body, could result in pimples on the chin. Even Tara's Great-Aunt Arupa had known the dangers of this mood. Had she not gone mad from despair?

Standing outside Kapoor's one afternoon in early June she thought it best to return to New York. She had seen three children eat rice and yoghurt off the sidewalk. And this not in some furtive alley or slum, but on Park Street, where girls like Tara walked. Her friends told her the children were hardy, that they were used to such life, that they were not like "us people." And more painful than the words of her friends had been the joy on the faces of the children as they devoured their rice and yoghurt. She wished she could talk to Joyonto Roy Chowdhury, but he had disappeared from the Catelli and the waiters would not disclose his whereabouts.

Sanjay hinted there was something vaguely unpatriotic about her depression. He ordered a plate of cheese *pakoras* and suggested she had surely been depressed in New York too. It was outrageous, he believed, to blame it all on Calcutta. The others ordered the "Superdeliteful Snakes" from the menu, and ignored Tara's moods.

"I'd like a cold coffee."

"I want an American Pride and *samosas.*"

"What's that?"

"It's a tall, fuzzy drink. Pink at the bottom."

"Fizzy?" asked Tara.

Their snubs brought out minor viciousness in Tara. She insisted on correcting the grammatical errors of her friends, made jokes about their mannerisms, then waited to be shunned. But the group did not desert her. They decided Tara's depression was really boredom and boredom was the affliction of their class. They made new and heroic efforts to humor her. They wrote long letters to David, who wrote back to Tara that the letters were priceless. They planned a picnic at the Botanical Gardens and canceled it only when the Bengal Tiger insisted that the gardens were no longer safe from *goondahs*. They talked of moonlit drives and fancy dress balls and finally settled for a picnic on the factory premises of Banerjee & Thomas [Tobacco] Co., Ltd.

The group was charmed by its decision. It felt it finally had a focus. It met several times at Kapoor's to decide about the date for the picnic. Sanjay and Pronob were busy men after all, they couldn't go dashing off without canceling appointments or rescheduling others. The girls scribbled names of guests and telephone numbers on paper napkins at the restaurant.

"What about Suniti?"

"What nonsense! She didn't invite us to hers!"

"What about Roma Sen?"

"What nonsense! She married her weird Nigerian and went off at least a month ago."

"How dare you say that. She was such a nice girl, no?"

The friends expressed their disapproval of Roma Sen's marriage, then continued with the guest list. They were racial purists, thought Tara desperately. They liked foreigners in movie magazines—Nat Wood and Bob Wagner in faded *Photoplays*. They loved Englishmen like Worthington at the British Council. But they did not approve of foreign marriage partners. So much for the glamour of her own marriage. She had expected admiration from these friends. She had wanted them to consider her marriage an emancipated gesture. But emancipation was suspicious—it presupposed bondage. In New York she had often praised herself, especially when it was time to clean the toilet or bathtub. She had watched the bubbly blue action of the toilet cleanser, and had confided to David that at home there was a woman just to clean bathrooms. There was no heroism for her in New York. It appeared there would be no romance, no admiration in Calcutta either. It had been foolish, she knew, to expect admiration. The years away from India had made her self-centered. She took everything, the heat, the beggars, as personal insults and challenges. That explained her pained response to the children too, but the others had remained calm. She would try to imitate the others. She feared she might break down and cry in Kapoor's Restaurant.

"I'd like an iced coffee, please," said Tara to the waiter.

16

During the week of preparations for the picnic Tara felt very close to her father. Though he remained pot-bellied and authoritarian all day battling business competitors, he seemed to reserve his best energy for the evenings when he sat with his family in the verandah and planned the details of the guest list. On those evenings Tara thought she could see in her father the young man he once must have been. At twenty, she knew, the Bengal Tiger had published a short story about a Brahmin boy in love. And just before the Second World War, when he had been "recently foreign-returned," German girls had sent him picture post cards with illegible inscriptions. Talking about the picnic seemed to return to him the romance of those younger years.

"This is like the olden times, no?" the Bengal Tiger often said as he sat on the brocaded swing and looked at his daughter. "All these years we're feeling lonely without you. Now we'll have fun!"

From the start, however, the picnic at the guest house was destined to be a failure. For instance, it was discovered just as the cars were about to leave for the picnic that there was not enough room for all the guests, servants, mattresses, sheets and bolsters. At least three servants had to crouch in the luggage area of an old station wagon, which meant that their best holiday turbans were badly crushed. Pronob complained bitterly about the smallness of Indian cars and wished India had raised a company like General Motors.

Barrackpore Trunk Road goes right past the main gates of Banerjee & Thomas [Tobacco] Co., Ltd. It is a commercial artery, clogged with bicycles, automobiles, lorries, buses, bullock carts, pushcarts, motor scooters and pedestrians. It offers the Bengali traveler a delightful opportunity for chauvinism as it winds past warehouses, factories and other impressive landmarks. Sanjay and Pronob wittily pointed out the industrial charms of the landscape to Tara, but she was too distracted by the pushcarts to listen to them. Once she counted two children and twenty enormous sacks of potatoes on a single cart, a single frail man jogging with it down the highway.

"I simply love B.T. Road," cried Nilima as the car Pronob's group was in avoided one pothole after another. "It gives me a tremendous sense of freedom!" She liked to think of herself as a passionate girl. Her passion increased with each dangerous semicircle described by the chauffeur as he overtook lorries driven by hairy Sikhs, bell-less bicycles, and slow Hindustan Motors ambassadors. Then the car ran over broken glass and ground to a halt with a flat tire.

The entire convoy stopped. The older picnickers exclaimed that it was a dangerous area for flat tires, that the chauffeur surely could have been more careful. Pronob's driver, they suddenly recalled, was Moslem. They sat on leather-topped *morahs* by the roadside while a servant poured them buttermilk from a thermos. "Oh dear! Right in the heart of Dar-jipara! Why did this have to happen?" Darjipara was Moslem.

Sanjay and Pronob, anxious to show off, proposed they all go over to a lorry-drivers' teashop. But they were quickly put in their places by the girls. "What nonsense! You chaps must think we're the Rock of Gibral-tar! That's the surest way to get cholera and jaundice and whatnot."

Nilima, temporarily exposed to the stares of cyclists and pedestrians on Barrackpore Trunk Road, said, "*Eesh,* how dare they look at us like that?" and her sensitivity was appreciated by Pronob. Some of the older women spoke in whispers about the Moslem onlookers who had crowded around to watch the chauffeur change the flat tire.

"Look how near to us they've come!"

"Such smelly people. I think I'm going to faint right now."

"One moment please. Can you faint in the car instead?"

"We ought to ban beef-eating. That's what makes them smell so foul."

"We people are withering and dying and these people are getting fat and oily. How come they never practice birth control?"

Tara listened quietly. She was not particularly disturbed by the whis-pered remarks; only the force of their sentiment startled her. She could muster little passion herself. Her own, fraught with explanations and constantly reviewed, seemed all too pale and perishable. She felt quite cut off from the fidgeting women on *morahs* and looked to see if her mother was complaining like the others. But Arati was busy counting bedrolls and bolsters on the roof of a car to make sure nothing had fallen off. Then Sanjay strolled up to the women. Tara saw his face darken with what a rival journalist had recently labeled his "pseudo-liberal wrath." She heard him use English phrases like "communalism" and "race riots" and the older women scattered quickly to their cars. Tara wanted to explain to Sanjay that he was wrong to bully them with English words, that she knew he too was often malicious in his editorials. But when he appealed to her, she thought of David and his earnest magazines, and had to smile at Sanjay to show her approval. Meanwhile the chauffeur responsible for this panic and self-analysis among the picnickers prodded the slashed tire, spat forcefully on it and finally com-pleted his job.

The excitement over the flat sustained everyone till they reached the factory premises of Banerjee & Thomas [Tobacco] Co., Ltd. The front gates of the factory were black and formidable. If the reports of Barrack-pore residents were to be believed these gates were electrically wired. Three gatekeepers in khaki uniform stood at attention in one narrow kiosk. The gate and its keepers were frail and inoffensive, but the imag-ination of the lower-class neighbors, seeking abuse or release, had made of them a necessary nightmare.

As the procession approached, the three *durwans* leaped out of the kiosk and unlocked the chained and padlocked entrance while virile picnickers smoked impatiently in their cars. Inside the factory premises some laborers waved tiny posies of factory flowers; others pushed their children forward from behind the legs of their elders. Young women like Nilima and Reena were moved by the performance of the children. They threw coins at them from their windows and addressed them as "little darlings" to show their affection. Then the entire procession disappeared in the direction of the guest house.

The guest house was separated from the factory buildings and the animal sheds by a large artificial pond, dug by the original owner of the garden house at the express wishes of his widowed mother. Though the pond owed its origin to the whim of a rich old woman, its main function now was to shield the Bengal Tiger's guests from the curious eyes of his laborers. In the evenings the *durwans* swam in that pond in order to perform all necessary and religious ablutions. Over the years, three *durwans* had drowned while performing such ablutions. A small boat was tied to a tree near the steps of the *ghat*. It had been given to Tara as a birthday gift by an uncle who had devoted himself to punting on the Cam for one fearfully expensive term. The boat had sprung a leak and been useless from the start.

The pond was surrounded by a circular driveway, canopied by living arches of pink and orange bougainvillea creepers. The guest house itself was adequately shaded by sturdy mango and *devdaru* trees. The spot where the guest house now stood had once been a wild garden taken over by creepers, bushes, trees, strange snakes and birds. When Banerjee & Thomas [Tobacco] Co., Ltd. bought the garden house, they had to clear all that, even the prize magnolias, *champaks*, grapefruits and cobras. Occasionally, on the hottest days of the summer, snakes still slithered to the guest house patio, and had to have their heads smashed by the Bengal Tiger's brave *durwans*.

The guest house itself had been designed by a friend of a jovial shareholder. From the day of its formal inauguration, people had complained that the guest house was airless, almost claustrophobic, totally unsuited to hot weather. Later it had come out that the young "architect" was an Algerian candy salesman who had fled to India to escape the retribution of the F.L.N.

The patio of the guest house overlooked an outdoor swimming pool. It was a splendid-looking pool, with marble trim and a deep blue interior. It had just one drawback: a primitive drainage system which had been devised by the same candy seller. The beautiful pool was strictly out of bounds of *durwans* and laborers.

On the other side of the swimming pool was the recreation club, a small, separate building consisting of two rooms and a yard. The recrea-

tion club was flanked on two sides by a lawn-tennis court and a badminton court, both recent additions for the Company Executives' Recreation Association. No executive, however, seemed to want to cross the
pond and play tennis or badminton there. It was sufficient for them to
know such facilities existed and that the board of directors cared for
their welfare.

The large band of picnickers burst on this scene of bungalows, gardens and water.

"Welcome! Welcome!" shouted the recreation officer, while the guests
investigated their surroundings and the servants snatched bedrolls from
the roofs of cars. "I am waiting since dawn! I cannot describe to you
my pleasure!"

"What is this nonsense?" asked the Bengal Tiger. "Since dawn is too
bad! I instructed head office we would be here ten-thirty eleven sharp."

"Poor Recreation-*babu!*" consoled Tara's mother. "What an unhappy
mix-up!" She advised her husband to take the matter up with "the boys"
at the head office.

"No, please. No mention. No scolding for head office boys. I myself
have just arrived."

The recreation officer had a vigilant desire to please; pleasing he
regarded as a point of honor.

To Tara's friends a picnic meant a great deal of sitting around in deep
canvas chairs and grumbling about the weather. Distressed by this
inertia, Tara tried to interest Pronob, Sanjay and Nilima in tennis.
Pronob was dressed for tennis, she thought, except for his absurd red
ascot. He kept slapping his white-cottoned thighs as he told jokes about
the recreation officer. The recreation officer, when pressed by Tara, could
produce only two rackets, so Tara and Nilima had to return to the canvas
chairs. The children of the guest house staff, ordered to act as ball boys
for the day, blocked all view of the players. If it had been possible,
thought Tara, the ball boys would have recovered the ball in midair.

Reena and Nilima did not appear to expect anything more from a picnic than the gratification of their desire for chilled mangoes and papayas.
Everything was perfect, except for Tara, still in her mood, who sat
beside them.

"What is this?" asked Nilima. "You are unwell? You look so hot and
bothered." She suggested a swim to cool off. Besides, Nilima was anxious
to show off the swimsuit Tara had brought her from New York.

She was soon joined by Sanjay, Pronob and Reena. But for Tara swimming was no good either. She was depressed at this first sight of her
friends in swimming attire. She felt there was something unnatural or
absurdly heroic about their posture. The soft edges of their bottoms
escaping the grip of the western bathing suit had no business being seen
by servants. Nilima ran with flapping thighs around the pool and her

swimsuit was duly admired by the others. Tara pleaded to be excused. She said she had never learned to swim though she had made several beginnings. Sanjay called her a "spoilsport" and offered to teach her.

The journalist was very handsome as he stood at the edge of the pool. He had a hairless brown chest and a charmingly brave air. "Just let yourself go," he said. "That's dead right. Relax. Walk toward me. No, no. Relax. How is it they didn't teach you to relax in America?"

Tara clung to the side of the pool, jumpy and cantankerous. The pool water, piped in from the bigger pond, was tepid and unwholesome. Water-logged twigs and mango leaves floated on the surface, and a surprising number of dead bugs. The blue bottom of the swimming pool tried its best to make the water seem attractive, and was embarrassed by its own failure.

Soon other picnickers jumped in and tried improbable stunts.

"This is nothing. When we were kids we swam across rivers!" bragged their mothers, who had spent their childhoods in Pachapara. Now they were too old and dignified to wear bathing suits, and saris became transparent in water. "Swimming in pools is for the birds," said Hari Lal's granddaughter.

Tara sat on a shallow step and watched Sanjay show off.

"You'll kill yourself! Why do you want to do a thing like that?"

"Don't dive! Don't dive! Tell him, someone!"

Her waist and thighs were washed by the sun-warmed water. Sanjay was standing on a giant cement fountain that was shaped like a lotus. He struck a comically romantic pose.

"Look at me!" he shouted to her. He probably meant look, what a good sport I am, look at my body, at this model of Bengali culture. Then, gleaming, hairless and brown, he leaped and hit the water.

"He'll kill himself!" screamed his mother.

"How he dares! What a daredevil!"

"Why isn't he coming up?"

"Sanjay, are you all right?"

This crisis gave Tara ghoulish pleasure. Was she about to experience a tragic accident? Would Sanjay suddenly drown just to please her? David was not capable of such extravagant emotion. He would consider fooling around on top of giant cement lotuses quite ridiculous. She thought this freak happening would permanently affect her attitude toward the group.

"Poor Tara is hysterical! Someone get the factory doctor!"

The guest house servants appeared on the patio. "Lunch is ready," they said.

"Shut up, you idiots! How is it servants have no feelings anymore?" sighed Nilima.

"Sanjay-*baba* is drowning," Reena explained to everyone.

Then the journalist erupted from the water, hair and shoulders plastered with soggy leaves. "I heard you! Fooled you that time, didn't I? Fooled every single one of you!"

"What a lark! He was only fooling us."

"Just trying to see if I was loved, that's all!"

"*Narayan! Narayan!* What a close shave! It's mentioned in his horoscope!" said his mother.

"Do you think you *are* loved?" asked Tara, but Sanjay did not hear her. He was still on the giant lotus, arms raised above his head, ready to take off.

"Lunch is ready," repeated the guest house servants.

Lunch was served on the patio. The Bengal Tiger insisted it was a very simple meal, that he had not had enough time to attend to the menu. But the flushed faces of the cooks and the noise of heavy utensils being scrubbed in the kitchen reassured the picnickers.

The guests attacked heaps of fragrant snow-white Dehra Dun rice on English bone-china platters.

"How is it we do not get this kind of rice?"

"There are ways, my dear."

"And these beautiful platters? Tara brought them for you?"

Tara, who had brought few gifts for her parents, was distressed by this attention.

"I'm sorry," she began, "I really wasn't able . . ."

"You should see all the beautiful things she got us," interrupted her mother. Love was at times measured by gifts, and Tara and her parents knew they loved each other.

The rice was garnished with shrimps, peas, nuts and raisins. Surrounding the platters of rice was a ring of roast ducklings, which when alive had paddled in the factory's pond.

"We have madcap *Americawallah* doctor," laughed the Bengal Tiger. "Too strict and diet-conscious. You can blame him for the simple fare."

The roast duck was more spicy and delicious than any roast duck Tara had ever tasted. Ten crisp, brown birds sat in beds of cumin, coriander, ginger, tumeric and other more dangerous spices left unmentioned by the head cook of the guest house kitchen staff.

"Is everything satisfactory?" asked the ulcerous recreation officer. "Is De Souza's duck all right? These men can be so dumb sometimes, sir."

"Everything is perfect, Recreation-*babu*. How is it you cannot forget everything and eat like the rest of us?"

"But tell me truthfully, sir. Are the potatoes bouncy enough?"

"They're perfect, absolutely perfect. Grab a plate and try one." The picnickers pushed six huge and greasy potatoes on a plate for the recreation officer.

Pronob and Sanjay were partial to the tossed salad which had been grown on the factory premises. But the older women considered their taste a sad aberration. "What is this nonsense that you fill yourselves with grass and leaves? Eat more roast duck!"

Tara watched the food disappear, not just the main dishes, but the incidentals, like shredded cucumber in spicy yoghurt, oily and wafer thin *papads*, pickles, chutneys, sweet and sour *dal*. She wondered at the frailness of her own stomach. She had never enjoyed her food like the others. She had never entered into the spirit of feasts. In New York she and David usually skipped lunch; David was given to fatness and dedicated to diets. Dinners were fixed on the run. David had been amused by her parents' chronicle of birthday menus in aerogrammes. How can they eat so much? It's obscene! he had said. But eating was not a matter for amusement, Tara realized. Nothing was merely amusing in Calcutta. She would have to write David that eating was a class protection, that it had been unfair of him to laugh.

Tara arranged lunch on her plate, choosing carefully from the display of colors, shapes and smells. The children, ball boys and Coke carriers of an earlier hour, had disappeared, no doubt waiting with their fathers in the kitchen for the platters to be returned so they too could pick them over and carry off their loot.

"You're very lucky to have a cook like De Souza," complimented the picnickers. "How much do you pay him? Two hundred rupees a month? *Plus* uniform?"

"Two hundred is not much," said the Bengal Tiger. "But he likes company service. You know how they feel nowadays about domestic work."

The men and women began to talk seriously about the servant crisis. They did not mind the servants' stealing a little from the day's grocery total, but they did mind their joining the Domestic Worker's Union. In their agitation they exchanged new stories about rape and riot. They reminded each other that Mrs. General Pumps Gupta had been abused twice on her way to the Metro Cinema in recent months.

"How is it the lower classes have such a good time? It's just us people who have to suffer!"

They grew shrill about labor problems in factories and tea gardens. They advised Pronob and his group to apply for immigration to Canada and America.

"Kanu! Nandi Lal!" shouted the recreation officer. "Bring out the dessert."

Tara, who had finished her rice *pilau* and duck, waited for further tragedy or danger. Sanjay in the swimming pool had provided an anticlimax. Some turning point was surely yet to occur. Tragedy, of course, was not uncommon in Calcutta. The newspapers were full of epidemics, collisions, fatal quarrels and starvation. Even murders, beheadings of landlords in front of their families. But now she looked for tragedy in closer quarters. Stretching before her was the vision of modern India. Though this was a Sunday the air was thick with industrial pollution. Across the pond, chimneys vomited smoke and fire. Tara fanned herself while analyzing her fears. Little splinters from the hand fan irritated her palms, which she had softened in childhood with fresh buffalo cream in the hope of an outstanding marriage. She had to admit her soft hands had not got her too far.

After the five separate dessert courses had been cleared, the picnickers belched with satisfaction and heartburn, then retired for the siesta hour.

"Good idea, sir," advised the recreation officer.

"You overfed us," admonished the Bengal Tiger. "The America-trained doctor will have a hundred *lakh* fits when he hears."

"But sir, what is this life if full of restraint, we have to watch and watch our weight?"

"Jolly good," said the picnickers. "Did you hear that? Recreation-*babu*'s got a sense of humor! He's playing games with

> *What is this life, if full of care,*
> *We have no time to stand and stare."*

"Like you, sirs, I learned it for my Inter-Science English Literature paper."

Everyone laughed, even those older women who had not been sent to college by their conservative fathers.

"Ah, those were the days," sighed an aging picnicker. "I remember learning it by heart. W. H. Davies, 'Leisure.' "

Temporarily their sense of panic, their racial and class fears disappeared. Delicately they reconstructed another Calcutta, one they longed to return to, more stable, less bitter. Buoyed by their memories of happier years, they retired indoors, the women confined to two rooms, the men to the rest of the guest house and the bar.

The afternoon sun, though sly and malcontent, had lost some of its earlier vigor. It deceived the picnickers into putting down their defenses so that they were no longer watchful of the landscape or of each other. Some actually fell asleep with mouths astonishingly open. Others dreamed of the days when they had written odes to snowdrops and skylarks. They slept on makeshift bedrolls and mattresses, no longer alarmed by the possibility of revolution in Calcutta.

While the picnickers slept, a thin little water snake, perhaps more curious than the others, wriggled through the network of drainage pipes and invaded the restricted pool. The water snake played with the mosquitoes on the surface. It ate the dead bugs that had escaped the nets of the alert *durwans*. It zigzagged among the mango leaves and twigs and swam in circles in the warm water. Then Tara thought she felt the floor move, and her own bedding, and this terrified her. "This is it!" said Tara. "This is the end. I'm shaking all over. Why don't the others wake up?"

She swung her narrow feet, pale brown and now slipperless, on the cement floor. She thought she should be close to some overwhelming knowledge in these last hours. Elegant bodies were all around her. She thought of Joyonto Roy Chowdhury dressed in British clothes of another era. The vibrations excited her. She felt ready for death. She'd been brought nearer to it all summer.

"I'm ready," she said, raising her arms in a theatrical gesture. She pleated her cotton sari over her breasts, and stepped over the bodies of picnickers.

As Tara emerged from her darkened sleeping quarters, she had to squint to avoid damaging her eyes in the glare. Everything appeared to be quite normal. The silence and the orderliness around pool and patio enraged her. She felt cheated. Her temples were cool, and the floor beneath her was once again firm. It had been just another anticlimax. She moved from chair to chair in case some meaning or point had been hidden by mistake under one of the cushions. Then over the marble edge of the swimming pool, she saw it. She saw that thing. She saw the snake.

"Help!" she screamed. "Help me, someone! Help!"

The little water snake had darted to the center of the pool.

"Mummy! Daddy! Help! Hurry and call the servants!"

Durwans armed with sticks and daggers arrived at once.

"Help!" the *durwans* shouted. "Where's Recreation-*babu*? Get him here quick! Hurry! Help!"

The commotion brought out most of the picnickers. They stood in groups on the patio, asking each other what possibly could have happened to cause such alarm.

"*Hai hai!* Someone must have drowned! I knew this would happen!"

"A picnic was a bad idea!"

Then they discovered the little snake.

"It'll go away," said the older women.

"We'll jump in and get it," offered Pronob and Sanjay as they stripped off their shirts.

At this point the recreation officer, who had been soothing his ulcers with antacid, arrived from his quarters. "No, sirs," he said to the two young men. "You will get wet." Then he turned to the two servants nearby. "Jump in quickly. Jump in and grab that filthy thing."

The servants took off their khaki factory uniforms and dove into the swimming pool of the guest house. It was an emergency after all.

"I have got it, sir," said one of the servants. "It's only a water snake. Quite harmless."

"Kill it!" screamed Tara. "Kill it! I can't stand snakes."

"No, no! It's bad to kill harmless snakes," answered the older women. "Its mate will return and take revenge on us."

The Bengal Tiger saved the situation. "Just throw the bloody snake in the big pond. It'll all be okay. And De Souza, don't just stand there like a statue. Make tea for all of us."

Order had been restored by the Bengal Tiger. The picnickers were satisfied the Bengal Tiger had done it again. He had removed the trouble to a safer place. He had not killed the snake.

"Why is it you became so hysterical?" the Bengal Tiger asked his daughter. "I think you don't eat enough. That's why you're nervous. I'm more and more convinced that your David isn't a provider like us people.'" He advised Tara to remain in Calcutta till she was at least ten pounds heavier.

The hungry picnickers ransacked all the ice chests for Coca-Cola and Fanta. They drained the guest house teapots. They did justice to De Souza's hard pink cakes and cream puffs.

"We're ready to go home," they said at last. "Thank you so much, Dr. Banerjee. It was an absolutely smashing picnic. How is it we do not do this more often?"

They tipped De Souza and the *durwans*. They lavished endearments on the servants' children. Then they piled into their cars.

"Why do I keep making a fool of myself?" Tara asked.

PART THREE

1

"Eesh!" said Reena. "How the Catelli has changed!"

The statement was unfair. Very little had changed at the Catelli-Continental in the last fifteen years. The last European proprietor had added a thin band of national orange and green to the white turbans on the waiters. And in 1953, when a Marwari millionaire had bought the Catelli, the Prince Albert Room had been renamed the Ashoka Banquet *Ghar*.

"Goodness gracious!" said Reena. "The flowerpots have been re-arranged."

"So what!" said Tara.

"Am I right in thinking you are being rude to me?"

"Yes."

"Such rudeness! It is not like you at all. Gosh! That's what happens when Bengali girls go to America."

Though Tara did not believe in intense friendships, she wanted Reena to understand her need for rest. She wanted to tell her friend that little things had begun to upset her, that of late she had been outraged by Calcutta, that there were too many people sprawled in alleys and store-fronts and staircases. She longed for the Bengal of Satyajit Ray, children running through cool green spaces, aristocrats despairing in muisc rooms of empty palaces. She hated Calcutta because it had given her kids eating yoghurt off dirty sidewalks.

"How is it you've changed too much, Tara?" Reena asked. "I mean this is no moral judgment or anything, but you've become too self-centered and European."

So it had to come at last, thought Tara. A quarrel was about to occur. And over such an issue, imagine calling her of all people a European!

"That's a goddamn lie!"

"Goddamn?" asked Reena. "I've never heard of that one. I know damn by itself. Goddamn is worse?"

"It's a lie. You are lying about me right to my face. How can you do that? How dare you?"

Such passion did not frighten Reena. The nuns had certified her as a "thoroughly sensible girl." She was ready to cope with Tara's outrage. She wondered if "goddamn" was spelled with one *d* or two. "You see, how you always make things too personal? I was just making an objective analysis of you and you get all het up."

Tara felt painfully misunderstood. Her education had ruined her for quarrels and showdowns. No one, it was assumed, would dare to argue with a St. Blaise's girl. Now she was ready to retreat into grudges that would ferment over the years. "But it *is* personal! You're calling me mean and selfish. How can you expect me to be perfectly calm?"

"Well, you *are* a goddamn egoist. Don't you remember the way you reacted to those children on Park Street? They were just sitting and eating and you had the goddamn cheek to turn it into something personal."

"Don't *you* think of beggars as your responsibility?"

"Why should I, you silly-billy? They're paid professionals, probably paid by a big, fat goddamn Marwari."

"Doesn't it bother you that someone's hired these children to beg?"

"It doesn't bother me *personally*, no. I always give alms."

Tara wanted to go on with the argument, she felt she owed it to herself and to David to go on, but she was alarmed by Reena's distortions.

"Why are you always thinking about yourself?" continued Reena. "Why don't you worry about the suffering of your friends, for instance?"

"My friends suffer?"

"What do you think? Of course they do. As proof I'll tell you a secret about Pronob."

On this trip Tara had discovered moods in Pronob that were quite out of keeping with the moods of the group. He was angry quite often or impatient with the endless coffee sessions at Moonlight, Venetia or Kapoor's. He fumed at having to accept the existence of workers' unions. He said things had been much easier for businessmen when his father was young.

"I think Pronob is in love with Nilima," said Reena. "I've seen him eye-make at her on several occasions."

Tara had not been prepared for this secret.

"That's all?" she asked, deflating the conspiratorial look on Reena's face.

"You are not satisfied with Pronob's eye-making? You want him to be downright lecherous. My God! You are a real fusspot."

It was the word "fusspot" that calmed Tara. What a curious tie language was! She had forgotten so many Indian-English words she had once used with her friends. It would have been treacherous to quarrel with Reena after that.

And so they spoke of Pronob's meetings with the Jaycees and hoped the guest list for American exchange students had been finalized for the year. And they recalled other foreign houseguests Pronob had billeted with them in the past.

"Do you remember when we took the whole Australian bunch to Kolaghat?"

"The toilet paper incident?"

"That was really priceless! Wow! Those Australian boys shouting 'Paper! Paper!' and our village servants chasing them in the woods with 'No paper, no paper, only water, sir.'"

The plight of the Australians had seemed uncontrollably funny to the girls at the time. But, in between paroxysms now, she thought of her panic at having to open a milk carton at Horn and Hardart her first night in America. What terror she had felt when faced by machines containing food, machines she was sure she could not operate, or worse still did not dare!

"Serves them right for wanting to see the *real* India," giggled Reena. "These foreigners just want to take snaps of bullock carts and garbage dumps. They're not satisfied with modern people like us."

Tara wondered what David would do if he ever came to India. He was not like her. Would he sling his camera like other Americans and photograph beggars in Shambazar, squatters in Tollygunge, prostitutes in Free School Street, would he try to capture in color the pain of Calcutta? She thought he would pass over the obvious. Instead he would analyze her life and her friends in the lens of his Minolta. He would group the family carefully, Mummy in new cotton sari on cane chair, Daddy in "bush coat" beside her, she herself on a *morah* in dead center, with servants, maids, and chauffeur in the background smiling fixedly at the camera. He would go with her to the Calcutta Club, take pictures of doctors and lawyers playing canasta. He would explode his flash bulbs at Pronob's parties, and regret he did not own a tape recorder. No, she feared, he was wiser than she cared to admit to herself. Perhaps he would not do these things either. He would land unannounced at Howrah Station and say to the coolie wearing a number, I'd like to see the real India. None of this, of course, helped her relations with Reena.

Afraid she might become hysterical at the Catelli or that she might resort to bitter remarks about friends who loved her, Tara returned to the problems of Pronob and the Jaycees, who had to find homes for eighteen teen-age guests from America. I must get busy, she told herself. I must try to care.

"I'd be very happy to help you in any way I can when your guest is here. Do you know where he's from?"

"Los Angeles. He has a nice Irish name. McDowell."

"In the States you can't always tell. It's not like here."

There it was again, the envy for Reena's world that was more stable, more predictable than hers. A Banerjee in that world could only be a Bengali Brahmin, no room for nasty surprises. Her instinct was to say something mean that would ruin Reena's confidence in herself, that would make her see that Calcutta would no longer support girls like her.

"I'm sure he's Irish. How can a McDowell be anything else? In any case, I'm willing to take my chances with this boy rather than two girls from Columbus, Ohio."

"What does your mother feel about all this?"

"Come on, you know her. Of course, she expects disaster. She thinks I'll follow your example and marry an American *mleccha*."

And again that bitterness, that instinct for destruction of smug people like Reena. She had never thought of David as a *mleccha*, an outcaste, not good enough for girls like Reena. She was numb with anger against Reena's mother.

"I don't like that last remark. Look, Reena—how *dare* you call David a *mleccha*? How dare your mother of all people talk like that about something that does not concern her?"

"What are you talking about? Of course my marriage concerns my mother."

"But how dare you call my husband a *mleccha*?"

"Don't get so excited, my dear. We are very modernized Indians, we don't give two hoots about caste. You should learn to face facts, that's all."

It was useless to pursue this anger. Reena and the others were surrounded by an impregnable wall of self-confidence. Through some weakness or fault, Tara had slipped outside. And reentry was barred.

"Would *you* marry a non-Brahmin?"

"Don't be silly. It's unthinkable that I should break my parents' hearts."

Amusing stories about Reena's mother helped to revive Tara. The poor woman was trying out stews and roasts on her family for fear McDowell would find curries uncivilized or ulcerous. She had stocked up on imported canned pork sausages, soups, packaged jelly crystal desserts. She had drawn a line only at beef; she was a good Hindu after all. Reena laughed louder than Tara, repeating details about her mother's efforts that she considered particularly foolish or extreme. The girls laughed with the relief of men who have just escaped disaster. While they laughed, clutching their stomachs, heaving masses of black hair, an elderly gentleman in blazer touched Tara's shoulder.

"Jolly good, Mrs. Cartwright," said the man. "Jolly good to see you again. I was afraid you had disappeared."

"Hello, Mr. Roy Chowdhury. I was so worried about *you*. Reena, I'd like to meet Mr. Roy Chowdhury, who knows Daddy. This is Reena Mukherjee."

"How do you do, Miss Mukherjee. Do I know your father?"

"I haven't the slightest. It doesn't really matter."

After Reena had made her report, Tara knew Pronob and his group would say of her that she was crazy to talk to weird men in the Catelli-Continental. They would say to her wisely, Calcutta has changed, my girl; it's not safe to talk to any strangers, not even at a place as decent as the Continental. They would tell her violent stories of pickpockets and rape, and remind her again of poor Mrs. General Pumps Gupta at the Metro Cinema.

"I thought you would never come back to the Catelli. I thought, Mrs. Cartwright, you had perhaps disappeared."

"What a strange word to use. I don't think I like it at all. Tara, we really should be going now. We are supposed to join the rest of the crowd."

"It *is* a strange word," agreed Tara. "Sort of chilling, you know."

"Mysteries and death. Dear Mrs. Cartwright, do they excite you?"

Tara had no idea what the old man meant by his question. She looked to Reena for help but the girl was cleaning her thumbnails, her pruned eyebrows locked in an expression of ill humor.

"Are you too one of us?" he asked.

"One of you?"

"He means are you also a weirdo," whispered Reena.

"Yes, one of us, Mrs. Cartwright. An addict of violence and murder, in fiction I hasten to add."

Tara felt he was probably speaking in puns, her need to complicate was so great each time the old man appeared. The old man wearing a blazer in the summer heat harassed her notions of the plausible. He spoke knowledgeably of Hercule Poirot and Perry Mason, while Tara recalled a *tantric* singer near funeral pyres and a snake in Barrackpore swimming in the guest house waters.

"I'm sorry I left in such a hurry that day," she said. "I don't know what came over me."

"No need to apologize. You did the only sensible thing if you know what I mean."

"What's all this?" interrupted Reena. And Tara, noting the girl's sudden interest, foresaw stories and misunderstandings that would surround this encounter. There was no way she could explain that a quiet hour by the funeral ghat had conspired with the pain within her till she had been forced to exclaim that it was no use, that it was hopeless, that things in Calcutta would never get any better.

"For today, ladies," Tara heard the absurdly dapper man declare, "I have a very simple plan in mind."

"We don't have time for plans today, I'm afraid, "said Tara. "But if we did, what had you in mind?" She herself did not like adventures, especially if they came to a bad end as they always seemed to in Calcutta. But she needed incidents to make much of in letters to David. David was painfully western; he still complained of her placidity. Things "happened" only when they began and ended. He wrote her that he worried she wasn't doing anything. He didn't mean working on Katherine Mansfield, but just reading and thinking and getting the most out of her vacation. He said he thought she spent too much time talking to bigots, why didn't she write him of things that really mattered?

"I'd like to take you to my place in Tollygunge."

"Mr. Roy Chowdhury, really!"

"What a lot of cheek he has!"

"What kind of girls do you take us for?" Reena confessed later that she had assumed at once the old man intended improper designs on them. After all they were both reasonably good-looking, almost beautiful if one overlooked small imperfections of teeth and ear.

"No, no, ladies. I'm gravely misunderstood. I mean no evil by my invitation."

Tara admitted in her letter to David that if she had been in New York and the old man an American, his invitation would have been merely sporting. But, at the Catelli-Continental, she shared the outrage that inflamed her companion.

"It's your fault," whispered Reena. "With your American husband, this chap thinks he can make these horrible proposals to us."

"It's *not* my fault. You're insulting my husband. You're insulting me."

"Ladies, ladies, please. Your whispering's giving me the jitters. I meant no harm at all." He explained he had a house and large compound in Tollygunge. He did not live there because it had been taken over by refugees and squatters. In any case, he had a roomy flat on Park Street, close to Kapoor's Restaurant. He thought it might amuse Mrs. Cartwright to drive with him across town to see his squatters. The other young lady, of course, was also most welcome.

"Is it a *bustee?*" asked Tara. She recalled frustrating moments at Vassar, when idealistic dormitory neighbors had asked her to describe the slums of India. "Are you taking us to see a *real bustee?*"

"It's a *bustee* of a sort."

"Do the squatters pay you rent?"

"Certainly not. I, dear lady, do not take from the poor."

Tara realized her last question had wounded the old man far more than her earlier suspicions about his honor. He stood in his sockless oxfords, the last insulted scion of a *zamindar* family, owner of tea estates in Assam, and he quivered. "To give, Mrs. Cartwright, is more pleasing than to receive."

He was pompous, of course. Besides, Reena and the others were quite right, Tara knew; Calcutta had become more dangerous than she remembered. It would be stupid to ride through the city with Mr. Roy Chowdhury to look at insolent strangers. But she wanted to trust the eccentric old man, who had without preliminaries shown her the funeral pyres.

"We've got to get going now," said Reena. "Really, my dear, don't you have any sense of time? We've got to rest for Sanjay's party tonight."

Tara's wish to trust the old man doubled with every obstacle offered by Reena. If Mr. Roy Chowdhury had been a little more cocky she might have responded differently. But she thought she could defend herself against any threat from a sockless man in a blazer. So she whispered to Reena that they had done the man an injustice, that good manners demanded they accompany him to Tollygunge.

"I want to go on record," Reena objected loudly, "as being totally opposed to this trip. It'll come to a bad end. I'm going for the sole purpose of protecting my friend here." Then she went to telephone Tara's and her own mother with invented excuses about going to the movies with an old St. Blaise's girl.

The trip to Tollygunge was preceded by the usual confusion about which car or cars to take. Tara was no longer bothered by such confusion. She had come to expect it; she assumed that even a phone call meant several bad connections in Calcutta. This, she guessed, was an extraordinary trip worthy of several arguments and false starts. In the end they agreed that they would all travel in Tara's Rover, while Joyonto's chauffeur would run an errand for the widowed Roy Chowdhury aunt, then go to his own *bustee* for lunch.

Tollygunge had once promised to be a splendid residential area, smarter than Ballygunge and without the upstart snobbery of New Alipore. The land had stretched for miles, unmarked by factory chimneys or swamps, broken only by groups of coconut trees. Friends of Tara's parents had bought land there in the forties. You should look into it, Banerjee-*babu*, they had advised, land is best investment, buy now before it all disappears. But the Bengal Tiger had procrastinated. Then had come the partition, and squatters, and finally riots.

The road to Tollygunge was circuitous. At first it was *pukka*, black and hardtopped, though very uneven, full of cracks and bumps. It crossed tramlines and railway tracks. It edged half-finished apartment houses where tubercular men shouted slogans from verandahs. Then, as it neared Joyonto's compound, the rod was *kutcha*, dry, brown and dusty before the monsoons. It was flanked by huts, cow sheds and stalls. The dust and squalor forced the young ladies from Camac Street to roll up their windows.

Had Tara visualized at the start of the journey this exposure to ugliness and danger, to viruses that stalked the street, to dogs and cows scrapping in garbage dumps, she would have refused Joyonto's invitation. She would have remained at the Catelli, sipping espresso and reading old issues of *The New Yorker*. Now she wondered what had made it so easy to come.

Finally when the vast compound of Joyonto Roy Chowdhury came into view, Tara thought her chauffeur had made a mistake, it seemed to her so dreary, a wall overgrown with weeds and grass. The opposite side of the street was more interesting. There was a movie house there, two bicycle shops hung with chains and wheels, and a teashop combined with medical clinic. Reena stared at the long line of moviegoers sitting on the sidewalk, and refused to get out of the car at first. Above the squatting moviegoers were giant posters of Hindi film stars, all looking sadly Jewish, Tara noticed; New York had tamed the fierce Semitic charms of Raj Kapoor and Waheeda Rehman. In India, Susie Goldberg would be a goddess. She slid out of her car and saw a very black man near her feet throwing kisses at a gigantic picture of Saira Banu in miniskirt. Then she heard Reena announce she would be sick if they did not go home at once.

Mr. Roy Chowdhury tried to head off Reena's sickness by offering to take the young women to the little teashop. Customers sat on uncomfortable wooden chairs, staring at a blackboard on which the proprietor had scrawled: *Try our Vegitable patty (Finest in World)* . . . *4as. pr. pc.*

and Mutton Kofta Curry (Extra Hot) . . . *12as. per odr.* But Tara, who would have liked to say yes to show her friends she was sporting, feared the large flies clinging to tea rings on tables and found herself declining Joyonto's offer. Reena, who had not entertained the lunch invitation seriously, did not bother to answer at all. Only the chauffeur, who had been given lunch *baksheesh* by Tara, was anxious to taste the extra hot curry of mutton.

"Enough of detours then," snapped the old man. "Let's get to my squatters."

There were no formal gates, only a gap in the wall; also several holes in the wall, jagged and varied openings, where bricks had obviously been pried loose to build hovels or stalls.

"I'm sorry there isn't a gate," apologized the host. "The refugees arrived before the construction men had a chance to really get started."

Tara was bewildered by her first view of the large and dusty compound. She thought if she had been David she would have taken out notebook and pen and entered important little observations. All she saw was the obvious. Goats and cows grazing in the dust, dogs chasing the friskier children, men sleeping on string beds under a banyan tree. Children playing with mud beside a cracked tube well. Rows of hovels and huts.

"This was to have been my rose garden," Joyonto said.

The huts were made of canvas cloth, corrugated tin, asbestos sheets, bamboo poles, cardboard pieces and occasional bricks torn loose from compound walls. Posters were used as building material by the more desperate squatters. Saira Banu in ski slacks hung upside down on one wall. DEEPAK GHOSE LIBERATES, CAPITALISM ENSLAVES, announced handbills on many other walls. There were no doors to these hovels. Tara could imagine David asking quite naturally if he might go inside and take a look. But she did not dare look too closely at them herself. Though they were open, these homes seemed to her secretive, almost evil.

Tara concentrated on the children playing near a tube well. Most of them were naked. They threw themselves on the tube well's rusty arm, then ran to sit under its spout before the water trickled down. Some of them were holding bananas black with flies. Sometimes they put them down in the mud so they could play with the tube well. She saw a pretty girl in torn bloomers giggle as water sprayed her. She thought the girl would be perfect for adoption ads in western periodicals: *For only a dollar fifty a day you can make this beautiful Indian girl happy. She*

THE TIGER'S DAUGHTER / 621

has no mother or father . . . She wanted to adopt all the children playing with water.

"This is criminal!" said Reena. "What is this? How is it they do this to your private personal property?"

"I'm afraid there's nothing I can do about this," answered Joyonto.

Now Tara thought she was beginning to understand what Pronob had once called a pain in his stomach. She thought she now knew the meaning of Camac Street and its paraphernalia of spacious lawns, padlocks, chains and triple bolts.

"This is too much! Can't you throw them out? I mean bodily throw them out?"

"Eviction notices get torn up the moment they are served." Joyonto Roy Chowdhury seemed interested in other dramas. He nibbled the lapel of his blazer and walked ahead of the girls. "Come, Mrs. Cartwright. Come let me show you what should have been my vegetable garden."

Tara and Reena followed the goatlike old man past the tube well. *Bustee*-dwellers started at them. Tara thought they had sly eyes and impudent ears. She thought she saw obsessive distrust on their faces—anger against people who were obviously not squatters.

"I told you we shouldn't have come, Tara. I told you it was dangerous to talk to strangers."

The young men of the *bustee* closed around the little party. They were shirtless and muscular. They had sun-bleached matter hair. They spat on the ground as they stared at the girls.

"Ladies, let me handle this my own way if you please," said Joyonto. Then he raised his manicured fingernails in an exaggerated show of despair. "The weather is unbearable, isn't it, sirs? I wish the rains would come."

It occurred to Tara that the next moment could very likely involve her in some tragedy or violence. She did not want to die, though getting hurt by vulgar hands and being left to bleed on the duty yard would be much worse. She thought she loved David very much, and death or mutilation before she had told him that would be unbearable. If she died in the *bustee* she knew her parents would blame David. They would say that he was not like "us people," that he let his wife wander into danger. She thought again how much she loved David and how impossible it was to tell him that in the aerogrammes bought by the *durwans* of the Bengal Tiger.

"Are you the rent collector? Mister, just tell your boss we want to spit on his face," shouted a young man with a scar.

"Deepak Ghose liberates, capitalism enslaves," chorused the others.

"No," said the old man. "I am not the rent collector. Would I bring these two nice ladies with me to collect rent?"

Then the young men accused Joyonto of being a reporter. They struck matches to light their *biris* (Tara noticed the matches had been manufactured by Pronob's company), and they threatened to burn Calcutta. But Joyonto told them quietly that they were not reporters.

"How is that?" asked the young men. "You are really just looking around?" They offered, like tourist guides at official ruins, to show their *bustee* to the old man. They sang film songs as they led the way, even imitated love scenes between Raj Kapoor and Vijayantimala. They pushed aside children playing with a bucket of water. A naked ugly girl threw water on Tara and ran away giggling to the door of her hut.

"Chase her! Chase the *pugli!*" shouted the young men. "One *lakh* pardons. She's a *pugli*, she's mad."

"Don't worry," assured Joyonto. "It's nothing serious."

But Tara could not dismiss the incident as casually as the old man. There was to be no major drama, no sensational excitement, she understood that now. No big crises that she could later point to and say: that was when I became a totally different person. She would only suffer relentless anticlimaxes, which Joyonto would dismiss as nothing at all.

"I want to go back," said Tara. "I'm afraid I might catch a cold from this damp sari."

"But we have just begun, big sister," said the muscular young men. "You haven't yet seen the *pukka* house. The bathing area for ladies. The temple."

"I've seen enough, thank you," said Tara. "It's been a most unusual trip. Thank you very much."

Joyonto Roy Chowdhury, however, refused to let her go. He discarded good manners. "You can't leave," he insisted. "I'm not worried about my transportation back home. It is you I'm worried about."

Reena was a few feet ahead of them, notebook in hand, entering names and details she procured cunningly from the *bustee* children. She looked efficient and self-confident, an old man's secretary doing routine jobs for her boss.

"This compound, Mrs. Cartwright, was meant for eight separate mansions." Joyonto's voice was louder now, the English accent less pronounced. He was like a guide at some obscure, vastly sacred shrine, as if he were recounting history and not the failure of his own fortune. "There was to be a house for me, all on one floor, you understand. A museum, you understand, for all the things I bought in auctions."

Reena, still ahead, notebook in hand, had not missed the explanations of her host. "What about the other seven?" she asked.

Tara attributed Reena's new energy to her instinct for self-protection;

it could not possibly be penance. Perhaps Reena felt if she could write it all down, she would calculate and avoid future confrontations.

"I'm partial to family compounds," Joyonto cried, yet louder. "The others were to be for my nephews and nephews-in-law."

Then the young men led the sightseers to a brick house. It was still incomplete. A hundred bamboo poles supported the second floor. But already the house looked dilapidated, fit for a demolition crew. A rusty cement mixer lay on its side before the house. Here too the walls were pocked with holes where loose bricks had been pulled away by other *bustee*-dwellers. The young men said that they would be honored to have the guests inspect this house.

The house was shaking with voices: of mothers scolding children, women fighting in the kitchen, young men wrestling in tiny rooms and old men smoking in open hallways. There must have been two families to each room. Others spilled out into the courtyard and the porches. The men and women who lived in this decaying brick house had more confidence than the inhabitants of huts and hovels. Some of their young men had enrolled in and dropped out of evening college. Some were businessmen who hawked safety pins and hair ribbons all day. They made the rules of the *bustee* and they enforced them.

"I was going to build a swimming pool right in front of this house," Joyonto said, now calmly.

"You were wise not to," said Tara.

Reena kicked the rusty cement mixer. Perhaps it confirmed to her that Joyonto was prodigal and a danger to her class. Perhaps she saw in that decaying machinery the end of her own dreams of technological progress. "It's criminal," she said. "If we start giving in to these people once there'll be no way to stop them."

Joyonto waited for her to finish, then turned to the rough young men. "It's been a satisfactory trip," he said, tipping them lavishly.

Though there was a note of finality in Joyonto's voice, the drama of the day had not been completed. It was time for the little party to leave. They had made excursions to the ladies' bathing area and the temple, and now they were going through the motions of farewell.

"We'll be late for Sanjay's party if we don't hurry," Reena said.

The squatters and their children were walking back with the visitors. For them, too, it had been a satisfactory day. Suddenly a little girl in faded party dress, her arms covered with muddy bandages, detached herself from the other children. She blocked Tara's way. Except for its size there was nothing childish in the little girl's face. It had already assumed the lines of disappointment that it would retain. The body, rectangular and skinny under the party dress, would no doubt thicken a little with unlovely handling but it was already the body of a stunted young woman. She came forward, shrill and angry, circling the visitors like a bird of prey till they responded with embarrassed endearments and nods of the head. The little girl raised her arms, making exit impossible for Tara and her friends. The arms quivered with hatred and Tara, who was only inches away, saw blood spreading on the bandage. There were sores on the little girl's legs, sores that oozed bloody pus with each shiver of hatred. How horrible, thought Tara, the kid's got leprosy, she's being eaten away!

"I want that!" screamed the little girl. "I want a sari just like that! I want that! I want that!"

It is harder to damage others than to damage oneself. Tara, who had been carefully trained to discipline mind and body by the nuns at St. Blaise's, lost her composure at that moment, and had to be dragged quickly to the Rover. No one was sure what exactly had happened. On going over the incident in Camac Street or at the Catelli-Continental the girls remembered outstanding details, but with each telling the chronology changed. Had Tara fallen on the child in order to beat her to silence? Or had the child thrown herself on Tara and tugged at her *dhakai* sari with bloody, poisonous hands? Reena insisted she had heard Tara scream, *Don't touch me, don't touch me!* She said that she had seen Tara claw like a maniac at the spot that the girl had soiled with her bandages. Tara only knew she had seen the muscular men pin down the offensive girl and fling her out of the room. A pail of water had been brought to Tara as a token of amendment. The mother of the little girl had threatened to beat her daughter. A five-rupee note had been offered guiltily to the child, and the money accepted on her behalf by two virile young men.

In the car, revived by smelling salts the faithful chauffeur kept in the glove compartment for just such emergencies, Tara had worried about making a fool of herself. "I'm sorry I ruined the trip for you people. I don't know what came over me. I saw that girl with leprosy and I just lost my head."

Reena had tried to comfort her friend. "It probably wasn't leprosy! Don't worry about it. It's infectious only if you have an open wound. I've heard from my medical-college uncle leprosy is a very hard disease to catch."

Joyonto alone had maintained an indifferent silence.

Tara remembered being grateful to the chauffeur for taking charge of the situation. "I go straight to Camac Street double fast," the man had said. He had deposited the girls on the steps of the Bengal Tiger's house so that they could gaze at the deserted lawns, wander through the empty marble rooms, linger on the spacious verandahs, bathe themselves in the "English" style bathroom, and regain their composure before the maid brought them tea and sandwiches.

But more than anything else Tara remembered Reena just before they had parted from Joyonto in the car. Reena had drawn herself up like a tremulous Brahminical Joan of Arc. "Here are the names I took down, Mr. Roy Chowdhury. It's your duty to serve them new eviction notices. Good-bye."

2

A husband is a curious animal. His presence is discovered by a series of stratagems. Advertisements are inserted in newspapers like the *Calcutta Patrika* and the *Reader* of Bombay. "Wanted: suitable bride-groom for tall, very fair, excessively beautiful Bengali Brahmin girl of respectable family; age 20; groom must be foreign-returned, earning four-figure salary." Or: "Wanted: beautiful, very fair bride for brilliant Kayastha boy, 38, Class 1 govt. officer, father retd. High Court Justice. Only respectable parties need apply."

"You are not trying hard enough," Tara's mother had often complained to the Bengal Tiger while Tara had sat over her homework, pigtails sliding over the poems of Alice Meynell.

"There's plenty of time, don't worry. I always take care of everything, don't I?"

Tara recalled how this tableau had embarrassed her greatly in those days. She was anxious to fall in love, good heavens! There was nothing wrong with her. But marriage meant certain physical mysteries, centering, as best as she could determine, on or near the navel. She had been grateful that the Bengal Tiger, so fierce in the business world, had procrastinated in this small personal thing.

"You are supposed to wear out fourteen pairs of shoes looking for a *jamai*," Tara's mother had complained. "I'm afraid you're taking your responsibilities too lightly. You'll live to regret it."

"How is it you want to part with Taramoni?" the Bengal Tiger had countered. "Finding suitable match is man's job. Leave me alone or else."

These conversations always ended in arguments or headaches. A few months before Tara left for Vassar things had come to such a pass that her mother would prepare debates, practicing her speech in the privacy of the prayer room with prime opening sentences and calls on the gods for reinforcement. Then she would cook persuasive meals for the Bengal Tiger and finally the subject of marriage.

The groom is an easy target. He waits in his room after a day at the office and a shower and light refreshment, for female relatives to bring him photographs of beautiful women. He scrutinizes the faces, tensed by strong lights, not smiling for that would be mistaken for boldness, nor yet really glum for that would be taken as a sour disposition. Do you like this one? The father is a high court judge, the women whisper. Or what about this one? Her father is a civil servant. No, he replies with studied calm, her nose is too long, and that girl has no breasts.

When the choice is made and the bargaining over furniture, ornaments, number of towels to be given, sheets and pillowcases, underwear for the groom, clothes for the female relatives, all settled with maximum discontent, then the Brahmin priest appears with the tools of his trade. And after a fire has been lit, and the gods appealed to, and the bridal couples' clothes joined in a knot amidst applause from witnesses, when the guests have been fed, and the servants tipped and scolded, when the children have fallen asleep in their party dresses, then the groom takes his bride, a total stranger, and rapes her on a brand new, flower-decked bed.

"Why don't we get a *ghar jamai?*" Tara's mother once said. "Some poor but honest boy, very brilliant of course. We could teach him about the business, and Tara would not have to go away."

"Shut up, Mummy. I do not need advice from a female!"

One day in Madison, sighting a young man in an elevator, Tara had murmured to herself, "My goodness! How easy, I'm in love!" and had completed her father's business. But a husband is a creature from whom one hides one's most precious secrets. Tara had been dutifully devious in her marriage. She had not divulged her fears of *mleccha* men. Did they bathe twice a day? Did they eat raw beef? Did they too have to hiccup and belch? The white foreigners she had talked to in Calcutta had been mainly diplomats or businessmen out for the evening in their best tropical dress, anxious to please, or at least careful not to offend. The tiresome Australians who had been driven to distraction by the absence of toilet paper in a village, she preferred to forget.

Now there would be no brilliant boys, no invitations, no priests, no fires, no blessings. She was a married woman, victim of a love match. David knew nothing of Calcutta, Camac Street, the rows of gods, the power and goodness of the Bengal Tiger. She could not trust herself to explain; some things could not be explained. The security of a traditional Bengali marriage could not be explained, not to David Cartwright, not by Tara Benerjee.

Toward the end of her second year in the States, when she'd been deep in the problems of Hawthorne and his scarlet woman, Tara had received an important communication from her father. The importance was obvious enough: her father had taken up all the space in the aerogramme, leaving no room for her mother, not even a line for the customary blessings for "all great success in your term papers and other brainy things."

"We have made sound progress [the letter had said], regarding your

marriage. There is one Dr. Amya Chakravorty, very fine boy, Ph.D. in Chemistry (Heidelberg), earning modest but promising salary from Govt. Boy's father is educated man, middle-class, not rich, a professor at the University, and a member of University Senate, but money thank goodness is not at all our problem.

"Anyway, we have initiated serious talks through your Uncle Bibhuti (who unfortunately is still unemployed, by the way), and things appear to be going smoothly so far. However, all plans have not been finalized as yet. The main hurdles, boy's willingness for marriage and dowry settlement, have been already covered with all due satisfaction to parties concerned. We have shown your colored snap to the boy in question. We have no studio photograph of yourself, a grave oversight on our part, but with the grace of God, this snap you sent us (sitting with friends at Princeton Homecoming Game) has proved adequate. I myself do not care for it too much, you look like you are suffering from rigors of cold weather, but your Mummy says that one is the best.

"Dr. Chakravorty, the prospective jamai *under discussion, will be leaving for Chicago in three weeks' time. On some research-cum-training project. All your Mummy and I can say is that this opportunity is heaven-sent. We are modern progressive people, we do not in any way wish to force you into marriage. We shall leave the rest of this matter in your hands, and of course to Fate. The boy will come to see you for a weekend during next Xmas hols. If you both like each other then, then all will be well. We have already ascertained his favorable reaction to your snap, and have from his father more or less firm commitment.*

"Do not act with any undue haste, or any degree of unnaturalness. Whatever God does is for the best. Or as the lovely lady would say: Que será, será.

"If you should decide in consultation with the boy in question, that this is it, then wire us immediately. You may get engaged on the spot, but no marriage. Preparations are being made here for grandest ever wedding ceremony. No holes barred! Needless to say all your relatives, big and small, rich and poor, close and near, are extremely excited. As is old Recreation-babu of the factory, who plans to supervise the feeding of the guests.

"One small word of advice from your mother. She insists I add that you do not kill yourself with overstudy this semester or next. It is essential you try to look your best for the Xmas hols. No doubt you will get A grade in your papers without much effort anyway.

"Que será, será. Take it easy. Drink plenty of milk in your daily diet. You do not know how lucky you are to have unadulterated food: America is indeed the land of milk and honey; if I were younger I would sell my business and emigrate to a poultry farm in the Midwest. Good-bye and Godbless.

"P.S. Dr. Chakravorty is foreign-returned and very brilliant boy, everybody likes him. I shall relate to you small anecdote of his liveliness and intelligence. Your Mummy and I took him for dinner and heart-to-heart chat at Sun Sun Restaurant. He was full of jokes, making witty cracks. When it was time to order, the Chinese waiters tried to get us to buy huge quantities of each item, but the clever boy cut them short and ordered only two plates of each, because he knew the size of each plate was immense. The waiters were entirely cowed by Dr. Chakravorty. Your Mummy and I were favorably impressed by this touching incident."

The letter had thrown Tara into utter confusion. She could guess from the closing paragraphs of the letter that her parents wanted her to give up her studies for at least two months in case it ruined her perfect wrinkle-free complexion. At every possible opportunity she shut the door to her room and tried to study her old book on flower arrangement. As for singing, playing the *sitar* or cooking gourmet dishes, she felt she had been very inadequately trained.

"Que será, será!" she consoled herself.

In the affairs of the heart or marriage, there was no doubt that Tara at the time was incredibly inept. As it turned out, things did indeed disintegrate. But, at least on this one occasion, Tara was not to blame.

Dr. Chakravorty, the prospective *jamai* who had been promised future control of Banerjee and Thomas [Tobacco] Co., Ltd. as well as the boss's daughter, arrived in due time in Chicago. There he met a Polish girl from the South Side, a limping divorcée who was kind to him on his first day, who taught him to be aggressive, to desire not just position and wealth, but sex for the asking; who confessed one Sunday in November that she was pregnant, and whom he dutifully married.

"Que será, será," advised Tara's father when Professor Chakravorty of the Calcutta University's senate broke the news hesitantly to the Bengal Tiger.

"Yes," agreed Tara, returning to her essay on Hawthorne.

Now, bewildered in Camac Street, still unable to share her fears with the young man in the elevator, she wrote him a letter that she knew he would find exasperating.

"It's hard to explain what's happening to me here, David. Or for that matter what's happening to the city itself. I don't know where to begin. There's no plot to talk about. Maybe that's the whole trouble, nothing really has happened.

"Mummy and Daddy are fine. They're starting another diet. But the cook's gone crazy over the blender I brought home. In fact, so far we've blown two electric fuses.

"Oh, this will interest you, I think. I saw a real bustee the other day. Mr. Roy Chowdhury, that's the old man who drinks coffee at the Catelli, took Reena and me to see his bustee. Absolutely incredible, David. I mean you can't imagine how horrible it was. Like seeing it at the movies or something, certainly not like the beggars everywhere on the streets. Anyway I don't think I want to talk about it. Enough to say that poverty is an art your people will never master.

"The weather's absolutely beastly right now. My parents are talking about a week's hols. in Darjeeling (that's the hill station on the Himalayas, I must've mentioned it before), and I hope we can go very soon. Of course it'll be unbearably hot when we come back. Anyway, at least the rains shan't be far away.

"Do you remember my friend Sanjay, the newspaper chap? Well, he had a beautiful piece on 'The Denigration of My Beloved City: Calcutta' a few days ago. Really great. Unfortunately lacking in his usual wit, but so moving, I can't tell you. Would you like me to send you the clipping by air mail? If I can find the paper, that is—the maid here is neurotic about tidiness.

"By the way, did I tell you the picnic to the factory was incredibly tedious? Even Pronob and his group failed to be their usual scintillating selves. Though Sanjay tried hard. I mean he pretended he was drowning in order to make us laugh. I had one terrible moment I must confess. A water snake managed to invade our swimming pool. No, I better not talk about this any further. A snake in a swimming pool, you'll say! Calcutta is a jungle! Of course, it is a jungle, but not in the way you're thinking. Just be glad you're not part of this mess. I don't think you could begin to comprehend these problems.

"All this doesn't mean I'm undermining your hang-ups of course. But at least you people can go to your analyst and he can tell you what's the source of your problem. We can't do that. I haven't heard Daddy mention any psychiatrist friends, not one. Maybe we don't need them. Our mess is too complicated, I'm afraid.

"I could go on and on, David, but I must stop now and arrange the flowers for tonight's dinner guests. I know you're saying right now how can I worry about flowers when people are dying on the streets of Calcutta, how can I be so callous, etc., I know that's exactly what you're saying to yourself. Well, all I can reply is that nothing my parents could give up would possibly change the life of the poor. India is not a banana republic, there aren't any landlord classes you could simply execute or exile. We're all involved in each other's fates.

"Well, I really must stop now. There's no more space in the aerogramme. You can't imagine how I look forward to your letters, though they're not always as affectionate as I'd like them to be. No, I'm only

*joking, your letters are perfect. Good-bye. Look after yourself. Love,
Tara."*

So Tara confided secrets in her letters to her husband, but managed
quite deftly not to give her own feelings away. She thought there was
no way she could describe the visions that had failed her at the guest
house picnic. Such events could not be described to David, who expected everything to have some meaning or point.

It was not a toppling or sliding of identities that Tara wanted to
suggest to David, but an alarming new feeling that she was an apprentice
to some great thing or power. If she were pressed to tell more precisely
the nature of that power, she would have to remain silent. It was so
vague, so pointless, so diffuse, this trip home to India.

The eccentricities of overseas mail service made it impossible for
Tara's correspondence with David to follow any pattern of confession,
reproof and rebuttal. Two days after she had mailed her letter to her
husband, she received from him several angry letters.

The letters seemed to Tara to make the same points. David was
outraged. He accused her of "stupid inanities," and "callousness." He
thought the customs she praised merely degraded the poor in India. He
had started to read Segal's book on India, and he wrote: "With Segal,
I shudder." Tara had not heard of this book, and in passing she wondered if it meant David was having trouble with his fifth chapter. David
wanted her to take a stand against injustice, against unemployment,
hunger and bribery. He made horrible analogies between her Calcutta
and Czarist Russia on the eve of revolution. He told her that he thought
from the omissions in her letters that a bloody struggle was inevitable,
that perhaps Calcutta did not deserve any better. In the face of such
outrage Tara knew she could never tell David that the misery of her
city was too immense and blurred to be listed and assailed one by one.
That it was fatal to fight for justice; that it was better to remain passive
and absorb all shocks as they came.

There were also occasional lines of local gossip in David's letters.
Tara clung to them because they did not tax her conscience. She
learned, with some malicious pleasure, that Susie had separated from
Phil and that Phil had taken an instructor's job at Montana State; and
that Susie had a part in "The Tragedy of Motherhood," which Tara
assumed was guerrilla theater. Such news did not demand that she
share her husband's faith in democracy. In the early months of marriage
she had insisted rituals were useful and democracy not always the
right answer. But finding that these objections exasperated David and
fatigued her, she had given in smiling, not hearing another word.

She put away the letters in her suitcase, and retired to the verandah.

It was still unbearably hot, though the rest of the house had been clamped down under cool-smelling rose sprays and damp coconut coir blinds. She sat in the center of the Sears garden hammock, and traced leafy designs with her forefinger. The lizards were out in numbers, still and prehistoric, fastened to the walls of the verandah.

She thought about Calcutta. Not of the poor sleeping on main streets, dying on obscure thoroughfares. But of the consolation Calcutta offers. Life can be very pleasant here, thought Tara.

3

Every morning between yoga and ablutions, it was rumored among Bengalis in Calcutta, Mr. Tuntunwala repeated his dearest sentiment. "Heart's matters," he was believed to say as he held his breath for several seconds, "heart's matters are for idiots and women." Tara heard him express that sentiment late one evening by the steps of the boathouse at Dhakuria Club while Chinese lanterns threw red and yellow lights on his monkeyish little face.

Her presence at the club that evening was almost accidental. She had run into Sanjay at the Catelli-Continental and been asked to accompany him to the club for an exciting assignment. He was covering a political rally for the *Calcutta Observer;* it was to be a rally for P. K. Tuntunwala, who had recently emerged as the strongest conservative candidate. She gladly accompanied Sanjay, thinking how he had changed from witty assistant editor to mad prophet in the last few weeks. In his editorials he wept for Calcutta, *this cudgeled and bleeding city that brings me a taste of cannibalism and ashes.* He called P. K. Tuntunwala, Esq. *the hero of all heroes, the only savior who can pull us people out of the burning and monstrous mouth.* If Calcutta were to be saved, he often told the group, then all other candidates must fail.

On the way over to the club in his Fiat, Sanjay remarked to Tara, "If strength is love, and I believe it is, then Tuntunwala can love very, very surely."

The group did not quite share Sanjay's devotion to the political candidate. Pronob, for instance, laughed at the idea that Calcutta was nearing any violent catastrophe. Nor did he see Tuntunwala as a savior. "That man is money-minded, he'd charge too much," he usually added. "Look at the way he runs his factories and mills! Look at the way he slave-drives his workers! Of love he knows nothing; I can tell you he is a mistake."

Tara found all this talk about love quite disconcerting during a political campaign. She had expected "integrity" to be an issue, and "political acumen," even "personal magnetism and charisma" perhaps, but Sanjay and Pronob kept returning to love instead. On a wall outside the club, in fresher and more assertive white, one political slogan had effaced all others: MAO BRINGS DEATH, NIXON BRINGS LIFE.

The management of the Dhakuria Club had put up banners and posters for Tuntunwala's rally. GHOSE UNLEASHES EMOTION: TUNTUN-WALA LEASHES FRUSTRATION. LANDOWNERS OF CALCUTTA UNITE! There were balloons and ribbons and a brass band that played "Three Coins in the Fountain." Tuntunwala himself displayed awesome energy greeting guests at the club's entrance, belching out his orders to bring out more ice cream and *papadoms*, scattering malicious exclamations against "Those *goondahs!* Those weritable hooligans!" and picking his teeth for the cameras.

His energy did not win over the entire crowd at the club's pavilion. Some, like Pronob, remained suspicious or hostile, though they paid substantial sums to Tuntunwala's campaign fund. They regretted bitterly they could not find a savior within their own circle. They seized trivial incidents—the candidate's crude and clumsy way with silverware, his fractured Bengali and eccentric English, his insulting way with their aunts and cousins—to justify their hatred.

Sanjay was glad of this opportunity to meet the man he had decided would save Calcutta. He cornered the candidate between the boathouse and the pavilion and dramatically threw away the questionnaire his secretary had slipped into his briefcase. Tara, who had been held up on the pavilion by friends of her mother, ran down the path to the boathouse so she could join them. Sanjay's photographer had just finished posing the candidate beside an arrangement of Chinese lanterns.

"First of all, sir," said Sanjay, "let me ask you. What is your exact stand on redistribution of land?"

"Those who work hard can make paradise out of a desert, no?" Then, without pausing, he said, "Mrs. Cartwright, I'm so moved to see you here. You're beautiful as usual, especially when you're a little out of breath."

"What is your stand on the resettlement of refugees?" asked an old man from a Bengali newspaper.

"May I remind you," screamed Mr. Tuntunwala, "if you men get too tricky I shall cut off this interview this very second!"

Tara had been flattered by his aside to her. She was eager to help him. He was a man of such energy, so aggressive, so brittle and ferocious that next to him businessmen like Pronob seemed flabby. And the Bengal Tiger, she thought, what of my father? And she wanted to cry. She watched Tuntunwala whip out charts and clippings from the pocket of his vest to force a point. But she thought that of all the journalists present only Sanjay, pale and fanatical, would write of him as "the savior of the moment."

"And what, sir, is your position on cow slaughter?" asked Sanjay.
"Only those cows that deserve to be slaughtered should be slaughtered. When you find one, let us know, okay?"

"Why do you think *lakhs* and *lakhs* of people riot in Calcutta?" asked
a young man from *The Rebel Speaks*, a weekly with a small circulation.

"Because there are *lakhs* and *lakhs* of chinless and morally weak persons today."

"But what of frustration, Mr. Tuntunwala?" persisted the young man.
"I ask you, what of poverty and outrage?"

The young man's questions brought out all the ferocity of Tuntunwala's character. Shadows, deep and fierce, gathered in that fistlike face.
Sanjay's photographer crouched with his camera ready to capture the
candidate's wrath. So Tara, recovering the artful innocence she had been
taught by the St. Blaise's nuns, asked her little question.

"What of love, Mr. Tuntunwala?" she asked softly. "What of the
refugees and love?"

At first the candidate seemed pleased, as if he thought she were
playing charming games with him. Then he picked his teeth with a
show of arrogance and said, "Heart's matters, Mrs. Cartwright, are for
idiots and women. I do not knowingly stray into heart's matters."

All of this was reported in the *Calcutta Observer*. "As for love,"
Sanjay wrote, "a question raised by an impudent, unaccredited western
reporter, Mr. Tuntunwalal had a single, clear ringing response. The age
of love has passed long ago," Sanjay rhapsodized. "The needs of Calcutta are for confidence, investment, and enforcement." Perhaps Sanjay,
in his madness, believed it. Perhaps Tuntunwala, in a politician's privilege, had added it later. Perhaps Sanjay, in the presence of the candidate, had only heard Tara's Americanized voice. Tara was beginning
to see it clearly. The campaign, the articles, the bitterness, were merely
to confirm it. Pronob and his friends sipping lemonade at the club were
bankrolling one doom to forestall another. But this, however near, was
still to come.

Just then there were noises by the lily pool in the center of the club
grounds. Little sparks went off. Pink and green and blue flames danced
on the grass. Children who had been eating ice cream all evening
clapped their hands and asked for more fireworks. Sanjay took notes
for his paper. The man from *The Rebel Speaks* laughed.

"What is this thing?" demanded Tuntunwala. "Call out the special
guards!"

Then there were more bangs, more flames and sparks. Women began
to scream. A waiter switched off the verandah lights. There was only
panic and confusion, children crying for their mothers, men trying to
reach telephones in the dark. "Bombs!" shouted Pronob. "How dare
those chaps plant bombs in the club!"

Tara was flung to the ground by Tuntunwala, who ordered her to crouch against an upturned boat for protection. She waited for the flash, the bone-shattering explosion that would end it all. They've won, she thought, amazed. She was praying. Then she opened her eyes, and saw Tuntunwala squatting in front of her. He seemed perfectly calm; in fact he seemed to welcome this opportunity to display new mastery. He instructed her to stay put until he reappeared. He yelled to the public not to worry—P. K. Tuntunwala was still alive, still in charge. Soon the lights had been restored. A waiter and the journalist from *The Rebel Speaks* were apprehended by the candidate's special guards. Tara was ordered to emerge from her hideout.

"To think, Mrs. Cartwright, you might have been killed because of my political career!"

When the police arrived Tuntunwala's bodyguards handed over the two alleged criminals. There were many helpful shoves and pushes from respectable campaign leaders as the police led the men away. Even the children wanted to get in the act. They took bony little swings at the handcuffed men. As the journalist was being pushed toward a truck, Tuntunwala excused himself from Tara and ran to block his path. To the accompaniment of flash bulbs, he threw away his toothpick and slapped the journalist in the face. Then the procession continued to the truck. The truck left for the police station.

A crowd had formed around the political candidate. This man is an enemy, thought Tara, savior or not. She had seen terrifying hate on his face the instant before he had slapped the young man from the newspaper, and now he was being praised for his courage. Sanjay had begun to tell her of the editorial he would write later that night. "Industrialist with spunk," he began. "Say what you will, the man has charisma." An older man from a Bengali-language daily kept irritating everyone with his suspicions that the bombs had been rigged by the campaign managers to insure the correct degree of drama. He too was led out of the club by a special bodyguard.

"If only I didn't believe in heart's matters," said Tara to Sanjay, who was too busy taking notes on the size of scorch marks on the grass to pay attention to her.

Two sticks of dynamite were found in the box. "Thank God they bungled the fuse," said one of the bodyguards.

"One moment, Mrs. Cartwright," called Tuntunwala from the club's pavilion. "Mr. Sanjay Basu will be shown much dastardly detail about tonight's attack. I suggest you take my car and a bodyguard home now. Who knows what else might happen here!"

Tuntunwala had not exaggerated the dangers of the club. In the early part of the summer when she had seen the rioters only from the roof of the Catelli-Continental she had thought life in Calcutta could be a succession of exciting confrontations. But now she was impressed by the city's physical dangers. Now after the bomb or fireworks at the pavilion, after the crouching and shivering in the boathouse, she understood the group's fierce desire for protection. She had seen enough; she was no longer curious. Between the boredom of the group and the newfound zealousness of Sanjay, there was deadness. She thought again of the old man in a blazer and she prayed for his preservation, and hers.

When Tuntunwala's car, chauffeur and bodyguard arrived for her at the club gates she was thankful that he wanted to protect her.

"Driver, take *memsahib* to Camac Street," ordered Tuntunwala. The unflattering light magnified the candidate's ferocious ugliness. Tara thought she saw him slowly bring down his left eyelid and wink at her.

4

Reena received a picture of young McDowell a week before his arrival. To her astonishment Washington McDowell turned out to be black. She and her mother argued at great length about the diet of "the African," as her mother insisted on calling him. They were certain he was a ferocious beef-eater. In despair they telephoned Tara, who was expected to be an authority on all matters dealing with "Europeans," even black ones. "Ribs!" Tara informed them curtly, and then hung up.

Reena's mother was so upset she seriously considered calling off the whole thing. Especially since other families had gotten American boys who could sing movie songs like "Que Será, Será" and say a few phrases in imperfect Bengali to delight their host and hostess. She was not familiar with the ways of Africans, had only seen them in Tarzan movies, and now there was not enough time to learn.

Reena, of course, thought of herself as a great deal more sophisticated than her mother. Her mother had come from an orthodox family and had not gone to school past grade eight, but Reena was a St. Blaise's girl in addition to being modern. She'd read Conrad at St. Blaise's and tried to keep an open mind.

The day of Washington McDowell's visit to Calcutta coincided with a minor citywide riot. The price of rice had gone up overnight, and though no general strike had been declared it was rumored that the followers of Deepak Ghose would take to looting grocery stores and overturning cars. Bringing young McDowell home from the Dum Dum Airport would be both difficult and dangerous. Sanjay offered to use his influential friends and broadcast an appeal not to give a bad impression to important African dignitaries. But Tuntunwala suggested

636 / INTERNATIONAL SHORT NOVELS

that such an appeal would be imprudent. The *durwans* of Camac Street where Tara and Reena were neighbors offered to accompany the *missy-babas* to the airport. But the Bengal Tiger, who had come to feel *durwans* were useless in a violent city, instead taped two red crosses to Reena's Fiat and advised her father to pose as a doctor on call for that day. Reena's father borrowed a stethoscope, packed his wife, Reena and Tara in the back seat, and left for the airport at daybreak.

When the passengers finally arrived no one except perhaps Tara was prepared for the "Africanness" of the young McDowell. His hair grew in a foot-wide halo around his face. Tara tried to whisper the word "Afro," but Reena's family was too stunned to listen. He looked about sixteen and he seemed to the Indians to be at least eight feet tall. In truth he was six foot seven and still growing, a high school basketball star on scholarship to Berkeley. He had long legs like Bamboo poles which were partially covered with jeans on which several messages had been scrawled. He wore a colorful Indian shirt and beads and a peace symbol.

"What is this thing that Pronob has given us?" asked Reena's mother as she sat tightly balled in a plastic armchair at the airport lounge.

The project officer, who was a Rotarian and a slight friend of Reena's father, brought young McDowell over to them.

"Hi!" shouted Washington McDowell. He called Reena's parents Mom and Pop from the first moment. The whole party was quickly supplied with Cokes by the project officer, who explained that Tara lived in New York and would be of "veritable and invaluable service" to McDowell. Then they were left to wait out the riot at the airport. The project officer himself had a meeting in town, and so intended to borrow a purser's uniform and sneak out in an airlines coach.

"We are very, very ashamed about this riot business," said Reena's father. "I cannot think what you must be feeling."

Young McDowell assured Mom and Pop and Reena that he thought the riots were a gas. They asked him the only questions they'd ever asked Americans—such as how did he like India?—and he told them that he couldn't take the heat. Everything in California was air-conditioned.

"What do you know of our culture?" Reena's mother asked. It was, for the moment, an innocent question delivered like an accusation.

"I knew an Indian cat back in school used to groove on Ravi Shankar records. Little guy blacker than I am—you know him?"

"Probably South Indian," said Tara.

"Name kinda like Submarine."

"Subramanian?" Tara asked.

"We are a very large country," said Reena's father. "This Subramanian chap is Madrasi. We have never even been to Madras it is so far away."

"India is a whole continent," Reena's mother put in, now more aggressively.

"Yeah—O.K." said Washington McDowell. "But all the way over on the plane they were asking me to sing Johnny Mathis."

"How silly they are," said Reena. Reena, through the mediumship of Carefree Kevin of Radio Ceylon, had once written a letter to Johnny Mathis. "Your voice is much deeper than Johnny Mathis's. You should sing Andy Williams' songs. Will you sing 'Moon River'?"

"Andy Williams, huh? Wait'll I play the records I brought."

Reena's mother kept prompting Tara to ask Washington McDowell if he liked chilled tomato cocktail. "You ask, please, you ask. He won't understand my English," the woman said each time in English. "Tell him we have very, very chilled tomato cocktail in the house. Tell him it'll be served under the garden umbrella as soon as we get home."

Reena's father called Pronob from the airport and was offered the assistance of a police escort. He turned the offer down, judging it to be too conspicuous and therefore potentially dangerous. Pronob then advised him to wait till four when the rioters were expected to disperse, and to form a convoy of host families for the ride to town.

Promptly at four the host families led by Reena's Fiat left Dum Dum. It was difficult to fit all of Washington McDowell into a packed Fiat. Reena's mother worried the African would get cramps. But she worried even more that Reena would be crushed indecently against a strange and gigantic male.

"Push over here," she directed her daughter. "There is too much room here." Reena found herself sitting on Tara's lap.

The street outside the airport looked wider than it had on the way out. It was deserted except for groups of mild youngsters playing cricket. Storefronts were pulled down and padlocked. Banks were protected by collapsible metal shutters. People watched anxiously from the windows of their homes. The ditches were dry and cracked at either side of the road. Once Tara believed she saw a man lying in the ditch but she thought it best not to exclaim in case it alarmed young McDowell.

In Shambazar the convoy ran into its first hint of trouble. The lead car was stopped by a band of fierce-looking youths. They made rude comments to Reena's mother, ripped the stethoscope off Reena's father and shouted, "*Masai*—that doesn't fool us. We weren't born yesterday, you know." "Hey, stop the car, man!" said Washington McDowell. Then he emerged, knees first, from the Fiat. They stared at him in wonder. They had never seen hair like a stiff halo. They had never seen clothes that carried slogans like a Shambazar wall. McDowell had a strange walk. His hips reached the eye level of the fierce-looking youngsters. They watched the loose rotation of McDowell's hips as he walked around the Fiat and shook hands with everyone. "Now you cats gonna get with it! I want some noise. I want some chanting, man. You guys gotta get a little class in your riots or else you ain't gettin' no-where." He taught them to raise clenched fists and shout "Brown is beautiful!" He read them jokes from his sweatshirt and jeans and he was hysterically applauded.

"Right out!" the boys shouted.

"*On*, man. *On*," said McDowell. "Now I want you all to come over here and apologize to Mom and Pop and Reena. You were right—he ain't no doctor."

One young man raised a penknife.

"No, man—cool it. Pop's brought me here all the way from America so's I can study how to help. How can I help if I don't even get home from the airport, huh?"

Washington McDowell's performance was repeated before each bar-ricade. "*Arré*—this fellow is better than a Patton tank with our *goon-dahs*," Reena's father beamed. By the time the Fiat had reached Camac Street Tara had the feeing that the whole city was standing with clenched fists and yelling "Right on, right out."

"We're very, very ashamed," apologized Reena's mother. "Tell him, Tara, tell him I cannot describe how ashamed I am about those horrible people. Tell him he'll get his chilled cocktail right away."

The servants in Reena's house, like most servants on Camac Street, were easy to shock. The female servants took one look at the new house guest and ran screaming inside the house. Reena's family allowed McDowell to pretend he had noticed nothing unusual about his recep-tion. While Reena sat on the lawn and told the visitor she knew some-thing about his people from having read *The Negro of the Narcissus* at St. Blaise's, her parents rushed to the kitchen to give the servants a scolding. It was an uncomfortable time for Tara. She had been asked to be a bridge between Washington McDowell and Camac Street during the crucial hours before dinner was served. Reena's father had invited Tara's parents and Sanjay Basu to dinner to lighten her load. Tara, who knew very few blacks in New York and was invariably frightened by those she saw, wondered what further conversation she could practice on young McDowell. He's *so* American, she thought, even more than David. But the visitor couldn't relate to her—she was just another Indian and the fact of an apartment on the fringes of Harlem, an American husband and passport, simply didn't register. She frightened him. But he looked so relaxed and comfortable on Reena's lawn that she found it hard to ask him small questions about his family or home-town.

He said he was from L.A. "Watts?" she asked.

"Yeah," he said, and she realized too late that she'd offended him.

It was impossible to be a bridge for anyone; she wished someone had made her duties clearer for the evening. Reena seemed to be getting on extremely well on her own, urging the guest to teach her new phrases and songs. Bridges had a way of cluttering up the landscape.

After a while the dinner guests arrived. McDowell had tried to spruce himself a bit for dinner by adding a colorful headband to his Afro. The Bengal Tiger was the first to hold out his hand.

"Never mind," he said. "We're ordinary middle-class people. For the next fortnight you'll be like our boy. No formalities. no shyness."

Arati and Reena's mother looked pained and slightly embarrassed all evening as if they both suffered from menopausal nervous disorders. Reena's father tried to establish a party note by reminiscing about his "student days in the foreign." He sang a few bars from "Chattanooga Shoe Shine Boy" and stood up to do his Bing Crosby imitation. But young McDowell appeared to be on the verge of a headache, so "Pop" had to run up to get his chest of homeopathic medicine instead of performing his emergency song-and-dance routine. Headaches were the plague of Camac Street society; Washington McDowell had gained some acceptance.

"Tara, you tell him homeopathic medicine is best in the world," said Reena's mother. "Tell him it's safe enough to give to pregnant women."

"I don't need no pills, thanks," said Washington McDowell.

"He doesn't need any pills," Sanjay repeated in case the others had not understood McDowell's accent.

The assistant editor of the *Calcutta Observer* was dressed in a three-button suit from Jordan Marsh, a raw-silk shirt, an English tie and Ganesh cuff links. He believed nice ties like that went a long way to save difficult situations. He had run out of his imported aftershave lotion, otherwise that nicety too would have been preserved. The young man had prepared very seriously for the evening at Reena's. In addition to dressing sharply he had honed his favorite opinions, elaborated them sedately on the way over, and now awaited the right pause to launch them. He felt his whole journalistic career had somehow been a preparation for this encounter. It was a good thing the black boy suffered from a headache. The boy had listened politely to the vulgar conversation of the older generation. Now he would seize the headache as his opportunity to withdraw with McDowell to the privacy of the verandah.

"Come, Washington. I think you need some fresher air."

The older men looked at him in relief. They lit their cigarettes and admired the smooth way the young editor had extricated them from a frightening situation. There was no need to struggle on in English.

They began a passionate and technical discussion of import restrictions and licenses.

"A marvelous idea!" agreed Reena as she followed Sanjay and McDowell to the verandah, leaving Tara no choice but to join her.

In the verandah outside Sanjay leaned against a bamboo trellis and tried to adjust his prepared ideas and delivery to the larger audience. He preferred a confidential man-to-man talk in which young McDowell would have given him the lowdown on America and he would have been frank, if necessary even bitter, in his comments about India and especially Calcutta. The boy had strange hair. Sanjay himself did not believe in long hair or careless manners or anything that detracted from a professional man's career. But the sight of McDowell's hair released him from his usual guardedness with foreigners. A man with hair like that could never be a *sahib*, and that in itself was pleasant.

The assistant editor stared shyly at the teen-age visitor, then handed him a clipping of a recent editorial he had written for his paper.

"I'd be delighted to have your opinion, my dear sir."

"We're in the midst of a bloodcurdling election campaign," explained Reena. "All those *goondahs* who stopped us are on the *other* side, of course."

Tara sensed the moment required her "bridging" functions. McDowell's sympathies were probably with the *goondahs*. It would be impossible to explain to Reena that Washington McDowell *was* the other side, that when he returned to Watts he would make fun of Camac Street girls like Reena, that one day at Berkeley perhaps he too would slash cars and riot. She was saved from refereeing the situation by Washington McDowell, who had started to stumble aloud through Sanjay's editorial.

"Some venerable gentlemen in this country have declared that democracy is suffering a crisis in Calcutta at present. That our democracy is in danger is an indisputable fact. Those who are not convinced of the dangerous crisis should be referred to the bizarre and inexplicable (fortunately foiled) violence during a recent campaign rally for the Independent Opposition candidate. It is inconceivable that in this day and age of Calcutta's enlightenment a militant majority should try to impose its fierce will on a responsible tax-paying minority. Does not a minority have rights? Does not the minority have feelings? We ask these painful questions because the vocal majority will not ask them. It is unjust to asume that wealth and indifference go hand in hand. Anyone who assumes that the multimillionaire Tuntunwala is disdainful of the have-nots should be referred to the fifty hospital beds he has donated to the Sarada Devi Ladies' Hospital, the specialized equipment to Physical Handicap Clinic, etc., and to the countless donations he has made

to temples, schools, orphanages and other suchlike charities. The mali-
cious campaign unleashed by certain other political figures to disfigure
the reputation of Tuntunwala will only serve to strengthen this man's
determination to succeed. Malice will not harm Tuntunwala, nor hate
wither his tremendous energy."

Washington McDowell read through the clipping slowly and painfully, hesitating over occasional words and tugging at his Indian beads.

"Do you like it? I mean do you get it all?" Sanjay was anxious to
explain the point and tone. He had come prepared to expand on topics
like urban land reform, peaceful coexistence, unarmed neutrality, Five-
Year Plans, the abuse of Hindus in East Pakistan. His mind was
crowded with mathematical trivia about literacy percentages, crop in-
creases, and bank interest rates, because Tara had warned him of the
Americans' respect for statistics. Sheltered girls like Reena and Tara
had no head for numbers. They could be counted on to be quite beautiful, intuitive and charming. Sometimes they could make almost brilliant
comments on literature. But the responsibility for facts, dates and numbers rested with him alone. His head was bursting with tabulated figures. Graphs, economic maps and charts had suddenly attained the pro-
portions of a vision.

"I have *one* important question, man," Washington McDowell said
solemnly, dropping his voice and placing a hand on Sanjay's shoulder.
"Don't people here use any deodorants?"

Sanjay felt betrayed by the black visitor. He had been near a crisis—
nowadays Calcutta brought him frequently close to crises—and he had
hoped to give flesh to his new vision. A crisis would occur again, but
he was sure the vision would disappear. Next time he would merely be
a dogmatic journalist who stated facts with shrill emphasis and bored
everyone with his ideas. No longer in a mood for international candor,
he sat heavily in a canvas easy chair.

"We don't need deodorants, Washington," Reena said. "We people
take three baths a day. We leave scents and deodorants to Europeans."

Washington McDowell looked to the right and left in the verandah,
brought his knees up to his chin, shook his Afro head till the headband
slipped below his ears, and giggled for the first time. Tara decided there
was no point in telling McDowell that Reena had not meant her remark
to be either amusing or malicious.

Sanjay rose stiffly from his easy chair. "You no doubt have questions
about the caste system?" He did not intend to let the matter rest with
deodorants and daily baths. "You no doubt think us primitive racialists
because of our castes?" He was beginning to recover his British Council

debating manner. "My dear sir, you probably think we are beastly toward our little *harijans*. But let me assure you, sir, that is an unfortunate and preposterous deception, let me assure you . . ."

"There is no caste system in India," interrupted Reena.

"It was technically abolished after the independence," added Tara.

Tara was disturbed that their talk had taken such a turn. It was going on longer than it should have. She wished Reena's servants would announce dinner. But Sanjay was pleased with the new flippant-yet-dignified personality he had resumed. He pressed on with more questions that could have been mistaken for answers.

"No doubt McDowell, my boy, you think of us as an undemocratic and underdeveloped nation? No doubt you think we're a race of philosophers and fire walkers? You think we'll never get on because we're poor at figures and facts?"

"Goodness," interrupted Reena. "Tonight you're really in form, Sanjay!"

"Well, let *me* ask you a serious question that I hope, sir, merits an honest answer. Is there discrimination in America?" Sanjay sank back in his chair, finger tips together as if he were praying for the return of his vision.

"Oh, isn't he too much! How to do anything with Sanjay when he gets in one of those moods!"

"You putting me on?" McDowell asked. The phrase, new for Reena, who devoured foreign colloquialisms and trivia, successfully diverted the conversation.

"Because racial discrimination was abolished after *our* independence. It says right there on the paper—All men are created equal. Yes, sir."

Tara felt sorry for Sanjay, who continued to sit with his finger tips together, a debater defected by the refinement of his own words.

"There *is* discrimination, you know," Tara assured him. But it was no good. He had wanted to hear that admission from Washington McDowell. Having bungled her main duties for the evening she now concentrated on comforting the ruffled editor.

Reena and McDowell were arguing playfully in a corner. Exclamations reached Tara now and then. "You would really shoot? With a gun?" And from McDowell the words that had become so common. *Pigs. Honky.* Reena giggled with each new word.

Tara complimented Sanjay on his editorial and agreed enthusiastically that Tuntunwala was a forceful candidate. If only he could arrange a debate between Ghose and Tuntunwala!

"What you need, Sanjay," Tara explained, "is some kind of confrontation scene. You know what I mean? Some kind of drama involving

Ghose and Tuntunwala. Very few witnesses, but a lot of coverage by reporters."

The sophisticated editor was not to be appeased by Tara's earnest suggestions. He felt from that evening on he would be a failure. He would not convince anyone with his words. Lizards scurried on the wall behind his chair. He pulled up a stake from a potted creeper and teased the lizards. "I am only a chronicler of events, my dear girl," Sanjay said slowly without looking at Tara. "You want me to manipulate destinies? I'll have to leave that to chaps like Tuntunwala."

By the time the "European" lentil soup was served, Reena had mastered the radical style, and Sanjay had begun to depress everyone with his comments. "This boy's not the joker he pretends to be," Sanjay repeated to anyone who would listen to him during dinner. "The boy knows the importance of my question. I've been keeping up with foreign magazines. I know discrimination still exists. He can't fool me. We aren't the only backward country!"

Reena's father admitted later that the dinner had not been a success.

A week after young McDowell's arrival in Calcutta Tara received a frantic call from Reena's mother.

"You are our lone *Americawali!* Can you come quickly right now? I cannot tell you over the phone the shame that has happened."

Tara canceled her plans for going to an Uttam Kumar movie with Nilima in order to help Reena's mother. She had accepted the responsibility of bridging problems between McDowell and his host family partially because it made her feel noble and competent and partially because he was familiar and American. The younger of the two *durwans* escorted her next door to Reena's house, and Tara was met on the lawn by the distraught woman.

"I thought you would try to hurry at least," complained Reena's mother. "Reena might come back any minute."

She led Tara through a series of halls and small rooms, up a narrow back staircase and through more small rooms into her private sitting room. Like Tara's house Reena's house was too large for the needs of the family, and looked permanently empty and middle-aged. Reena's older sister, who lived in a mining town near Jamshedpur, came once a year to visit with her two boys. But her boys were so well behaved that they too failed to make the house seem smaller or more cosy.

The sitting room, which Reena's mother had learned to call "my den" from an old issue of an American interior decorating magazine, was furnished exuberantly. Pink Sankhera sofas and chairs were burdened with overstuffed cushions in red, green, yellow and blue printed raw silk. Pale madras checks of blue and orange draped the windows and polka-dotted Swiss organza covered all tabletops. On the wall hung mounted prints of Mogul paintings, Radha and Krishna surrounded by monkeys and peacocks and framed scenic views of Lac Leman, Matterhorn and Lausanne.

"Have some mango nectar," ordered the distracted mother, pointing to a brass tray full of light refreshment. "Go on, have some guavas or papayas."

Tara ate obediently as she waited for the catastrophe. The woman beside her appeared to be marshaling her emotions into place as she sat on the pink Sankhera sofa, a tightly bloused mother in despair.

"I need your advice," Reena's mother began in intimidating tones. "I have always loved Americans. I have told Reena's father I wish India could become the forty-ninth state in the U.S."

The pause was obviously for rhetorical effect. When Tara seemed about to interrupt she was waved to silence by a regally tragical gesture.

"I repeat again that I have always loved Americans. I say to you now in all frankness I stood by your mother when your wedding telegram arrived and everyone was crying."

"Just a minute," began Tara. "I want to discuss that."

But Reena's mother had no time that afternoon for small battles. She had reserved her phrases and resentments for some other drama. "I love all things American, yes. But I don't like that boy!"

Tara felt ill. This love of America by a plump Bengali mother on Camac Street was more than she could bear. She put her mango nectar down in a hurry and spilled some nectar on the frilly Swiss organza tablecloth.

"Don't worry about it. It doesn't matter at all. Today I've time only for very, very important matters."

"What's wrong with McDowell?"

"Reena calls him Wash!"

"Is that terribly bad?"

"What can be worse?" Reena's mother assumed she could not depend on Tara's sympathy, so she tried to work on Tara's guilt. "Utter shame. Utter disgrace for us. How can I tell you how serious it is?"

The strategy obviously worked. Tara saw the hunched figure in the little pink sofa and she cursed herself for not warning Pronob and the project officer that foreigners could cause havoc in Camac Street, Calcutta. In recent weeks she had timidly observed Reena's mother at parties and had been shocked at the ignorance of the woman. No other word could describe the coarseness and vulgarity of her remarks. At first Tara had chosen words like "simple" or "naive," but gradually she had realized that Reena's mother had made a talisman out of her ignorance.

"Where's Reena?"

"How to conceal anything from you! I better explicitly explain."

"Explain what?"

"I suspect hanky-panky business between that boy and my girl!" This revelation was accompanied by unstifled gasps from the outraged maternal breast.

"I'm sorry but I still don't get it."

"You expect me to be crude? I'm saying that I fear Reena is in love with the African. I'm saying that I think they're up to no good."

The woman had heard whispered conversations between McDowell and Reena in the verandah; she claimed words like "sex" had floated to her chair hidden by a curtain.

"I blame myself, don't worry. What can a young girl do? She has her natural urges. I should have been more careful."

"But auntie, that's preposterous. Reena has no such urges."

"My Reena's a good girl. She's too innocent for such things. *Hai Bhagwan!* What if she's prematurely pregnant?"

The mother's self-berating was interrupted by the slamming of a car door. "That boy is a traitor!" finished Reena's mother. That was to remain her final judgment. But before Reena walked in through the door of the small sitting room she prepared a gently tragic smile to greet the young woman.

Reena seemed more blithe and agile than Tara had ever seen her.

"Hello there," she said, surprised to see her mother alone with Tara. "Right on, both of you!"

"Where have you been?"

"I think we've lost him to the students, Mother. He said he was going to room with one of the boys at the coffee shop!"

"He's out of his mind! Call the project officer!"

"Seriously. They got all involved talking about pickets and things. And he just wandered off. He got lost. He said goodbye and just got lost, you know what I mean?"

Reena's mother had no intention of investigating for herself the meaning of the situation. She hurried out of the room to make urgent telephone calls to her husband. For a long time Tara sat lost. She tried to explain to Reena that young McDowell had been one of the *others* from the very beginning. Only his slogan, his outlandish appearance, his knowledge of music had deceived Reena. She tried to soften things for her friend. "In America a girl like you and a boy like McDowell would never have met—so it's natural that he's gone away."

"Power to the people," said Reena sadly.

Reena's mother had been wrong of course about the "hanky-panky business." But the visit of Washington McDowell left other more permanent scars on Camac Street. The residents were pained by Mc-Dowell's easy desertion. Over gin and tonic they sometimes talked of it as "a thoughtless betrayal." Only Tara insisted it had not been thoughtless; it had been inevitable, a minimal act of gratitude from the other side.

PART FOUR
1

When the weather in Calcutta turns beastly, when the air conditioning breaks down in efficient hotels like the Catelli, when dance combos in nightclubs halt their music so the drummer can wipe his chin, when bullocks in harness collapse in busy streets, then prominent Bengali families collect their children and their servants and vacation for a fortnight in Himalayan Darjeeling.

Hemmed in by mountain ranges, Darjeeling spreads itself a little higher each year till from a distance the newest hotels and houses are hardly visible among the forests. In the days of the British Raj, choleric Englishmen and their wives fled to Darjeeling at the first hint of insubordinate May. Homesick subalterns and captains had called it "the queen of hill stations" and had tried to make of its stubborn landscape a bit of England. The westernized Indian had shortened Darjeeling to Darj and endowed it with the comforts of a newer, stranger exile.

On clear mornings, viewed from a bend in the narrow-gauge railway tracks, Darjeeling does look vaguely European. Little wooden houses hang perilously from green crags, mountain flowers bloom in window boxes, ladies in tweed suits peer from behind lace curtains and schoolboys in gym shorts play rugby and cricket.

The town itself is clearly divided into two sections: the upper and the lower. The upper town is picturesque in a guidebook way. There are clubhouses, boarding schools, a mall edged by rows of wooden benches, a park for nursemaids and children, an observatory, luxury hotels and the chalets of very rich men from the plains. The upper town is landscaped by pine trees and mountain streams. Flowers are grown to prodigious size in the park by municipal workmen. On cool fresh mornings when the vacationer recalls the Calcutta of the sweltering plains, Upper Darjeeling seems to him not a bit of England but a bit of paradise instead.

The lower town is dominated by the bazaar. From the bazaar radiate dirty alleys and steep trails. It is not considered beautiful by fashionable Bengali men and women. But tourists eager to finish their rolls of film take the Cart Road down to Lower Darjeeling and spend the day examining stalls, monasteries, yogis and tribal dens. Here the trees have been cut down to make room for people and business. Mountain streams have been diverted to purify shops and hovels. There are no flowers here, only pretty weeds that cover the sides of occasional mountains. Anonymous holy men sit bent in improbable positions in the middle of the mountain trails. Near the bazaar are two Hindi movie houses and posters advising people to have no more than two children. The streets are crowded with tribal urchins in tattered jackets, bowlegged donkeys hauling firewood up steep mountain trails, and occasional palanquins for arthritic businessmen. The lower town looks like any other town in the plains, except that it is smaller and poorer and that it high up in the Himalayan mountains.

2

Nilima was the first in Pronob's group to leave for Darjeeling. Her family owned a modest house on Cart Road near the mall, but her father preferred to rent that house to tenants and occupy "a two-bedroom suite with fantastic view and all further amenities" at the Kinchen Janga Hotel. Pronob went up next. His father had returned from Benares for two weeks to consult a heart specialist, so Pronob took advantage of his presence in Calcutta to leave the Flame Co., Ltd., for a short spell. Pronob always stayed at the Chatterly Hotel though the food there was bad. Every year after the first two days he threatened to change hotels, but he never did, and the Chatterly management had grown very fond of him. Reena's and Tara's family left last of all. The Bengal Tiger had been busy addressing shareholders, and Reena's father liked company.

Hill stations were not recommended as resorts to the Bengal Tiger. He suffered from high blood pressure and fierce nosebleeds. But for two weeks in the year the Bengal Tiger was foolish and romantic. He loved the Himalayas; he had written three poems set in Darjeeling in his early twenties, and as a middle-aged man he returned every summer to those hills. Tara was happy at the thought of going up to Darjeeling. The small violence at the Dhakuria Club had unnerved her more than she cared to admit and her failure with Washington McDowell still tortured her with guilt. McDowell was rumored to be somewhere in Shambazar, safe from Rotarians, diarrhetic but active. She felt protected in the mountains. She heard her father say to the doctor over the phone, "*Arré*, doctor-*babu*, que será, será. If I must die then let me die in the mountains where the air at least is fresh," and Tara thought she too could die in Darjeeling quite happily.

The journey to Darjeeling was not a difficult one. It involved a short Dakota hop to Siliguri and then a steep climb in the airline's limousine. The morning that Tara went up to Darjeeling she thought the mountains were particularly splendid. The limousine curled past tribal women doing their laundry in mountain streams and dirty children running among pine trees, past a tiny train filled with Bengali families who sat on their baggage and waved back at them. Sometimes there were dynamite scars where mountains had been blown up to lay the tracks and narrow highways. The chauffeur occasionally pointed to boulders heaped at the side of the road and detailed the date of that landslide and the number of deaths or injuries it had caused.

Besides the families of Reena and Tara, the limousine carried a tall, white girl, a mustached old Englishman and his Anglo-Indian secretary. The two mothers whispered in Bengali throughout the journey. The Anglo-Indian secretary shivered in her thin cardigan, and the Englishman remained aloof and slightly malicious to the end. The tall white girl seemed friendly and exclaimed to herself all the way to Darjeeling. Tara felt sure the girl was American, but after her failure with young McDowell she was reluctant to respond to overtures by *sahibs*. The white girl was the first to be let out. The other passengers watched her leap out of the limousine with mannish energy, carry her own suitcase, and knock on the door of the Everest View Tourist Lodge, which seemed to them a low-class boarding house too close to the bazaar.

"She will not get fresh air there," said Arati. "Tara, why didn't you tell her that boarding house is too close to the bazaar? The poor girl will get sick!"

Then the limousine pulled up before the rock gardens of the Kinchen Janga Hotel, and coolies grabbed suitcases and picnic baskets.

"Sir," said the chauffeur to the evil-looking Englishman, who sat stiffly with his sick secretary in the front seat. "This is the first-class super-best hotel in Darjeeling. As good, sir, as the Mount Everest Hotel, the Pine-View, the Windermere and the Snow-Vista. *Sahib*, here running hot and cold water twenty-four hours per day, and all nice amenities. Plus famous view of Kinchenjunga range from bed every morning.

"The Chatterly please," said the evil-looking man. "And hurry."

The two families were welcomed by the hotel manager, who rushed outside at the sound of the limousine.

"*Arré arré*, Dr. Banerjee *sahib*! We're honored by your party's humble visit, sir! Make my hotel your home as long as you like. I have arranged special housie night for you people, and beauty contest and suchlike for the young ladies."

It was eight or nine years since Tara had been to Darjeeling. Scaling the mountain with foreigners in the airline's limousine, she had been very apprehensive. As a schoolgirl she had loved the hill station, had breathed deep like the others and murmured, "Oh how fresh the air is!" But this time things would no doubt be less perfect.

"Thank you, manager *sahib*," said Tara's mother. "The mountains are beautiful as always. In the mountains I feel God is physically present."

After tea in the main lounge, where Reena commented on the growing number of Marwaris in decent hotels, the girls telephoned Nilima and Pronob. Pronob sounded lonely, anxious for the latest news from the plains. He complained that the dining room in his hotel was musty and the meals too British and that he was a fool to come every year to Darjeeling. Nilima's mood was more ambiguous. She talked quickly on the telephone as if she were afraid that the others might try to ask her a question.

"We're in the west wing," Nilima said. "A simply marvelous suite overlooking the old palace. Ma wants me to do up my hair now because she's invited shoals of people before dinner and I'm supposed to impress them. We went to Tiger Hill last Sunday and that was simply super though we had to get up in the middle of the night to reach the right spot in time to see the sunrise. Just fantastic, I can't tell you what it was like, it was that great. I'll probably see you in the dining room tonight. We are table eight, don't forget." Then she hung up on her friends.

The two girls changed into pretty afternoon silk saris and worried that Nilima seemed to be avoiding them. They guessed that Nilima's mother was probably trying to clinch a marriage deal during the fortnight's holiday, when she could consult Nilima's father without competing with the family business. But they were astonished that Nilima refused to confide in them.

On the way to the mall after tea Reena and Tara thought they were passing the entire summer population of Darjeeling. Everyone had turned out in their holiday best to stroll near the mall and chat with people one avoided in the plains. There were women in bright georgettes and short woolen jackets. Men in tweed suits or gabardine raincoats left over from their student days in England or on the Continent. Children in ski slacks clinging to gnarled old horses and nursemaids in hand-me-down cardigans running behind them. Servants in summer liveries walking with solemn fat spaniels.

Tara was moved by her first full view of the hill station. The holidayers walked up and down the mall in solid groups of ten and twelve, or rode around the observatory on slow and retired racehorses. A band in singular but impressive uniform played "When Irish Eyes Are Smiling" from a permanent stand. Once she caught sight of Nilima talking earnestly to a bespectacled young man in a vest while a bevy of relatives from both sides stood self-consciously near a dry fountain ten feet away. Tara tried to catch Nilima's eye, and failed; so she called out to her friend and Reena waved. But Nilima pointedly ignored them.

"She's embarrassed by us!" Tara exploded. "What's the matter with her? Why is she avoiding us?"

"She's embarrassed of *you*, not me, my dear," Reena said. "She probably thinks that little man will run away if he finds out one of her friends arranged her own marriage."

Tara found both the snub and its explanation believable and infuriating. She was just an eccentric and imprudent creature whose marriage had barred her from sharing the full confidence of her St. Blaise's friends.

There had been a time, Tara remembered, when Darjeeling had meant quiet walks along mountain trails with Giribala the maid and Rajah the cocker. The Himalayan resort had released adolescent happiness; strolling to Ghum with Pronob and Reena and listening to Buddhist monks chant strange phrases. Once Darjeeling had meant not an annual ritual to be rigorously executed, but a time of escape from the inexorable plains.

"Hello there!" shouted a fat man in a navy beret as he eased the girls from the thick of the strollers to the edge of the mall. It was Pronob, barely recognizable in his winter dress. As a younger man he had wanted to study painting in Paris, but his father considered a term at Cambridge more prudent for a future match-firm magnate. His overcoat, beret, scarf and gloves were relics of that brief period at Cambridge and a Paris weekend. "Isn't this a crazy place?" He stood with his arms around his two friends.

"I can't think why we come here! You should see the jam at our hotel!"

So it had come again. They exchanged their annual regret at having come up, their disappointment with their hotels, their anger at the social improprieties of Calcutta acquaintances, of greetings unacknowledged and dining etiquette appallingly mismanaged. Tara invited Pronob to join them for the housie game later that evening and Pronob appeared delighted to accept. She wondered what prevented him from making new friends at his own hotel.

Suddenly the crowds parted directly in front of them, and a big red-headed girl in green pants and turtleneck sweater emerged like a tractor before them. Other vacationers had stopped walking and were staring fixedly at the white girl who had forced her way through their ranks. "Hi!" she said, holding out her hand to Tara. "We came up together in the car this morning. I'm Antonia Whitehead."

It was hard for Tara to determine what was so startling about Antonia as she introduced herself and her friends. They had all seen white women before. There were still some little Englishwomen in Darjeeling, all widows of ex-colonels who called India "bloody hell" but who had opted to stay on after India's independence. It was perhaps Antonia Whitehead's size that made her so different. And the athletic way she was so well put together. They had never seen such brutal health.

Antonia Whitehead led Pronob and the two girls out of the mall and the crowds parted again. They lingered for a moment near a bench where a cluster of Bengali children fell over each other trying to make room for them. But Antonia did not sit down; the pause, Tara realized, had been merely to emphasize some point the girl had made.

"Isn't this place great?" the American girl said, raising her arms in an extravagant gesture that made her little breasts jiggle inside the green turtleneck.

Weeks later, in response to a letter to the *Calcutta Observer*, Sanjay would write an impassioned editorial on Antonia Whitehead:

"It has been said that she is really a blessing in disguise, that she is a missionary defrocked, that she is Deepak Ghose's special lady-friend. But I say to you she is dangerous. She is like a snake tightly coiled. I say to you get rid of her before she spreads further discontent. She talks in Shambazar of 'democratization' and 'politicization,' of parity and socioeconomic balance. But I urge you Calcatians to throw out this perilous lady before it is too late."

But that would come weeks later, after the rains had come down, and the revolution had broken in earnest. In the mountains of Darjeeling, where one was close to the gods, Antonia Whitehead simply wanted to be a friend. That first afternoon, it was more early evening than after-noon, she accompanied Reena, Tara and Pronob to Smith's Super Snack Counter and bared her heart to the three Indians over faintly rank ham sandwiches.

The history of Antonia Whitehead was simple. She had been born in Buffalo and had lived there with her parents till her father died of a heart attack and her mother remarried. Her dislike of her stepfather had freed her for travel. At fifteen she had become a missing person, had found herself first in San Francisco, later in Arizona, still later in Singapore and finally in Calcutta, which she said she wanted to call home.

Pronob started to loosen up at Smith's Super Snack Counter. He

652 / INTERNATIONAL SHORT NOVELS

leaned closer to the white girl than etiquette permitted and he asked a mildly flirtatious question. "And pray what brings a lovely lady like you to our country?"

"Oh, Pronob, what a silly question!" Reena exploded. "Of course we know she's here to seek peace and real happiness! Everyone comes here for that."

Antonia Whitehead laughed. Her laugh revealed gigantic, even teeth. Those teeth had no doubt been tamed by dentists in Buffalo, but next to dainty Reena's or Tara's they looked like the Himalayan ranges. "Reena, you're putting me on. I'm here," she said, turning seriously to Pronob and letting her red hair touch his Parisian beret, "really, I'm here because India needs help. The third world has to be roused to help itself."

And there it was, Tara realized. A small crisis without point perhaps, without emphasis or accent. But it was a crisis, distinct and serious, nevertheless. Pronob's face grew livid, though a girl from Buffalo could not be expected to notice changes of color under his brown smoothness. She resented the threat that Antonia Whitehead presented as she sat incomparably earnest and equine in a diner at Darjeeling. In this white girl with red hair Tara saw a faint rubbing of herself as she had been her first weeks in Calcutta, when her responses too had been impatient, menacing and equally innocent.

"I don't think you mean that," Pronob said. "I think you have a typically American sense of humor. I like a sense of humor. Will we see more of you after this day?"

"I'm dead serious, Pronob. And, of course, you'll see more of me. I thought you would never ask me for a date."

The matter of national need and individual utility rested there. Pronob offered to meet Antonia at the Everest View Tourist Lodge at seven, take her out to dinner at his hotel, then walk with her to the Kinchen Janga for an evening of housie and modest excitement.

"I don't like it," Tara confided to Reena as the girls returned to the hotel to change for dinner. "I *know* the type, believe me." And Reena had giggled. Like Washington McDowell, this American girl would supply her with phrases. "You poor silly-billy fusspot," she said.

3

Tara's misgivings lasted all night; the next morning she decided it would be better if she left Pronob and Reena for a few hours and accompanied her mother to a local shrine instead. It was not as if she had not warned her friends. Their wit—or what was left of it—would have to see them through.

Tara's mother, given to religious dreams, had learned to consider shrines as physical extensions of her dreaming self. Her fondest hope was to see a vision while wide awake. Quite logically she had made temples her natural targets.

"Where is this shrine, Mummy?" Tara called from the tiny dressing room as she finished her preparations for a possible holy moment.

"Do you think your mother knows her right from her left? You'll have to ask people on the way," remarked the Bengal Tiger from the living room, where he was being massaged by a servant.

"All these years and he still thinks I'm ignorant!"

"You ask her what number house this shrine is. Go on, ask her what street and see if she knows."

"If God wants me to visit him today He'll find a way," said Arati. Then in a conspiratorial dash to the dressing room she told Tara she knew the shrine was in the lower town somewhere. "Are you sure you want to come with us?" The "us" represented a maidservant and herself. "If you go, the maid can stay back."

"Are you sure you really want to go?" the Bengal Tiger asked.

"Yes." After the bad starts at Aunt Jharna's, the afternoons at the Catelli, after an old man had shown her his ruins and a handcuffed young man had been slapped in the face, she thought she had little to lose. Calcutta was the deadliest city in the world; alarm and impatience were equally useless.

"I'm so happy that I can't describe it," her mother wept. "It was so hard to know from your letters your feelings."

The Bengal Tiger, who was still being pummeled by a frail servant with firm hands, was moved by the conversation he had with some difficulty overheard. "What is this? You still believe? You're our little girl again? How to express this fantastic happiness?" He leaped off the Victorian sofa where he had been lying face down, took out a sandalwood icon of Narayan from his overcoat pocket, and rubbed it gently against Tara's forehead.

The joy of her parents released Tara's poor atrophied senses. Her early encounters with religion had been restricted to little more than bedtime mythological tales, dressing up for the Durga Pujah feast days and hearing her friends recite the Act of Perfect Contrition at St. Blaise's. She knew any truly religious experience required self-abandon, even frenzy. She had committed herself to an unusually holy experience: a visit to the ashram of Mata Kananbala Devi, whom devotees came to see not only from all over India, but from America and England as well.

If through intuition or prophetic dream Tara's mother had divined the full importance of Tara's visit to the shrine, she would have insisted on consulting palmists and horoscopes to determine the most propitious instant for such an outing. She believed in good and bad days, even good and bad hours within good days. The Bengal Tiger often joked that Arati did not cut her toenails when the planets were in the wrong places. But Tara's mother was on a mission in Darjeeling. She abandoned herself to fate and called for a double palanquin so Tara and she could hurry to Mata Kananbala Devi's temporary residence.

The palanquin was like an uncovered sedan chair. It was carried by four *pahari* tribesmen. As a vehicle it was not particularly comfortable, but Arati's rheumatism was bad that morning, and the palanquin was the only alternative to walking.

"I feel sort of conspicuous in this thing, Mummy," Tara objected. "It's almost like a rickshaw, and I could never ride in a rickshaw."

"You are being sensitive." Her mother looked perfectly gracious in the palanquin, dwarfing porters and pillows. "Besides, you would be far more conspicuous running behind me and the coolies."

They set off uphill from the Kinchen Janga Hotel past little wooden houses where potty Englishwomen in wide-brimmed hats and garden gloves tended flowers, past little teashops above souvenir stalls and shops that sold photographic equipment, till finally the road widened, and the palanquin was at the mall.

"Let us go around the mall once," decided Tara's mother. "I'd like to say hello to my friends and perhaps invite someone to come with us to see the Mata."

"But I don't want to run into anyone I know when I'm in this awful thing!"

"You are just too sensitive," soothed her mother. "It is a sickness to worry too much about other people's feelings."

The older woman sat back among the cushions, which had a permanently stale odor. Every now and then she raised her hand and waved to old friends, or ordered the palanquin stopped so she could exchange comments about her health and Darjeeling's weather with acquaintances who seemed anxious to pay her homage.

Embarrassed and sullen, Tara began to realize that passers-by envied her mother and her. Their glances, their whispers, their sudden veering of bodies or horses, showed respect rather than scorn, and Tara was amazed. It had been so long since she'd been admired by anyone. She did not deserve that admiration; she had done nothing outstanding.

Their carriage was suddenly interrupted by explosive laughter at the mall. Antonia Whitehead in purple jumpsuit and felt hat was pointing to their palanquin and shaking Pronob by his lapels. Her gestures were amused, not angry, though the crowd in the mall considered such distinctions in the white girl unimportant. The holidayers stood in large messy groups, unwilling to get mixed up in any incident but eager to enjoy from a distance whatever drama the girl might generate.

"What's that?" Antonia Whitehead shouted. "What the hell are they riding, Pronob?"

"It is a palanquin," said Tara's mother with dignity. She had raised herself a little from the smelly cushions. "I'm sure you don't have it in the States."

Tara would have made some pitiful joke and blushed purplish brown in answer to Antonia's question. But her mother, though deeply offended by the white girl's laugh, had defended her palanquin and her country with simple restraint.

"You do look awfully funny in that thing, Tara," Pronob remarked. He sounded bitter, as if he had permitted himself to referee a match between unequals and was ashamed because he could anticipate the consequences.

"With my pains, you prefer she lets me walk? No cars are allowed, you know that."

"Where're you going in that rickshaw?" Antonia asked.

"It is not a rickshaw," Tara's mother objected. "It is a palanquin." (That evening, while the Kinchen Janga Band played "Around the World in Eighty Days," Arati would say of Antonia Whitehead: "How can you trust that girl? She looks like a boy. How can you trust a girl without hips?" But now she was more guarded.)

The destination of the palanquin was reluctantly disclosed by Tara. Her parents considered it unwise to talk of shrines and pilgrimages in front of foreigners. They'd not even mention their *kirtans* or *pujahs* in letters to her and David. In revealing the purpose of their ride in the palanquin Tara felt she was betraying her whole family.

"All faith leads to the same god. Faith is all that counts," said Arati simply.

Tara thought her disclosure would be greeted with silence or witty contempt. She waited for the jokes to come so she could look dignified like her mother and say firmly to the others that she thought God was within reach even in Darj and that she really must be on her way.

"Pronob, I want to see this shrine," said Antonia Whitehead.

"You will not like it at all," Arati said. "It's near the bazaar. Very hot and very dirty. Why don't you go and roller-skate? Exercising is good for your health."

In the end, however, the party of four set off on Cart Road down the side of the hill. The *paharis* sang as they carried the two women. They were followed by Antonia and Pronob on foot arguing affectionately, and an undetermined number of silent *pahari* children.

It took the coolies approximately twenty minutes to lead the procession down to the bazaar. Seeing a giant purple *memsahib* in their party, the coolies lingered in front of stalls where tribal women in braids sold ornaments.

The procession stopped once at a large confectioner's, where Tara's mother bought four dozen orange and black sweetmeats, then continued down the crowded alleys till they reached a bright pink house next to a sari shop.

"This is the shrine," Tara's mother said, making preparatory motions for descent. "This is where Kananbala Mata lives."

The four visitors pushed through the unlocked front door and found themselves in a chamber that resembled a Victorian drawing room rather than a Hindu shrine.

"Mummy, are you sure we are at the right address?"

"Of course, I'm sure. I'm good with facts and figures no matter what your daddy says. I got ninety-six percent in maths in my Matriculation Exam. I think the Mata doesn't live in a temple but in a private place."

The arrival of a Nepali servant with holy marks on his forehead reassured them. The servant seemed uncertain of the white girl, but when Antonia folded her hands in a *namaste*, he threw her obsequious glances. "You have come for *dashan* with the Mata Devi? This way please. I'm her *Chela* Number One, otherwise known as Chief *Chela*. Hand me your sweetmeats please, I will make certain the Mata Devi gets them."

Chief *Chela*, who suffered from a visible skin disease, grabbed the four confectioners' boxes from Arati's hand. Tara disliked physical defects and worried about germs polluting the sweetmeats, which the *chela* had taken to be blessed. The man led them to an inner, more austere chamber. This place was bare of furniture except for a wooden bed against a whitewashed wall. Large portraits of saints and deceased patrons covered the walls. These portraits were garlanded with tinseled marigolds. Rows of worshipers sat on an extravagantly patterned rug, and shook their bodies in time to a religious tune that existed in their heads. Some had brought their children; these children left puddles on the rug or ate dried fruits from a plate.

Tara's mother walked to a modest seat far from the empty bed, where Kananbala Mata would eventually relax and bless her audience. The worshipers who had arrived very early for the morning *darshan* welcomed the arrival of the newcomers as a diversionary incident. They tightened their haunches to make room for the new guests. They discussed Antonia quite freely, detailing in astonished tones the vagaries of her outward appearance.

Suddenly there came the sound of feet behind the curtained door, the jingling of gold bangles, and for a second everyone in the room fell silent. A woman appeared at the door, she was short and fair and very beautiful. She paused briefly at the entrance and a quickness passed from body to body. The worshipers forgot to stare at Antonia. They were no longer housewives, daughters or parents, no longer vulgar or complaining women. They rang little brass bells or blew conch shells or shouted, "Ma, Ma, Mata!" The woman stepped over the worshipers' hands and legs and took up her position between bolsters on the bed.

Tara found herself shouting "Ma, Ma, Mata!" with the rest. She found it easy suddenly to love everyone, even Antonia Whitehead, who was the only person standing in the entire room. It was not Kananbala Mata who moved her so much as the worshipers themselves. They stretched their arms toward the woman, whose skin was the color of saffron rice. They tried to touch her, her plump toes, her wet hair that dripped on the bolster and mattress. And some succeeded. The woman did not move at all after taking up her position on the wooden bed. She did not look at her followers, who now seemed convinced they too had shared her radiance. Kananbala Mata fixed her gaze on the iron bars of the window, beyond which was a view of the bazaar, and beyond that the mountains where God rested.

Warm and persistent tears rose in Tara's heart. She forgot her instinctive suspicions, her fears of misunderstandings and scenes, she forgot her guardedness and atrophy in that religious moment. "Ma, Ma, Mata!" she shouted with the rest. Then some rose to their feet. Others threw posies of mountain flowers in the direction of Kananbala's holiness.

"Chief Chela begs your blessing, Mata Devi. On behalf of these worshipers, Chief Chela requests permission to present sweetmeats and other odds and ends."

Tara felt her mother's large body quiver beside her. She felt close to her mother, and to the other worshipers, close even to the Chela with the skin disease, so moving was the experience. Some new and reckless emotion made tiny incisions in her body, and forced her inhibitions to evaporate through the window that overlooked the mountains. Now, like her mother, she too believed in miracles and religious experiences. She knew men could walk on fire and sleep on beds of nails. Click went Antonia Whitehead's Instamatic camera. Antonia was getting it all down in true color so she could show it later to her friends. Click, click went Mata Kananbala's bangles as she hid her face from such homage.

"I'm just a housewife from East Bengal. Go home, you people, go home and worship yourselves."

"Chief Chela begs you, Mata Devi. Bless these sweetmeats and bowed heads."

"Go home and think of heart's matters. That's all I can say today."

The religious moment was over too quickly. Mata Kananbala officially blessed the gathering, canceled her afternoon *darshan* appointments, and left.

"Chief *Chela* bids all worshipers to partake of humble feast. All proceed to dining room with caution on your left."

In the dining room, paneled after some incongruous British style, the Hindu worshipers ate sweetmeats and peaches distributed by the Chief, *Chela*, who took time off to scratch his diseased hands.

Antonia Whitehead had not been impressed. She said clearly and rather loudly that she had witnessed a depressing performance. What India needed, she exclaimed, was less religious excitement and more birth-control devices. She hated confusion of issues, she said. Indians should be more discerning. They should demand economic reforms and social upheavals and throw out the Chief *Chela* as pledge of future success.

"You're making fun of us," Arati interrupted. "What do you know of the beautiful feelings I had in that room? What can you understand of the love I just felt?"

"She didn't mean that as a personal insult, Mummy," Tara explained.

"I do not insult her. How dare she do this to me then?"

Antonia Whitehead would not be silenced. She spoke of the need for artesian wells in the rainless villages, of improved farming techniques and better-trained doctors and nurses.

"You shut up," shouted Tara's mother. "If I knew better English I would show you how you were misrepresenting us. You have no right to be in this place."

Tara came quickly to her mother's rescue. "Antonia, you are making an utter fool of yourself!"

She recalled again her own bad starts and mistakes. To Pronob and his group at the Catelli she must have seemed as naive and dangerous as Antonia. There was no way to warn the girl, no way they could be friends. "You're being quite idiotic about this thing," Tara repeated as Antonia turned away in disgust. Tara sensed that Pronob had given Antonia a wink, or at the least a fleeting smile.

4

Beauty contests were new at the Kinchen Janga Hotel. They had been introduced by Mr. Patel, the new manager, who had received his hotel training at Cornell. Since taking over the failing business, he had crowned a Holi Festival Queen, a Pan-Indian Hill Station Queen and a Queen of the Pujah Holidays. The beauty contests did not help registration necessarily, but Mr. Patel believed in the establishment of traditions for his hotel. He hoped the Kinchen Janga would in time acquire an international reputation as a "fun place."

On the last Saturday before the June rains, Mr. Patel organized one of his many annual beauty contests. He hired old men, "refugees from terror in Tibet," he liked to inform his foreign clients, and gave them sandwich boards proclaiming a Miss Himalaya Contest.

"Will you invite me to the contest at your hotel tonight?" Pronob asked Tara. "I'd like to invite Antonia as my guest."

Tara, who bore reticent and ladylike grudges, gave him two tickets that had been issued as invitations to avoid complicated entertainment taxes.

"You don't expect her to win, do you?" teased Reena. " I didn't know you ever took out ugly women."

"She's not up too tight like you girls," Pronob retorted.

The mothers in Darjeeling were thrown into a panic by the promised beauty contest. Though they disapproved of such contests in principle, they worked very hard with creams and cucumbers and carrot juices to make their daughters lovelier. They regarded the event as a perfect opportunity to present a beautiful daughter to families on the market for brides, perfect because all preliminary negotiations could be handled with informality during the holidays.

The beauty contest should have been a happy and fruitful occasion for everyone. But a small incident on the afternoon of the contest almost ruined it for Tara.

It was a flimsy thing. Even Antonia Whitehead with her passion for accuracy could not reconstruct the chronology of those few disturbing seconds. When the Bengal Tiger was told of the incident he displayed unusual anger. "That Pronob is a nogood fool! Next time send for me quickly, let me handle it. That Pronob is fat and useless!" He assigned a servant to accompany Tara in the future whenever she went out of the hotel.

The afternoon began like any other. Tara accompanied Pronob and Antonia on horseback around the Observatory Hill, so they could admire the gray-blue beauty of the plains below, and then they struck out on little-used trails. That afternoon the riders discovered a lopsided grave erected by an Englishman for his "beloved friend," a Dalmatian, poisoned by a native servant. On the way back a band of rather scruffy holidayers in ill-fitting sweaters blocked their bridle path. At first Tara assumed the men had accidentally strayed off the sidewalk. But the holidayers came closer and closer, darting playfully between the three horses. They made rude comments about Tara and Antonia, blew them noisy kisses and slapped each other furiously on the back.

"You are so beautiful," shouted the frail and cunning holidayers in

Bengali. "For love of you, we want to die. Come ride over us. Put us out of our misery, you arrogant, lovely women." They pretended to collapse with pain near Tara's horse, then picked themselves up and laughingly brushed her legs. From torn pockets they pulled out little cameras and took countless snapshots of Tara, who sat stiff and outraged on horseback.

"Do something!" Tara yelled at Pronob. "They can't take my picture! Strangers can't take my picture!"

The thought of those crude men lingering over her photograph, tracing the lines of her face, of her turtleneck and breeches, was more than she could bear. She wished she had not come to the mountains.

"Don't get so excited," cautioned Pronob. "There's probably no film in these cameras. They're just teasing you, old girl. If you ignore them, they'll get bored and go away."

The holidayers forgot Antonia. They aimed their cameras at Tara; some tried to separate her horse from the others. They tickled its tail with leafy branches. "Come, my beauty," they coaxed. "We want to see you in action."

A small hatless man touched her boot. Another managed a quick pat of the knee. Terrified horse and rider sprang into the thick of holidayers, who laughed and whistled all the louder as they jumped out of the way.

"Smile, please. Little more action."

"This camera's better. Please, sideface needed here."

"Blow a kiss here, lady. And one for my shy friend, it's his first visit to the mountains."

Two men tried to pull the reins out of Tara's hand while the others shouted obscene encouragement from the sidewalk.

"How dare you? How dare you?" Tara's shrill scream fanned the mountain sides. It was obvious Pronob and Antonia would not rescue her. She wondered what her father would have done if he had been present. Of course such disaster would not have occurred at all then.

Tara kicked one of the two men in the stomach. She lifted her foot again and again out of the stirrup, and kicked the muscular resilient abdomen. The men did not go way. They stood there, arrogant and sullen. Some shook their fists, others spat at the horse's head.

"You'll pay for this!" they screamed. "We never forget! We'll get all the likes of you! We'll be your judge and executioner! You won't have long to wait!" The men squeezed each other off the sidewalk and back on to the bridle path, so caught up were they in their dreams of revenge. Then Pronob took them by surprise. He charged in their midst, and they scattered down the sides of the mountain.

"Race back to the mall," he said over his shoulder to Tara. He had no advice for Antonia. Antonia Whitehead could look after herself.

As they sped toward the mall, Tara and Pronob felt very close to each other. Pronob seemed to want to do something heroic for her; he was moved by her helplessness. Nasty things always happened to nice people, that was the trouble in Calcutta. He could think of half a dozen shrewish housewives, mothers and sisters of his friends, who deserved to be looted or raped, but only the quiet ones were assaulted. When Antonia later complained that she thought Tara had handled the incident disgracefully and viciously, Pronob was very short with her. He invited Tara to join Antonia and himself for tea with a rather pointed graciousness.

An hour later the Bengal Tiger recounted the story of abuse to his friends in the lounge of the Kinchen Janga Hotel. The friends were fathers themselves. They looked harassed in spite of the invigorating breezes. They went over the tragedy of Mrs. General Pumps Gupta, who had never quite recovered from her ill-treatment. They mentioned a new story about someone's cousin-in-law, who had been looted on Red Road, then left carless.

"Disgraceful," they chorused in helpless rage. "Our Calcutta has gone to a hell."

This incident prevented Tara from looking her best for the beauty contest. She could not be a candidate anyway; she was a married woman. Mr. Patel, the hotel manager, tried to compensate for the afternoon by selecting her as a judge for the contest.

That evening dinner was served early to give the waiters enough time to ready the dining hall for the evening spectacle. Young girls skipped their dessert and fruits and left early to change. Older men and women lingered over their cups of Nescafé and had to be practically ejected.

"The contest's really for non-Bengali girls," the older women exclaimed. "Ours are too shy."

"It was better in the olden days. No contest madness. Why, we did not see *him* till the wedding day."

"No, no, we must keep up with the times," some men objected. "The girls go to college now. They're much older than you were."

"That's the whole trouble. They're too old, they decide for themselves. That's how tragedies happen."

"At least there's still some respect for old age. My son, he has a son of his own now, but he'd never dare smoke in front of *him* or myself."

"Don't worry. Soon the left-of-leftists will teach our sons disrespect."

"It's already happened. Don't you know what happened to the Bengal Tiger's daughter today?"

"Well, she made a love match. Surely she can look after herself?"

Soon the band, made up of four retired nightclub musicians, began to tune their instruments and drown out those lingering, frightened voices.

The musicians, Mr. Patel's third choice, had been hired considerably below the going rates, so they did not feel compelled to enjoy themselves. They opened the evening with a halfhearted rendition of "Que Será, Será," then eased themselves into "Green Sleeves" and "Goodnight, Irene."

A few Anglo-Indian boys in Elvis Presley hairstyles and girls wearing frilly party dresses got up to dance. They were quickly joined by some Punjabi couples and half a dozen progressive-looking Bengalis. Tara was not sure what was expected of her as a judge. She took out her notebook and pencil to make observations about possible queen candidates.

Antonia and Pronob arrived rather early and joined the Bengal Tiger's party. They made no reference to the riding mishap, though they did retell amusing stories about the dog's grave they had visited. Antonia looked particularly unfortunate in a dress. Earlier in the afternoon the turtleneck and pants had given her an air of alacrity; now she was swaddled muscularly in a chiffon evening dress. She had also experimented with Indian eye shadow, and her lips were brutally red. While Reena's father was going over his favorite story about the boarding house in London where he had stayed as a student, Antonia Whitehead pushed back her chair and embarrassed Pronob into inviting her to dance.

"I have known that boy's family since he was so high," said Reena's father. "I think I ought to tell him he is making a regrettable mistake."

"No, Daddy, I think he's enjoying himself," answered Reena. "He can't be free with us Bengali girls like that. So he's taking advantage."

The Bengal Tiger's party watched the two young people as they walked closer to the platform where the halfhearted band was amusing itself. They were deeply moved, even the Bengal Tiger; they longed to warn young Pronob before he hurt himself, but they were afraid he would get angry or worse still would laugh at them.

Nilima and her family arrived quite early too, but they sat at a table far away. Nilima's hair was piled high above her head, giving her a fulsome Nefertiti effect. Little black tendrils, unhappily too curly, hung about her ears to soften the rectangular face. The face itself was tiny, turned sickly gray by white powder for the night of the contest. The eyelids, gently painted, made the eyes appear much larger than the face.

"What on earth are they doing to her?" exclaimed the Bengal Tiger.

The answer was simple. Nilima's mother, a somewhat unsubtle woman, had hoisted her daughter on a barstool high above the other diners, so Nilima would be seen by the parents of eligible Bengali men.

"She's going about it all wrong," Tara's mother said.

"Well, *you* didn't have to worry about such problems!" Reena's mother retorted.

That was true; her marriage had done her parents little good except to increase their fortitude. She heard her father immediately come to the rescue with praise of David, calling him "a very, very brilliant boy and so lovable," though Reena's mother merely wriggled her bosom and turned away. Tara wondered if her father really meant what he was saying about David. Down in the plains, ten days before, she had heard him describe David as "such a good and lovable boy" to an audience of distant and disapproving relatives, while a servant in khaki shorts had rubbed his neck tense with tobacco problems. Now her father was following up the praise of David with loud and vigorous dreams about his old age.

"Yes, I'll sell the firm," the Bengal Tiger shouted. "It means nothing to me. I'll buy a poultry farm in America. I'll go to America. I have initiative. Taramoni and David will live with us and help. We'll have happy-go-lucky days again."

The dance music might have lessened the misery Tara felt as she heard her father's emotional rebuke to the vulgar woman. But the musicians were taking a break. They stood in a corner of the platform, smoking cheap little cigarettes and comparing callouses. The dancers, still full of unutilized energy, swayed noiselessly in twos during this enforced rest.

"What a dashed nuisance!" exploded Pronob. "Why must they quit playing when I'm just getting the hang of it?"

Only Antonia Whitehead was undisturbed by the musicians' break. She had plans for a livelier evening than the band had provided. She led Pronob back to the table like a puppy on a leash, stroked his head once or twice, then walked purposefully to the microphone on the stage.

"What's she doing to our mike?" yelled the leader of the musicians. His assistants shook their frail and alarmed fists at Miss Whitehead. But Antonia was too busy trying to look sexy to be frightened by them.

"Please, please, dear lady," pleaded Mr. Patel, slipping tiny homeopathic pills into his mouth. He felt a responsibility toward his resident guests; the ugly girl in chiffon was likely to offend them.

"What's this? What's going to happen?" asked the dancers as they backed away from the stage.

In response to the whispered questions Antonia rubbed her fingers slowly over the straps of her evening dress, and let them slip a little so that even from that distance raw lines were revealed on each shoulder. Occasionally she brought her fingers to her hair, fluffed it slyly, then pressed a strand against her lips. She closed her eyes now and then, and rocked gently from side to side. It was an evil moment for the audience. The dancers and diners were stupefied, some staring greedily at the figure on the stage, others looking fixedly at the designs on their china

plates. They were afraid of an unleashed energy; the swaying and rocking, they believed, was only the prologue to stranger events. And they
waited for some miracle or sign to save them from this new threat.

The sign came very quickly. It came from the Bengal Tiger himself.
"Sing, Miss Whitehead. Sing for us, please," he said.

"Bravo!" shouted the others. "Bravo! Sing, please. Accompaniment!
Accompaniment!"

Antonia Whitehead straightened up on the stage. She became efficient
and businesslike at once, consulted the four musicians, hummed a few
bars, then threw back her head and sang lustily. Her song was well
received, and so she refused to surrender the mike, sang several more
songs, and finally blew kisses from her perch at Mr. Patel and his guests.

"She's more diligent than those musicians," said the audience. "Surely
Patel will give her a cut of those men's salary?" The band seized their
instruments again, this time as if they would use their guitars and cellos
to nudge the young woman off the stage. But Antonia gave them each a
perfunctory little kiss and jumped to the floor by herself.

The audience bravoed her all over again, some playboy types even
tried to squeeze her hand as she walked by their tables. The feelings of
the Anglo-Indian dancers were closer to hero-worship than affection. In
their cross-cultural eyes she was a dream made flesh. After Antonia's
performance they felt anything was possible. They too might leap on the
stage and seize the mike and force the Indian audience to listen. If
Antonia had not been so far out of their reach, they would have hugged
her, they thought, to show their gratitude.

"I can sing like that too, man," said Victoria Fernandez, the prettiest
of the Anglo-Indian girls at the dance. "Man, my grandmother was the
toast of London."

"Victoria, you sing like some kind of angel," agreed her friends. "If
they saw you in England they'd make you a star in two days." They
threw their thin and supple bodies into new, energetic dance steps.

"I'm going to the States, man. I'm going to save my moolah and buy
a one-way ticket," all the young men said.

"They appreciate good singing there. Here my talents are quite
unappreciated."

Mr. Patel dismissed his earlier apprehensions of the evening as quite
unwarranted. He had a habit of cupping his pudgy hands over his mouth
and shouting for attention whenever he wanted to address more than
two of his guests. He could be seen on the stage now, cupping his hands.
Tara feared the time for her to act as judge had arrived. She quickly took
out a notebook from the purse she had bought at foolhardy expense
from Saks Fifth Avenue to impress her Calcutta friends.

"Could I draw your humble minds to my direction, please," began

Mr. Patel. "I remind you, ladies and gentlemen, tonight is the night of the Kinchen-Janga Miss Himalaya Beauty Queen Contest. The winner of tonight's activities, that lucky young lady, will compete in the Pan-Hill-Station Deluxe Beauty Queen Contest."

The dancers on the floor pounded with their shoes and Mr. Patel had to restrain their gaiety with a look he reserved for obstreperous non-resident guests.

"We have decided to run this contest in a most democratic way. All men, no matter what age, will write the name of the most beautiful lady on a slip of white paper to be passed out by the waiters. Only ladies who are heavenly looking and unmarried, please. The judges will come with me, and count the slips when they have been collected . . ."

He read out the list of judges with appropriate flattering appositions for each name. Tara was listed as the "exquisite and intellectual daughter of very big industrial magnate." In addition to Tara, there was a Calcutta High Court judge, the wife of a Bengali diplomat, a heart specialist, and a Marwari real estate agent.

"The band will play dance music, and all heavenly ladies and their partners will please dance near the stage so we can get a good look before.we cast our momentous votes."

Victoria Fernandez and her friends, buoyed up by their frilly petti-coats and dresses, floated to the center of the dance floor. They executed difficult dance steps before the band had had a chance to warm up and really get started. They displayed certifiable self-confidence as they waited for the male guests to come up and find out their first names. Some Indian girls were also on the floor, progressive and tomboyish if hair and deportment could still be regarded as an Indian woman's inner index. They had allowed themselves to be led near the stage after nom-inal persuasion by male admirers and parents, and now they made a pleasing dynamo of energy and grace. But their western dance move-ments seemed lamentably related to *Bharat natyam* and *Kathakali*, which they had been taught by stern long-haired dancing masters since the age of nine or ten.

"What about the bathing suit bit?" Antonia Whitehead asked in a loud voice. "You can't have a real beauty contest in clothes like that."

Mr. Patel, who prided himself as an open-minded hotel manager, was upset by the suggestion. It sounded obscene to him; he wished he had not heard it, or better still that it had not been made. On the other hand, Miss Whitehead, he acknowledged, was a real American and could be expected to know how beauty contests were run; his professionalism was at stake.

"What should I do?" he asked the panel of judges.

"You could dismiss her case," advised the High Court judge.

"I think we should try not to be overtly rude to the foreign young lady," the diplomat's wife mediated. "We should, in my opinion, ignore her comments, and just carry on as if nothing has been said. You might also ask that stupid band to play a little louder, Mr. Patel. That'll cut down the possibilities of more such comments from nonresident guests."

"But why not a bathing suit contest?" Tara demanded. "That's a legitimate demand if you are going to judge a person's physical appearance."

"Really, Mrs. Cartwright. I think your years abroad have robbed you of feminine propriety or you are joking with us. You know as well as I do our modest Indian girls would not submit to such disgrace." The heart specialist was genuinely offended.

"No, no," shouted the Marwari real estate agent, who begged old editions of *Playboy* from his more westernized friends. "Let the girls wear bathing suits. The modest ones should not be in the contest anyway."

"But," said Mr. Patel, not wishing to take sides in spite of his prudish prejudices, "none of these ladies have their swimsuits with them. I'm sure they did not expect to swim tonight."

"Then let them wear their birthday suits. That suits me jolly okay." The Marwari's rejoinder, made a little too close to the microphone, carried to the audience and totally destroyed its illusions of beauty and love.

The Indian dancers rushed back to their seats, wrapping their gorgeous saris tightly around midriffs and plump breasts.

"That crude beast!" whispered angry parents. "That horrible deviate!" Their faces wore a uniform outrage.

The evening had again changed its direction. What had been intended as a harmless imitation of western contests had first become threatening, then suddenly soured. Mr. Patel admitted he did not know how to cope with the problem.

Victoria Fernandez was perhaps the only one prepared to meet the challenge. She did not return to her table. Instead, with flaring nostrils and arrogantly plucked eyebrows, she stood ready for any change in the rules of the contest. The greasy young men and women, her friends, formed a protective circle around her. The band, caught up in the beauty of its own music, remained totally calm in the face of such hatred. It sat like a tropical island, solid though buffeted, and played "I Feel Pretty" with touching recklessness.

"Man, I'm going to see this through," vowed Victoria Fernandez. "I'm thirty-six, twenty, thirty-eight. you know. Bring me a bathing costume, Mr. Patel. I don't scare so easily. Get me a costume and I'll be ready in two secs."

Victoria Fernandez was not destined to win that night. She was pretty and graceful, ambitious and sporting, and such qualities may generally be rewarded in beauty contests. But the evening had turned evil. It deepened the audience's capacity for shock and increased Antonia Whitehead's playfulness. Antonia began to tease Pronob, to whom earlier that morning she had given her paperback copy of the Kama Sutra. Ignoring the feelings of the people at her table, she described in detail what she called "the erotic vagaries" of Khajuraho and the Krishna legends. Pronob was by nature a nervous young man. The incidents of the early afternoon coupled with the evil of the evening totally undermined his strength.

"You aren't going to do anything foolish, are you?" he begged.

"Don't worry, Pronob." But Antonia's answer was not meant to comfort Pronob. She strode to the center of the hall, laughing and unzipping her dress as she went, then let it fall in a loop around her sandals till she was revealed to the world in her body stocking: an immense column of white flesh.

Next day the young men admitted that Antonia Whitehead had a commendable body. Their eyes were dull and glazed as they recalled the slipping of her floral chiffon dress. Then they reminded each other that the young woman had manly shoulders, tight little hips and negligible breasts, that her complexion was rude and savage, unsoothed by fresh cream or cucumber slices. But though they knew she was no apsara or Indian angel, they claimed that in their minds Darjeeling from that moment on somehow blended with the vision of an almost naked Miss Whitehead.

The competition for beauty queen lasted only a second. The white girl in body stocking galvanized noble emotions in the dining hall. Pride, humiliated sensitiveness, shock, fear locked the dim and dusky faces, demanding from Mr. Patel some last show of justice or revenge. Only the band, maliciously unresponsive to such feelings, continued to play "Lemon Tree" at its slow and tedious pace.

Mr. Patel was not equal to the responsibilities of the evening. He tried to behave naturally, cupping his hands, but allowing only rebellious ohs and ahs to escape. Then the Bengal Tiger jumped to his feet, his face like a sun in eclipse, lethal if viewed without a shade. He grabbed the damask cloth off his table, scattering crystal and champagne, pilau, pakoras and jeweled purses. He dragged the cloth with its spreading stains to the middle of the hall where Antonia Whitehead stood like a challenge, then he flung it over her pale and knotted shoulders. And each one in the room, dancers and diners alike, resident and nonresident guests, loved the Bengal Tiger for his quick reflexes and his infinite resourcefulness. They applauded him madly, shouting "Bravo!" and "Encore!" while some sensitive older women wept into handkerchiefs they had in happier days embroidered and tatted.

"What's happening to us?" cried the Bengal Tiger, having returned

Antonia Whitehead to Pronob at the far end of his table. "I came here to rest. To breathe fresh air. What is this thing that has happened?" Then, pointing a stern finger at Mr. Patel, he instructed, "Manager-*babu*, please disqualify all contestants. Ladies and gentlemen, we better go to sleep. Otherwise all will be lost, our common sense and our happy-go-luckiness."

He gathered his party together, claimed his daughter from the judges' stand, where the Marwari sat sheepishly cleaning his fingernails with a toothpick, and he left.

"I must think of a new gimmick," said Mr. Patel to himself. He helped the waiters clear the dining room of guests and contestants. Then he waited for the rains so he could return to the plains, where he felt his life was infinitely more predictable and therefore safe.

5

The Bengal Tiger and his family returned to Calcutta the day before the rains were scheduled to start in Darjeeling.

"Hill diarrhea on top of everything else would be too much!"

The mountains had been magnificent, of course. But the holiday had been dismal. They had meant to see the sunrise from Tiger Hill, and drive down for a day to Kalimpong, but somehow the chance to do these things had never arisen. They came down to the plains unrefreshed by the fortnight in the hills.

In Calcutta the Bengal Tiger was quickly absorbed into his office routine. There were orders to track down and supply; junior executives to scold, dismiss and reinstate; import licenses to renew; and government officials to cajole. That left the Bengal Tiger little time to see to the emotional maladjustments of his family.

Tara and her mother worried that the Bengal Tiger would work himself sick. They tried to lure him away to Doris Day matinees on weekdays, but the Bengal Tiger appeared very displeased each time the women swooped into his office brandishing tickets for him. They schemed to save him from himself as they bought new saris or raised money for honest charities, but the Bengal Tiger remained bitterly uncooperative. Finally Arati planned a long weekend visit to Nayapur, a new township in a complex of coal mines, steel foundries and plants for hydroelectricity. At first the Bengal Tiger seemed enthusiastic about the weekend trip. He was anxious to show off Bengal's industrial progress to his daughter, and he instructed his secretary to reserve rooms for his party in the Nayapur Guest House. But two days before the Banerjees were scheduled to leave a business tangle developed and the Bengal Tiger had to fly to Delhi for a week. It was unthinkable for Tara's mother to leave her husband in the unloving hands of hotel servants, especially when his blood pressure was inordinately high after the holiday. She arranged for Aunt Jharna and her clubfooted little girl to move into Camac Street for a week.

Pronob's group feared that Tara would acquit herself badly with her aunt and suggested the whole group go off to Nayapur for an unusual weekend trip. Though their parents were unhappy (the mothers were convinced mixed picnics led to improperly romantic dreams), they entrusted Tara, the only married person, with the moral responsibilities of the picnic. When two maids were added to help Tara in her chaperoning duties, even Nilima was allowed by her mother to join the party.

Within days the whole city seemed to know of the projected trip to Nayapur. The Calcutta editor of the *Feminine Weekly* called the Bengal Tiger for permission to cover the weekend, and was told off roundly. Till the last minute before departure Pronob hoped Antonia Whitehead would accompany him. But Antonia had already left for a village in Bihar, saying, "Your friends put me off, Pronob. I've got work to do."

Nayapur can look gorgeous when viewed from the right angle. It spreads across scarred little hills and forests. The view is limitless and quite devastating. There are shiny roofs, long stretches of plate glass windows reflecting unbearable sunlight, chimneys, fires, smoke, trolleys, trucks.

Pronob's group arrived in Nilima's old Dodge station wagon very early on Friday morning. They followed erratic arrows that led to the Nayapur Guest House and reached a large bungalow hung with stiffly welcoming signs. The guest house seemed quite full; they had the feeling they had walked into a circus or a trap, and that the Calcutta editor of the *Feminine Weekly* was lying in wait for them inside the bungalow. They recognized Mr. Tuntunwala immediately. He was standing in the verandah surrounded by serious men in *dhoti*. When he noticed the newcomers, he forsook the serious men and thanked Sanjay for a recent editorial the young man had devoted to him. He shook hands with Tara, pointedly ignored Nilima and Reena, and invited everyone to his suite for lemonade.

The *chowkidar* and the *chowkidar's* cousin, a recent arrival from his village, showed Pronob's group to their rooms. The girls were given one large room in the west wing, and the young men two rooms in the east wing. The *chowkidar's* cousin, who spoke ambitious though scanty English, offered to bring the guests hot water for baths "and all special amenities."

Except for Tara, the group was reluctant to sample the industrial wonders of Nayapur. They ordered bucketfuls of hot water at seventy-five *naye paise* a bucket, breakfasted lightly on tea and eggs, then dedicated themselves to gin rummy. Tara, who disliked cards and had never mastered rummy or bridge, was rescued unexpectedly by Tuntunwala from her chaperoning duties.

"May I show you the township, Mrs. Cartwright?" he asked, pointing to a Land Rover parked in the shade of a mango tree. "It will honor me."

Tara, in spite of herself, was flattered by the attentions of a national hero. Tuntunwala had come to Nayapur to plan strategy for the final weeks of his election campaign. He left his advisers arguing nastily over brochures in a corner of the verandah, and helped Tara into the Land Rover.

The countryside was overwhelming. Gigantic tracts had been gouged out of green and romantic hills. Symmetrical layers had been cut into the earth. Bulldozers, tractors, caterpillars, cement mixers, the equipment of industrial progress, were reduced to the size of roaches in that layered distance. After a while Tara noted little clumps of buildings, neatly numbered and painted, lit with neon, decorated with signboards that indicated the way to reservoirs, foundries and dams. There were little residential colonies also—small houses and gardens arranged in tidy files. The colonies appeared sensible and dispassionate in the exaggerated violence of a landscape being fitted for industry and progress.

Tuntunwala stopped the Land Rover on a rise and asked Tara if the view before her compensated for the bumps and lurches on the drive through unpaved trails. "It is truly a dignified place, don't you think, Mrs. Cartwright?"

Tara could come up with no appropriate words to his questions, and so said nothing.

"You don't like it?"

"Oh yes, I do. I'm just . . ."

"If there is an emotion to express one can always find a way of expressing it, Mrs. Cartwright. Perhaps you don't have an emotion to express?"

"I love it, I love it. I'm terribly impressed."

"I want you to do one thing, please. I want you to shut your eyes tightly and remember this scene in your head. This is my favorite scene and I want to give you this memory as a present."

Tara was amused that a man like Tuntunwala was capable of such imaginative games. She shut her eyes obediently and dismissed any suspicions she had initially entertained about him. She did not know then that Tuntunwala had spoken very literally. Later he would commission an artist to paint him that landscape, and a bodyguard would deliver it to the Bengal Tiger's residence.

"You know, when I first started to come here this was a weritable jungle." He had told her she could open her eyes if she felt the scene had firmly impressed itself on her brain. "I could pick out small animals with my headlights. And once—no, I'm not joking—I shot a tiger near here, very decent-sized chap." Then because Tara looked unconvinced, he added, "If fate wills I can show you the selfsame tiger skin in my house one day?"

"I don't think fate will will any such thing."

"You're telling me I'm too bold a beggar, no? I'm sorry I offend you. I must curb my foolish impulses. Forget what I said about tiger skin, please."

Small talk was impossible between them. As long as they remained awed by the landscape they disposed of their fears of each other or their instinctive distrustfulness. But words required tact; words without tact left terrible consequences.

"What's that building there?" Tara asked, indicating a shiny roof at random.

Tuntunwala seized her question with gratitude and explained the function of that building, and of other buildings not indicated; he detailed the number, size and purpose of knobs, buttons, levers, charts and graphs that were inside those buildings. Tara quickly lost all interest, though she continued to supply him with well-timed questions. Tuntunwala was enchanted by his explanations. A procession of possibilities— what urbanization could mean for the rural electorate—must have passed through his head. He turned to her with increasing passion. "We can put electricity in every hut if the voters listen to me. In fact, we can put a TV set in every hut if I'm elected."

"But think of the ads for bad breath, Mr. Tuntunwala."

"Call me by my good name please. Call me Pintoo because you are my friend."

"Think of the ads for deodorants and detergents."

Then he returned to making exclamations about the landscape. "It is such a fine and moving place! I experience redoubtable mental peace here. Looking at this scene I say to myself, India will be safe."

A prophetic light had overwhelmed the man. He leaned closer in the uncomfortable Land Rover and confided to Tara his dreams for industrial progress. Any remark that she could make she knew would be insufficient or inappropriate.

"We must make all our own machinery. We must do that before anything else."

"Don't you think you ought to worry about feeding the voters first?"

"You are for heart's matters, dear lady. You'd be no good in my Cabinet."

When they returned from the drive Tara discovered Pronob and his group had gone to an Uttam Kumar matinee in Nayapur's only movie theater.

"They have left you alone to cope with my wiles, Mrs. Cartwright?"

"Oh, no, they have left one of the maids. Besides, I'm the chaperon. *My* reputation is not at stake."

"And chaperons are irreproachable? Then there can be no scandal to my escorting you into the dining room while your friends are away?"

The waiter, who doubled as *chowkidar* to receive guests on their arrival at the bungalow, brought two handwritten menus, and stood beside their table with noticeable nervousness.

"Veg or non-veg?"

"Bring out both!" commanded Tuntunwala. "We're here on holiday, we mean to indulge ourselves."

The *chowkidar*'s cousin flexed his muscles and saluted. "Very good, *sahib*. I bring *brinjal* curry, *dal* and *loochi* to begin with. But chicken curry excellent. I tried little bit in kitchen."

"Shut your mouth," whispered the sophisticated *chowkidar*. "My cousin-brother stupid villager. He did not try any food in the kitchen."

"Bring out the veg and the non-veg," repeated the National Personage.

The food when it appeared looked peppery and hot. Tara assumed it was delicious only because Tuntunwala devoured it at incredible speed. The long and bumpy ride in the Land Rover had given her a sick headache. Now the sight of the vegetarian and non-vegetarian meals being put away by a thin and temporarily amiable man accelerated her nausea. At first she was afraid to leave the table for fear of unnecessarily offending her lunch partner, but by the time the chicken had been ruthlessly chewed and its bones ground fine and discarded, she knew she would have to excuse herself and rush to the toilet.

"But you haven't touched your food yet!" Then he realized from the expression on Tara's face that perhaps more than food was involved in her illness. "You're not feeling well!"

Tuntunwala took charge at once. He led her out of the public dining room with authority while diners stared at him in anticipation of scandal or excitement. Tara was glad of his sympathy and even more of his offer of a homeopathic medicine that would cure her sick headache. He invited her to his suite to pick up the medicine. They were followed by the maid left behind in the guest house in case she was needed by Tara. The maid had fallen asleep before Tara returned from her drive, and she now blamed herself tearfully for whatever might have happened.

The Marwari's suite was the only air-conditioned one in the Nayapur Guest House. It also appeared to be better furnished than Tara's room. Tuntunwala settled Tara on a sofa that may have been meant for midgets, then went to the bathroom to mix the homeopathic drink. At Tara's feet the maid cursed herself extravagantly for having fallen asleep and permitted some undetermined calamity to overwhelm her mistress.

"Just stop making so much noise. The *missybaba* needs rest. Wait quietly in the verandah and I'll call you back when you are needed."

The man's tone was so authoritative, it did not occur to the maid to question the proprieties of his suggestion. Tara knew she should protest. Yet she couldn't. It would be useless to storm out now. She was tired, and sick; she was curious and impatient. She could wait a few minutes longer. If she were a more aggressive young woman, better able to protect herself like Antonia Whitehead, she knew she would have walked out of the suite with the maid. But she was neither forceful nor impulsive. At that moment the Marwari appeared to her strong, sensible and curiously akin to the Bengal Tiger and Hari Lal Banerjee.

While Tuntunwala held a glass of fetid yellow liquid in front of her Tara thought she loved David desperately. How absurd that she had feared she was incapable of affection! How pathetic that she had worried about sinking into Calcutta's vast sadness! She saw a procession of children eating yoghurt off Park Street, rude men chasing horses in Darjeeling, a marcher subdued near the Catelli, and she whispered, "It isn't possible in Bengal. We're sensitive, we're sentimental, it can't happen to Bengalis."

But Tuntunwala had decided to ignore her tender feelings. "Please try to relax. Please continue to sit tight. I'll rub some Vicks VapoRub on your forehead. I've found it excellent for all headaches and nervous crises."

Tara gathered herself primly on the small sofa. "No thanks," she said. But Tuntunwala was accustomed only to acquiescence, to disposing of business empires and petty destinies without advice or apology. He dismissed her "No thanks" with a sympathetic nod, and began rubbing Vicks VapoRub indulgently on her forehead. Tara resorted to small talk; it had ruined an entente between them earlier in the day and she thought she could count on her tactlessness to do so again. "What are you *really* doing here this weekend, Mr. Tuntunwala?"

"Planning strategy."

"You expect to win?"

"In heart's matters, yes."

She was hurt by his confidence. She turned away from him and worried that the lunch of uneaten chicken, the headache, the homeopathic drink and the Vicks VapoRub had led only to this pitiful attempt at promiscuity. Then Tuntunwala changed to a gentler tone.

"Please, please," he said, clutching Tara with sticky fingers. "I'm given to unfortunate impulses. You can't surely break from me now?"

"Really!"

"There is no time for coy preliminaries. You're liberated and advanced and I admire you greatly."

"Admiration is no reason for yielding to what you suggest!"

"I do not think you will leave, Mrs. Cartwright—how will you explain it to your maid?"

The Marwari sat on the arm of Tara's sofa, looking most unhappy. Then slowly the disappointment paled and was succeeded by dull anger. "I think you have no choice," he said, putting away the jar of Vicks.

In another Calcutta such a scene would not have happened. Tara would not have walked into the suite of a gentleman for medicine, and a gentleman would not have dared to make such improper suggestions to her. But except for Camac Street, Calcutta had changed greatly; and even Camac Street had felt the first stirrings of death. With new dreams like Nayapur Tara's Calcutta was disappearing. New dramas occurred with each new bulldozer incision in the green and romantic hills. Slow learners like Tara were merely victims.

6

The seduction of Tara had been tastefully executed by Tuntunwala, and the maid in the corridor remained ignorant of all untoward details. There were no apologies or recriminations. Tuntunwala assumed that "heart's matters" were unimportant. He invited her to join him for tea, then went to the next room to confer with the serious men in *dhoti* who were planning his campaign. Tara's first reaction had been to complain to Sanjay and Pronob, to tell them Tuntunwala was a parasite who would survive only at their expense. But the outrage soon subsided, leaving a residue of unforgiving bitterness. She realized she could not share her knowledge of Tuntunwala with any of her friends. In a land where a friendly smile, an accidental brush of the fingers, can ignite rumors—even lawsuits—how is one to speak of Mr. Tuntunwala's violence? The others would have to make their own compromises. Tara wrote them a note saying that she had suddenly taken ill. Then, accompanied by the useless maid, she left immediately for Camac Street by train.

In Camac Street her parents found her bitterness inexplicable. She talked constantly of returning to David, and in their efforts to encourage her to remain longer with them they suggested intellectual pastimes like poetry readings and visits to the nuns at St. Blaise's. Their love for her was so great that they arranged a coffee-house poet to read in their own house. The deliberately dirty and vituperous young man recited his anatomical verses on the lawn, then demanded some cutlets and sweetmeats for the other "Hungry Generation" poets in his mess.

The nuns at St. Blaise's were more sympathetic than the avantgarde poet. They seemed to Tara browner than she remembered, their accents more Indian than she had expected. They fluttered around her in the parlor, anxious for news and for snaps of her husband. They were hysterical with pleasure when she produced a passport-size photograph of an amused young man in glasses; then she read them a paragraph from David's latest letter because she considered his observation frighteningly appropriate.

"I have been reading a biography of William James, with all of his innumerable trips through the Continent. The trips you describe in India seem so nineteenth centuryish, so beware of highwaymen, my dear . . ."

Mother Peter Ignatius was distraught with pleasure at the revelation of photograph and confidential letter; she begged permission to include the paragraph in the alumna column of the school magazine she edited. Then the nuns showed her embroidered sandwich covers, lace doilies, tablecloths and pillowcases that the "poor girls" had made in a branch of their convent to assure her that nothing had changed at St. Blaise's. Tara was moved to buy a dozen doilies, then with bitter regret she left the nuns standing on the school steps. All her early ideas of love, fair play and good manners had come from those women. Now as she saw them in their quaint formation on the steps of St. Blaise's, they seemed to her people in a snapshot, yellow and faded.

David's letters during the monsoons also intensified her depression. He wrote that he had been reading Ved Mehta's journals on India, and that even in New York they brought home to him the dangers that surrounded her every day. He told Tara he saw Calcutta as the collective future in which garbage, disease, and stagnation are man's estate. "Survival to the lower forms, insects and sludgeworms." Though the Bengal Tiger tried to protect her from the excesses of the city, Tara told her parents that she was preparing to return to David and the United States.

On the first rainless day in August Tara went to the Air India office and reserved a seat for herself on a flight to New York leaving at the end of the week. Then, because she was given to serious and sentimental farewells, she telephoned Reena, Pronob and Sanjay to meet her at the Catelli-Continental that afternoon so she could break the news to them.

The Bengal Tiger and his wife were helpless in the face of Tara's new and implacable determination. They brightened up a little when Sanjay came in his Fiat to drive their daughter to the Catelli-Continental. They hoped the group would succeed in delaying Tara's departure. It was seven years since they had last seen her, and they convinced themselves that they would never see her again. They watched the PRESS sticker on Sanjay's car disappear from their compound, and because they were affectionate and clannish they hoped life would be kinder to Tara than it had been to them. They called for an early tea and prayed that the riots would not interrupt the last days of Tara's holiday.

In the car Tara was careful not to respond with cynicism to Sanjay's praise of Tuntunwala as a candidate. She felt she had made her peace with the city, nothing more was demanded. If she were to stay, she thought, there would be other concessions, other deals and compromises, all menacing and unbearably real, waiting to be made.

The crowds on the way to the hotel seemed more than usually impertinent. At traffic lights and intersections they threatened to overturn the car and burn its occupants. The refugees on the sidewalk were gathering together their pots and pans and children, rolling up sleeping mats and putting away coins. They seemed to be taking precautions against some foreseeable damage.

Under a striped umbrella of the Catelli-Continental Pronob told the group he had heard rumors that a procession was on its way to the *maidan*, that it would go right by the hotel and rally near the monument. The waiters completed the details. A boy had been run over by a tram and killed; he had been carrying a heavy can of oil for his mother when his foot slipped on the tracks. An angry crowd had tried to lynch the tram conductor, and when the police had frustrated them by arresting the man, the crowd had lain in wait for the next tram, dragged its conductor out and beaten him to death. Now the crowd, still unappeased and swelling, were marching over to the *maidan's* monument.

Tara realized the moment was inappropriate for the breaking of sentimental news. A mob was approaching Chowringee from the south. The young men in front were armed with bamboo poles and axes. Some of them wore handkerchiefs knotted over their heads. At times they lifted the kerchiefs to wipe sweat off their foreheads and necks. Some carried whistles, which they blew shrilly to punctuate slogans. Their gestures were those of rebellious children rather than political militants. Many joked and laughed and ate peanuts from paper cones. Tara's friends were furious; they told each other it had been a bad idea to meet at the Catelli on such a day.

A contingent of policemen soon appeared. They looked very spruce, still in starched turbans and short pants, twirling their *lathi* and fingering their belts. A group of young and beardless marchers darted out of the procession and punched two policemen. But they were driven back far into the mob, bleeding from cuts on their faces or heads. The marshals of the procession shouted orders to each other, argued vociferously, then scolded the groups nearest them. A young woman in braids threw down her cardboard sign and sat on the curb to rest. There were children among the marchers, and they were holding new toys, perhaps liberated from shops on the way. A toothless old man walking his dog beside the marchers was persuaded to carry an extra pennant.

The excitement of the riot overwhelmed Reena. She stood by the parapet, exclaiming at the mob and encouraging the policemen. Then she waved in the direction of a very handsome young man in uniform, leaning against the side of a police jeep.

Reena pointed to his revolver and the little swagger stick he carried and addressed him as "old Popo," because he had roomed with her cousin at college. He was too far away, of course, to hear her. But she cupped her hands and leaned over the parapet. "Right on!" she shouted. "Power to old Popo! Right on, I say!"

The discovery of "old Popo" in the mob reassured Pronob's group that fair play would still prevail in Calcutta that day. At first the anonymity of the rioters had frightened them. But now that they had recognized a face in that confusion of marchers and policemen they felt reasonably sure they could predict how the day would end. They called the waiter to their table to order more coffee, then settled down to enjoying the spectacle below them.

"You know, I'm beginning to think I was wrong about that Tuntunwala chap," confessed Pronob as he waited for the Catelli waiter to bring him an espresso. "If he's elected, things like this won't happen again."

Tara agreed with him, but with pointed nastiness, and was rebuked by Sanjay. In recent weeks the editor had relied solely on fierce passion to convince his readers that Tuntunwala was a prophet.

"This is no time for petty suspicions, Tara. This is crisis time for all of us, so be sensible if nothing else."

A frail woman in the street hurled a soda bottle against a confectioner's window on Chowringhee Avenue. Soon dirty men and children were running in and out of the store, carrying fancy cakes shaped like hearts or diamonds, some with marzipan clowns or brides on them. They tossed cookies to each other, let them fall into the street, then darted between legs to collect them in handkerchiefs and save them for hungrier moments. A very dark man in striped boxer shorts carried a radio on his head and danced in and out of his line in the procession. Suddenly there was a loud explosion, and the man fell flat on his back, and someone else picked up the radio and disappeared into an alley. Quickly and violently all cars were being stopped by either the marchers or the police. Passengers were ordered to run to safety, so they abandoned their cars in the middle of the street. In the distance a car was still smoking and handcuffed boys were being pushed into police trucks. A motorcyclist, moving slowly and noisily down the length of the procession, was shoved by a marcher from behind; he fell on the street and his motorcycle careened into the mob without him. There were screams and curses. People surged out of the way of the motorcycle. A young man lifted a boy who had been knocked unconscious by the machine. Slogans were shrill and triumphant around the young man holding the boy. The marshals waved the crowd on. The *maidan* was slowly filling.

Tara was not immune to such casual madness. She plunged into terrified chatter about airplane tickets and reservations and David and Katherine Mansfield. An agitated waiter in a torn turban pleaded with the patrons of the Catelli to go home before the hotel was sacked. Diners overturned delicate rattan chairs in their anxiety to be first in the elevator. Apprenhensive managers walked from table to table, asking, "Was the service satisfactory, sir? No need to panic. This hotel is burglar-proof and safer than the streets." A little girl cried into her ice-cream cone as she ran with her mother to the fire exit. Young women in pale georgette saris stood on glass-topped tables weeping inconsolably. A businessman in a three-piece suit took off his socks and shoes to make his getaway easy. An old man in a blazer sitting beside a potted palm counted change from his pocket for the waiter's tip.

The threat of riot seemed to bring out the best in Pronob. He was suddenly full of passionate sententiousness. He talked of "Calcutta's final curtain," of "mad dogs and beasts" and "heroic survivors" as he organized his group for a dash down the staircase and into Sanjay's car parked across the street. Fat women wearing diamonds dug their elbows under Tara's chin. A pudgy boy in sailor outfit was pushed against the railing and started to cry when the balloon he had been holding burst at the end of its long string. "Bang on!" Reena kept whispering as she carved a path for herself and her friends among the thick and frightened bodies. Halfway down the carpeted staircase Tara's jeweled aqua sandals came apart and she tripped. Pronob pulled her up and dragged her down the rest of the way. He flung the torn sandal on the receptionist's counter as the crowd pushed him toward the Catelli's doorway. There were posters of Tuntunwala on the counter top, brochures and flags announcing his candidacy. A beardless young man resembling Tuntunwala but without the older man's hardness or authority stood behind the counter, waving to the Catelli patrons to behave sensibly.

When Pronob escorted his group to the door of the hotel, a splinter mob tried to force him back into the foyer. They were fierce men and women. They smashed glass panels with bricks they had brought with them. They struck the doorkeeper again and again; just before he fell the doorkeeper shouted to Pronob to hurry back inside the hotel.

"Press! Press!" shouted Sanjay. The crowd parted slightly, absorbed the four friends, then disgorged them on the other side of the street. They ran to Sanjay's Fiat as the mob pressed against the sides of the car, pointed to soda bottles and bamboo sticks, and shook tiny fists at the four people inside. Then a bomb exploded somewhere. A storefront collapsed. Looters carried off sheets and towels. Sullen policemen arrived swinging *lathi*. Marchers kicked Sanjay's Fiat as they ran toward the steps of the hotel. There was no way Sanjay could back his car out into the street. The friends crouched in the little car with doors locked and windows rolled tight. Now and then a stone or broken bottle hurled against a door and chipped paint off the Fiat. The empty taxi on their left was dented badly, its tires slashed and headlights missing. Young boys were working on it methodically, carrying out detachable ashtrays and light bulbs, and destroying what they could not carry. On the other side of the street a bus was burning slowly. People spat on the windows of Sanjay's car, rattled the locked door handles and made obscene gestures at the girls crying inside.

A confrontation was shaping up outside the Catelli-Continental. The doorkeeper lay on his side under the striped awning and a beggar girl with tangled hair sat on his high stool instead. Tuntunwala suddenly came out of the hotel. He stood on the steps, stubborn and dispassionate. "Old Popo" was conferring seriously with him. Rows of constables were called and lined up near the doorway. They held their *lathi* horizontally and the mob withdrew a few feet. A middle-aged man in an undershirt and loose pajamas threw a stone through the open door and was wrestled to the ground before he had barely finished throwing.

Tara watched Tuntunwala guarding the entrance of the Catelli-Continental and thought of something even lower than a parasite, something that had evolved beyond the need for higher forms. In that moment of terror, in a closed car before a mob, she felt she was being used by some force that was too large for her to manage.

"Have you seen *Pather Panchali?*" she asked.

"What a stupid question! Who hasn't?"

"Do you remember all that greenery? Do you remember Apu running through those forests?" Tara asked.

"I remember the greenery in black and white."

"What's happened to those forests, Pronob? What killed them?"

"Really, Tara! How dare you talk such nonsense at a time like this!"

"Old Popo" was shouting into a megaphone. "Please fall back, everyone. Please fall back. This hotel is the private property of Mr. Tuntunwala."

The crowd surged backward and forward, then retreated toward the line of cars parked across the street.

"Please fall back or we will be forced to adopt drastic measures. This is a warning."

Two marchers jumped on the hood of Sanjay's Fiat as the crowd pushed back farther and farther. From the *maidan* someone hurled a brick and it crashed through the windshield of the dented taxi.

Then an old man in a blazer rushed out of the Catelli-Continental. He was stopped by Tuntunwala and a constable, but the old man shook himself free and snatched the megaphone from Popo's hand.

"Mrs. Cartwright!" he shouted. "Are you there, dear lady? Are you still there somewhere?"

"What's wrong with him?"

"*Here I am* . . . Mrs. Cartwright . . . *an old man* . . . The year of the puppy is over, do you understand? The age of snakes is coming but the boy doesn't know it yet."

"He's absolutely daft!"

"*We who seven years ago spoke of honor,* Madam . . ."

"Here, you, give that thing back to me!"

"Crows are picking at corpses, Mrs. Cartwright. The fires we saw are frozen."

"Tara, that's your weird friend out there!"

"You can't allow him to continue like this, Inspector! He's a veritable nuisance!"

"Can you hear me? Can you hear? Already half of Calcutta, surely half of . . . *bats with baby faces.*"

"Will you do it or shall I call my bodyguards?"

"*I have no ghosts,* Mrs. Cartwright."

"Sir, it's my job, and I'll have you know I take all my jobs very seriously."

"Kisses were tattooed on our foreheads. Rust on walls can kill, did you guess that?"

"Oh, for heaven's sake, Tara, your friend's going to make Tuntunwala look like a fool!" exclaimed Sanjay.

"Why doesn't he get out of the way?"

"They'll hurt him! They've no choice!"

"*After such knowledge* . . . tail devoured by head as always . . . and then . . ."

"He's crazy. You want me to hit a crazy man, sir?"

"He's not a madman at all. I weritably believe he's been sent by the other side."

"Dear Madam, you *I shored against my ruins.* Have you left? Where are the jets?"

"Okay, you had your chance. Now I'll call my own guards."

There was a scuffle on the steps of the Catelli-Continental. Amplified and distorted groans came through the megaphone, which was now lying on the sidewalk under the striped awning. Four men in livery had wrestled the old man to the ground. His ascot had come undone, and his gray hair was dusty. The men in livery played with him a bit, then threw him lightly like a handball into the mob, and the mob fell on him immediately.

They were not kind to Joyonto Roy Chowdhury, those marchers in undershirts and ragged *dhoti*. They kicked him and scratched him and tossed him from line to line. A bruise spread across his face, and there was a cut under his chin. They tore off his blazer, and flung the brass buttons at his cheek. Giggling youths tried the blazer on for size, made funny faces to each other, then ripped it viciously with pocketknives.

"My God! They're not content to kill him!"

"Your friend's a bloody fool, Tara! But I can't let them do this to him!"

"Pronob! Don't, please! There's nothing you can do."

"How dare they do that to an old man like him!"

"Pronob! What is this nonsense, please? They'll get you too!"

But Pronob was out of the car before anyone could stop him. He got only two steps away when the mob seized him. A soda bottle burst against Pronob's head. He had no time to scream. Tara had not seen so much blood on a friend before; a fat man bleeds profusely. They punched him while he was still bleeding. Pronob fell against the side of the taxi and they kept punching. He would never know that his gesture had been useless, that "Old Popo" had rescued Joyonto before the crowd could kill him.

Above Chowringhee Avenue the vision that had teased Tara all summer, the vision that had made Joyonto sometimes feel almost holy, bounced off banners and picket signs, boxed the ears of a looting urchin and pinched the bottom of a female revolutionary, and spread hysteria in the city.

And Tara, still locked in a car across the street from the Catelli-Continental, wondered whether she would ever get out of Calcutta, and if she didn't, whether David would ever know that she loved him fiercely.